STAR TREK

BEST OF KLINGONS

STAR TREK #1-4

WRITTEN BY
MIKE W. BARR

ART BY
TOM SUTTON and RICARDO VILLAGRAN

COLORS BY
MICHELE WOLFMAN

LETTERS BY
JOHN COSTANZA

EDITS BY
MARV WOLFMAN

BLOOD WILL TELL

WRITTEN BY
SCOTT TIPTON and DAVID TIPTON

ART BY
DAVID MESSINA

ART ASSIST BY
ELENA CASAGRANDE

COLORS BY
ILARIA TRAVERSI

LETTERS BY
NEIL UYETAKE and ROBBIE ROBBINS

COVER BY THE SHARP BROS. • COVER COLORS BY HI-FI
COLLECTION EDITS BY JUSTIN EISINGER AND ALONZO SIMON
COLLECTION DESIGN BY CHRIS MOWRY

Star Trek created by Gene Roddenberry.

Special thanks to Risa Kessler and John Van Citters of CBS Consumer Products for their invaluable assistance.

IDW founded by Ted Adams, Alex Garner, Kris Oprisko, and Robbie Robbins |

Ted Adams, CEO & Publisher
Greg Goldstein, President & COO
Robbie Robbins, EVP/Sr. Graphic Artist
Chris Ryall, Chief Creative Officer/Editor-in-Chief
Matthew Ruzicka, CPA, Chief Financial Officer
Alan Payne, VP of Sales
Dirk Wood, VP of Marketing
Lorelei Bunjes, VP of Digital Services

Become our fan on Facebook **facebook.com/idwpublishing**
Follow us on Twitter **@idwpublishing**
Check us out on YouTube **youtube.com/idwpublishing**
www.IDWPUBLISHING.com

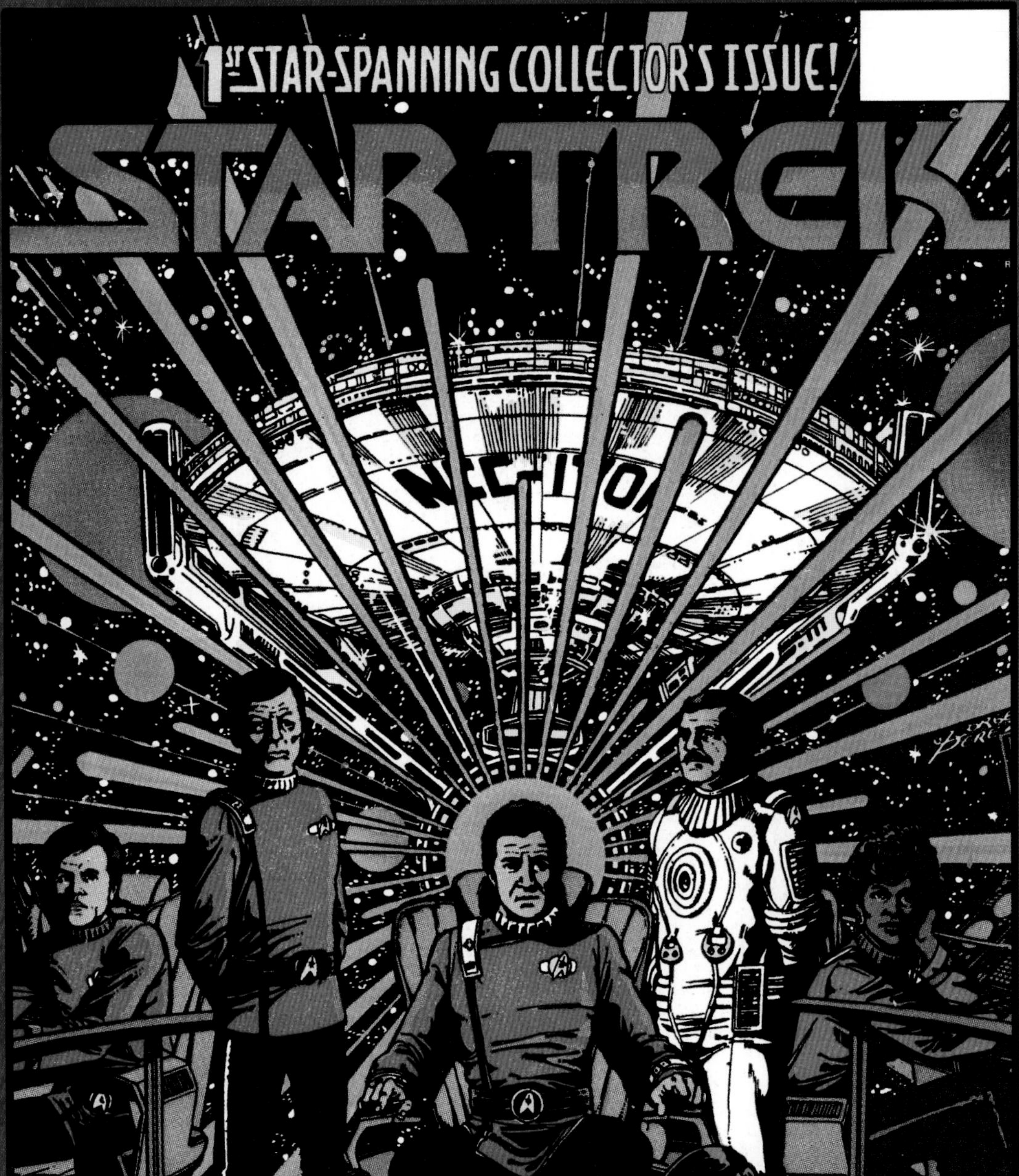
1ST STAR-SPANNING COLLECTOR'S ISSUE!
STAR TREK
NCC-1701

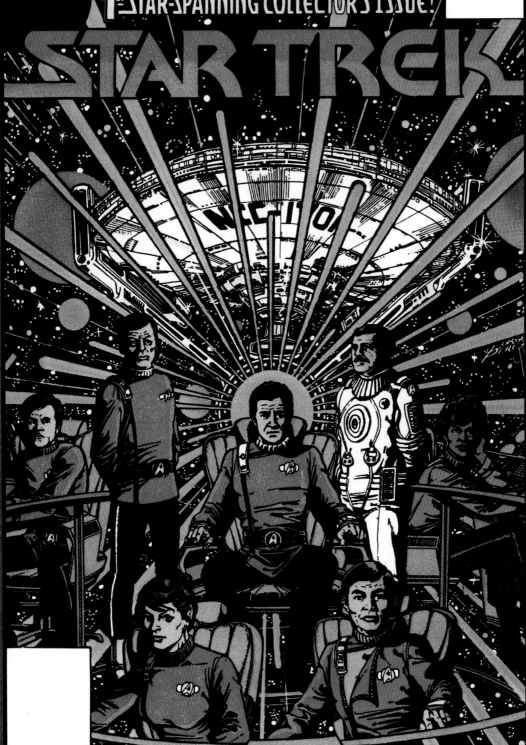

STAR TREK®

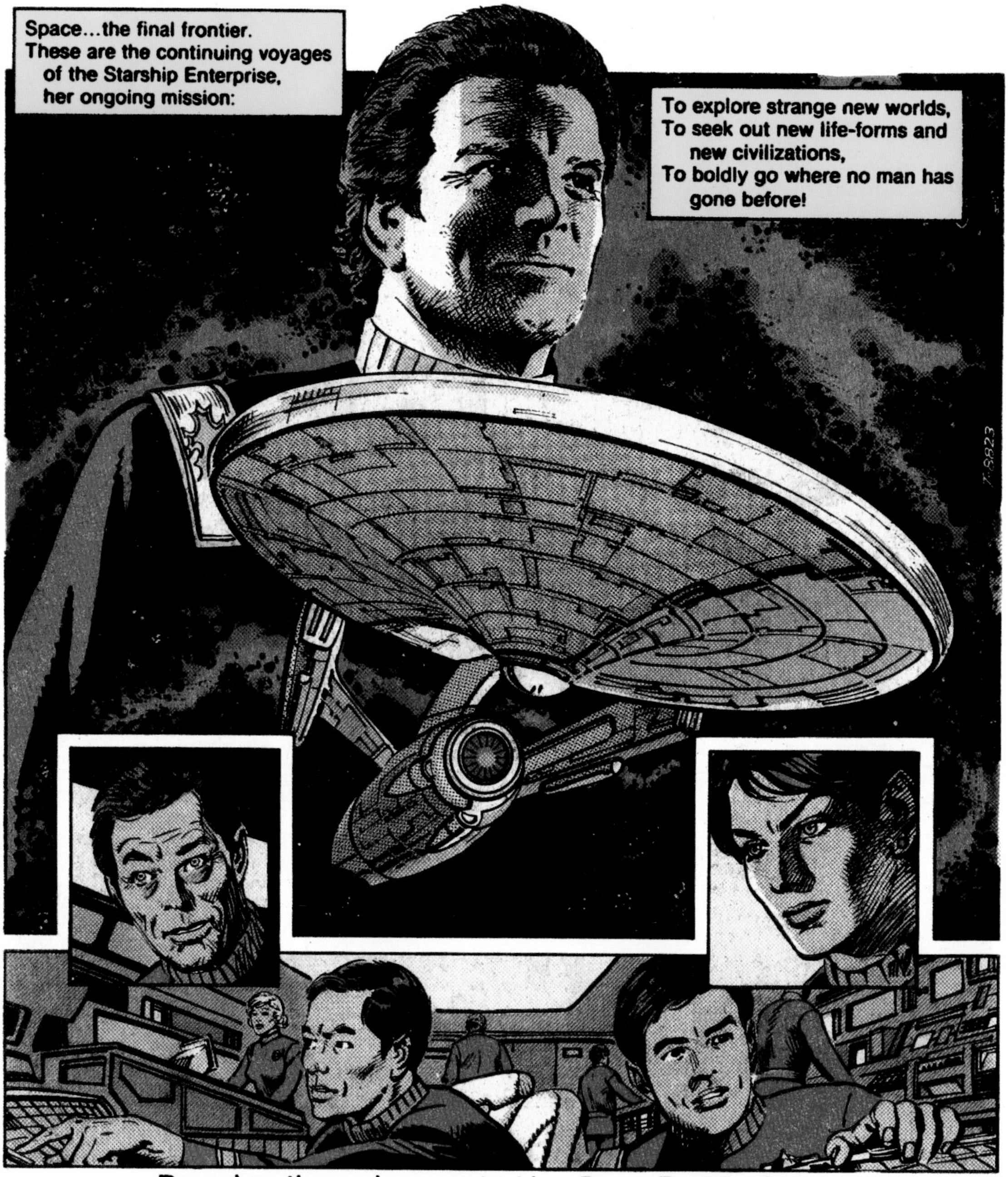
Space...the final frontier.
These are the continuing voyages of the Starship Enterprise, her ongoing mission:
To explore strange new worlds, To seek out new life-forms and new civilizations, To boldly go where no man has gone before!

Based on the series created by **Gene Roddenberry**

MIKE W. BARR * **TOM SUTTON & RICARDO VILLAGRAN**
Writer — Artists

JOHN COSTANZA * **MICHELE WOLFMAN** * **MARV WOLFMAN**
Letterer — Colorist — Editor

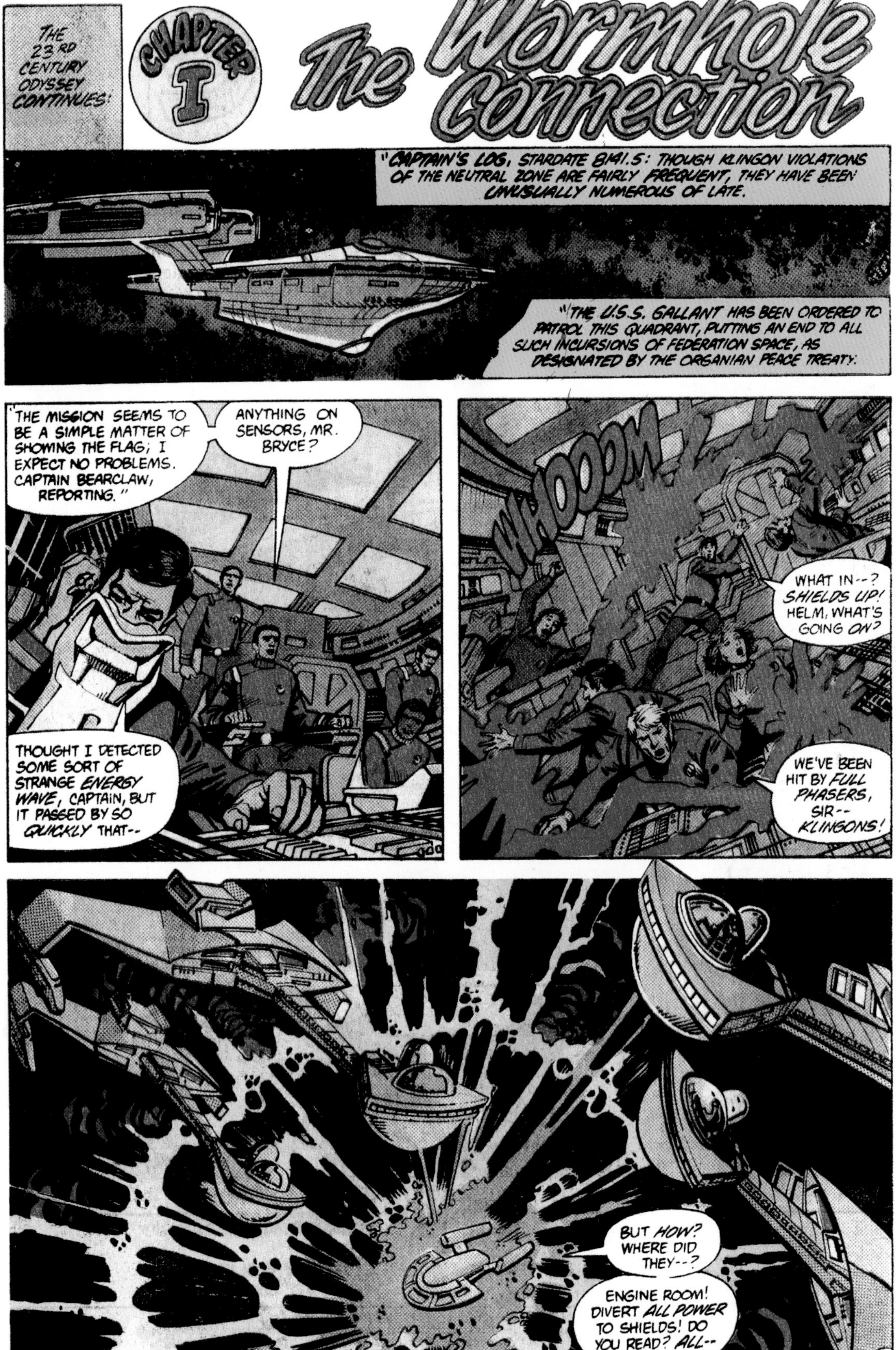
THE 23RD CENTURY ODYSSEY CONTINUES:
CHAPTER I
The Wormhole Connection
"CAPTAIN'S LOG, STARDATE 8141.5: THOUGH KLINGON VIOLATIONS OF THE NEUTRAL ZONE ARE FAIRLY FREQUENT, THEY HAVE BEEN UNUSUALLY NUMEROUS OF LATE.
"THE U.S.S. GALLANT HAS BEEN ORDERED TO PATROL THIS QUADRANT, PUTTING AN END TO ALL SUCH INCURSIONS OF FEDERATION SPACE, AS DESIGNATED BY THE ORGANIAN PEACE TREATY.
"THE MISSION SEEMS TO BE A SIMPLE MATTER OF SHOWING THE FLAG; I EXPECT NO PROBLEMS. CAPTAIN BEARCLAW, REPORTING."
ANYTHING ON SENSORS, MR. BRYCE?
THOUGHT I DETECTED SOME SORT OF STRANGE ENERGY WAVE, CAPTAIN, BUT IT PASSED BY SO QUICKLY THAT--
WHOOOM
WHAT IN--? SHIELDS UP! HELM, WHAT'S GOING ON?
WE'VE BEEN HIT BY FULL PHASERS, SIR-- KLINGONS!
BUT HOW? WHERE DID THEY--?
ENGINE ROOM! DIVERT ALL POWER TO SHIELDS! DO YOU READ? ALL--
2

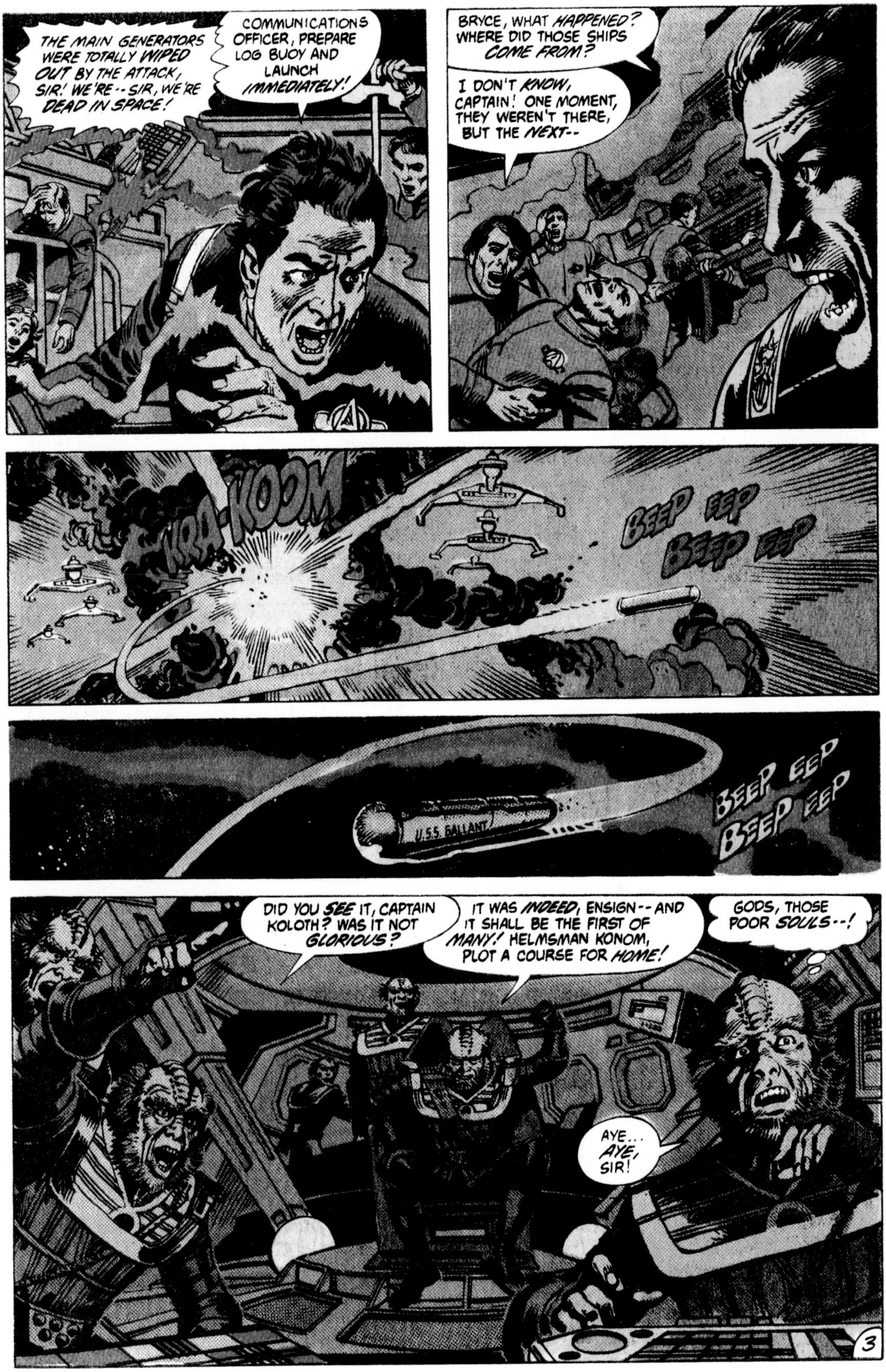
THE MAIN GENERATORS WERE TOTALLY WIPED OUT BY THE ATTACK, SIR! WE'RE--SIR, WE'RE DEAD IN SPACE!
COMMUNICATIONS OFFICER, PREPARE LOG BUOY AND LAUNCH IMMEDIATELY!
BRYCE, WHAT HAPPENED? WHERE DID THOSE SHIPS COME FROM?
I DON'T KNOW, CAPTAIN! ONE MOMENT, THEY WEREN'T THERE, BUT THE NEXT--
KRA-KOOM
BEEP EEP
BEEP EEP
U.S.S. GALLANT
BEEP EEP
BEEP EEP
DID YOU SEE IT, CAPTAIN KOLOTH? WAS IT NOT GLORIOUS?
IT WAS INDEED, ENSIGN--AND IT SHALL BE THE FIRST OF MANY! HELMSMAN KONOM, PLOT A COURSE FOR HOME!
GODS, THOSE POOR SOULS--!
AYE... AYE, SIR!
3

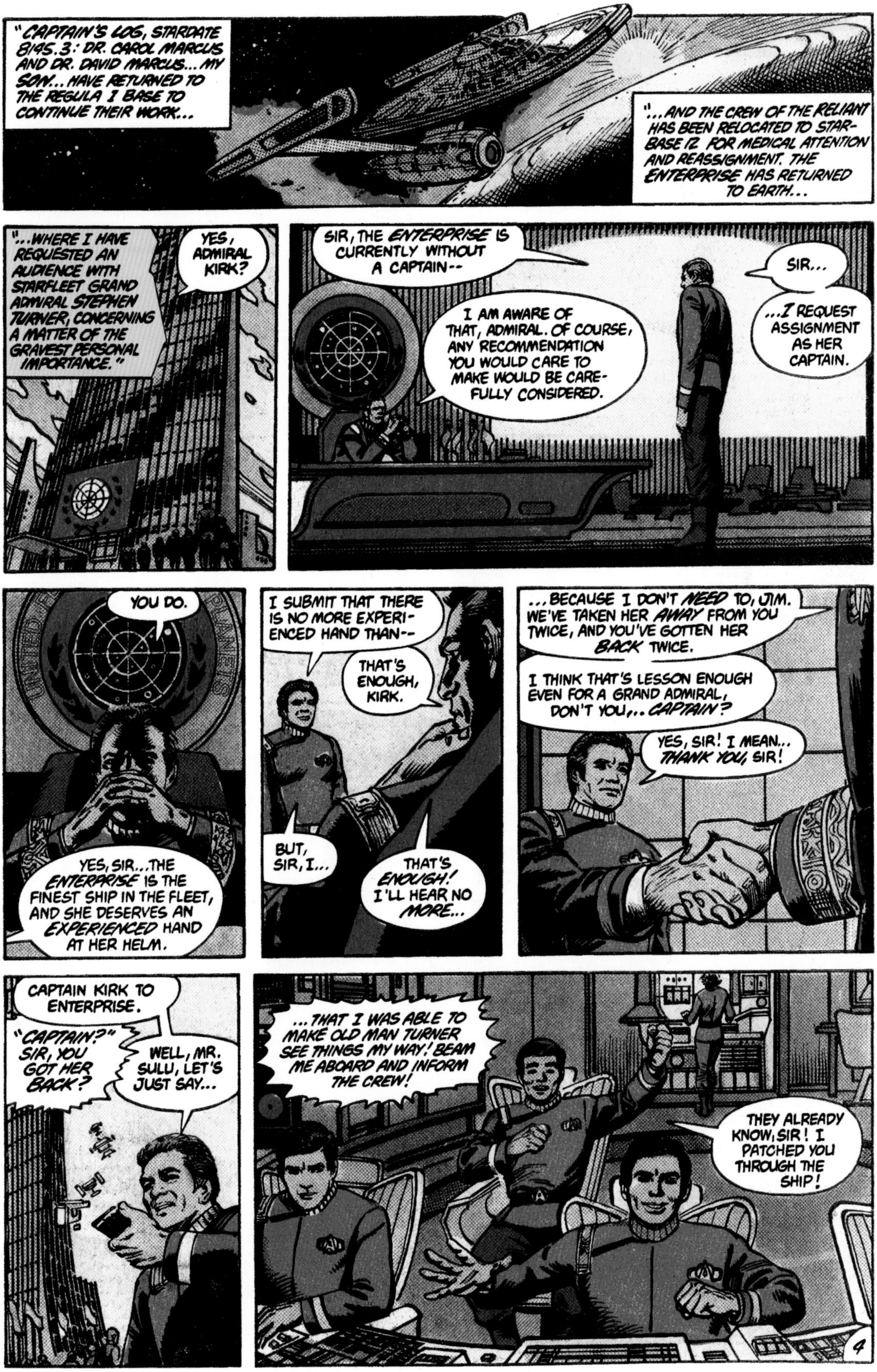
"CAPTAIN'S LOG, STARDATE 8195.3: DR. CAROL MARCUS AND DR. DAVID MARCUS... MY SON... HAVE RETURNED TO THE REGULA I BASE TO CONTINUE THEIR WORK...
"...AND THE CREW OF THE RELIANT HAS BEEN RELOCATED TO STARBASE 12 FOR MEDICAL ATTENTION AND REASSIGNMENT. THE ENTERPRISE HAS RETURNED TO EARTH...
"...WHERE I HAVE REQUESTED AN AUDIENCE WITH STARFLEET GRAND ADMIRAL STEPHEN TURNER, CONCERNING A MATTER OF THE GRAVEST PERSONAL IMPORTANCE."
YES, ADMIRAL KIRK?
SIR, THE ENTERPRISE IS CURRENTLY WITHOUT A CAPTAIN--
I AM AWARE OF THAT, ADMIRAL. OF COURSE, ANY RECOMMENDATION YOU WOULD CARE TO MAKE WOULD BE CAREFULLY CONSIDERED.
SIR...
...I REQUEST ASSIGNMENT AS HER CAPTAIN.
YOU DO.
YES, SIR... THE ENTERPRISE IS THE FINEST SHIP IN THE FLEET, AND SHE DESERVES AN EXPERIENCED HAND AT HER HELM.
I SUBMIT THAT THERE IS NO MORE EXPERIENCED HAND THAN--
THAT'S ENOUGH, KIRK.
BUT, SIR, I...
THAT'S ENOUGH! I'LL HEAR NO MORE...
...BECAUSE I DON'T NEED TO, JIM. WE'VE TAKEN HER AWAY FROM YOU TWICE, AND YOU'VE GOTTEN HER BACK TWICE.
I THINK THAT'S LESSON ENOUGH EVEN FOR A GRAND ADMIRAL, DON'T YOU,.. CAPTAIN?
YES, SIR! I MEAN... THANK YOU, SIR!
CAPTAIN KIRK TO ENTERPRISE.
"CAPTAIN?" SIR, YOU GOT HER BACK?
WELL, MR. SULU, LET'S JUST SAY...
...THAT I WAS ABLE TO MAKE OLD MAN TURNER SEE THINGS MY WAY! BEAM ME ABOARD AND INFORM THE CREW!
THEY ALREADY KNOW, SIR! I PATCHED YOU THROUGH THE SHIP!
4

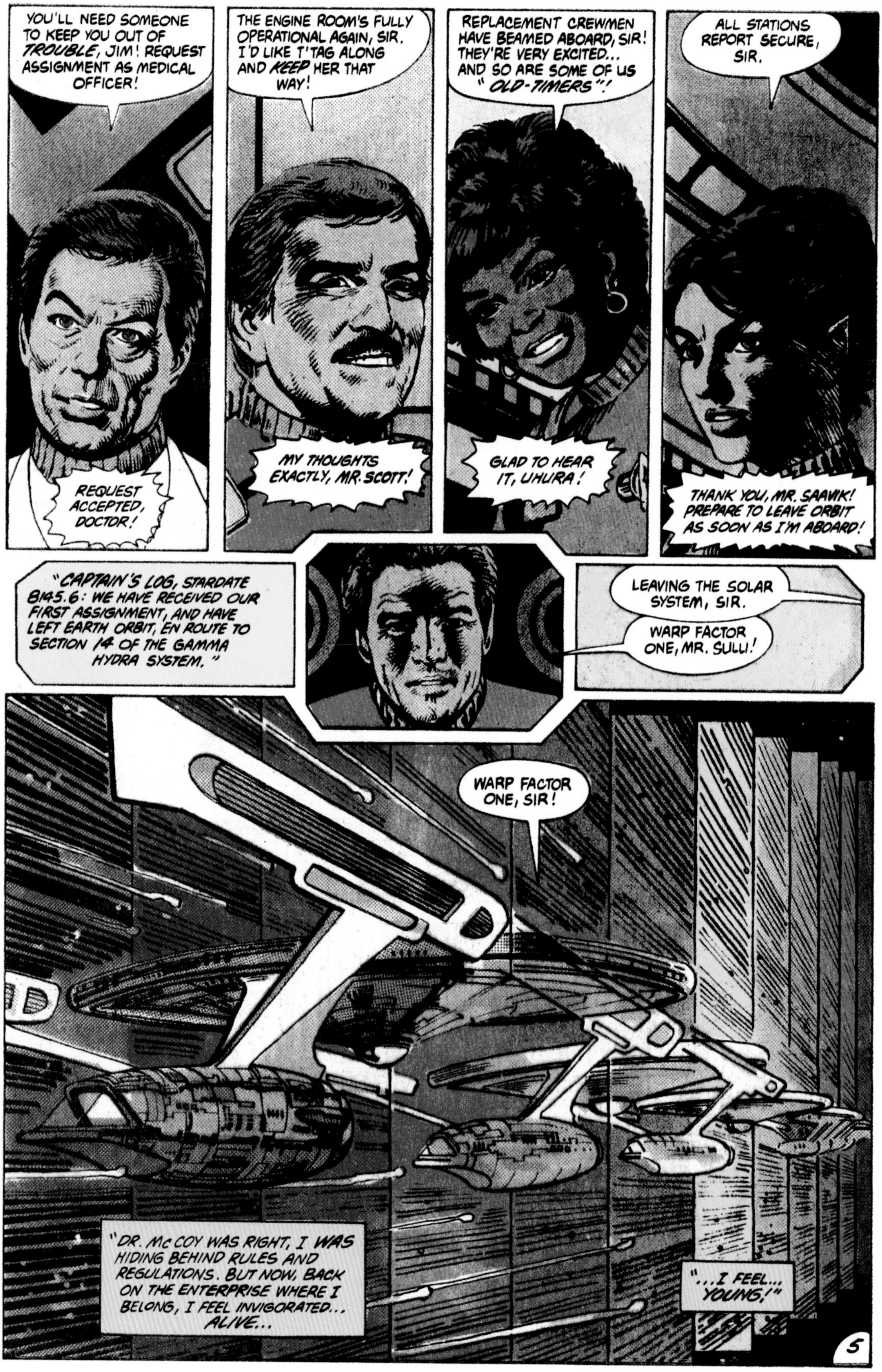

YOU'LL NEED SOMEONE TO KEEP YOU OUT OF TROUBLE, JIM! REQUEST ASSIGNMENT AS MEDICAL OFFICER!
REQUEST ACCEPTED, DOCTOR!
THE ENGINE ROOM'S FULLY OPERATIONAL AGAIN, SIR. I'D LIKE T'TAG ALONG AND KEEP HER THAT WAY!
MY THOUGHTS EXACTLY, MR. SCOTT!
REPLACEMENT CREWMEN HAVE BEAMED ABOARD, SIR! THEY'RE VERY EXCITED... AND SO ARE SOME OF US "OLD-TIMERS"!
GLAD TO HEAR IT, UHURA!
ALL STATIONS REPORT SECURE, SIR.
THANK YOU, MR. SAAVIK! PREPARE TO LEAVE ORBIT AS SOON AS I'M ABOARD!
"CAPTAIN'S LOG, STARDATE 8145.6: WE HAVE RECEIVED OUR FIRST ASSIGNMENT, AND HAVE LEFT EARTH ORBIT, EN ROUTE TO SECTION 14 OF THE GAMMA HYDRA SYSTEM."
LEAVING THE SOLAR SYSTEM, SIR.
WARP FACTOR ONE, MR. SULU!
WARP FACTOR ONE, SIR!
"DR. McCOY WAS RIGHT, I WAS HIDING BEHIND RULES AND REGULATIONS. BUT NOW, BACK ON THE ENTERPRISE WHERE I BELONG, I FEEL INVIGORATED... ALIVE...
"...I FEEL... YOUNG!"
5

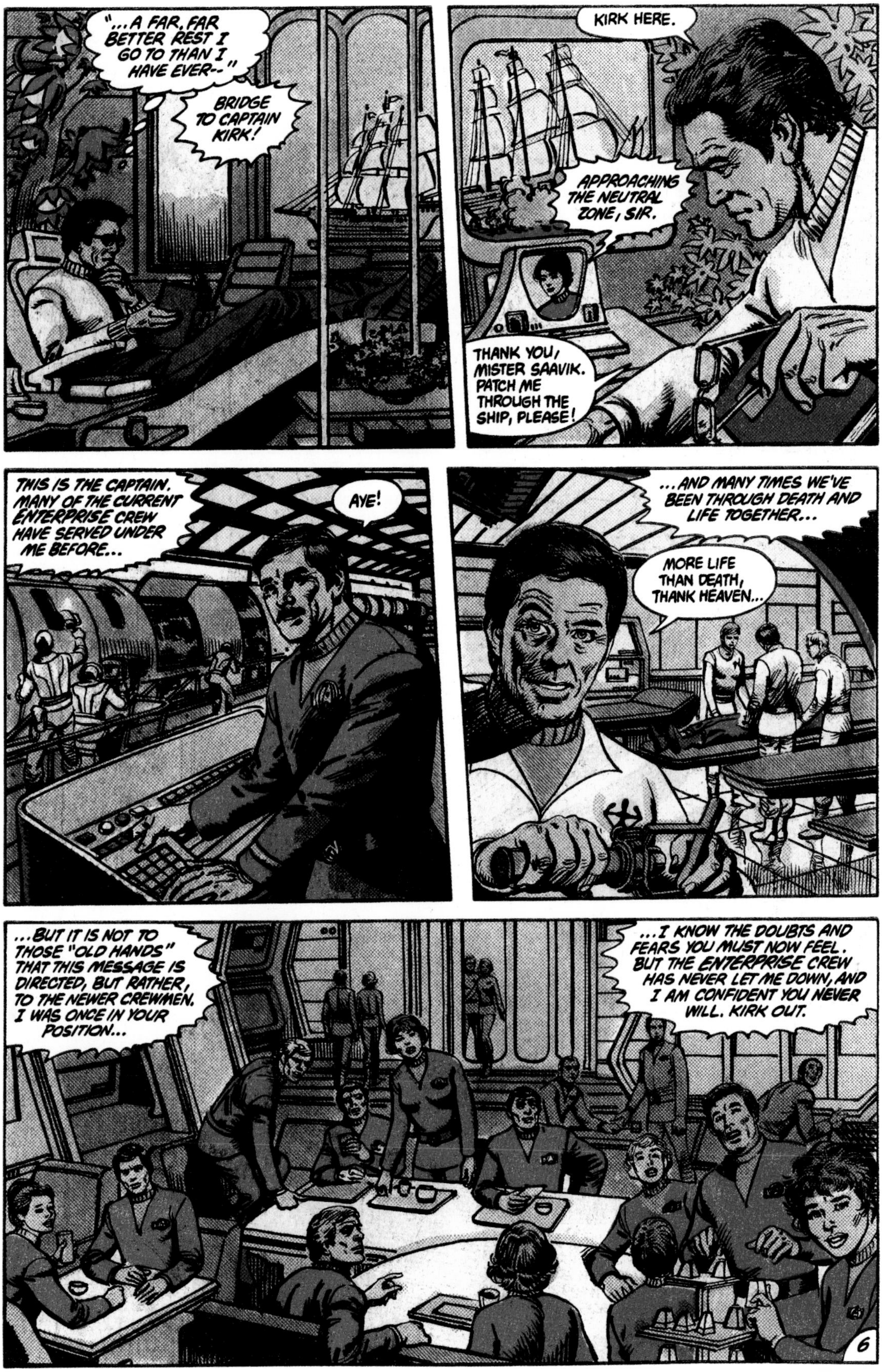
"...A FAR, FAR BETTER REST I GO TO THAN I HAVE EVER--"
BRIDGE TO CAPTAIN KIRK!
KIRK HERE.
APPROACHING THE NEUTRAL ZONE, SIR.
THANK YOU, MISTER SAAVIK. PATCH ME THROUGH THE SHIP, PLEASE!
THIS IS THE CAPTAIN. MANY OF THE CURRENT ENTERPRISE CREW HAVE SERVED UNDER ME BEFORE...
AYE!
...AND MANY TIMES WE'VE BEEN THROUGH DEATH AND LIFE TOGETHER...
MORE LIFE THAN DEATH, THANK HEAVEN...
...BUT IT IS NOT TO THOSE "OLD HANDS" THAT THIS MESSAGE IS DIRECTED, BUT RATHER, TO THE NEWER CREWMEN. I WAS ONCE IN YOUR POSITION...
...I KNOW THE DOUBTS AND FEARS YOU MUST NOW FEEL. BUT THE ENTERPRISE CREW HAS NEVER LET ME DOWN, AND I AM CONFIDENT YOU NEVER WILL. KIRK OUT.
6

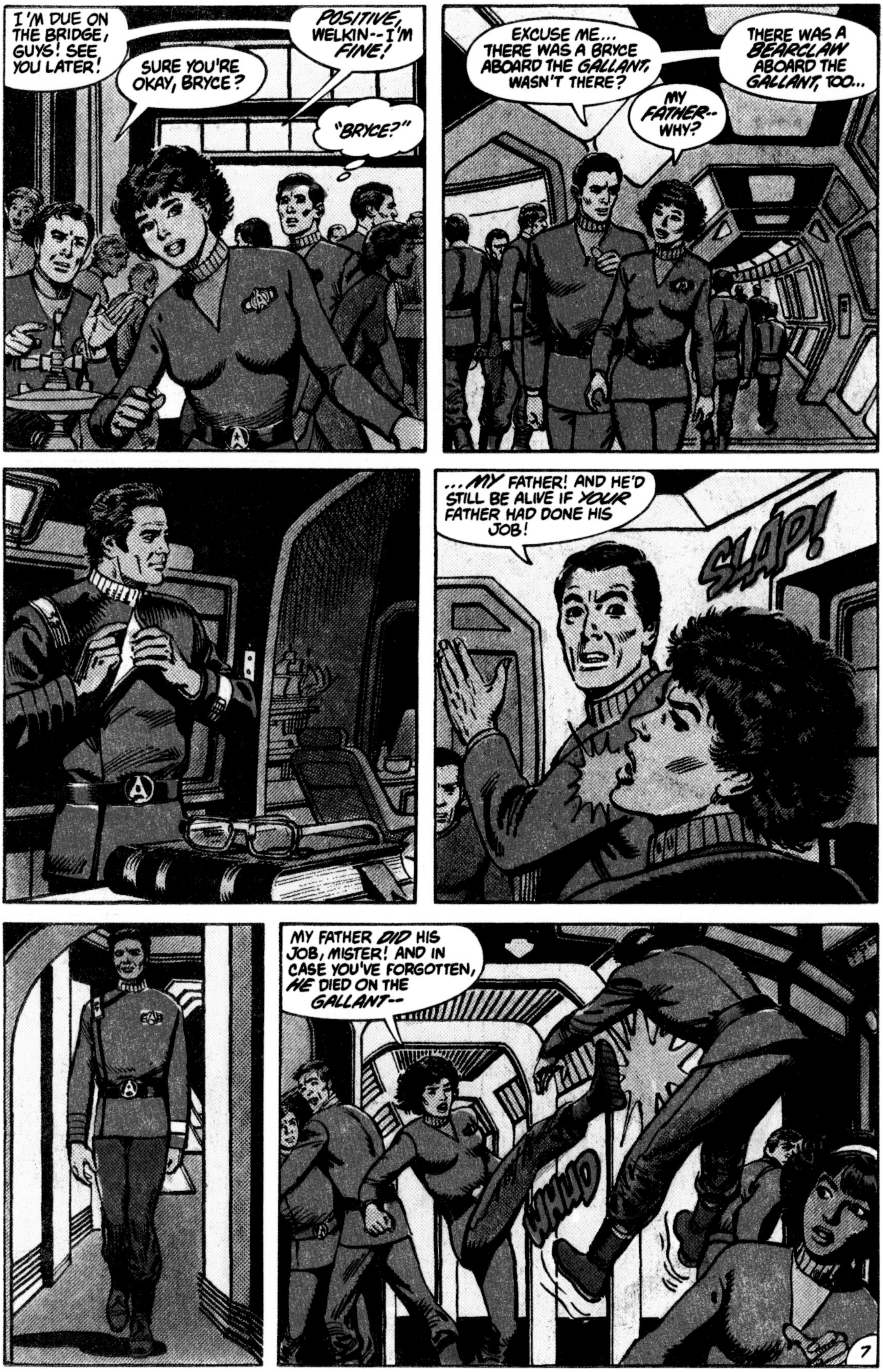
I'M DUE ON THE BRIDGE, GUYS! SEE YOU LATER!
SURE YOU'RE OKAY, BRYCE?
POSITIVE, WELKIN--I'M FINE!
"BRYCE?"
EXCUSE ME... THERE WAS A BRYCE ABOARD THE GALLANT, WASN'T THERE?
MY FATHER-- WHY?
THERE WAS A BEARCLAW ABOARD THE GALLANT, TOO...
...MY FATHER! AND HE'D STILL BE ALIVE IF YOUR FATHER HAD DONE HIS JOB!
SLAP!
MY FATHER DID HIS JOB, MISTER! AND IN CASE YOU'VE FORGOTTEN, HE DIED ON THE GALLANT--
WHUD
7

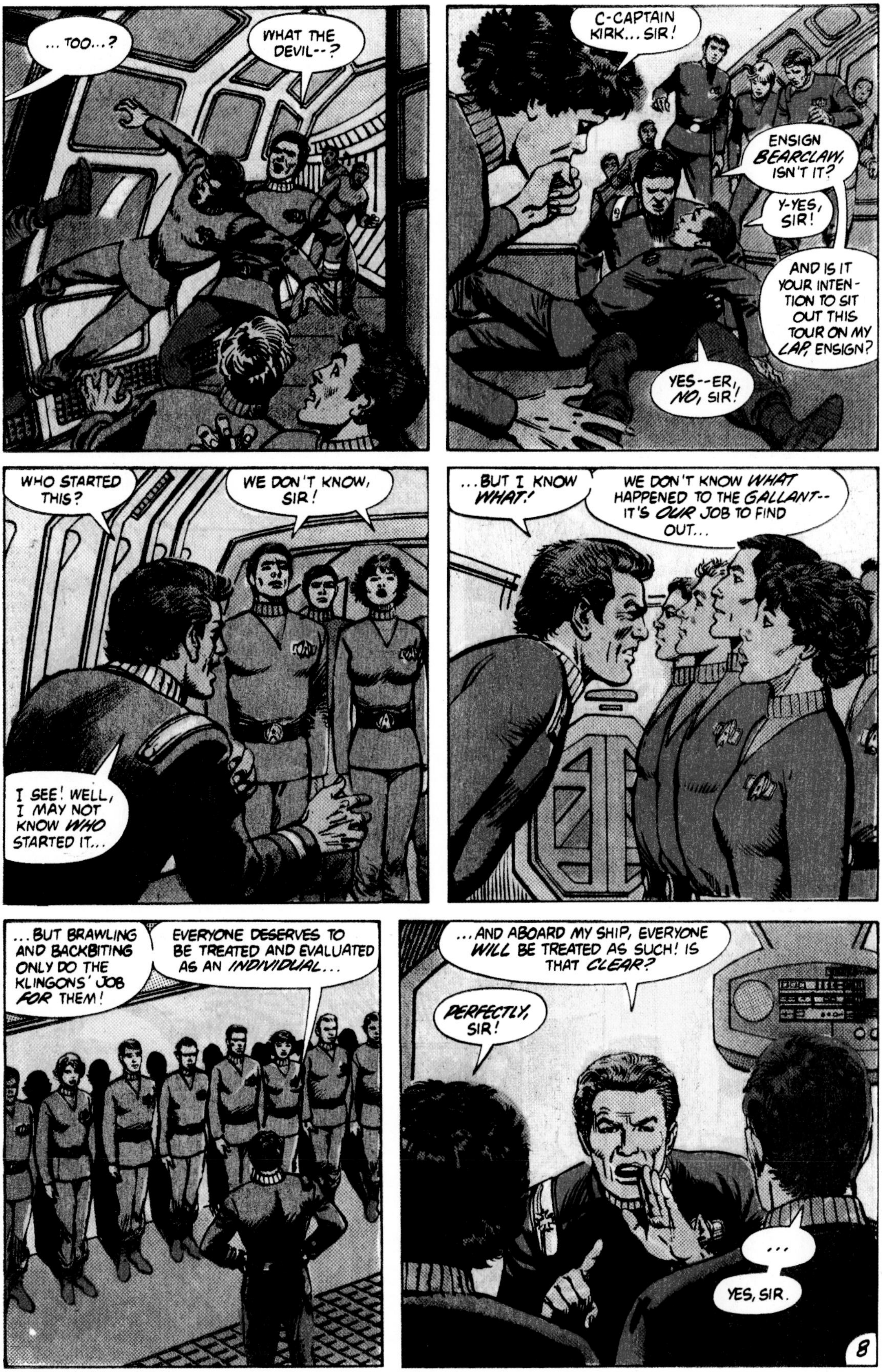

...TOO...?
WHAT THE DEVIL--?
C-CAPTAIN KIRK...SIR!
ENSIGN BEARCLAW, ISN'T IT?
Y-YES, SIR!
AND IS IT YOUR INTENTION TO SIT OUT THIS TOUR ON MY LAP, ENSIGN?
YES--ER, NO, SIR!
WHO STARTED THIS?
WE DON'T KNOW, SIR!
I SEE! WELL, I MAY NOT KNOW WHO STARTED IT...
...BUT I KNOW WHAT!
WE DON'T KNOW WHAT HAPPENED TO THE GALLANT-- IT'S OUR JOB TO FIND OUT...
...BUT BRAWLING AND BACKBITING ONLY DO THE KLINGONS' JOB FOR THEM!
EVERYONE DESERVES TO BE TREATED AND EVALUATED AS AN INDIVIDUAL...
...AND ABOARD MY SHIP, EVERYONE WILL BE TREATED AS SUCH! IS THAT CLEAR?
PERFECTLY, SIR!
...
YES, SIR.
8

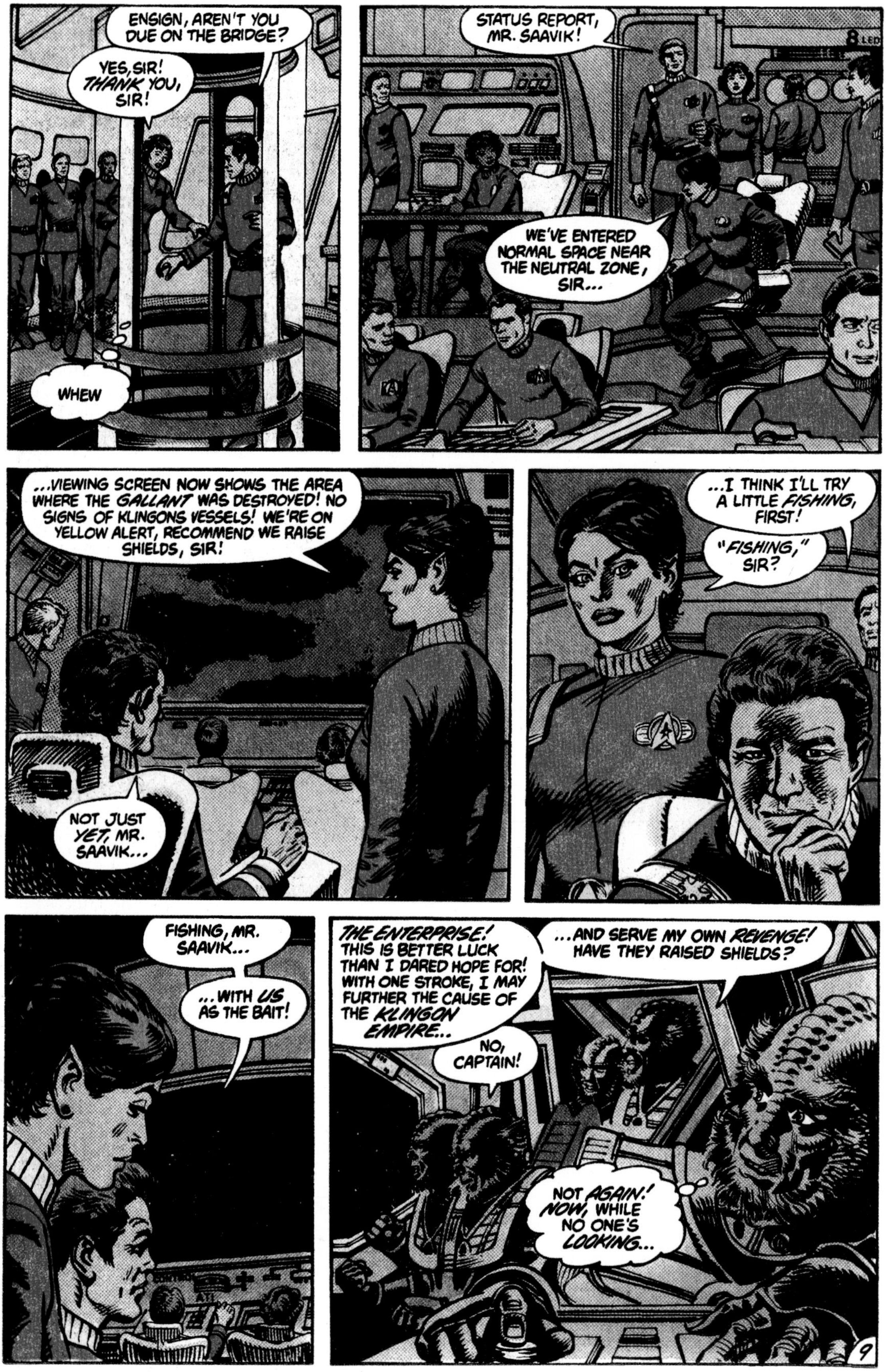
ENSIGN, AREN'T YOU DUE ON THE BRIDGE?
YES, SIR! THANK YOU, SIR!
WHEW
STATUS REPORT, MR. SAAVIK!
WE'VE ENTERED NORMAL SPACE NEAR THE NEUTRAL ZONE, SIR...
...VIEWING SCREEN NOW SHOWS THE AREA WHERE THE GALLANT WAS DESTROYED! NO SIGNS OF KLINGONS VESSELS! WE'RE ON YELLOW ALERT, RECOMMEND WE RAISE SHIELDS, SIR!
NOT JUST YET, MR. SAAVIK...
...I THINK I'LL TRY A LITTLE FISHING, FIRST!
"FISHING," SIR?
FISHING, MR. SAAVIK...
...WITH US AS THE BAIT!
THE ENTERPRISE! THIS IS BETTER LUCK THAN I DARED HOPE FOR! WITH ONE STROKE, I MAY FURTHER THE CAUSE OF THE KLINGON EMPIRE...
...AND SERVE MY OWN REVENGE! HAVE THEY RAISED SHIELDS?
NO, CAPTAIN!
NOT AGAIN! NOW, WHILE NO ONE'S LOOKING...
9

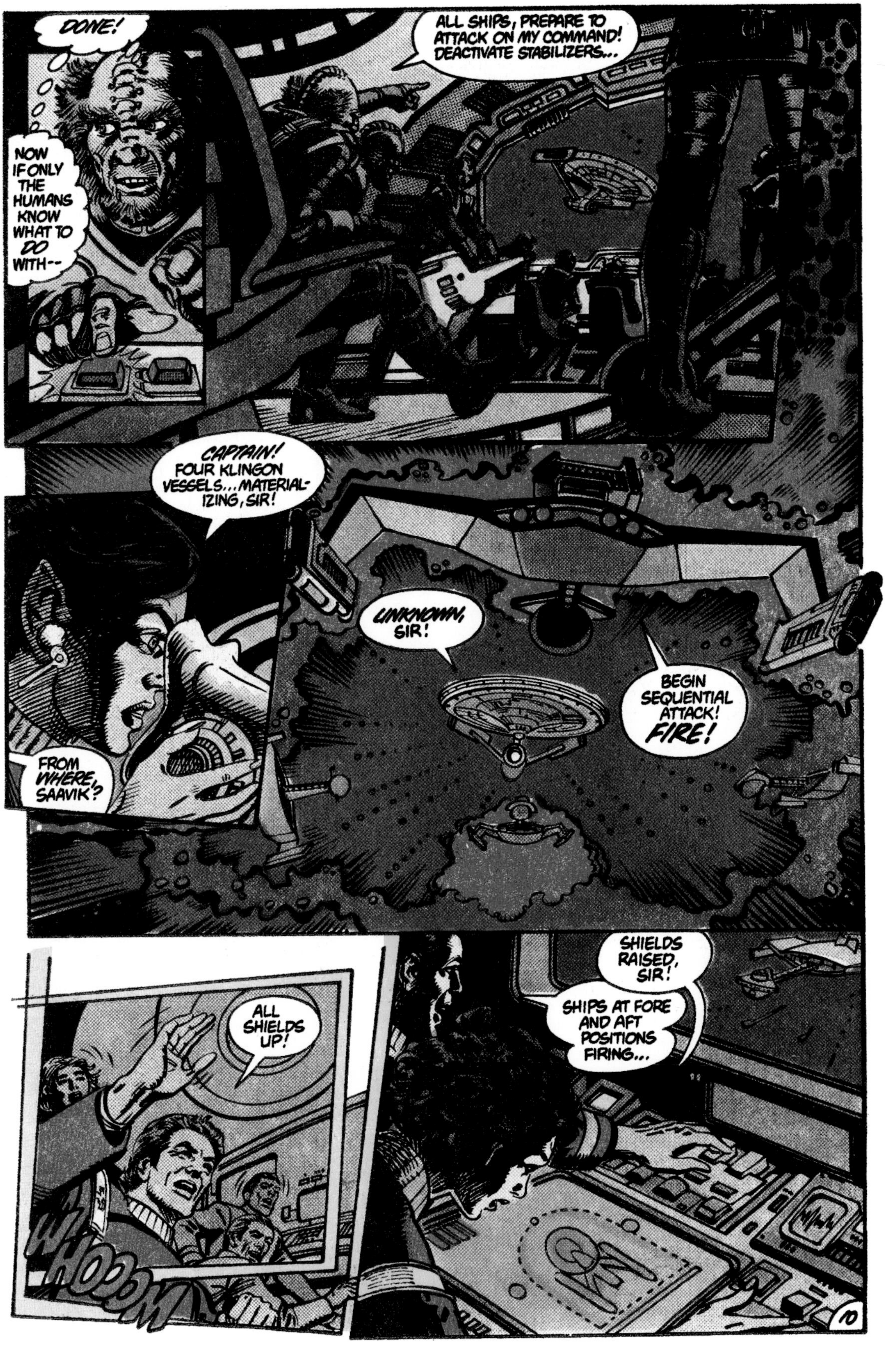
DONE!
NOW IF ONLY THE HUMANS KNOW WHAT TO DO WITH--
ALL SHIPS, PREPARE TO ATTACK ON MY COMMAND! DEACTIVATE STABILIZERS...
CAPTAIN! FOUR KLINGON VESSELS...MATERIALIZING, SIR!
FROM WHERE, SAAVIK?
UNKNOWN, SIR!
BEGIN SEQUENTIAL ATTACK! FIRE!
ALL SHIELDS UP!
WHOOOM
SHIELDS RAISED, SIR!
SHIPS AT FORE AND AFT POSITIONS FIRING...
10

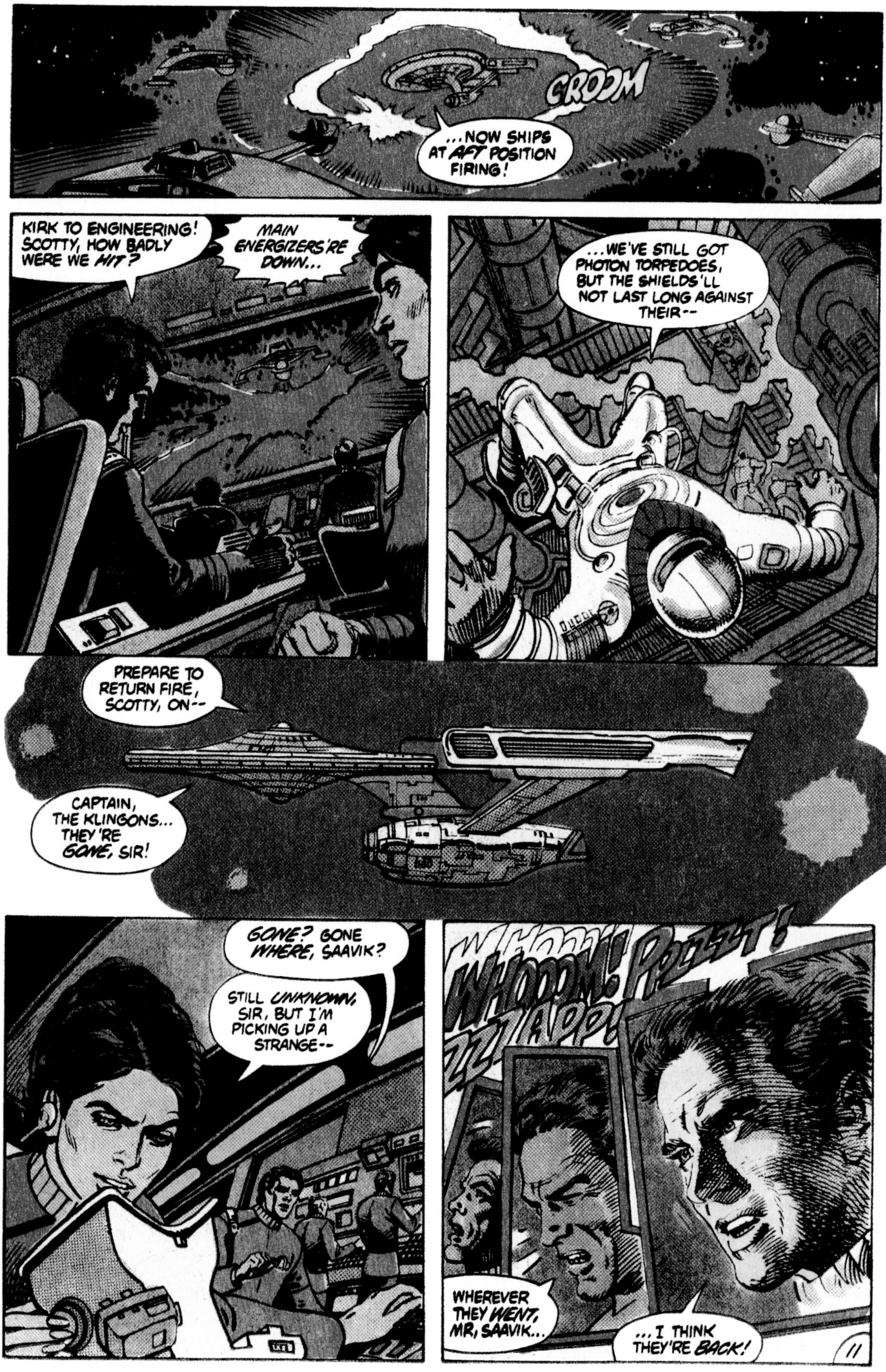
CROOM
...NOW SHIPS AT AFT POSITION FIRING!
KIRK TO ENGINEERING! SCOTTY, HOW BADLY WERE WE HIT?
MAIN ENERGIZERS'RE DOWN...
...WE'VE STILL GOT PHOTON TORPEDOES, BUT THE SHIELDS'LL NOT LAST LONG AGAINST THEIR--
PREPARE TO RETURN FIRE, SCOTTY, ON--
CAPTAIN, THE KLINGONS... THEY'RE GONE, SIR!
GONE? GONE WHERE, SAAVIK?
STILL UNKNOWN, SIR, BUT I'M PICKING UP A STRANGE--
WHOOOM! PZZZT!
WHEREVER THEY WENT, MR. SAAVIK...
...I THINK THEY'RE BACK!
11

THAT SALVO WAS TO OUR *TAIL*, SIR-- KLINGONS *AHEAD* OF US FIRING NOW!

WHOOM

ENGINEERING, *ALL POWER* TO SHIELDS!

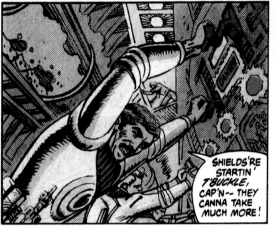

SHIELDS'RE STARTIN' *T'BUCKLE*, CAP'N-- THEY *CANNA* TAKE MUCH MORE!

AFT SHIPS FIRING AGAIN, SIR!

THEY'RE ONE-TWOING US, MR. SULU...

...MAYBE WE CAN *USE* THAT...!

MR. SULU-- ON MY COMMAND, *DROP* AFT SHIELDS!

?

Y-YES, SIR!

...AND, MR. CHEKOV, PREPARE TO FIRE *AFT PHOTON TORPEDOES!*

AYE, KEPTIN!

CAPTAIN, DO YOU THINK--

WHEN I NEED A COMMENT FROM *YOU*, MR. SAAVIK, I'LL *ASK* FOR IT! IS THAT CLEAR?

YES... SIR.

12

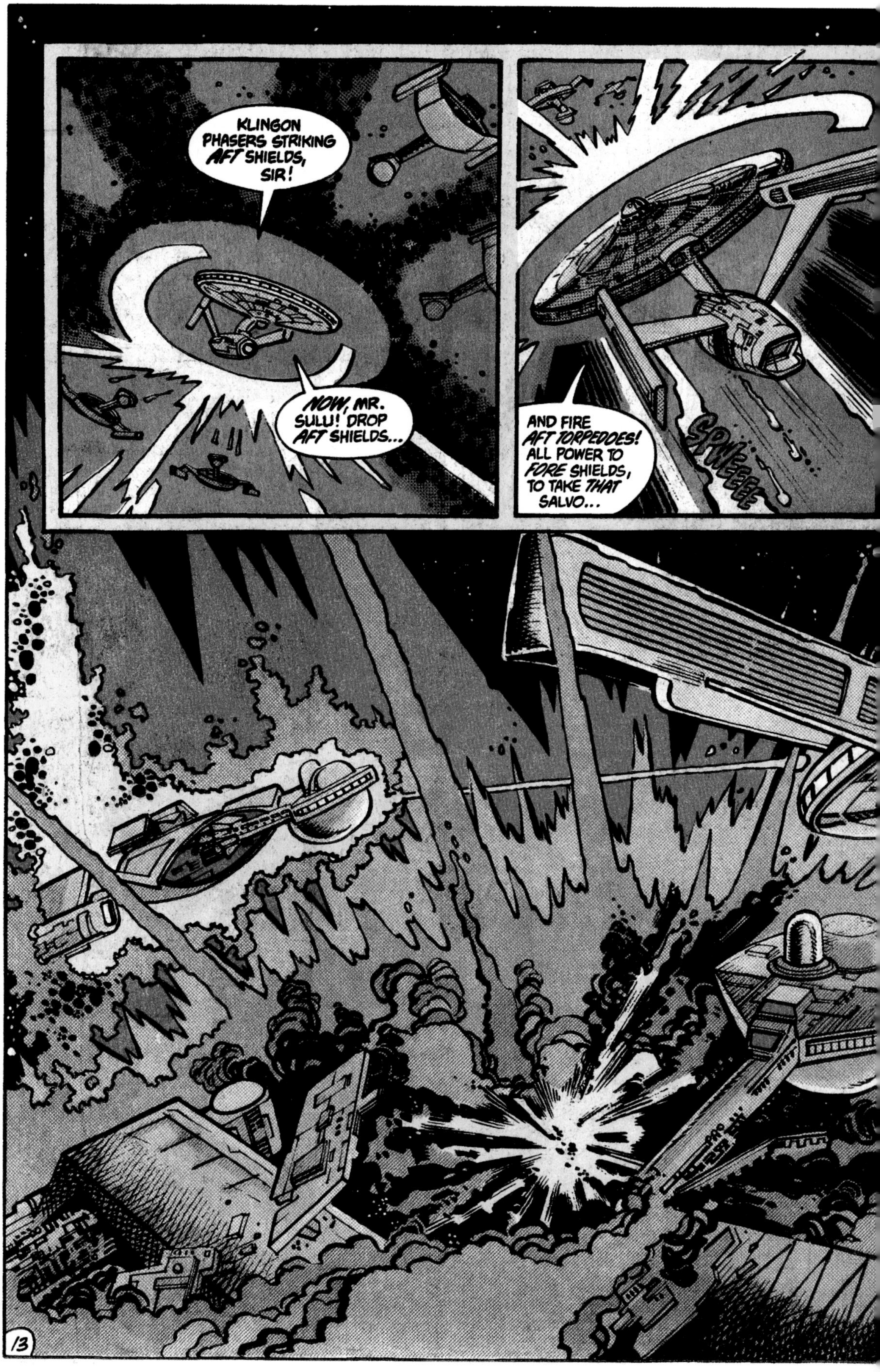
KLINGON PHASERS STRIKING AFT SHIELDS, SIR!
NOW, MR. SULU! DROP AFT SHIELDS...
AND FIRE AFT TORPEDOES! ALL POWER TO FORE SHIELDS, TO TAKE THAT SALVO...
SPWEEEEE
13

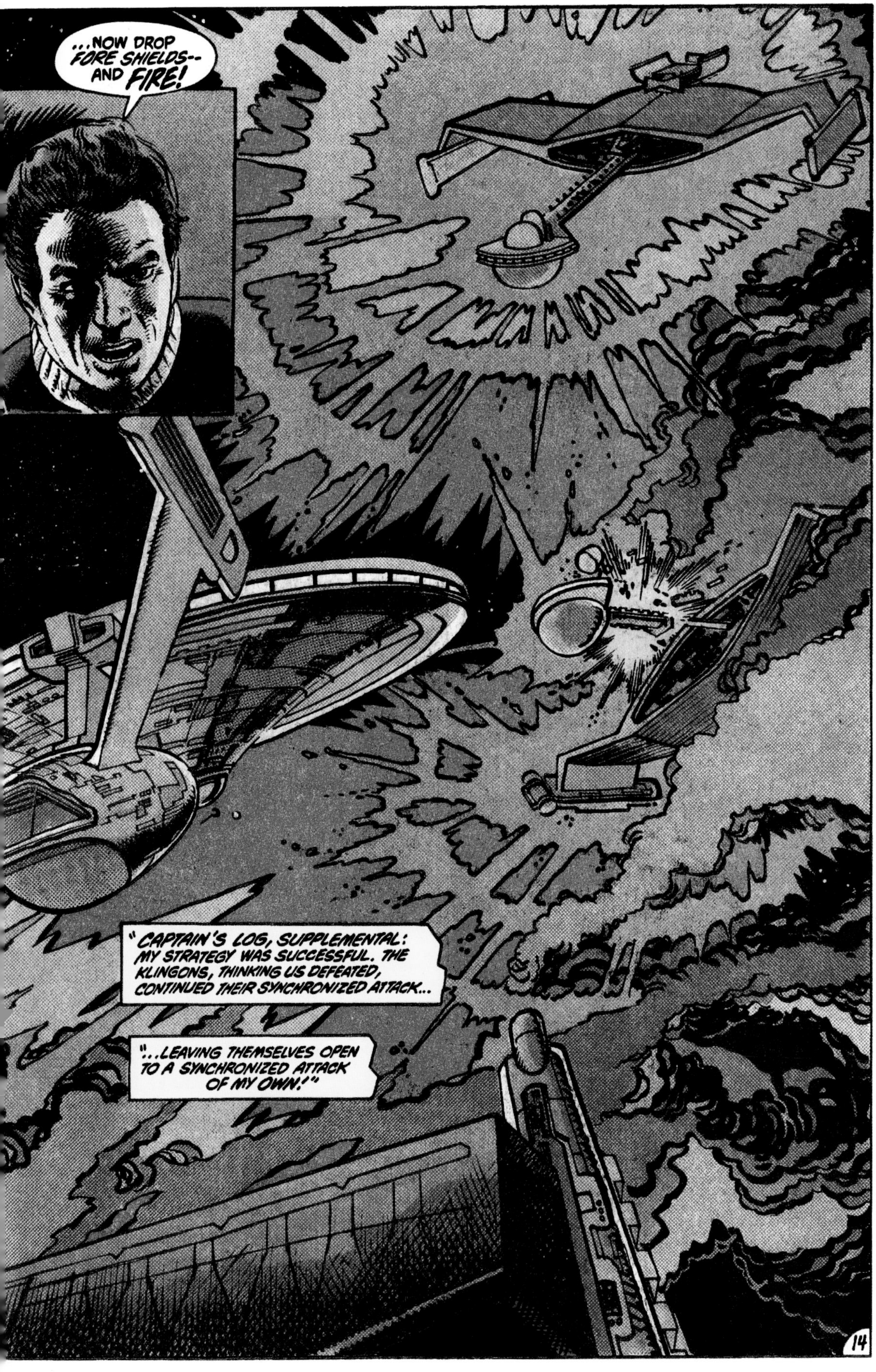
...NOW DROP FORE SHIELDS-- AND FIRE!
"CAPTAIN'S LOG, SUPPLEMENTAL: MY STRATEGY WAS SUCCESSFUL. THE KLINGONS, THINKING US DEFEATED, CONTINUED THEIR SYNCHRONIZED ATTACK...
"...LEAVING THEMSELVES OPEN TO A SYNCHRONIZED ATTACK OF MY OWN!"
14

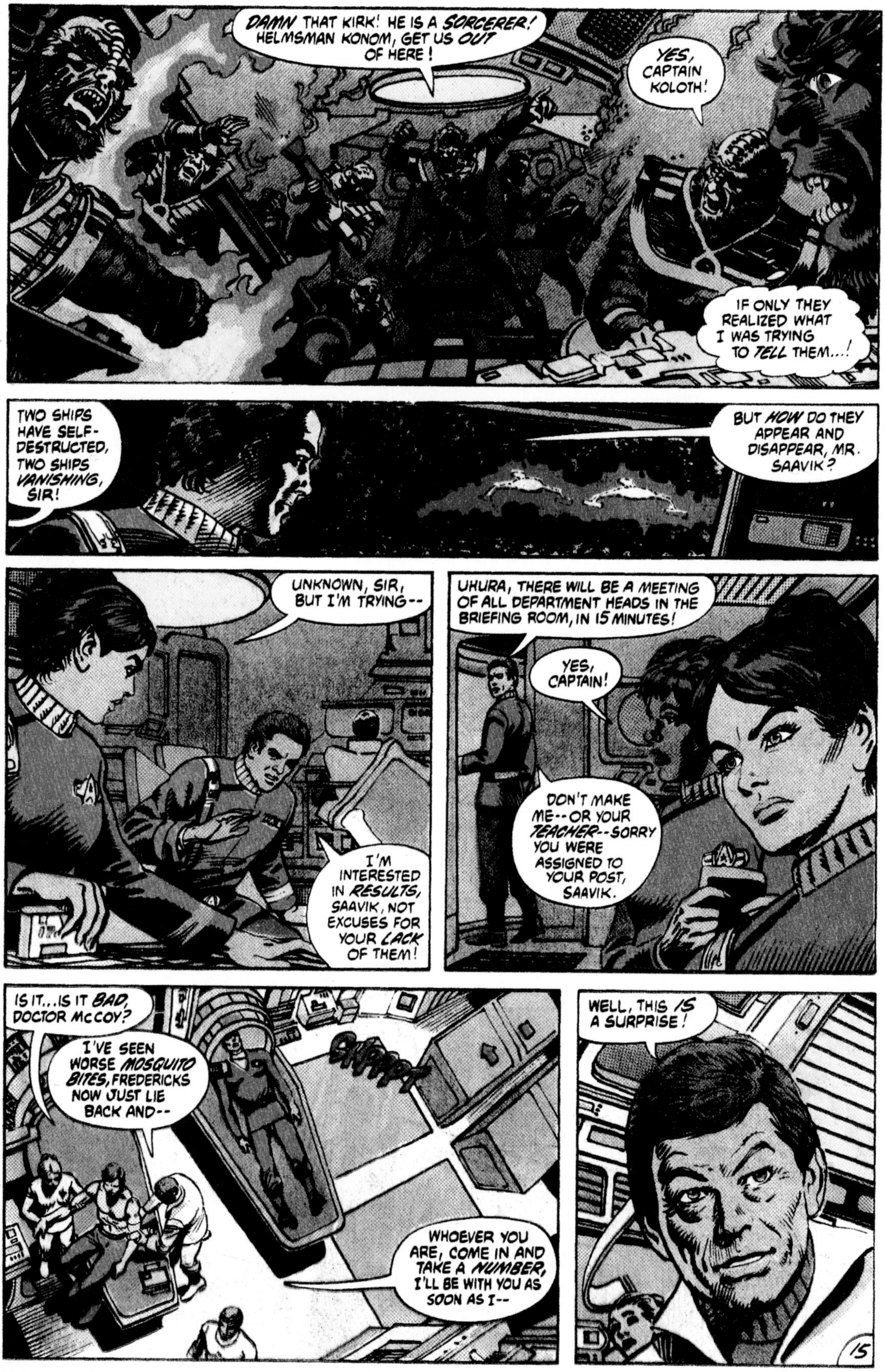
DAMN THAT KIRK! HE IS A SORCERER! HELMSMAN KONOM, GET US OUT OF HERE!
YES, CAPTAIN KOLOTH!
IF ONLY THEY REALIZED WHAT I WAS TRYING TO TELL THEM...!
TWO SHIPS HAVE SELF-DESTRUCTED, TWO SHIPS VANISHING, SIR!
BUT HOW DO THEY APPEAR AND DISAPPEAR, MR. SAAVIK?
UNKNOWN, SIR, BUT I'M TRYING--
I'M INTERESTED IN RESULTS, SAAVIK, NOT EXCUSES FOR YOUR LACK OF THEM!
UHURA, THERE WILL BE A MEETING OF ALL DEPARTMENT HEADS IN THE BRIEFING ROOM, IN 15 MINUTES!
YES, CAPTAIN!
DON'T MAKE ME--OR YOUR TEACHER--SORRY YOU WERE ASSIGNED TO YOUR POST, SAAVIK.
IS IT...IS IT BAD, DOCTOR McCOY?
I'VE SEEN WORSE MOSQUITO BITES, FREDERICKS NOW JUST LIE BACK AND--
WHOEVER YOU ARE, COME IN AND TAKE A NUMBER, I'LL BE WITH YOU AS SOON AS I--
WELL, THIS IS A SURPRISE!
15

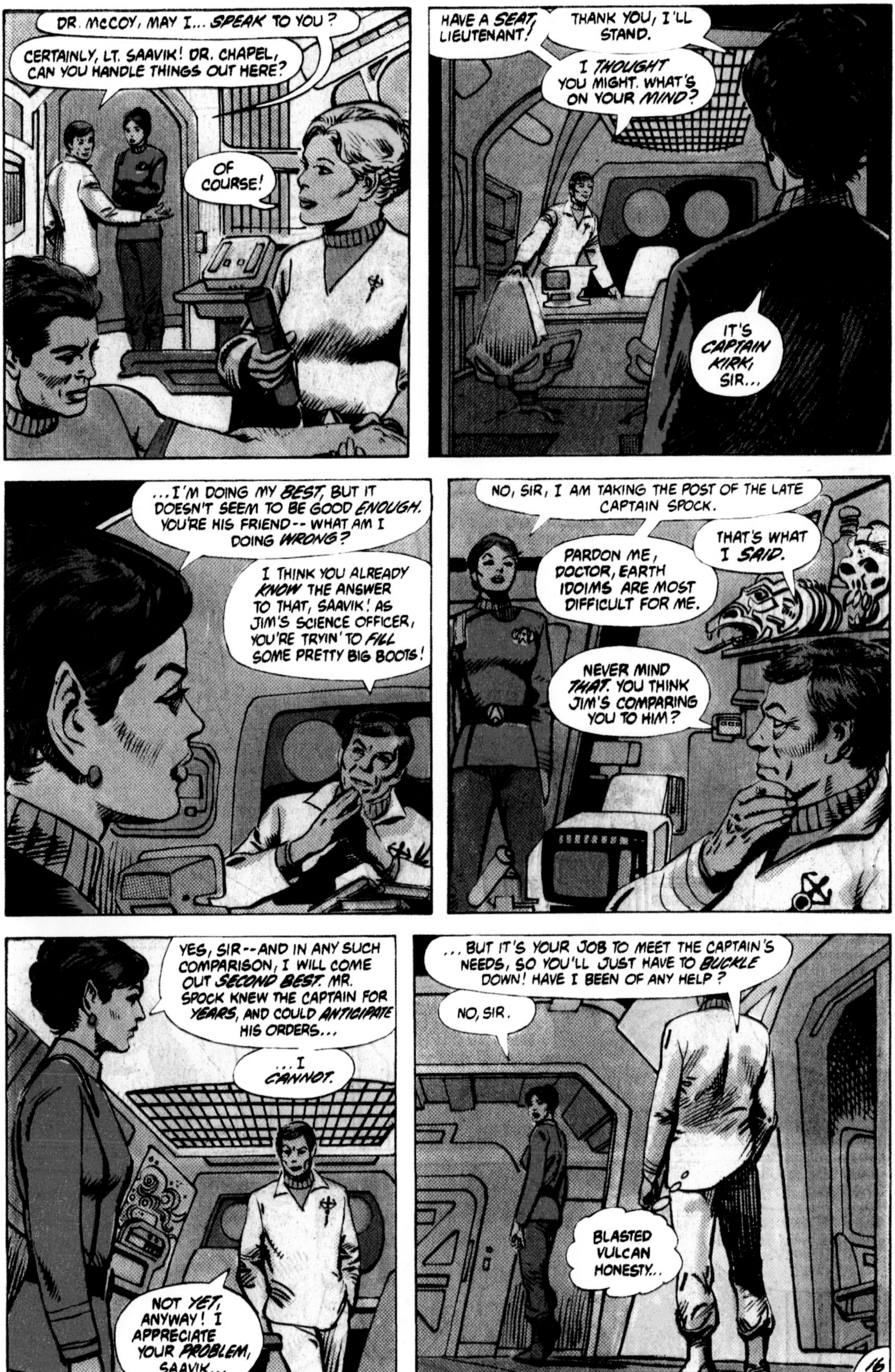
DR. McCOY, MAY I... SPEAK TO YOU?
CERTAINLY, LT. SAAVIK! DR. CHAPEL, CAN YOU HANDLE THINGS OUT HERE?
OF COURSE!
HAVE A SEAT, LIEUTENANT!
THANK YOU, I'LL STAND.
I THOUGHT YOU MIGHT. WHAT'S ON YOUR MIND?
IT'S CAPTAIN KIRK, SIR...
...I'M DOING MY BEST, BUT IT DOESN'T SEEM TO BE GOOD ENOUGH. YOU'RE HIS FRIEND-- WHAT AM I DOING WRONG?
I THINK YOU ALREADY KNOW THE ANSWER TO THAT, SAAVIK! AS JIM'S SCIENCE OFFICER, YOU'RE TRYIN' TO FILL SOME PRETTY BIG BOOTS!
NO, SIR, I AM TAKING THE POST OF THE LATE CAPTAIN SPOCK.
PARDON ME, DOCTOR, EARTH IDOIMS ARE MOST DIFFICULT FOR ME.
THAT'S WHAT I SAID.
NEVER MIND THAT. YOU THINK JIM'S COMPARING YOU TO HIM?
YES, SIR--AND IN ANY SUCH COMPARISON, I WILL COME OUT SECOND BEST. MR. SPOCK KNEW THE CAPTAIN FOR YEARS, AND COULD ANTICIPATE HIS ORDERS...
...I CANNOT.
NOT YET, ANYWAY! I APPRECIATE YOUR PROBLEM, SAAVIK...
...BUT IT'S YOUR JOB TO MEET THE CAPTAIN'S NEEDS, SO YOU'LL JUST HAVE TO BUCKLE DOWN! HAVE I BEEN OF ANY HELP?
NO, SIR.
BLASTED VULCAN HONESTY...
16

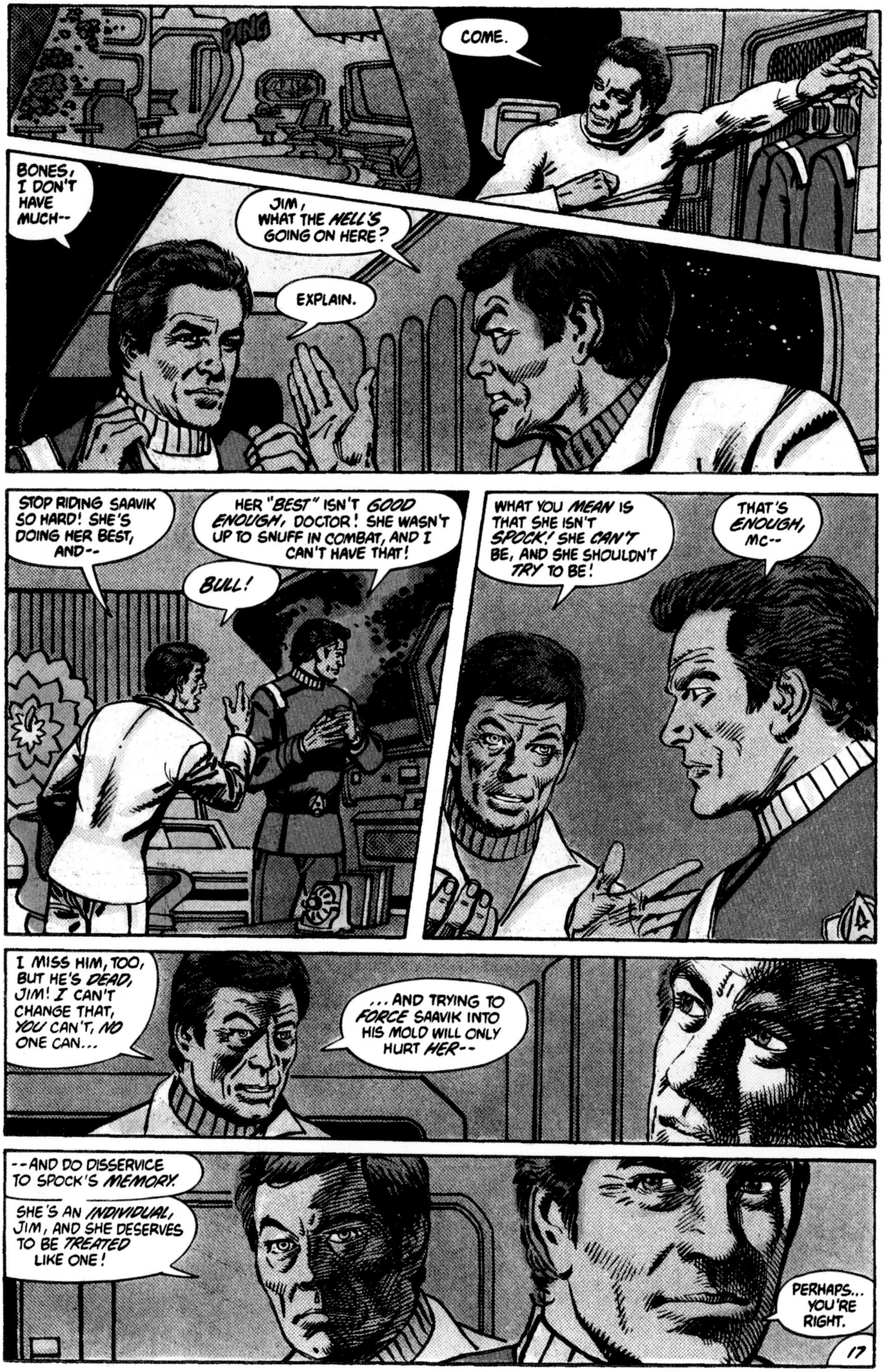
PING
COME.
BONES, I DON'T HAVE MUCH--
JIM, WHAT THE HELL'S GOING ON HERE?
EXPLAIN.
STOP RIDING SAAVIK SO HARD! SHE'S DOING HER BEST, AND--
HER "BEST" ISN'T GOOD ENOUGH, DOCTOR! SHE WASN'T UP TO SNUFF IN COMBAT, AND I CAN'T HAVE THAT!
BULL!
WHAT YOU MEAN IS THAT SHE ISN'T SPOCK! SHE CAN'T BE, AND SHE SHOULDN'T TRY TO BE!
THAT'S ENOUGH, MC--
I MISS HIM, TOO, BUT HE'S DEAD, JIM! I CAN'T CHANGE THAT, YOU CAN'T, NO ONE CAN...
...AND TRYING TO FORCE SAAVIK INTO HIS MOLD WILL ONLY HURT HER--
--AND DO DISSERVICE TO SPOCK'S MEMORY.
SHE'S AN INDIVIDUAL, JIM, AND SHE DESERVES TO BE TREATED LIKE ONE!
PERHAPS... YOU'RE RIGHT.
17

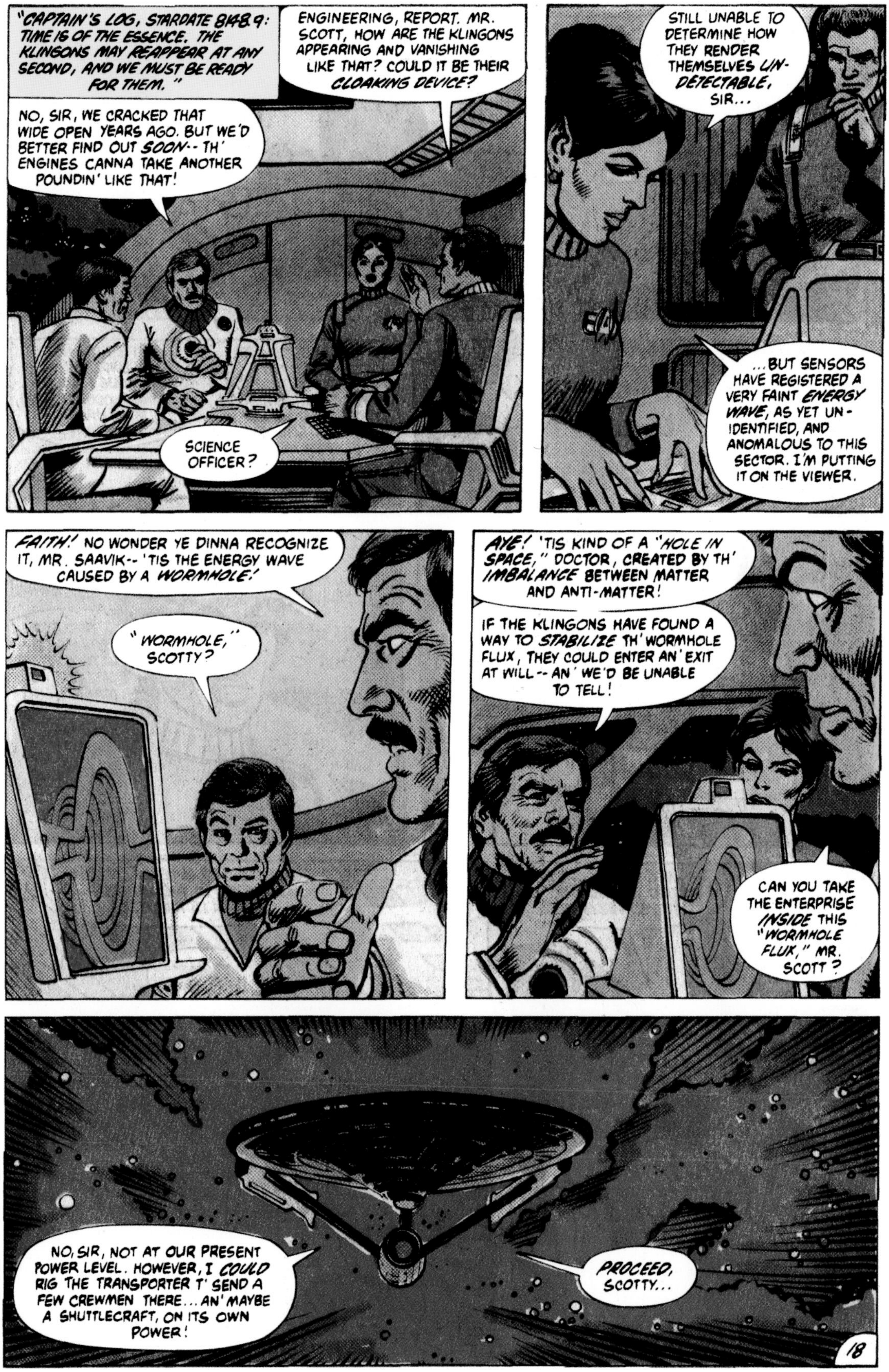
"CAPTAIN'S LOG, STARDATE 8148.9: TIME IS OF THE ESSENCE. THE KLINGONS MAY REAPPEAR AT ANY SECOND, AND WE MUST BE READY FOR THEM."
ENGINEERING, REPORT. MR. SCOTT, HOW ARE THE KLINGONS APPEARING AND VANISHING LIKE THAT? COULD IT BE THEIR CLOAKING DEVICE?
NO, SIR, WE CRACKED THAT WIDE OPEN YEARS AGO. BUT WE'D BETTER FIND OUT SOON -- TH' ENGINES CANNA TAKE ANOTHER POUNDIN' LIKE THAT!
SCIENCE OFFICER?
STILL UNABLE TO DETERMINE HOW THEY RENDER THEMSELVES UN-DETECTABLE, SIR...
...BUT SENSORS HAVE REGISTERED A VERY FAINT ENERGY WAVE, AS YET UN-IDENTIFIED, AND ANOMALOUS TO THIS SECTOR. I'M PUTTING IT ON THE VIEWER.
FAITH! NO WONDER YE DINNA RECOGNIZE IT, MR. SAAVIK -- 'TIS THE ENERGY WAVE CAUSED BY A WORMHOLE!
"WORMHOLE," SCOTTY?
AYE! 'TIS KIND OF A "HOLE IN SPACE," DOCTOR, CREATED BY TH' IMBALANCE BETWEEN MATTER AND ANTI-MATTER!
IF THE KLINGONS HAVE FOUND A WAY TO STABILIZE TH' WORMHOLE FLUX, THEY COULD ENTER AN' EXIT AT WILL -- AN' WE'D BE UNABLE TO TELL!
CAN YOU TAKE THE ENTERPRISE INSIDE THIS "WORMHOLE FLUX," MR. SCOTT?
NO, SIR, NOT AT OUR PRESENT POWER LEVEL. HOWEVER, I COULD RIG THE TRANSPORTER T' SEND A FEW CREWMEN THERE... AN' MAYBE A SHUTTLECRAFT, ON ITS OWN POWER!
PROCEED, SCOTTY...
18

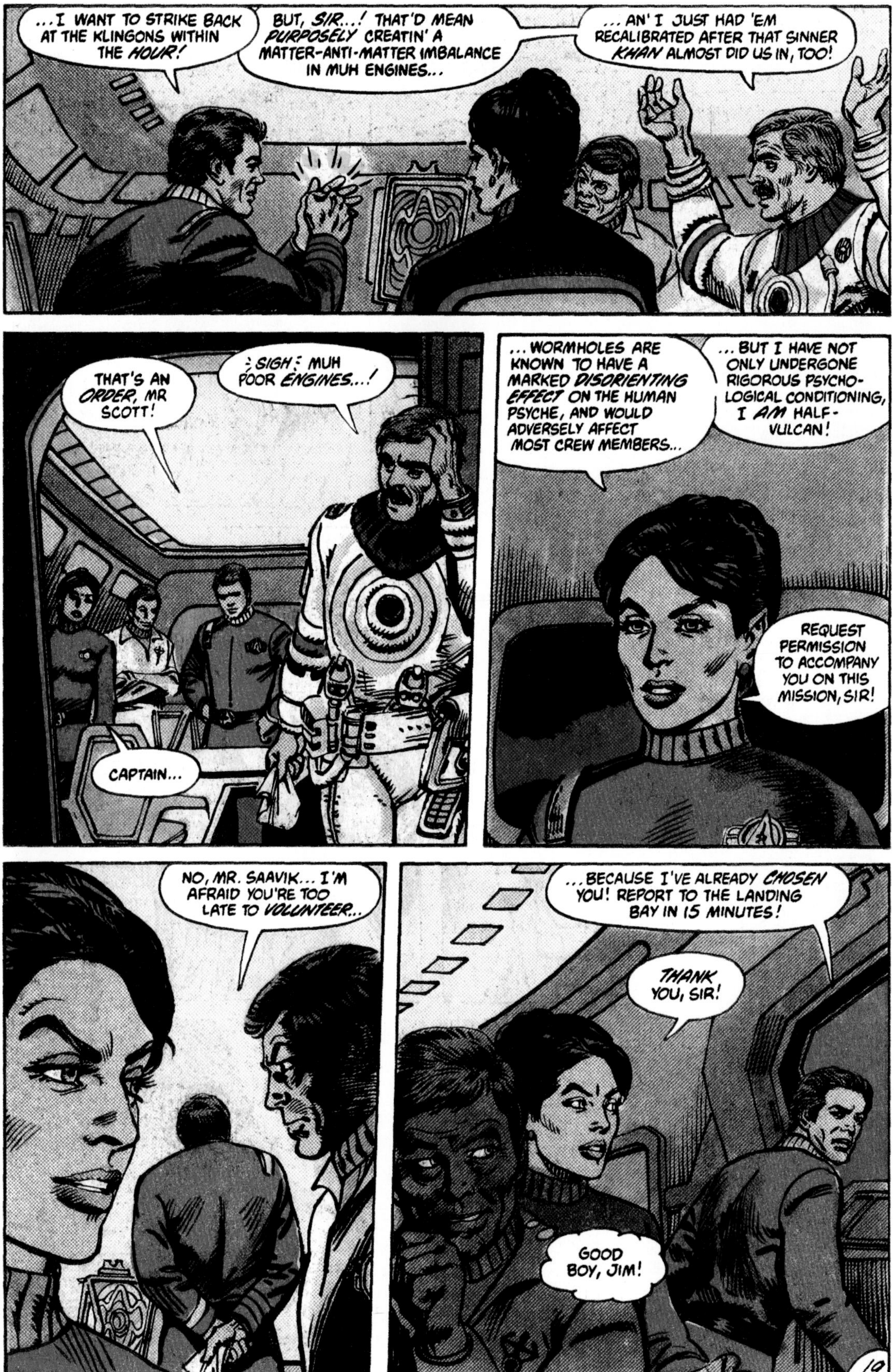
...I WANT TO STRIKE BACK AT THE KLINGONS WITHIN THE HOUR!
BUT, SIR...! THAT'D MEAN PURPOSELY CREATIN' A MATTER-ANTI-MATTER IMBALANCE IN MUH ENGINES...
...AN' I JUST HAD 'EM RECALIBRATED AFTER THAT SINNER KHAN ALMOST DID US IN, TOO!
THAT'S AN ORDER, MR SCOTT!
SIGH MUH POOR ENGINES...!
CAPTAIN...
...WORMHOLES ARE KNOWN TO HAVE A MARKED DISORIENTING EFFECT ON THE HUMAN PSYCHE, AND WOULD ADVERSELY AFFECT MOST CREW MEMBERS...
...BUT I HAVE NOT ONLY UNDERGONE RIGOROUS PSYCHO-LOGICAL CONDITIONING, I AM HALF-VULCAN!
REQUEST PERMISSION TO ACCOMPANY YOU ON THIS MISSION, SIR!
NO, MR. SAAVIK... I'M AFRAID YOU'RE TOO LATE TO VOLUNTEER...
...BECAUSE I'VE ALREADY CHOSEN YOU! REPORT TO THE LANDING BAY IN 15 MINUTES!
THANK YOU, SIR!
GOOD BOY, JIM!
19

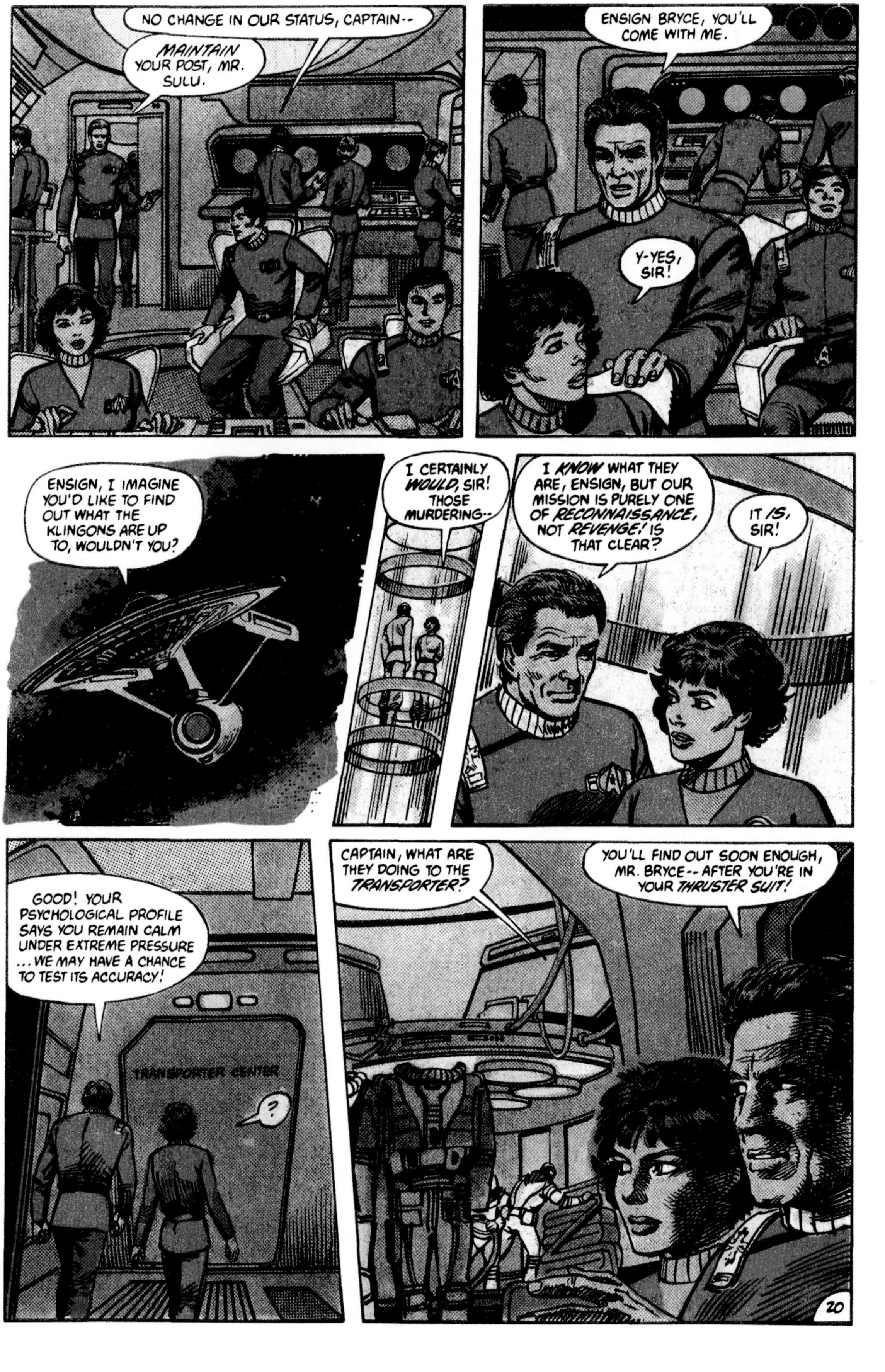
NO CHANGE IN OUR STATUS, CAPTAIN--
MAINTAIN YOUR POST, MR. SULU.
ENSIGN BRYCE, YOU'LL COME WITH ME.
Y-YES, SIR!
ENSIGN, I IMAGINE YOU'D LIKE TO FIND OUT WHAT THE KLINGONS ARE UP TO, WOULDN'T YOU?
I CERTAINLY WOULD, SIR! THOSE MURDERING--
I KNOW WHAT THEY ARE, ENSIGN, BUT OUR MISSION IS PURELY ONE OF RECONNAISSANCE, NOT REVENGE! IS THAT CLEAR?
IT IS, SIR!
GOOD! YOUR PSYCHOLOGICAL PROFILE SAYS YOU REMAIN CALM UNDER EXTREME PRESSURE ...WE MAY HAVE A CHANCE TO TEST ITS ACCURACY!
TRANSPORTER CENTER
?
CAPTAIN, WHAT ARE THEY DOING TO THE TRANSPORTER?
YOU'LL FIND OUT SOON ENOUGH, MR. BRYCE-- AFTER YOU'RE IN YOUR THRUSTER SUIT!
20

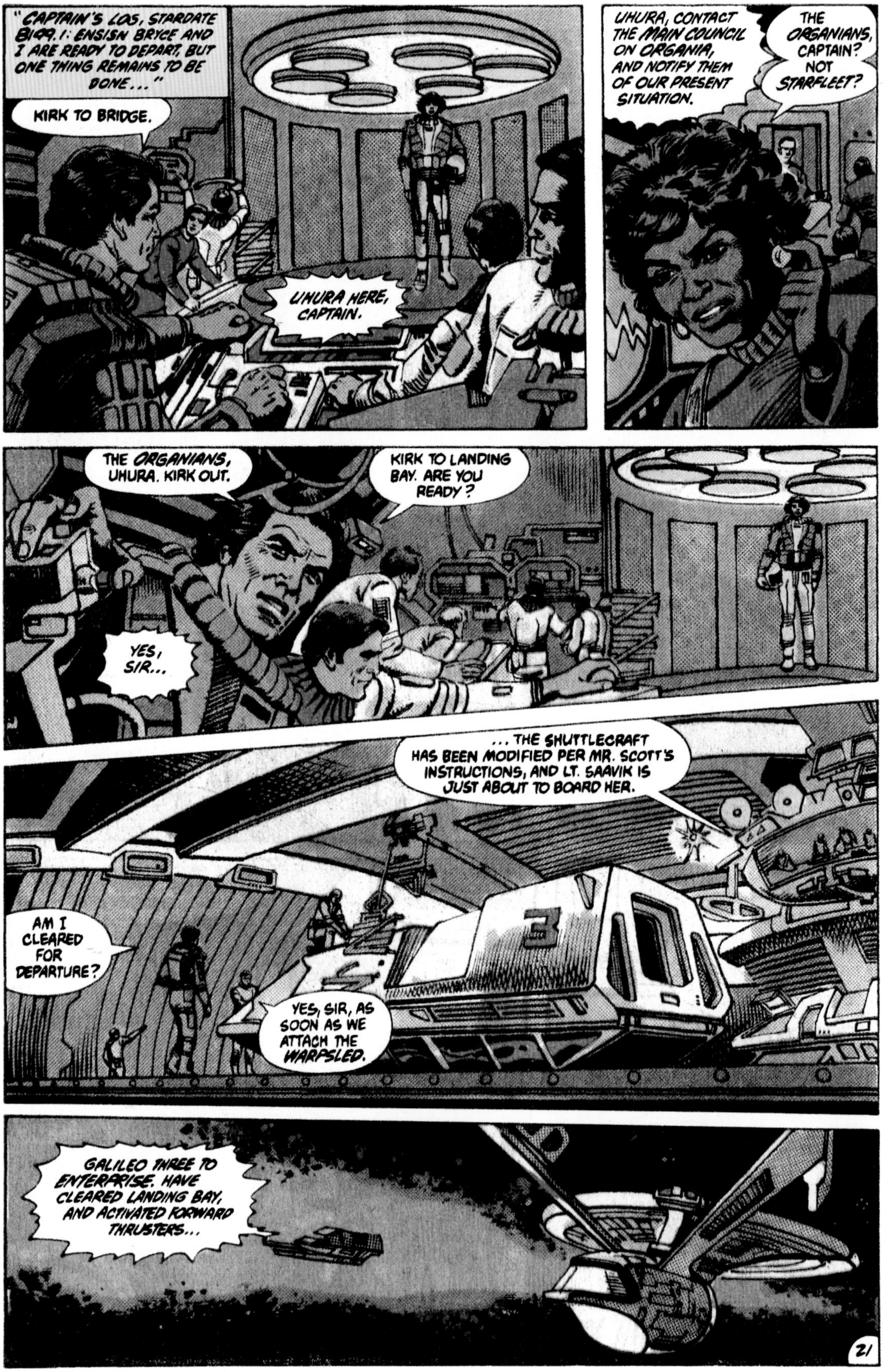
"CAPTAIN'S LOG, STARDATE 8149.1: ENSIGN BRYCE AND I ARE READY TO DEPART, BUT ONE THING REMAINS TO BE DONE..."
KIRK TO BRIDGE.
UHURA HERE, CAPTAIN.
UHURA, CONTACT THE MAIN COUNCIL ON ORGANIA, AND NOTIFY THEM OF OUR PRESENT SITUATION.
THE ORGANIANS, CAPTAIN? NOT STARFLEET?
THE ORGANIANS, UHURA. KIRK OUT.
KIRK TO LANDING BAY. ARE YOU READY?
YES, SIR...
...THE SHUTTLECRAFT HAS BEEN MODIFIED PER MR. SCOTT'S INSTRUCTIONS, AND LT. SAAVIK IS JUST ABOUT TO BOARD HER.
AM I CLEARED FOR DEPARTURE?
YES, SIR, AS SOON AS WE ATTACH THE WARPSLED.
3
GALILEO THREE TO ENTERPRISE. HAVE CLEARED LANDING BAY, AND ACTIVATED FORWARD THRUSTERS...
21

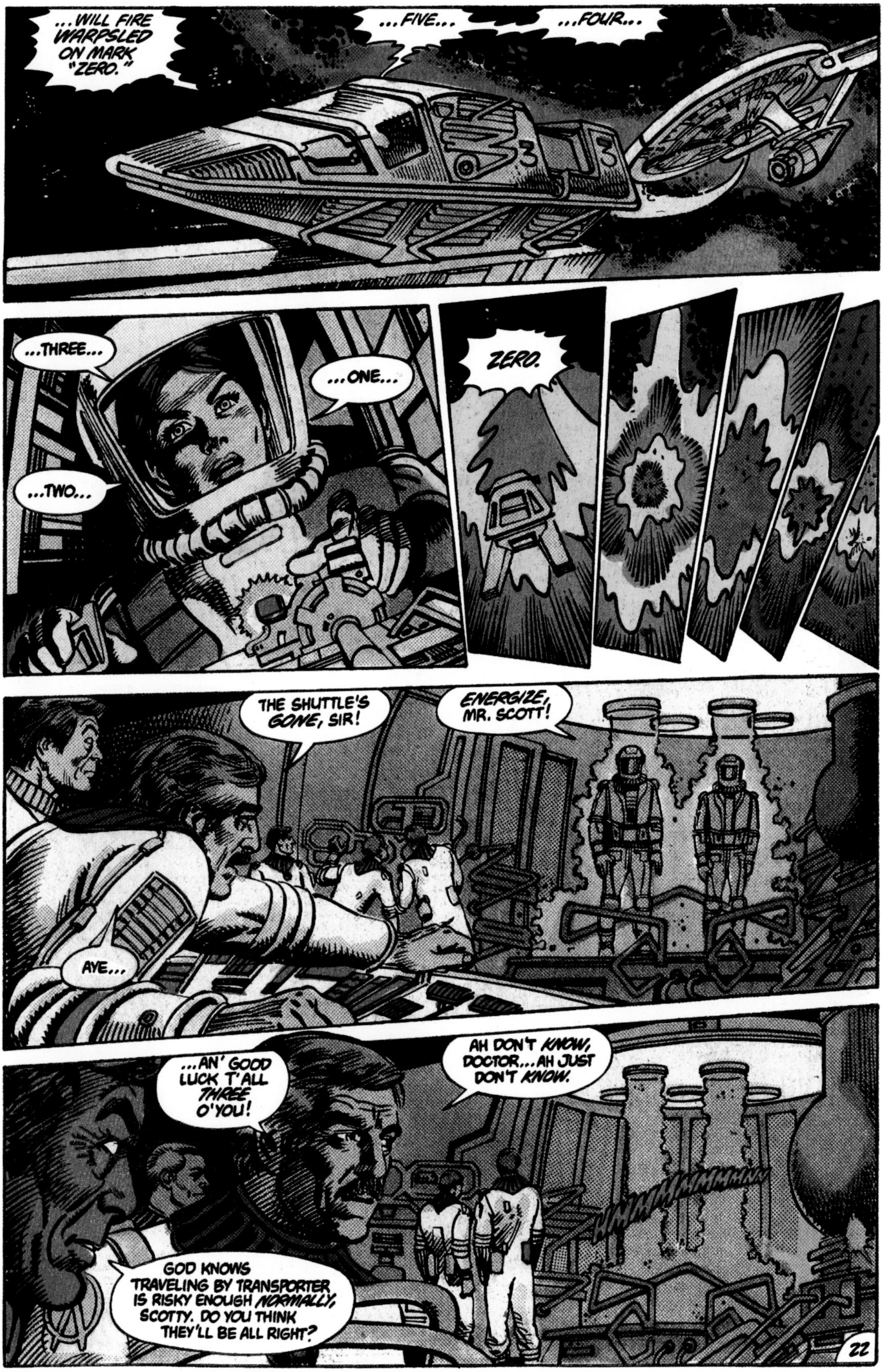
...WILL FIRE WARPSLED ON MARK "ZERO."
...FIVE...
...FOUR...
...THREE...
...TWO...
...ONE...
ZERO.
THE SHUTTLE'S GONE, SIR!
ENERGIZE, MR. SCOTT!
AYE...
...AN' GOOD LUCK T'ALL THREE O'YOU!
AH DON'T KNOW, DOCTOR...AH JUST DON'T KNOW.
GOD KNOWS TRAVELING BY TRANSPORTER IS RISKY ENOUGH NORMALLY, SCOTTY. DO YOU THINK THEY'LL BE ALL RIGHT?
22

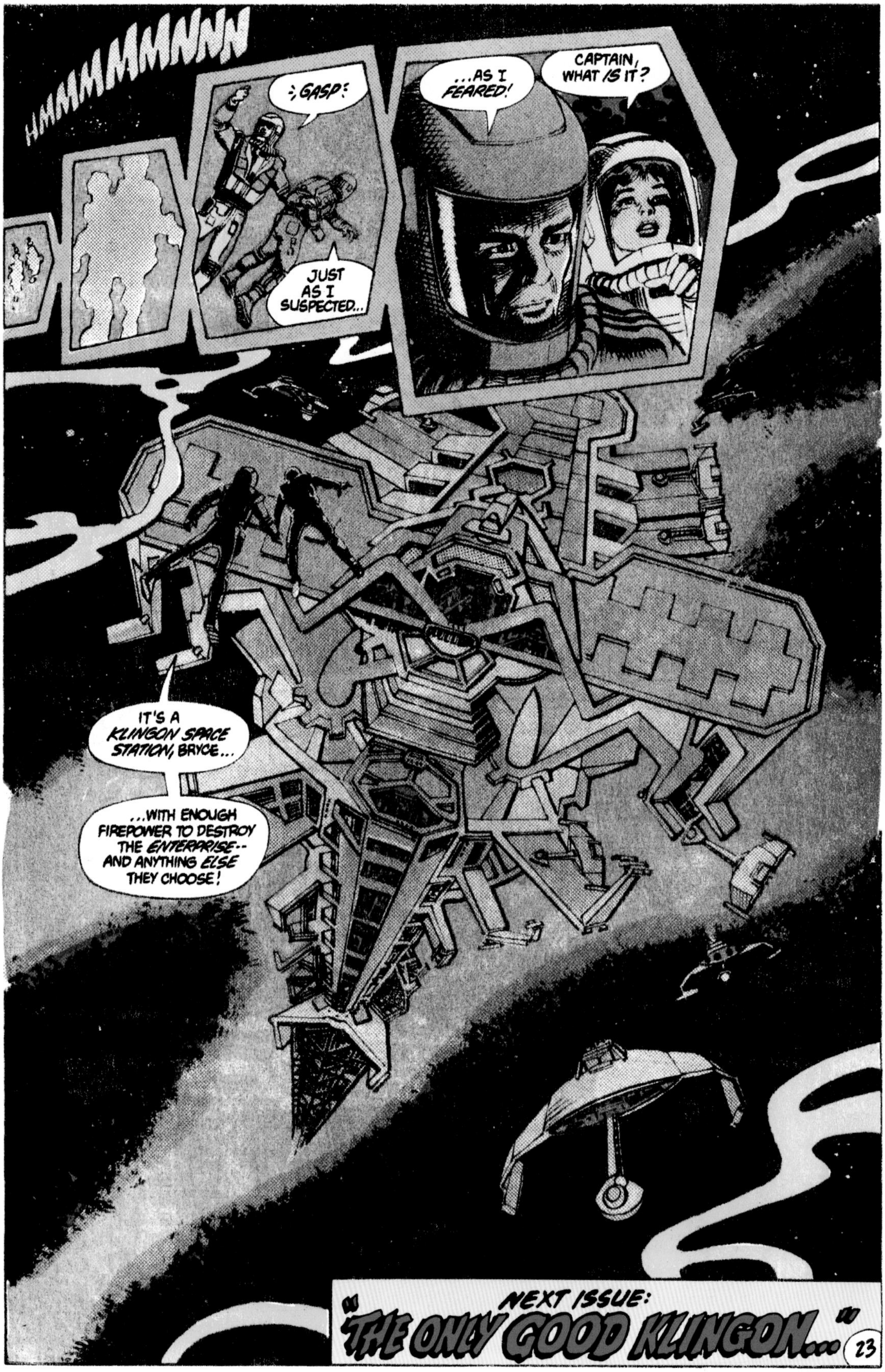
HMMMMMMNNN
:GASP:
JUST AS I SUSPECTED...
...AS I FEARED!
CAPTAIN, WHAT IS IT?
IT'S A KLINGON SPACE STATION, BRYCE...
...WITH ENOUGH FIREPOWER TO DESTROY THE ENTERPRISE-- AND ANYTHING ELSE THEY CHOOSE!
NEXT ISSUE:
"THE ONLY GOOD KLINGON..."
23

STAR TREK™

Based on the series created by **Gene Roddenberry**

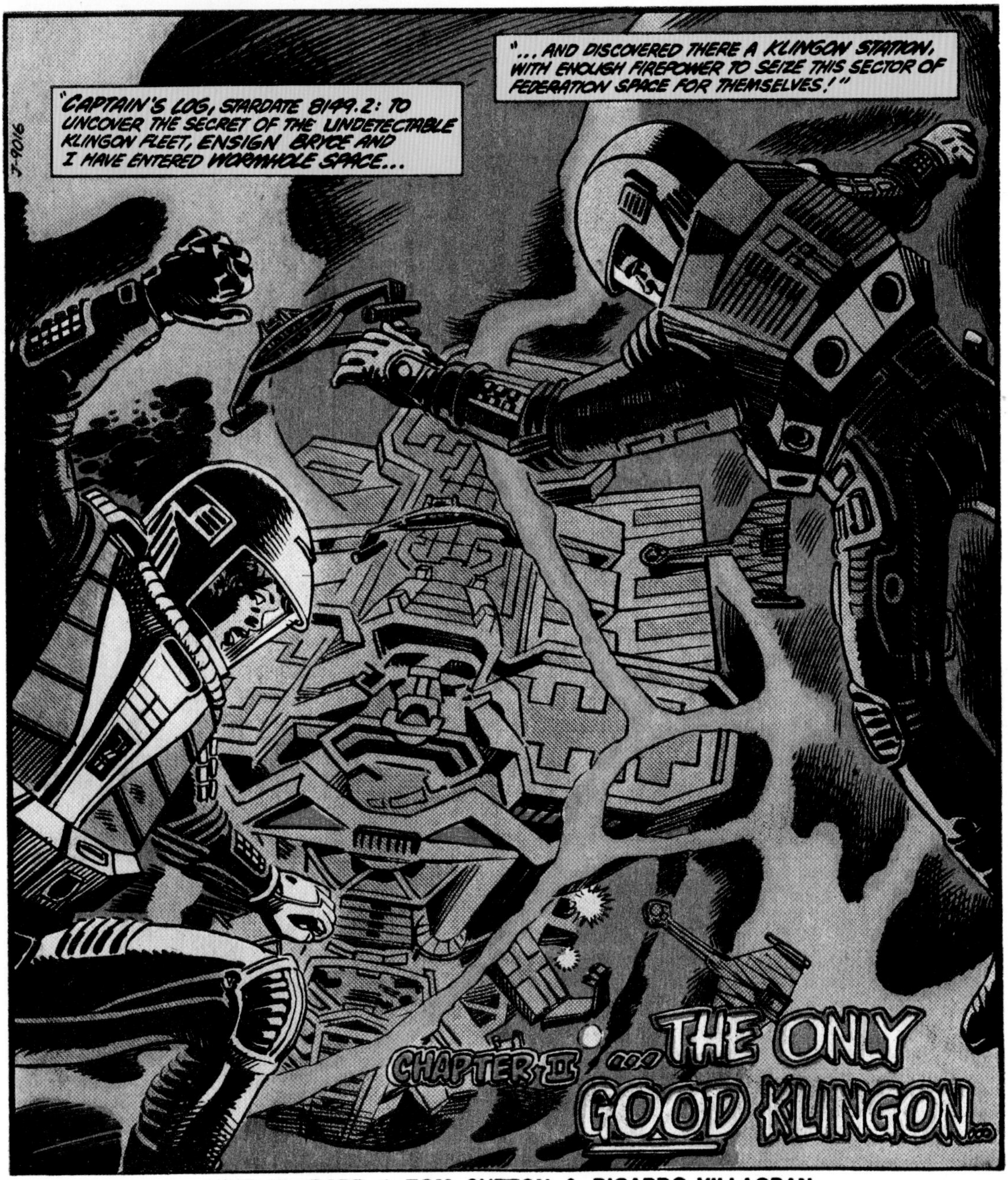
"CAPTAIN'S LOG, STARDATE 8149.2: TO UNCOVER THE SECRET OF THE UNDETECTABLE KLINGON FLEET, ENSIGN BRYCE AND I HAVE ENTERED WORMHOLE SPACE...
"...AND DISCOVERED THERE A KLINGON STATION, WITH ENOUGH FIREPOWER TO SEIZE THIS SECTOR OF FEDERATION SPACE FOR THEMSELVES!"
J-9016
CHAPTER II ...THE ONLY GOOD KLINGON...

MIKE W. BARR * **TOM SUTTON & RICARDO VILLAGRAN**
Writer — Artists

JOHN COSTANZA * **MICHELE WOLFMAN** * **MARV WOLFMAN**
Letterer — Colorist — Editor

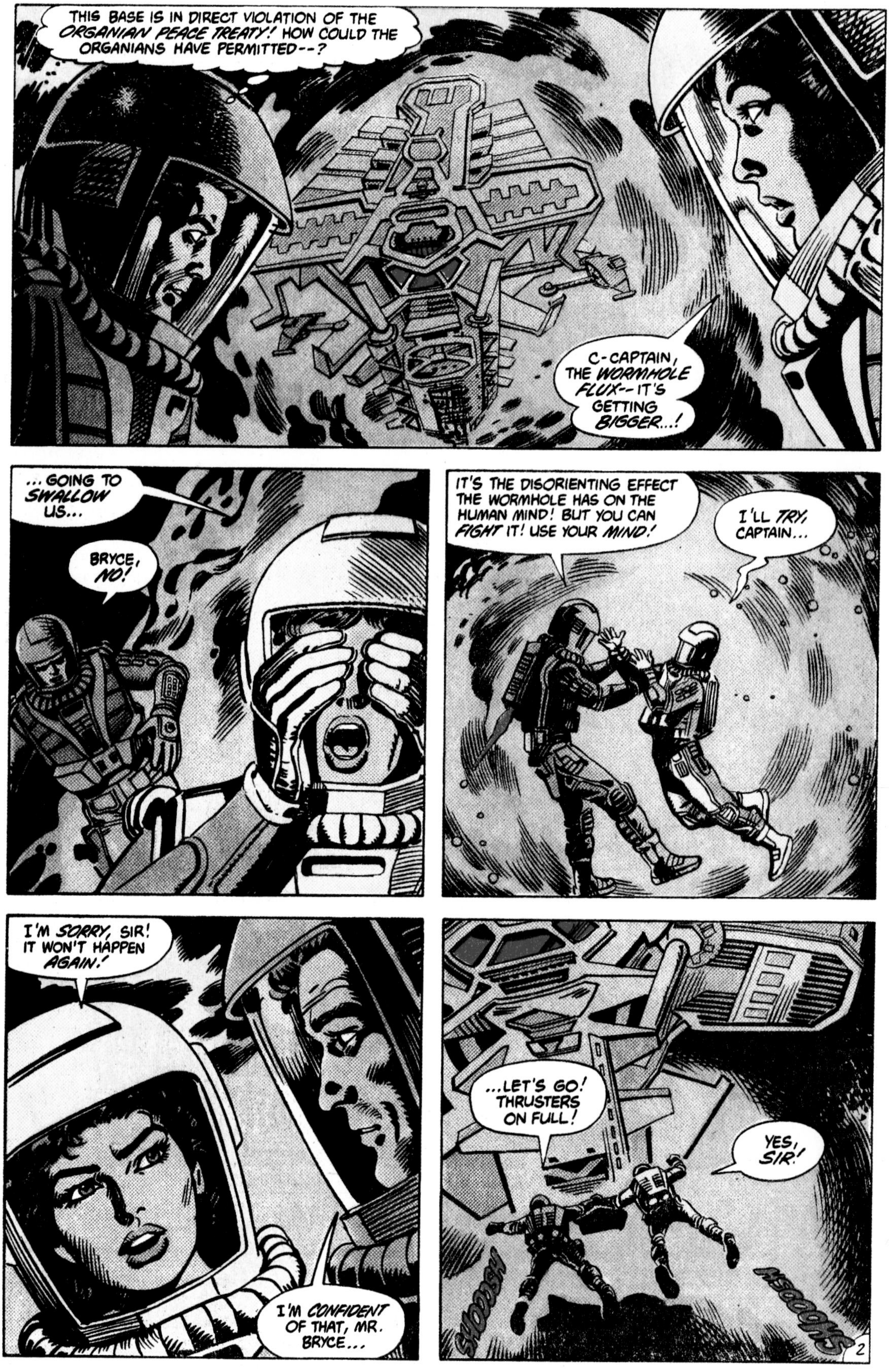

THIS BASE IS IN DIRECT VIOLATION OF THE ORGANIAN PEACE TREATY! HOW COULD THE ORGANIANS HAVE PERMITTED--?
C-CAPTAIN, THE WORMHOLE FLUX-- IT'S GETTING BIGGER...!
...GOING TO SWALLOW US...
BRYCE, NO!
IT'S THE DISORIENTING EFFECT THE WORMHOLE HAS ON THE HUMAN MIND! BUT YOU CAN FIGHT IT! USE YOUR MIND!
I'LL TRY, CAPTAIN...
I'M SORRY, SIR! IT WON'T HAPPEN AGAIN!
I'M CONFIDENT OF THAT, MR. BRYCE...
...LET'S GO! THRUSTERS ON FULL!
YES, SIR!
SHOOOSH
SHOOOOSH
2

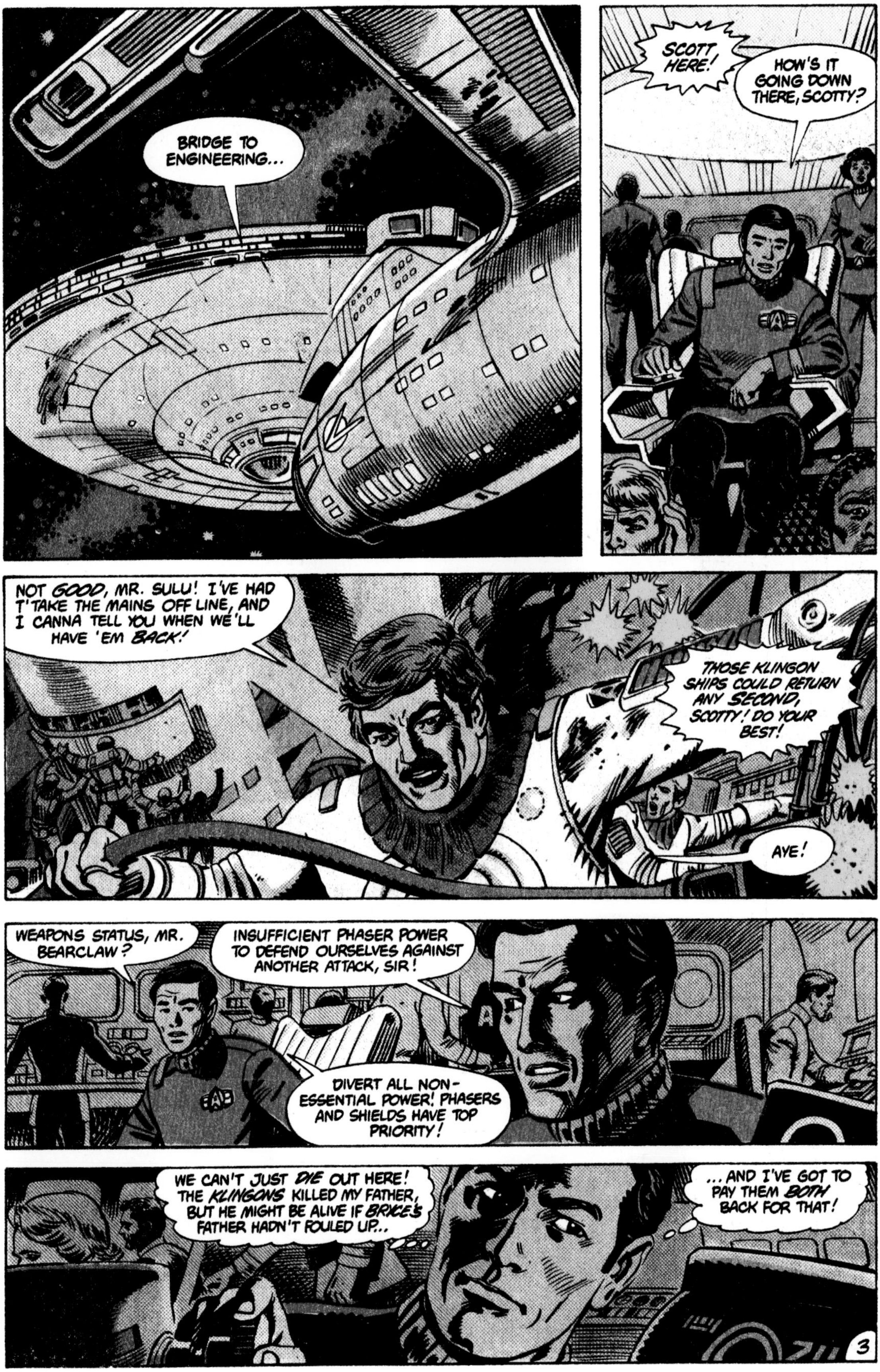
BRIDGE TO ENGINEERING...
SCOTT, HERE!
HOW'S IT GOING DOWN THERE, SCOTTY?
NOT GOOD, MR. SULU! I'VE HAD T'TAKE THE MAINS OFF LINE, AND I CANNA TELL YOU WHEN WE'LL HAVE 'EM BACK!
THOSE KLINGON SHIPS COULD RETURN ANY SECOND, SCOTTY! DO YOUR BEST!
AYE!
WEAPONS STATUS, MR. BEARCLAW?
INSUFFICIENT PHASER POWER TO DEFEND OURSELVES AGAINST ANOTHER ATTACK, SIR!
DIVERT ALL NON-ESSENTIAL POWER! PHASERS AND SHIELDS HAVE TOP PRIORITY!
WE CAN'T JUST DIE OUT HERE! THE KLINGONS KILLED MY FATHER, BUT HE MIGHT BE ALIVE IF BRYCE'S FATHER HADN'T FOULED UP...
...AND I'VE GOT TO PAY THEM BOTH BACK FOR THAT!
3

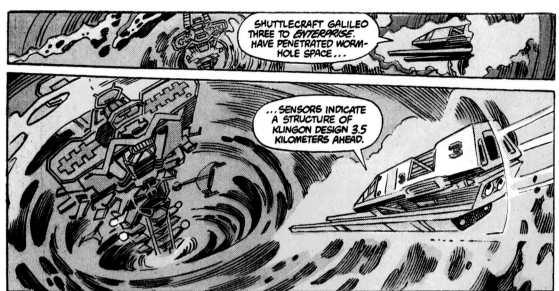

SHUTTLECRAFT *GALILEO* THREE TO *ENTERPRISE.* HAVE PENETRATED WORM- HOLE SPACE...

...SENSORS INDICATE A STRUCTURE OF KLINGON DESIGN 3.5 KILOMETERS AHEAD.

NOW BEGINNING RECONNAISSANCE SURVEY OF STRUCTURE...

...LIEUTENANT SAAVIK OUT.

WHAT'S WRONG, UHURA?

MR. SAAVIK'S *TRANSMISSION*-- SHE DIDN'T EVEN *SCRAMBLE* IT! THE KLINGONS ARE SURE TO PICK IT UP, TOO!

SHE DID THAT ON *PURPOSE,* UHURA...TO DRAW ATTENTION TO HERSELF--AND *AWAY* FROM THE CAPTAIN!

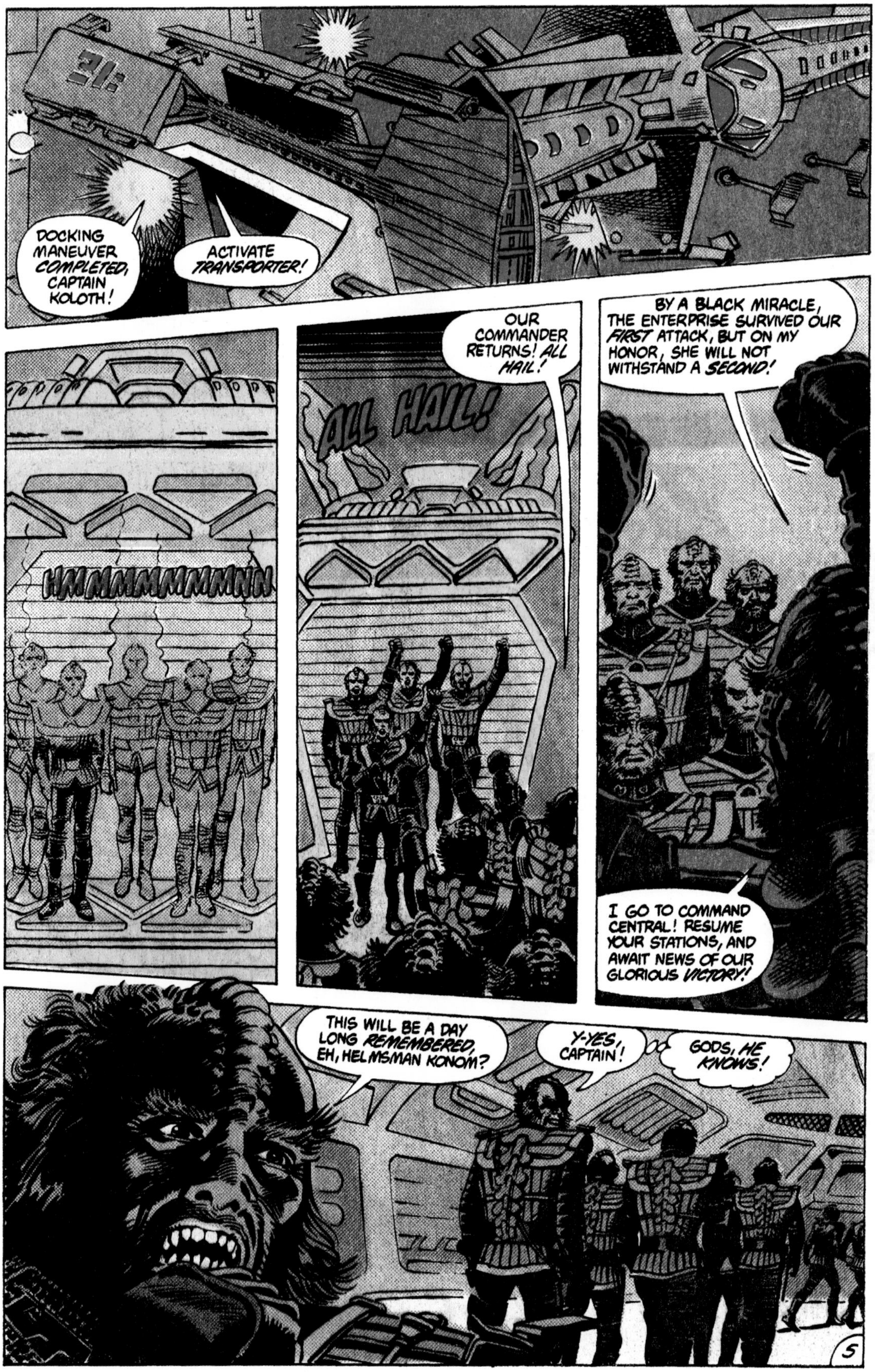
DOCKING MANEUVER COMPLETED, CAPTAIN KOLOTH!
ACTIVATE TRANSPORTER!
HMMMMMMMNN
OUR COMMANDER RETURNS! ALL HAIL!
ALL HAIL!
BY A BLACK MIRACLE, THE ENTERPRISE SURVIVED OUR FIRST ATTACK, BUT ON MY HONOR, SHE WILL NOT WITHSTAND A SECOND!
I GO TO COMMAND CENTRAL! RESUME YOUR STATIONS, AND AWAIT NEWS OF OUR GLORIOUS VICTORY!
THIS WILL BE A DAY LONG REMEMBERED, EH, HELMSMAN KONOM?
Y-YES, CAPTAIN!
GODS, HE KNOWS!
5

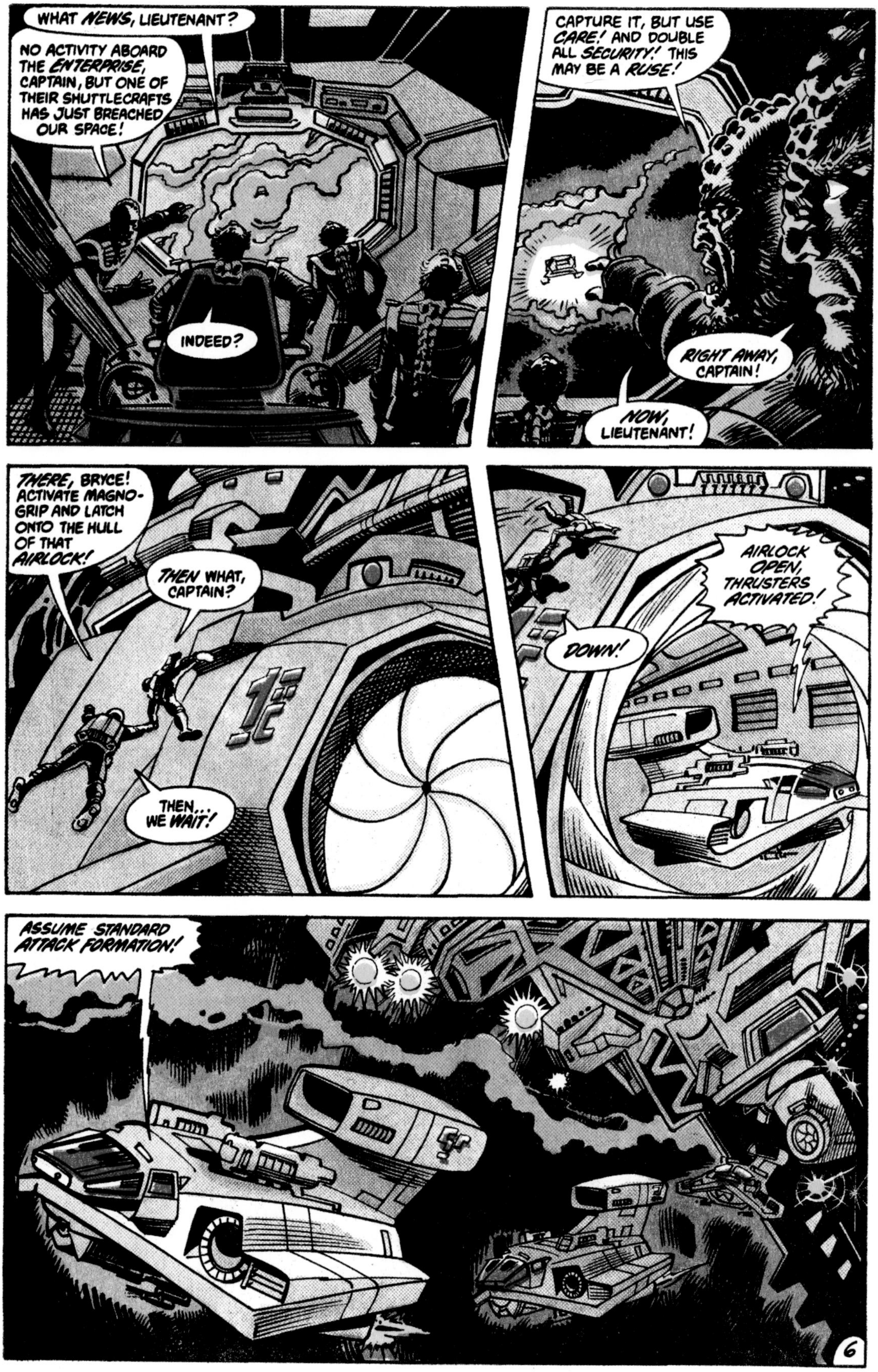
WHAT NEWS, LIEUTENANT?
NO ACTIVITY ABOARD THE ENTERPRISE, CAPTAIN, BUT ONE OF THEIR SHUTTLECRAFTS HAS JUST BREACHED OUR SPACE!
INDEED?
CAPTURE IT, BUT USE CARE! AND DOUBLE ALL SECURITY! THIS MAY BE A RUSE!
RIGHT AWAY, CAPTAIN!
NOW, LIEUTENANT!
THERE, BRYCE! ACTIVATE MAGNO-GRIP AND LATCH ONTO THE HULL OF THAT AIRLOCK!
THEN WHAT, CAPTAIN?
THEN... WE WAIT!
AIRLOCK OPEN, THRUSTERS ACTIVATED!
DOWN!
ASSUME STANDARD ATTACK FORMATION!
6

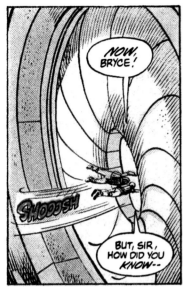

NOW, BRYCE!

SHOOSH

BUT, SIR, HOW DID YOU KNOW--

HOW DID I KNOW THIS AIRLOCK WOULD OPEN?

YES, SIR.

LET'S JUST SAY, MR. BRYCE, THAT I ARRANGED A LITTLE DIVERSION!

GOOD, THEY'VE REPRESSURIZED! PHASERS ON STUN!

YES--

GRZZZZ

AGGGGH!

CAPTAIN!

KLLNK

WHUMP

WE HAVE THEM NOW!

LOOK OUT, THAT ONE STILL--

UNNNN!

BRYCE, YOUR THRUSTER SUIT--!

MMMM

7

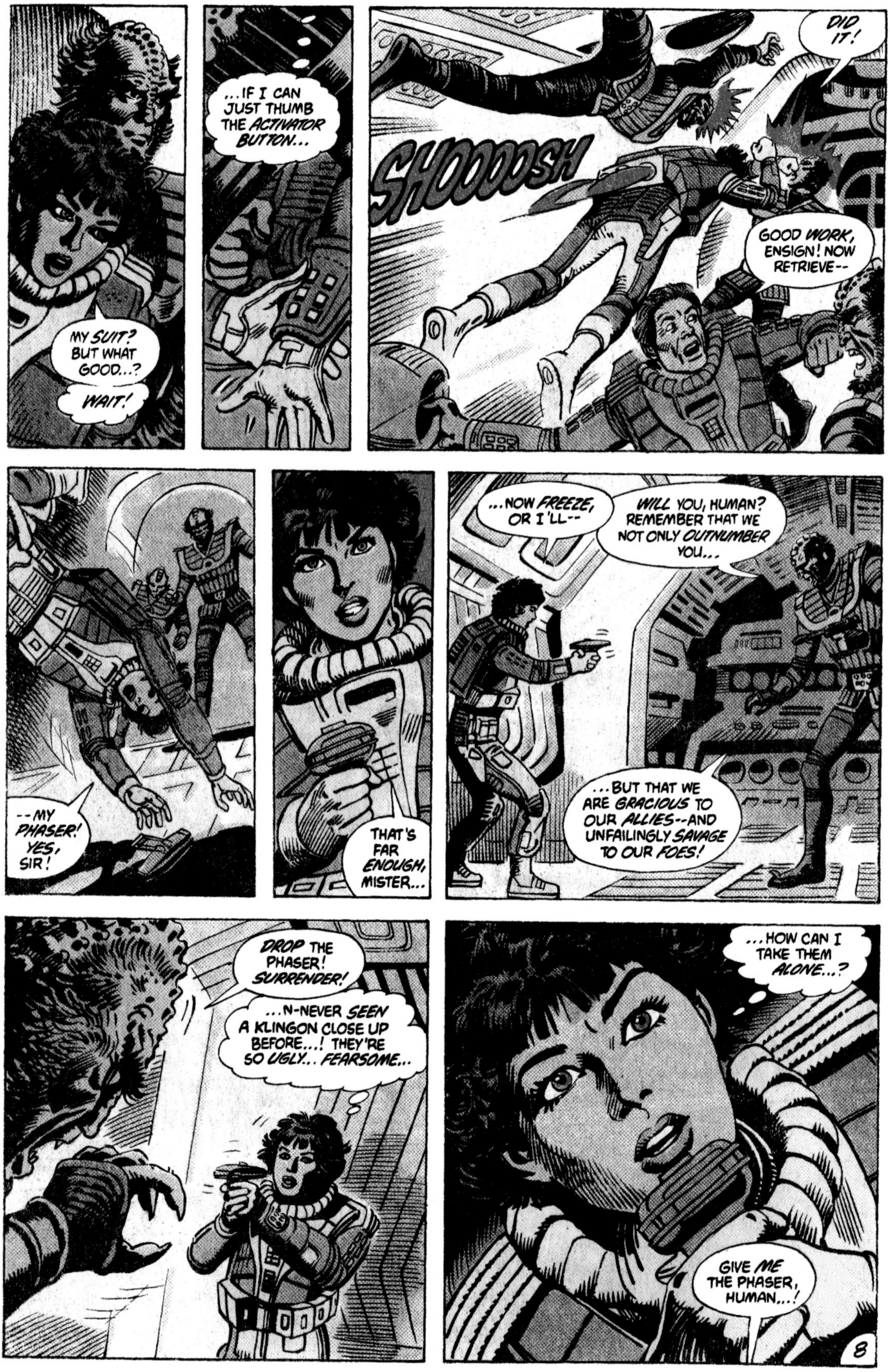

MY SUIT? BUT WHAT GOOD...?
WAIT!
...IF I CAN JUST THUMB THE ACTIVATOR BUTTON...
SHOOOOSH
DID IT!
GOOD WORK, ENSIGN! NOW RETRIEVE--
--MY PHASER! YES, SIR!
THAT'S FAR ENOUGH, MISTER...
...NOW FREEZE, OR I'LL--
WILL YOU, HUMAN? REMEMBER THAT WE NOT ONLY OUTNUMBER YOU...
...BUT THAT WE ARE GRACIOUS TO OUR ALLIES--AND UNFAILINGLY SAVAGE TO OUR FOES!
DROP THE PHASER! SURRENDER!
...N-NEVER SEEN A KLINGON CLOSE UP BEFORE...! THEY'RE SO UGLY... FEARSOME...
...HOW CAN I TAKE THEM ALONE...?
GIVE ME THE PHASER, HUMAN...!
8

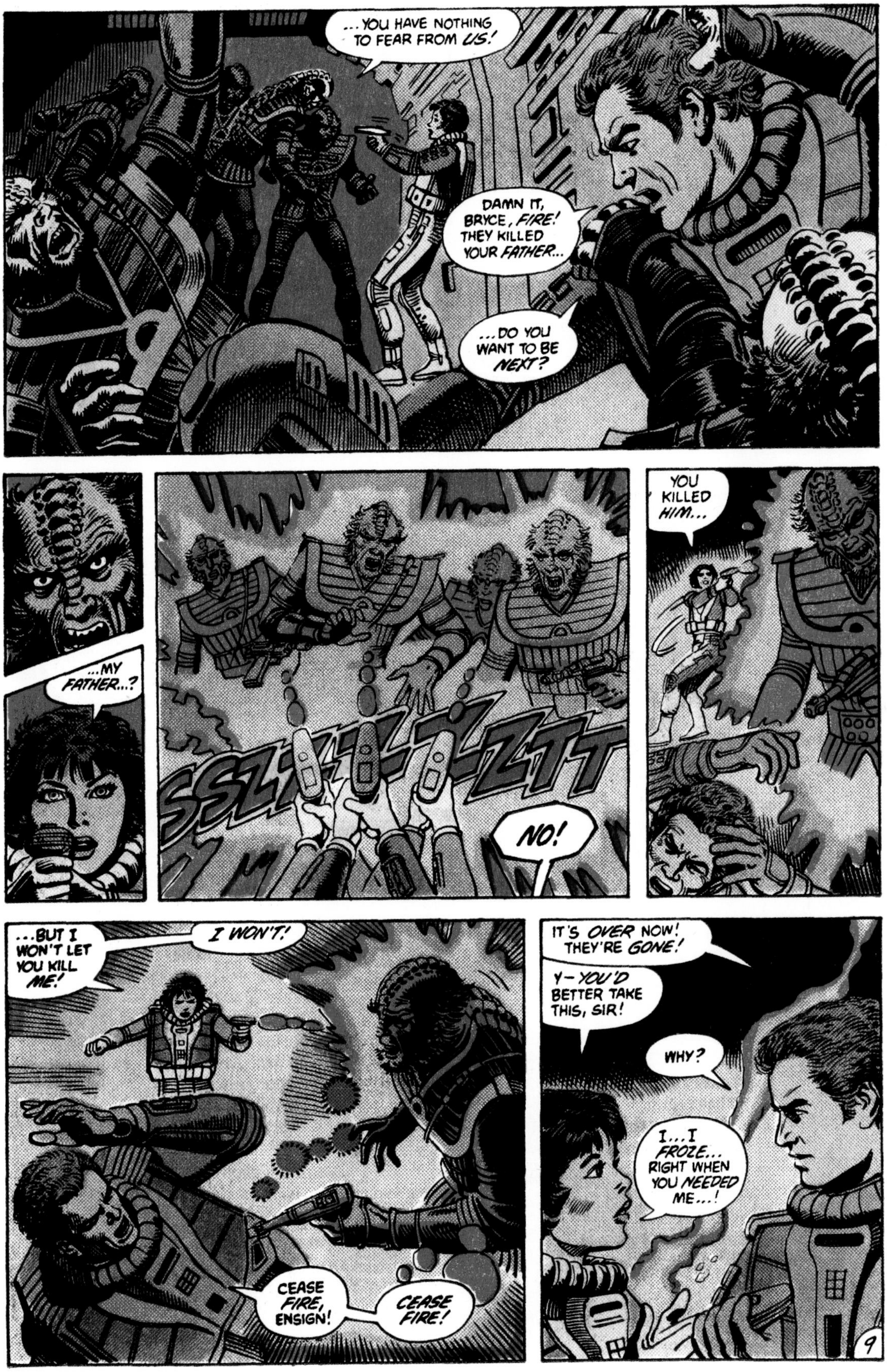
...YOU HAVE NOTHING TO FEAR FROM US!
DAMN IT, BRYCE, FIRE! THEY KILLED YOUR FATHER...
...DO YOU WANT TO BE NEXT?
...MY FATHER...?
SSZZZZZ-ZTT
NO!
YOU KILLED HIM...
I WON'T!
...BUT I WON'T LET YOU KILL ME!
CEASE FIRE, ENSIGN!
CEASE FIRE!
IT'S OVER NOW! THEY'RE GONE!
Y-YOU'D BETTER TAKE THIS, SIR!
WHY?
I...I FROZE... RIGHT WHEN YOU NEEDED ME...!
9

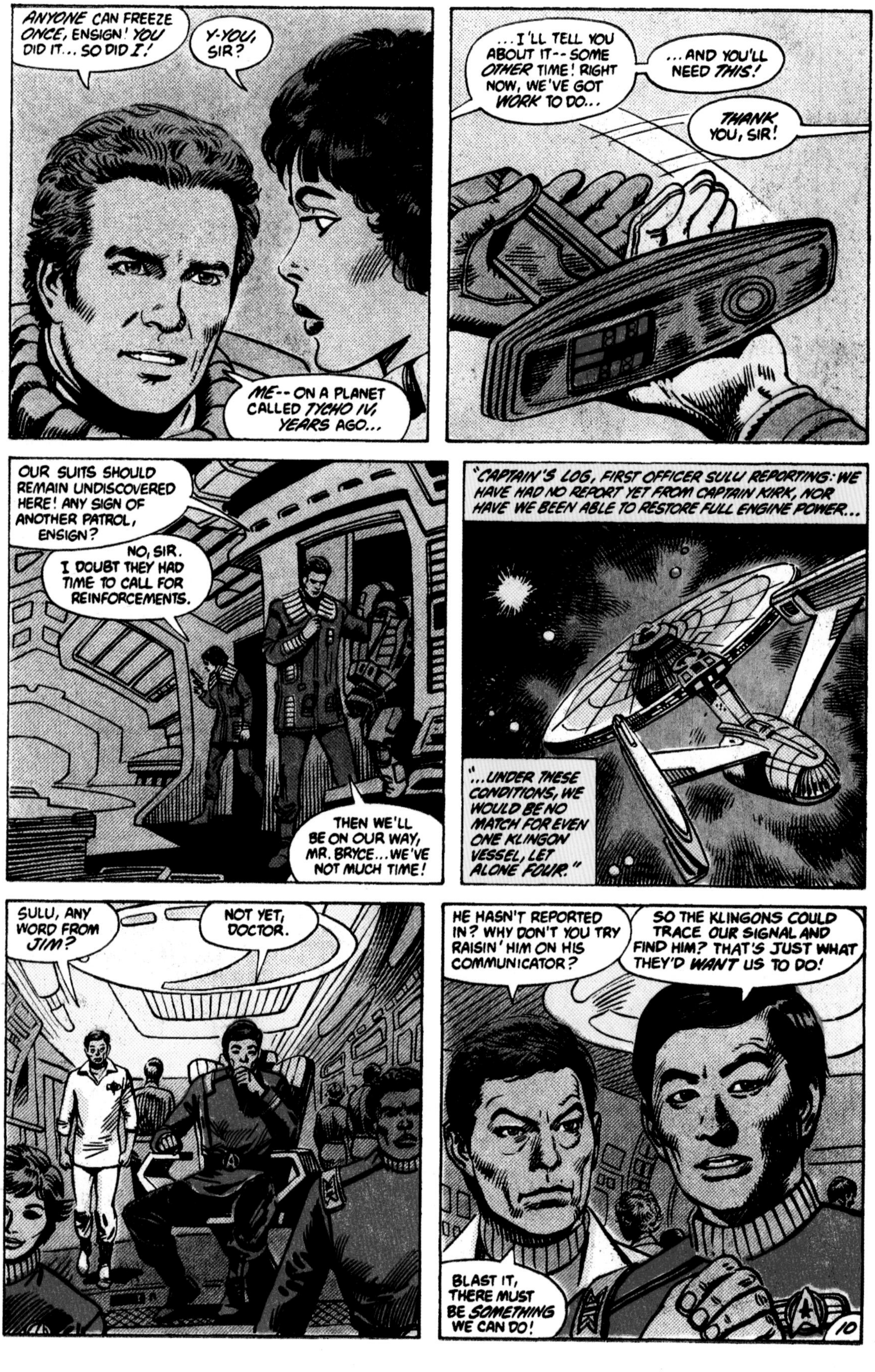
ANYONE CAN FREEZE ONCE, ENSIGN! YOU DID IT... SO DID I!
Y-YOU, SIR?
ME-- ON A PLANET CALLED TYCHO IV, YEARS AGO...
...I'LL TELL YOU ABOUT IT-- SOME OTHER TIME! RIGHT NOW, WE'VE GOT WORK TO DO...
...AND YOU'LL NEED THIS!
THANK YOU, SIR!
OUR SUITS SHOULD REMAIN UNDISCOVERED HERE! ANY SIGN OF ANOTHER PATROL, ENSIGN?
NO, SIR. I DOUBT THEY HAD TIME TO CALL FOR REINFORCEMENTS.
THEN WE'LL BE ON OUR WAY, MR. BRYCE... WE'VE NOT MUCH TIME!
"CAPTAIN'S LOG, FIRST OFFICER SULU REPORTING: WE HAVE HAD NO REPORT YET FROM CAPTAIN KIRK, NOR HAVE WE BEEN ABLE TO RESTORE FULL ENGINE POWER...
"...UNDER THESE CONDITIONS, WE WOULD BE NO MATCH FOR EVEN ONE KLINGON VESSEL, LET ALONE FOUR."
SULU, ANY WORD FROM JIM?
NOT YET, DOCTOR.
HE HASN'T REPORTED IN? WHY DON'T YOU TRY RAISIN' HIM ON HIS COMMUNICATOR?
SO THE KLINGONS COULD TRACE OUR SIGNAL AND FIND HIM? THAT'S JUST WHAT THEY'D WANT US TO DO!
BLAST IT, THERE MUST BE SOMETHING WE CAN DO!
10

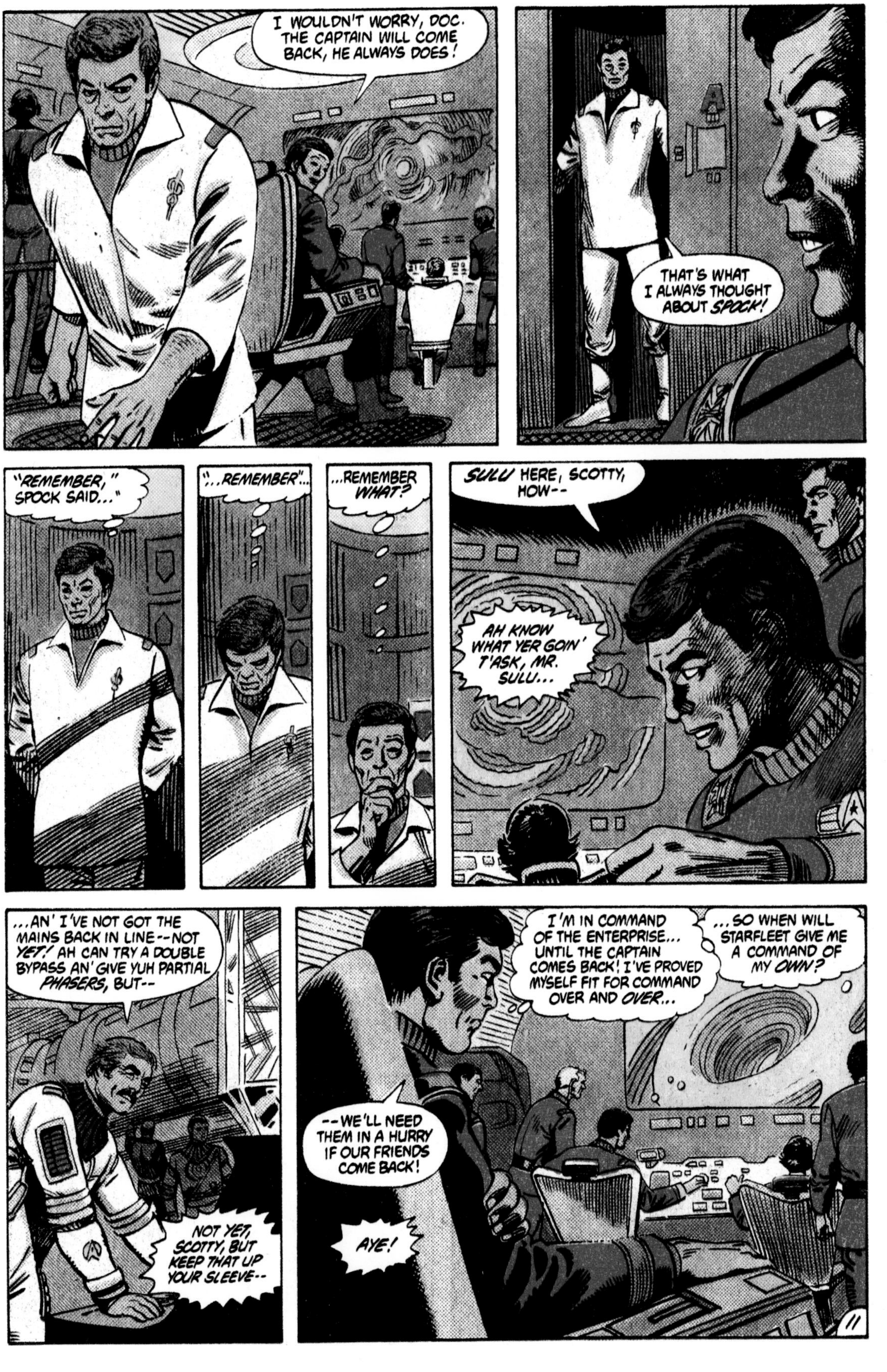
I WOULDN'T WORRY, DOC. THE CAPTAIN WILL COME BACK, HE ALWAYS DOES!
THAT'S WHAT I ALWAYS THOUGHT ABOUT SPOCK!
"REMEMBER," SPOCK SAID..."
"...REMEMBER"...
...REMEMBER WHAT?
SULU HERE, SCOTTY, HOW--
AH KNOW WHAT YER GOIN' T'ASK, MR. SULU...
...AN' I'VE NOT GOT THE MAINS BACK IN LINE--NOT YET! AH CAN TRY A DOUBLE BYPASS AN' GIVE YUH PARTIAL PHASERS, BUT--
NOT YET, SCOTTY, BUT KEEP THAT UP YOUR SLEEVE--
--WE'LL NEED THEM IN A HURRY IF OUR FRIENDS COME BACK!
AYE!
I'M IN COMMAND OF THE ENTERPRISE... UNTIL THE CAPTAIN COMES BACK! I'VE PROVED MYSELF FIT FOR COMMAND OVER AND OVER...
...SO WHEN WILL STARFLEET GIVE ME A COMMAND OF MY OWN?
11

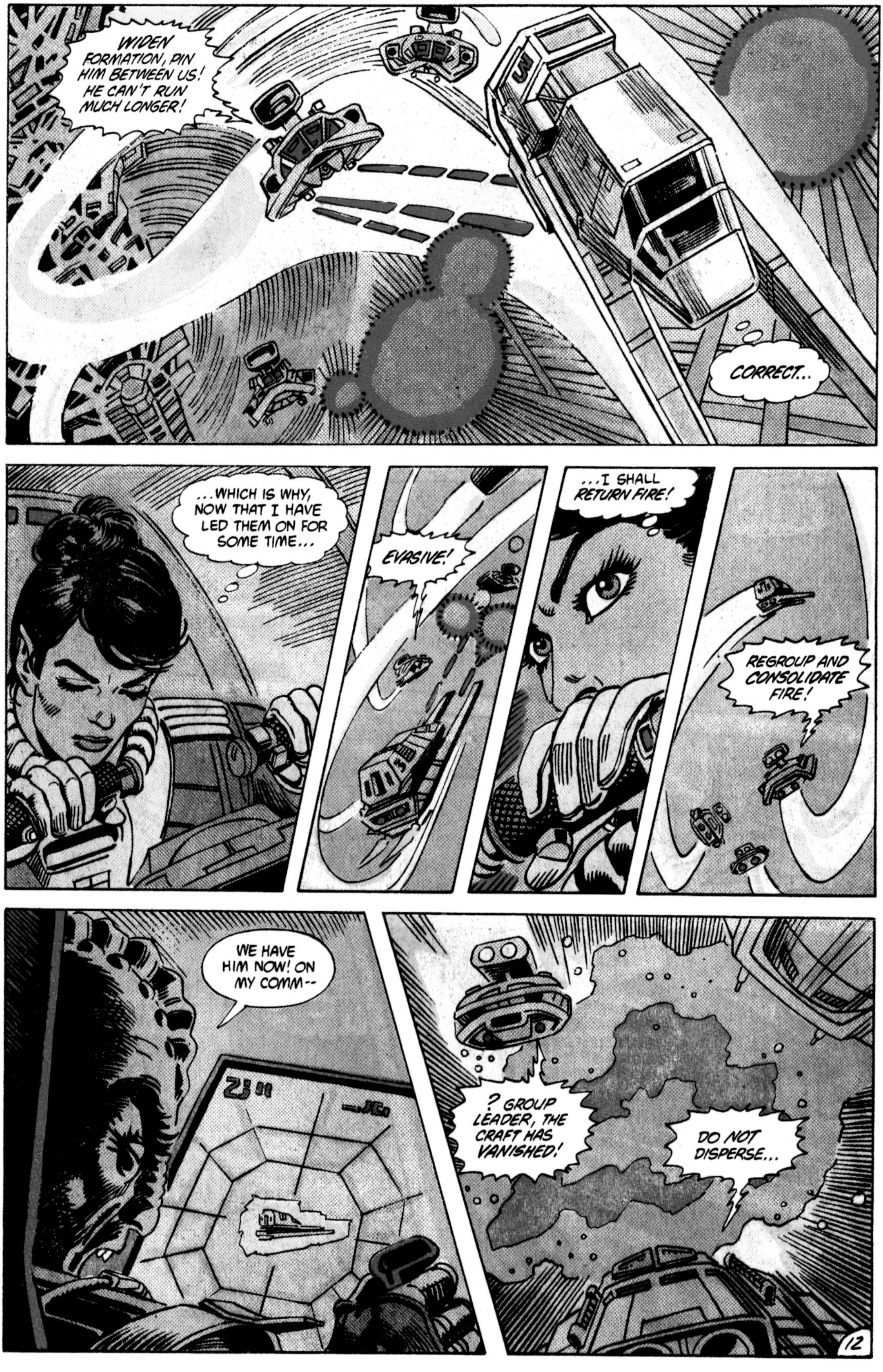
WIDEN FORMATION, PIN HIM BETWEEN US! HE CAN'T RUN MUCH LONGER!
CORRECT...
...WHICH IS WHY, NOW THAT I HAVE LED THEM ON FOR SOME TIME...
EVASIVE!
...I SHALL RETURN FIRE!
REGROUP AND CONSOLIDATE FIRE!
WE HAVE HIM NOW! ON MY COMM--
? GROUP LEADER, THE CRAFT HAS VANISHED!
DO NOT DISPERSE...
12

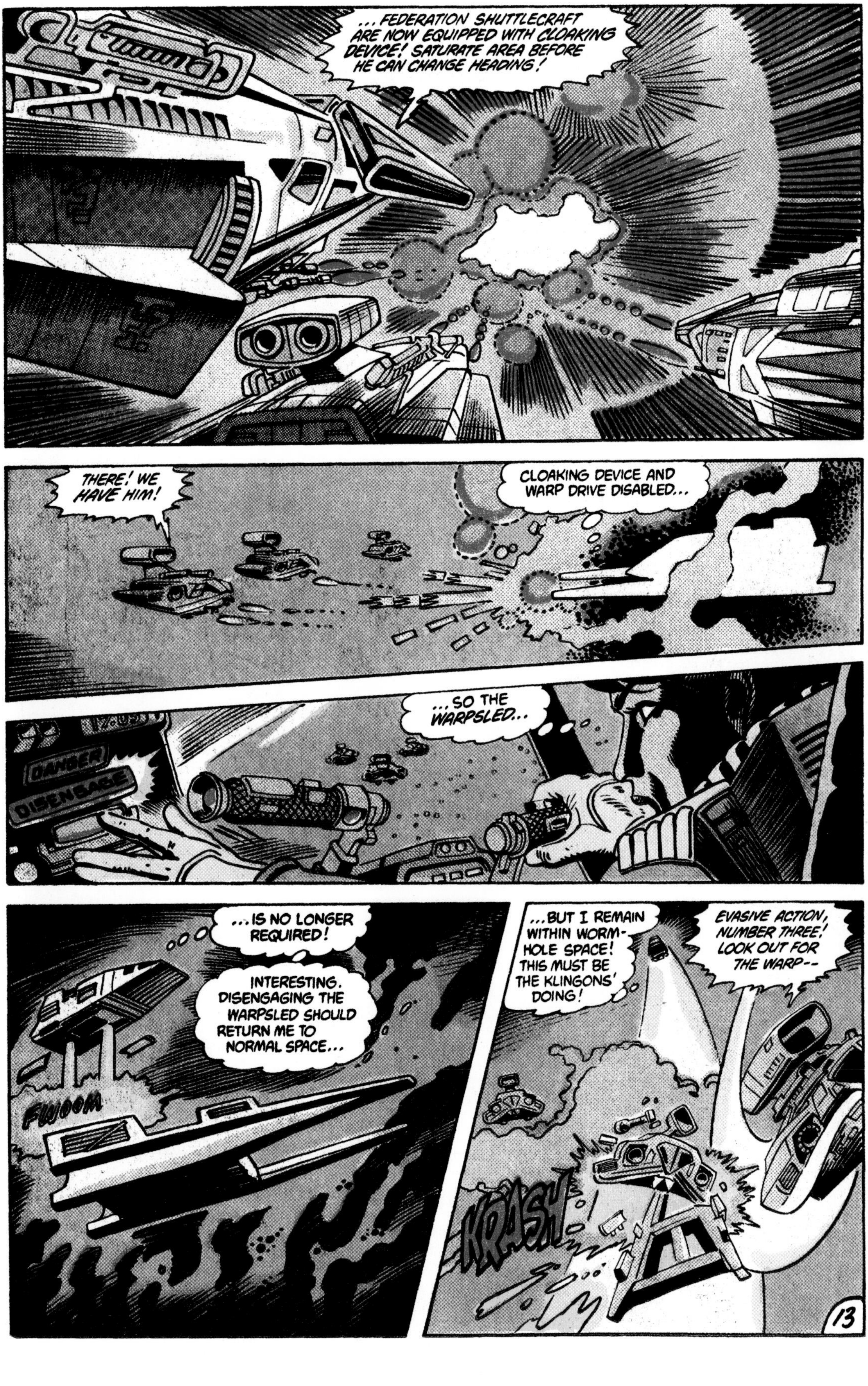
...FEDERATION SHUTTLECRAFT ARE NOW EQUIPPED WITH CLOAKING DEVICE! SATURATE AREA BEFORE HE CAN CHANGE HEADING!
THERE! WE HAVE HIM!
CLOAKING DEVICE AND WARP DRIVE DISABLED...
DANGER
DISENGAGE
...SO THE WARPSLED...
...IS NO LONGER REQUIRED!
INTERESTING. DISENGAGING THE WARPSLED SHOULD RETURN ME TO NORMAL SPACE...
FWOOM
...BUT I REMAIN WITHIN WORM-HOLE SPACE! THIS MUST BE THE KLINGONS' DOING!
EVASIVE ACTION, NUMBER THREE! LOOK OUT FOR THE WARP--
KRASH
13

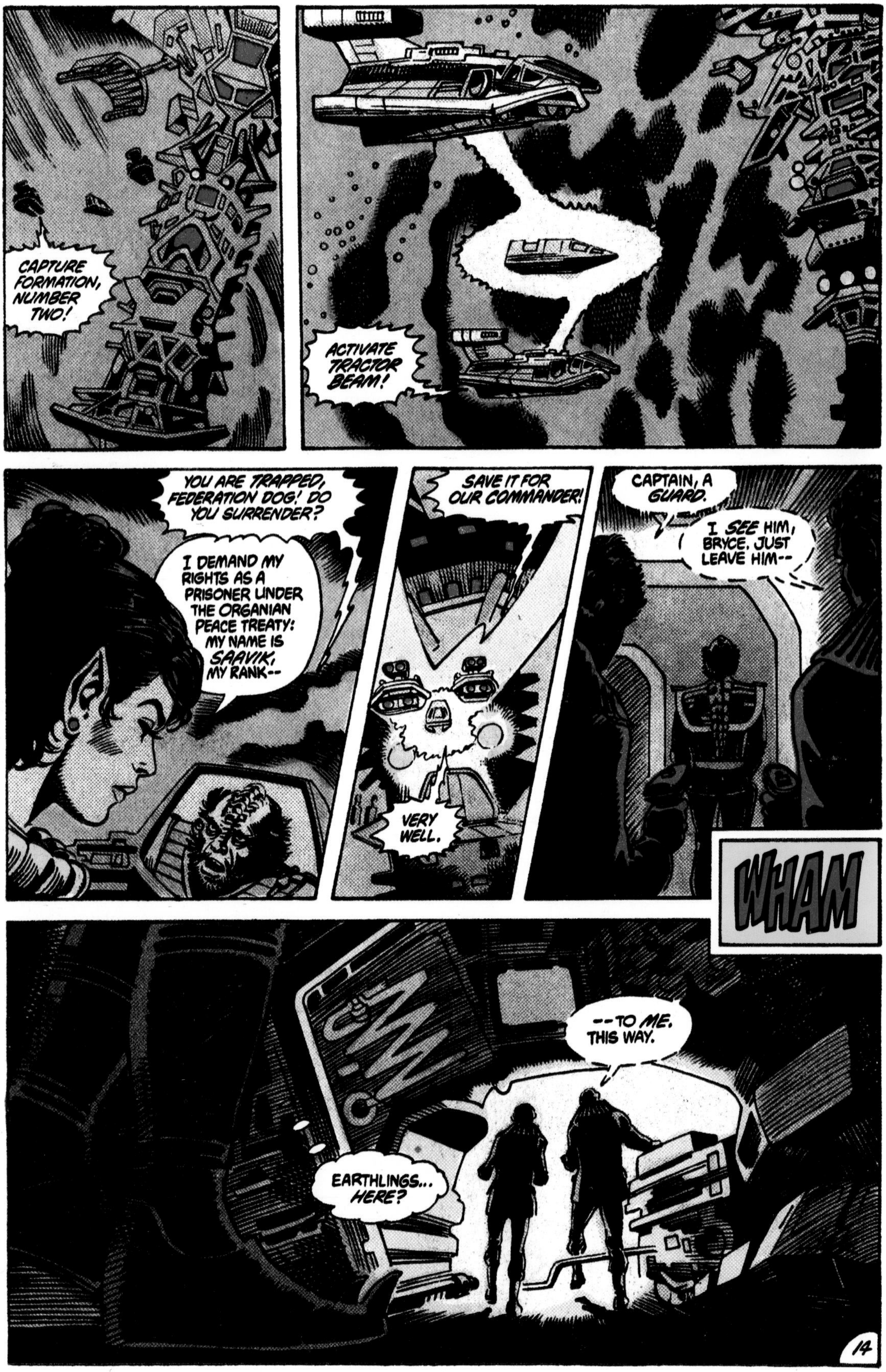
CAPTURE FORMATION, NUMBER TWO!
ACTIVATE TRACTOR BEAM!
YOU ARE TRAPPED, FEDERATION DOG! DO YOU SURRENDER?
I DEMAND MY RIGHTS AS A PRISONER UNDER THE ORGANIAN PEACE TREATY: MY NAME IS SAAVIK, MY RANK--
SAVE IT FOR OUR COMMANDER!
VERY WELL.
CAPTAIN, A GUARD.
I SEE HIM, BRYCE. JUST LEAVE HIM--
WHAM
--TO ME. THIS WAY.
EARTHLINGS... HERE?
14

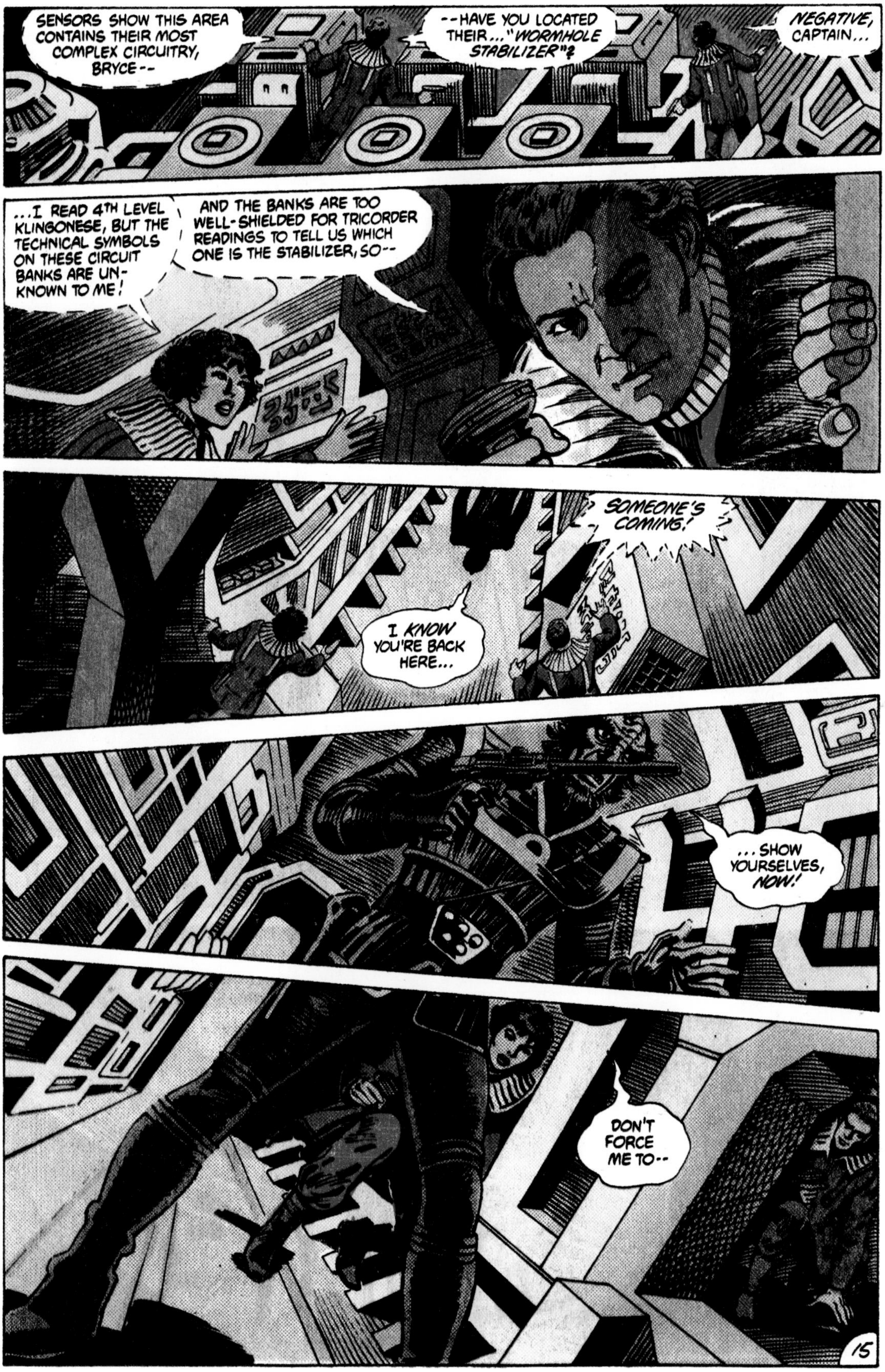
SENSORS SHOW THIS AREA CONTAINS THEIR MOST COMPLEX CIRCUITRY, BRYCE--
--HAVE YOU LOCATED THEIR..."WORMHOLE STABILIZER"?
NEGATIVE, CAPTAIN...
...I READ 4TH LEVEL KLINGONESE, BUT THE TECHNICAL SYMBOLS ON THESE CIRCUIT BANKS ARE UNKNOWN TO ME!
AND THE BANKS ARE TOO WELL-SHIELDED FOR TRICORDER READINGS TO TELL US WHICH ONE IS THE STABILIZER, SO--
SOMEONE'S COMING!
I KNOW YOU'RE BACK HERE...
...SHOW YOURSELVES, NOW!
DON'T FORCE ME TO--
15

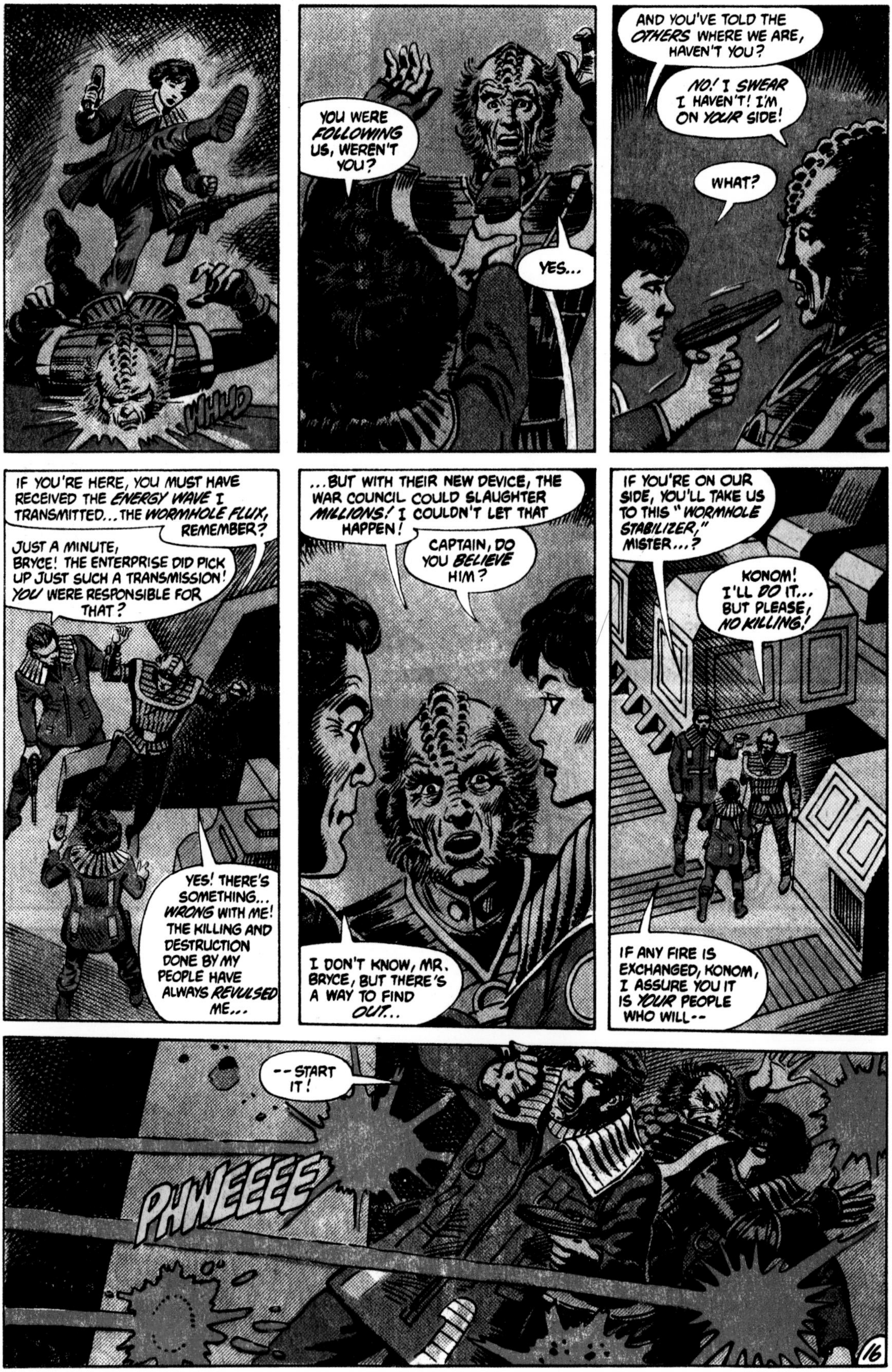
WHUD
YOU WERE FOLLOWING US, WEREN'T YOU?
YES...
AND YOU'VE TOLD THE OTHERS WHERE WE ARE, HAVEN'T YOU?
NO! I SWEAR I HAVEN'T! I'M ON YOUR SIDE!
WHAT?
IF YOU'RE HERE, YOU MUST HAVE RECEIVED THE ENERGY WAVE I TRANSMITTED... THE WORMHOLE FLUX, REMEMBER?
JUST A MINUTE, BRYCE! THE ENTERPRISE DID PICK UP JUST SUCH A TRANSMISSION! YOU WERE RESPONSIBLE FOR THAT?
YES! THERE'S SOMETHING... WRONG WITH ME! THE KILLING AND DESTRUCTION DONE BY MY PEOPLE HAVE ALWAYS REVULSED ME...
...BUT WITH THEIR NEW DEVICE, THE WAR COUNCIL COULD SLAUGHTER MILLIONS! I COULDN'T LET THAT HAPPEN!
CAPTAIN, DO YOU BELIEVE HIM?
I DON'T KNOW, MR. BRYCE, BUT THERE'S A WAY TO FIND OUT...
IF YOU'RE ON OUR SIDE, YOU'LL TAKE US TO THIS "WORMHOLE STABILIZER," MISTER...?
KONOM! I'LL DO IT... BUT PLEASE, NO KILLING!
IF ANY FIRE IS EXCHANGED, KONOM, I ASSURE YOU IT IS YOUR PEOPLE WHO WILL--
--START IT!
PHWEEEE
16

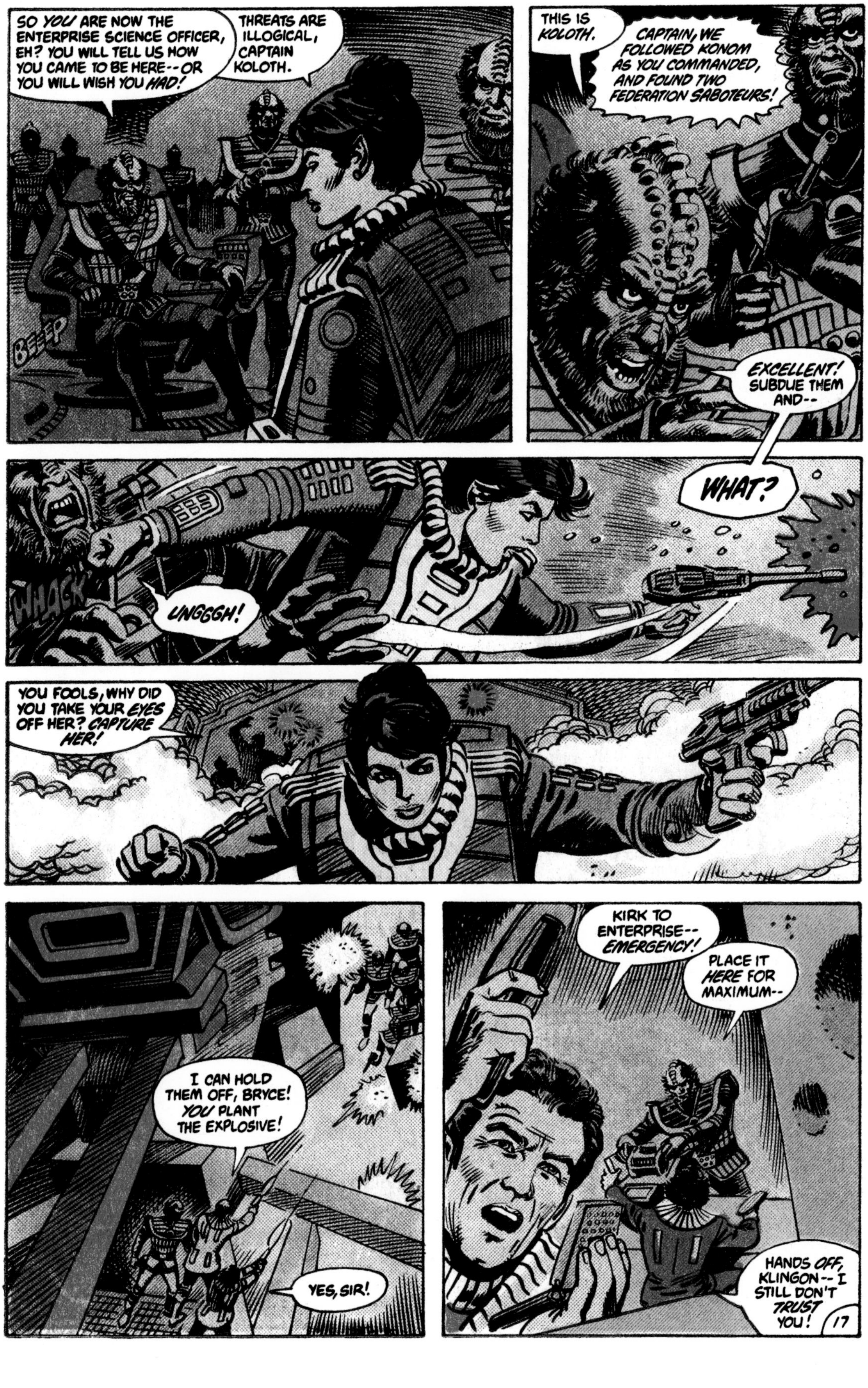
SO YOU ARE NOW THE ENTERPRISE SCIENCE OFFICER, EH? YOU WILL TELL US HOW YOU CAME TO BE HERE--OR YOU WILL WISH YOU HAD!
THREATS ARE ILLOGICAL, CAPTAIN KOLOTH.
BEEEP
THIS IS KOLOTH.
CAPTAIN, WE FOLLOWED KONOM AS YOU COMMANDED, AND FOUND TWO FEDERATION SABOTEURS!
EXCELLENT! SUBDUE THEM AND--
WHAT?
WHACK
UNGGGH!
YOU FOOLS, WHY DID YOU TAKE YOUR EYES OFF HER? CAPTURE HER!
I CAN HOLD THEM OFF, BRYCE! YOU PLANT THE EXPLOSIVE!
YES, SIR!
KIRK TO ENTERPRISE-- EMERGENCY!
PLACE IT HERE FOR MAXIMUM--
HANDS OFF, KLINGON-- I STILL DON'T TRUST YOU!
17

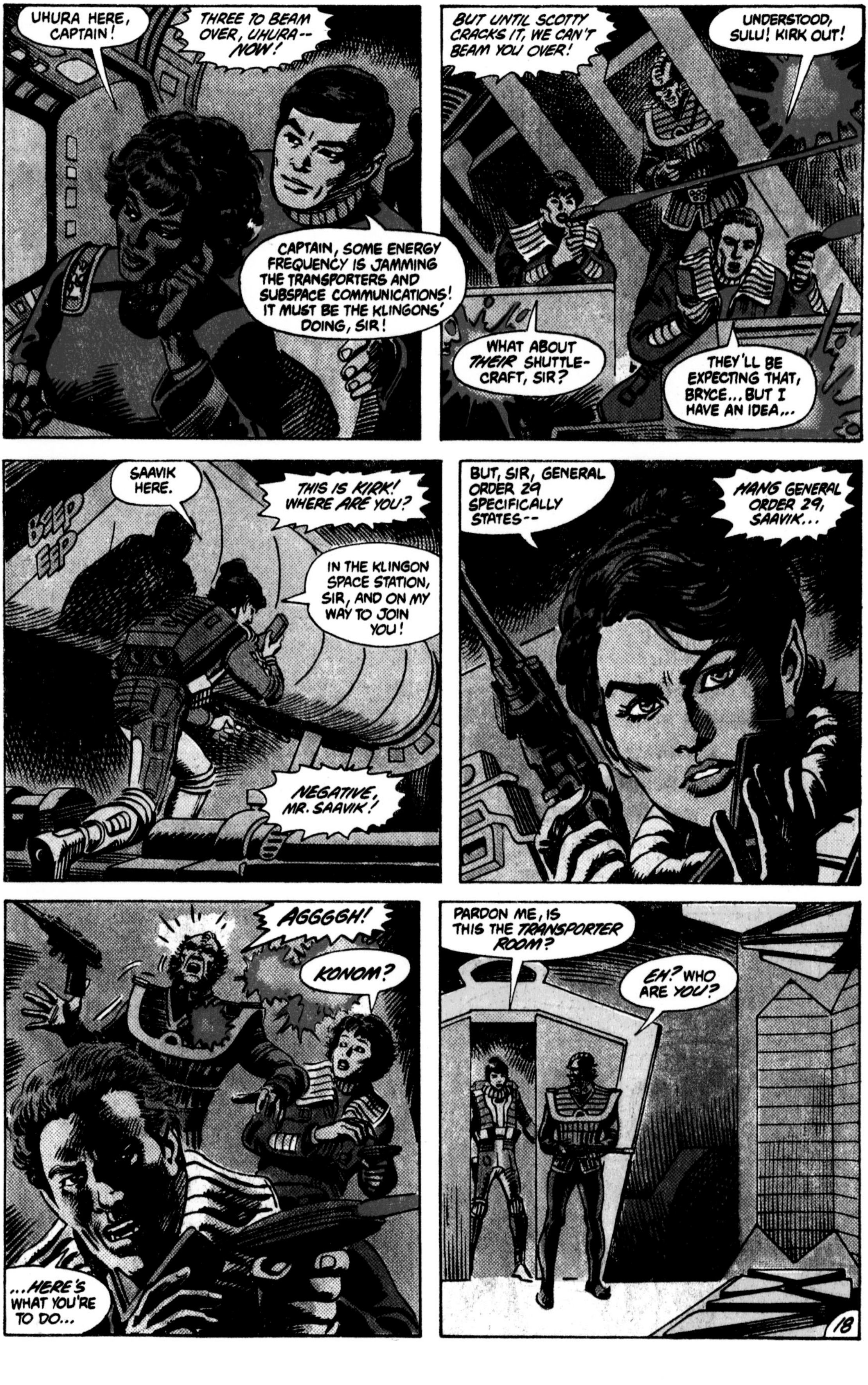
UHURA HERE, CAPTAIN!
THREE TO BEAM OVER, UHURA-- NOW!
CAPTAIN, SOME ENERGY FREQUENCY IS JAMMING THE TRANSPORTERS AND SUBSPACE COMMUNICATIONS! IT MUST BE THE KLINGONS' DOING, SIR!
BUT UNTIL SCOTTY CRACKS IT, WE CAN'T BEAM YOU OVER!
UNDERSTOOD, SULU! KIRK OUT!
WHAT ABOUT THEIR SHUTTLE-CRAFT, SIR?
THEY'LL BE EXPECTING THAT, BRYCE... BUT I HAVE AN IDEA...
SAAVIK HERE.
BEEP EEP
THIS IS KIRK! WHERE ARE YOU?
IN THE KLINGON SPACE STATION, SIR, AND ON MY WAY TO JOIN YOU!
NEGATIVE, MR. SAAVIK!
BUT, SIR, GENERAL ORDER 29 SPECIFICALLY STATES--
HANG GENERAL ORDER 29, SAAVIK...
AGGGGH!
KONOM?
...HERE'S WHAT YOU'RE TO DO...
PARDON ME, IS THIS THE TRANSPORTER ROOM?
EH? WHO ARE YOU?
18

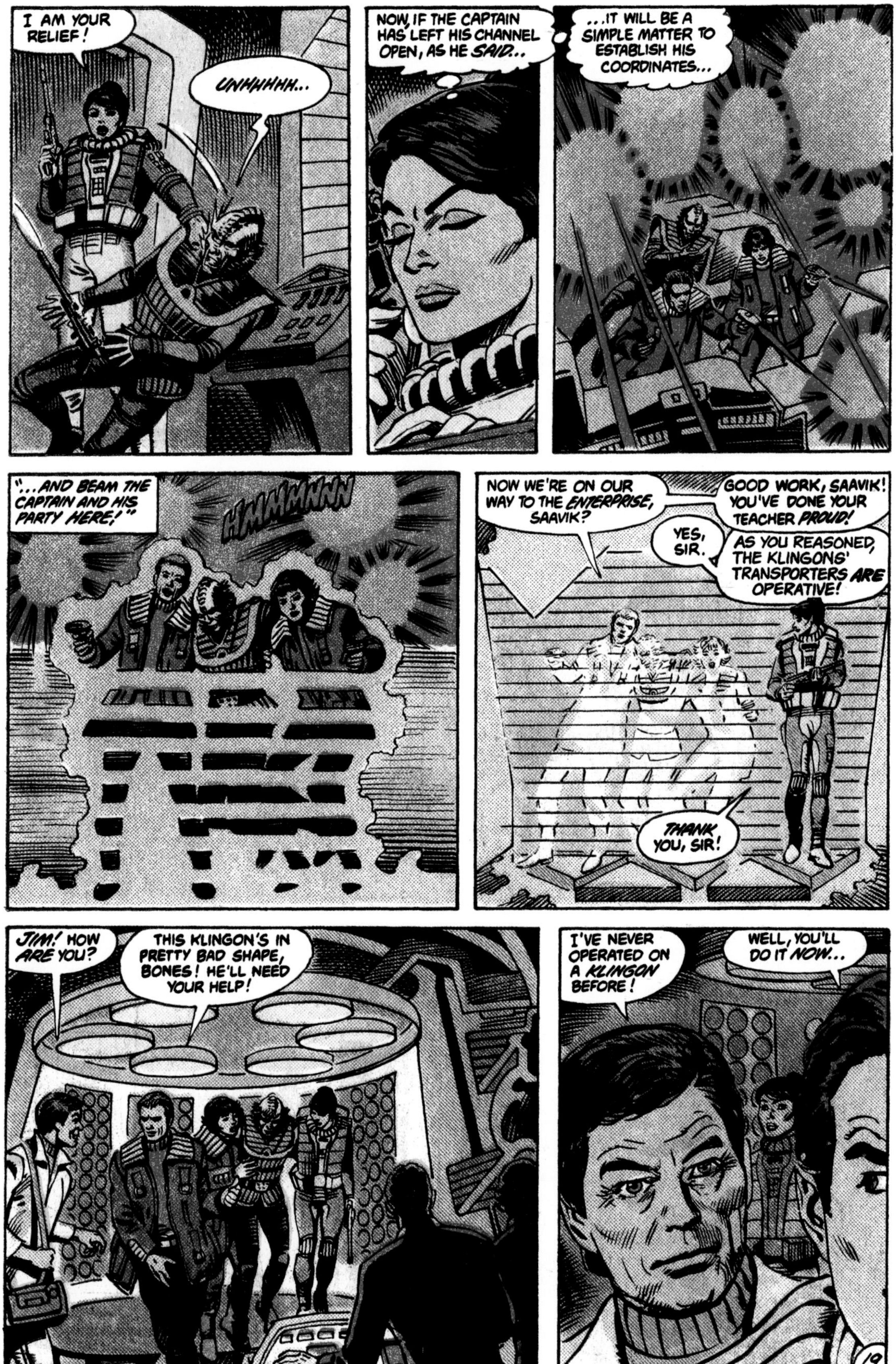
I AM YOUR RELIEF!
UNHHHHH...
NOW, IF THE CAPTAIN HAS LEFT HIS CHANNEL OPEN, AS HE SAID...
...IT WILL BE A SIMPLE MATTER TO ESTABLISH HIS COORDINATES...
"...AND BEAM THE CAPTAIN AND HIS PARTY HERE!"
HMMMNNN
NOW WE'RE ON OUR WAY TO THE ENTERPRISE, SAAVIK?
YES, SIR.
GOOD WORK, SAAVIK! YOU'VE DONE YOUR TEACHER PROUD!
AS YOU REASONED, THE KLINGONS' TRANSPORTERS ARE OPERATIVE!
THANK YOU, SIR!
JIM! HOW ARE YOU?
THIS KLINGON'S IN PRETTY BAD SHAPE, BONES! HE'LL NEED YOUR HELP!
I'VE NEVER OPERATED ON A KLINGON BEFORE!
WELL, YOU'LL DO IT NOW...
19

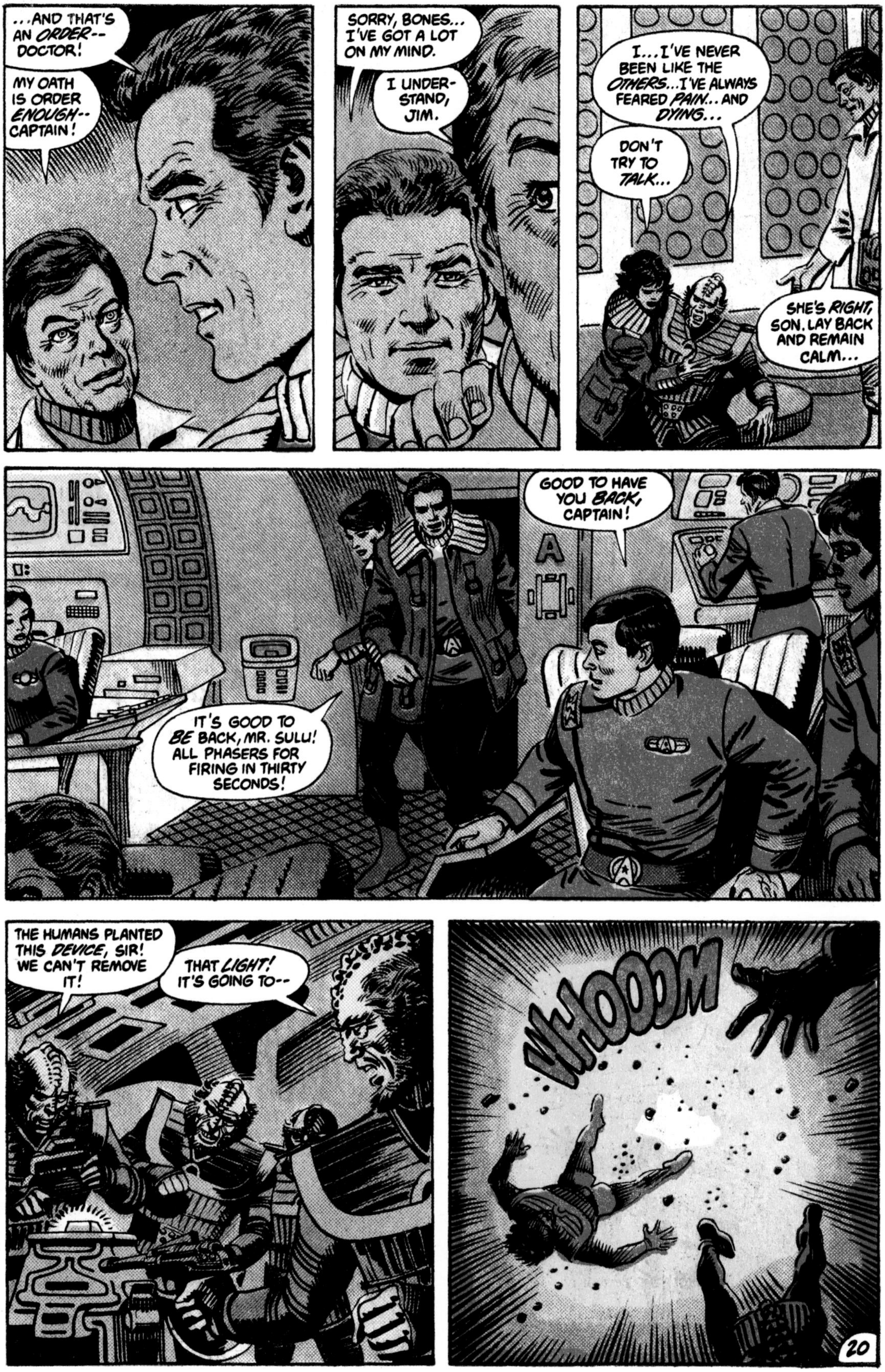
...AND THAT'S AN ORDER-- DOCTOR!
MY OATH IS ORDER ENOUGH-- CAPTAIN!
SORRY, BONES... I'VE GOT A LOT ON MY MIND.
I UNDERSTAND, JIM.
I... I'VE NEVER BEEN LIKE THE OTHERS... I'VE ALWAYS FEARED PAIN... AND DYING...
DON'T TRY TO TALK...
SHE'S RIGHT, SON. LAY BACK AND REMAIN CALM...
GOOD TO HAVE YOU BACK, CAPTAIN!
IT'S GOOD TO BE BACK, MR. SULU! ALL PHASERS FOR FIRING IN THIRTY SECONDS!
THE HUMANS PLANTED THIS DEVICE, SIR! WE CAN'T REMOVE IT!
THAT LIGHT! IT'S GOING TO--
WHOOOM
20

ALL HANDS, *BATTLE STATIONS!* THE WORM-HOLE STABILIZER HAS BEEN *DESTROYED!* WE WILL REENTER--

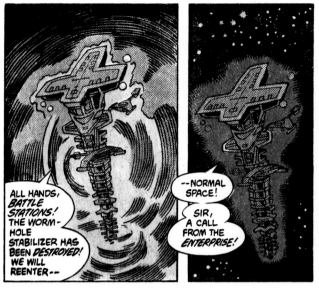

--NORMAL SPACE!

SIR, A CALL FROM THE *ENTERPRISE!*

THIS IS *CAPTAIN JAMES T. KIRK,* KOLOTH! GIVE IT UP, IT'S *OVER!*

OVER?

I THINK *NOT,* CAPTAIN... AS YOU AND YOUR ACCURSED *FEDERATION* WILL SOON FIND OUT!

FOR AS YOU KNOW, WE KLINGONS *LIVE* BY OUR OWN RULES...

...AND *DIE* BY THEM, AS WELL!

KLIK

FWOOOOOM

21

47

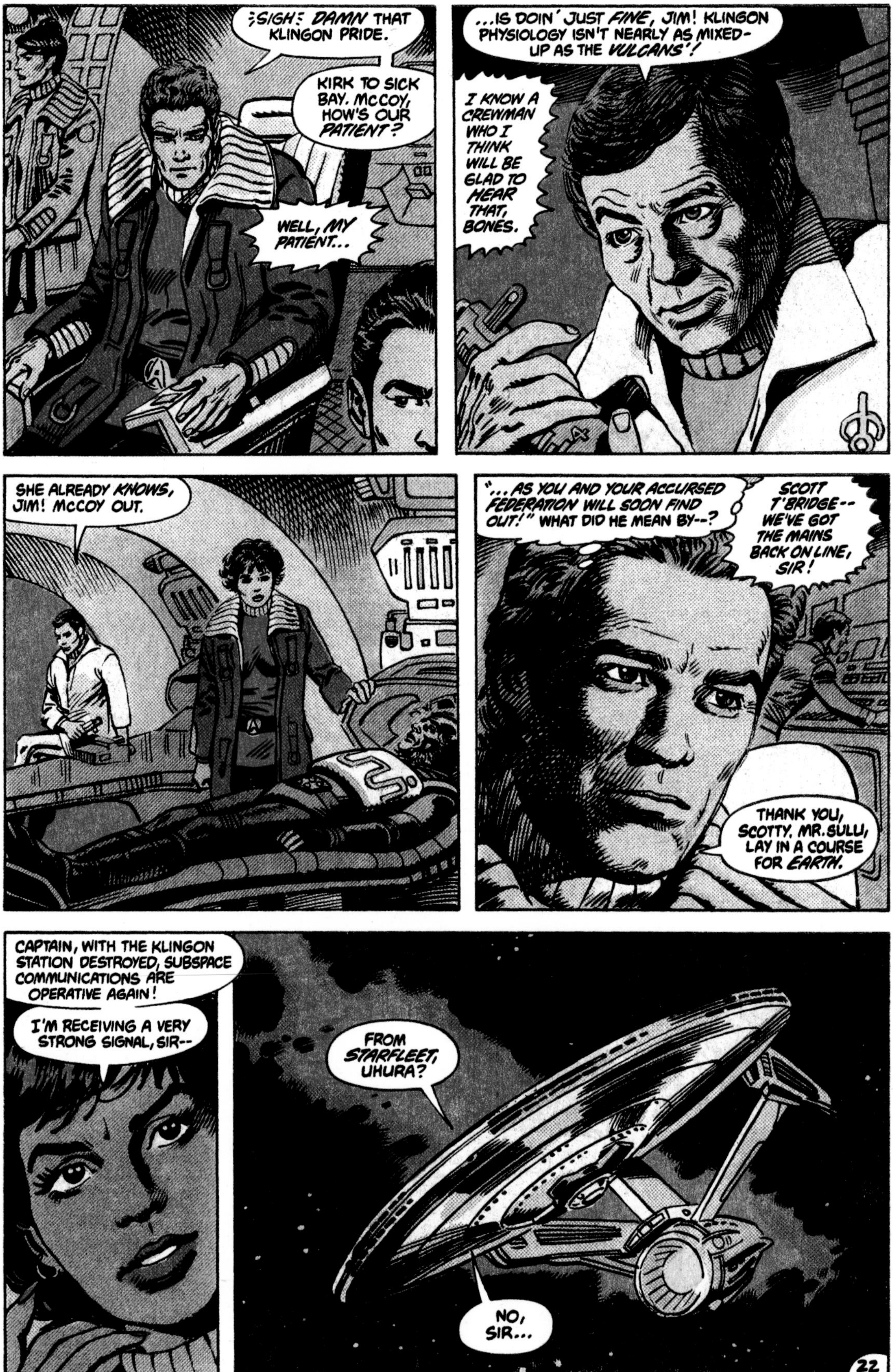
:SIGH: DAMN THAT KLINGON PRIDE.
KIRK TO SICK BAY. McCOY, HOW'S OUR PATIENT?
WELL, MY PATIENT...
...IS DOIN' JUST FINE, JIM! KLINGON PHYSIOLOGY ISN'T NEARLY AS MIXED-UP AS THE VULCANS'!
I KNOW A CREWMAN WHO I THINK WILL BE GLAD TO HEAR THAT, BONES.
SHE ALREADY KNOWS, JIM! McCOY OUT.
"...AS YOU AND YOUR ACCURSED FEDERATION WILL SOON FIND OUT!" WHAT DID HE MEAN BY--?
SCOTT T'BRIDGE-- WE'VE GOT THE MAINS BACK ON LINE, SIR!
THANK YOU, SCOTTY. MR. SULU, LAY IN A COURSE FOR EARTH.
CAPTAIN, WITH THE KLINGON STATION DESTROYED, SUBSPACE COMMUNICATIONS ARE OPERATIVE AGAIN!
I'M RECEIVING A VERY STRONG SIGNAL, SIR--
FROM STARFLEET, UHURA?
NO, SIR...
22

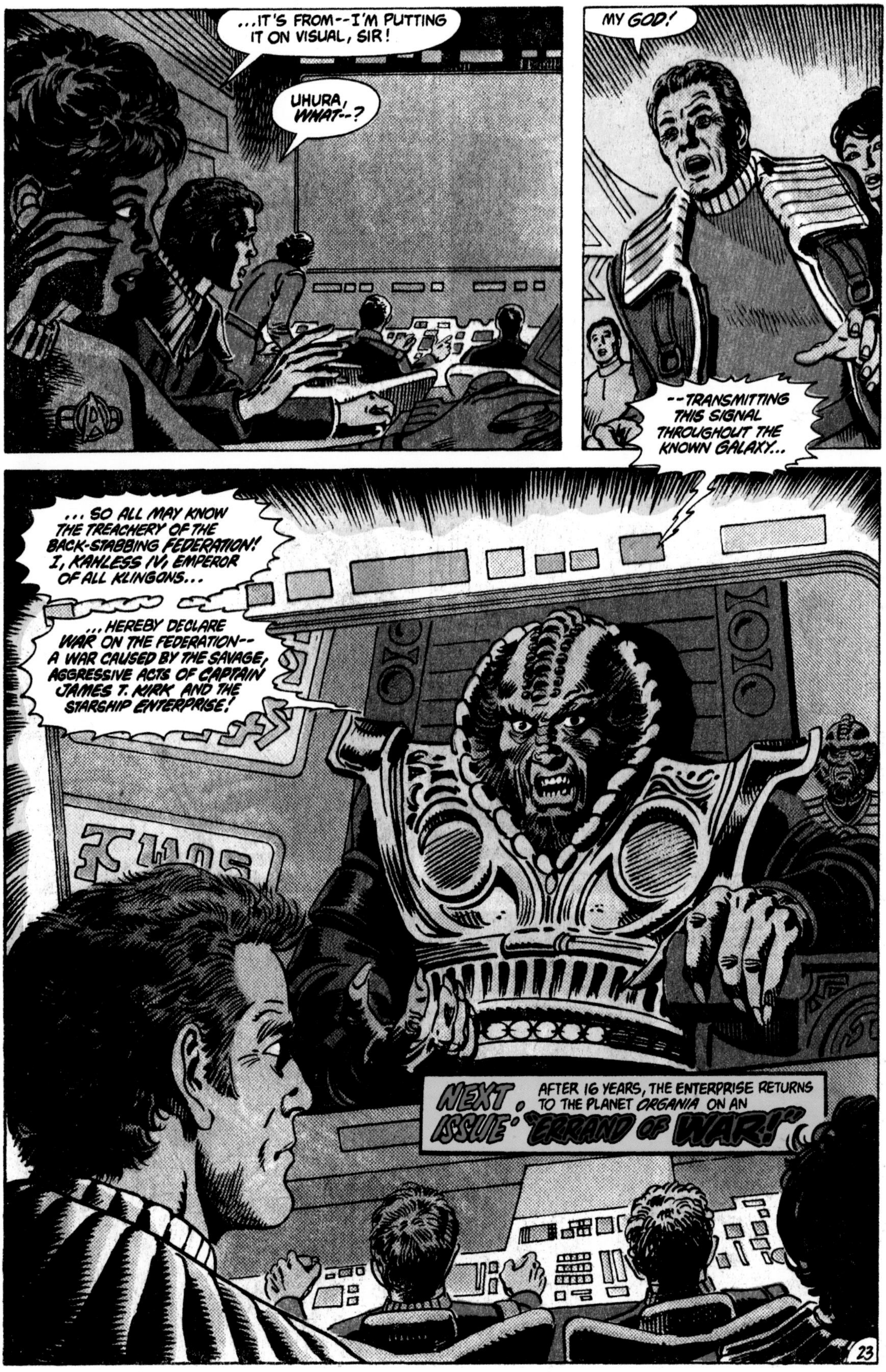
...IT'S FROM--I'M PUTTING IT ON VISUAL, SIR!
UHURA, WHAT--?
MY GOD!
--TRANSMITTING THIS SIGNAL THROUGHOUT THE KNOWN GALAXY...
... SO ALL MAY KNOW THE TREACHERY OF THE BACK-STABBING FEDERATION! I, KAHLESS IV, EMPEROR OF ALL KLINGONS...
...HEREBY DECLARE WAR ON THE FEDERATION-- A WAR CAUSED BY THE SAVAGE, AGGRESSIVE ACTS OF CAPTAIN JAMES T. KIRK AND THE STARSHIP ENTERPRISE!
NEXT ISSUE: AFTER 16 YEARS, THE ENTERPRISE RETURNS TO THE PLANET ORGANIA ON AN "ERRAND OF WAR!"
23

STAR TREK®

Based on the series created by **Gene Roddenberry**

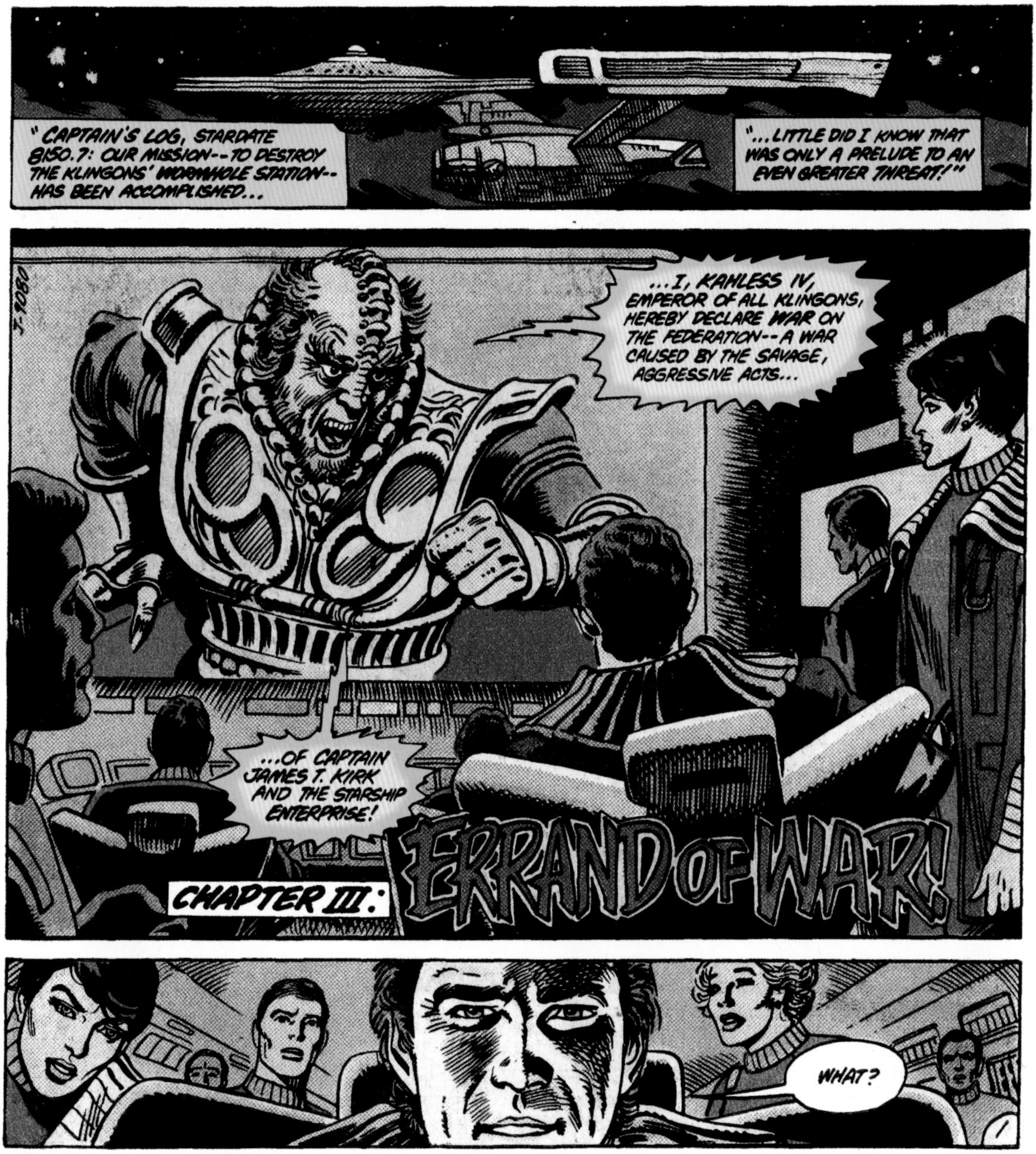

"CAPTAIN'S LOG, STARDATE 8150.7: OUR MISSION--TO DESTROY THE KLINGONS' WORMHOLE STATION--HAS BEEN ACCOMPLISHED...
"...LITTLE DID I KNOW THAT WAS ONLY A PRELUDE TO AN EVEN GREATER THREAT!"
...I, KAHLESS IV, EMPEROR OF ALL KLINGONS, HEREBY DECLARE WAR ON THE FEDERATION--A WAR CAUSED BY THE SAVAGE, AGGRESSIVE ACTS...
...OF CAPTAIN JAMES T. KIRK AND THE STARSHIP ENTERPRISE!
CHAPTER III: ERRAND OF WAR!
WHAT?

MIKE W. BARR * TOM SUTTON & RICARDO VILLAGRAN
Writer — Artists

JOHN COSTANZA * MICHELE WOLFMAN * MARV WOLFMAN
Letterer — Colorist — Editor

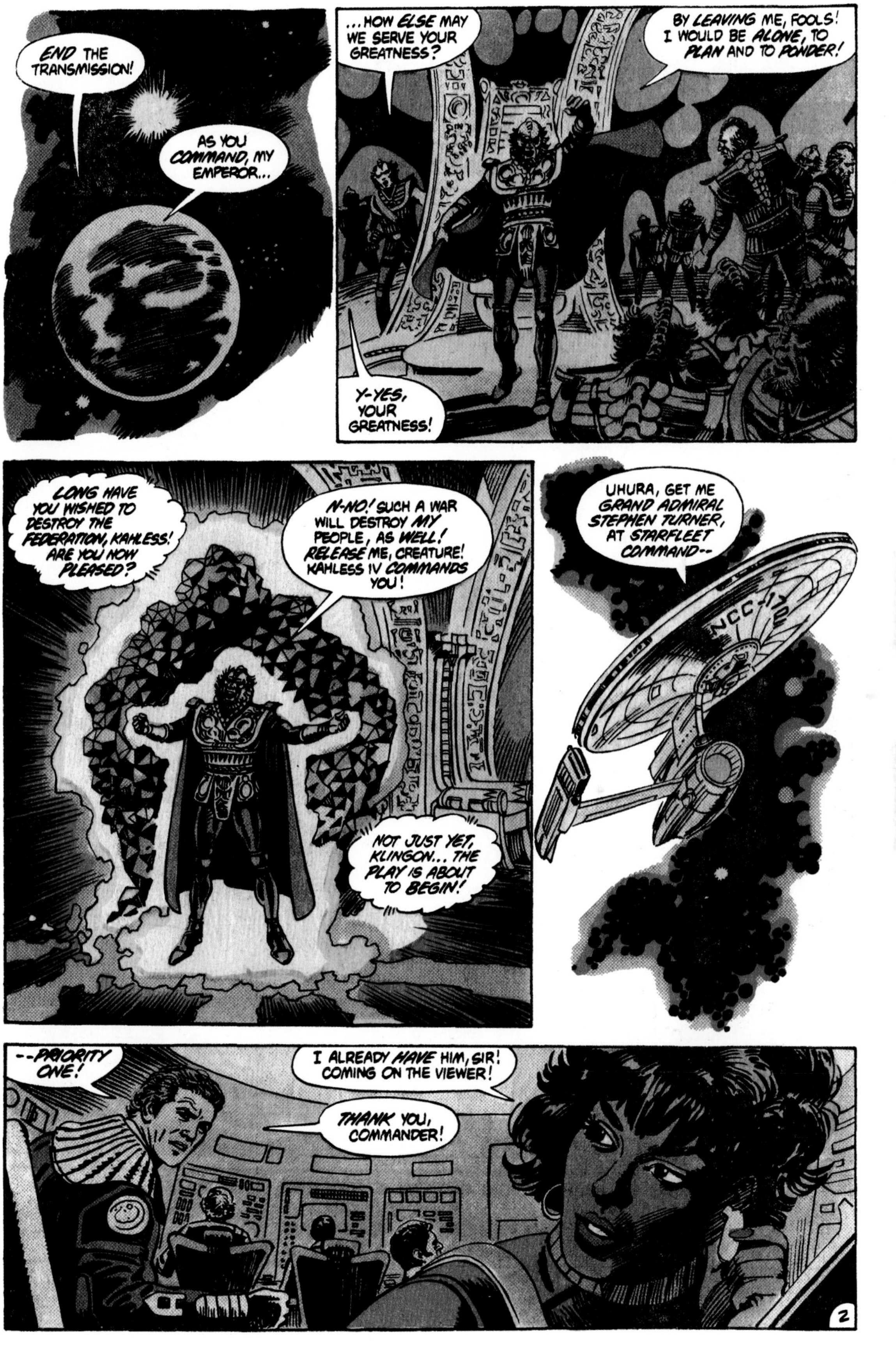
END THE TRANSMISSION!
AS YOU COMMAND, MY EMPEROR...
...HOW ELSE MAY WE SERVE YOUR GREATNESS?
BY LEAVING ME, FOOLS! I WOULD BE ALONE, TO PLAN AND TO PONDER!
Y-YES, YOUR GREATNESS!
LONG HAVE YOU WISHED TO DESTROY THE FEDERATION, KAHLESS! ARE YOU NOW PLEASED?
N-NO! SUCH A WAR WILL DESTROY MY PEOPLE, AS WELL! RELEASE ME, CREATURE! KAHLESS IV COMMANDS YOU!
NOT JUST YET, KLINGON... THE PLAY IS ABOUT TO BEGIN!
UHURA, GET ME GRAND ADMIRAL STEPHEN TURNER, AT STARFLEET COMMAND--
--PRIORITY ONE!
I ALREADY HAVE HIM, SIR! COMING ON THE VIEWER!
THANK YOU, COMMANDER!
2

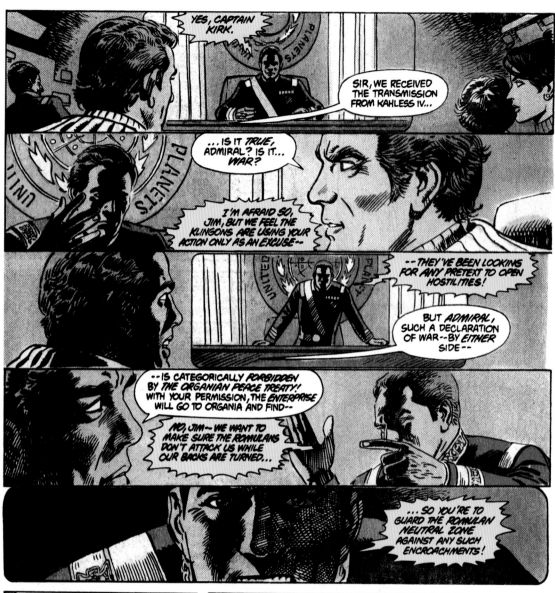

YES, CAPTAIN KIRK.

SIR, WE RECEIVED THE TRANSMISSION FROM KAHLESS IV...

...IS IT *TRUE*, ADMIRAL? IS IT... *WAR?*

I'M AFRAID SO, JIM, BUT WE FEEL THE KLINGONS ARE USING YOUR ACTION ONLY AS AN EXCUSE--

--THEY'VE BEEN LOOKING FOR *ANY* PRETEXT TO OPEN HOSTILITIES!

BUT *ADMIRAL*, SUCH A DECLARATION OF WAR--BY *EITHER* SIDE--

--IS CATEGORICALLY *FORBIDDEN* BY *THE ORGANIAN PEACE TREATY!* WITH YOUR PERMISSION, THE *ENTERPRISE* WILL GO TO ORGANIA AND FIND--

NO, JIM-- WE WANT TO MAKE SURE THE ROMULANS DON'T ATTACK US WHILE OUR BACKS ARE TURNED...

...SO YOU'RE TO GUARD THE *ROMULAN NEUTRAL ZONE* AGAINST ANY SUCH ENCROACHMENTS!

THE *ROMULAN*--! SIR, THAT'S 5,000 PARSECS OUT OF OUR WAY! I SUBMIT THE *ENTERPRISE* WOULD BE BETTER USED--

YOU WANTED YOUR *COMMAND* BACK, KIRK-- AND IF YOU WANT TO *KEEP* IT, YOU'LL OBEY ORDERS...*CAPTAIN!*

I...UNDERSTAND, ADMIRAL. KIRK OUT.

WHEW

3

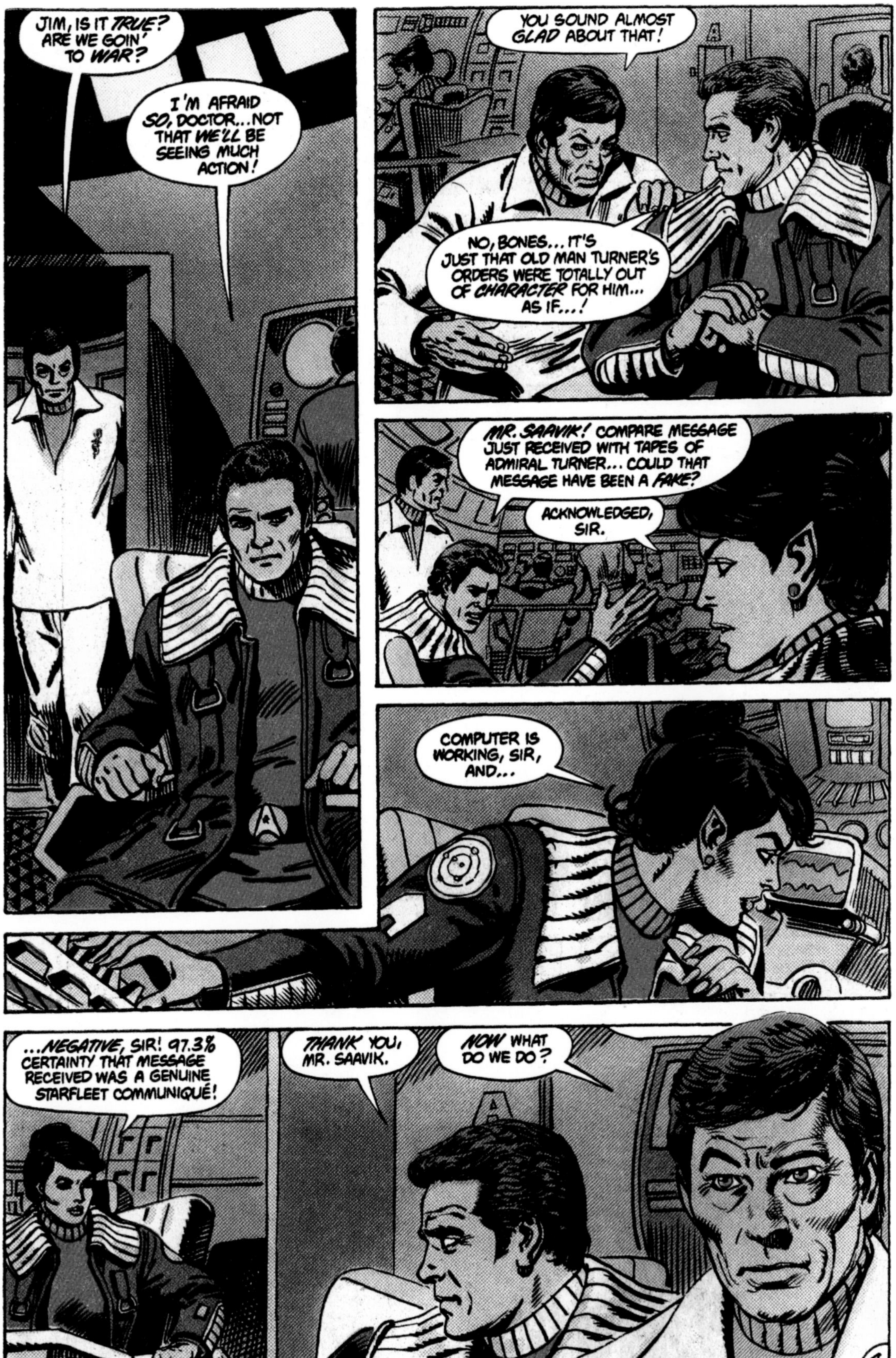
JIM, IS IT TRUE? ARE WE GOIN' TO WAR?
I'M AFRAID SO, DOCTOR... NOT THAT WE'LL BE SEEING MUCH ACTION!
YOU SOUND ALMOST GLAD ABOUT THAT!
NO, BONES... IT'S JUST THAT OLD MAN TURNER'S ORDERS WERE TOTALLY OUT OF CHARACTER FOR HIM... AS IF...!
MR. SAAVIK! COMPARE MESSAGE JUST RECEIVED WITH TAPES OF ADMIRAL TURNER... COULD THAT MESSAGE HAVE BEEN A FAKE?
ACKNOWLEDGED, SIR.
COMPUTER IS WORKING, SIR, AND...
...NEGATIVE, SIR! 97.3% CERTAINTY THAT MESSAGE RECEIVED WAS A GENUINE STARFLEET COMMUNIQUÉ!
THANK YOU, MR. SAAVIK.
NOW WHAT DO WE DO?
4

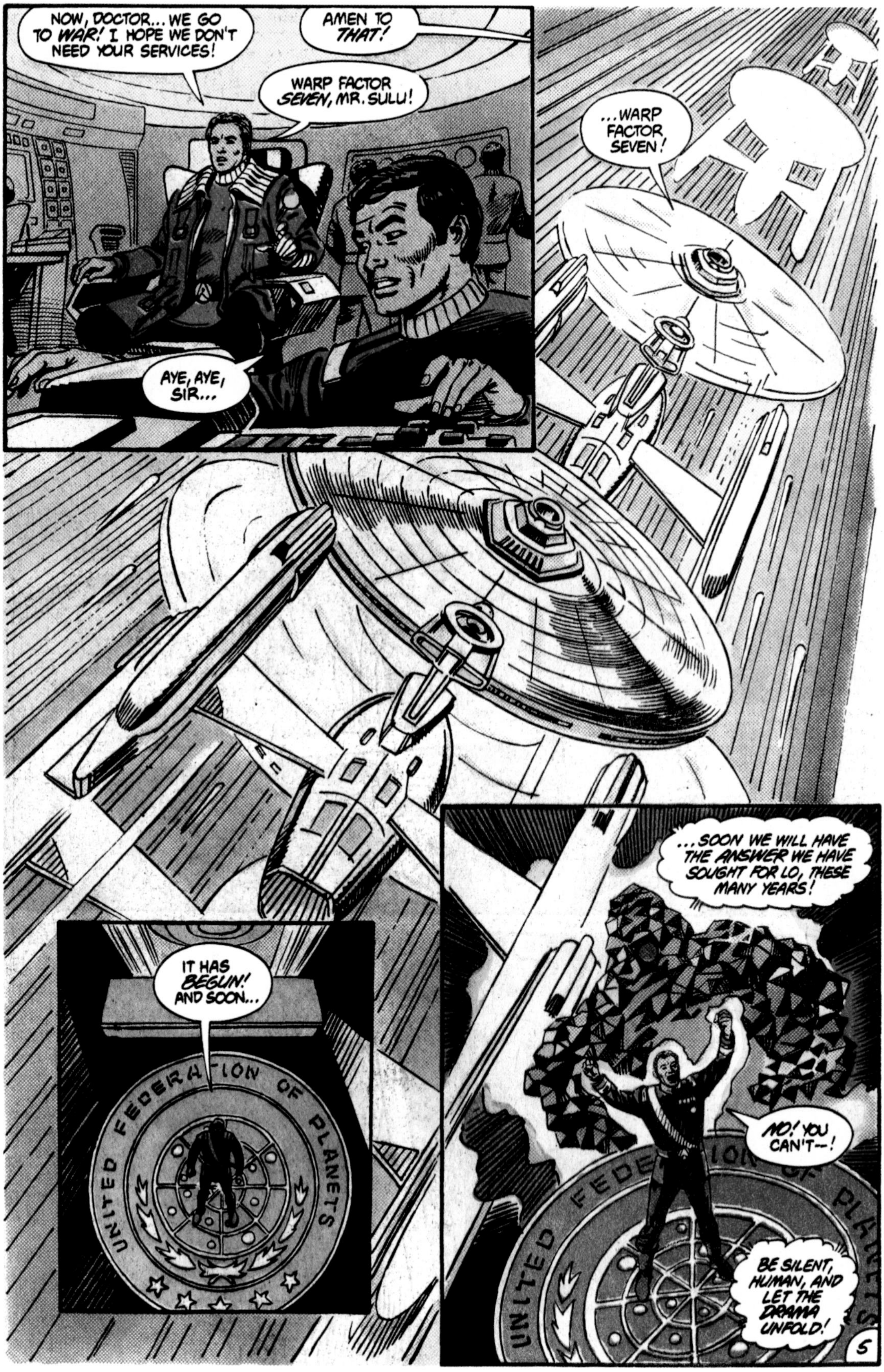
NOW, DOCTOR... WE GO TO WAR! I HOPE WE DON'T NEED YOUR SERVICES!
AMEN TO THAT!
WARP FACTOR SEVEN, MR. SULU!
AYE, AYE, SIR...
...WARP FACTOR SEVEN!
...SOON WE WILL HAVE THE ANSWER WE HAVE SOUGHT FOR LO, THESE MANY YEARS!
IT HAS BEGUN! AND SOON...
UNITED FEDERATION OF PLANETS
NO! YOU CAN'T--!
BE SILENT, HUMAN, AND LET THE DRAMA UNFOLD!
UNITED FEDERATION OF PLANETS
5

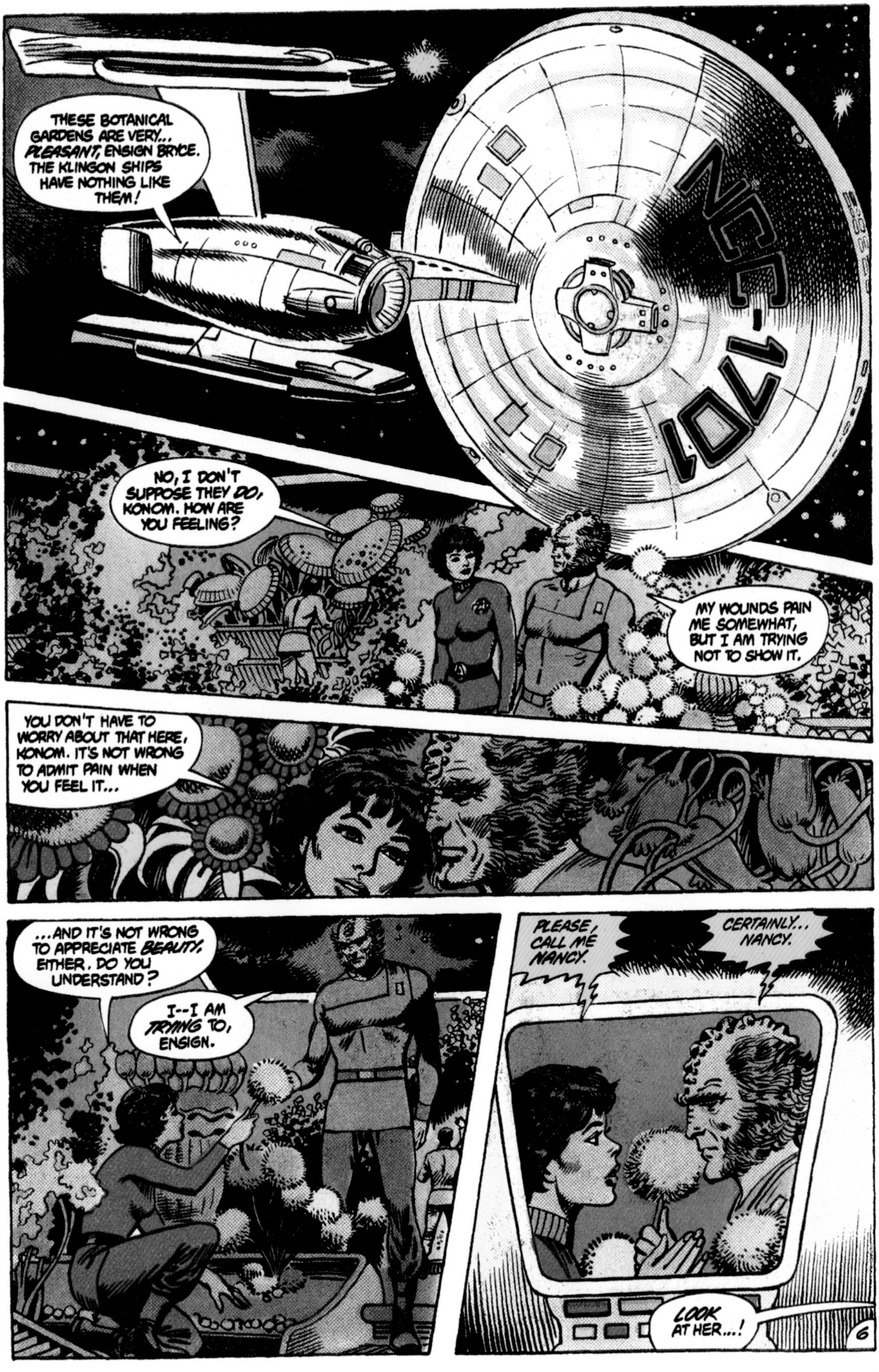
THESE BOTANICAL GARDENS ARE VERY... PLEASANT, ENSIGN BRYCE. THE KLINGON SHIPS HAVE NOTHING LIKE THEM!
NCC-1701
NO, I DON'T SUPPOSE THEY DO, KONOM. HOW ARE YOU FEELING?
MY WOUNDS PAIN ME SOMEWHAT, BUT I AM TRYING NOT TO SHOW IT.
YOU DON'T HAVE TO WORRY ABOUT THAT HERE, KONOM. IT'S NOT WRONG TO ADMIT PAIN WHEN YOU FEEL IT...
...AND IT'S NOT WRONG TO APPRECIATE BEAUTY, EITHER. DO YOU UNDERSTAND?
I--I AM TRYING TO, ENSIGN.
PLEASE, CALL ME NANCY.
CERTAINLY... NANCY.
LOOK AT HER...!
6

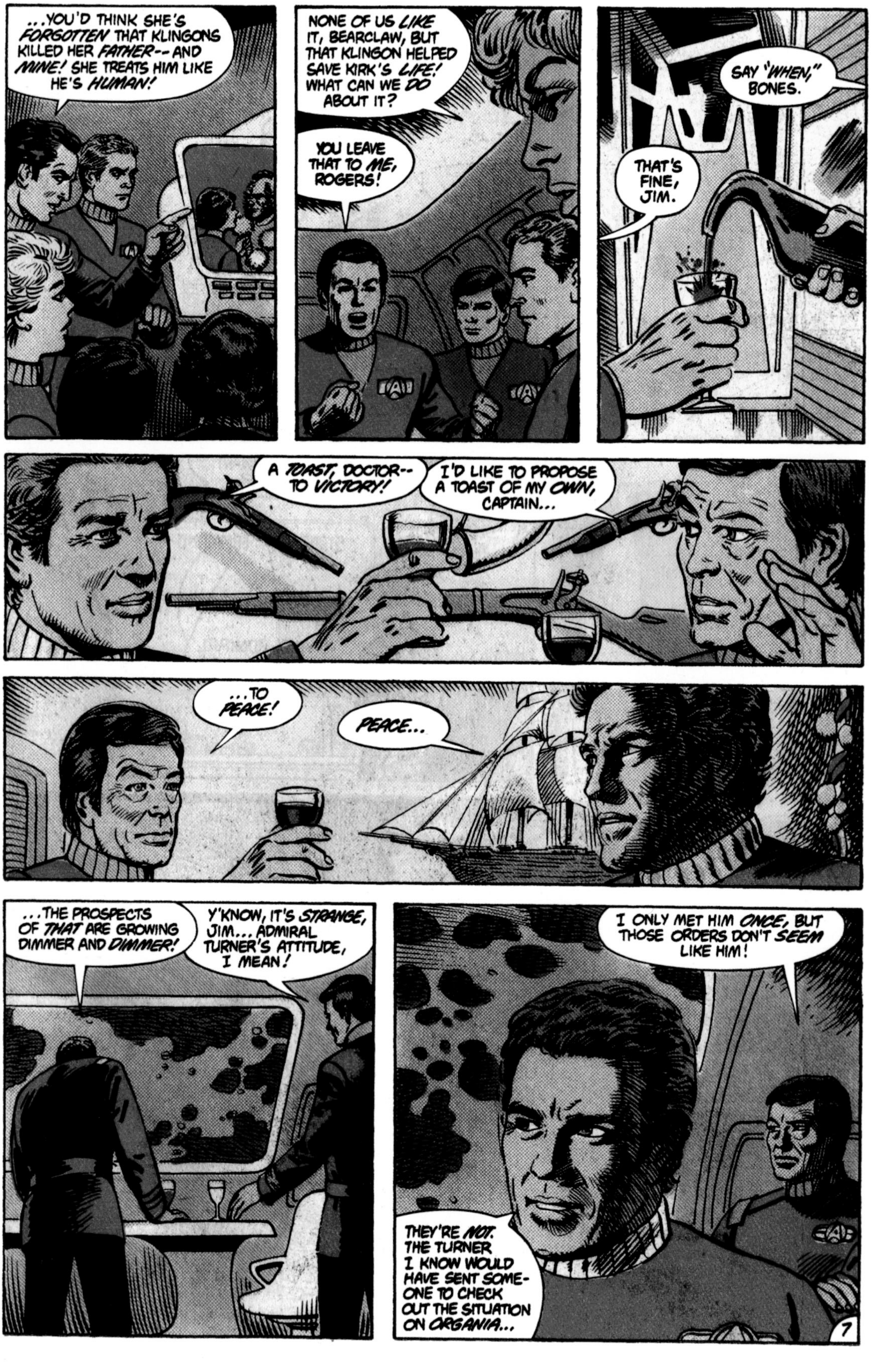
...YOU'D THINK SHE'S FORGOTTEN THAT KLINGONS KILLED HER FATHER-- AND MINE! SHE TREATS HIM LIKE HE'S HUMAN!
NONE OF US LIKE IT, BEARCLAW, BUT THAT KLINGON HELPED SAVE KIRK'S LIFE! WHAT CAN WE DO ABOUT IT?
YOU LEAVE THAT TO ME, ROGERS!
SAY "WHEN," BONES.
THAT'S FINE, JIM.
A TOAST, DOCTOR-- TO VICTORY!
I'D LIKE TO PROPOSE A TOAST OF MY OWN, CAPTAIN...
...TO PEACE!
PEACE...
...THE PROSPECTS OF THAT ARE GROWING DIMMER AND DIMMER!
Y'KNOW, IT'S STRANGE, JIM... ADMIRAL TURNER'S ATTITUDE, I MEAN!
I ONLY MET HIM ONCE, BUT THOSE ORDERS DON'T SEEM LIKE HIM!
THEY'RE NOT. THE TURNER I KNOW WOULD HAVE SENT SOME-ONE TO CHECK OUT THE SITUATION ON ORGANIA...
7

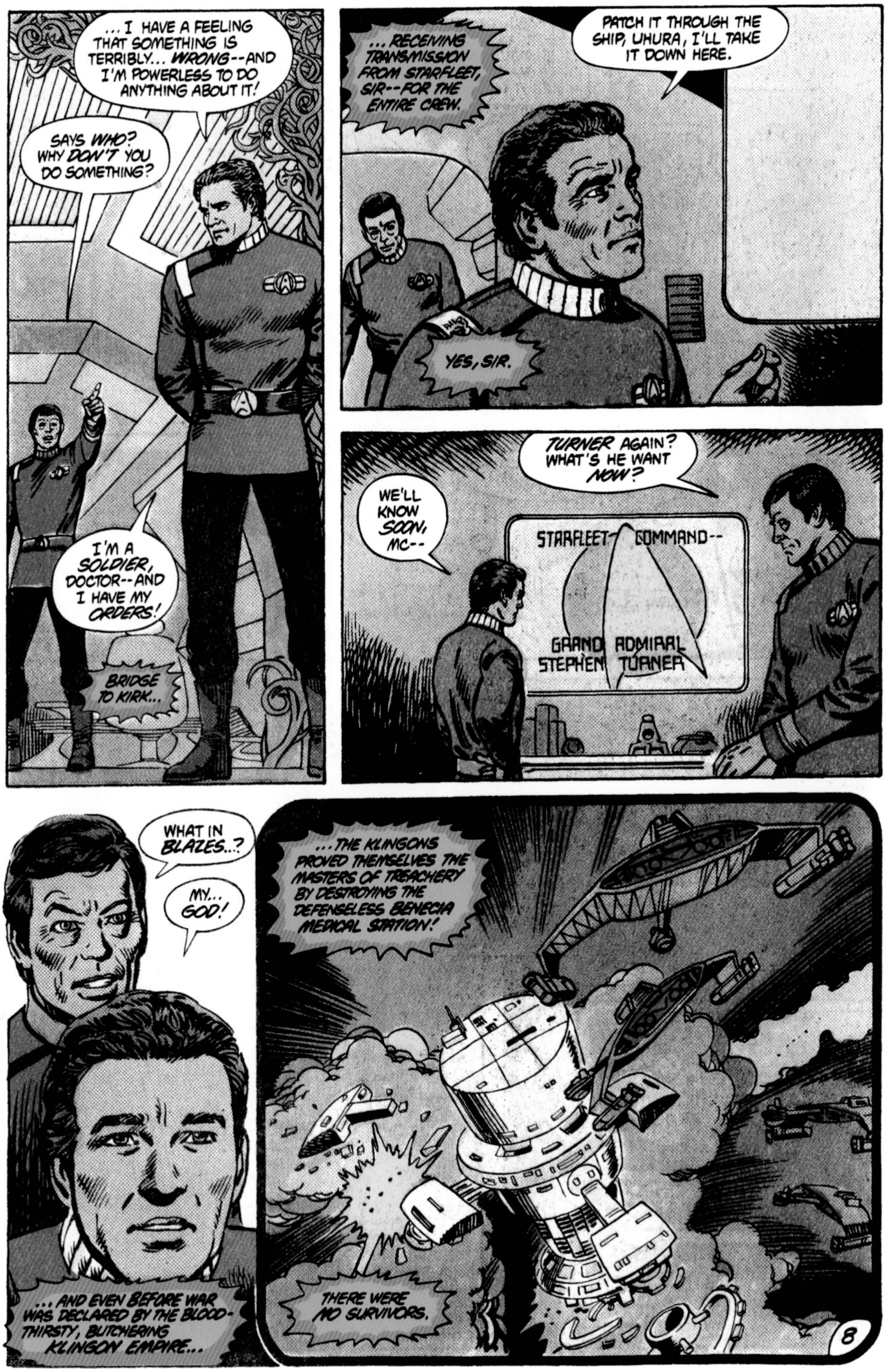
...I HAVE A FEELING THAT SOMETHING IS TERRIBLY... WRONG--AND I'M POWERLESS TO DO ANYTHING ABOUT IT!
SAYS WHO? WHY DON'T YOU DO SOMETHING?
I'M A SOLDIER, DOCTOR--AND I HAVE MY ORDERS!
BRIDGE TO KIRK...
...RECEIVING TRANSMISSION FROM STARFLEET, SIR--FOR THE ENTIRE CREW.
PATCH IT THROUGH THE SHIP, UHURA, I'LL TAKE IT DOWN HERE.
YES, SIR.
TURNER AGAIN? WHAT'S HE WANT NOW?
WE'LL KNOW SOON, MC--
STARFLEET COMMAND--
GRAND ADMIRAL STEPHEN TURNER
WHAT IN BLAZES...?
MY... GOD!
...AND EVEN BEFORE WAR WAS DECLARED BY THE BLOOD-THIRSTY, BUTCHERING KLINGON EMPIRE...
...THE KLINGONS PROVED THEMSELVES THE MASTERS OF TREACHERY BY DESTROYING THE DEFENSELESS BENECIA MEDICAL STATION!
THERE WERE NO SURVIVORS.
8

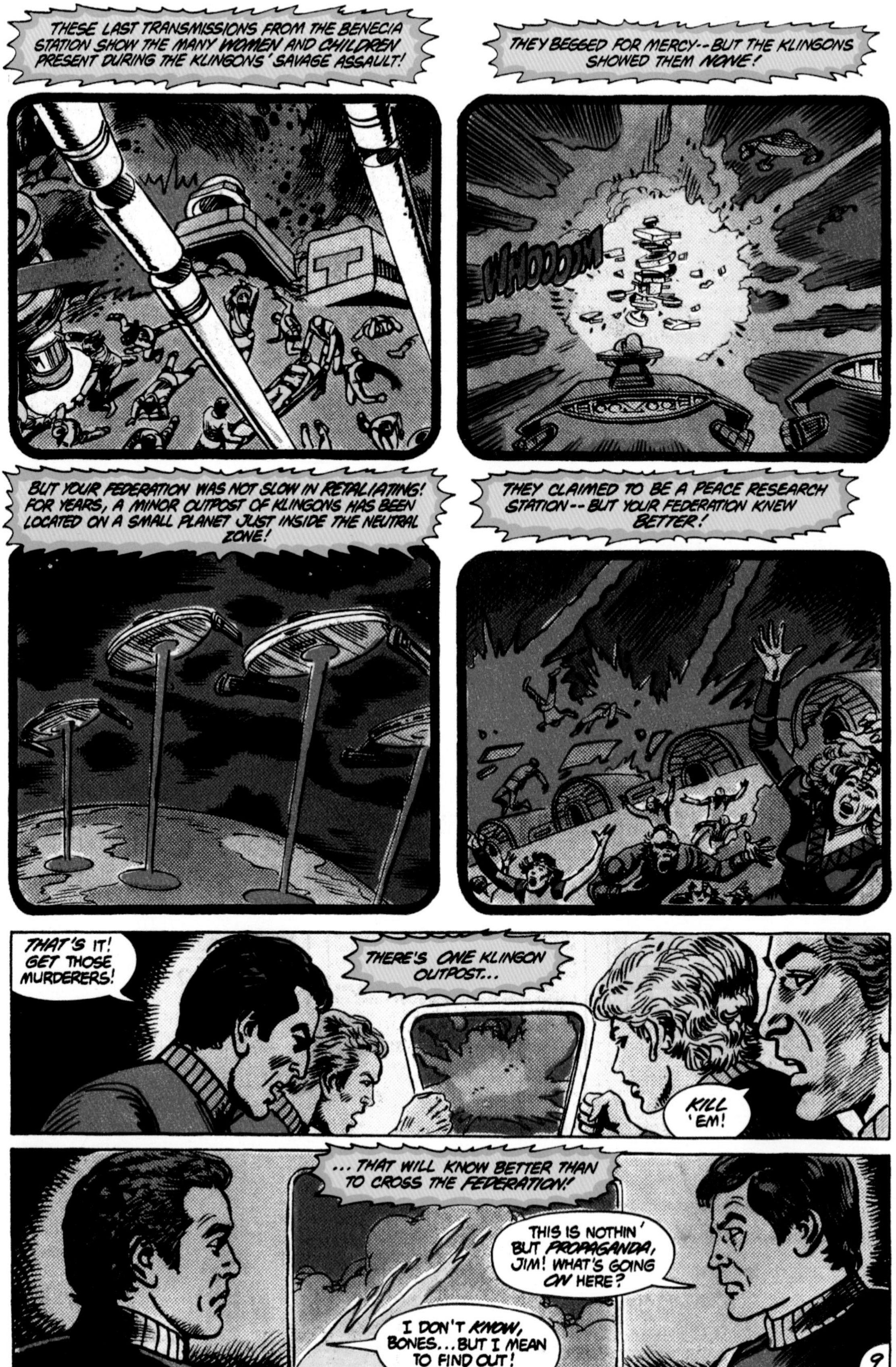
THESE LAST TRANSMISSIONS FROM THE BENECIA STATION SHOW THE MANY WOMEN AND CHILDREN PRESENT DURING THE KLINGONS' SAVAGE ASSAULT!
THEY BEGGED FOR MERCY--BUT THE KLINGONS SHOWED THEM NONE!
WHOOOOM
BUT YOUR FEDERATION WAS NOT SLOW IN RETALIATING! FOR YEARS, A MINOR OUTPOST OF KLINGONS HAS BEEN LOCATED ON A SMALL PLANET JUST INSIDE THE NEUTRAL ZONE!
THEY CLAIMED TO BE A PEACE RESEARCH STATION--BUT YOUR FEDERATION KNEW BETTER!
THAT'S IT! GET THOSE MURDERERS!
THERE'S ONE KLINGON OUTPOST...
KILL 'EM!
...THAT WILL KNOW BETTER THAN TO CROSS THE FEDERATION!
THIS IS NOTHIN' BUT PROPAGANDA, JIM! WHAT'S GOING ON HERE?
I DON'T KNOW, BONES...BUT I MEAN TO FIND OUT!
9

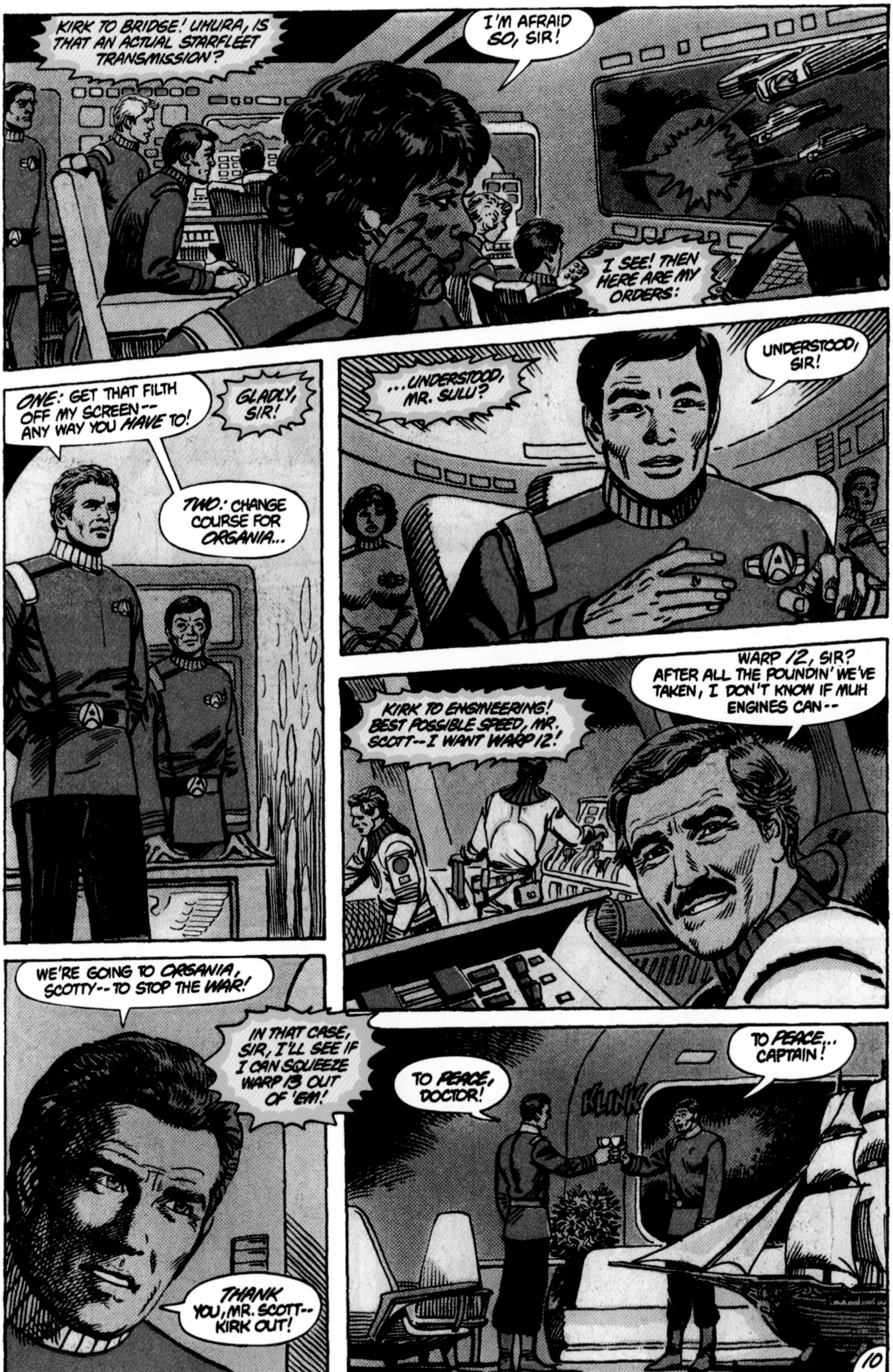
KIRK TO BRIDGE! UHURA, IS THAT AN ACTUAL STARFLEET TRANSMISSION?
I'M AFRAID SO, SIR!
I SEE! THEN HERE ARE MY ORDERS:
ONE: GET THAT FILTH OFF MY SCREEN-- ANY WAY YOU HAVE TO!
GLADLY, SIR!
TWO: CHANGE COURSE FOR ORGANIA...
...UNDERSTOOD, MR. SULU?
UNDERSTOOD, SIR!
KIRK TO ENGINEERING! BEST POSSIBLE SPEED, MR. SCOTT--I WANT WARP 12!
WARP 12, SIR? AFTER ALL THE POUNDIN' WE'VE TAKEN, I DON'T KNOW IF MUH ENGINES CAN--
WE'RE GOING TO ORGANIA, SCOTTY--TO STOP THE WAR!
IN THAT CASE, SIR, I'LL SEE IF I CAN SQUEEZE WARP 13 OUT OF 'EM!
THANK YOU, MR. SCOTT--KIRK OUT!
TO PEACE, DOCTOR!
TO PEACE... CAPTAIN!
KLINK
10

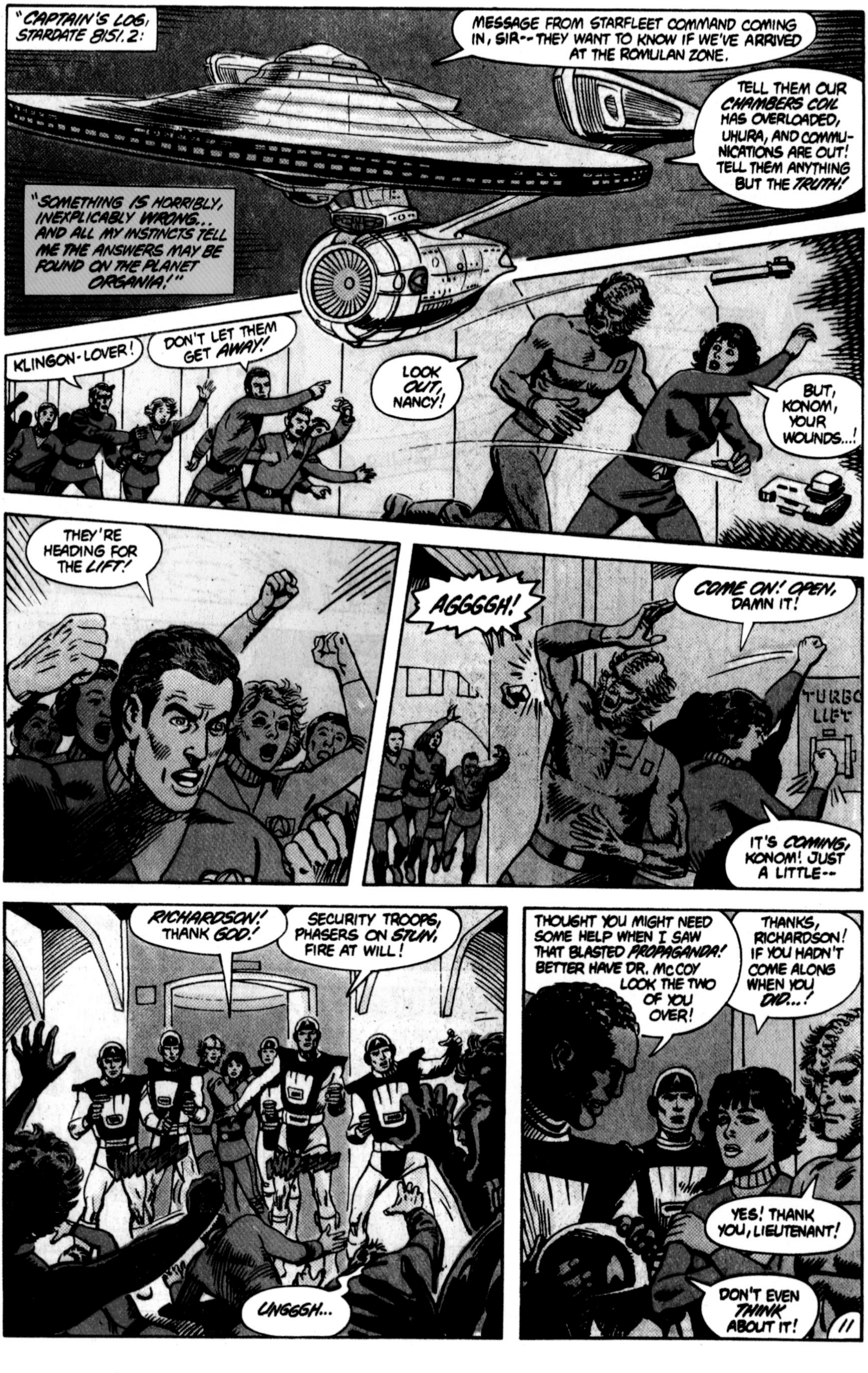
"CAPTAIN'S LOG, STARDATE 8151.2:
MESSAGE FROM STARFLEET COMMAND COMING IN, SIR-- THEY WANT TO KNOW IF WE'VE ARRIVED AT THE ROMULAN ZONE.
TELL THEM OUR CHAMBERS COIL HAS OVERLOADED, UHURA, AND COMMUNICATIONS ARE OUT! TELL THEM ANYTHING BUT THE TRUTH!
"SOMETHING IS HORRIBLY, INEXPLICABLY WRONG... AND ALL MY INSTINCTS TELL ME THE ANSWERS MAY BE FOUND ON THE PLANET ORGANIA!"
KLINGON-LOVER!
DON'T LET THEM GET AWAY!
LOOK OUT, NANCY!
BUT, KONOM, YOUR WOUNDS...!
THEY'RE HEADING FOR THE LIFT!
AGGGGH!
COME ON! OPEN, DAMN IT!
TURBO LIFT
IT'S COMING, KONOM! JUST A LITTLE--
RICHARDSON! THANK GOD!
SECURITY TROOPS, PHASERS ON STUN, FIRE AT WILL!
UNGGGH...
THOUGHT YOU MIGHT NEED SOME HELP WHEN I SAW THAT BLASTED PROPAGANDA! BETTER HAVE DR. McCOY LOOK THE TWO OF YOU OVER!
THANKS, RICHARDSON! IF YOU HADN'T COME ALONG WHEN YOU DID...!
YES! THANK YOU, LIEUTENANT!
DON'T EVEN THINK ABOUT IT!
11

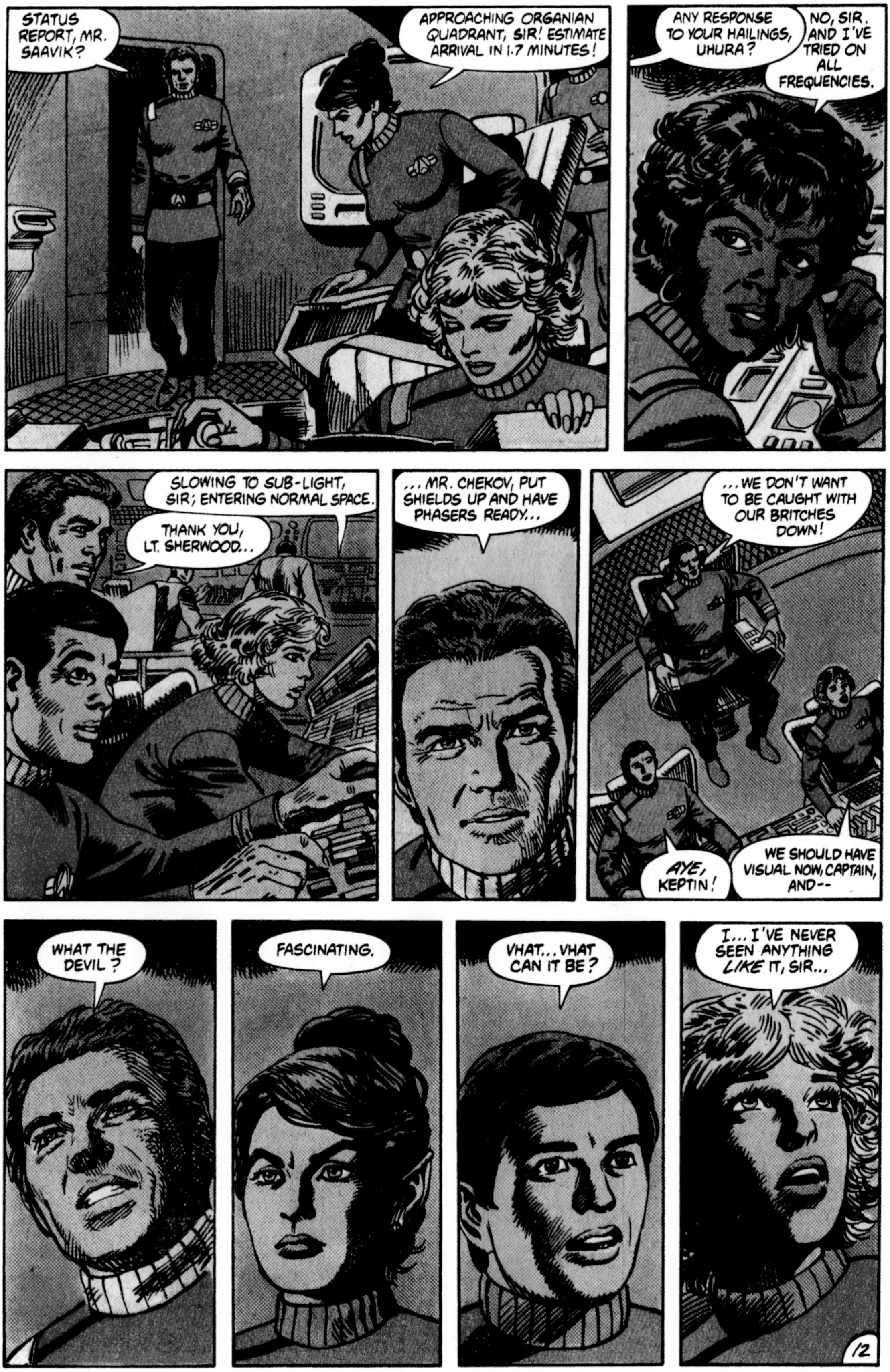
STATUS REPORT, MR. SAAVIK?
APPROACHING ORGANIAN QUADRANT, SIR! ESTIMATE ARRIVAL IN 1.7 MINUTES!
ANY RESPONSE TO YOUR HAILINGS, UHURA?
NO, SIR. AND I'VE TRIED ON ALL FREQUENCIES.
SLOWING TO SUB-LIGHT, SIR; ENTERING NORMAL SPACE.
THANK YOU, LT. SHERWOOD...
...MR. CHEKOV, PUT SHIELDS UP AND HAVE PHASERS READY...
...WE DON'T WANT TO BE CAUGHT WITH OUR BRITCHES DOWN!
AYE, KEPTIN!
WE SHOULD HAVE VISUAL NOW, CAPTAIN, AND--
WHAT THE DEVIL?
FASCINATING.
VHAT...VHAT CAN IT BE?
I... I'VE NEVER SEEN ANYTHING *LIKE* IT, SIR...
12

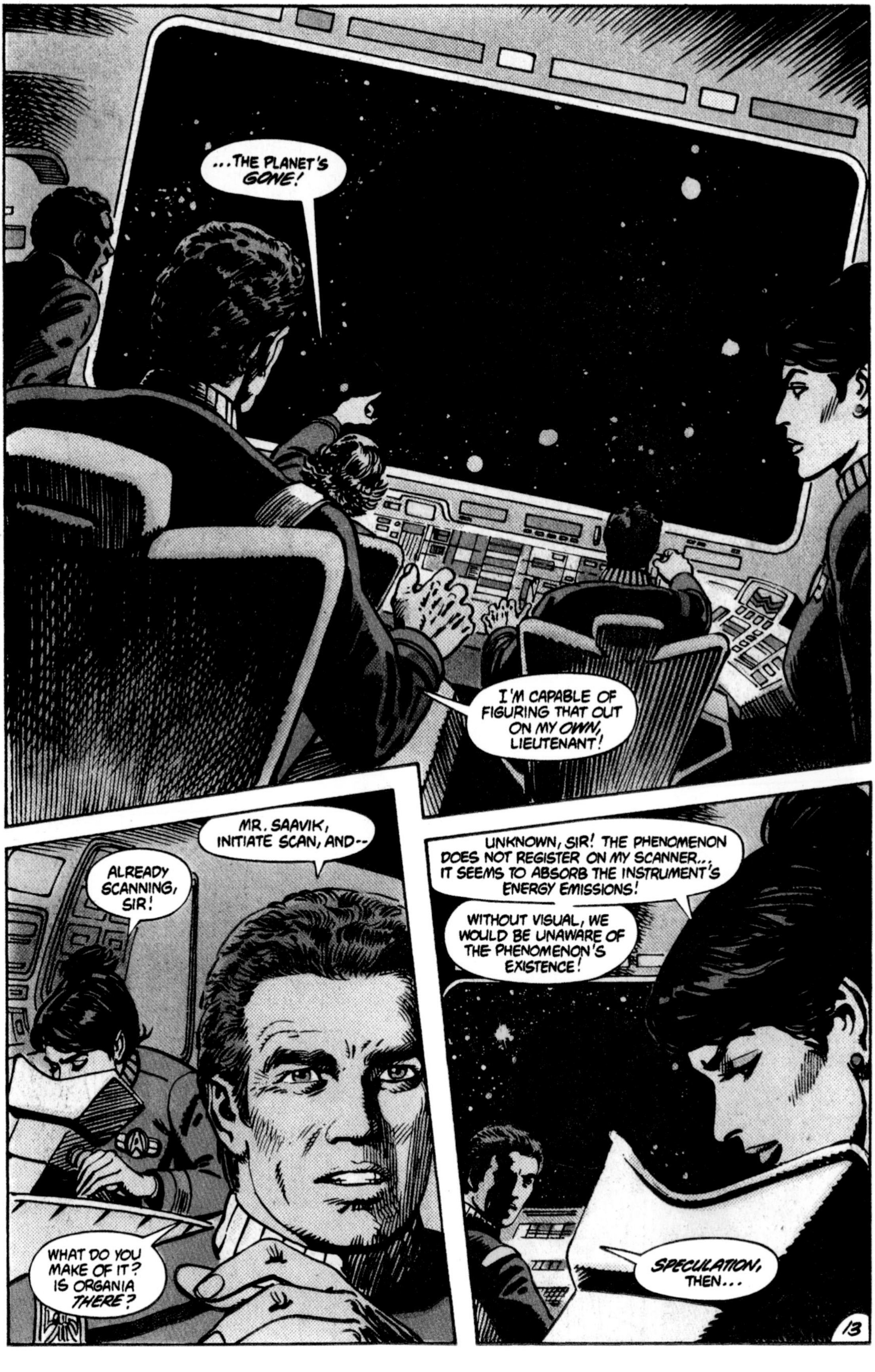
...THE PLANET'S GONE!
I'M CAPABLE OF FIGURING THAT OUT ON MY OWN, LIEUTENANT!
MR. SAAVIK, INITIATE SCAN, AND--
ALREADY SCANNING, SIR!
WHAT DO YOU MAKE OF IT? IS ORGANIA THERE?
UNKNOWN, SIR! THE PHENOMENON DOES NOT REGISTER ON MY SCANNER... IT SEEMS TO ABSORB THE INSTRUMENT'S ENERGY EMISSIONS!
WITHOUT VISUAL, WE WOULD BE UNAWARE OF THE PHENOMENON'S EXISTENCE!
SPECULATION, THEN...
13

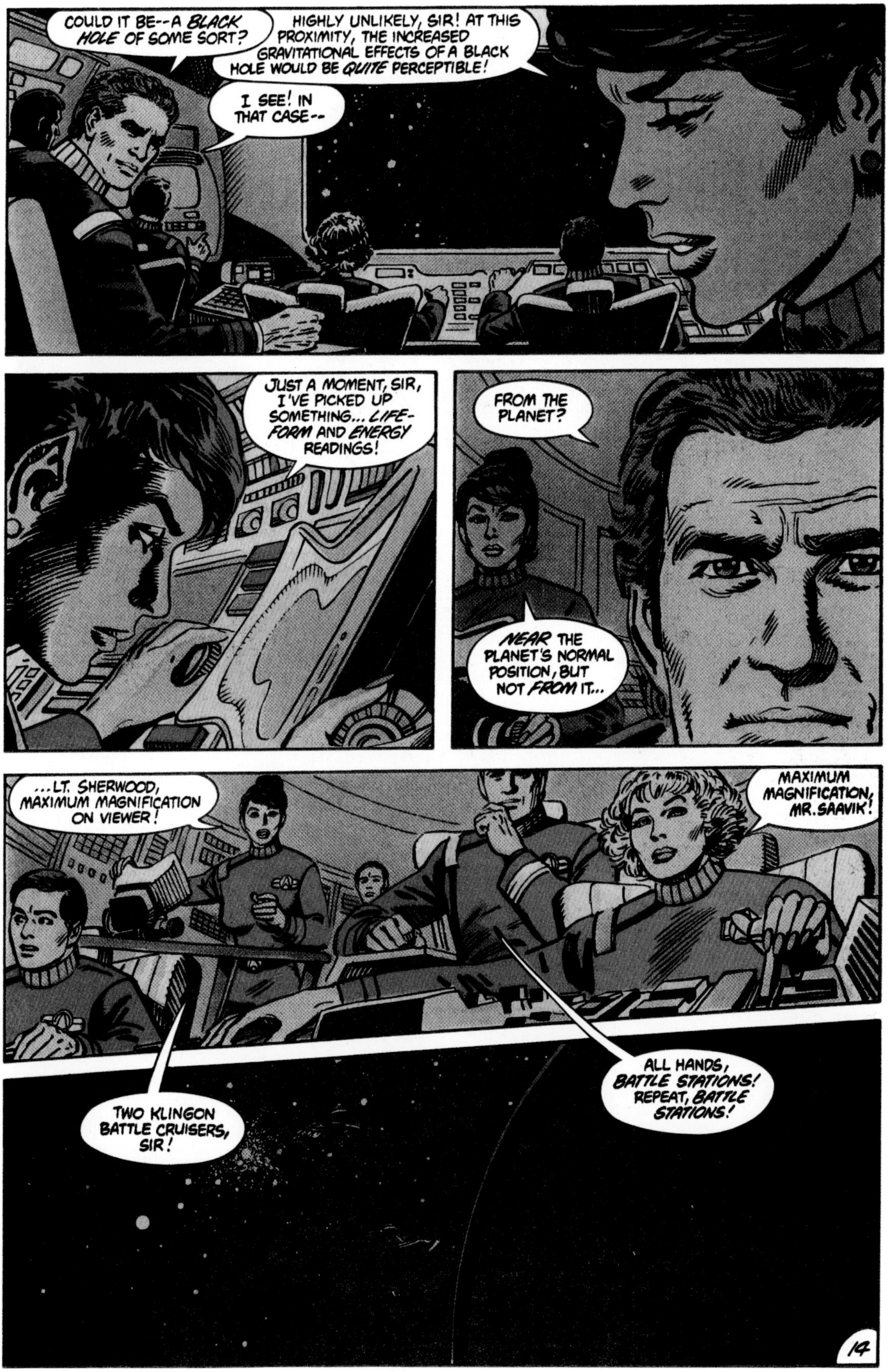
COULD IT BE--A BLACK HOLE OF SOME SORT?
HIGHLY UNLIKELY, SIR! AT THIS PROXIMITY, THE INCREASED GRAVITATIONAL EFFECTS OF A BLACK HOLE WOULD BE QUITE PERCEPTIBLE!
I SEE! IN THAT CASE--
JUST A MOMENT, SIR, I'VE PICKED UP SOMETHING... LIFE-FORM AND ENERGY READINGS!
FROM THE PLANET?
NEAR THE PLANET'S NORMAL POSITION, BUT NOT FROM IT...
...LT. SHERWOOD, MAXIMUM MAGNIFICATION ON VIEWER!
MAXIMUM MAGNIFICATION, MR. SAAVIK!
TWO KLINGON BATTLE CRUISERS, SIR!
ALL HANDS, BATTLE STATIONS! REPEAT, BATTLE STATIONS!
14

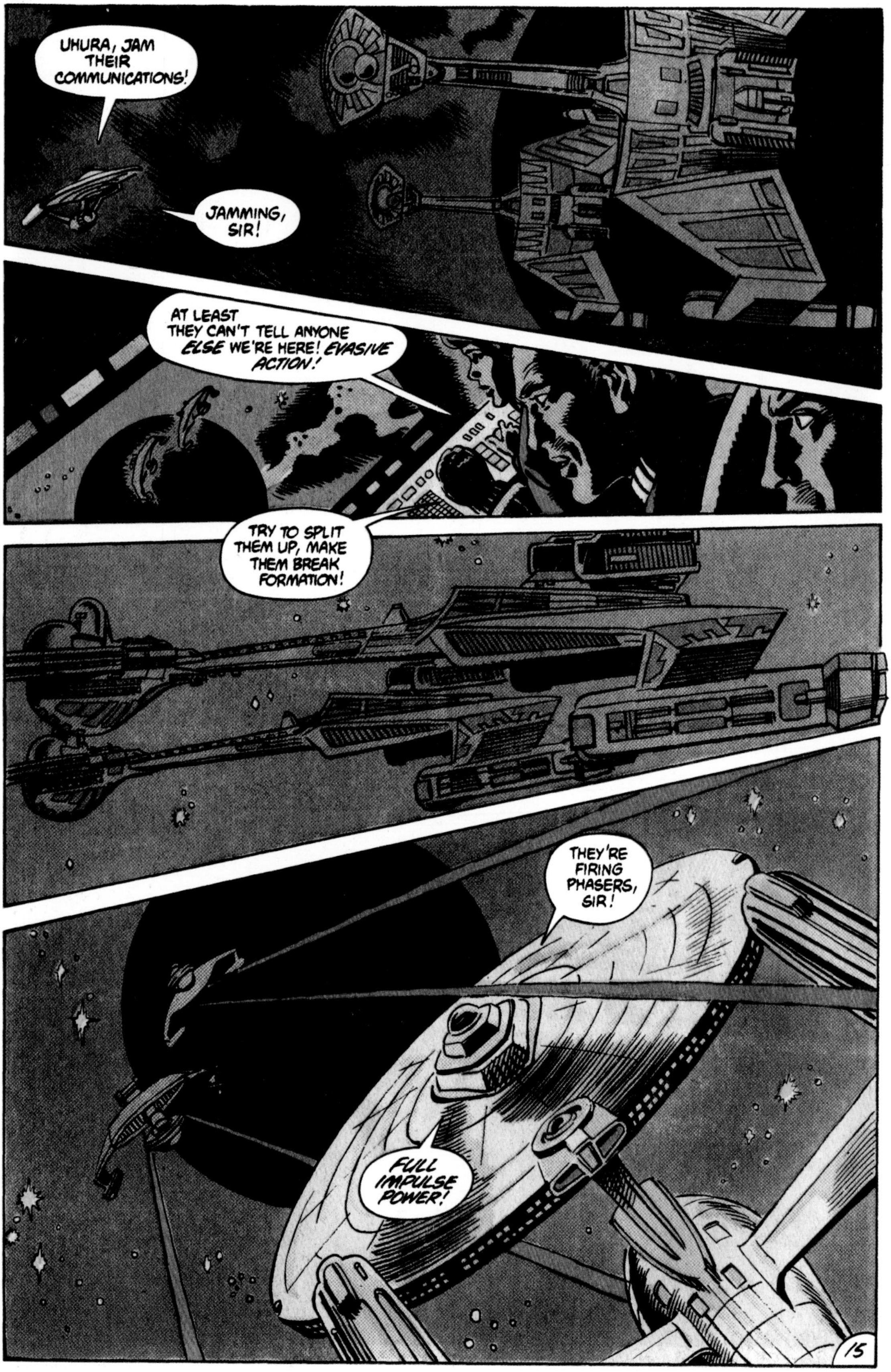
UHURA, JAM THEIR COMMUNICATIONS!
JAMMING, SIR!
AT LEAST THEY CAN'T TELL ANYONE ELSE WE'RE HERE! EVASIVE ACTION!
TRY TO SPLIT THEM UP, MAKE THEM BREAK FORMATION!
THEY'RE FIRING PHASERS, SIR!
FULL IMPULSE POWER!
15

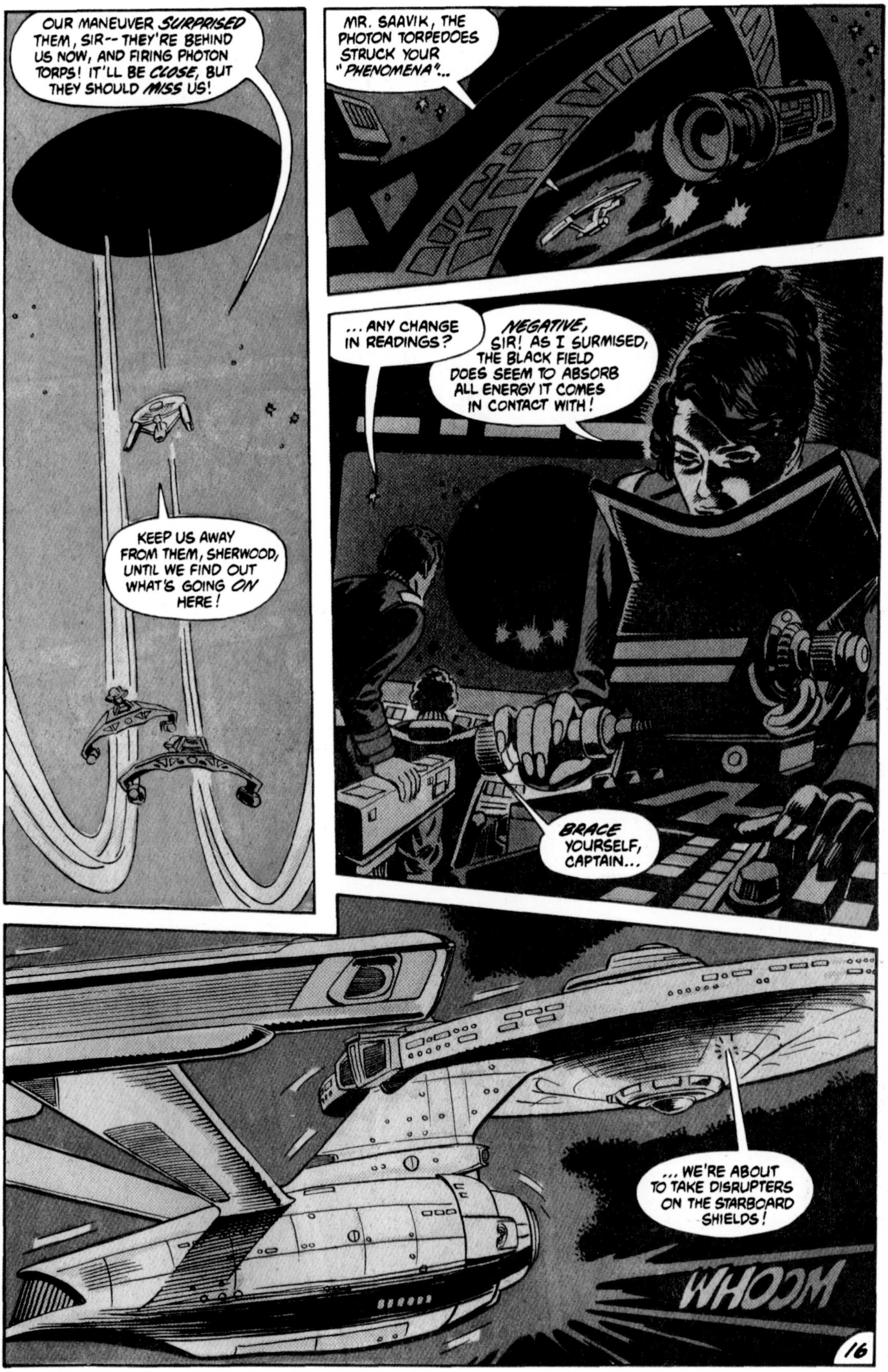
OUR MANEUVER SURPRISED THEM, SIR-- THEY'RE BEHIND US NOW, AND FIRING PHOTON TORPS! IT'LL BE CLOSE, BUT THEY SHOULD MISS US!
KEEP US AWAY FROM THEM, SHERWOOD, UNTIL WE FIND OUT WHAT'S GOING ON HERE!
MR. SAAVIK, THE PHOTON TORPEDOES STRUCK YOUR "PHENOMENA"...
... ANY CHANGE IN READINGS?
NEGATIVE, SIR! AS I SURMISED, THE BLACK FIELD DOES SEEM TO ABSORB ALL ENERGY IT COMES IN CONTACT WITH!
BRACE YOURSELF, CAPTAIN...
... WE'RE ABOUT TO TAKE DISRUPTERS ON THE STARBOARD SHIELDS!
WHOOM
16

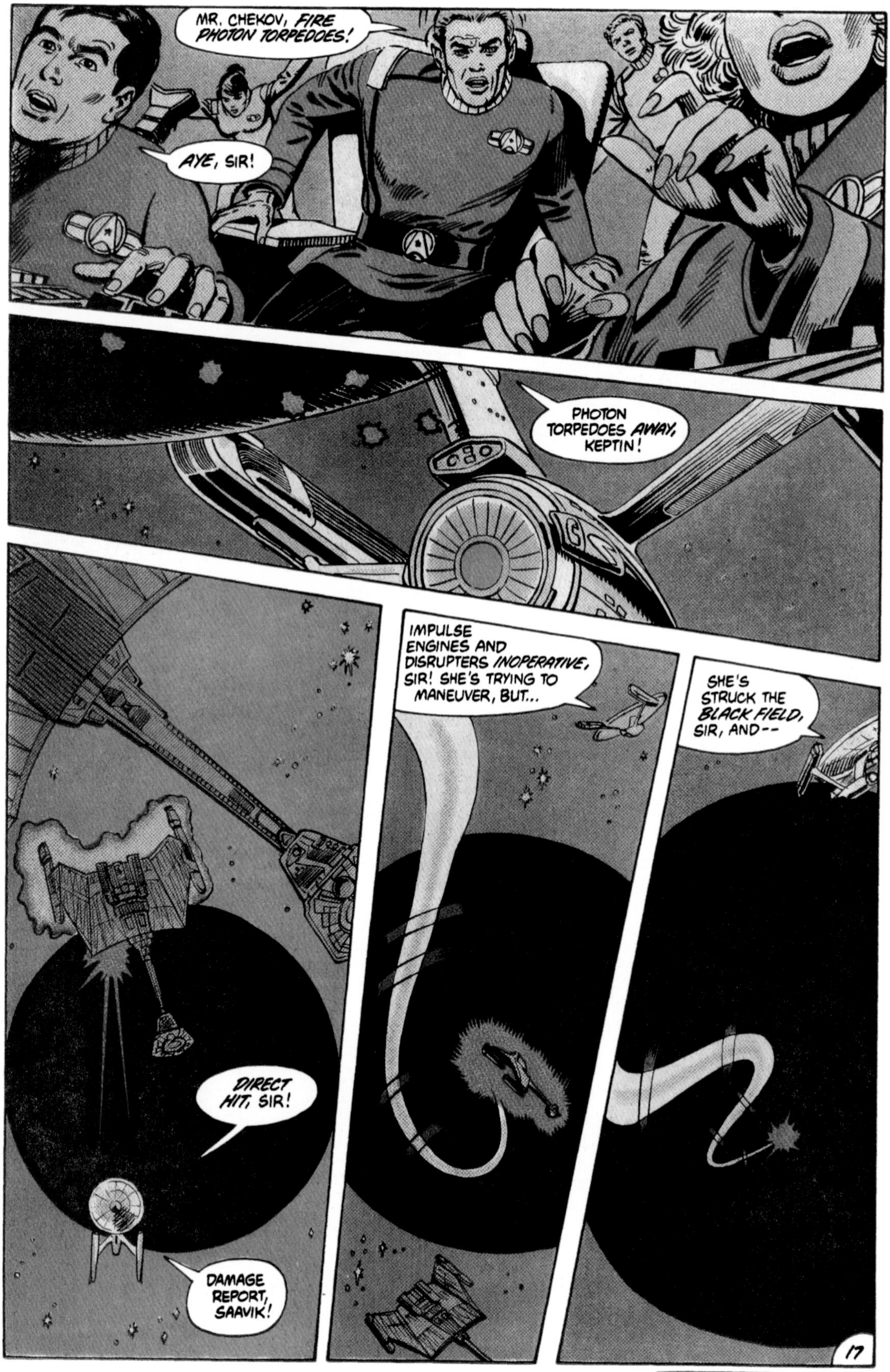
MR. CHEKOV, *FIRE PHOTON TORPEDOES!*
AYE, SIR!
PHOTON TORPEDOES *AWAY*, KEPTIN!
DIRECT HIT, SIR!
DAMAGE REPORT, SAAVIK!
IMPULSE ENGINES AND DISRUPTERS *INOPERATIVE*, SIR! SHE'S TRYING TO MANEUVER, BUT...
SHE'S STRUCK THE *BLACK FIELD*, SIR, AND--
17

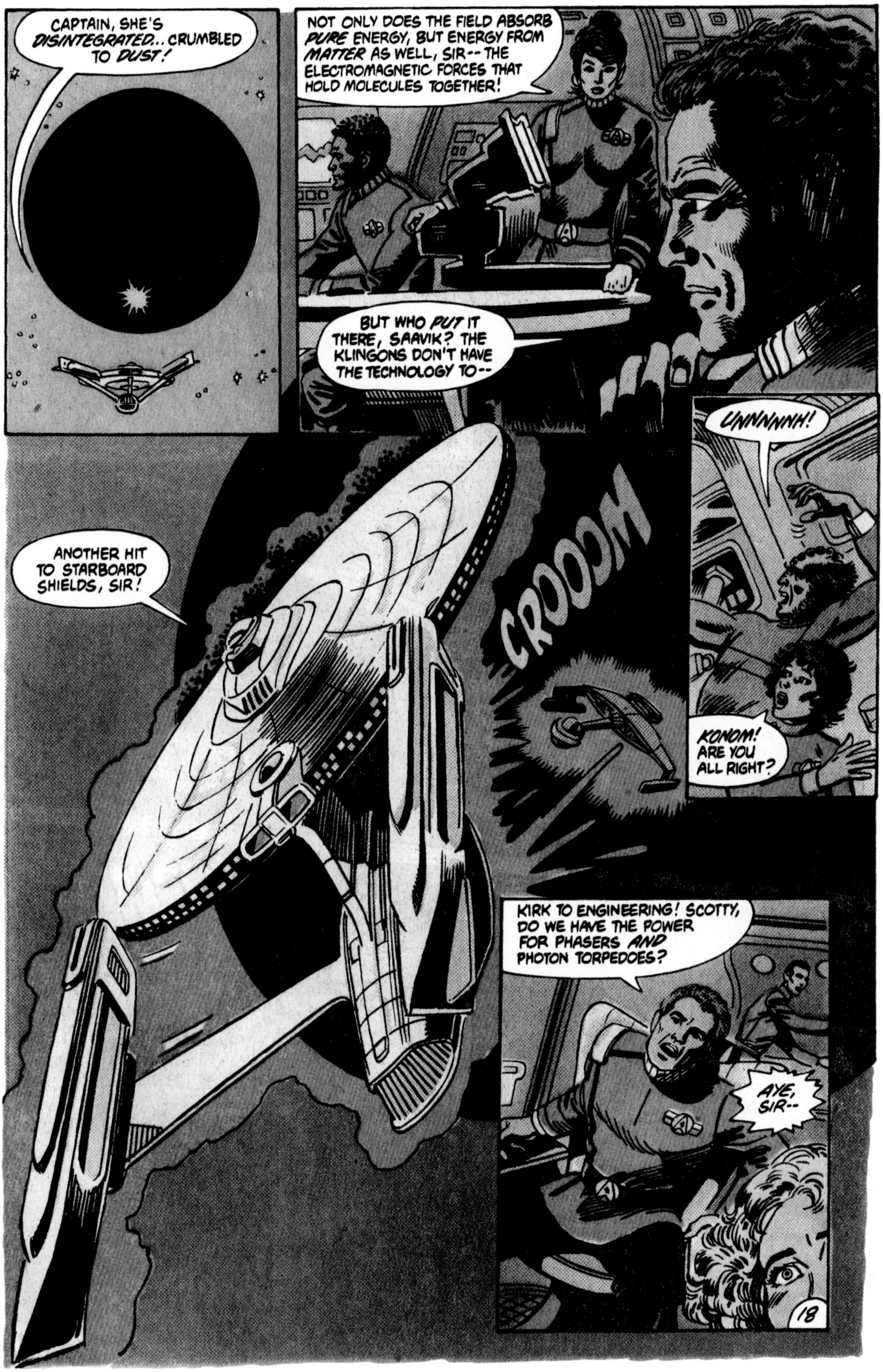
CAPTAIN, SHE'S DISINTEGRATED... CRUMBLED TO DUST!
NOT ONLY DOES THE FIELD ABSORB PURE ENERGY, BUT ENERGY FROM MATTER AS WELL, SIR-- THE ELECTROMAGNETIC FORCES THAT HOLD MOLECULES TOGETHER!
BUT WHO PUT IT THERE, SAAVIK? THE KLINGONS DON'T HAVE THE TECHNOLOGY TO--
ANOTHER HIT TO STARBOARD SHIELDS, SIR!
CROOOM
UNNNNNH!
KONOM! ARE YOU ALL RIGHT?
KIRK TO ENGINEERING! SCOTTY, DO WE HAVE THE POWER FOR PHASERS AND PHOTON TORPEDOES?
AYE, SIR--
18

--WE'VE NOT BEEN HIT THAT BADLY...

...NOT YET!

UNDERSTOOD, MR. SCOTT!

LT. SHERWOOD, LOCK ONTO THEIR *ENGINEERING* SECTION...

BUT, SIR, THEIR SHIELDS--

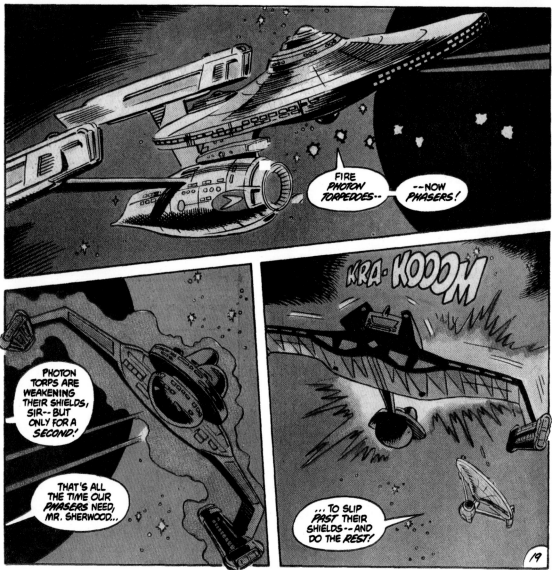

FIRE *PHOTON TORPEDOES*--

--NOW *PHASERS!*

PHOTON TORPS ARE *WEAKENING* THEIR SHIELDS, SIR-- BUT ONLY FOR A *SECOND!*

THAT'S ALL THE TIME OUR *PHASERS* NEED, MR. SHERWOOD...

KRA-KOOOM

... TO SLIP *PAST* THEIR SHIELDS-- AND DO THE *REST!*

19

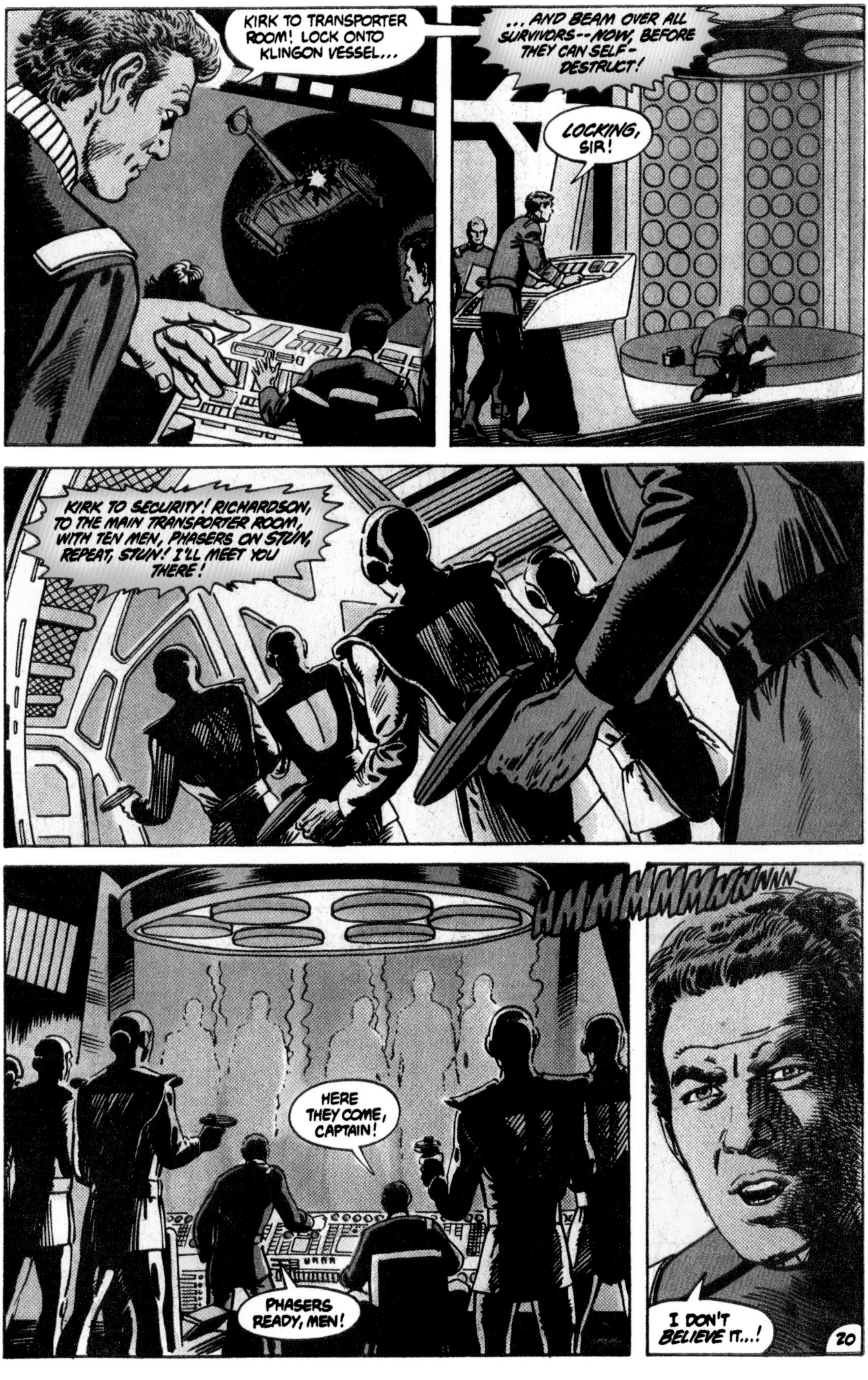
KIRK TO TRANSPORTER ROOM! LOCK ONTO KLINGON VESSEL...
...AND BEAM OVER ALL SURVIVORS--NOW, BEFORE THEY CAN SELF-DESTRUCT!
LOCKING, SIR!
KIRK TO SECURITY! RICHARDSON, TO THE MAIN TRANSPORTER ROOM, WITH TEN MEN, PHASERS ON STUN, REPEAT, STUN! I'LL MEET YOU THERE!
HMMMMMMNNNN
HERE THEY COME, CAPTAIN!
PHASERS READY, MEN!
I DON'T BELIEVE IT...!
20

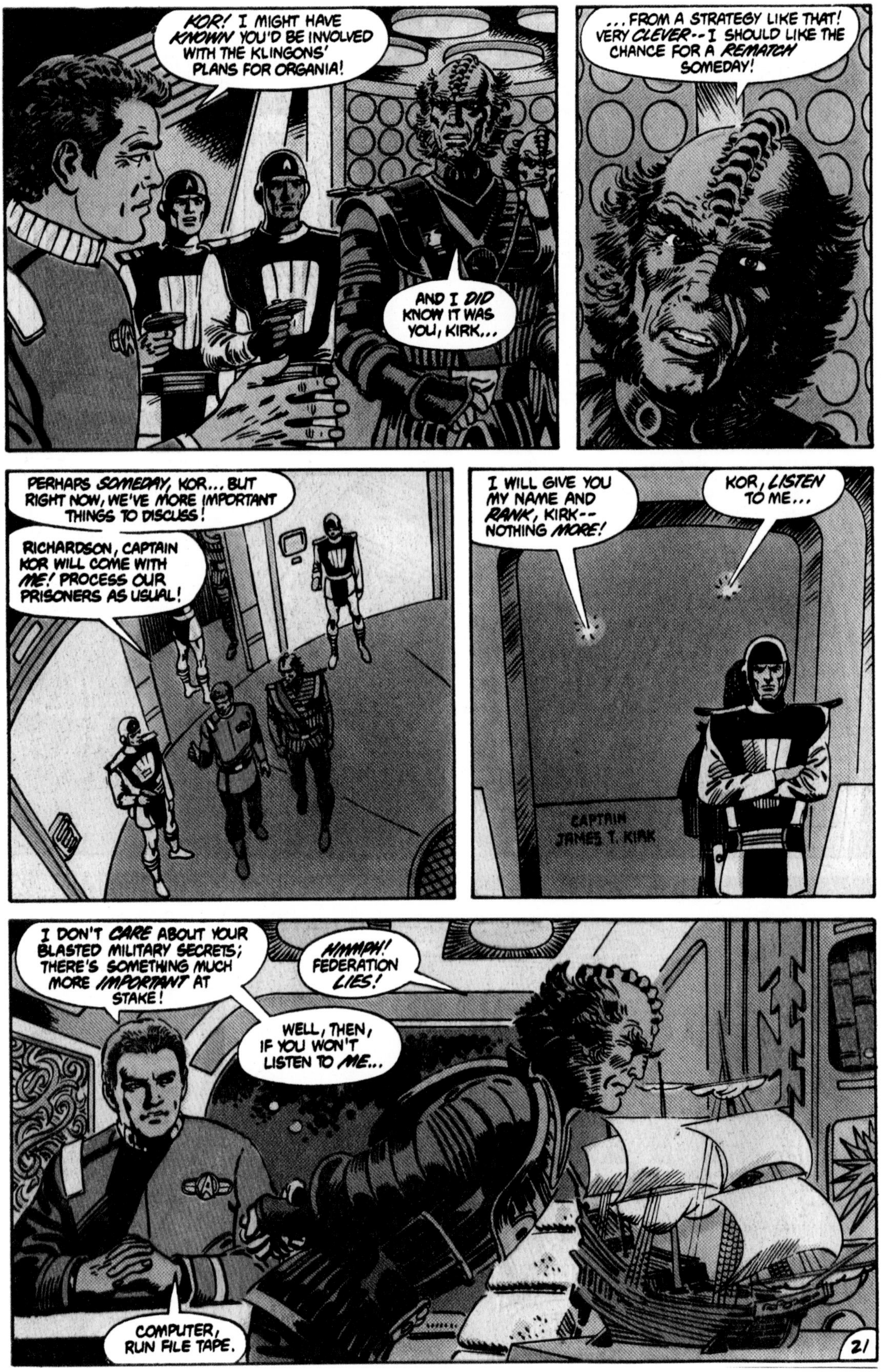
KOR! I MIGHT HAVE KNOWN YOU'D BE INVOLVED WITH THE KLINGONS' PLANS FOR ORGANIA!
AND I DID KNOW IT WAS YOU, KIRK...
...FROM A STRATEGY LIKE THAT! VERY CLEVER-- I SHOULD LIKE THE CHANCE FOR A REMATCH SOMEDAY!
PERHAPS SOMEDAY, KOR... BUT RIGHT NOW, WE'VE MORE IMPORTANT THINGS TO DISCUSS!
RICHARDSON, CAPTAIN KOR WILL COME WITH ME! PROCESS OUR PRISONERS AS USUAL!
I WILL GIVE YOU MY NAME AND RANK, KIRK-- NOTHING MORE!
KOR, LISTEN TO ME...
CAPTAIN
JAMES T. KIRK
I DON'T CARE ABOUT YOUR BLASTED MILITARY SECRETS; THERE'S SOMETHING MUCH MORE IMPORTANT AT STAKE!
HMMPH! FEDERATION LIES!
WELL, THEN, IF YOU WON'T LISTEN TO ME...
COMPUTER, RUN FILE TAPE.
21

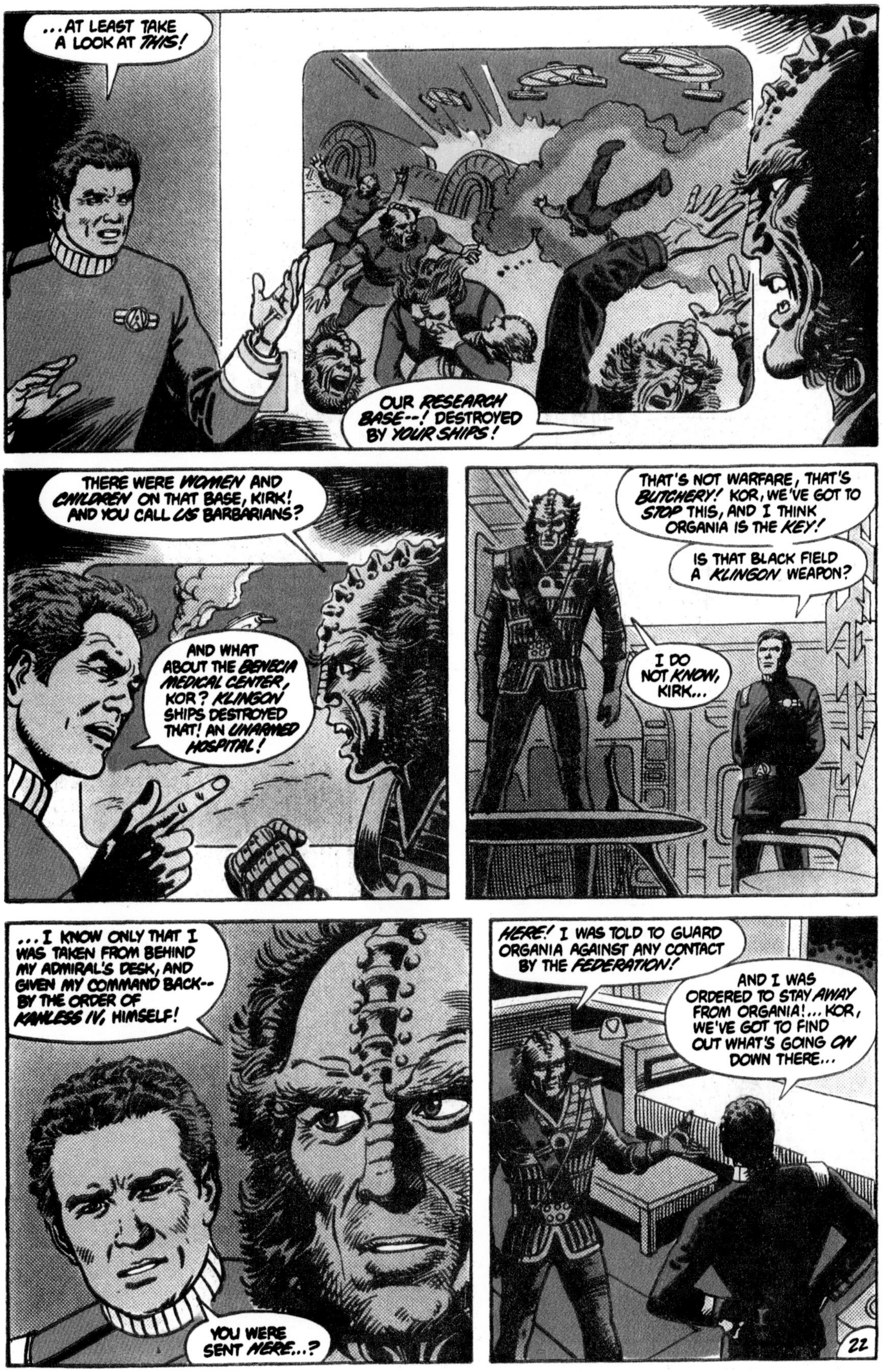
...AT LEAST TAKE A LOOK AT THIS!
OUR RESEARCH BASE--! DESTROYED BY YOUR SHIPS!
THERE WERE WOMEN AND CHILDREN ON THAT BASE, KIRK! AND YOU CALL US BARBARIANS?
AND WHAT ABOUT THE BENECIA MEDICAL CENTER, KOR? KLINGON SHIPS DESTROYED THAT! AN UNARMED HOSPITAL!
THAT'S NOT WARFARE, THAT'S BUTCHERY! KOR, WE'VE GOT TO STOP THIS, AND I THINK ORGANIA IS THE KEY!
IS THAT BLACK FIELD A KLINGON WEAPON?
I DO NOT KNOW, KIRK...
...I KNOW ONLY THAT I WAS TAKEN FROM BEHIND MY ADMIRAL'S DESK, AND GIVEN MY COMMAND BACK--BY THE ORDER OF KAHLESS IV, HIMSELF!
YOU WERE SENT HERE...?
HERE! I WAS TOLD TO GUARD ORGANIA AGAINST ANY CONTACT BY THE FEDERATION!
AND I WAS ORDERED TO STAY AWAY FROM ORGANIA!... KOR, WE'VE GOT TO FIND OUT WHAT'S GOING ON DOWN THERE...
22

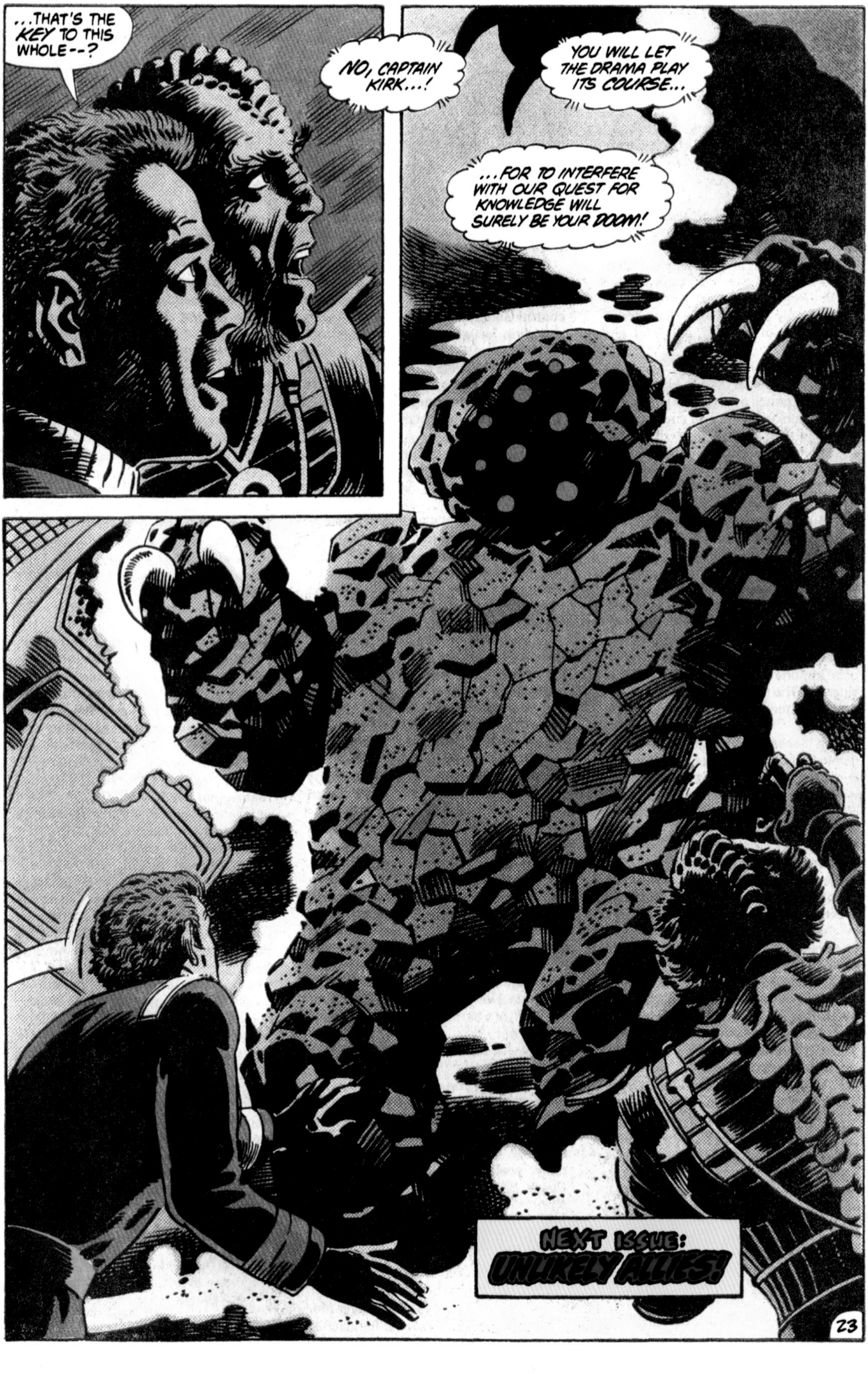
...THAT'S THE KEY TO THIS WHOLE--?
NO, CAPTAIN KIRK...!
YOU WILL LET THE DRAMA PLAY ITS COURSE...
...FOR TO INTERFERE WITH OUR QUEST FOR KNOWLEDGE WILL SURELY BE YOUR DOOM!
NEXT ISSUE: UNLIKELY ALLIES!
23

STAR TREK®

Based on the series created by **Gene Roddenberry**

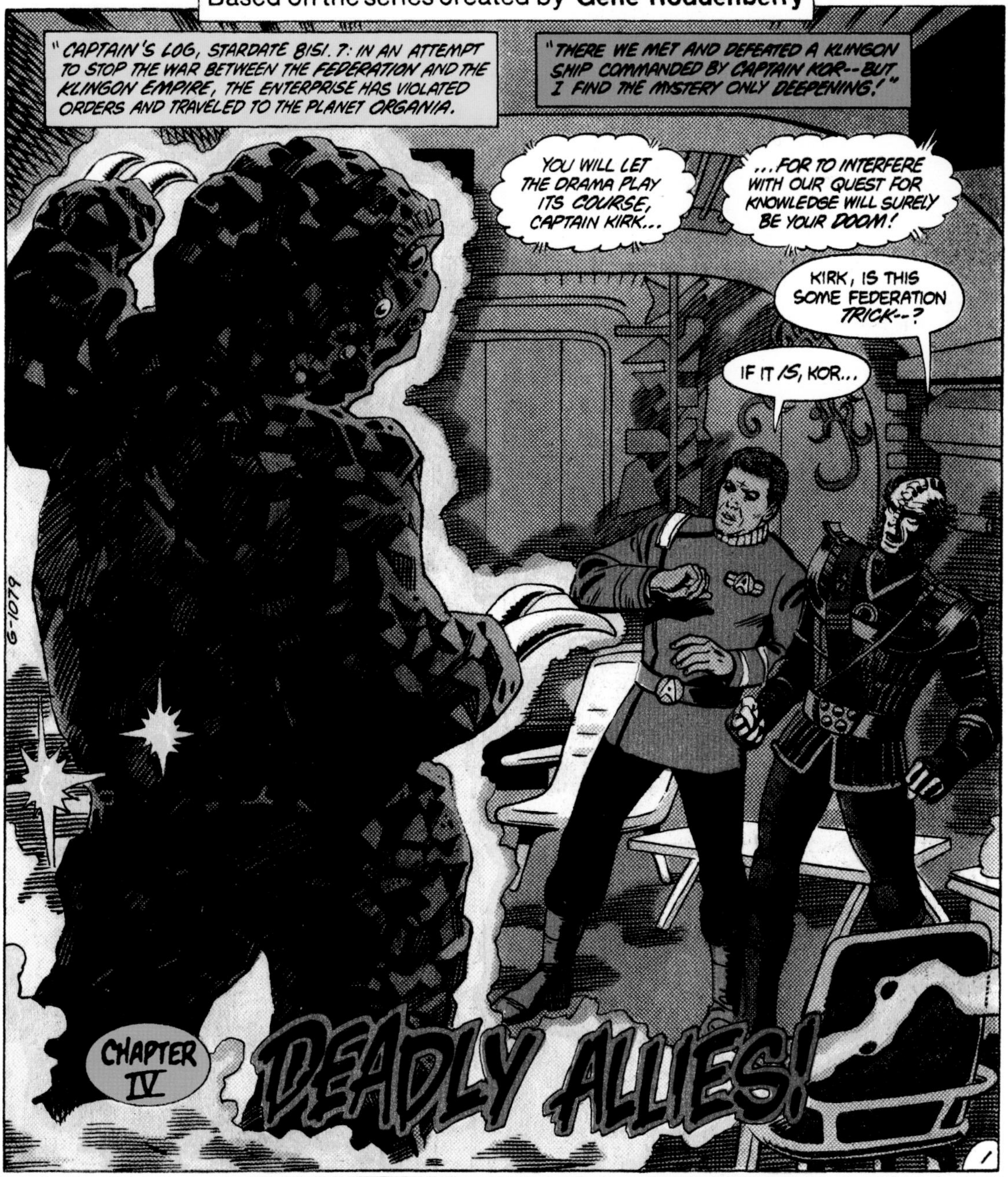

"CAPTAIN'S LOG, STARDATE 8151.7: IN AN ATTEMPT TO STOP THE WAR BETWEEN THE FEDERATION AND THE KLINGON EMPIRE, THE ENTERPRISE HAS VIOLATED ORDERS AND TRAVELED TO THE PLANET ORGANIA.
"THERE WE MET AND DEFEATED A KLINGON SHIP COMMANDED BY CAPTAIN KOR--BUT I FIND THE MYSTERY ONLY DEEPENING!"
YOU WILL LET THE DRAMA PLAY ITS COURSE, CAPTAIN KIRK...
...FOR TO INTERFERE WITH OUR QUEST FOR KNOWLEDGE WILL SURELY BE YOUR DOOM!
KIRK, IS THIS SOME FEDERATION TRICK--?
IF IT IS, KOR...
G-1079
CHAPTER IV
DEADLY ALLIES!
1

MIKE W. BARR * **TOM SUTTON & RICARDO VILLAGRAN**
Writer — Artists

JOHN COSTANZA * **MICHELE WOLFMAN** * **MARV WOLFMAN**
Letterer — Colorist — Editor

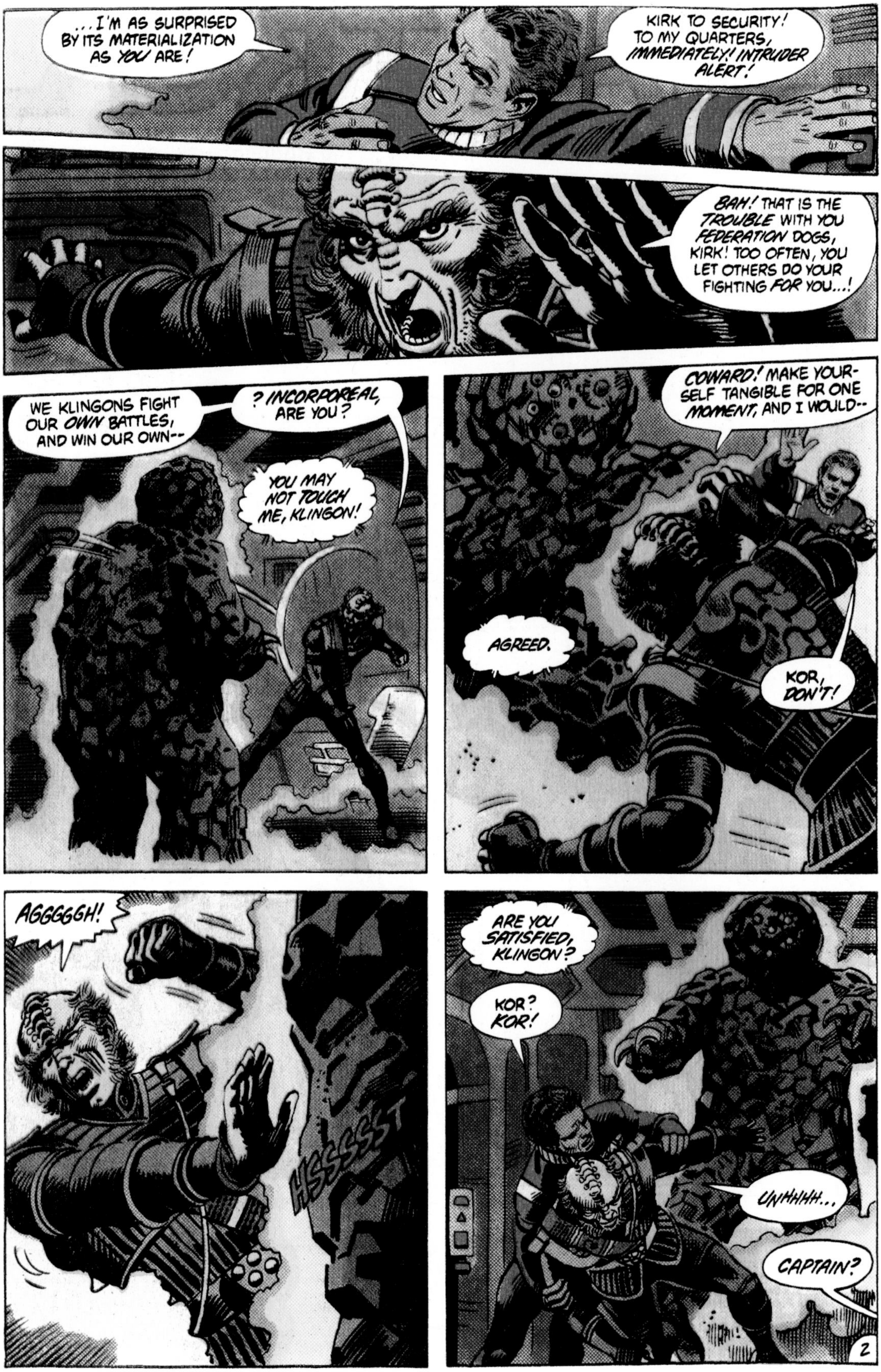

...I'M AS SURPRISED BY ITS MATERIALIZATION AS YOU ARE!
KIRK TO SECURITY! TO MY QUARTERS, IMMEDIATELY! INTRUDER ALERT!
BAH! THAT IS THE TROUBLE WITH YOU FEDERATION DOGS, KIRK! TOO OFTEN, YOU LET OTHERS DO YOUR FIGHTING FOR YOU...!
WE KLINGONS FIGHT OUR OWN BATTLES, AND WIN OUR OWN--
?INCORPOREAL, ARE YOU?
YOU MAY NOT TOUCH ME, KLINGON!
COWARD! MAKE YOURSELF TANGIBLE FOR ONE MOMENT, AND I WOULD--
AGREED.
KOR, DON'T!
AGGGGGH!
HSSSSST
ARE YOU SATISFIED, KLINGON?
KOR? KOR!
UNHHHH...
CAPTAIN?
2

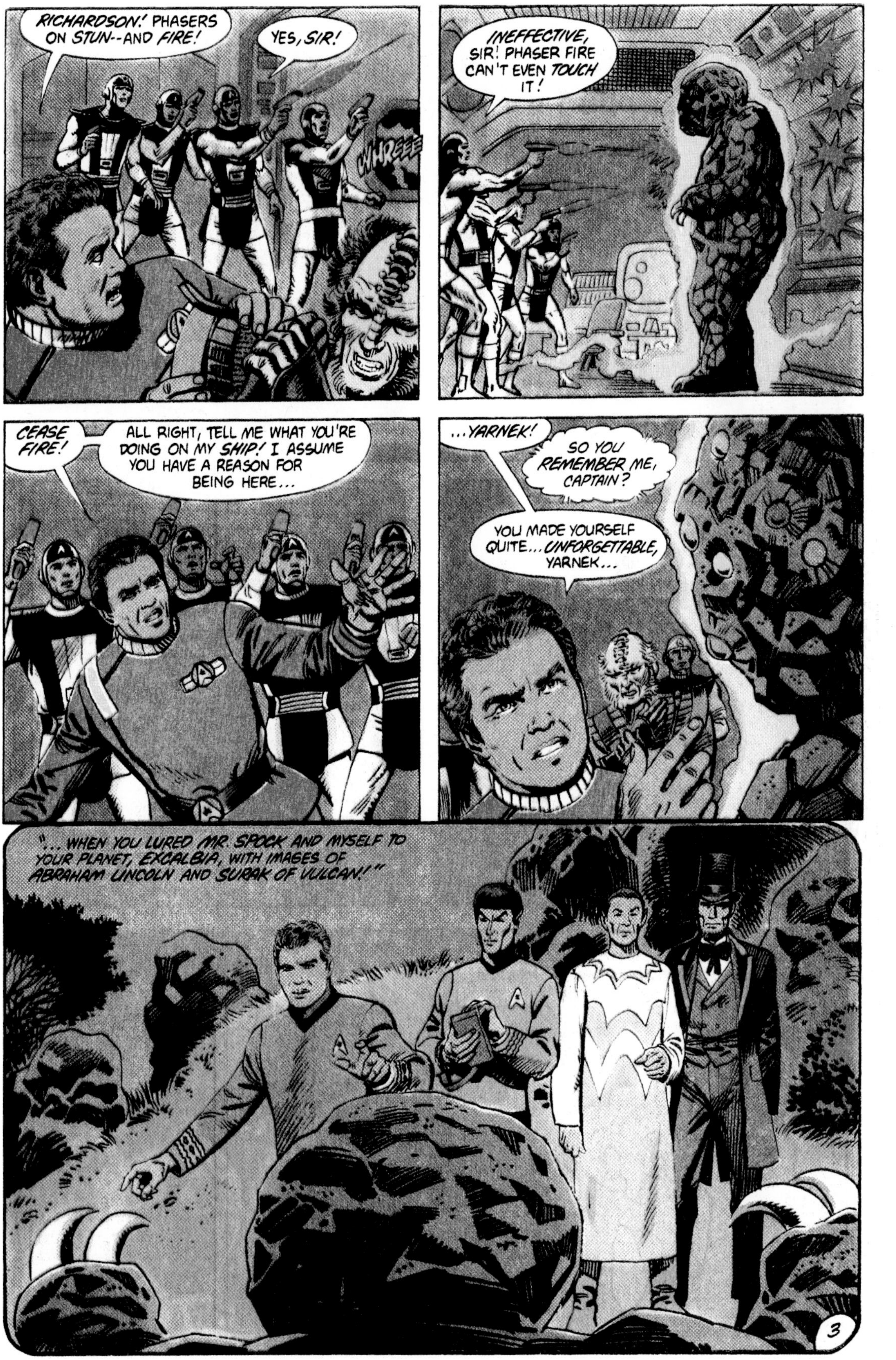
RICHARDSON! PHASERS ON STUN--AND FIRE!
YES, SIR!
WHREEE
INEFFECTIVE, SIR! PHASER FIRE CAN'T EVEN TOUCH IT!
CEASE FIRE!
ALL RIGHT, TELL ME WHAT YOU'RE DOING ON MY SHIP! I ASSUME YOU HAVE A REASON FOR BEING HERE...
...YARNEK!
SO YOU REMEMBER ME, CAPTAIN?
YOU MADE YOURSELF QUITE... UNFORGETTABLE, YARNEK...
"...WHEN YOU LURED MR. SPOCK AND MYSELF TO YOUR PLANET, EXCALBIA, WITH IMAGES OF ABRAHAM LINCOLN AND SURAK OF VULCAN!"
3

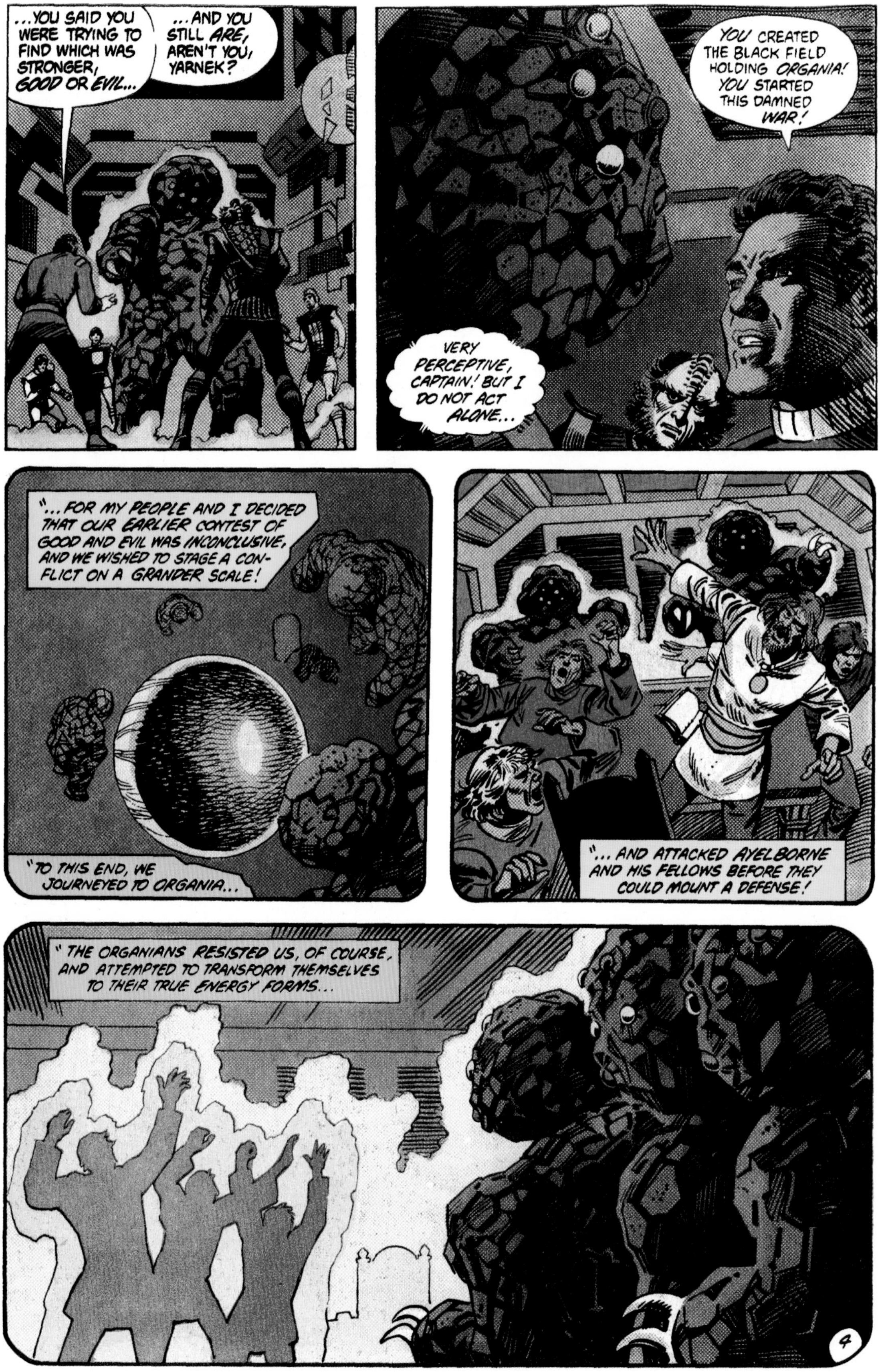

...YOU SAID YOU WERE TRYING TO FIND WHICH WAS STRONGER, GOOD OR EVIL...
...AND YOU STILL ARE, AREN'T YOU, YARNEK?
YOU CREATED THE BLACK FIELD HOLDING ORGANIA! YOU STARTED THIS DAMNED WAR!
VERY PERCEPTIVE, CAPTAIN! BUT I DO NOT ACT ALONE...
"...FOR MY PEOPLE AND I DECIDED THAT OUR EARLIER CONTEST OF GOOD AND EVIL WAS INCONCLUSIVE, AND WE WISHED TO STAGE A CONFLICT ON A GRANDER SCALE!
"TO THIS END, WE JOURNEYED TO ORGANIA...
"...AND ATTACKED AYELBORNE AND HIS FELLOWS BEFORE THEY COULD MOUNT A DEFENSE!
"THE ORGANIANS RESISTED US, OF COURSE, AND ATTEMPTED TO TRANSFORM THEMSELVES TO THEIR TRUE ENERGY FORMS...
4

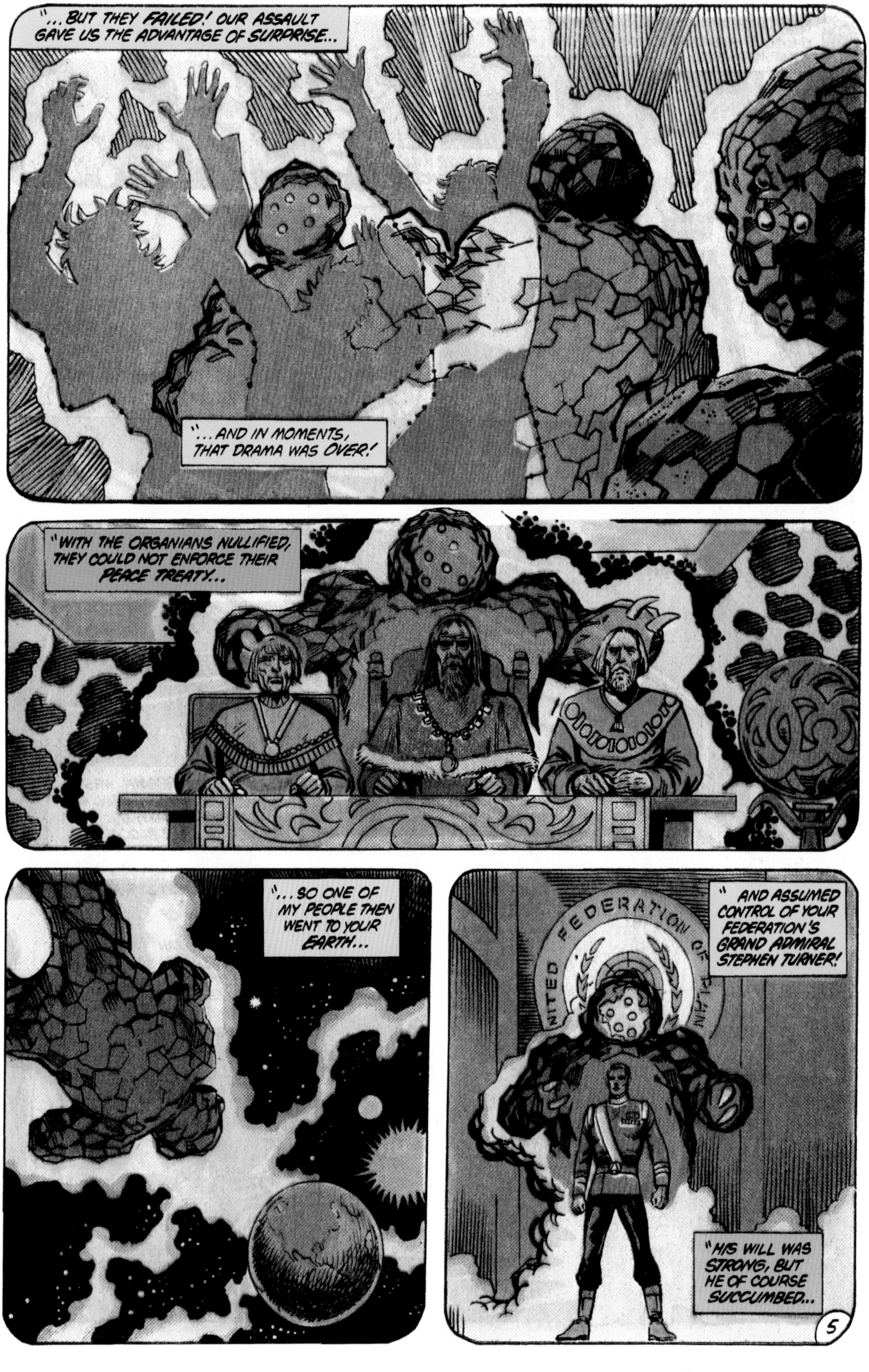
"...BUT THEY FAILED! OUR ASSAULT GAVE US THE ADVANTAGE OF SURPRISE...
"...AND IN MOMENTS, THAT DRAMA WAS OVER!
"WITH THE ORGANIANS NULLIFIED, THEY COULD NOT ENFORCE THEIR PEACE TREATY...
"...SO ONE OF MY PEOPLE THEN WENT TO YOUR EARTH...
" AND ASSUMED CONTROL OF YOUR FEDERATION'S GRAND ADMIRAL STEPHEN TURNER!
UNITED FEDERATION OF PLAN
"HIS WILL WAS STRONG, BUT HE OF COURSE SUCCUMBED...
5

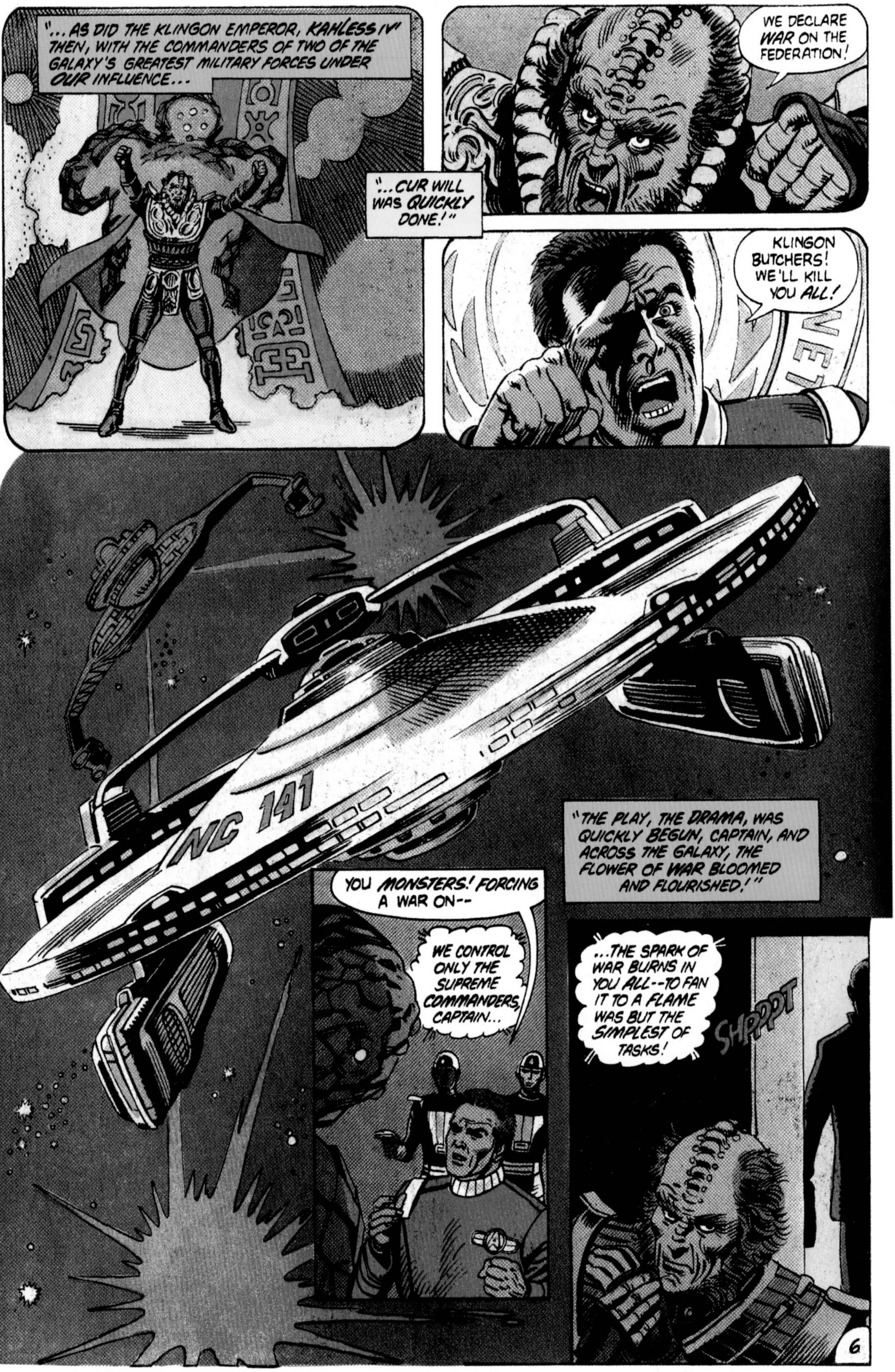
"...AS DID THE KLINGON EMPEROR, KAHLESS IV" THEN, WITH THE COMMANDERS OF TWO OF THE GALAXY'S GREATEST MILITARY FORCES UNDER OUR INFLUENCE...
WE DECLARE WAR ON THE FEDERATION!
"...CUR WILL WAS QUICKLY DONE!"
KLINGON BUTCHERS! WE'LL KILL YOU ALL!
NC 141
"THE PLAY, THE DRAMA, WAS QUICKLY BEGUN, CAPTAIN, AND ACROSS THE GALAXY, THE FLOWER OF WAR BLOOMED AND FLOURISHED!"
YOU MONSTERS! FORCING A WAR ON--
WE CONTROL ONLY THE SUPREME COMMANDERS, CAPTAIN...
...THE SPARK OF WAR BURNS IN YOU ALL--TO FAN IT TO A FLAME WAS BUT THE SIMPLEST OF TASKS!
SHPPPT
6

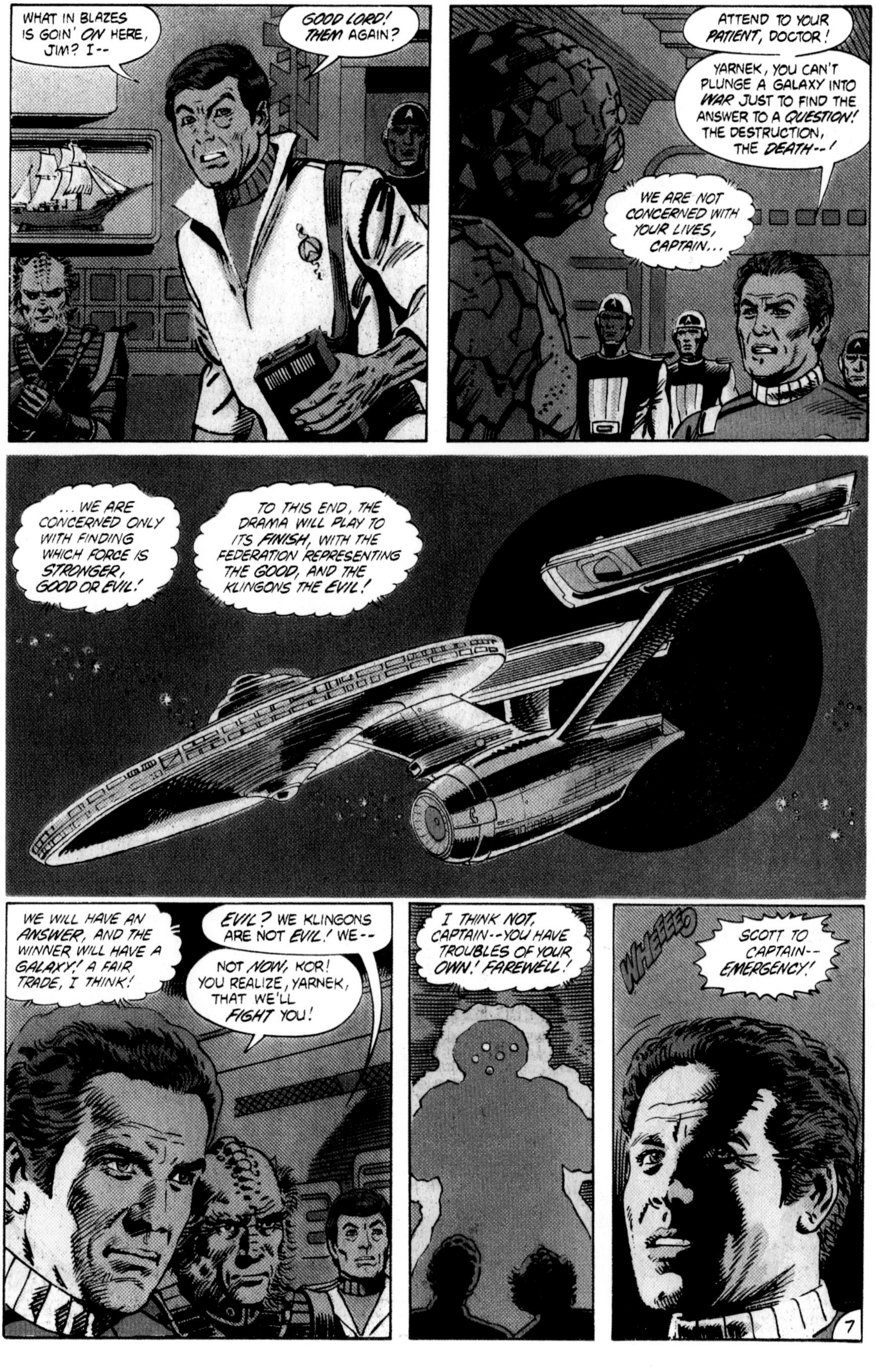

WHAT IN BLAZES IS GOIN' ON HERE, JIM? I--
GOOD LORD! THEM AGAIN?
ATTEND TO YOUR PATIENT, DOCTOR!
YARNEK, YOU CAN'T PLUNGE A GALAXY INTO WAR JUST TO FIND THE ANSWER TO A QUESTION! THE DESTRUCTION, THE DEATH--!
WE ARE NOT CONCERNED WITH YOUR LIVES, CAPTAIN...
...WE ARE CONCERNED ONLY WITH FINDING WHICH FORCE IS STRONGER, GOOD OR EVIL!
TO THIS END, THE DRAMA WILL PLAY TO ITS FINISH, WITH THE FEDERATION REPRESENTING THE GOOD, AND THE KLINGONS THE EVIL!
WE WILL HAVE AN ANSWER, AND THE WINNER WILL HAVE A GALAXY! A FAIR TRADE, I THINK!
EVIL? WE KLINGONS ARE NOT EVIL! WE--
NOT NOW, KOR! YOU REALIZE, YARNEK, THAT WE'LL FIGHT YOU!
I THINK NOT, CAPTAIN--YOU HAVE TROUBLES OF YOUR OWN! FAREWELL!
WHEEEEO
SCOTT TO CAPTAIN-- EMERGENCY!
7

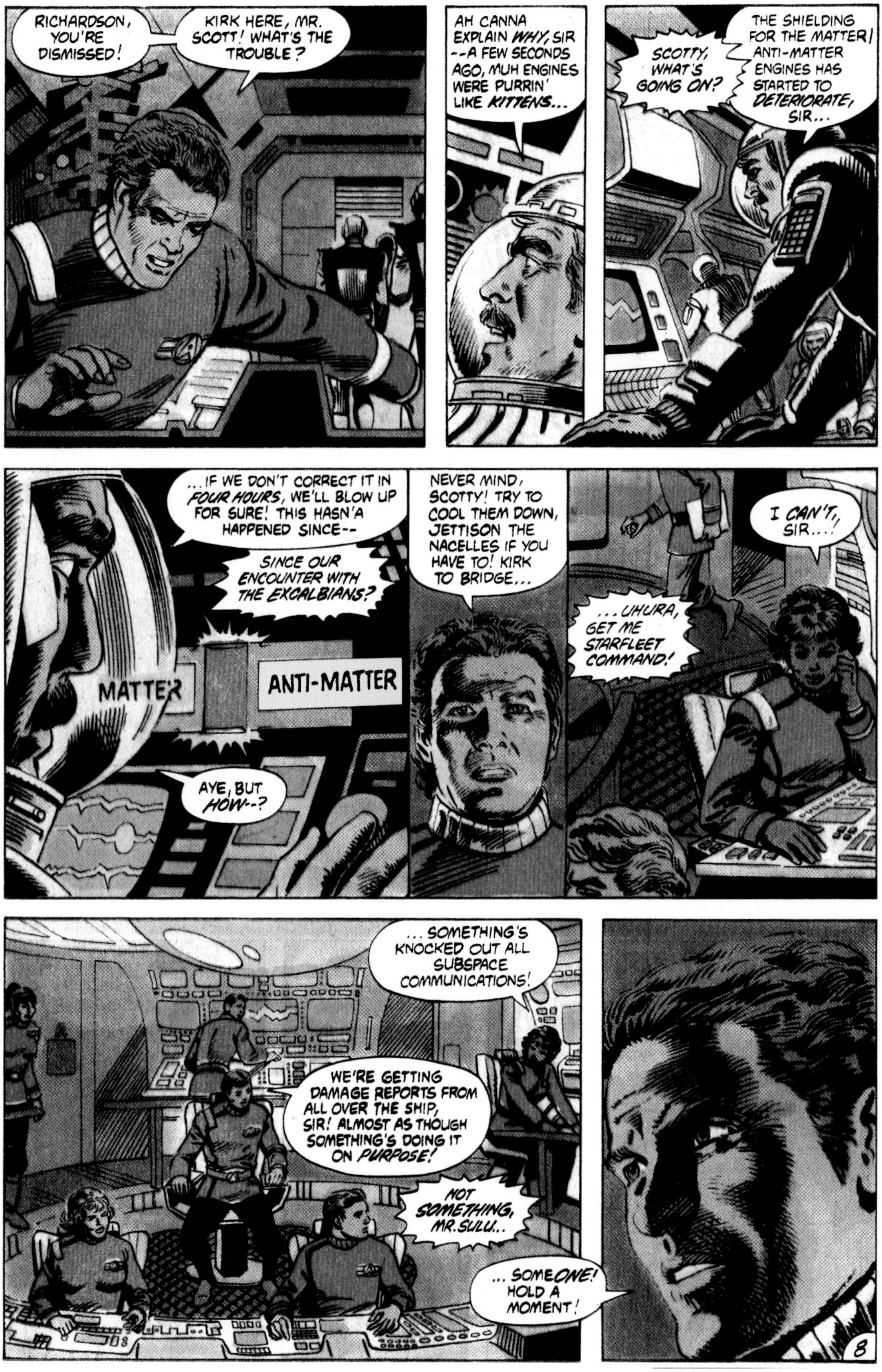
RICHARDSON, YOU'RE DISMISSED!
KIRK HERE, MR. SCOTT! WHAT'S THE TROUBLE?
AH CANNA EXPLAIN WHY, SIR --A FEW SECONDS AGO, MUH ENGINES WERE PURRIN' LIKE KITTENS...
SCOTTY, WHAT'S GOING ON?
THE SHIELDING FOR THE MATTER/ ANTI-MATTER ENGINES HAS STARTED TO DETERIORATE, SIR...
...IF WE DON'T CORRECT IT IN FOUR HOURS, WE'LL BLOW UP FOR SURE! THIS HASN'A HAPPENED SINCE--
SINCE OUR ENCOUNTER WITH THE EXCALBIANS?
MATTER
ANTI-MATTER
AYE, BUT HOW--?
NEVER MIND, SCOTTY! TRY TO COOL THEM DOWN, JETTISON THE NACELLES IF YOU HAVE TO! KIRK TO BRIDGE...
...UHURA, GET ME STARFLEET COMMAND!
I CAN'T, SIR...!
...SOMETHING'S KNOCKED OUT ALL SUBSPACE COMMUNICATIONS!
WE'RE GETTING DAMAGE REPORTS FROM ALL OVER THE SHIP, SIR! ALMOST AS THOUGH SOMETHING'S DOING IT ON PURPOSE!
NOT SOMETHING, MR. SULU...
...SOMEONE! HOLD A MOMENT!
8

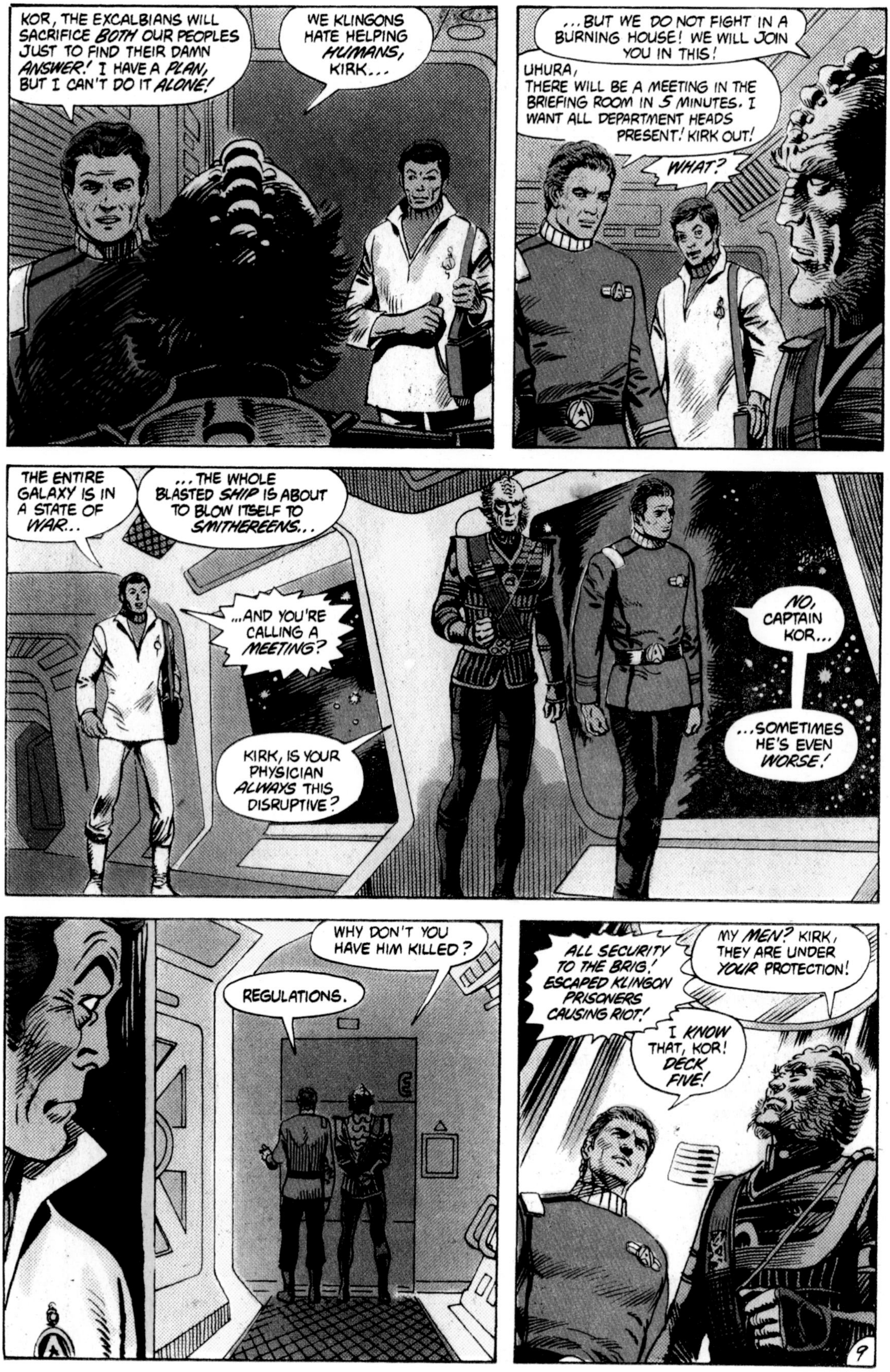
KOR, THE EXCALBIANS WILL SACRIFICE BOTH OUR PEOPLES JUST TO FIND THEIR DAMN ANSWER! I HAVE A PLAN, BUT I CAN'T DO IT ALONE!
WE KLINGONS HATE HELPING HUMANS, KIRK...
...BUT WE DO NOT FIGHT IN A BURNING HOUSE! WE WILL JOIN YOU IN THIS!
UHURA, THERE WILL BE A MEETING IN THE BRIEFING ROOM IN 5 MINUTES. I WANT ALL DEPARTMENT HEADS PRESENT! KIRK OUT!
WHAT?
THE ENTIRE GALAXY IS IN A STATE OF WAR...
...THE WHOLE BLASTED SHIP IS ABOUT TO BLOW ITSELF TO SMITHEREENS...
...AND YOU'RE CALLING A MEETING?
KIRK, IS YOUR PHYSICIAN ALWAYS THIS DISRUPTIVE?
NO, CAPTAIN KOR...
...SOMETIMES HE'S EVEN WORSE!
WHY DON'T YOU HAVE HIM KILLED?
REGULATIONS.
ALL SECURITY TO THE BRIG! ESCAPED KLINGON PRISONERS CAUSING RIOT!
MY MEN? KIRK, THEY ARE UNDER YOUR PROTECTION!
I KNOW THAT, KOR! DECK FIVE!
9

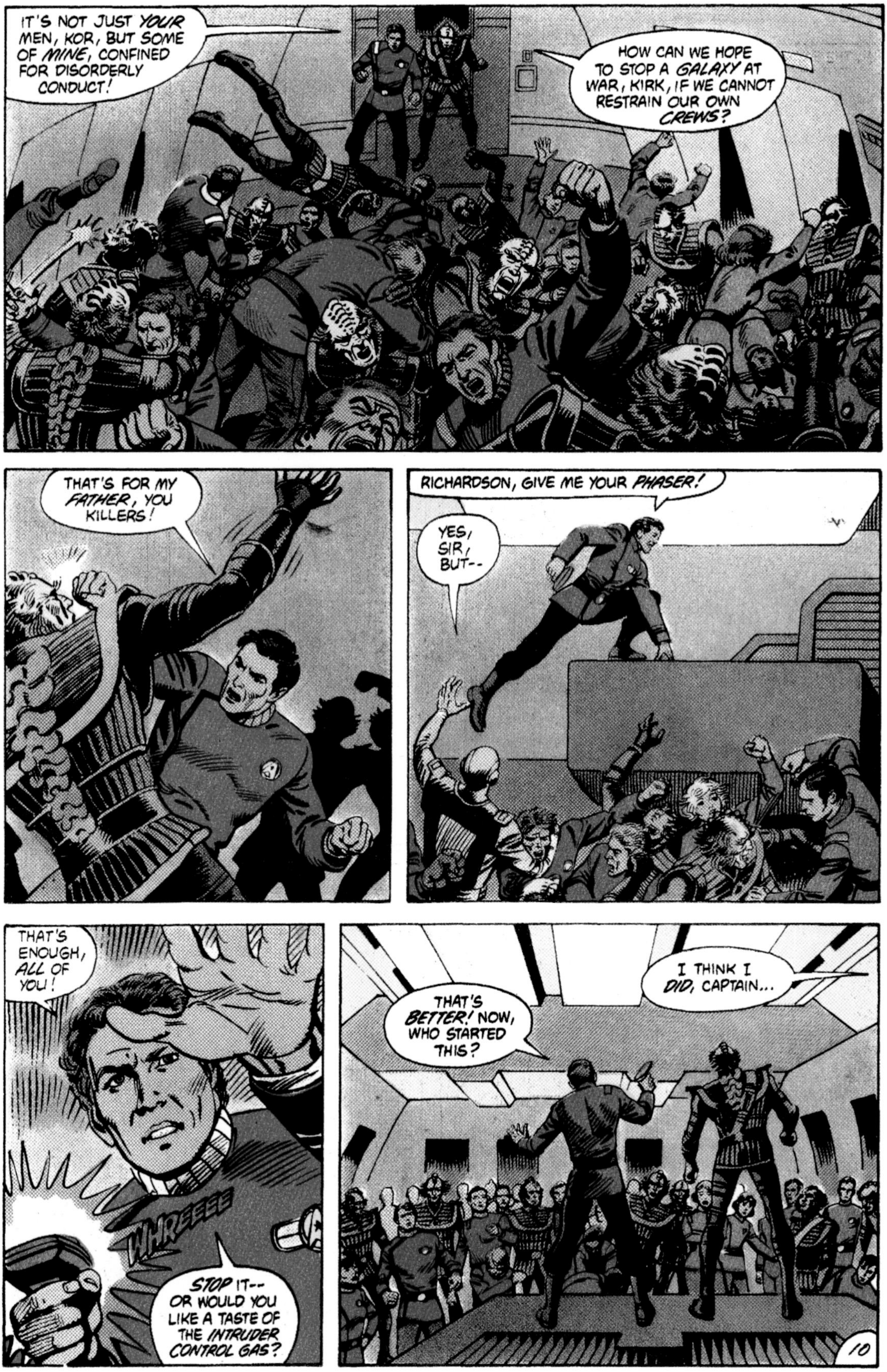
IT'S NOT JUST YOUR MEN, KOR, BUT SOME OF MINE, CONFINED FOR DISORDERLY CONDUCT!
HOW CAN WE HOPE TO STOP A GALAXY AT WAR, KIRK, IF WE CANNOT RESTRAIN OUR OWN CREWS?
THAT'S FOR MY FATHER, YOU KILLERS!
RICHARDSON, GIVE ME YOUR PHASER!
YES, SIR, BUT--
THAT'S ENOUGH, ALL OF YOU!
WHREEEE
STOP IT-- OR WOULD YOU LIKE A TASTE OF THE INTRUDER CONTROL GAS?
THAT'S BETTER! NOW, WHO STARTED THIS?
I THINK I DID, CAPTAIN...
10

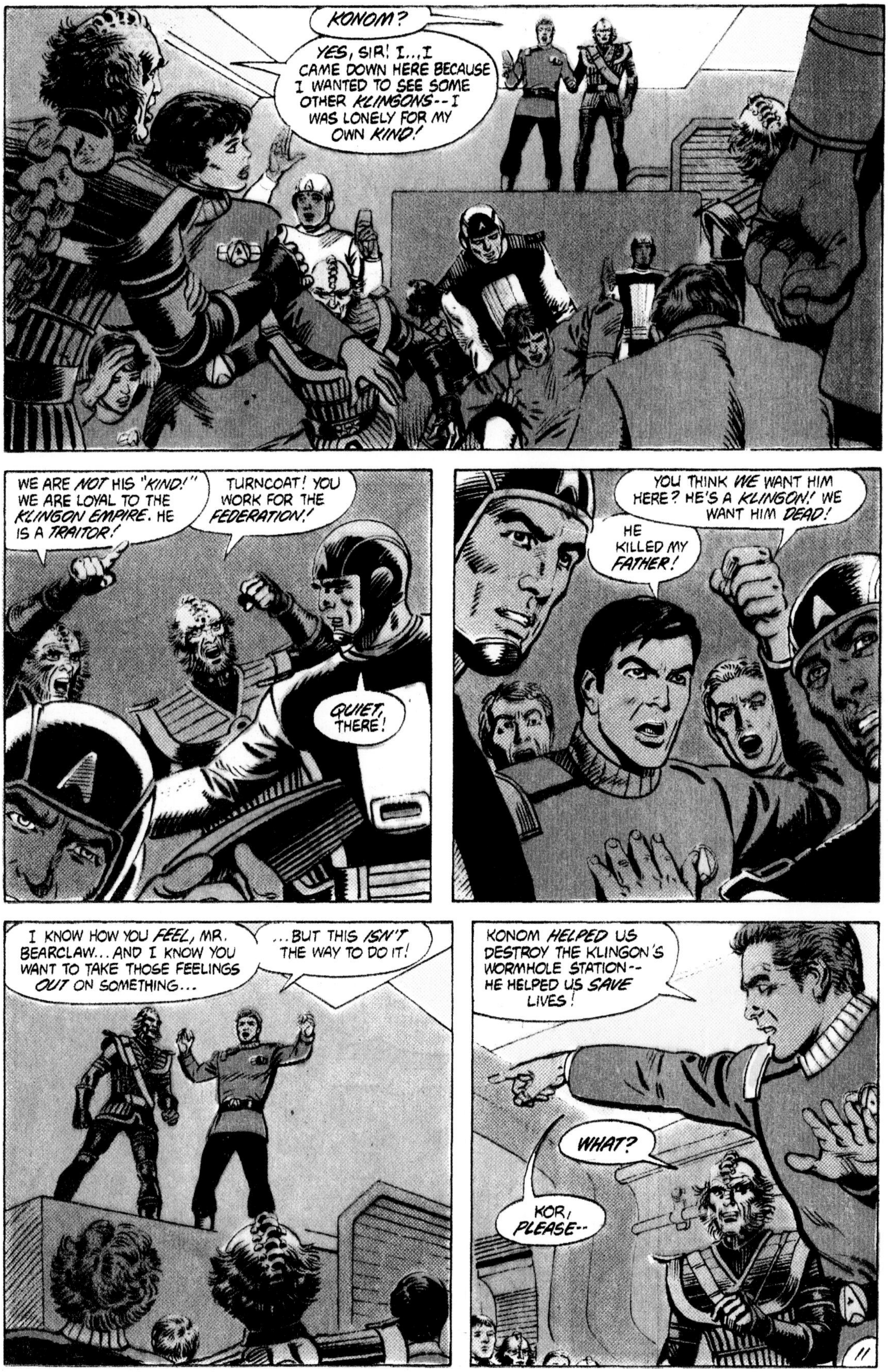
KONOM?
YES, SIR! I...I CAME DOWN HERE BECAUSE I WANTED TO SEE SOME OTHER KLINGONS--I WAS LONELY FOR MY OWN KIND!
WE ARE NOT HIS "KIND!" WE ARE LOYAL TO THE KLINGON EMPIRE. HE IS A TRAITOR!
TURNCOAT! YOU WORK FOR THE FEDERATION!
QUIET, THERE!
YOU THINK WE WANT HIM HERE? HE'S A KLINGON! WE WANT HIM DEAD!
HE KILLED MY FATHER!
I KNOW HOW YOU FEEL, MR. BEARCLAW... AND I KNOW YOU WANT TO TAKE THOSE FEELINGS OUT ON SOMETHING...
...BUT THIS ISN'T THE WAY TO DO IT!
KONOM HELPED US DESTROY THE KLINGON'S WORMHOLE STATION--HE HELPED US SAVE LIVES!
WHAT?
KOR, PLEASE--
11

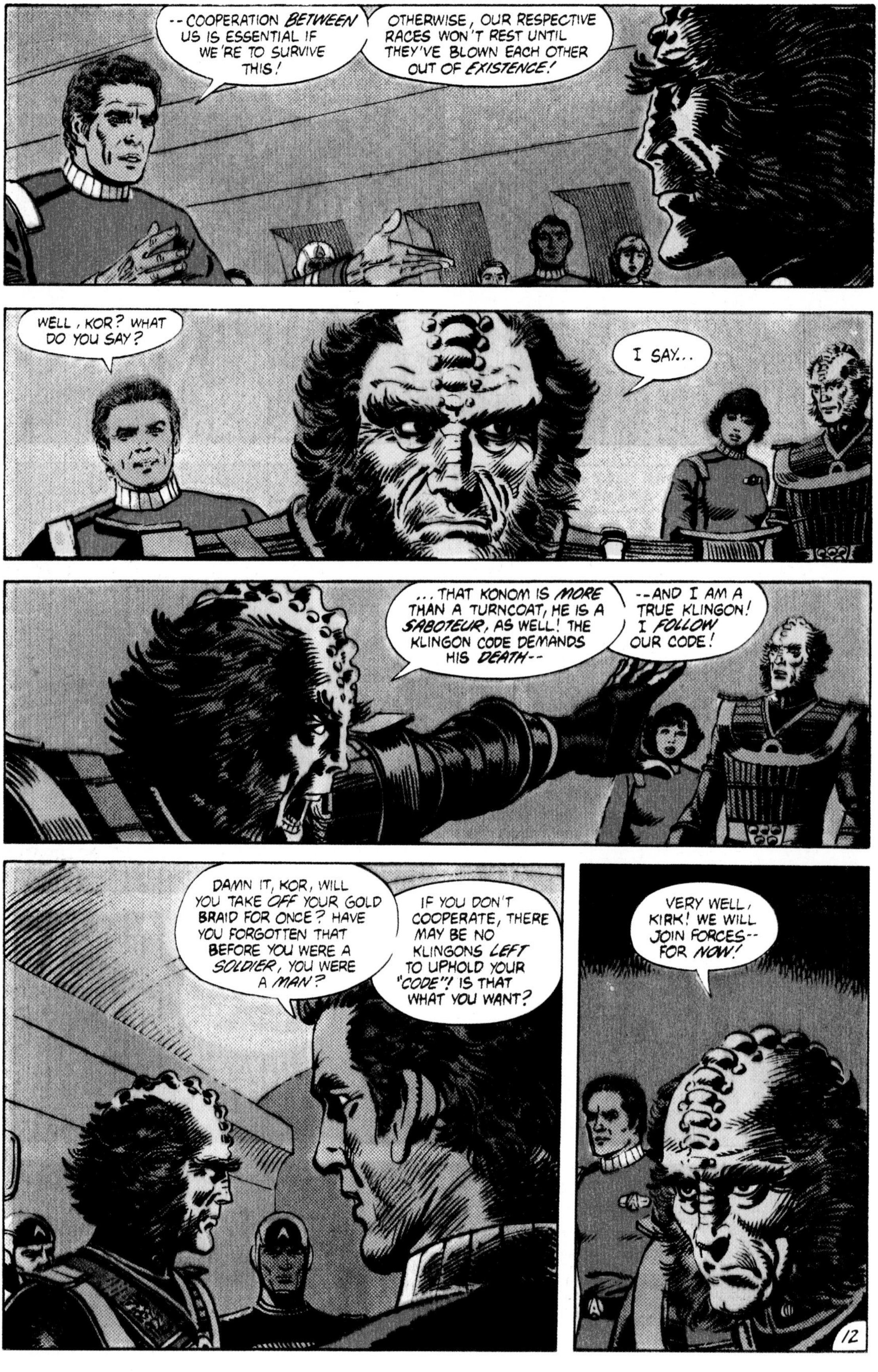
--COOPERATION BETWEEN US IS ESSENTIAL IF WE'RE TO SURVIVE THIS!
OTHERWISE, OUR RESPECTIVE RACES WON'T REST UNTIL THEY'VE BLOWN EACH OTHER OUT OF EXISTENCE!
WELL, KOR? WHAT DO YOU SAY?
I SAY...
...THAT KONOM IS MORE THAN A TURNCOAT, HE IS A SABOTEUR, AS WELL! THE KLINGON CODE DEMANDS HIS DEATH--
--AND I AM A TRUE KLINGON! I FOLLOW OUR CODE!
DAMN IT, KOR, WILL YOU TAKE OFF YOUR GOLD BRAID FOR ONCE? HAVE YOU FORGOTTEN THAT BEFORE YOU WERE A SOLDIER, YOU WERE A MAN?
IF YOU DON'T COOPERATE, THERE MAY BE NO KLINGONS LEFT TO UPHOLD YOUR "CODE"! IS THAT WHAT YOU WANT?
VERY WELL, KIRK! WE WILL JOIN FORCES-- FOR NOW!
12

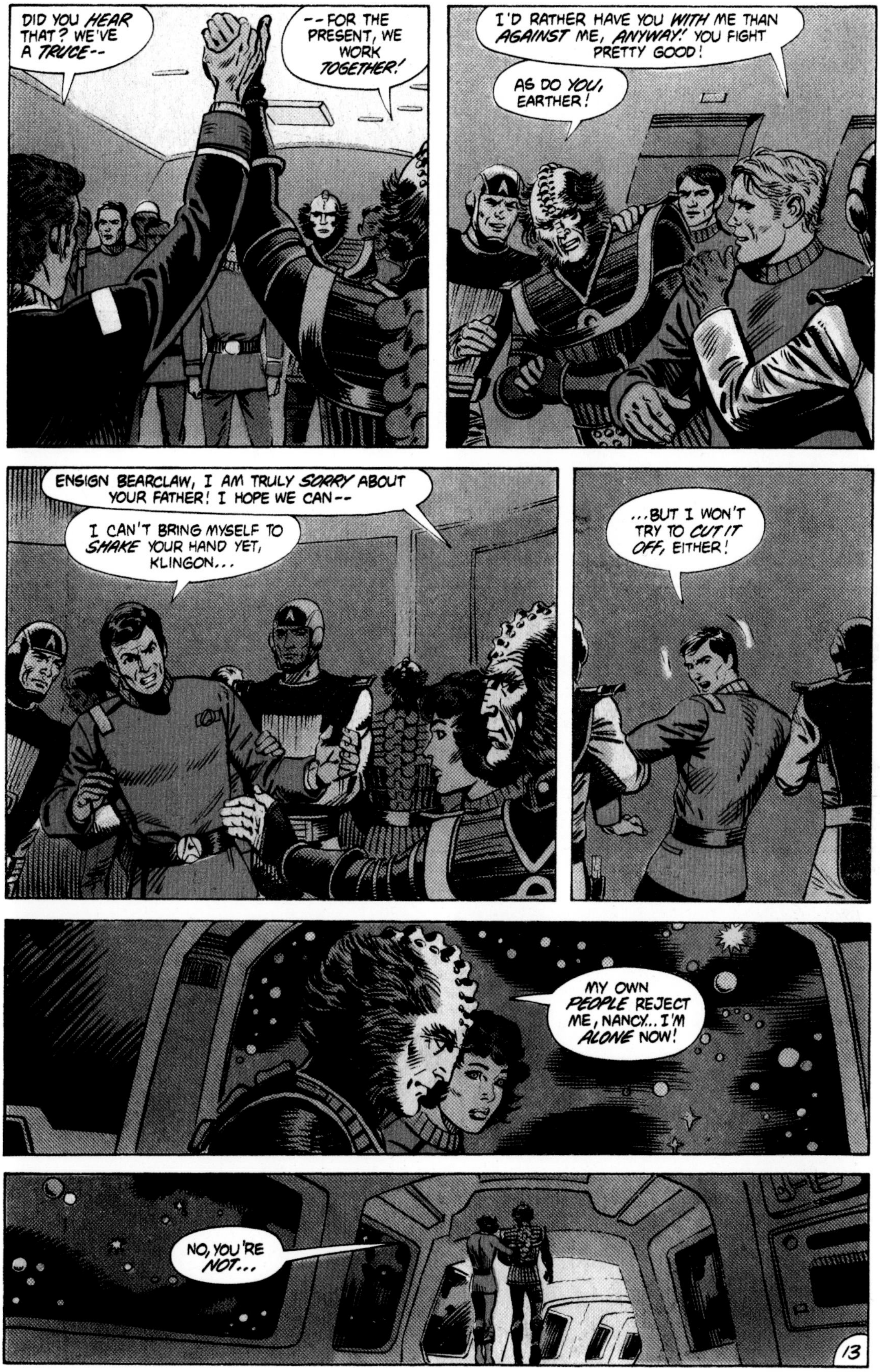
DID YOU HEAR THAT? WE'VE A TRUCE--
--FOR THE PRESENT, WE WORK TOGETHER!
I'D RATHER HAVE YOU WITH ME THAN AGAINST ME, ANYWAY! YOU FIGHT PRETTY GOOD!
AS DO YOU, EARTHER!
ENSIGN BEARCLAW, I AM TRULY SORRY ABOUT YOUR FATHER! I HOPE WE CAN--
I CAN'T BRING MYSELF TO SHAKE YOUR HAND YET, KLINGON...
...BUT I WON'T TRY TO CUT IT OFF, EITHER!
MY OWN PEOPLE REJECT ME, NANCY... I'M ALONE NOW!
NO, YOU'RE NOT...
13

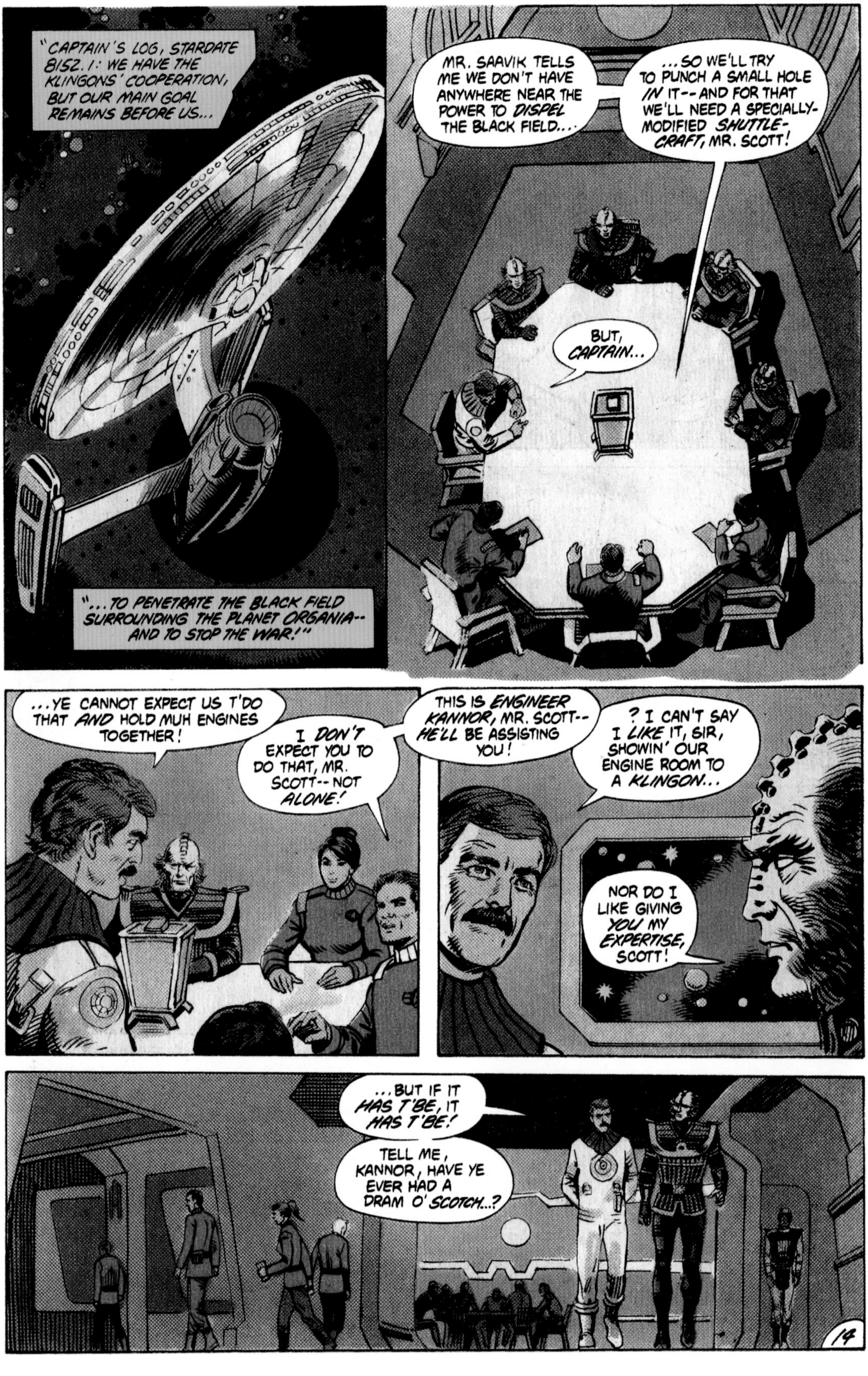
"CAPTAIN'S LOG, STARDATE 8152.1: WE HAVE THE KLINGONS' COOPERATION, BUT OUR MAIN GOAL REMAINS BEFORE US...
"...TO PENETRATE THE BLACK FIELD SURROUNDING THE PLANET ORGANIA-- AND TO STOP THE WAR!"
MR. SAAVIK TELLS ME WE DON'T HAVE ANYWHERE NEAR THE POWER TO DISPEL THE BLACK FIELD...
...SO WE'LL TRY TO PUNCH A SMALL HOLE IN IT--AND FOR THAT WE'LL NEED A SPECIALLY-MODIFIED SHUTTLE-CRAFT, MR. SCOTT!
BUT, CAPTAIN...
...YE CANNOT EXPECT US T'DO THAT AND HOLD MUH ENGINES TOGETHER!
I DON'T EXPECT YOU TO DO THAT, MR. SCOTT--NOT ALONE!
THIS IS ENGINEER KANNOR, MR. SCOTT--HE'LL BE ASSISTING YOU!
? I CAN'T SAY I LIKE IT, SIR, SHOWIN' OUR ENGINE ROOM TO A KLINGON...
NOR DO I LIKE GIVING YOU MY EXPERTISE, SCOTT!
...BUT IF IT HAS T'BE, IT HAS T'BE!
TELL ME, KANNOR, HAVE YE EVER HAD A DRAM O' SCOTCH...?
14

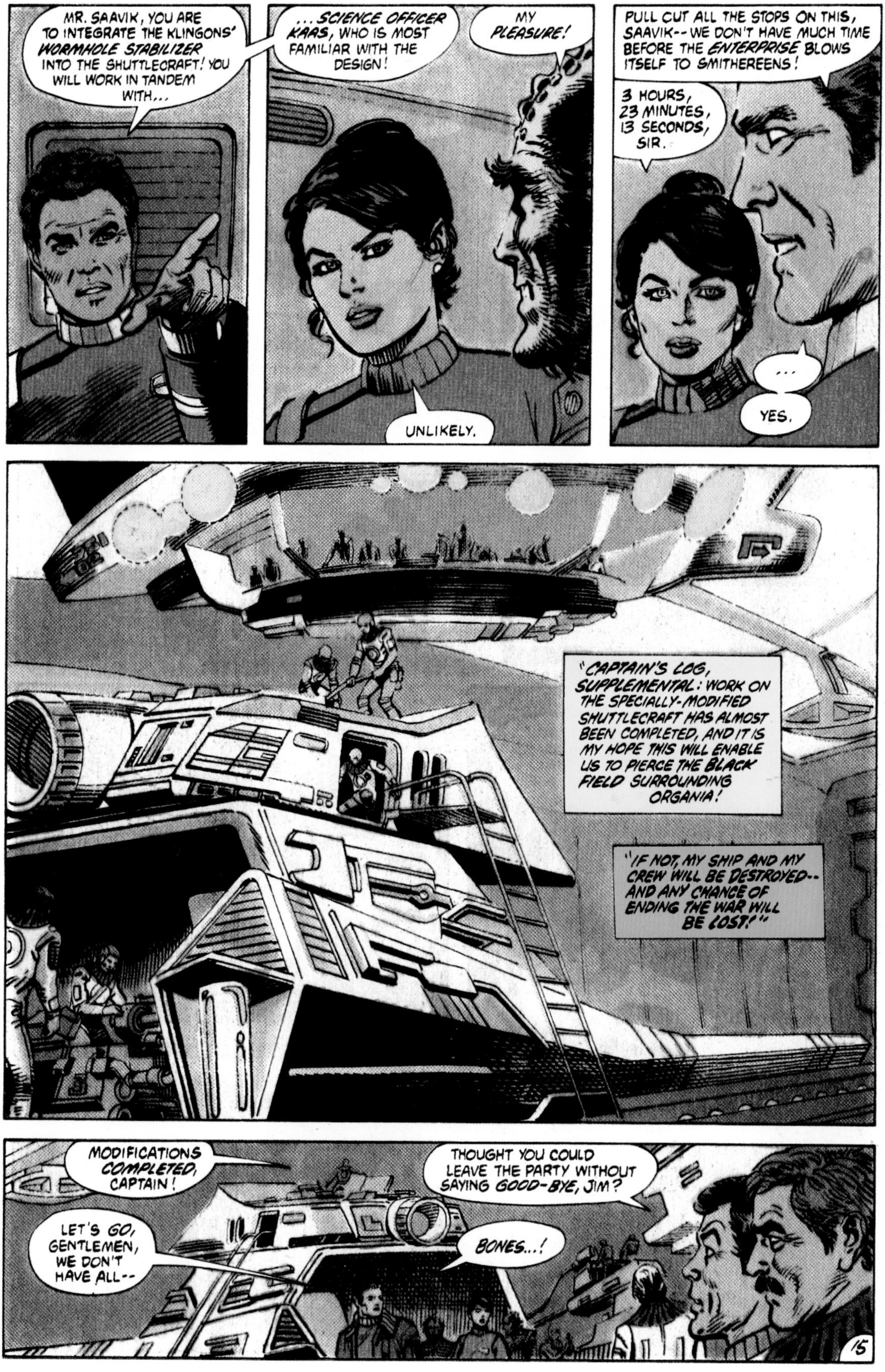

MR. SAAVIK, YOU ARE TO INTEGRATE THE KLINGONS' WORMHOLE STABILIZER INTO THE SHUTTLECRAFT! YOU WILL WORK IN TANDEM WITH...
...SCIENCE OFFICER KAAS, WHO IS MOST FAMILIAR WITH THE DESIGN!
MY PLEASURE!
UNLIKELY.
PULL OUT ALL THE STOPS ON THIS, SAAVIK--WE DON'T HAVE MUCH TIME BEFORE THE ENTERPRISE BLOWS ITSELF TO SMITHEREENS!
3 HOURS, 23 MINUTES, 13 SECONDS, SIR.
...
YES.
"CAPTAIN'S LOG, SUPPLEMENTAL: WORK ON THE SPECIALLY-MODIFIED SHUTTLECRAFT HAS ALMOST BEEN COMPLETED, AND IT IS MY HOPE THIS WILL ENABLE US TO PIERCE THE BLACK FIELD SURROUNDING ORGANIA!
"IF NOT, MY SHIP AND MY CREW WILL BE DESTROYED--AND ANY CHANCE OF ENDING THE WAR WILL BE LOST!"
MODIFICATIONS COMPLETED, CAPTAIN!
LET'S GO, GENTLEMEN, WE DON'T HAVE ALL--
THOUGHT YOU COULD LEAVE THE PARTY WITHOUT SAYING GOOD-BYE, JIM?
BONES...!
15

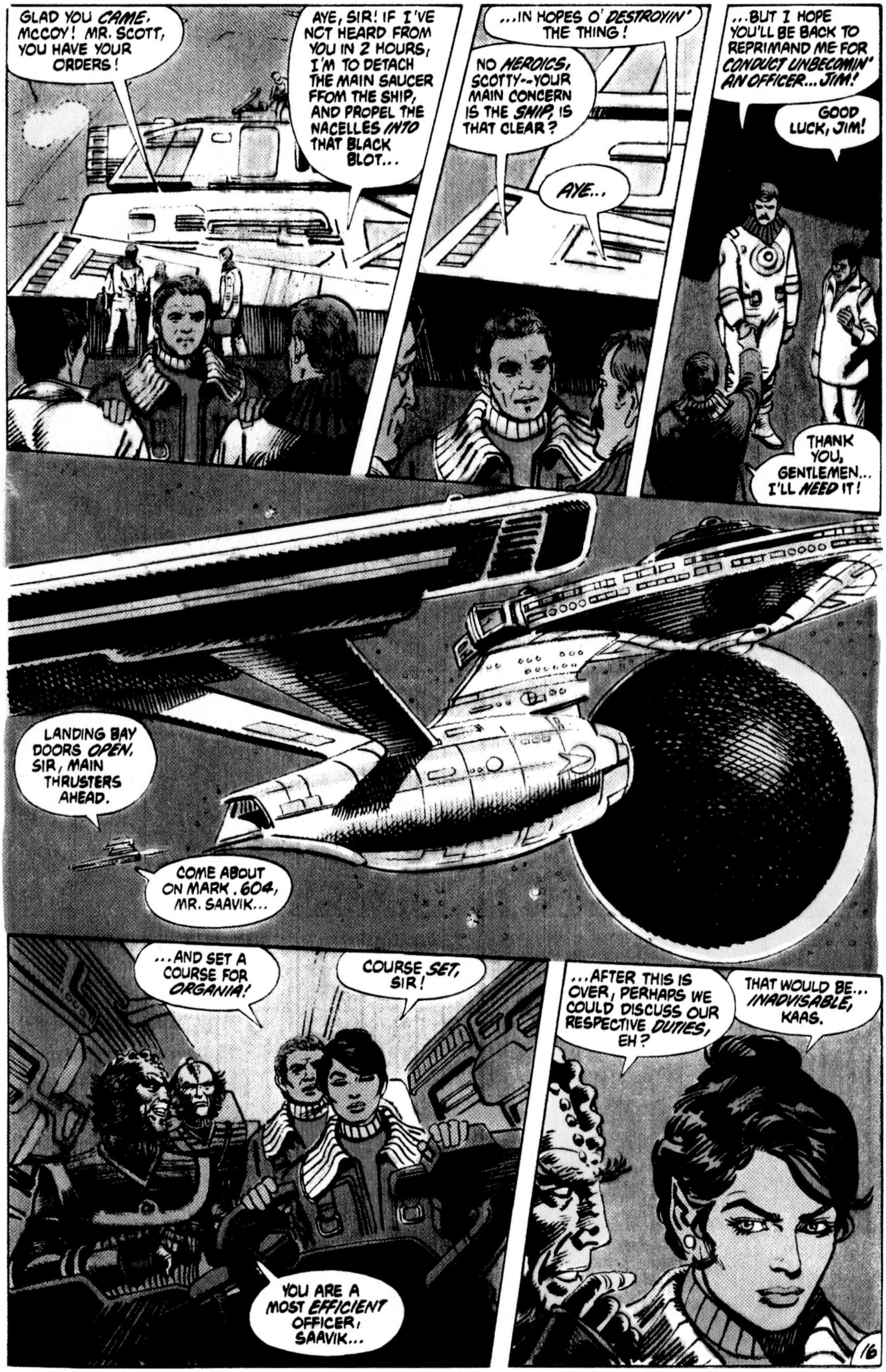
GLAD YOU CAME, McCOY! MR. SCOTT, YOU HAVE YOUR ORDERS!
AYE, SIR! IF I'VE NOT HEARD FROM YOU IN 2 HOURS, I'M TO DETACH THE MAIN SAUCER FFOM THE SHIP, AND PROPEL THE NACELLES INTO THAT BLACK BLOT...
...IN HOPES O' DESTROYIN' THE THING!
NO HEROICS, SCOTTY--YOUR MAIN CONCERN IS THE SHIP, IS THAT CLEAR?
AYE...
...BUT I HOPE YOU'LL BE BACK TO REPRIMAND ME FOR CONDUCT UNBECOMIN' AN OFFICER... JIM!
GOOD LUCK, JIM!
THANK YOU, GENTLEMEN... I'LL NEED IT!
LANDING BAY DOORS OPEN, SIR, MAIN THRUSTERS AHEAD.
COME ABOUT ON MARK .604, MR. SAAVIK...
...AND SET A COURSE FOR ORGANIA!
COURSE SET, SIR!
YOU ARE A MOST EFFICIENT OFFICER, SAAVIK...
...AFTER THIS IS OVER, PERHAPS WE COULD DISCUSS OUR RESPECTIVE DUTIES, EH?
THAT WOULD BE... INADVISABLE, KAAS.
16

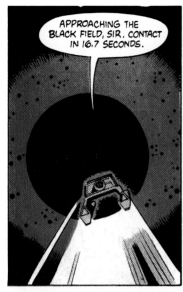

APPROACHING THE BLACK FIELD, SIR. CONTACT IN 16.7 SECONDS.

ACTIVATE *WORMHOLE STABILIZER,* MR. SAAVIK!

ACTIVATED, SIR, YOU REALIZE OUR CHANCES OF SUCCESS ARE ONLY--

PLEASE, MR. SAAVIK...

...IT'S A LITTLE *LATE* TO BE QUOTING THE ODDS! HERE WE GO!

STATUS REPORT?

OBVIOUSLY, WE DID *NOT* STRIKE THE BLACK FIELD, SIR. I READ AN *OXYGEN ATMOSPHERE* AHEAD. WE *MADE* IT, SIR!

GOOD WORK, MR. SAAVIK! BUT THAT'S ONLY THE FIRST STEP! PUT DOWN AT THE COORDINATES I GAVE YOU...

...AND WE'LL BEGIN STEP *TWO!*

ORGANIA! I HOPED NEVER TO SEE THIS MISERABLE PLANET AGAIN! I--

? KIRK, ON OUR *PREVIOUS* VISIT, THE DOORS *OPENED* ON OUR ARRIVAL!

SO THEY *DID,* KOR! BUT IT LOOKS LIKE *THIS* TIME...

17

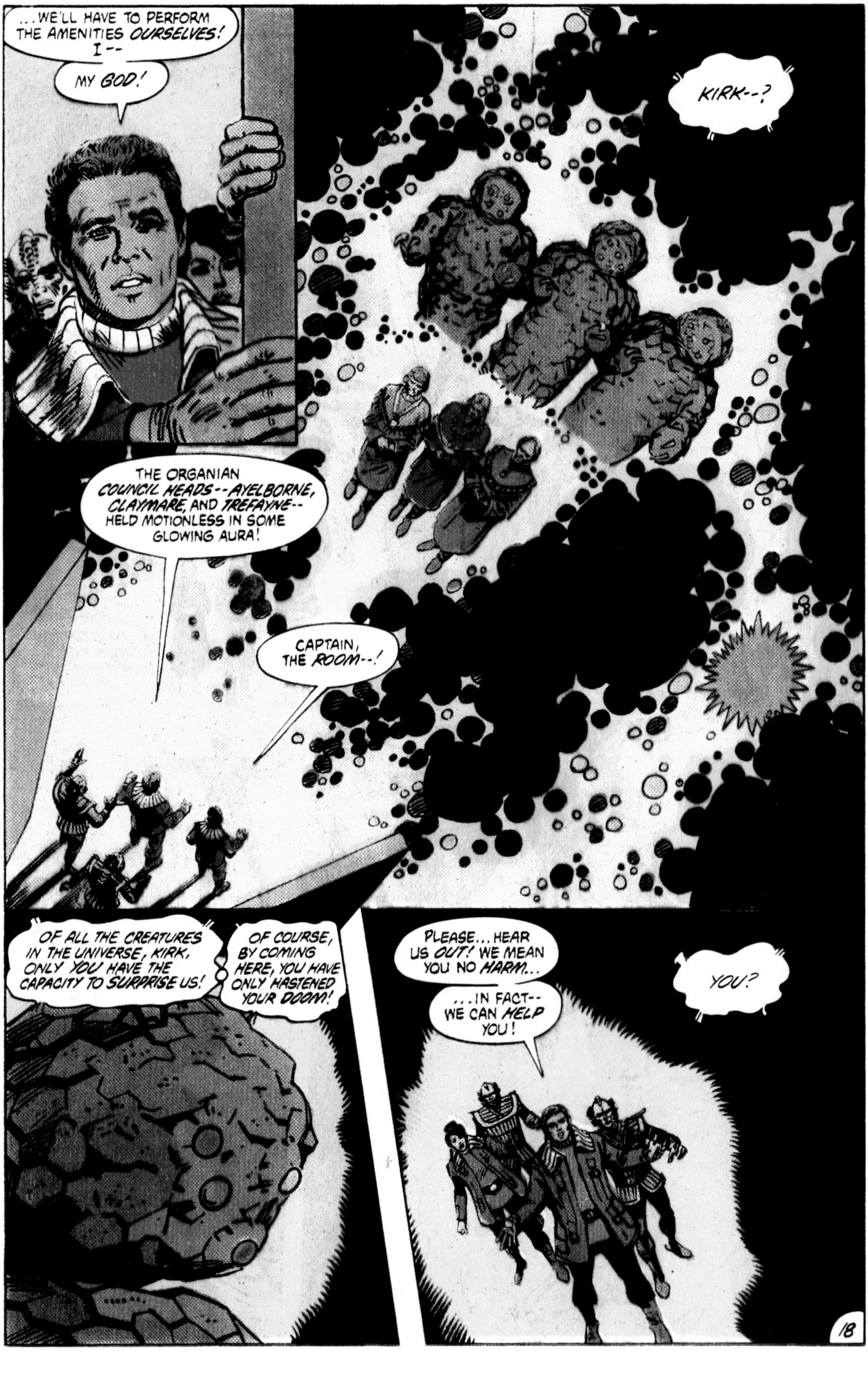
...WE'LL HAVE TO PERFORM THE AMENITIES OURSELVES! I--
MY GOD!
KIRK--?
THE ORGANIAN COUNCIL HEADS--AYELBORNE, CLAYMARE, AND TREFAYNE--HELD MOTIONLESS IN SOME GLOWING AURA!
CAPTAIN, THE ROOM--!
OF ALL THE CREATURES IN THE UNIVERSE, KIRK, ONLY YOU HAVE THE CAPACITY TO SURPRISE US!
OF COURSE, BY COMING HERE, YOU HAVE ONLY HASTENED YOUR DOOM!
PLEASE... HEAR US OUT! WE MEAN YOU NO HARM...
...IN FACT--WE CAN HELP YOU!
YOU?
18

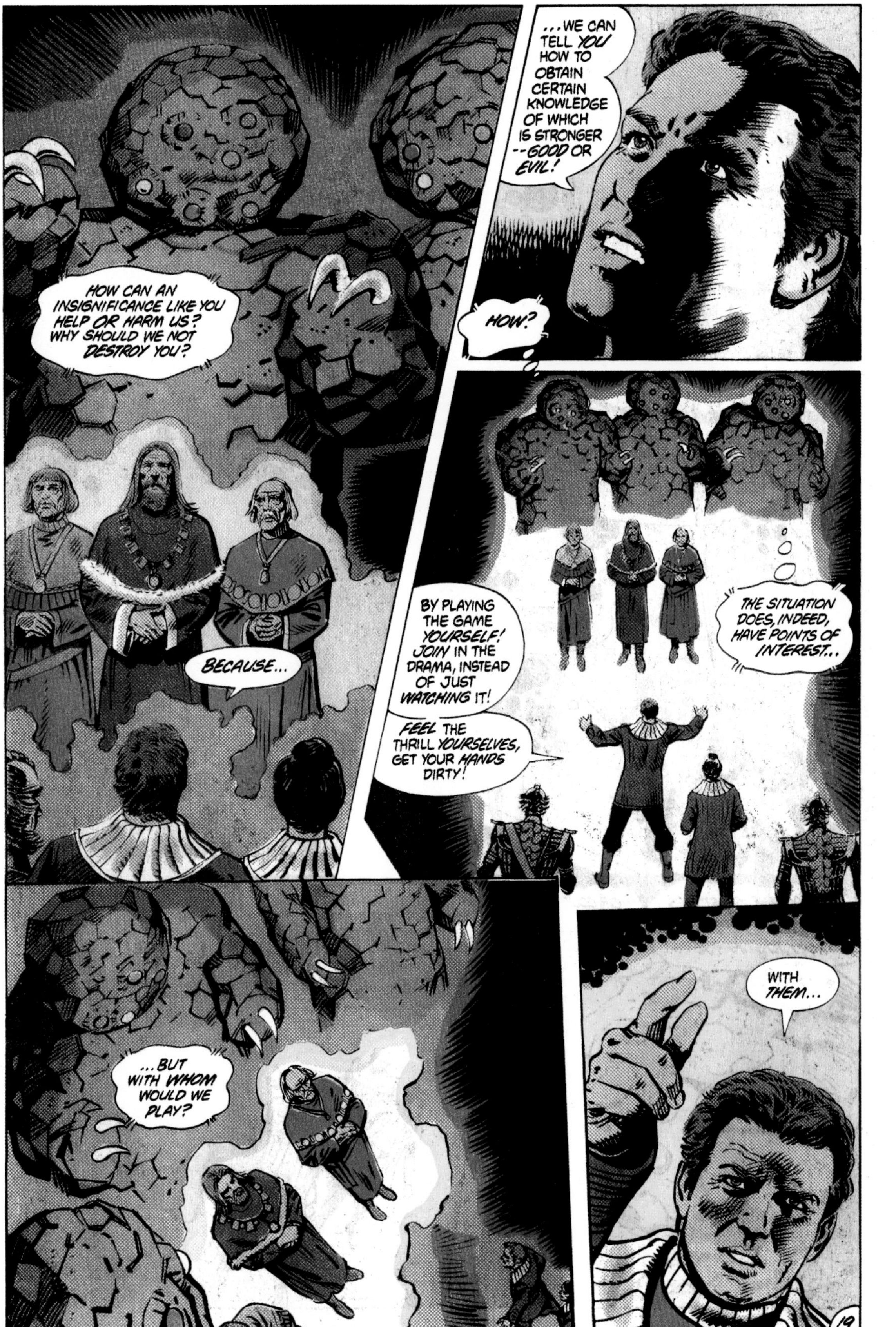
HOW CAN AN INSIGNIFICANCE LIKE YOU HELP OR HARM US? WHY SHOULD WE NOT DESTROY YOU?
BECAUSE...
...WE CAN TELL YOU HOW TO OBTAIN CERTAIN KNOWLEDGE OF WHICH IS STRONGER --GOOD OR EVIL!
HOW?
BY PLAYING THE GAME YOURSELF! JOIN IN THE DRAMA, INSTEAD OF JUST WATCHING IT!
FEEL THE THRILL YOURSELVES, GET YOUR HANDS DIRTY!
THE SITUATION DOES, INDEED, HAVE POINTS OF INTEREST...
...BUT WITH WHOM WOULD WE PLAY?
WITH THEM...
19

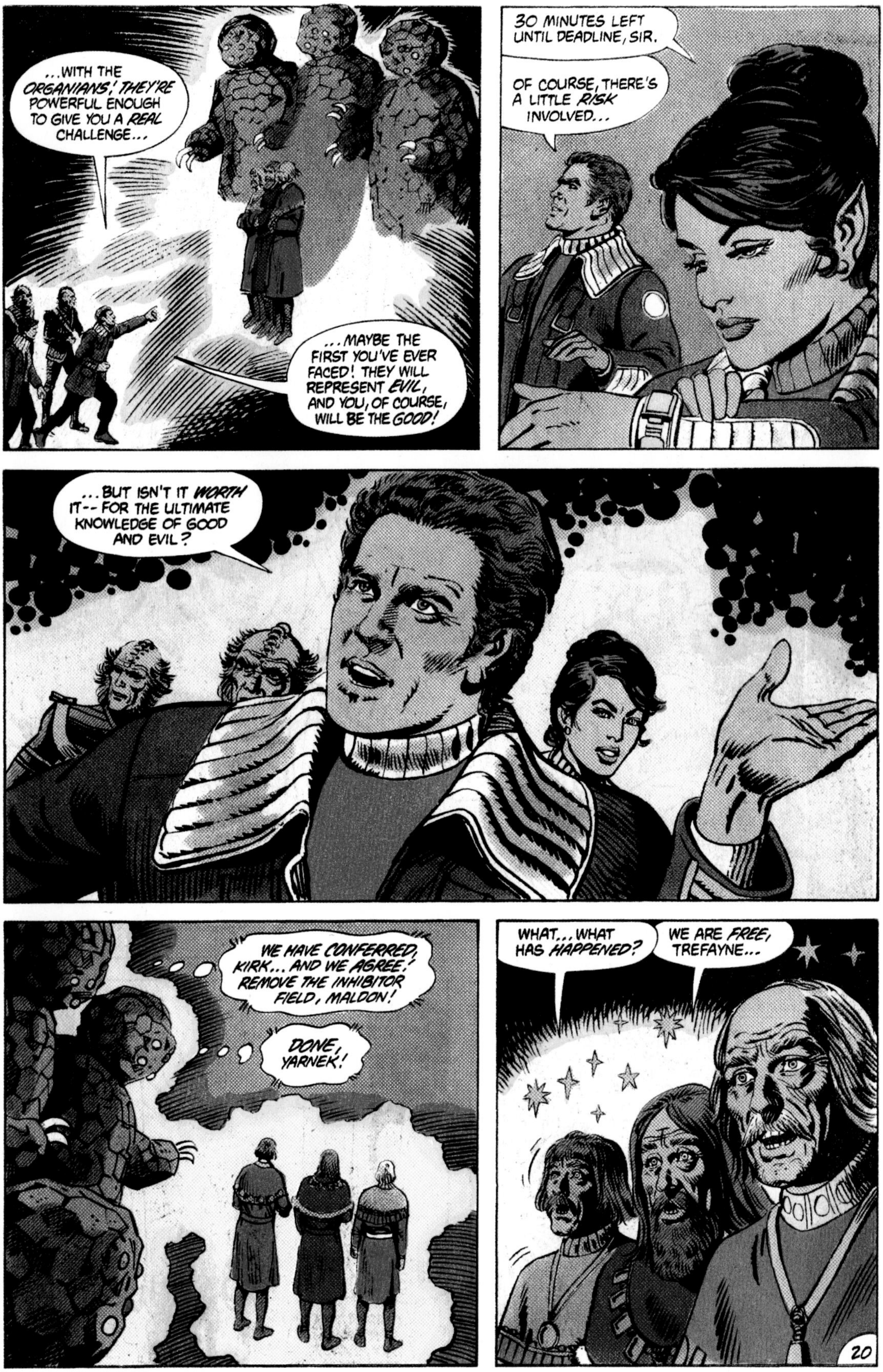
...WITH THE *ORGANIANS!* THEY'RE POWERFUL ENOUGH TO GIVE YOU A *REAL* CHALLENGE...
...MAYBE THE FIRST YOU'VE EVER FACED! THEY WILL REPRESENT *EVIL*, AND YOU, OF COURSE, WILL BE THE *GOOD!*
30 MINUTES LEFT UNTIL DEADLINE, SIR.
OF COURSE, THERE'S A LITTLE *RISK* INVOLVED...
...BUT ISN'T IT *WORTH* IT-- FOR THE ULTIMATE KNOWLEDGE OF GOOD AND EVIL?
WE HAVE CONFERRED, KIRK... AND WE AGREE! REMOVE THE INHIBITOR FIELD, MALDON!
DONE, YARNEK!
WHAT... WHAT HAS *HAPPENED?*
WE ARE *FREE*, TREFAYNE...
20

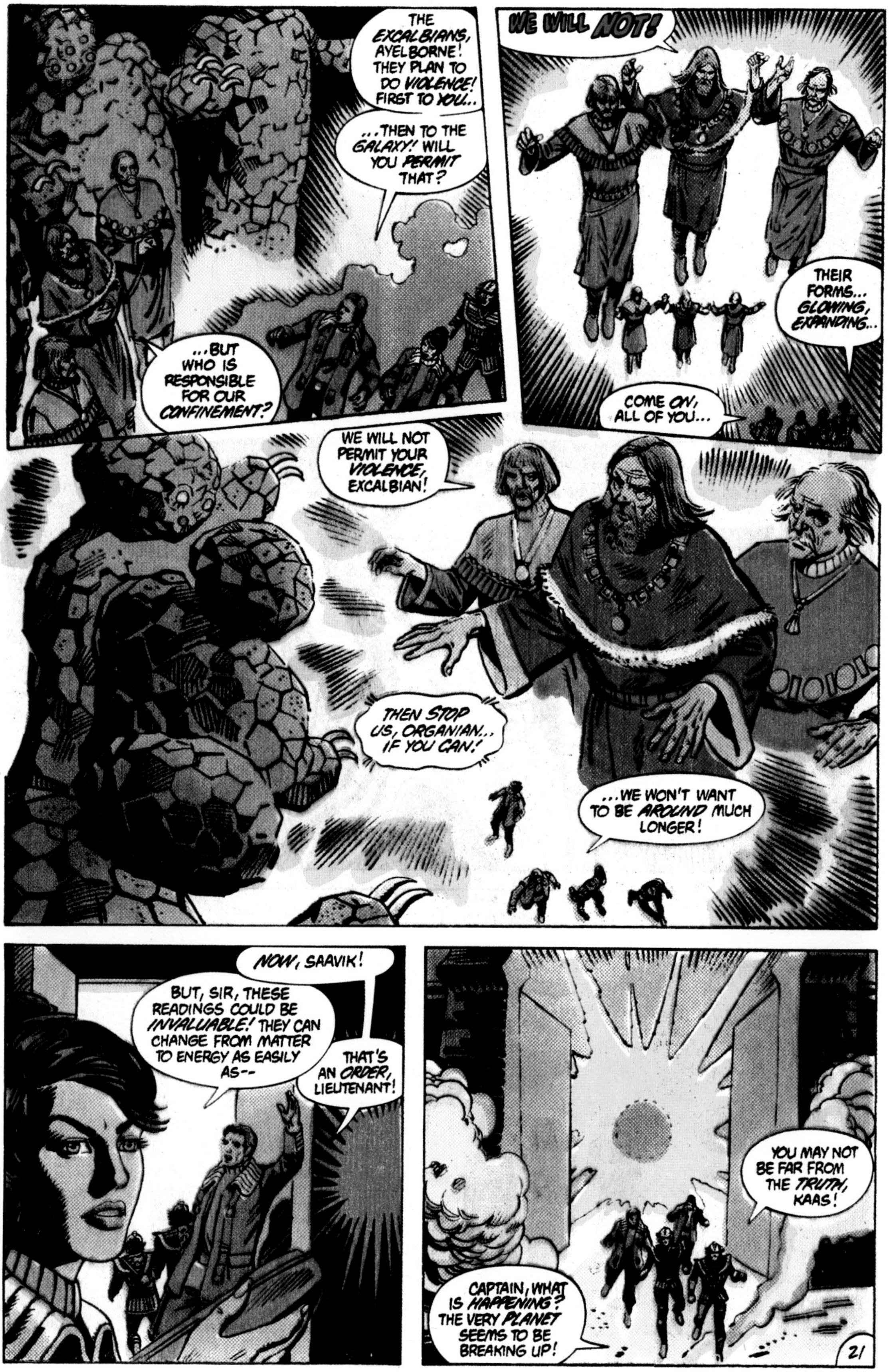
THE EXCALBIANS, AYELBORNE! THEY PLAN TO DO VIOLENCE! FIRST TO YOU..
...THEN TO THE GALAXY! WILL YOU PERMIT THAT?
...BUT WHO IS RESPONSIBLE FOR OUR CONFINEMENT?
WE WILL NOT!
THEIR FORMS... GLOWING, EXPANDING...
COME ON, ALL OF YOU...
WE WILL NOT PERMIT YOUR VIOLENCE, EXCALBIAN!
THEN STOP US, ORGANIAN... IF YOU CAN!
...WE WON'T WANT TO BE AROUND MUCH LONGER!
NOW, SAAVIK!
BUT, SIR, THESE READINGS COULD BE INVALUABLE! THEY CAN CHANGE FROM MATTER TO ENERGY AS EASILY AS--
THAT'S AN ORDER, LIEUTENANT!
YOU MAY NOT BE FAR FROM THE TRUTH, KAAS!
CAPTAIN, WHAT IS HAPPENING? THE VERY PLANET SEEMS TO BE BREAKING UP!
21

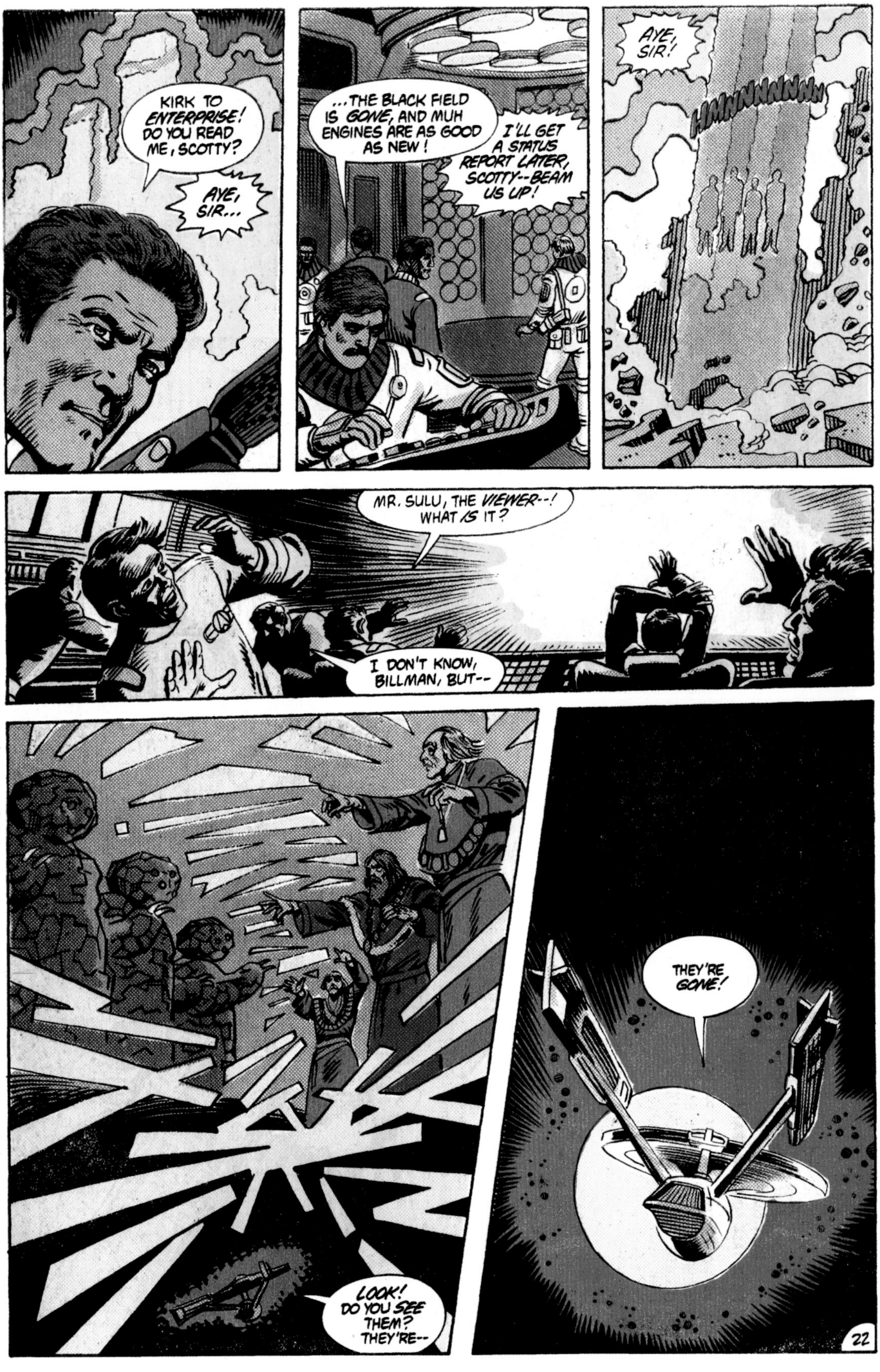
KIRK TO ENTERPRISE! DO YOU READ ME, SCOTTY?
AYE, SIR...
...THE BLACK FIELD IS GONE, AND MUH ENGINES ARE AS GOOD AS NEW!
I'LL GET A STATUS REPORT LATER, SCOTTY--BEAM US UP!
AYE, SIR!
HMNNNNNNNN
MR. SULU, THE VIEWER--! WHAT IS IT?
I DON'T KNOW, BILLMAN, BUT--
LOOK! DO YOU SEE THEM? THEY'RE--
THEY'RE GONE!
22

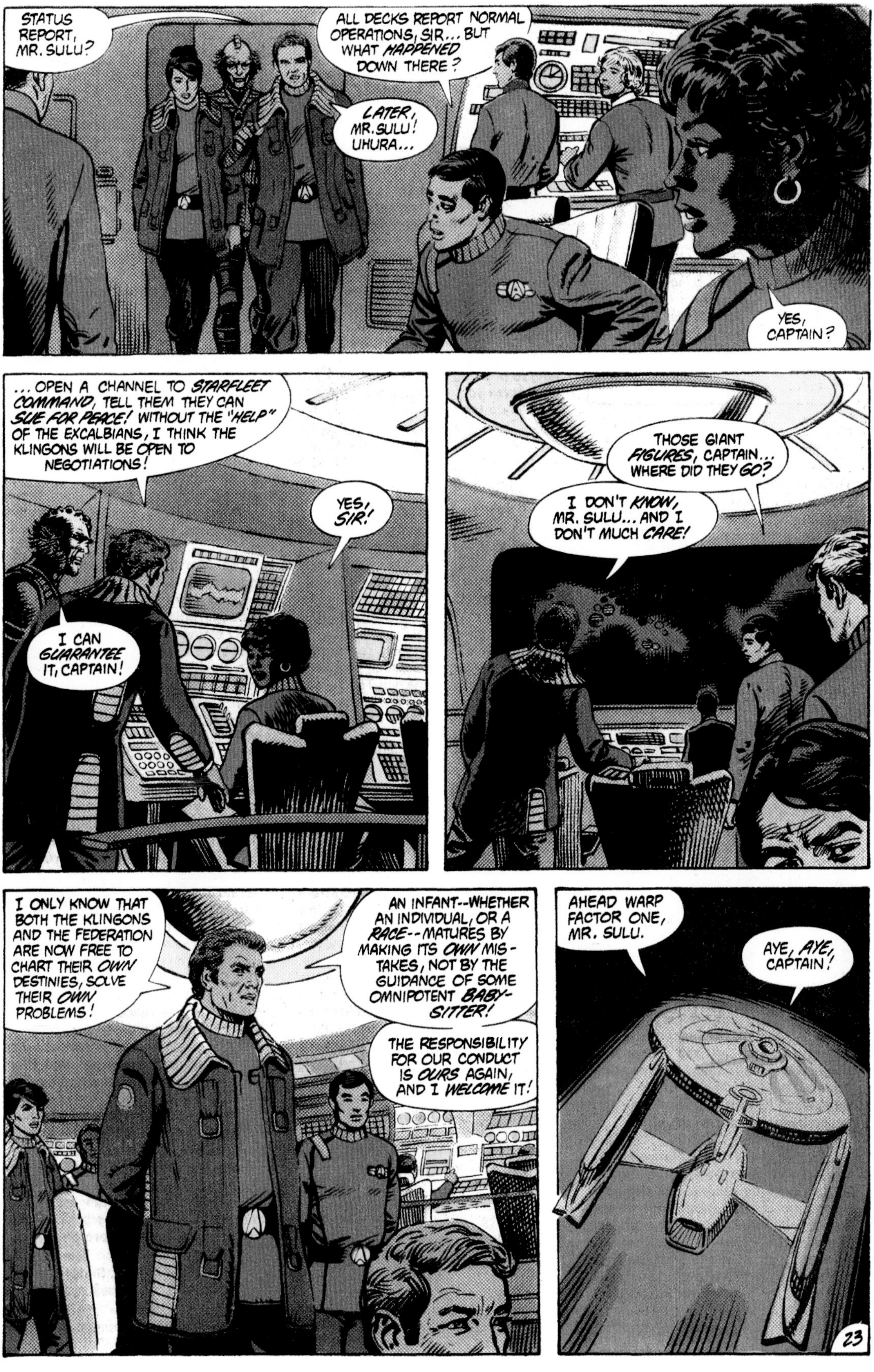
STATUS REPORT, MR. SULU?
ALL DECKS REPORT NORMAL OPERATIONS, SIR... BUT WHAT HAPPENED DOWN THERE?
LATER, MR. SULU! UHURA...
YES, CAPTAIN?
...OPEN A CHANNEL TO STARFLEET COMMAND, TELL THEM THEY CAN SUE FOR PEACE! WITHOUT THE "HELP" OF THE EXCALBIANS, I THINK THE KLINGONS WILL BE OPEN TO NEGOTIATIONS!
YES, SIR!
I CAN GUARANTEE IT, CAPTAIN!
THOSE GIANT FIGURES, CAPTAIN... WHERE DID THEY GO?
I DON'T KNOW, MR. SULU... AND I DON'T MUCH CARE!
I ONLY KNOW THAT BOTH THE KLINGONS AND THE FEDERATION ARE NOW FREE TO CHART THEIR OWN DESTINIES, SOLVE THEIR OWN PROBLEMS!
AN INFANT--WHETHER AN INDIVIDUAL, OR A RACE--MATURES BY MAKING ITS OWN MIS-TAKES, NOT BY THE GUIDANCE OF SOME OMNIPOTENT BABY-SITTER!
THE RESPONSIBILITY FOR OUR CONDUCT IS OURS AGAIN, AND I WELCOME IT!
AHEAD WARP FACTOR ONE, MR. SULU.
AYE, AYE, CAPTAIN!
23

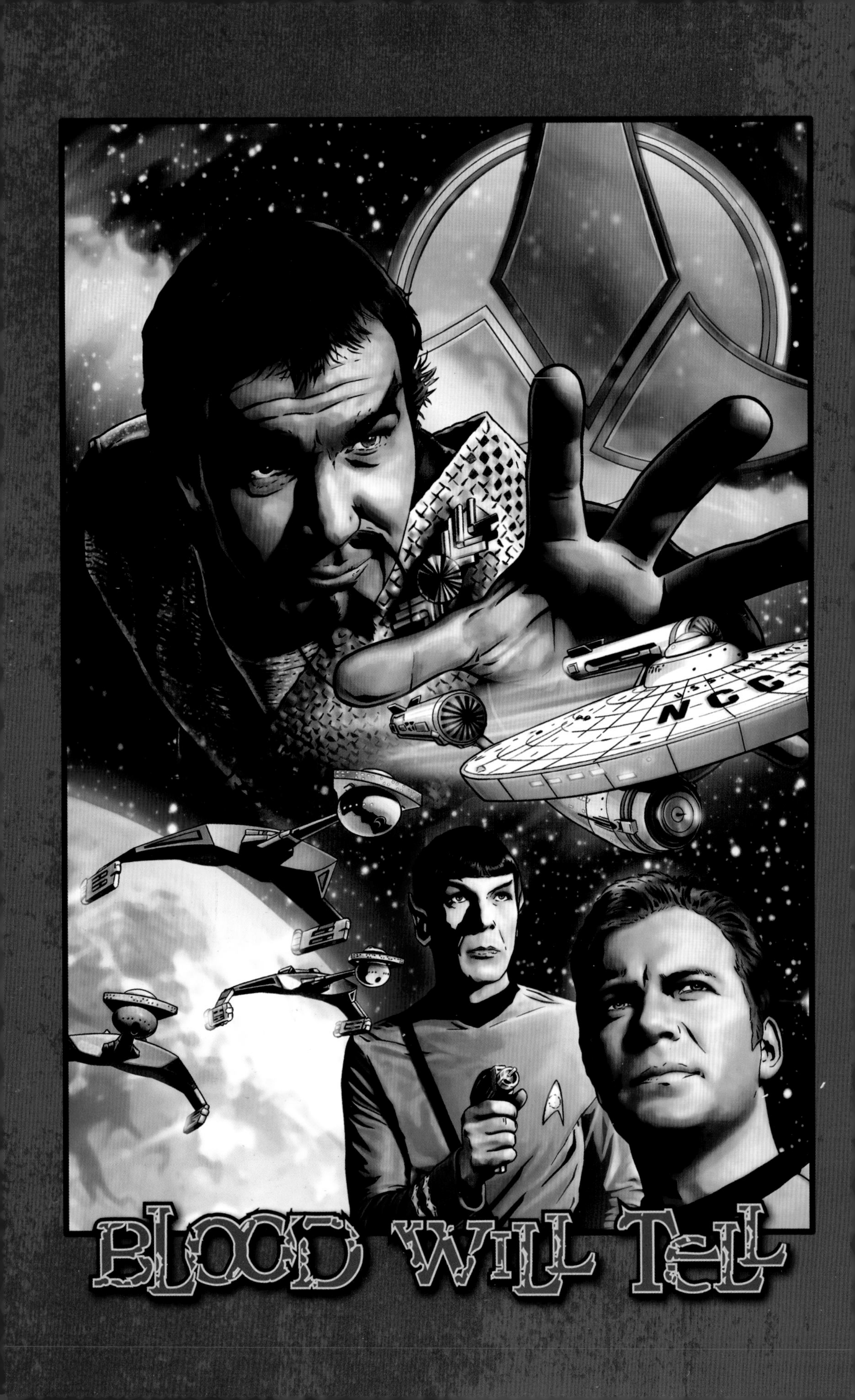
BLOOD WILL TELL

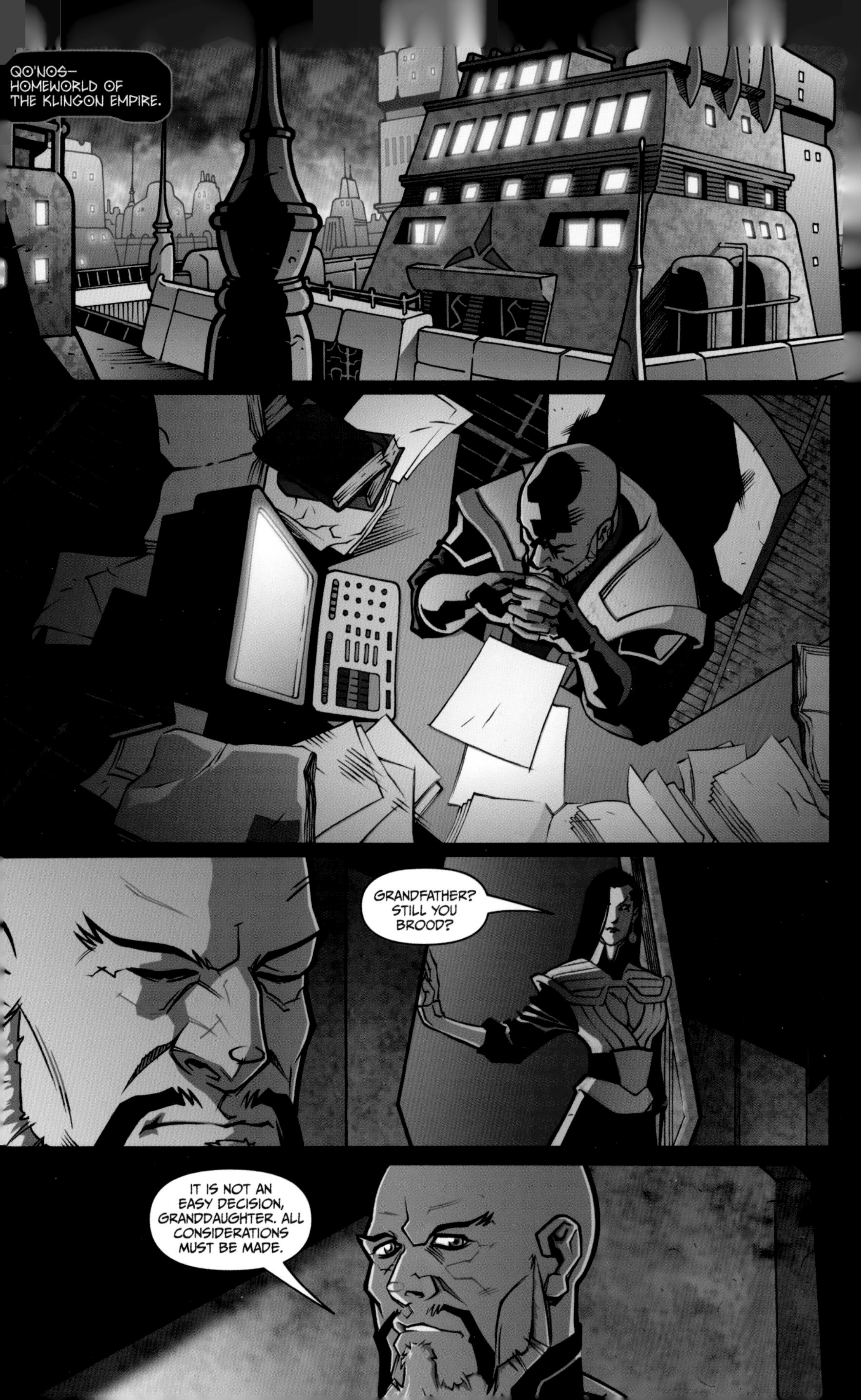

QO'NOS–
HOMEWORLD OF
THE KLINGON EMPIRE.
GRANDFATHER? STILL YOU BROOD?
IT IS NOT AN EASY DECISION, GRANDDAUGHTER. ALL CONSIDERATIONS MUST BE MADE.

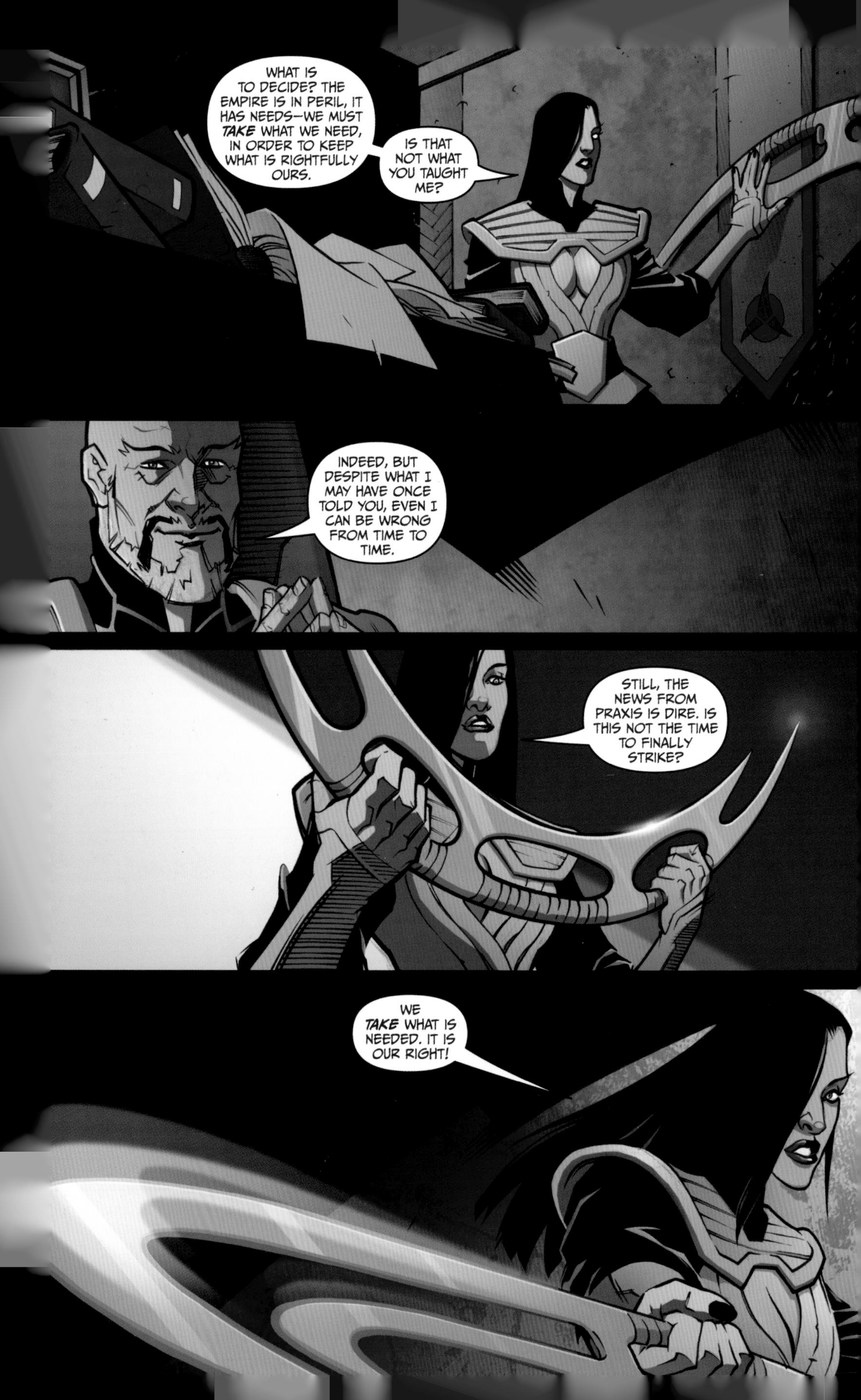
WHAT IS TO DECIDE? THE EMPIRE IS IN PERIL, IT HAS NEEDS—WE MUST *TAKE* WHAT WE NEED, IN ORDER TO KEEP WHAT IS RIGHTFULLY OURS.
IS THAT NOT WHAT YOU TAUGHT ME?
INDEED, BUT DESPITE WHAT I MAY HAVE ONCE TOLD YOU, EVEN I CAN BE WRONG FROM TIME TO TIME.
STILL, THE NEWS FROM PRAXIS IS DIRE. IS THIS NOT THE TIME TO FINALLY STRIKE?
WE *TAKE* WHAT IS NEEDED. IT IS OUR RIGHT!

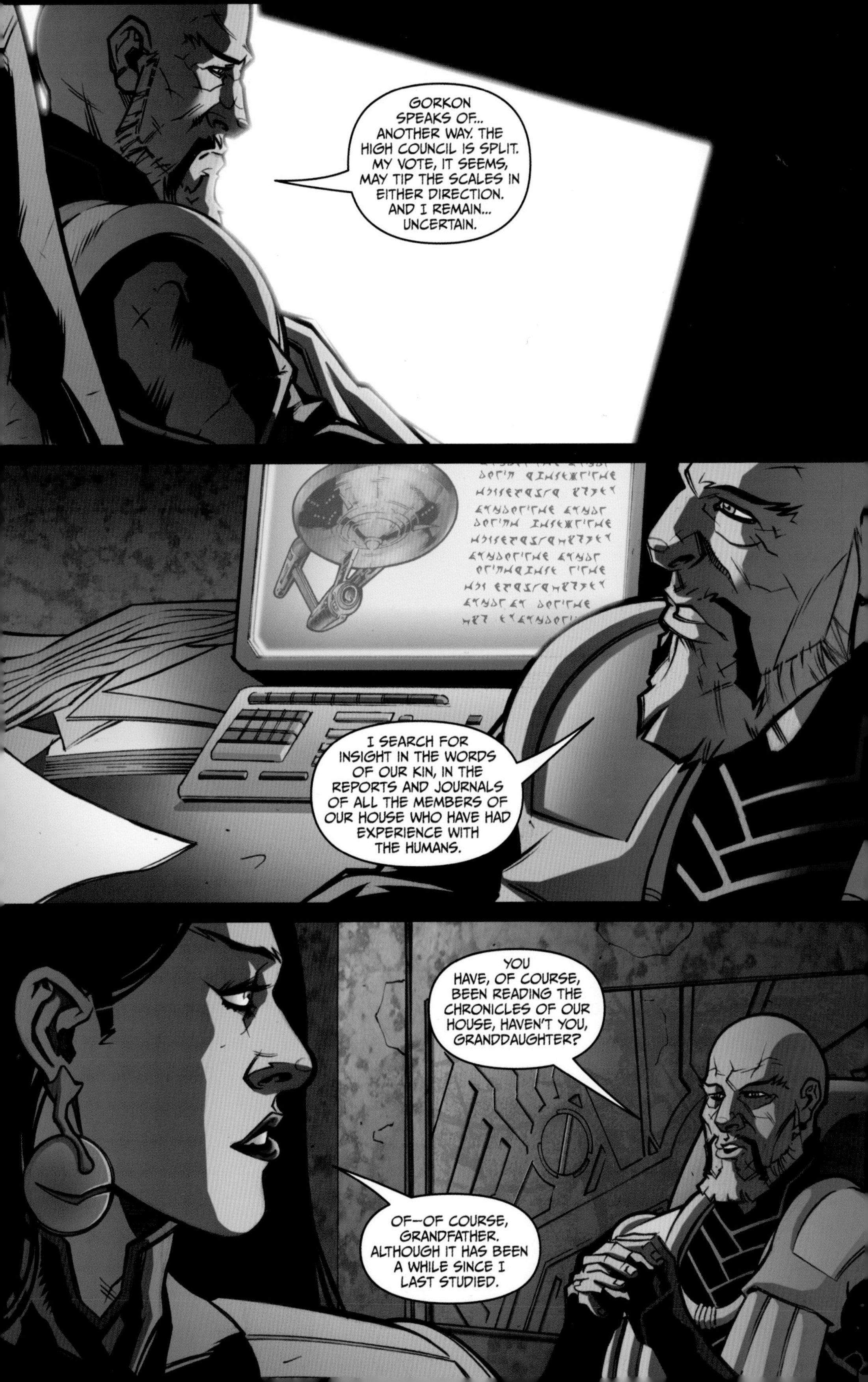
GORKON SPEAKS OF... ANOTHER WAY. THE HIGH COUNCIL IS SPLIT. MY VOTE, IT SEEMS, MAY TIP THE SCALES IN EITHER DIRECTION. AND I REMAIN... UNCERTAIN.
I SEARCH FOR INSIGHT IN THE WORDS OF OUR KIN, IN THE REPORTS AND JOURNALS OF ALL THE MEMBERS OF OUR HOUSE WHO HAVE HAD EXPERIENCE WITH THE HUMANS.
YOU HAVE, OF COURSE, BEEN READING THE CHRONICLES OF OUR HOUSE, HAVEN'T YOU, GRANDDAUGHTER?
OF--OF COURSE, GRANDFATHER. ALTHOUGH IT HAS BEEN A WHILE SINCE I LAST STUDIED.

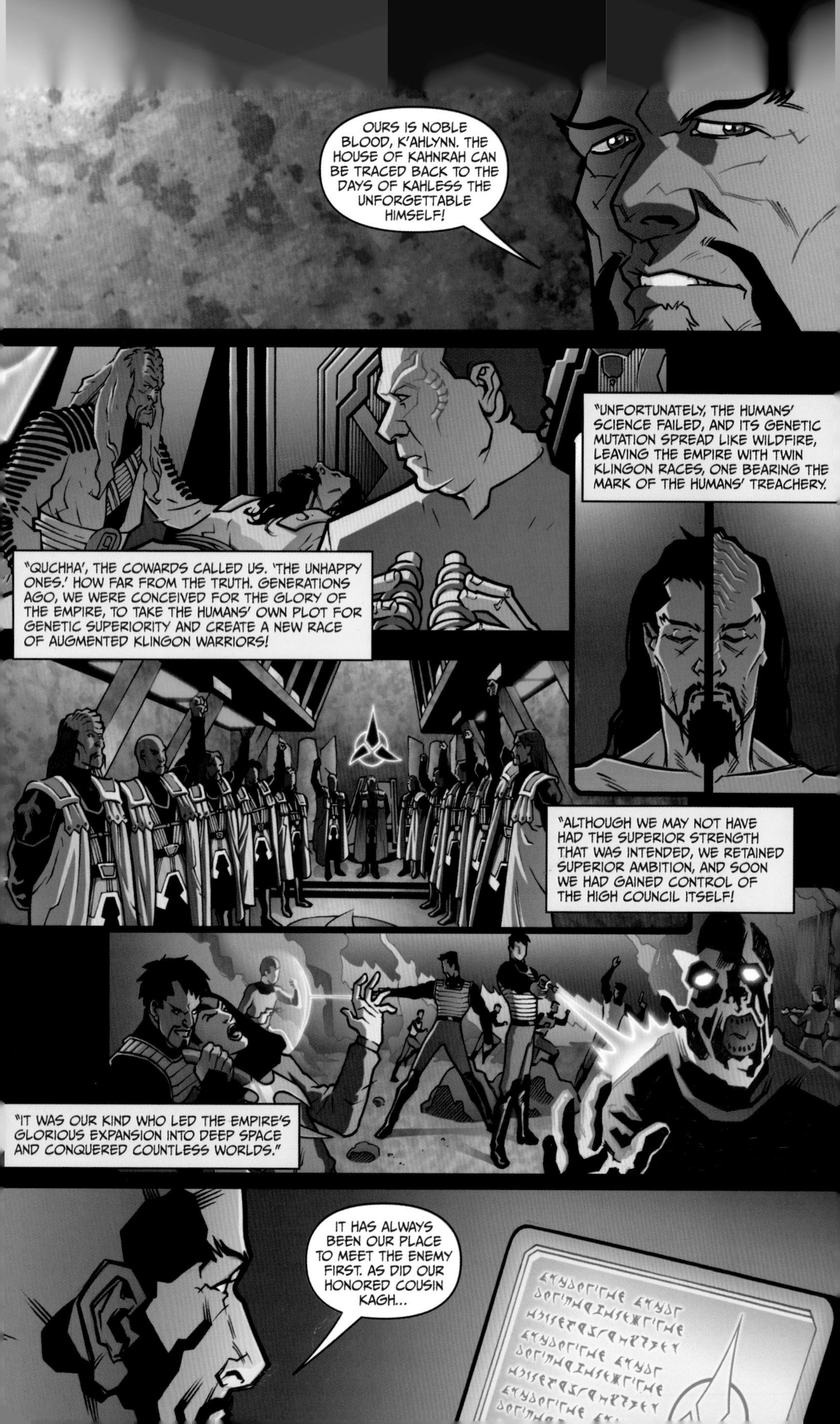
OURS IS NOBLE BLOOD, K'AHLYNN. THE HOUSE OF KAHNRAH CAN BE TRACED BACK TO THE DAYS OF KAHLESS THE UNFORGETTABLE HIMSELF!
"QUCHHA', THE COWARDS CALLED US. 'THE UNHAPPY ONES.' HOW FAR FROM THE TRUTH. GENERATIONS AGO, WE WERE CONCEIVED FOR THE GLORY OF THE EMPIRE, TO TAKE THE HUMANS' OWN PLOT FOR GENETIC SUPERIORITY AND CREATE A NEW RACE OF AUGMENTED KLINGON WARRIORS!
"UNFORTUNATELY, THE HUMANS' SCIENCE FAILED, AND ITS GENETIC MUTATION SPREAD LIKE WILDFIRE, LEAVING THE EMPIRE WITH TWIN KLINGON RACES, ONE BEARING THE MARK OF THE HUMANS' TREACHERY.
"ALTHOUGH WE MAY NOT HAVE HAD THE SUPERIOR STRENGTH THAT WAS INTENDED, WE RETAINED SUPERIOR AMBITION, AND SOON WE HAD GAINED CONTROL OF THE HIGH COUNCIL ITSELF!
"IT WAS OUR KIND WHO LED THE EMPIRE'S GLORIOUS EXPANSION INTO DEEP SPACE AND CONQUERED COUNTLESS WORLDS."
IT HAS ALWAYS BEEN OUR PLACE TO MEET THE ENEMY FIRST. AS DID OUR HONORED COUSIN KAGH...

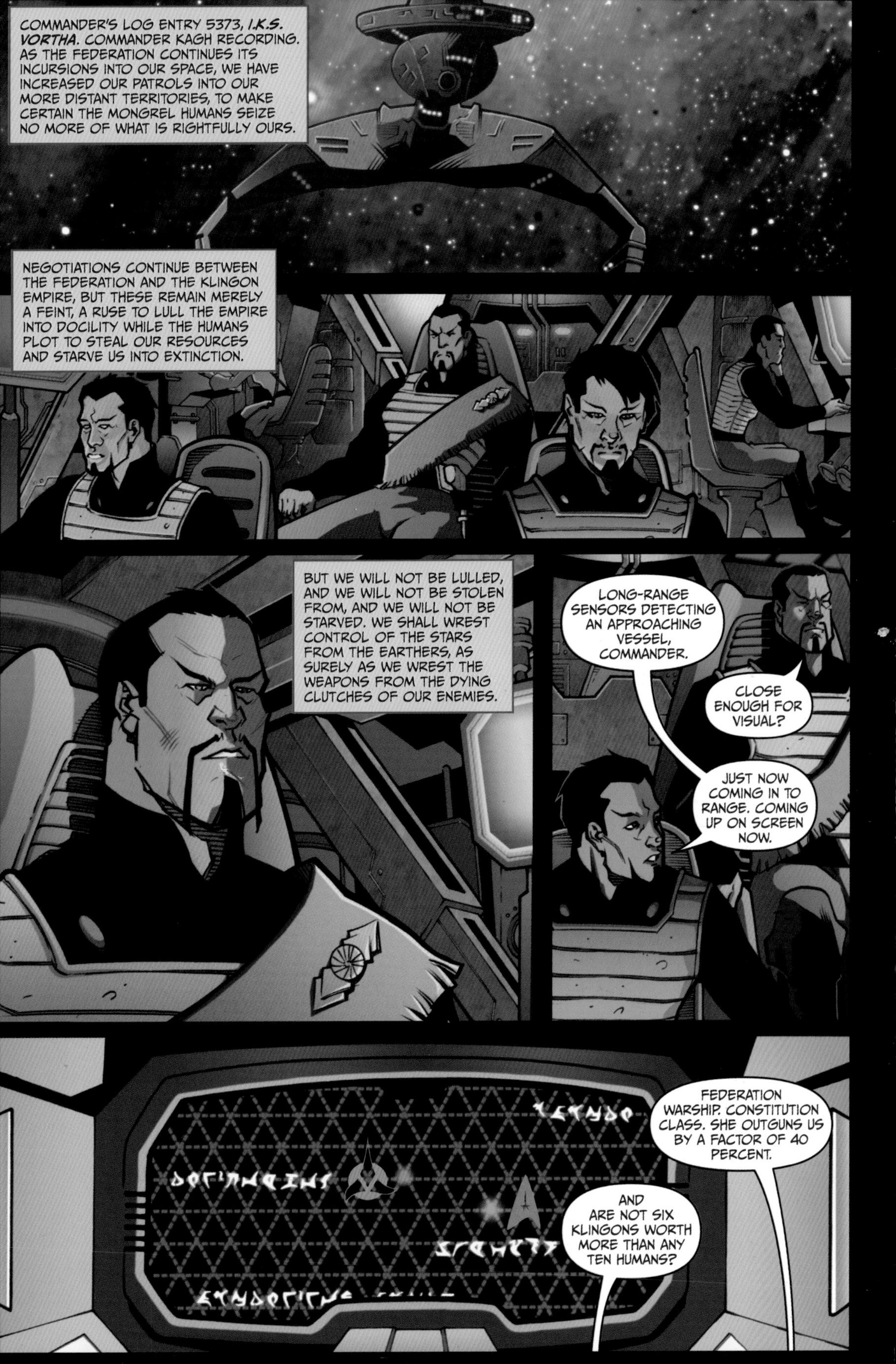
COMMANDER'S LOG ENTRY 5373, *I.K.S. VORTHA*. COMMANDER KAGH RECORDING. AS THE FEDERATION CONTINUES ITS INCURSIONS INTO OUR SPACE, WE HAVE INCREASED OUR PATROLS INTO OUR MORE DISTANT TERRITORIES, TO MAKE CERTAIN THE MONGREL HUMANS SEIZE NO MORE OF WHAT IS RIGHTFULLY OURS.
NEGOTIATIONS CONTINUE BETWEEN THE FEDERATION AND THE KLINGON EMPIRE, BUT THESE REMAIN MERELY A FEINT, A RUSE TO LULL THE EMPIRE INTO DOCILITY WHILE THE HUMANS PLOT TO STEAL OUR RESOURCES AND STARVE US INTO EXTINCTION.
BUT WE WILL NOT BE LULLED, AND WE WILL NOT BE STOLEN FROM, AND WE WILL NOT BE STARVED. WE SHALL WREST CONTROL OF THE STARS FROM THE EARTHERS, AS SURELY AS WE WREST THE WEAPONS FROM THE DYING CLUTCHES OF OUR ENEMIES.
LONG-RANGE SENSORS DETECTING AN APPROACHING VESSEL, COMMANDER.
CLOSE ENOUGH FOR VISUAL?
JUST NOW COMING IN TO RANGE. COMING UP ON SCREEN NOW.
FEDERATION WARSHIP. CONSTITUTION CLASS. SHE OUTGUNS US BY A FACTOR OF 40 PERCENT.
AND ARE NOT SIX KLINGONS WORTH MORE THAN ANY TEN HUMANS?

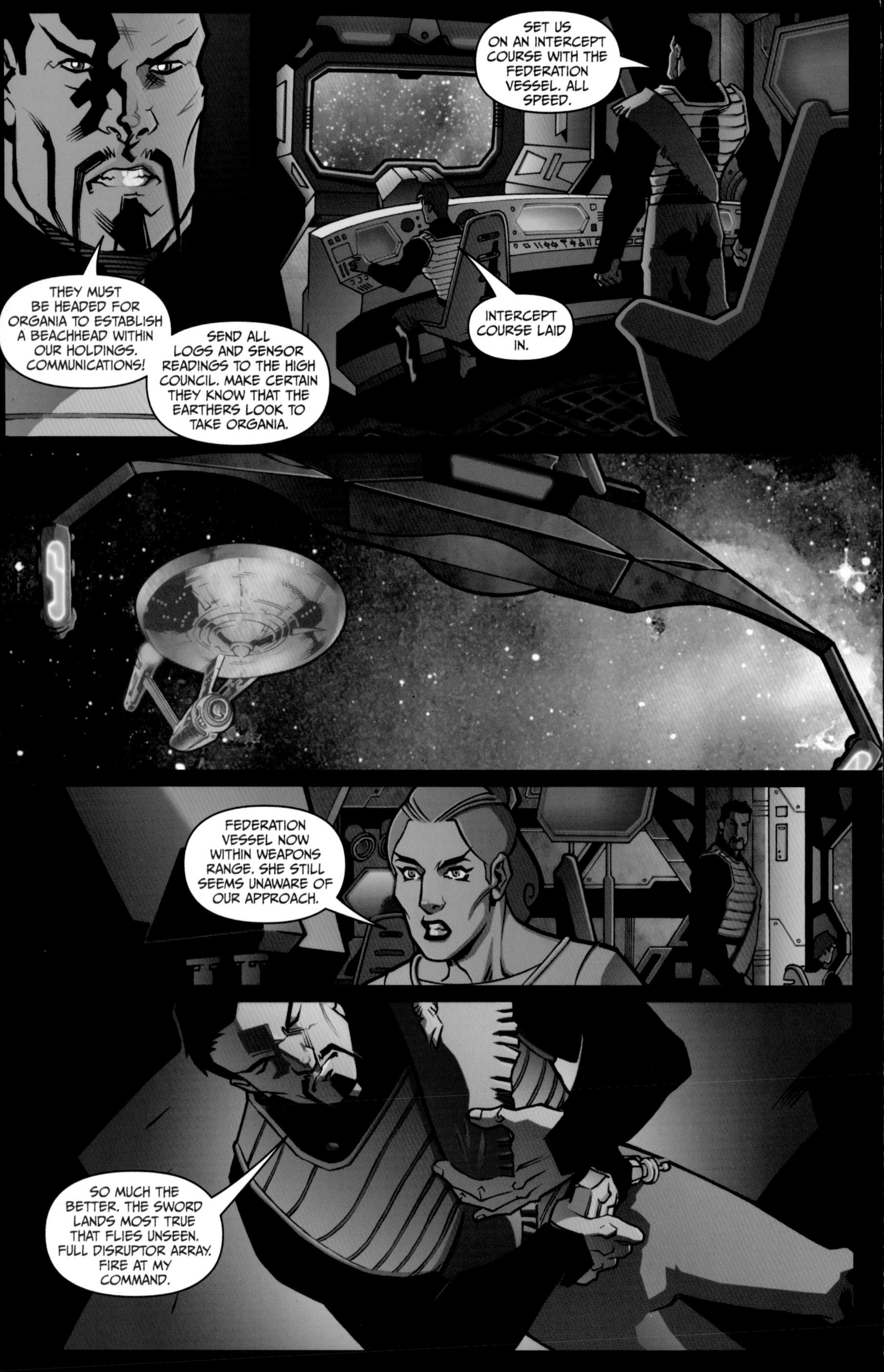

SET US ON AN INTERCEPT COURSE WITH THE FEDERATION VESSEL. ALL SPEED.
THEY MUST BE HEADED FOR ORGANIA TO ESTABLISH A BEACHHEAD WITHIN OUR HOLDINGS. COMMUNICATIONS!
SEND ALL LOGS AND SENSOR READINGS TO THE HIGH COUNCIL. MAKE CERTAIN THEY KNOW THAT THE EARTHERS LOOK TO TAKE ORGANIA.
INTERCEPT COURSE LAID IN.
FEDERATION VESSEL NOW WITHIN WEAPONS RANGE. SHE STILL SEEMS UNAWARE OF OUR APPROACH.
SO MUCH THE BETTER. THE SWORD LANDS MOST TRUE THAT FLIES UNSEEN. FULL DISRUPTOR ARRAY. FIRE AT MY COMMAND.

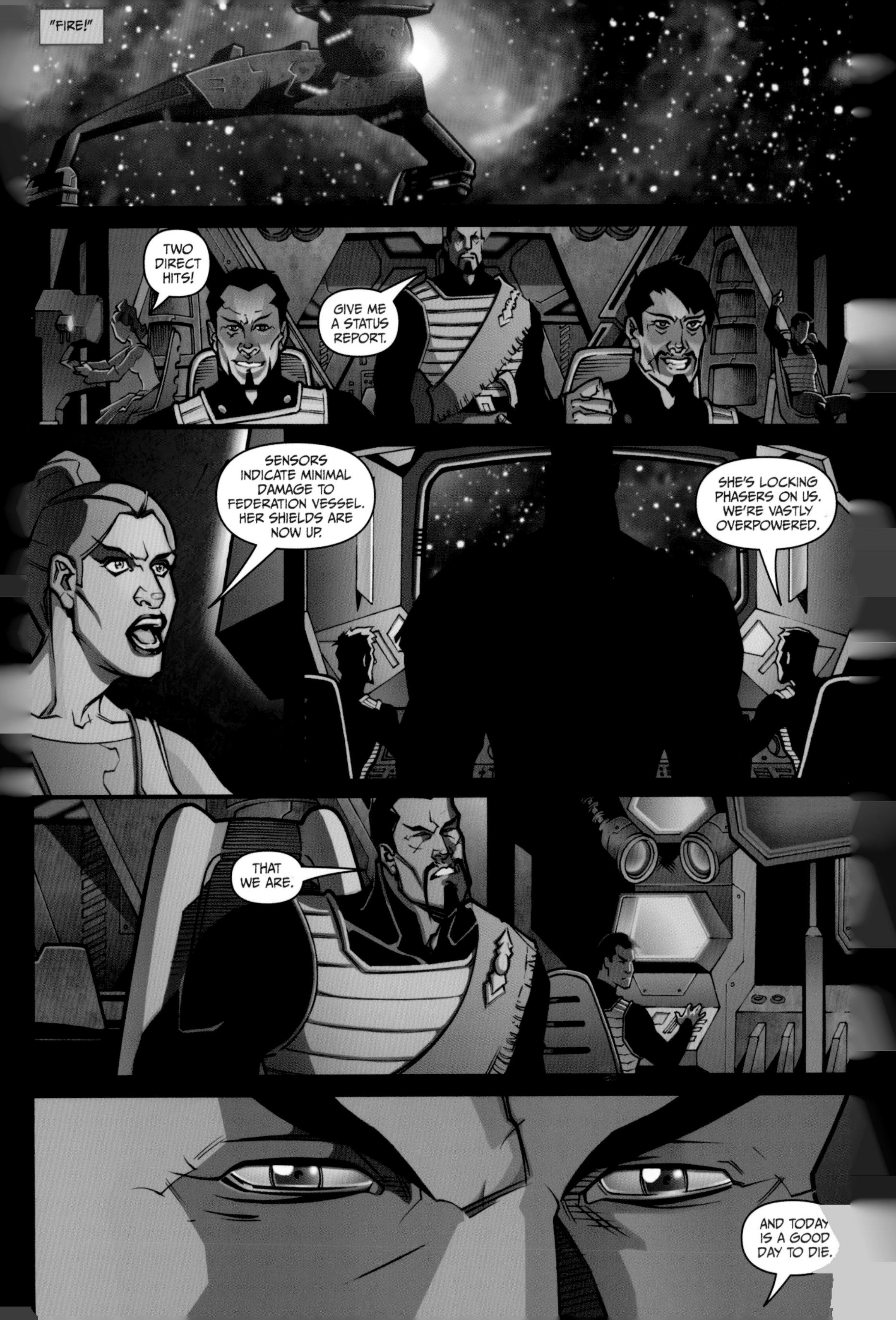
"FIRE!"
TWO DIRECT HITS!
GIVE ME A STATUS REPORT.
SENSORS INDICATE MINIMAL DAMAGE TO FEDERATION VESSEL. HER SHIELDS ARE NOW UP.
SHE'S LOCKING PHASERS ON US. WE'RE VASTLY OVERPOWERED.
THAT WE ARE.
AND TODAY IS A GOOD DAY TO DIE.

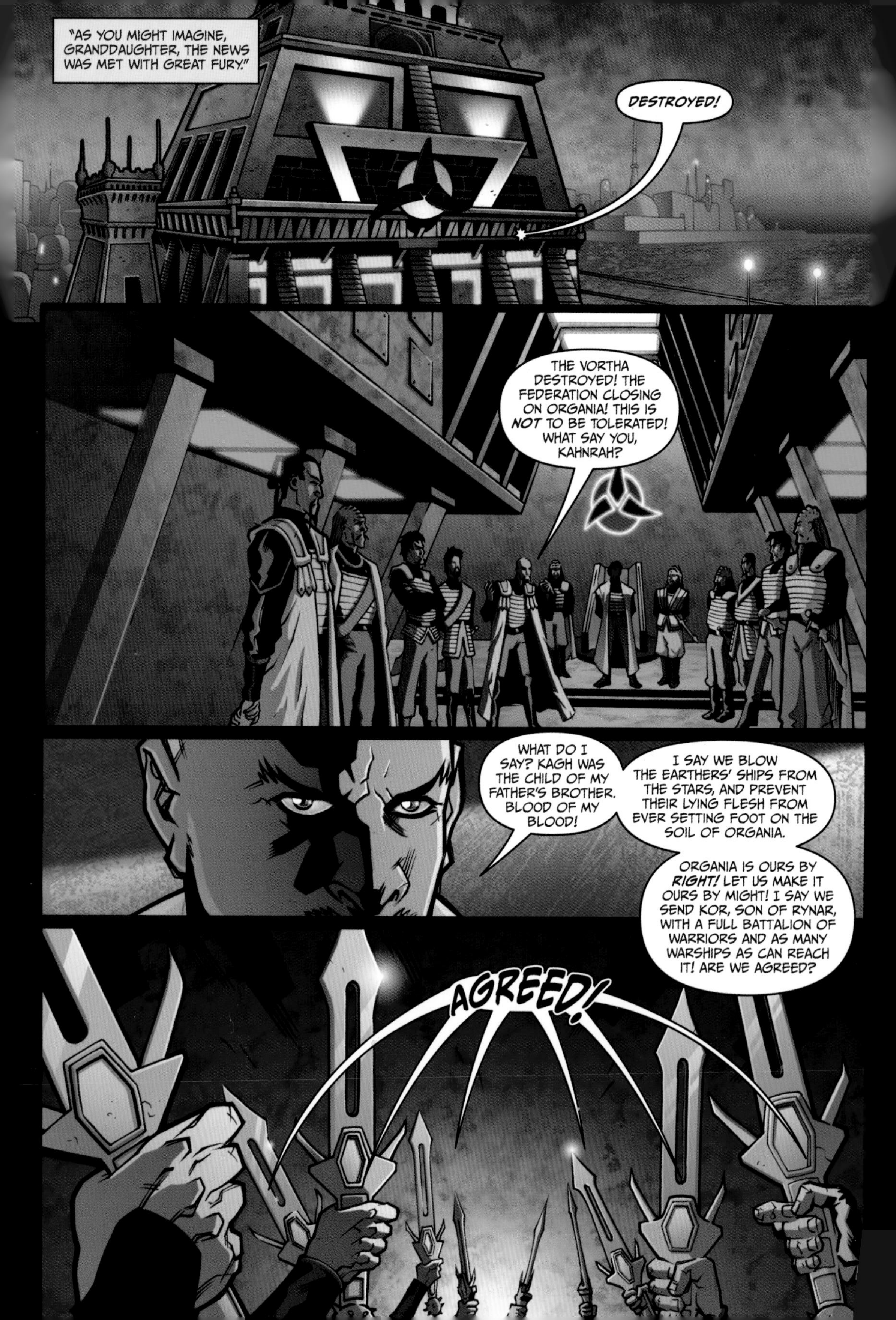
"AS YOU MIGHT IMAGINE, GRANDDAUGHTER, THE NEWS WAS MET WITH GREAT FURY."
DESTROYED!
THE VORTHA DESTROYED! THE FEDERATION CLOSING ON ORGANIA! THIS IS NOT TO BE TOLERATED! WHAT SAY YOU, KAHNRAH?
WHAT DO I SAY? KAGH WAS THE CHILD OF MY FATHER'S BROTHER. BLOOD OF MY BLOOD!
I SAY WE BLOW THE EARTHERS' SHIPS FROM THE STARS, AND PREVENT THEIR LYING FLESH FROM EVER SETTING FOOT ON THE SOIL OF ORGANIA.
ORGANIA IS OURS BY RIGHT! LET US MAKE IT OURS BY MIGHT! I SAY WE SEND KOR, SON OF RYNAR, WITH A FULL BATTALION OF WARRIORS AND AS MANY WARSHIPS AS CAN REACH IT! ARE WE AGREED?
AGREED!

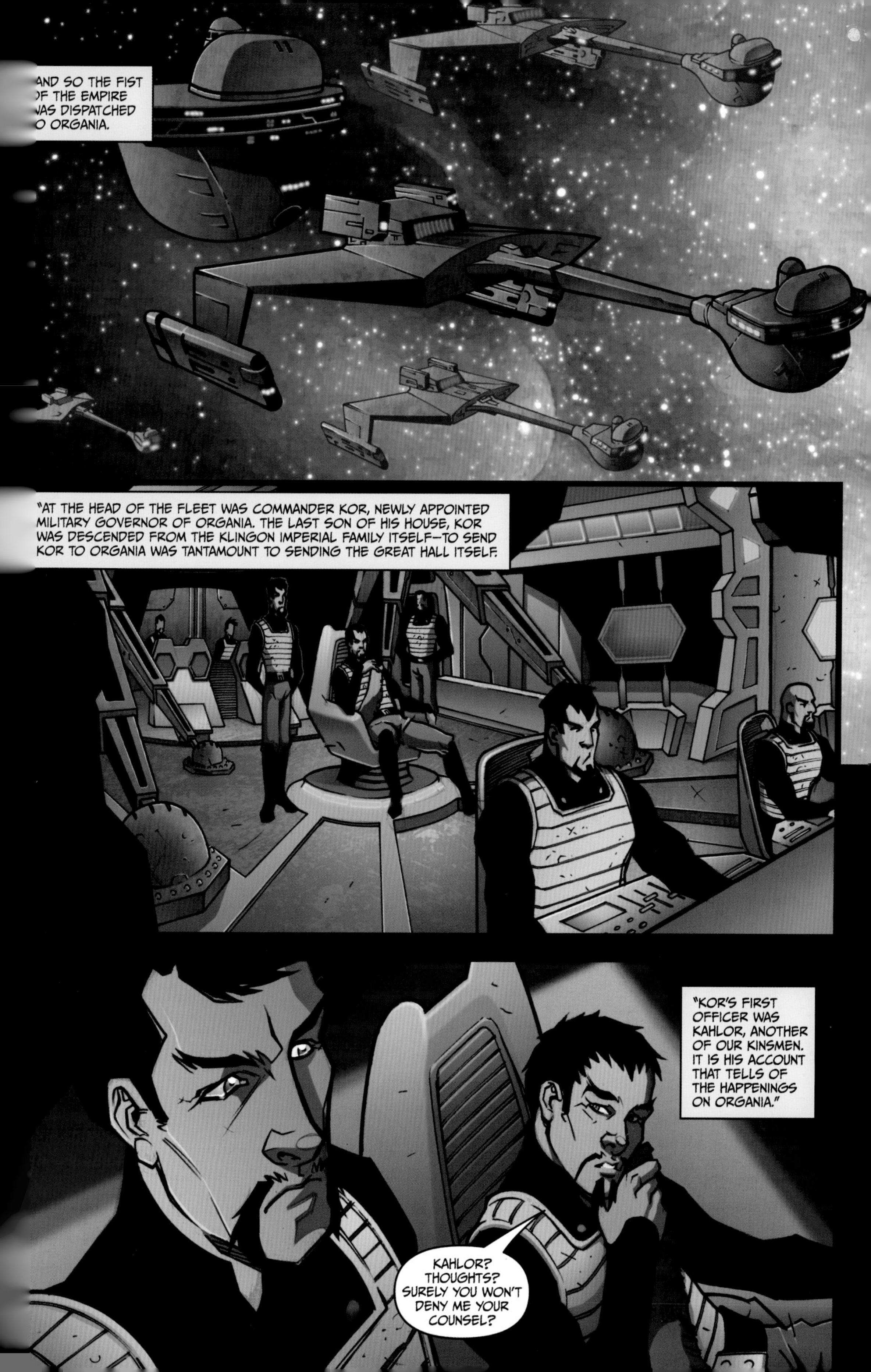
AND SO THE FIST OF THE EMPIRE WAS DISPATCHED TO ORGANIA.
"AT THE HEAD OF THE FLEET WAS COMMANDER KOR, NEWLY APPOINTED MILITARY GOVERNOR OF ORGANIA. THE LAST SON OF HIS HOUSE, KOR WAS DESCENDED FROM THE KLINGON IMPERIAL FAMILY ITSELF—TO SEND KOR TO ORGANIA WAS TANTAMOUNT TO SENDING THE GREAT HALL ITSELF.
"KOR'S FIRST OFFICER WAS KAHLOR, ANOTHER OF OUR KINSMEN. IT IS HIS ACCOUNT THAT TELLS OF THE HAPPENINGS ON ORGANIA."
KAHLOR? THOUGHTS? SURELY YOU WON'T DENY ME YOUR COUNSEL?

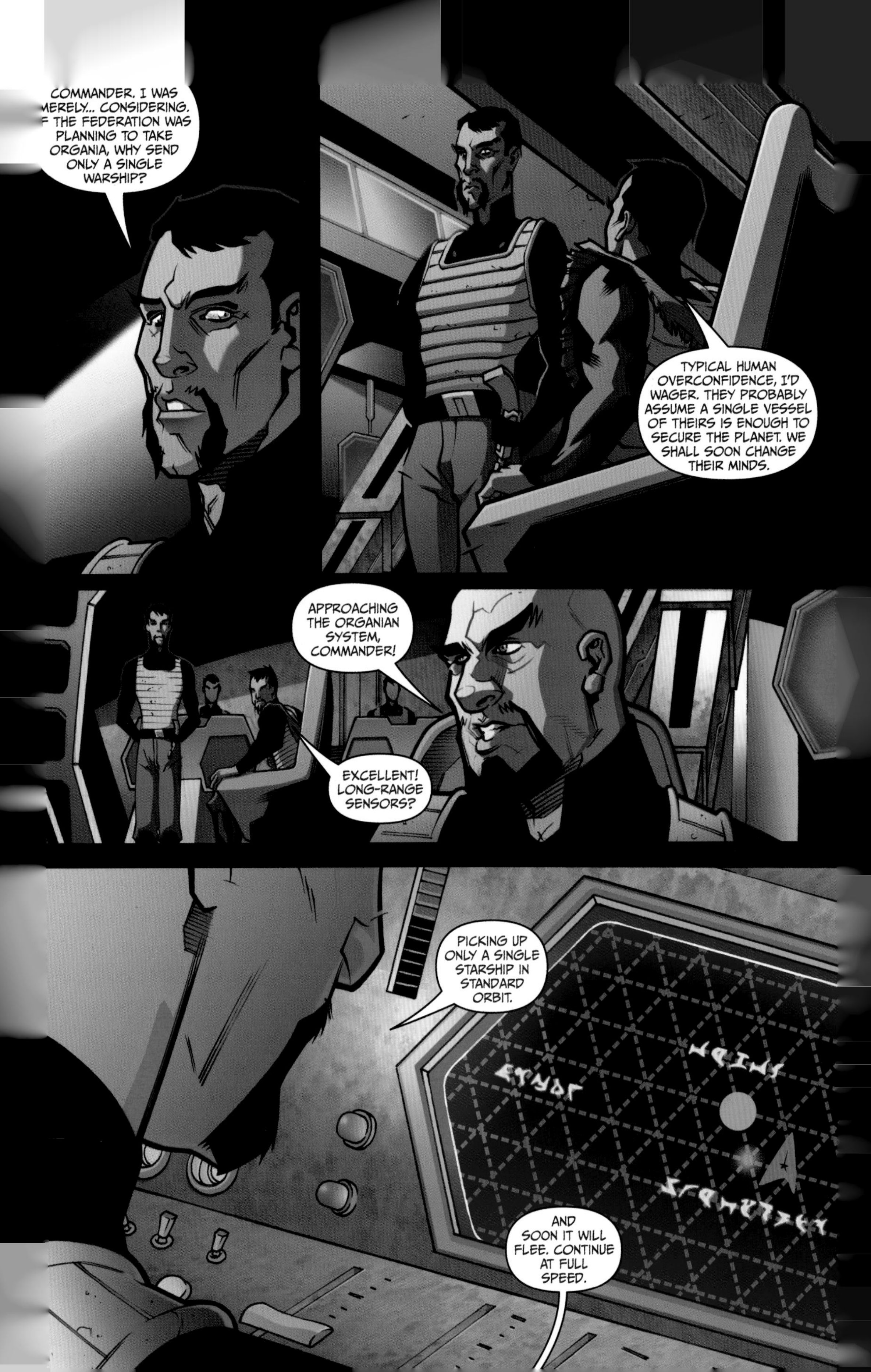
COMMANDER. I WAS MERELY... CONSIDERING. IF THE FEDERATION WAS PLANNING TO TAKE ORGANIA, WHY SEND ONLY A SINGLE WARSHIP?
TYPICAL HUMAN OVERCONFIDENCE, I'D WAGER. THEY PROBABLY ASSUME A SINGLE VESSEL OF THEIRS IS ENOUGH TO SECURE THE PLANET. WE SHALL SOON CHANGE THEIR MINDS.
APPROACHING THE ORGANIAN SYSTEM, COMMANDER!
EXCELLENT! LONG-RANGE SENSORS?
PICKING UP ONLY A SINGLE STARSHIP IN STANDARD ORBIT.
AND SOON IT WILL FLEE. CONTINUE AT FULL SPEED.

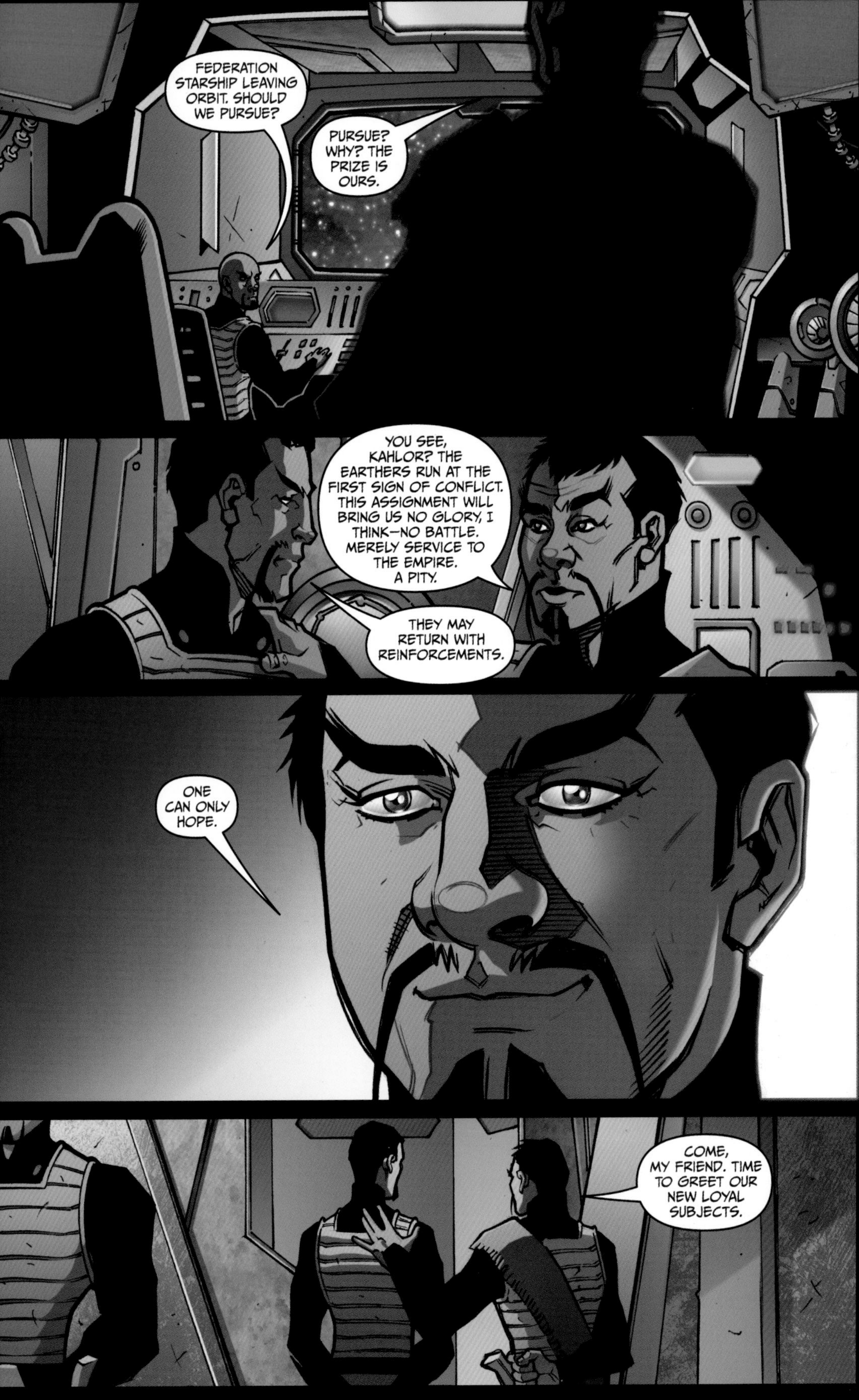
FEDERATION STARSHIP LEAVING ORBIT. SHOULD WE PURSUE?
PURSUE? WHY? THE PRIZE IS OURS.
YOU SEE, KAHLOR? THE EARTHERS RUN AT THE FIRST SIGN OF CONFLICT. THIS ASSIGNMENT WILL BRING US NO GLORY, I THINK—NO BATTLE. MERELY SERVICE TO THE EMPIRE. A PITY.
THEY MAY RETURN WITH REINFORCEMENTS.
ONE CAN ONLY HOPE.
COME, MY FRIEND. TIME TO GREET OUR NEW LOYAL SUBJECTS.

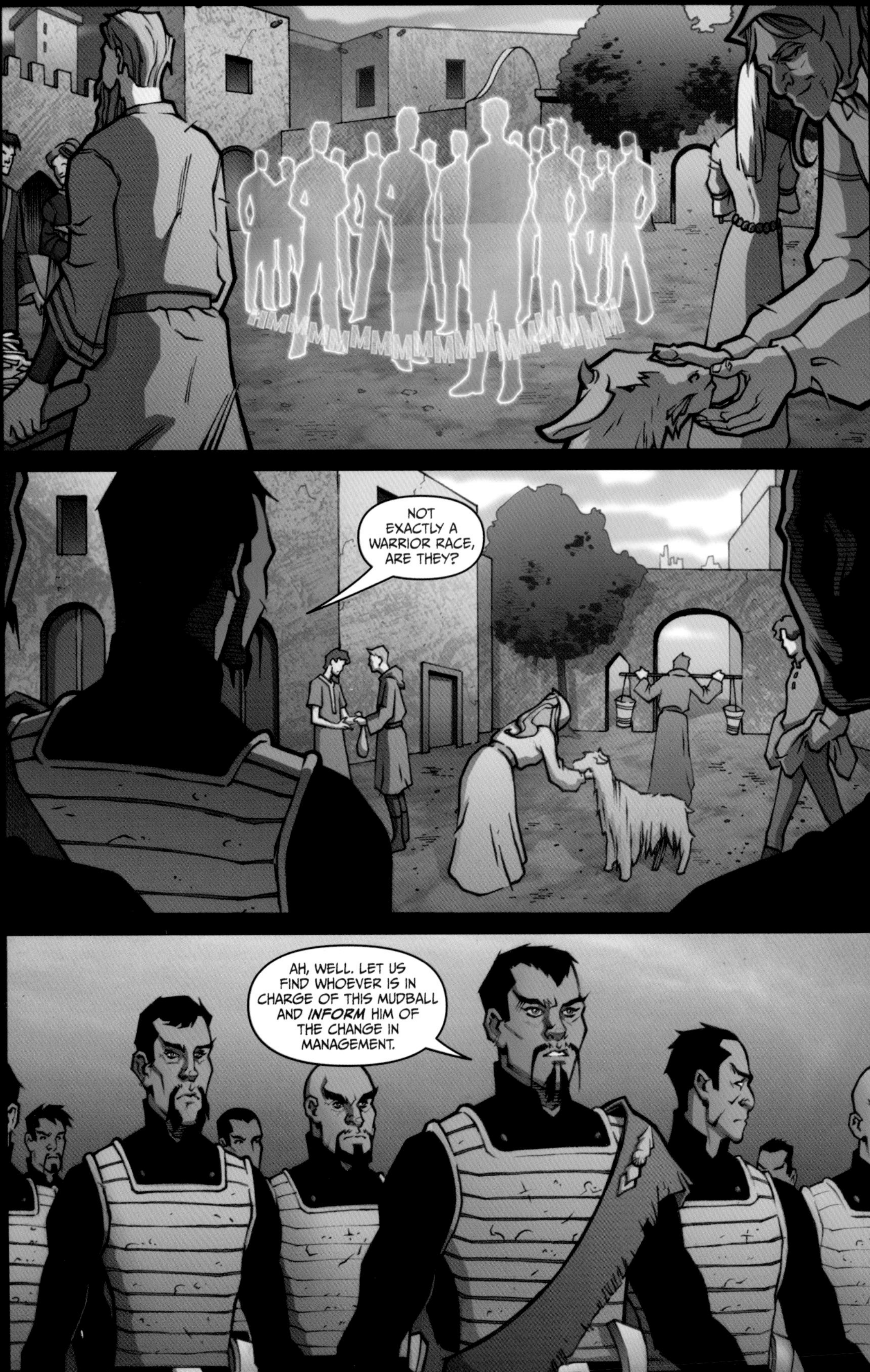
HMMMMMMMMMMMMMMMMM
NOT EXACTLY A WARRIOR RACE, ARE THEY?
AH, WELL. LET US FIND WHOEVER IS IN CHARGE OF THIS MUDBALL AND *INFORM* HIM OF THE CHANGE IN MANAGEMENT.

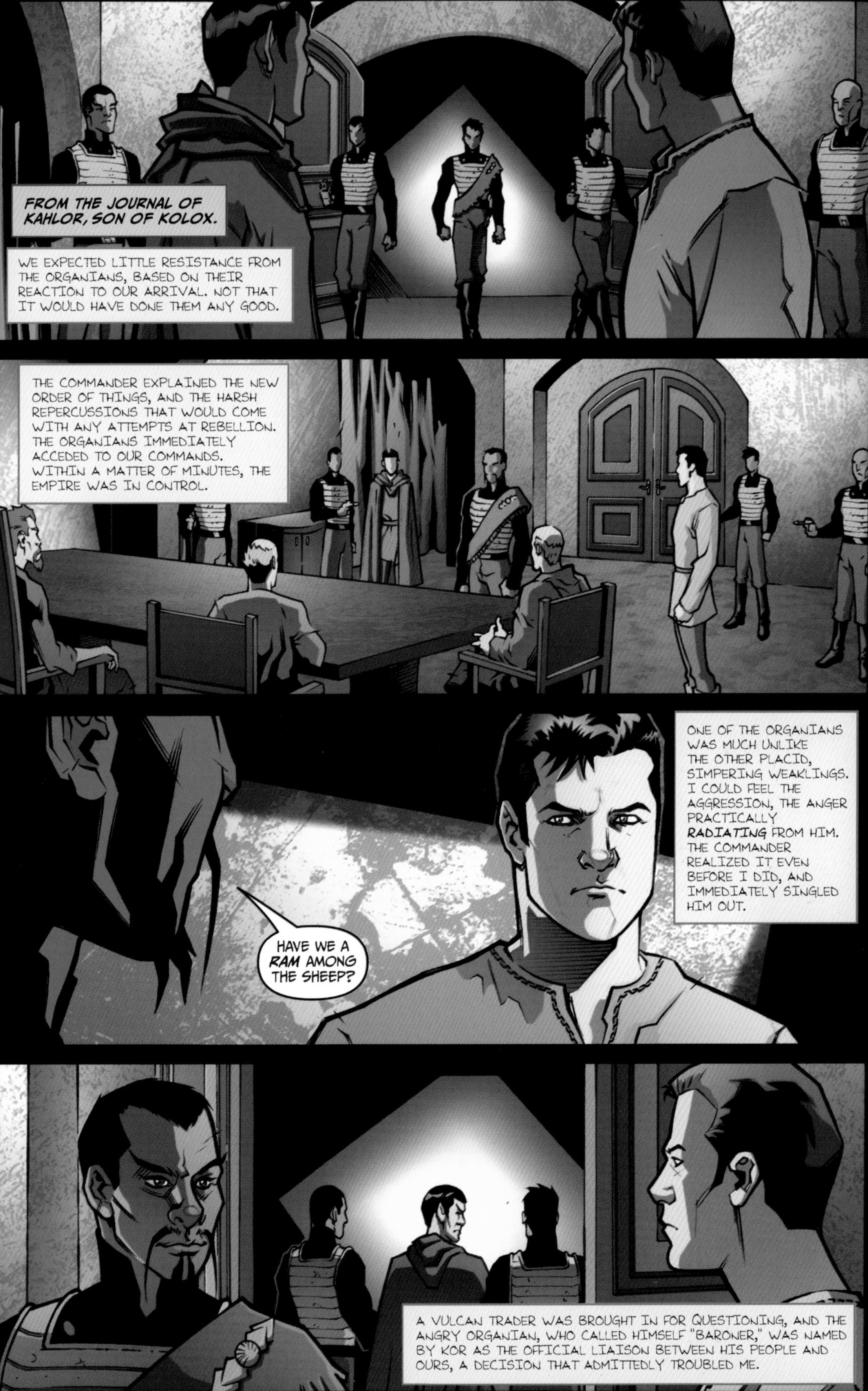

FROM THE JOURNAL OF KAHLOR, SON OF KOLOX.
WE EXPECTED LITTLE RESISTANCE FROM THE ORGANIANS, BASED ON THEIR REACTION TO OUR ARRIVAL. NOT THAT IT WOULD HAVE DONE THEM ANY GOOD.
THE COMMANDER EXPLAINED THE NEW ORDER OF THINGS, AND THE HARSH REPERCUSSIONS THAT WOULD COME WITH ANY ATTEMPTS AT REBELLION. THE ORGANIANS IMMEDIATELY ACCEDED TO OUR COMMANDS. WITHIN A MATTER OF MINUTES, THE EMPIRE WAS IN CONTROL.
ONE OF THE ORGANIANS WAS MUCH UNLIKE THE OTHER PLACID, SIMPERING WEAKLINGS. I COULD FEEL THE AGGRESSION, THE ANGER PRACTICALLY RADIATING FROM HIM. THE COMMANDER REALIZED IT EVEN BEFORE I DID, AND IMMEDIATELY SINGLED HIM OUT.
HAVE WE A RAM AMONG THE SHEEP?
A VULCAN TRADER WAS BROUGHT IN FOR QUESTIONING, AND THE ANGRY ORGANIAN, WHO CALLED HIMSELF "BARONER," WAS NAMED BY KOR AS THE OFFICIAL LIAISON BETWEEN HIS PEOPLE AND OURS, A DECISION THAT ADMITTEDLY TROUBLED ME.

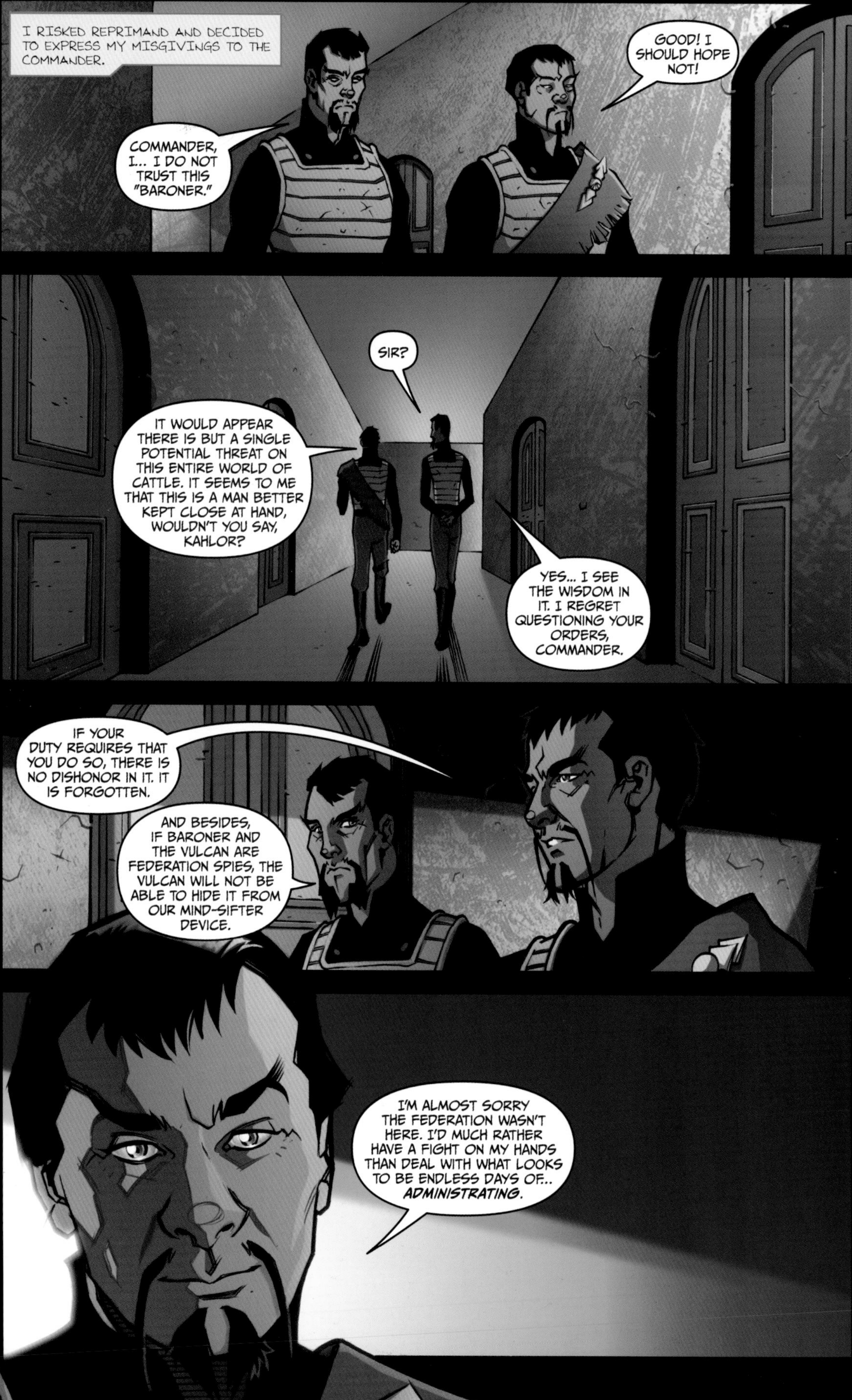
I RISKED REPRIMAND AND DECIDED TO EXPRESS MY MISGIVINGS TO THE COMMANDER.
COMMANDER, I... I DO NOT TRUST THIS "BARONER."
GOOD! I SHOULD HOPE NOT!
SIR?
IT WOULD APPEAR THERE IS BUT A SINGLE POTENTIAL THREAT ON THIS ENTIRE WORLD OF CATTLE. IT SEEMS TO ME THAT THIS IS A MAN BETTER KEPT CLOSE AT HAND, WOULDN'T YOU SAY, KAHLOR?
YES... I SEE THE WISDOM IN IT. I REGRET QUESTIONING YOUR ORDERS, COMMANDER.
IF YOUR DUTY REQUIRES THAT YOU DO SO, THERE IS NO DISHONOR IN IT. IT IS FORGOTTEN.
AND BESIDES, IF BARONER AND THE VULCAN ARE FEDERATION SPIES, THE VULCAN WILL NOT BE ABLE TO HIDE IT FROM OUR MIND-SIFTER DEVICE.
I'M ALMOST SORRY THE FEDERATION WASN'T HERE. I'D MUCH RATHER HAVE A FIGHT ON MY HANDS THAN DEAL WITH WHAT LOOKS TO BE ENDLESS DAYS OF... ADMINISTRATING.

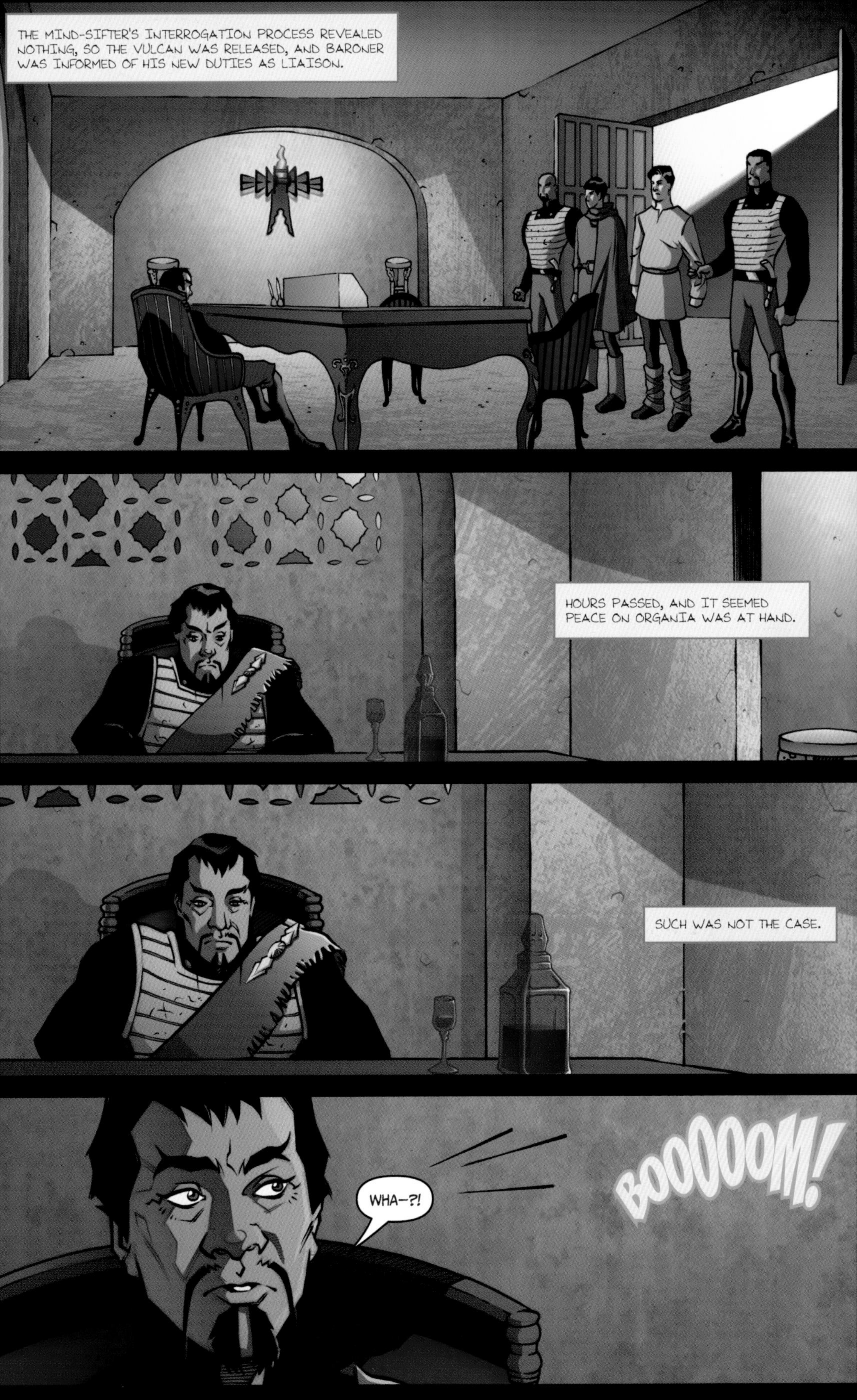
THE MIND-SIFTER'S INTERROGATION PROCESS REVEALED NOTHING, SO THE VULCAN WAS RELEASED, AND BARONER WAS INFORMED OF HIS NEW DUTIES AS LIAISON.
HOURS PASSED, AND IT SEEMED PEACE ON ORGANIA WAS AT HAND.
SUCH WAS NOT THE CASE.
WHA–?!
BOOOOOM!

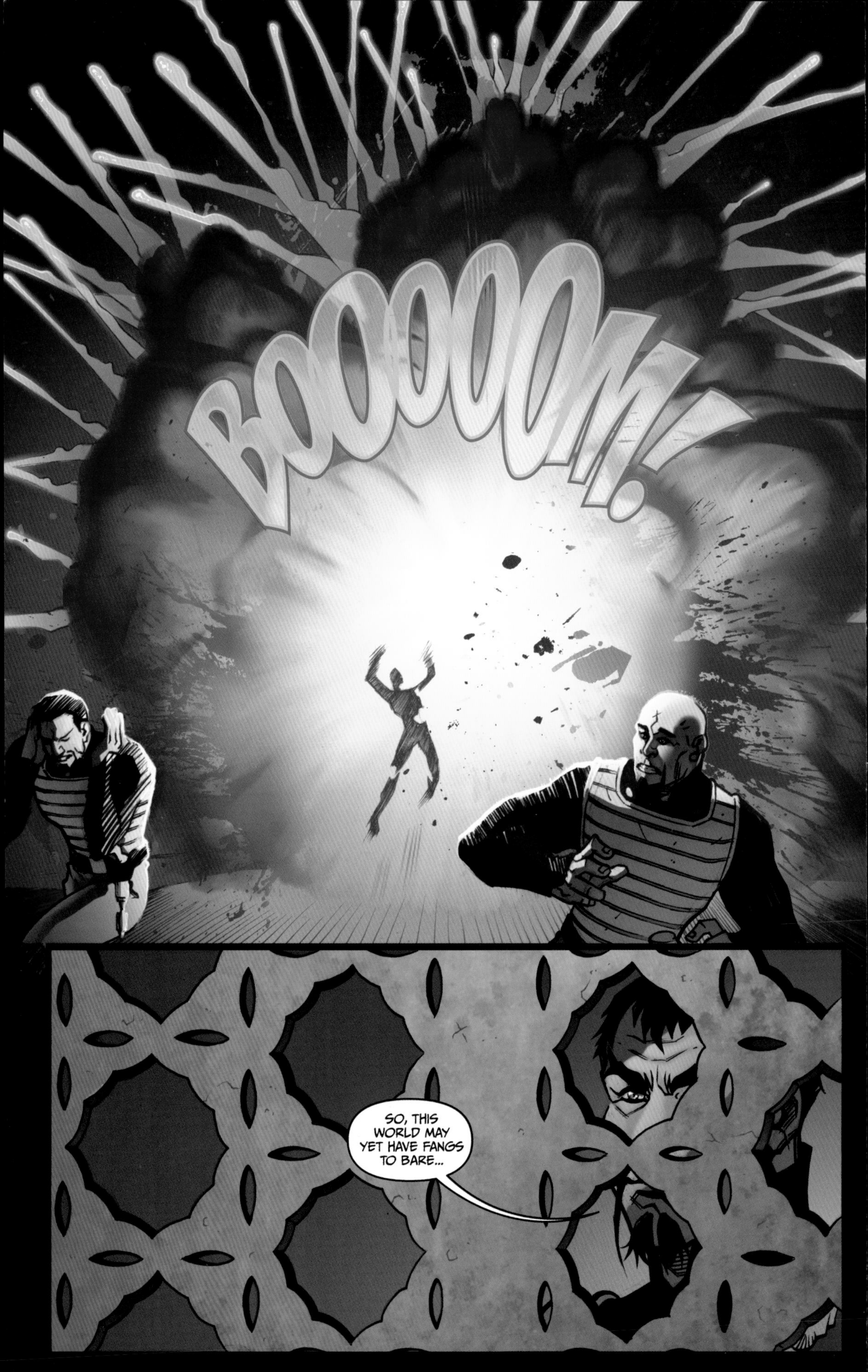
BOOOOOM!
SO, THIS WORLD MAY YET HAVE FANGS TO BARE...

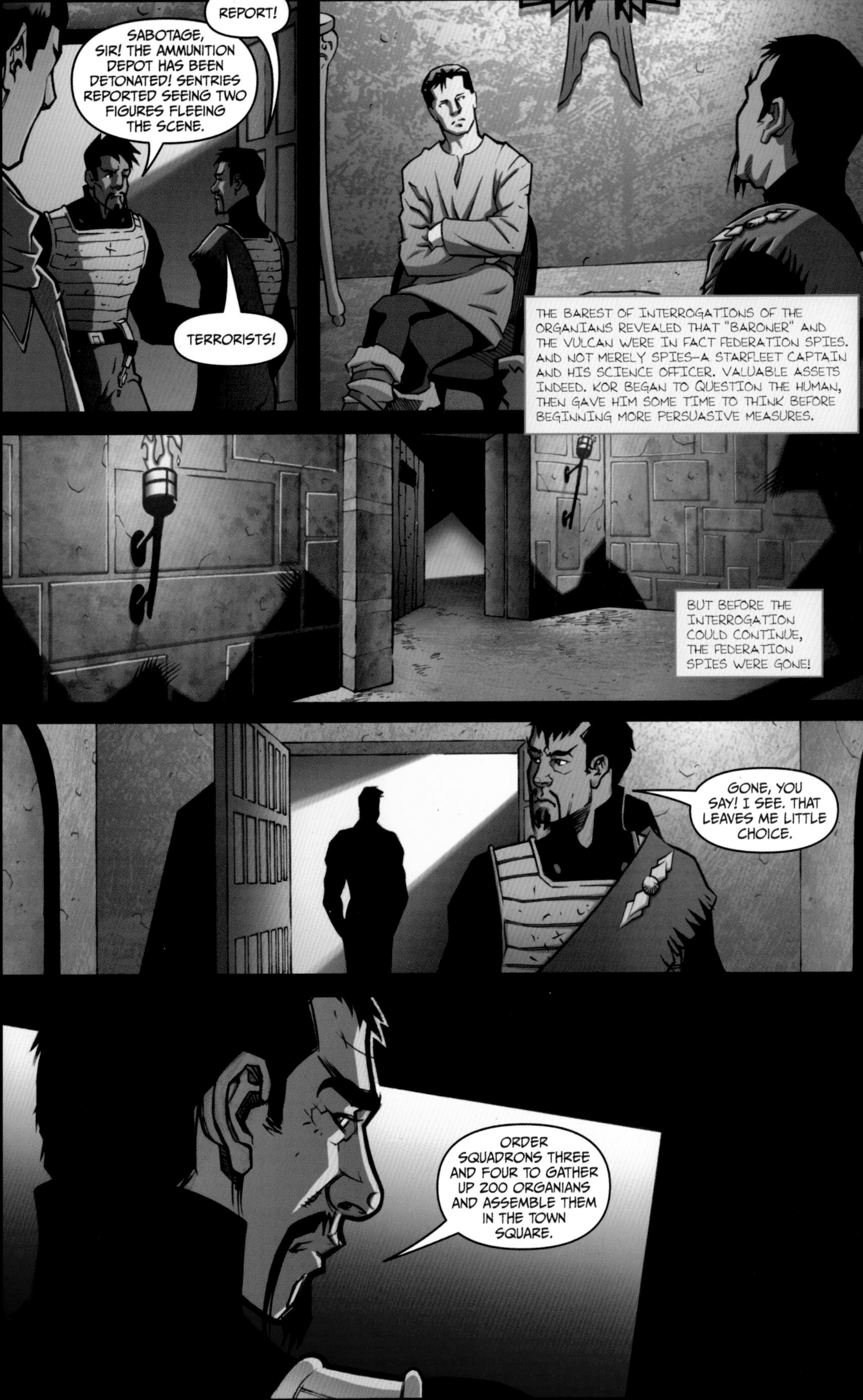
REPORT!
SABOTAGE, SIR! THE AMMUNITION DEPOT HAS BEEN DETONATED! SENTRIES REPORTED SEEING TWO FIGURES FLEEING THE SCENE.
TERRORISTS!
THE BAREST OF INTERROGATIONS OF THE ORGANIANS REVEALED THAT "BARONER" AND THE VULCAN WERE IN FACT FEDERATION SPIES. AND NOT MERELY SPIES—A STARFLEET CAPTAIN AND HIS SCIENCE OFFICER. VALUABLE ASSETS INDEED. KOR BEGAN TO QUESTION THE HUMAN, THEN GAVE HIM SOME TIME TO THINK BEFORE BEGINNING MORE PERSUASIVE MEASURES.
BUT BEFORE THE INTERROGATION COULD CONTINUE, THE FEDERATION SPIES WERE GONE!
GONE, YOU SAY! I SEE. THAT LEAVES ME LITTLE CHOICE.
ORDER SQUADRONS THREE AND FOUR TO GATHER UP 200 ORGANIANS AND ASSEMBLE THEM IN THE TOWN SQUARE.

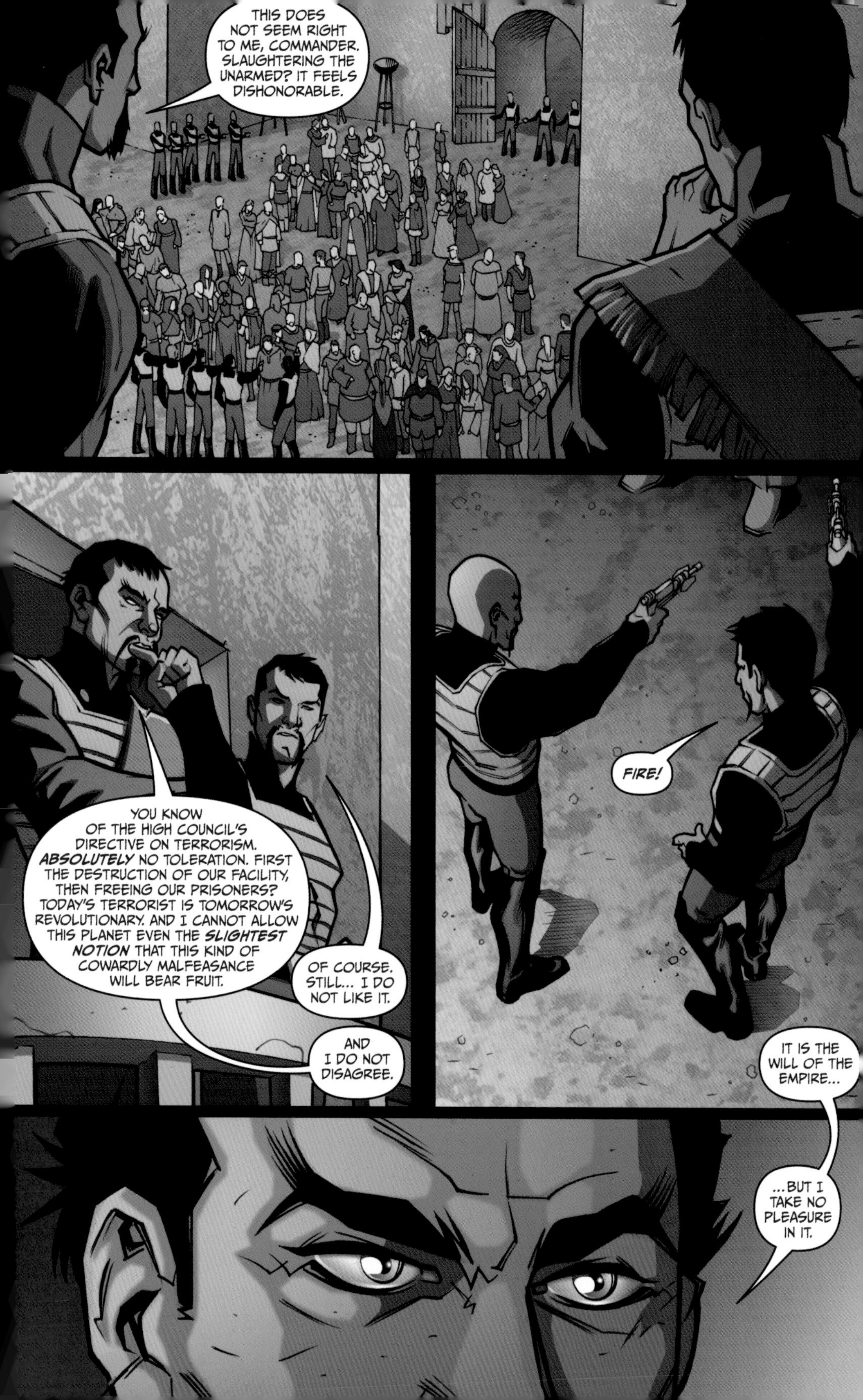
THIS DOES NOT SEEM RIGHT TO ME, COMMANDER. SLAUGHTERING THE UNARMED? IT FEELS DISHONORABLE.
YOU KNOW OF THE HIGH COUNCIL'S DIRECTIVE ON TERRORISM. ABSOLUTELY NO TOLERATION. FIRST THE DESTRUCTION OF OUR FACILITY, THEN FREEING OUR PRISONERS? TODAY'S TERRORIST IS TOMORROW'S REVOLUTIONARY. AND I CANNOT ALLOW THIS PLANET EVEN THE SLIGHTEST NOTION THAT THIS KIND OF COWARDLY MALFEASANCE WILL BEAR FRUIT.
OF COURSE. STILL... I DO NOT LIKE IT.
AND I DO NOT DISAGREE.
FIRE!
IT IS THE WILL OF THE EMPIRE...
...BUT I TAKE NO PLEASURE IN IT.

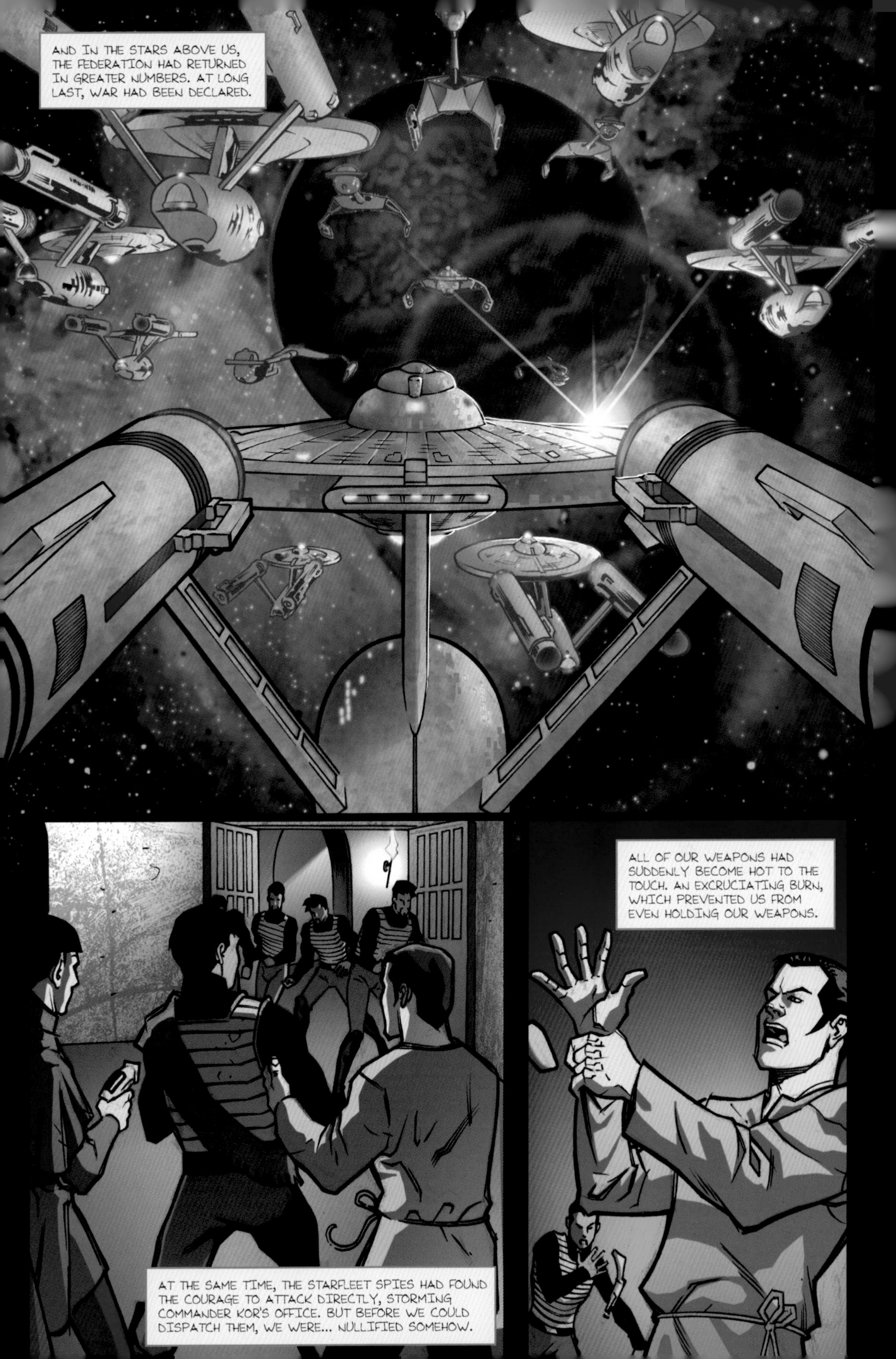
AND IN THE STARS ABOVE US, THE FEDERATION HAD RETURNED IN GREATER NUMBERS. AT LONG LAST, WAR HAD BEEN DECLARED.
AT THE SAME TIME, THE STARFLEET SPIES HAD FOUND THE COURAGE TO ATTACK DIRECTLY, STORMING COMMANDER KOR'S OFFICE. BUT BEFORE WE COULD DISPATCH THEM, WE WERE... NULLIFIED SOMEHOW.
ALL OF OUR WEAPONS HAD SUDDENLY BECOME HOT TO THE TOUCH. AN EXCRUCIATING BURN, WHICH PREVENTED US FROM EVEN HOLDING OUR WEAPONS.

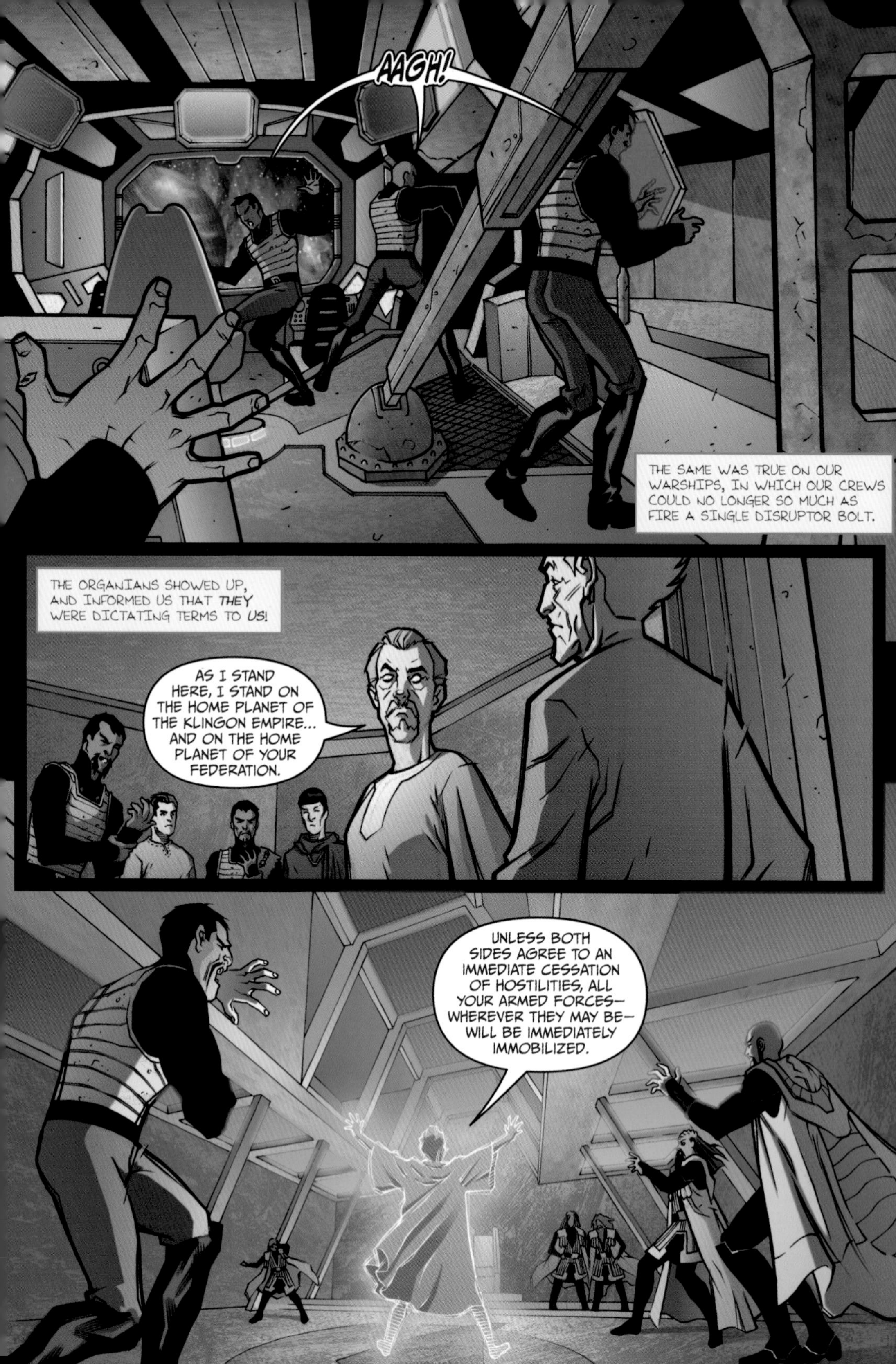
AAGH!
THE SAME WAS TRUE ON OUR WARSHIPS, IN WHICH OUR CREWS COULD NO LONGER SO MUCH AS FIRE A SINGLE DISRUPTOR BOLT.
THE ORGANIANS SHOWED UP, AND INFORMED US THAT THEY WERE DICTATING TERMS TO US!
AS I STAND HERE, I STAND ON THE HOME PLANET OF THE KLINGON EMPIRE... AND ON THE HOME PLANET OF YOUR FEDERATION.
UNLESS BOTH SIDES AGREE TO AN IMMEDIATE CESSATION OF HOSTILITIES, ALL YOUR ARMED FORCES—WHEREVER THEY MAY BE—WILL BE IMMEDIATELY IMMOBILIZED.

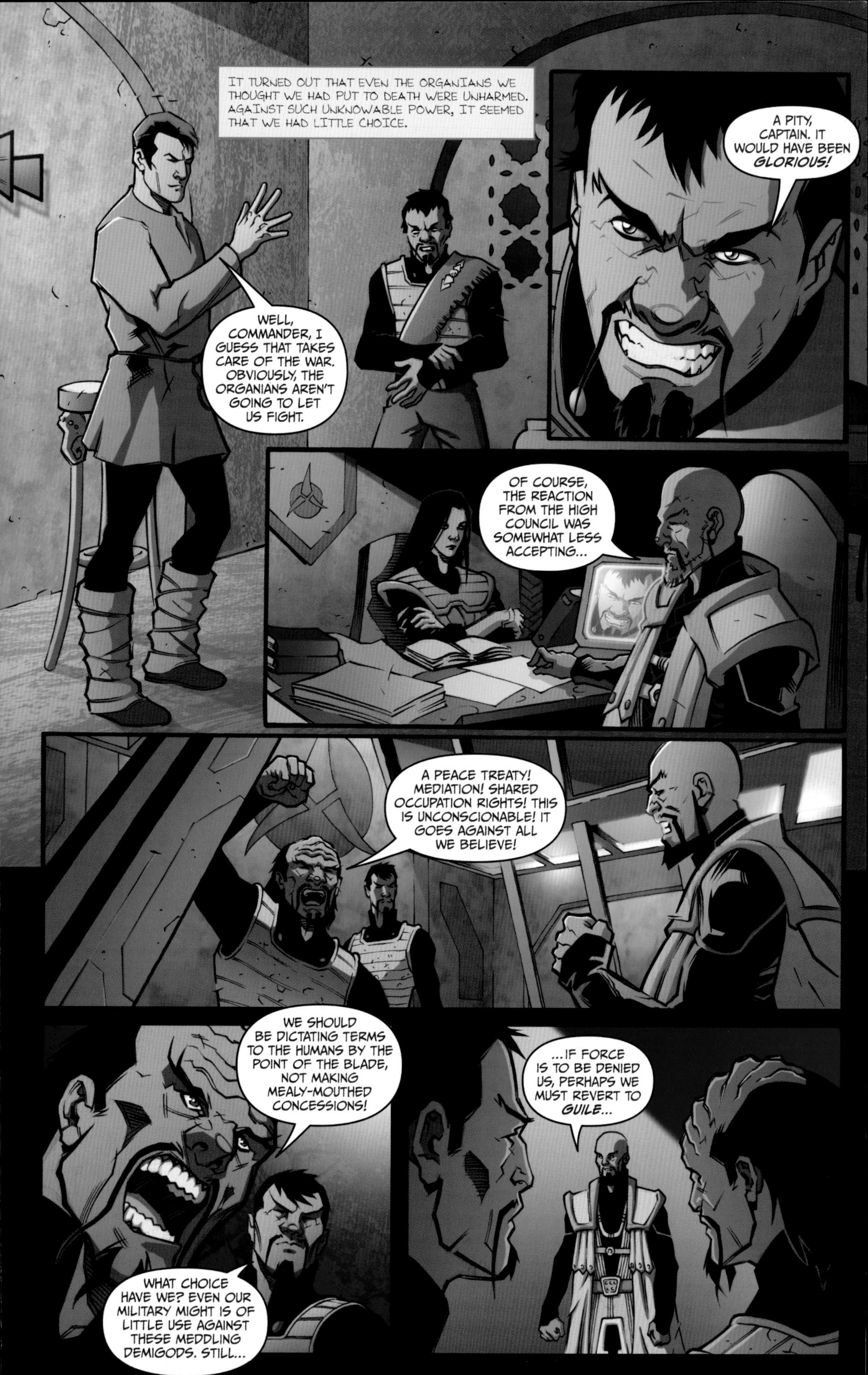
IT TURNED OUT THAT EVEN THE ORGANIANS WE THOUGHT WE HAD PUT TO DEATH WERE UNHARMED. AGAINST SUCH UNKNOWABLE POWER, IT SEEMED THAT WE HAD LITTLE CHOICE.
WELL, COMMANDER, I GUESS THAT TAKES CARE OF THE WAR. OBVIOUSLY, THE ORGANIANS AREN'T GOING TO LET US FIGHT.
A PITY, CAPTAIN. IT WOULD HAVE BEEN *GLORIOUS!*
OF COURSE, THE REACTION FROM THE HIGH COUNCIL WAS SOMEWHAT LESS ACCEPTING...
A PEACE TREATY! MEDIATION! SHARED OCCUPATION RIGHTS! THIS IS UNCONSCIONABLE! IT GOES AGAINST ALL WE BELIEVE!
WE SHOULD BE DICTATING TERMS TO THE HUMANS BY THE POINT OF THE BLADE, NOT MAKING MEALY-MOUTHED CONCESSIONS!
WHAT CHOICE HAVE WE? EVEN OUR MILITARY MIGHT IS OF LITTLE USE AGAINST THESE MEDDLING DEMIGODS. STILL...
...IF FORCE IS TO BE DENIED US, PERHAPS WE MUST REVERT TO *GUILE*...

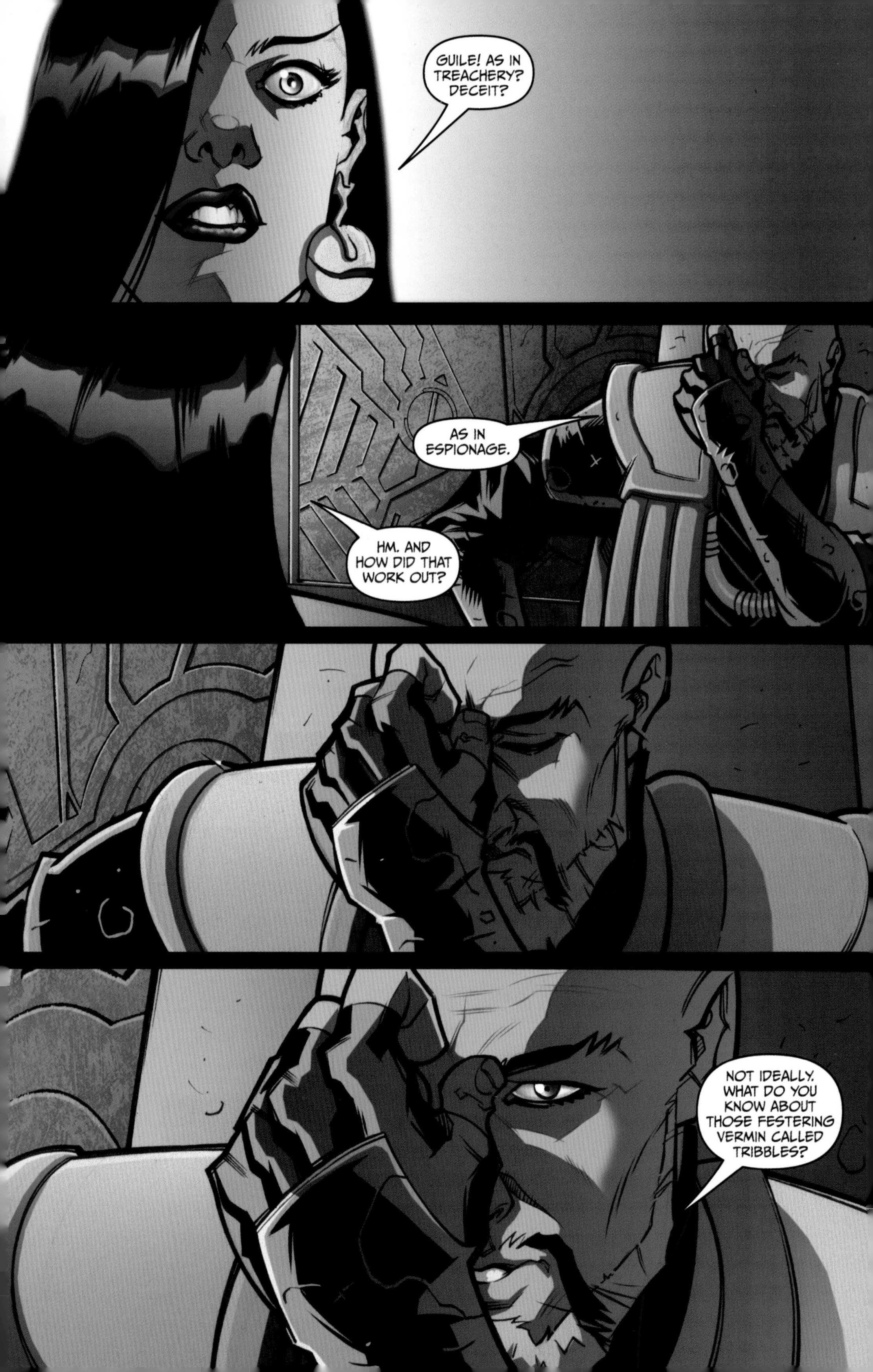
GUILE! AS IN TREACHERY? DECEIT?
AS IN ESPIONAGE.
HM. AND HOW DID THAT WORK OUT?
NOT IDEALLY. WHAT DO YOU KNOW ABOUT THOSE FESTERING VERMIN CALLED TRIBBLES?

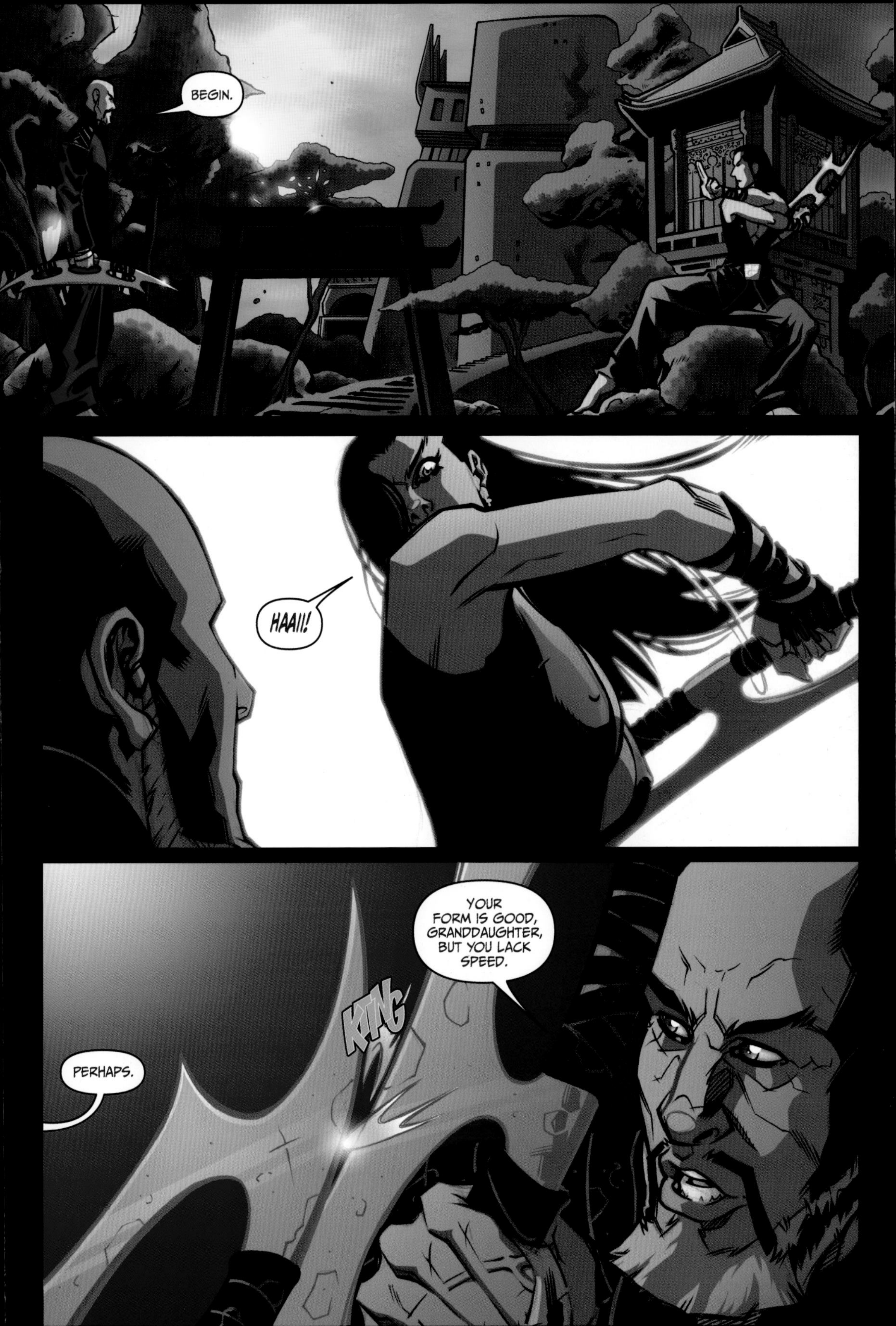
BEGIN.
HAAII!
YOUR FORM IS GOOD, GRANDDAUGHTER, BUT YOU LACK SPEED.
KTING
PERHAPS.

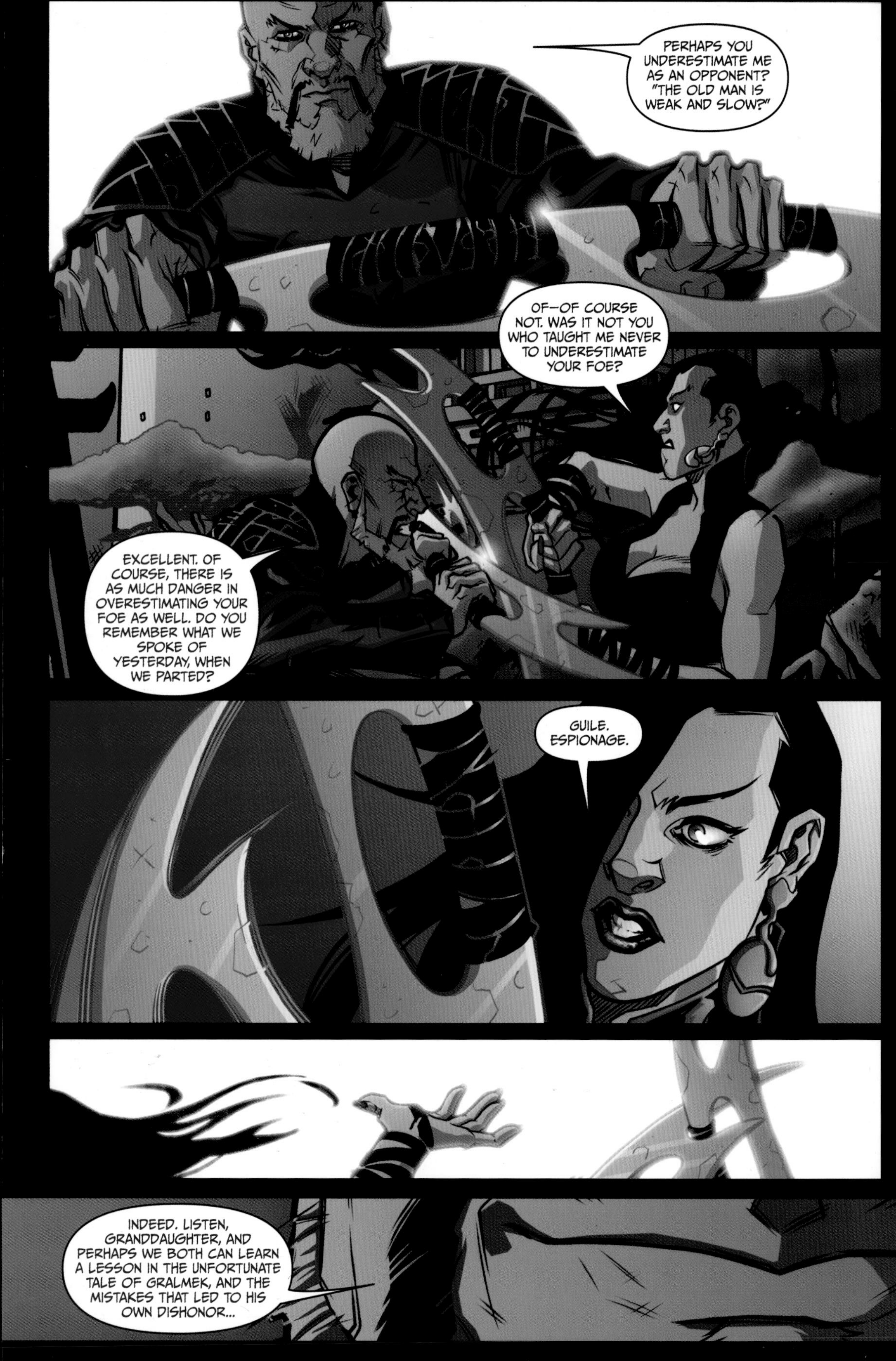
PERHAPS YOU UNDERESTIMATE ME AS AN OPPONENT? "THE OLD MAN IS WEAK AND SLOW?"
OF--OF COURSE NOT. WAS IT NOT YOU WHO TAUGHT ME NEVER TO UNDERESTIMATE YOUR FOE?
EXCELLENT. OF COURSE, THERE IS AS MUCH DANGER IN OVERESTIMATING YOUR FOE AS WELL. DO YOU REMEMBER WHAT WE SPOKE OF YESTERDAY, WHEN WE PARTED?
GUILE. ESPIONAGE.
INDEED. LISTEN, GRANDDAUGHTER, AND PERHAPS WE BOTH CAN LEARN A LESSON IN THE UNFORTUNATE TALE OF GRALMEK, AND THE MISTAKES THAT LED TO HIS OWN DISHONOR...

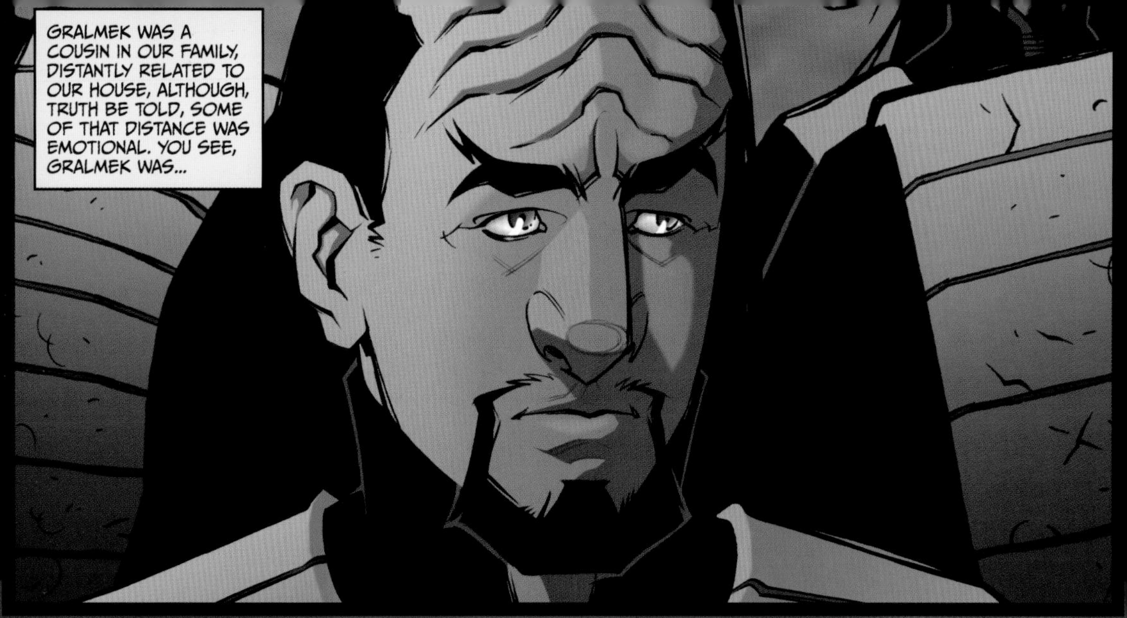
GRALMEK WAS A COUSIN IN OUR FAMILY, DISTANTLY RELATED TO OUR HOUSE, ALTHOUGH, TRUTH BE TOLD, SOME OF THAT DISTANCE WAS EMOTIONAL. YOU SEE, GRALMEK WAS...

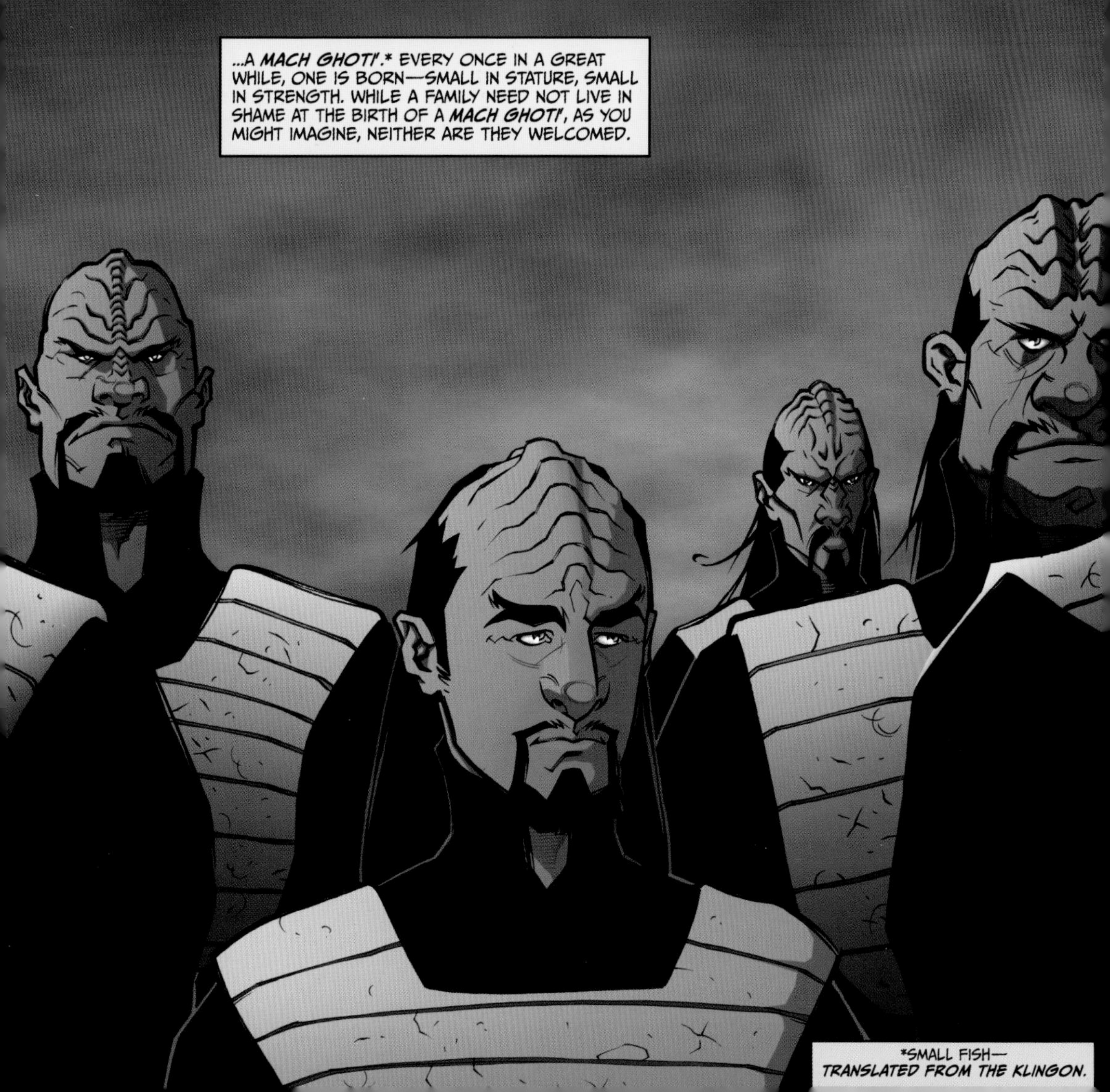
...A *MACH GHOTI'*.* EVERY ONCE IN A GREAT WHILE, ONE IS BORN—SMALL IN STATURE, SMALL IN STRENGTH. WHILE A FAMILY NEED NOT LIVE IN SHAME AT THE BIRTH OF A *MACH GHOTI'*, AS YOU MIGHT IMAGINE, NEITHER ARE THEY WELCOMED.
*SMALL FISH— *TRANSLATED FROM THE KLINGON.*

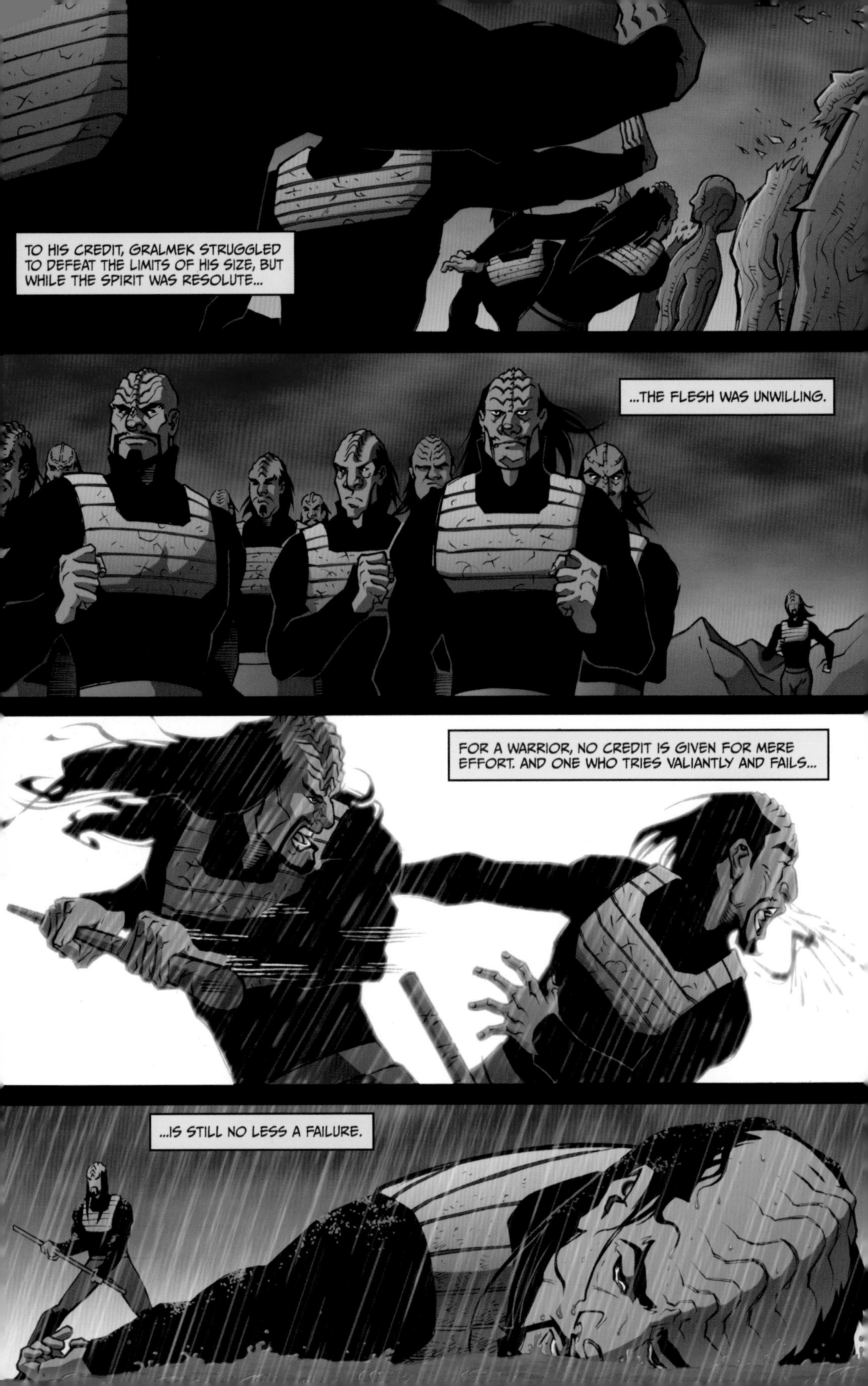
TO HIS CREDIT, GRALMEK STRUGGLED TO DEFEAT THE LIMITS OF HIS SIZE, BUT WHILE THE SPIRIT WAS RESOLUTE...
...THE FLESH WAS UNWILLING.
FOR A WARRIOR, NO CREDIT IS GIVEN FOR MERE EFFORT. AND ONE WHO TRIES VALIANTLY AND FAILS...
...IS STILL NO LESS A FAILURE.

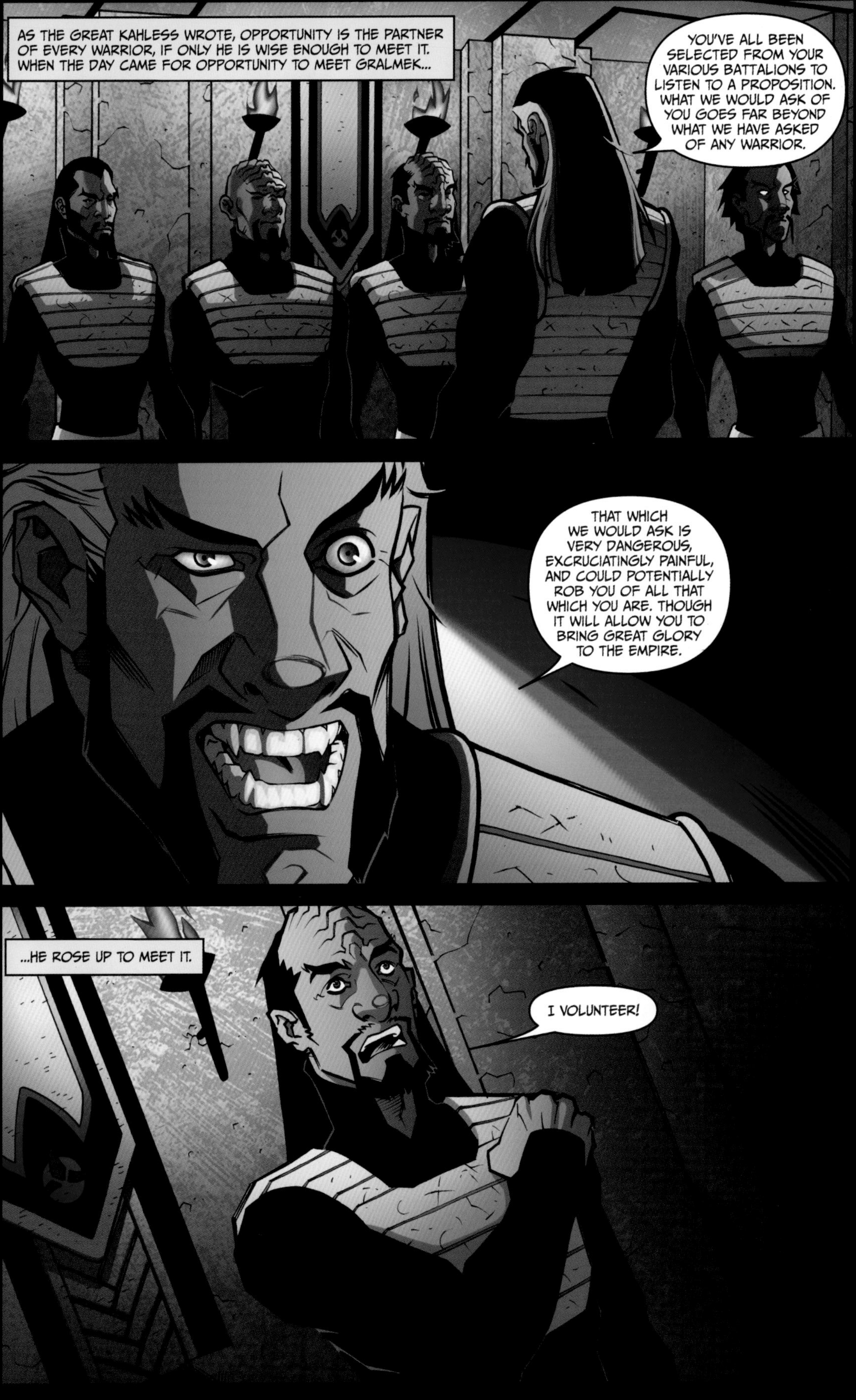

AS THE GREAT KAHLESS WROTE, OPPORTUNITY IS THE PARTNER OF EVERY WARRIOR, IF ONLY HE IS WISE ENOUGH TO MEET IT. WHEN THE DAY CAME FOR OPPORTUNITY TO MEET GRALMEK...
YOU'VE ALL BEEN SELECTED FROM YOUR VARIOUS BATTALIONS TO LISTEN TO A PROPOSITION. WHAT WE WOULD ASK OF YOU GOES FAR BEYOND WHAT WE HAVE ASKED OF ANY WARRIOR.
THAT WHICH WE WOULD ASK IS VERY DANGEROUS, EXCRUCIATINGLY PAINFUL, AND COULD POTENTIALLY ROB YOU OF ALL THAT WHICH YOU ARE. THOUGH IT WILL ALLOW YOU TO BRING GREAT GLORY TO THE EMPIRE.
...HE ROSE UP TO MEET IT.
I VOLUNTEER!

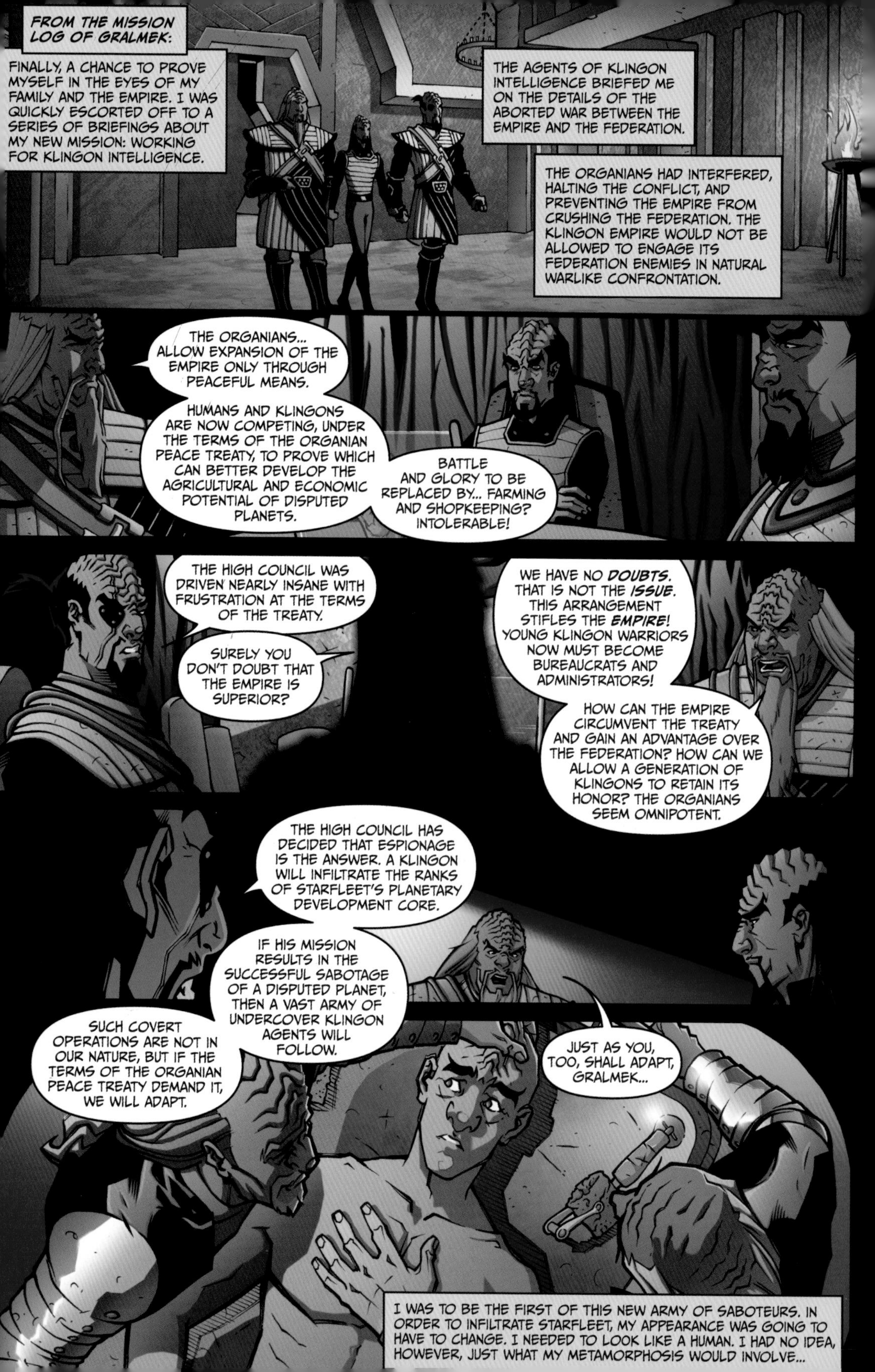
FROM THE MISSION LOG OF GRALMEK:
FINALLY, A CHANCE TO PROVE MYSELF IN THE EYES OF MY FAMILY AND THE EMPIRE. I WAS QUICKLY ESCORTED OFF TO A SERIES OF BRIEFINGS ABOUT MY NEW MISSION: WORKING FOR KLINGON INTELLIGENCE.
THE AGENTS OF KLINGON INTELLIGENCE BRIEFED ME ON THE DETAILS OF THE ABORTED WAR BETWEEN THE EMPIRE AND THE FEDERATION.
THE ORGANIANS HAD INTERFERED, HALTING THE CONFLICT, AND PREVENTING THE EMPIRE FROM CRUSHING THE FEDERATION. THE KLINGON EMPIRE WOULD NOT BE ALLOWED TO ENGAGE ITS FEDERATION ENEMIES IN NATURAL WARLIKE CONFRONTATION.
THE ORGANIANS... ALLOW EXPANSION OF THE EMPIRE ONLY THROUGH PEACEFUL MEANS.
HUMANS AND KLINGONS ARE NOW COMPETING, UNDER THE TERMS OF THE ORGANIAN PEACE TREATY, TO PROVE WHICH CAN BETTER DEVELOP THE AGRICULTURAL AND ECONOMIC POTENTIAL OF DISPUTED PLANETS.
BATTLE AND GLORY TO BE REPLACED BY... FARMING AND SHOPKEEPING? INTOLERABLE!
THE HIGH COUNCIL WAS DRIVEN NEARLY INSANE WITH FRUSTRATION AT THE TERMS OF THE TREATY.
SURELY YOU DON'T DOUBT THAT THE EMPIRE IS SUPERIOR?
WE HAVE NO *DOUBTS*. THAT IS NOT THE *ISSUE*. THIS ARRANGEMENT STIFLES THE *EMPIRE*! YOUNG KLINGON WARRIORS NOW MUST BECOME BUREAUCRATS AND ADMINISTRATORS!
HOW CAN THE EMPIRE CIRCUMVENT THE TREATY AND GAIN AN ADVANTAGE OVER THE FEDERATION? HOW CAN WE ALLOW A GENERATION OF KLINGONS TO RETAIN ITS HONOR? THE ORGANIANS SEEM OMNIPOTENT.
THE HIGH COUNCIL HAS DECIDED THAT ESPIONAGE IS THE ANSWER. A KLINGON WILL INFILTRATE THE RANKS OF STARFLEET'S PLANETARY DEVELOPMENT CORE.
IF HIS MISSION RESULTS IN THE SUCCESSFUL SABOTAGE OF A DISPUTED PLANET, THEN A VAST ARMY OF UNDERCOVER KLINGON AGENTS WILL FOLLOW.
SUCH COVERT OPERATIONS ARE NOT IN OUR NATURE, BUT IF THE TERMS OF THE ORGANIAN PEACE TREATY DEMAND IT, WE WILL ADAPT.
JUST AS YOU, TOO, SHALL ADAPT, GRALMEK...
I WAS TO BE THE FIRST OF THIS NEW ARMY OF SABOTEURS. IN ORDER TO INFILTRATE STARFLEET, MY APPEARANCE WAS GOING TO HAVE TO CHANGE. I NEEDED TO LOOK LIKE A HUMAN. I HAD NO IDEA, HOWEVER, JUST WHAT MY METAMORPHOSIS WOULD INVOLVE...

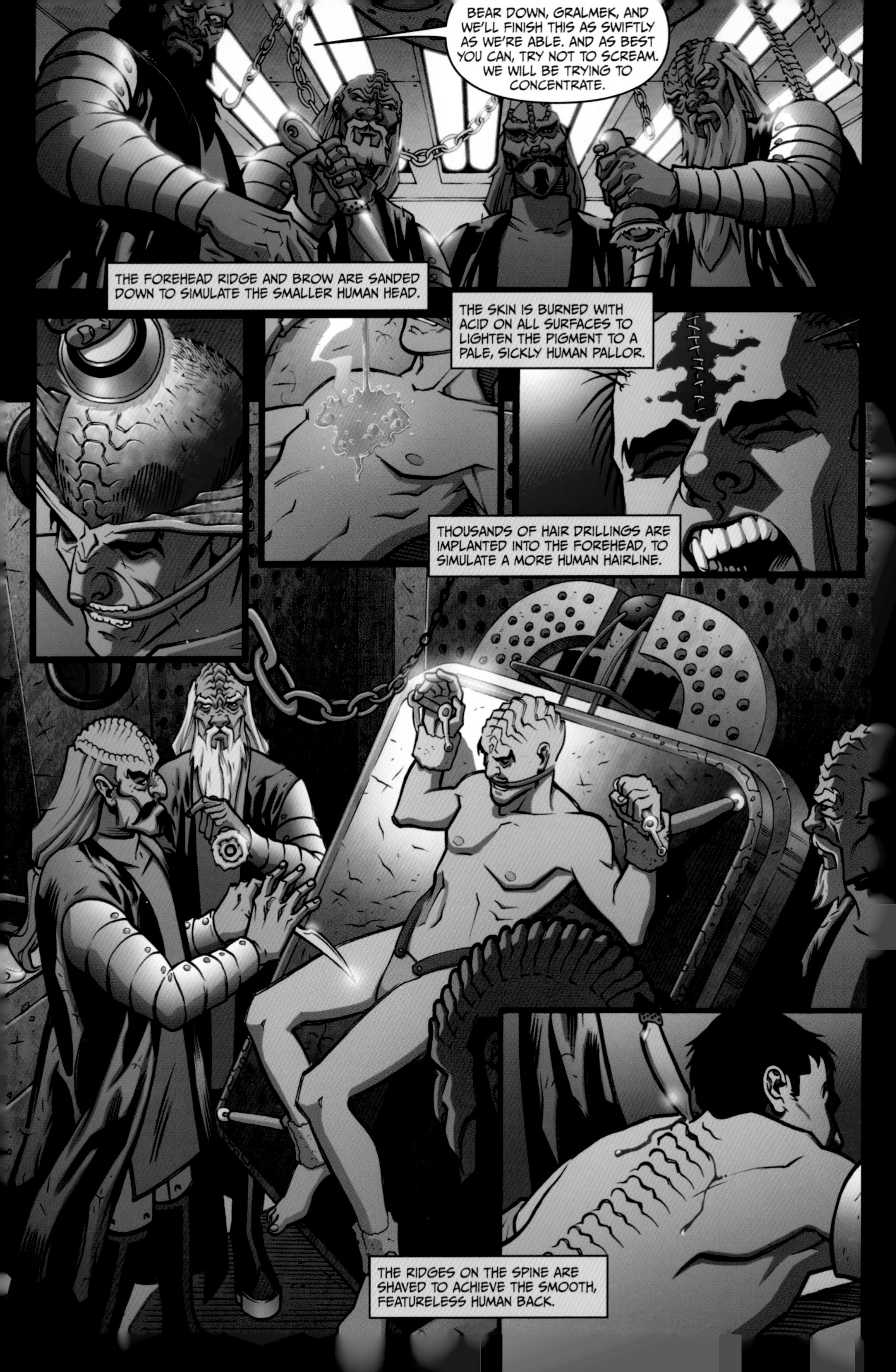
BEAR DOWN, GRALMEK, AND WE'LL FINISH THIS AS SWIFTLY AS WE'RE ABLE. AND AS BEST YOU CAN, TRY NOT TO SCREAM. WE WILL BE TRYING TO CONCENTRATE.
THE FOREHEAD RIDGE AND BROW ARE SANDED DOWN TO SIMULATE THE SMALLER HUMAN HEAD.
THE SKIN IS BURNED WITH ACID ON ALL SURFACES TO LIGHTEN THE PIGMENT TO A PALE, SICKLY HUMAN PALLOR.
THOUSANDS OF HAIR DRILLINGS ARE IMPLANTED INTO THE FOREHEAD, TO SIMULATE A MORE HUMAN HAIRLINE.
THE RIDGES ON THE SPINE ARE SHAVED TO ACHIEVE THE SMOOTH, FEATURELESS HUMAN BACK.

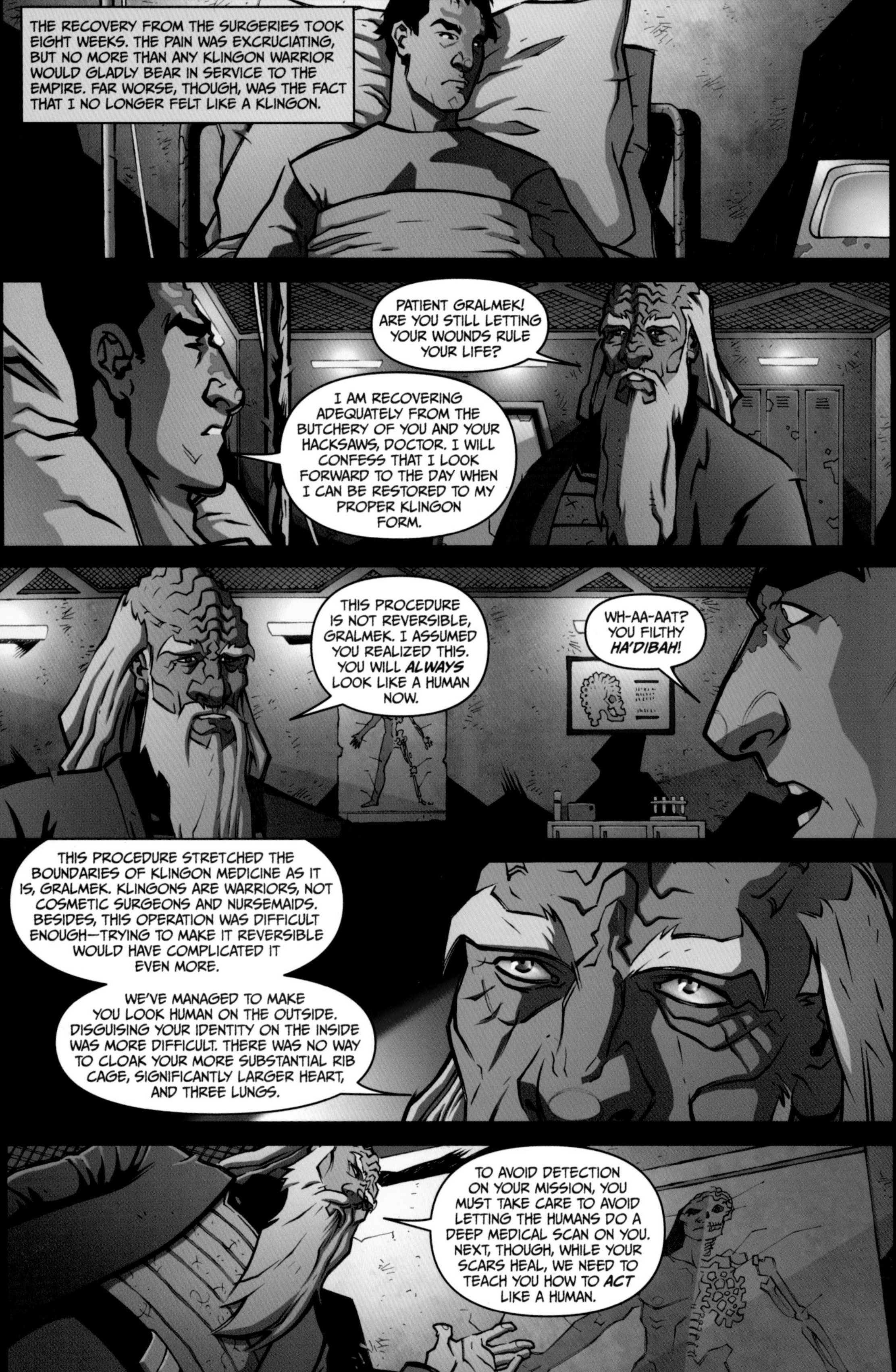
THE RECOVERY FROM THE SURGERIES TOOK EIGHT WEEKS. THE PAIN WAS EXCRUCIATING, BUT NO MORE THAN ANY KLINGON WARRIOR WOULD GLADLY BEAR IN SERVICE TO THE EMPIRE. FAR WORSE, THOUGH, WAS THE FACT THAT I NO LONGER FELT LIKE A KLINGON.
PATIENT GRALMEK! ARE YOU STILL LETTING YOUR WOUNDS RULE YOUR LIFE?
I AM RECOVERING ADEQUATELY FROM THE BUTCHERY OF YOU AND YOUR HACKSAWS, DOCTOR. I WILL CONFESS THAT I LOOK FORWARD TO THE DAY WHEN I CAN BE RESTORED TO MY PROPER KLINGON FORM.
THIS PROCEDURE IS NOT REVERSIBLE, GRALMEK. I ASSUMED YOU REALIZED THIS. YOU WILL *ALWAYS* LOOK LIKE A HUMAN NOW.
WH-AA-AAT? YOU FILTHY *HA'DIBAH*!
THIS PROCEDURE STRETCHED THE BOUNDARIES OF KLINGON MEDICINE AS IT IS, GRALMEK. KLINGONS ARE WARRIORS, NOT COSMETIC SURGEONS AND NURSEMAIDS. BESIDES, THIS OPERATION WAS DIFFICULT ENOUGH—TRYING TO MAKE IT REVERSIBLE WOULD HAVE COMPLICATED IT EVEN MORE.
WE'VE MANAGED TO MAKE YOU LOOK HUMAN ON THE OUTSIDE. DISGUISING YOUR IDENTITY ON THE INSIDE WAS MORE DIFFICULT. THERE WAS NO WAY TO CLOAK YOUR MORE SUBSTANTIAL RIB CAGE, SIGNIFICANTLY LARGER HEART, AND THREE LUNGS.
TO AVOID DETECTION ON YOUR MISSION, YOU MUST TAKE CARE TO AVOID LETTING THE HUMANS DO A DEEP MEDICAL SCAN ON YOU. NEXT, THOUGH, WHILE YOUR SCARS HEAL, WE NEED TO TEACH YOU HOW TO *ACT* LIKE A HUMAN.

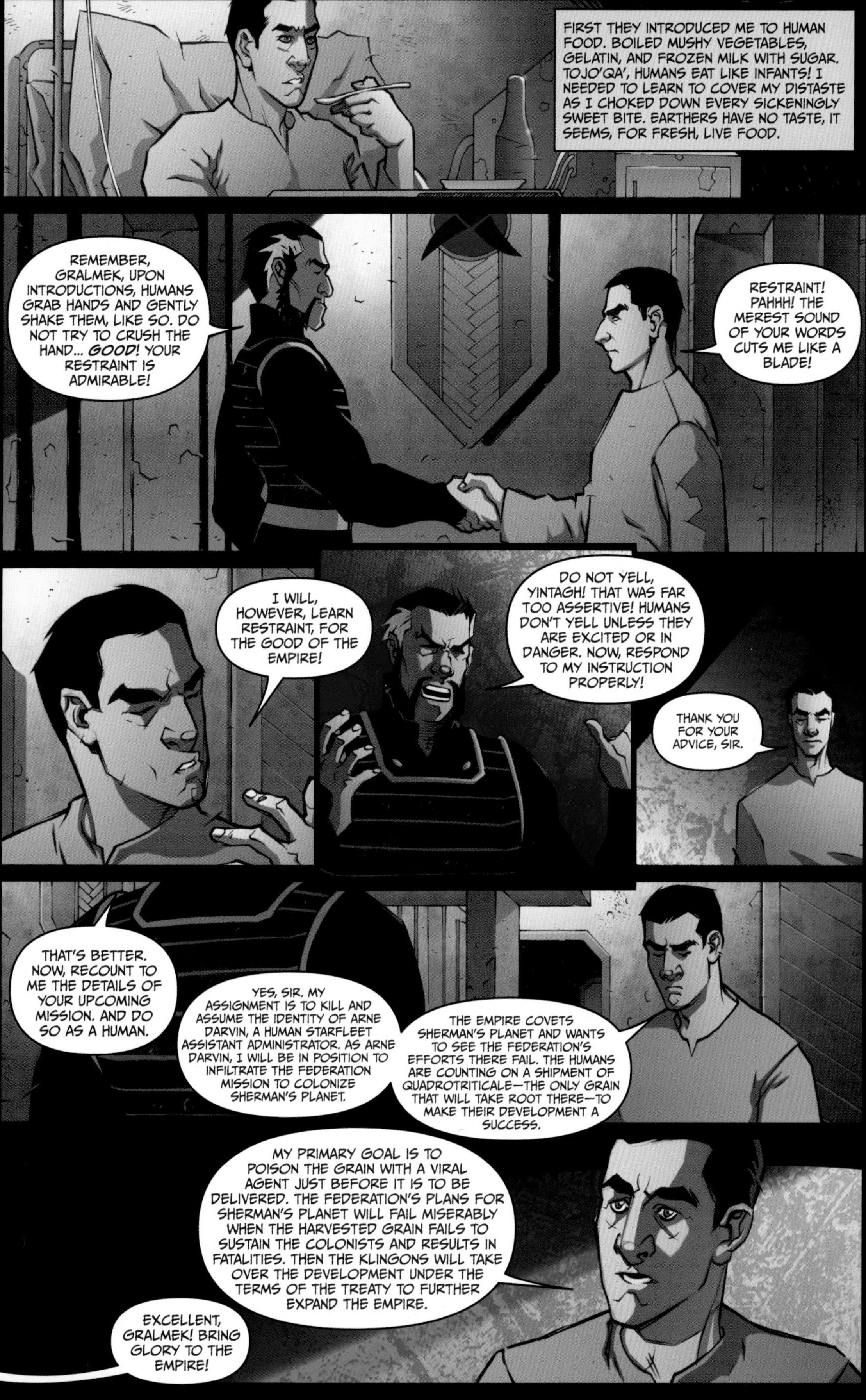
FIRST THEY INTRODUCED ME TO HUMAN FOOD. BOILED MUSHY VEGETABLES, GELATIN, AND FROZEN MILK WITH SUGAR. TOJO'QA', HUMANS EAT LIKE INFANTS! I NEEDED TO LEARN TO COVER MY DISTASTE AS I CHOKED DOWN EVERY SICKENINGLY SWEET BITE. EARTHERS HAVE NO TASTE, IT SEEMS, FOR FRESH, LIVE FOOD.
REMEMBER, GRALMEK, UPON INTRODUCTIONS, HUMANS GRAB HANDS AND GENTLY SHAKE THEM, LIKE SO. DO NOT TRY TO CRUSH THE HAND... GOOD! YOUR RESTRAINT IS ADMIRABLE!
RESTRAINT! PAHHH! THE MEREST SOUND OF YOUR WORDS CUTS ME LIKE A BLADE!
I WILL, HOWEVER, LEARN RESTRAINT, FOR THE GOOD OF THE EMPIRE!
DO NOT YELL, YINTAGH! THAT WAS FAR TOO ASSERTIVE! HUMANS DON'T YELL UNLESS THEY ARE EXCITED OR IN DANGER. NOW, RESPOND TO MY INSTRUCTION PROPERLY!
THANK YOU FOR YOUR ADVICE, SIR.
THAT'S BETTER. NOW, RECOUNT TO ME THE DETAILS OF YOUR UPCOMING MISSION. AND DO SO AS A HUMAN.
YES, SIR. MY ASSIGNMENT IS TO KILL AND ASSUME THE IDENTITY OF ARNE DARVIN, A HUMAN STARFLEET ASSISTANT ADMINISTRATOR. AS ARNE DARVIN, I WILL BE IN POSITION TO INFILTRATE THE FEDERATION MISSION TO COLONIZE SHERMAN'S PLANET.
THE EMPIRE COVETS SHERMAN'S PLANET AND WANTS TO SEE THE FEDERATION'S EFFORTS THERE FAIL. THE HUMANS ARE COUNTING ON A SHIPMENT OF QUADROTRITICALE—THE ONLY GRAIN THAT WILL TAKE ROOT THERE—TO MAKE THEIR DEVELOPMENT A SUCCESS.
MY PRIMARY GOAL IS TO POISON THE GRAIN WITH A VIRAL AGENT JUST BEFORE IT IS TO BE DELIVERED. THE FEDERATION'S PLANS FOR SHERMAN'S PLANET WILL FAIL MISERABLY WHEN THE HARVESTED GRAIN FAILS TO SUSTAIN THE COLONISTS AND RESULTS IN FATALITIES. THEN THE KLINGONS WILL TAKE OVER THE DEVELOPMENT UNDER THE TERMS OF THE TREATY TO FURTHER EXPAND THE EMPIRE.
EXCELLENT, GRALMEK! BRING GLORY TO THE EMPIRE!

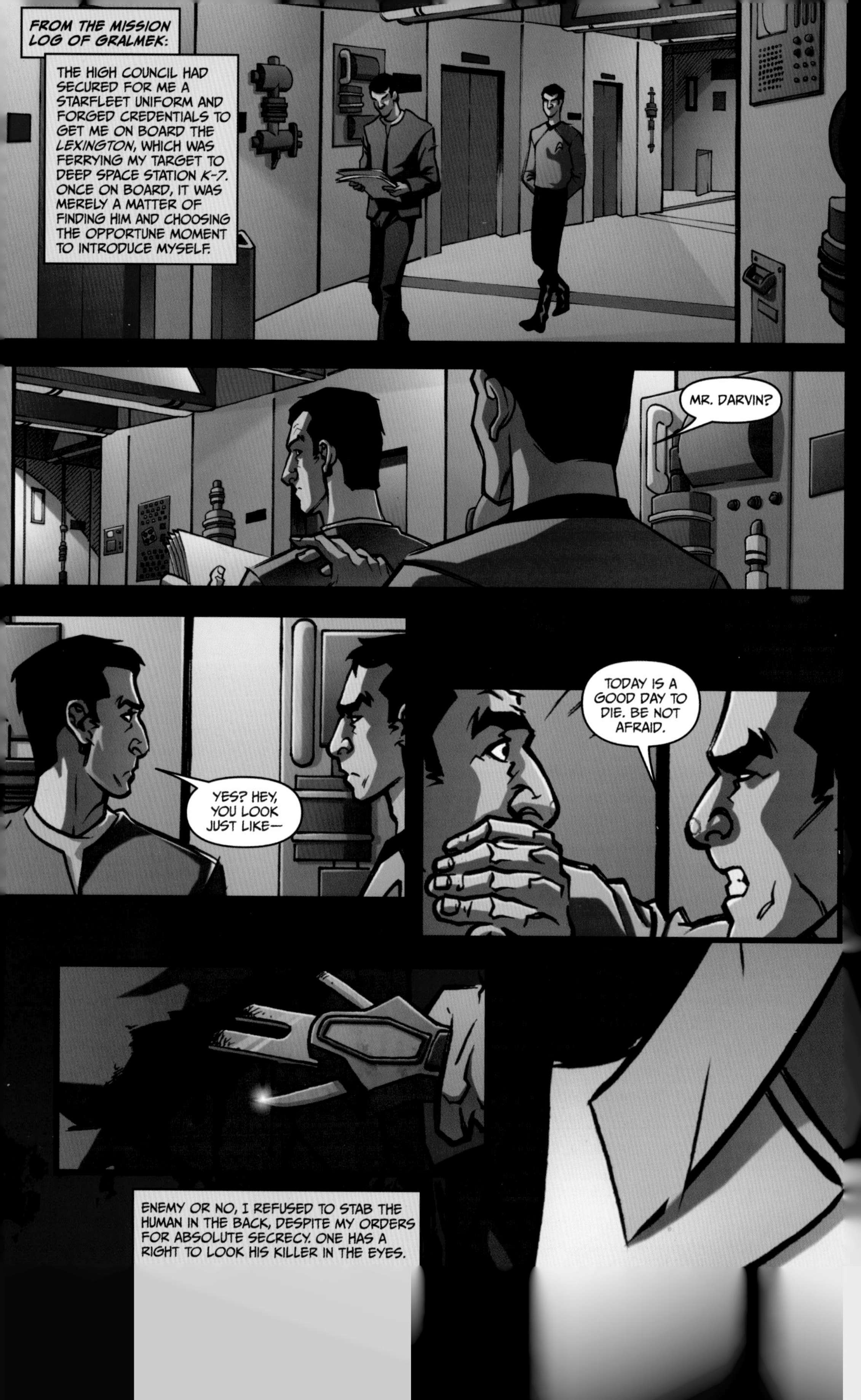
FROM THE MISSION LOG OF GRALMEK:
THE HIGH COUNCIL HAD SECURED FOR ME A STARFLEET UNIFORM AND FORGED CREDENTIALS TO GET ME ON BOARD THE *LEXINGTON*, WHICH WAS FERRYING MY TARGET TO DEEP SPACE STATION *K-7*. ONCE ON BOARD, IT WAS MERELY A MATTER OF FINDING HIM AND CHOOSING THE OPPORTUNE MOMENT TO INTRODUCE MYSELF.
MR. DARVIN?
YES? HEY, YOU LOOK JUST LIKE—
TODAY IS A GOOD DAY TO DIE. BE NOT AFRAID.
ENEMY OR NO, I REFUSED TO STAB THE HUMAN IN THE BACK, DESPITE MY ORDERS FOR ABSOLUTE SECRECY. ONE HAS A RIGHT TO LOOK HIS KILLER IN THE EYES.

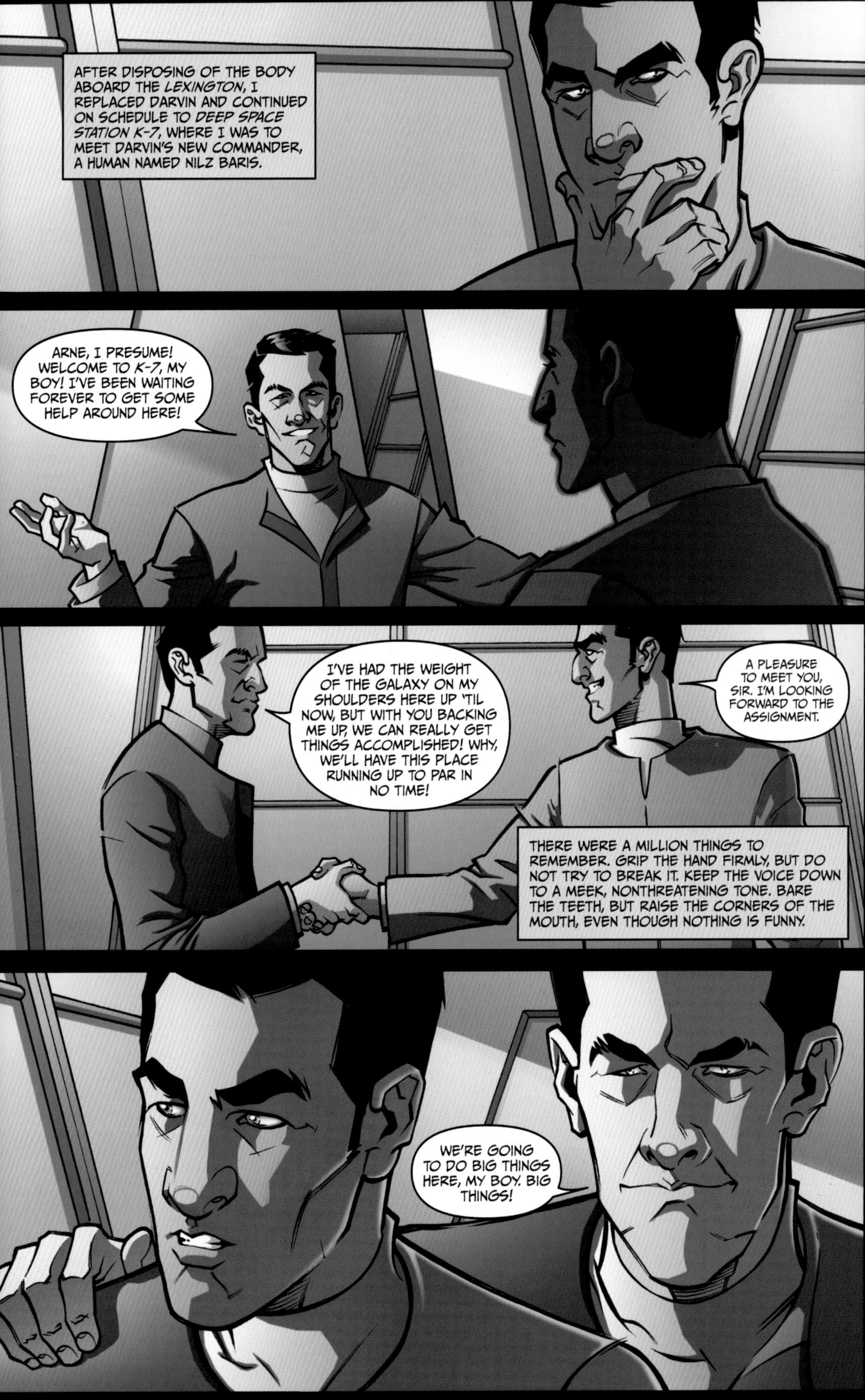

AFTER DISPOSING OF THE BODY ABOARD THE *LEXINGTON*, I REPLACED DARVIN AND CONTINUED ON SCHEDULE TO *DEEP SPACE STATION K-7*, WHERE I WAS TO MEET DARVIN'S NEW COMMANDER, A HUMAN NAMED NILZ BARIS.
ARNE, I PRESUME! WELCOME TO *K-7*, MY BOY! I'VE BEEN WAITING FOREVER TO GET SOME HELP AROUND HERE!
I'VE HAD THE WEIGHT OF THE GALAXY ON MY SHOULDERS HERE UP 'TIL NOW, BUT WITH YOU BACKING ME UP, WE CAN REALLY GET THINGS ACCOMPLISHED! WHY, WE'LL HAVE THIS PLACE RUNNING UP TO PAR IN NO TIME!
A PLEASURE TO MEET YOU, SIR. I'M LOOKING FORWARD TO THE ASSIGNMENT.
THERE WERE A MILLION THINGS TO REMEMBER. GRIP THE HAND FIRMLY, BUT DO NOT TRY TO BREAK IT. KEEP THE VOICE DOWN TO A MEEK, NONTHREATENING TONE. BARE THE TEETH, BUT RAISE THE CORNERS OF THE MOUTH, EVEN THOUGH NOTHING IS FUNNY.
WE'RE GOING TO DO BIG THINGS HERE, MY BOY. BIG THINGS!

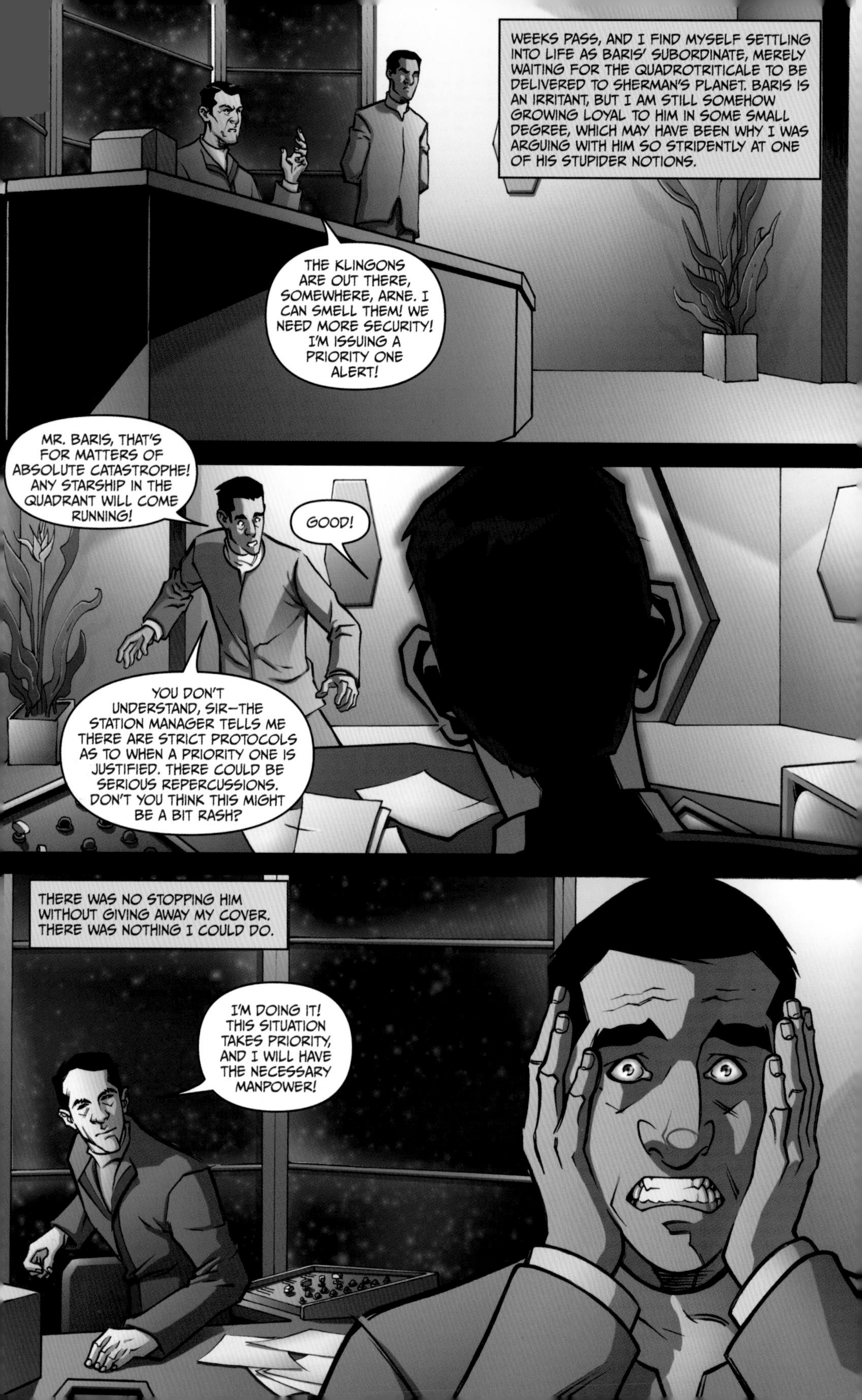
WEEKS PASS, AND I FIND MYSELF SETTLING INTO LIFE AS BARIS' SUBORDINATE, MERELY WAITING FOR THE QUADROTRITICALE TO BE DELIVERED TO SHERMAN'S PLANET. BARIS IS AN IRRITANT, BUT I AM STILL SOMEHOW GROWING LOYAL TO HIM IN SOME SMALL DEGREE, WHICH MAY HAVE BEEN WHY I WAS ARGUING WITH HIM SO STRIDENTLY AT ONE OF HIS STUPIDER NOTIONS.
THE KLINGONS ARE OUT THERE, SOMEWHERE, ARNE. I CAN SMELL THEM! WE NEED MORE SECURITY! I'M ISSUING A PRIORITY ONE ALERT!
MR. BARIS, THAT'S FOR MATTERS OF ABSOLUTE CATASTROPHE! ANY STARSHIP IN THE QUADRANT WILL COME RUNNING!
GOOD!
YOU DON'T UNDERSTAND, SIR—THE STATION MANAGER TELLS ME THERE ARE STRICT PROTOCOLS AS TO WHEN A PRIORITY ONE IS JUSTIFIED. THERE COULD BE SERIOUS REPERCUSSIONS. DON'T YOU THINK THIS MIGHT BE A BIT RASH?
THERE WAS NO STOPPING HIM WITHOUT GIVING AWAY MY COVER. THERE WAS NOTHING I COULD DO.
I'M DOING IT! THIS SITUATION TAKES PRIORITY, AND I WILL HAVE THE NECESSARY MANPOWER!

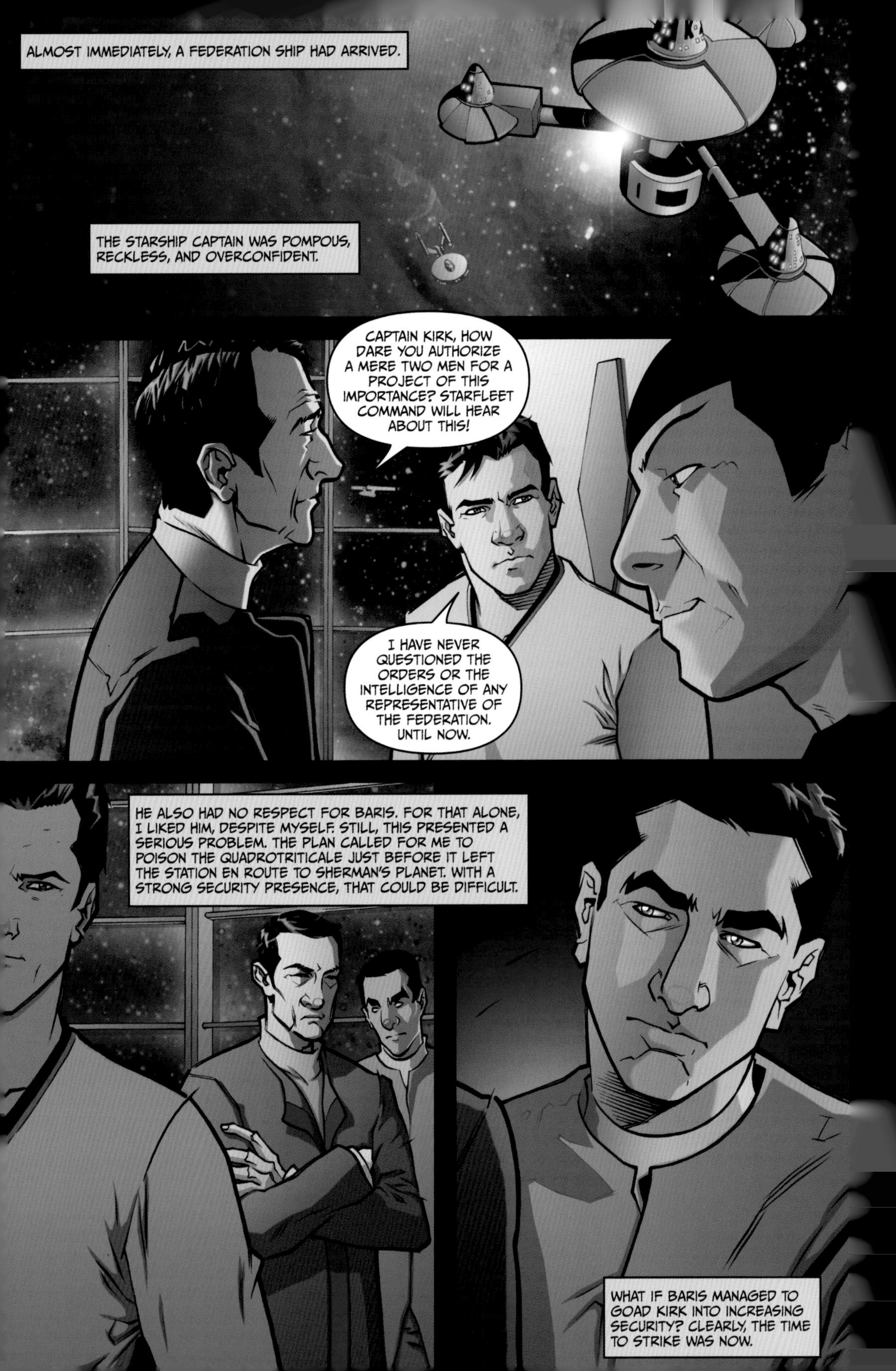
ALMOST IMMEDIATELY, A FEDERATION SHIP HAD ARRIVED.
THE STARSHIP CAPTAIN WAS POMPOUS, RECKLESS, AND OVERCONFIDENT.
CAPTAIN KIRK, HOW DARE YOU AUTHORIZE A MERE TWO MEN FOR A PROJECT OF THIS IMPORTANCE? STARFLEET COMMAND WILL HEAR ABOUT THIS!
I HAVE NEVER QUESTIONED THE ORDERS OR THE INTELLIGENCE OF ANY REPRESENTATIVE OF THE FEDERATION. UNTIL NOW.
HE ALSO HAD NO RESPECT FOR BARIS. FOR THAT ALONE, I LIKED HIM, DESPITE MYSELF. STILL, THIS PRESENTED A SERIOUS PROBLEM. THE PLAN CALLED FOR ME TO POISON THE QUADROTRITICALE JUST BEFORE IT LEFT THE STATION EN ROUTE TO SHERMAN'S PLANET. WITH A STRONG SECURITY PRESENCE, THAT COULD BE DIFFICULT.
WHAT IF BARIS MANAGED TO GOAD KIRK INTO INCREASING SECURITY? CLEARLY, THE TIME TO STRIKE WAS NOW.

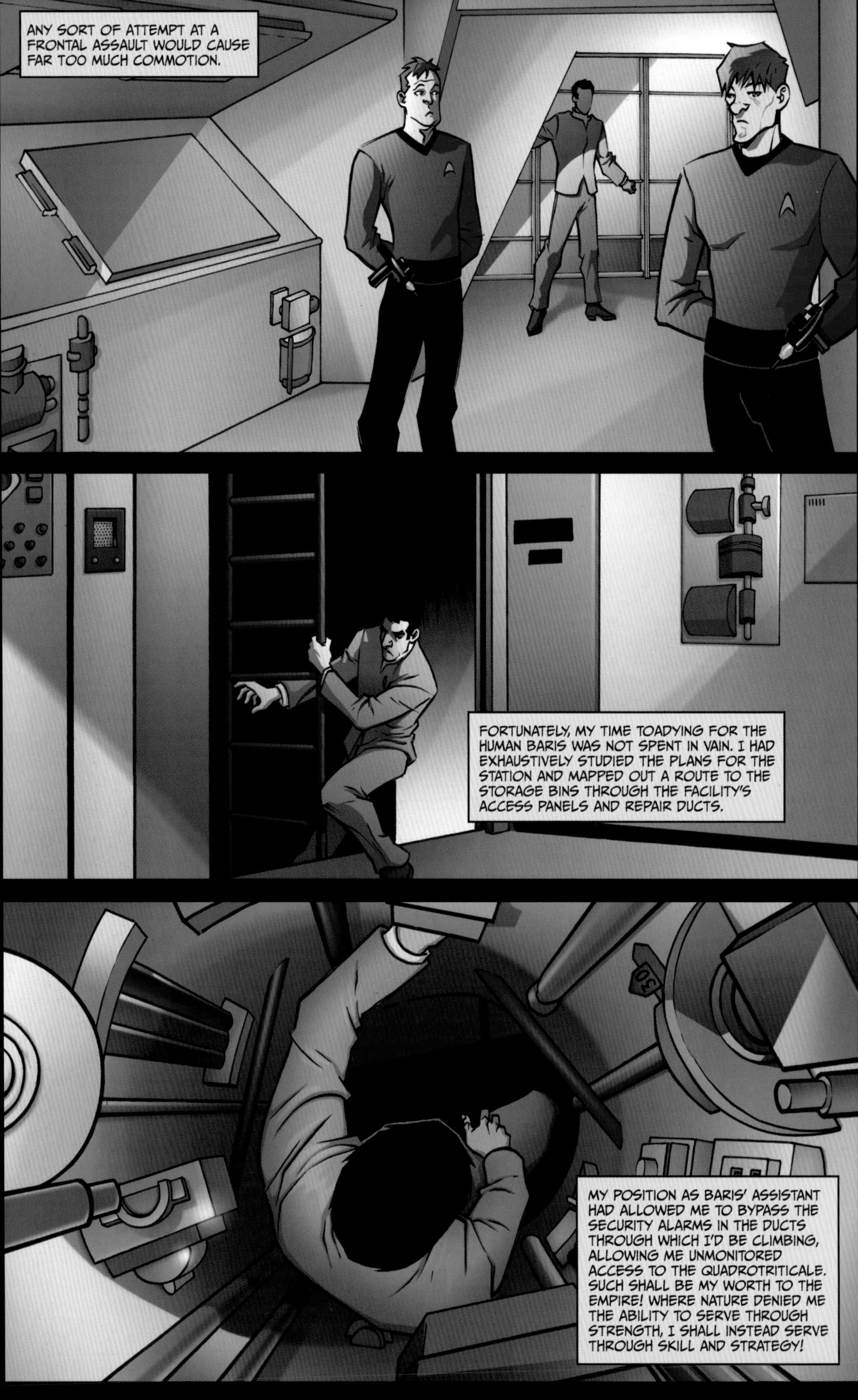
ANY SORT OF ATTEMPT AT A FRONTAL ASSAULT WOULD CAUSE FAR TOO MUCH COMMOTION.
FORTUNATELY, MY TIME TOADYING FOR THE HUMAN BARIS WAS NOT SPENT IN VAIN. I HAD EXHAUSTIVELY STUDIED THE PLANS FOR THE STATION AND MAPPED OUT A ROUTE TO THE STORAGE BINS THROUGH THE FACILITY'S ACCESS PANELS AND REPAIR DUCTS.
MY POSITION AS BARIS' ASSISTANT HAD ALLOWED ME TO BYPASS THE SECURITY ALARMS IN THE DUCTS THROUGH WHICH I'D BE CLIMBING, ALLOWING ME UNMONITORED ACCESS TO THE QUADROTRITICALE. SUCH SHALL BE MY WORTH TO THE EMPIRE! WHERE NATURE DENIED ME THE ABILITY TO SERVE THROUGH STRENGTH, I SHALL INSTEAD SERVE THROUGH SKILL AND STRATEGY!

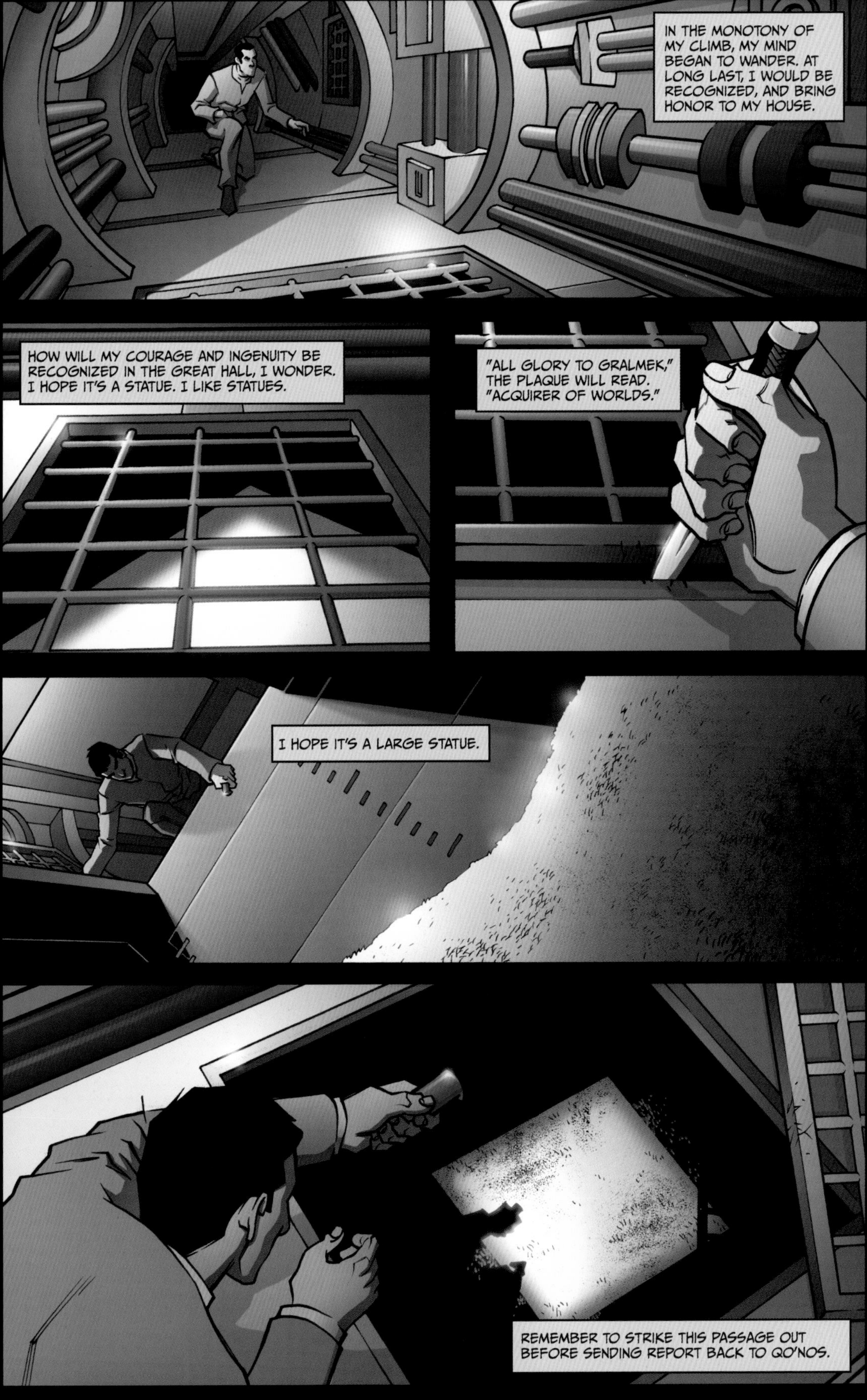
IN THE MONOTONY OF MY CLIMB, MY MIND BEGAN TO WANDER. AT LONG LAST, I WOULD BE RECOGNIZED, AND BRING HONOR TO MY HOUSE.
HOW WILL MY COURAGE AND INGENUITY BE RECOGNIZED IN THE GREAT HALL, I WONDER. I HOPE IT'S A STATUE. I LIKE STATUES.
"ALL GLORY TO GRALMEK," THE PLAQUE WILL READ. "ACQUIRER OF WORLDS."
I HOPE IT'S A LARGE STATUE.
REMEMBER TO STRIKE THIS PASSAGE OUT BEFORE SENDING REPORT BACK TO QO'NOS.

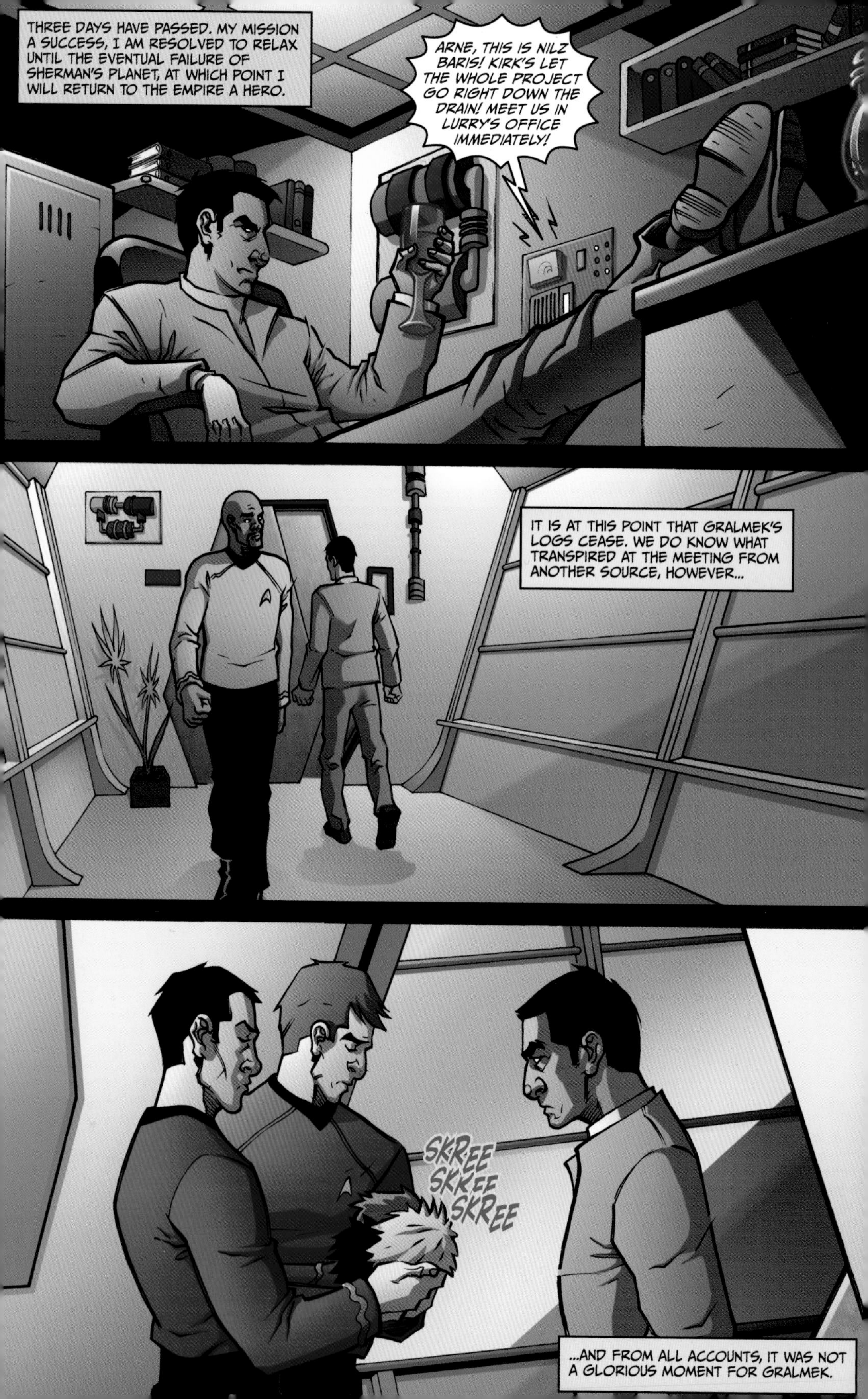
THREE DAYS HAVE PASSED. MY MISSION A SUCCESS, I AM RESOLVED TO RELAX UNTIL THE EVENTUAL FAILURE OF SHERMAN'S PLANET, AT WHICH POINT I WILL RETURN TO THE EMPIRE A HERO.
ARNE, THIS IS NILZ BARIS! KIRK'S LET THE WHOLE PROJECT GO RIGHT DOWN THE DRAIN! MEET US IN LURRY'S OFFICE IMMEDIATELY!
IT IS AT THIS POINT THAT GRALMEK'S LOGS CEASE. WE DO KNOW WHAT TRANSPIRED AT THE MEETING FROM ANOTHER SOURCE, HOWEVER...
SKREE SKREE SKREE
...AND FROM ALL ACCOUNTS, IT WAS NOT A GLORIOUS MOMENT FOR GRALMEK.

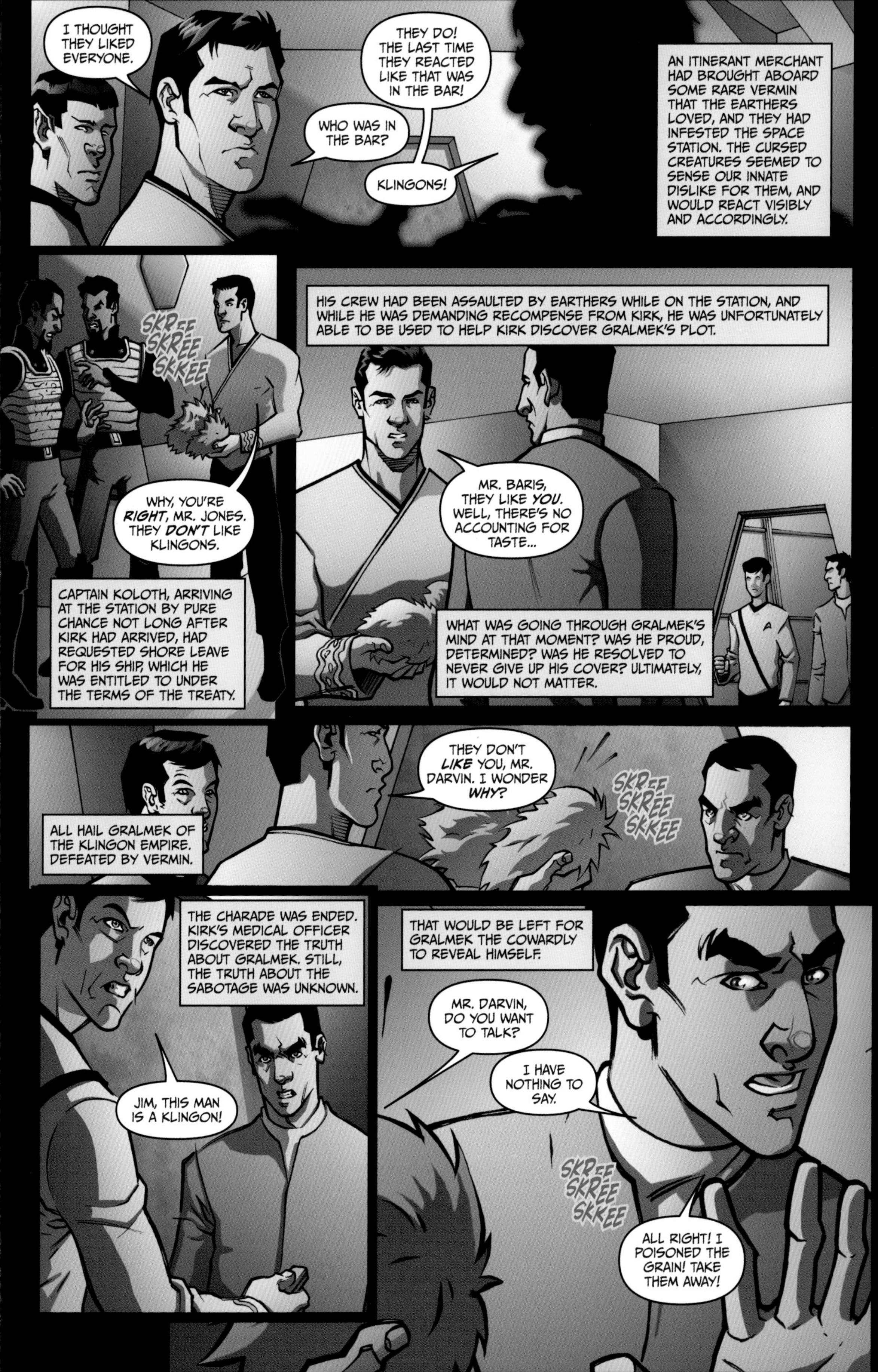
I THOUGHT THEY LIKED EVERYONE.
THEY DO! THE LAST TIME THEY REACTED LIKE THAT WAS IN THE BAR!
WHO WAS IN THE BAR?
KLINGONS!
AN ITINERANT MERCHANT HAD BROUGHT ABOARD SOME RARE VERMIN THAT THE EARTHERS LOVED, AND THEY HAD INFESTED THE SPACE STATION. THE CURSED CREATURES SEEMED TO SENSE OUR INNATE DISLIKE FOR THEM, AND WOULD REACT VISIBLY AND ACCORDINGLY.
SKREE SKREE SKKEE
WHY, YOU'RE RIGHT, MR. JONES. THEY DON'T LIKE KLINGONS.
CAPTAIN KOLOTH, ARRIVING AT THE STATION BY PURE CHANCE NOT LONG AFTER KIRK HAD ARRIVED, HAD REQUESTED SHORE LEAVE FOR HIS SHIP, WHICH HE WAS ENTITLED TO UNDER THE TERMS OF THE TREATY.
HIS CREW HAD BEEN ASSAULTED BY EARTHERS WHILE ON THE STATION, AND WHILE HE WAS DEMANDING RECOMPENSE FROM KIRK, HE WAS UNFORTUNATELY ABLE TO BE USED TO HELP KIRK DISCOVER GRALMEK'S PLOT.
MR. BARIS, THEY LIKE YOU. WELL, THERE'S NO ACCOUNTING FOR TASTE...
WHAT WAS GOING THROUGH GRALMEK'S MIND AT THAT MOMENT? WAS HE PROUD, DETERMINED? WAS HE RESOLVED TO NEVER GIVE UP HIS COVER? ULTIMATELY, IT WOULD NOT MATTER.
ALL HAIL GRALMEK OF THE KLINGON EMPIRE. DEFEATED BY VERMIN.
THEY DON'T LIKE YOU, MR. DARVIN. I WONDER WHY?
SKREE SKREE SKKEE
THE CHARADE WAS ENDED. KIRK'S MEDICAL OFFICER DISCOVERED THE TRUTH ABOUT GRALMEK. STILL, THE TRUTH ABOUT THE SABOTAGE WAS UNKNOWN.
JIM, THIS MAN IS A KLINGON!
THAT WOULD BE LEFT FOR GRALMEK THE COWARDLY TO REVEAL HIMSELF.
MR. DARVIN, DO YOU WANT TO TALK?
I HAVE NOTHING TO SAY.
SKREE SKREE SKKEE
ALL RIGHT! I POISONED THE GRAIN! TAKE THEM AWAY!

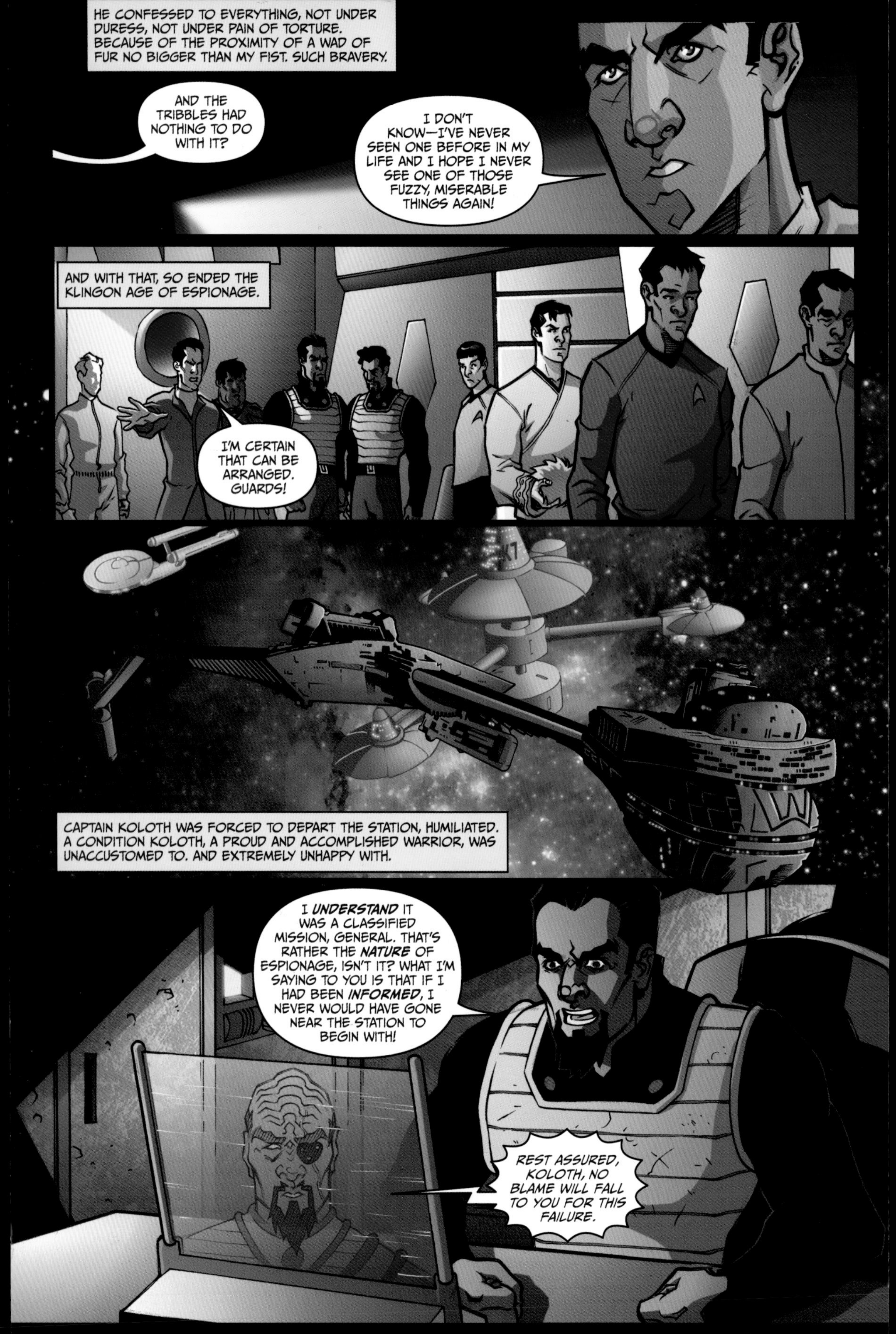
HE CONFESSED TO EVERYTHING, NOT UNDER DURESS, NOT UNDER PAIN OF TORTURE. BECAUSE OF THE PROXIMITY OF A WAD OF FUR NO BIGGER THAN MY FIST. SUCH BRAVERY.
AND THE TRIBBLES HAD NOTHING TO DO WITH IT?
I DON'T KNOW—I'VE NEVER SEEN ONE BEFORE IN MY LIFE AND I HOPE I NEVER SEE ONE OF THOSE FUZZY, MISERABLE THINGS AGAIN!
AND WITH THAT, SO ENDED THE KLINGON AGE OF ESPIONAGE.
I'M CERTAIN THAT CAN BE ARRANGED. GUARDS!
K7
CAPTAIN KOLOTH WAS FORCED TO DEPART THE STATION, HUMILIATED. A CONDITION KOLOTH, A PROUD AND ACCOMPLISHED WARRIOR, WAS UNACCUSTOMED TO. AND EXTREMELY UNHAPPY WITH.
I ***UNDERSTAND*** IT WAS A CLASSIFIED MISSION, GENERAL. THAT'S RATHER THE ***NATURE*** OF ESPIONAGE, ISN'T IT? WHAT I'M SAYING TO YOU IS THAT IF I HAD BEEN ***INFORMED***, I NEVER WOULD HAVE GONE NEAR THE STATION TO BEGIN WITH!
REST ASSURED, KOLOTH, NO BLAME WILL FALL TO YOU FOR THIS FAILURE.

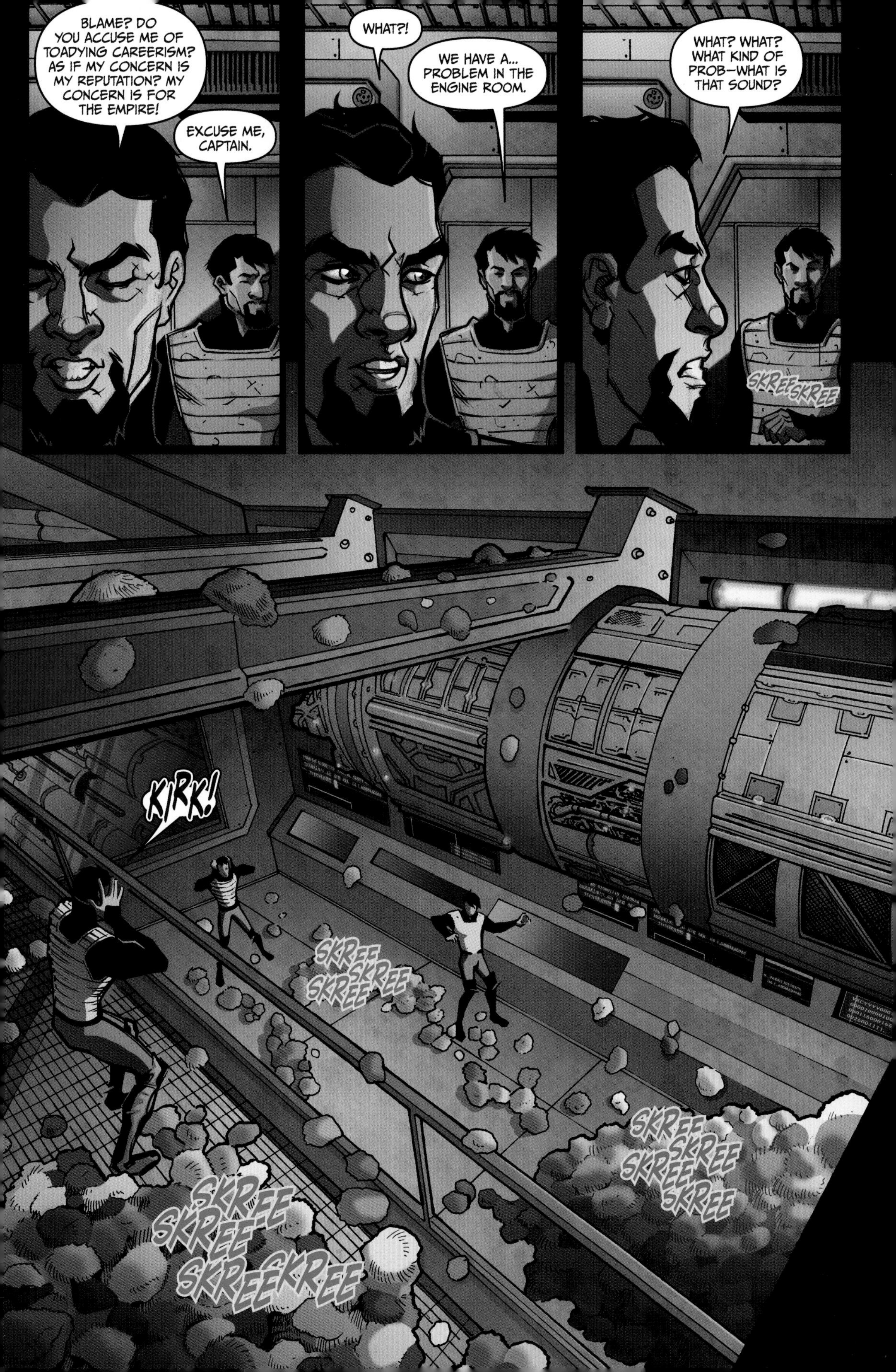
BLAME? DO YOU ACCUSE ME OF TOADYING CAREERISM? AS IF MY CONCERN IS MY REPUTATION? MY CONCERN IS FOR THE EMPIRE!
EXCUSE ME, CAPTAIN.
WHAT?!
WE HAVE A... PROBLEM IN THE ENGINE ROOM.
WHAT? WHAT? WHAT KIND OF PROB—WHAT IS THAT SOUND?
SKREESKREE
KIRK!
SKREE SKREE SKREE
SKREE SKREE SKREE SKREE SKREE
SKREE SKREE SKREESKREE

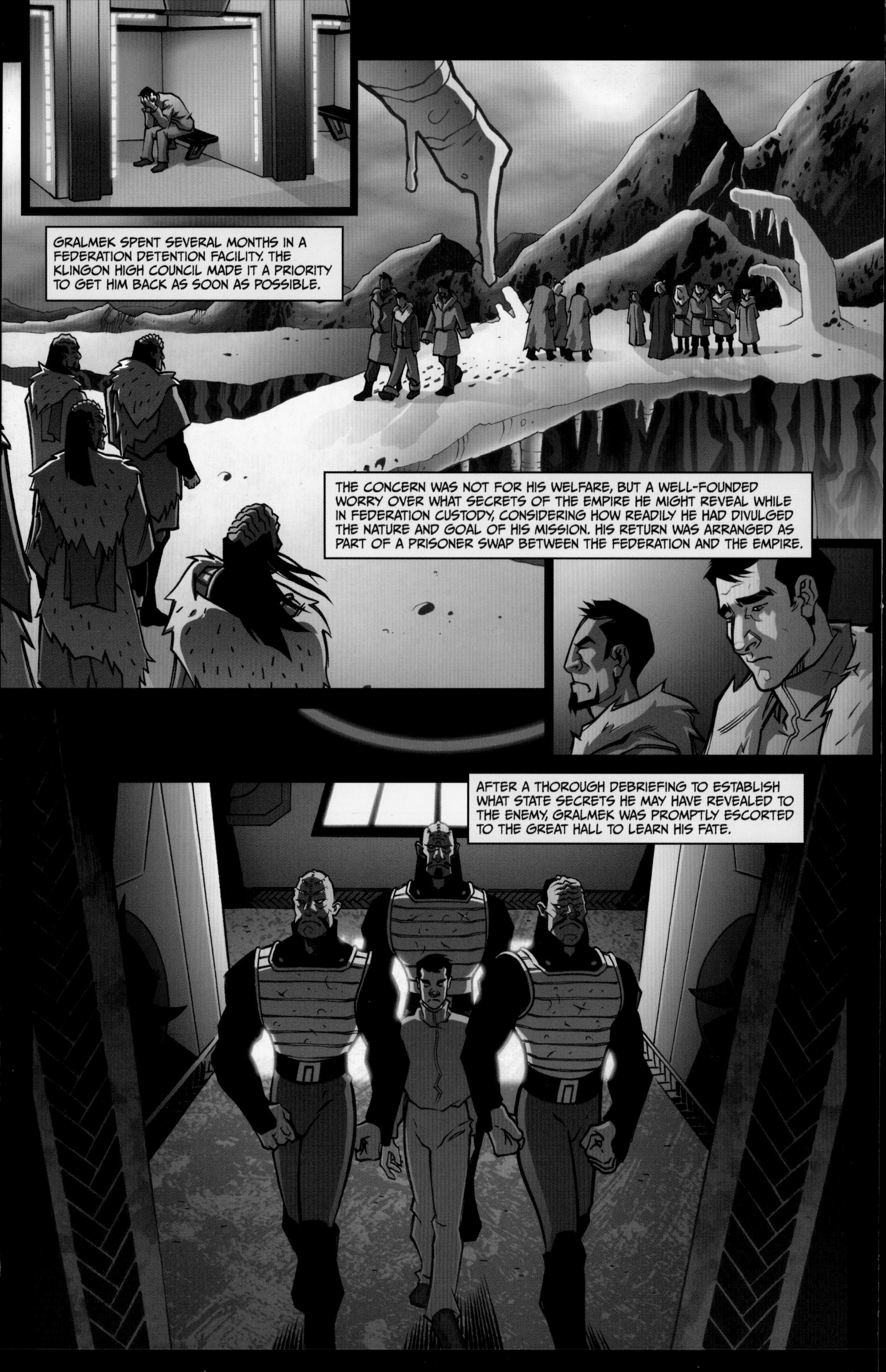
GRALMEK SPENT SEVERAL MONTHS IN A FEDERATION DETENTION FACILITY. THE KLINGON HIGH COUNCIL MADE IT A PRIORITY TO GET HIM BACK AS SOON AS POSSIBLE.
THE CONCERN WAS NOT FOR HIS WELFARE, BUT A WELL-FOUNDED WORRY OVER WHAT SECRETS OF THE EMPIRE HE MIGHT REVEAL WHILE IN FEDERATION CUSTODY, CONSIDERING HOW READILY HE HAD DIVULGED THE NATURE AND GOAL OF HIS MISSION. HIS RETURN WAS ARRANGED AS PART OF A PRISONER SWAP BETWEEN THE FEDERATION AND THE EMPIRE.
AFTER A THOROUGH DEBRIEFING TO ESTABLISH WHAT STATE SECRETS HE MAY HAVE REVEALED TO THE ENEMY, GRALMEK WAS PROMPTLY ESCORTED TO THE GREAT HALL TO LEARN HIS FATE.

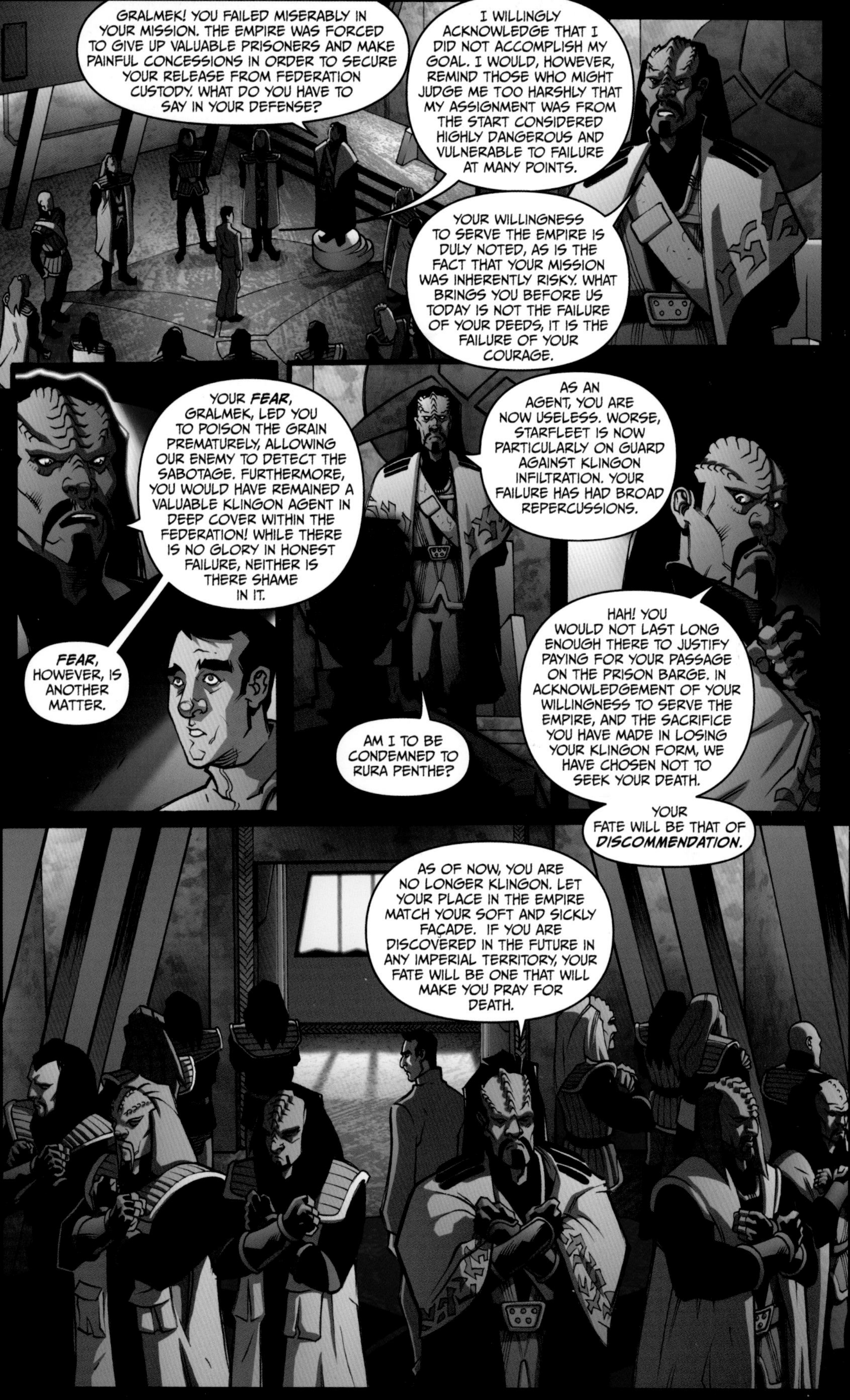
GRALMEK! YOU FAILED MISERABLY IN YOUR MISSION. THE EMPIRE WAS FORCED TO GIVE UP VALUABLE PRISONERS AND MAKE PAINFUL CONCESSIONS IN ORDER TO SECURE YOUR RELEASE FROM FEDERATION CUSTODY. WHAT DO YOU HAVE TO SAY IN YOUR DEFENSE?
I WILLINGLY ACKNOWLEDGE THAT I DID NOT ACCOMPLISH MY GOAL. I WOULD, HOWEVER, REMIND THOSE WHO MIGHT JUDGE ME TOO HARSHLY THAT MY ASSIGNMENT WAS FROM THE START CONSIDERED HIGHLY DANGEROUS AND VULNERABLE TO FAILURE AT MANY POINTS.
YOUR WILLINGNESS TO SERVE THE EMPIRE IS DULY NOTED, AS IS THE FACT THAT YOUR MISSION WAS INHERENTLY RISKY. WHAT BRINGS YOU BEFORE US TODAY IS NOT THE FAILURE OF YOUR DEEDS, IT IS THE FAILURE OF YOUR COURAGE.
YOUR *FEAR*, GRALMEK, LED YOU TO POISON THE GRAIN PREMATURELY, ALLOWING OUR ENEMY TO DETECT THE SABOTAGE. FURTHERMORE, YOU WOULD HAVE REMAINED A VALUABLE KLINGON AGENT IN DEEP COVER WITHIN THE FEDERATION! WHILE THERE IS NO GLORY IN HONEST FAILURE, NEITHER IS THERE SHAME IN IT.
FEAR, HOWEVER, IS ANOTHER MATTER.
AS AN AGENT, YOU ARE NOW USELESS. WORSE, STARFLEET IS NOW PARTICULARLY ON GUARD AGAINST KLINGON INFILTRATION. YOUR FAILURE HAS HAD BROAD REPERCUSSIONS.
AM I TO BE CONDEMNED TO RURA PENTHE?
HAH! YOU WOULD NOT LAST LONG ENOUGH THERE TO JUSTIFY PAYING FOR YOUR PASSAGE ON THE PRISON BARGE. IN ACKNOWLEDGEMENT OF YOUR WILLINGNESS TO SERVE THE EMPIRE, AND THE SACRIFICE YOU HAVE MADE IN LOSING YOUR KLINGON FORM, WE HAVE CHOSEN NOT TO SEEK YOUR DEATH.
YOUR FATE WILL BE THAT OF *DISCOMMENDATION.*
AS OF NOW, YOU ARE NO LONGER KLINGON. LET YOUR PLACE IN THE EMPIRE MATCH YOUR SOFT AND SICKLY FAÇADE. IF YOU ARE DISCOVERED IN THE FUTURE IN ANY IMPERIAL TERRITORY, YOUR FATE WILL BE ONE THAT WILL MAKE YOU PRAY FOR DEATH.

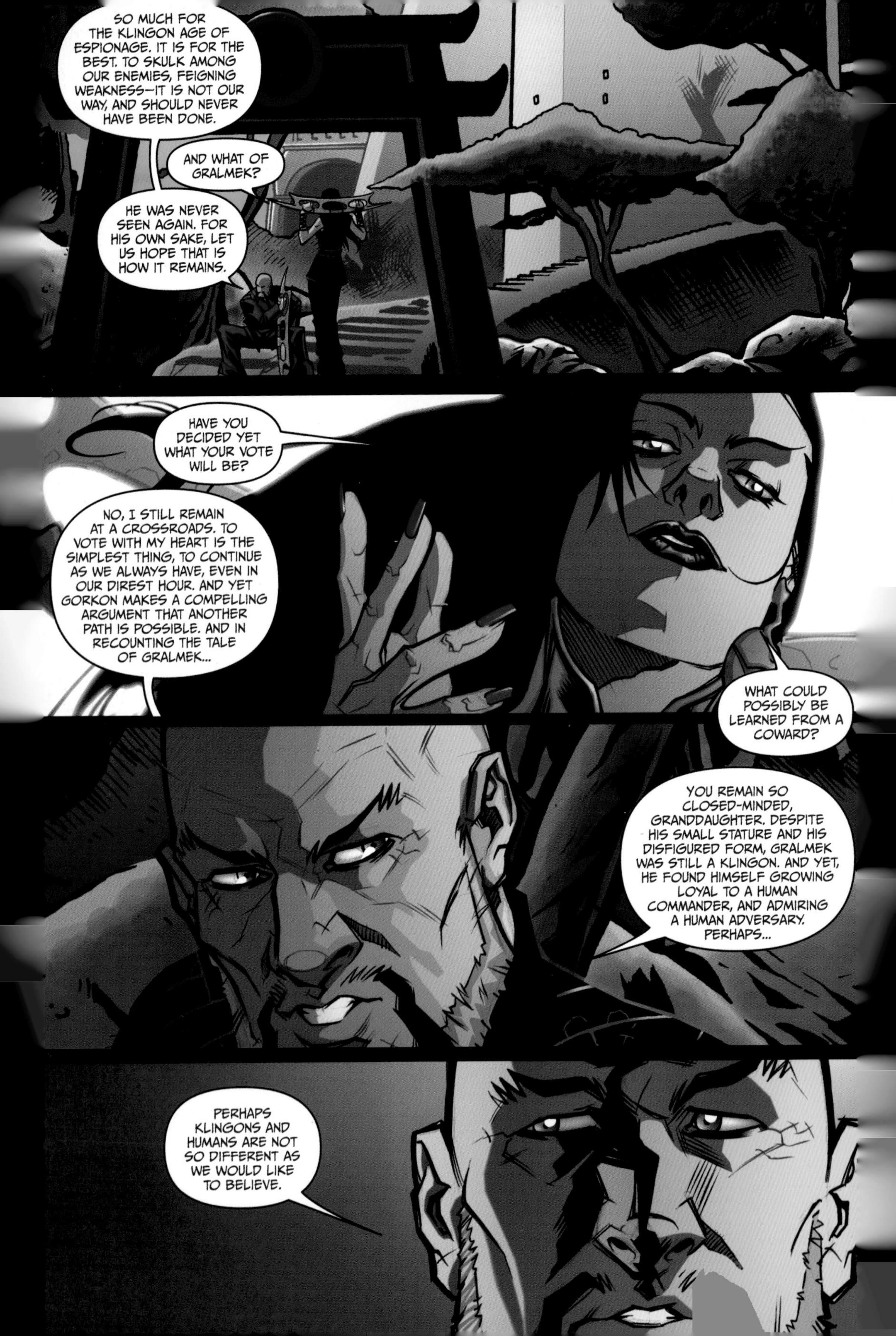
SO MUCH FOR THE KLINGON AGE OF ESPIONAGE. IT IS FOR THE BEST. TO SKULK AMONG OUR ENEMIES, FEIGNING WEAKNESS—IT IS NOT OUR WAY, AND SHOULD NEVER HAVE BEEN DONE.
AND WHAT OF GRALMEK?
HE WAS NEVER SEEN AGAIN. FOR HIS OWN SAKE, LET US HOPE THAT IS HOW IT REMAINS.
HAVE YOU DECIDED YET WHAT YOUR VOTE WILL BE?
NO, I STILL REMAIN AT A CROSSROADS. TO VOTE WITH MY HEART IS THE SIMPLEST THING, TO CONTINUE AS WE ALWAYS HAVE, EVEN IN OUR DIREST HOUR. AND YET GORKON MAKES A COMPELLING ARGUMENT THAT ANOTHER PATH IS POSSIBLE. AND IN RECOUNTING THE TALE OF GRALMEK...
WHAT COULD POSSIBLY BE LEARNED FROM A COWARD?
YOU REMAIN SO CLOSED-MINDED, GRANDDAUGHTER. DESPITE HIS SMALL STATURE AND HIS DISFIGURED FORM, GRALMEK WAS STILL A KLINGON. AND YET, HE FOUND HIMSELF GROWING LOYAL TO A HUMAN COMMANDER, AND ADMIRING A HUMAN ADVERSARY. PERHAPS...
PERHAPS KLINGONS AND HUMANS ARE NOT SO DIFFERENT AS WE WOULD LIKE TO BELIEVE.

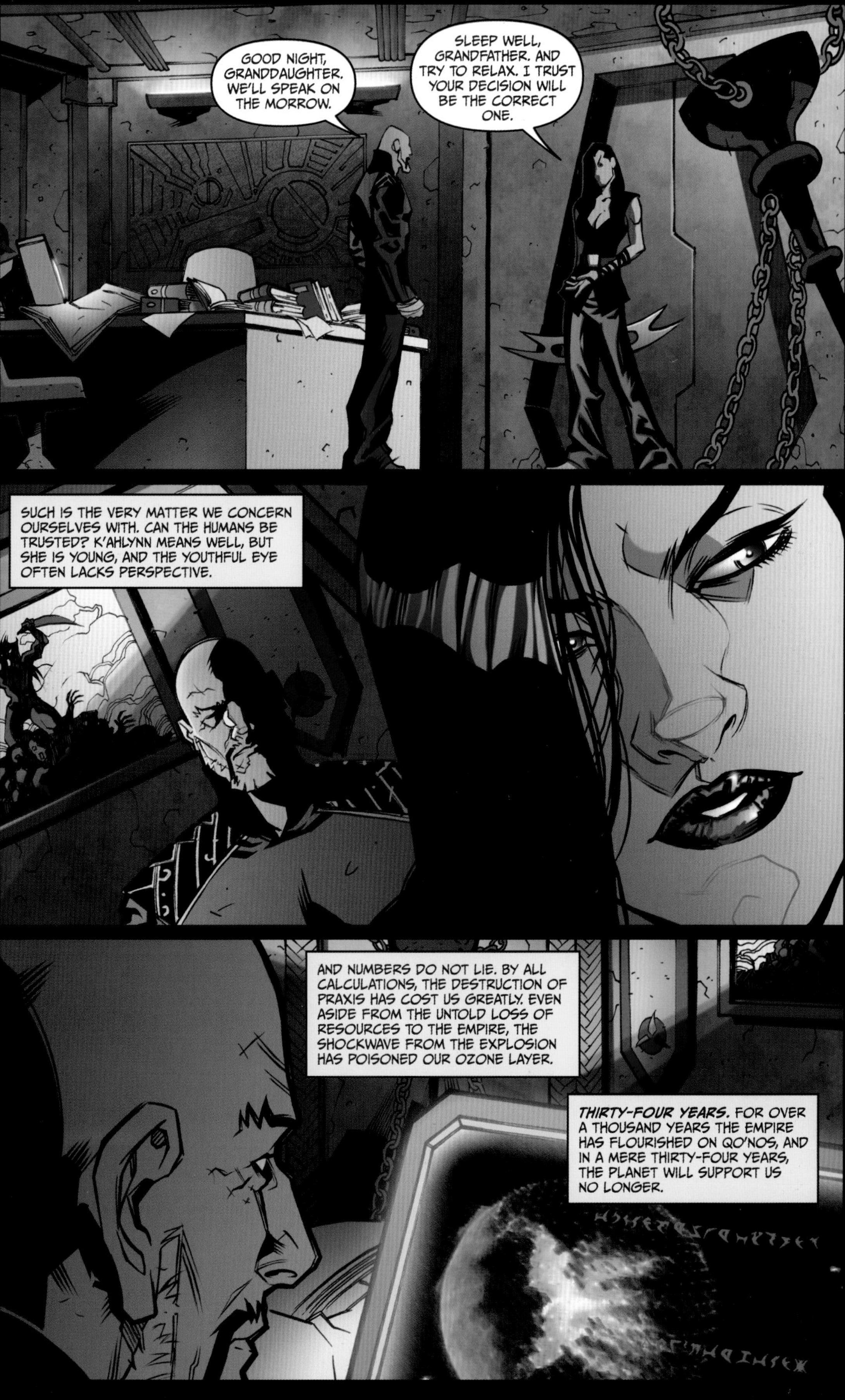
GOOD NIGHT, GRANDDAUGHTER. WE'LL SPEAK ON THE MORROW.
SLEEP WELL, GRANDFATHER. AND TRY TO RELAX. I TRUST YOUR DECISION WILL BE THE CORRECT ONE.
SUCH IS THE VERY MATTER WE CONCERN OURSELVES WITH. CAN THE HUMANS BE TRUSTED? K'AHLYNN MEANS WELL, BUT SHE IS YOUNG, AND THE YOUTHFUL EYE OFTEN LACKS PERSPECTIVE.
AND NUMBERS DO NOT LIE. BY ALL CALCULATIONS, THE DESTRUCTION OF PRAXIS HAS COST US GREATLY. EVEN ASIDE FROM THE UNTOLD LOSS OF RESOURCES TO THE EMPIRE, THE SHOCKWAVE FROM THE EXPLOSION HAS POISONED OUR OZONE LAYER.
THIRTY-FOUR YEARS. FOR OVER A THOUSAND YEARS THE EMPIRE HAS FLOURISHED ON QO'NOS, AND IN A MERE THIRTY-FOUR YEARS, THE PLANET WILL SUPPORT US NO LONGER.

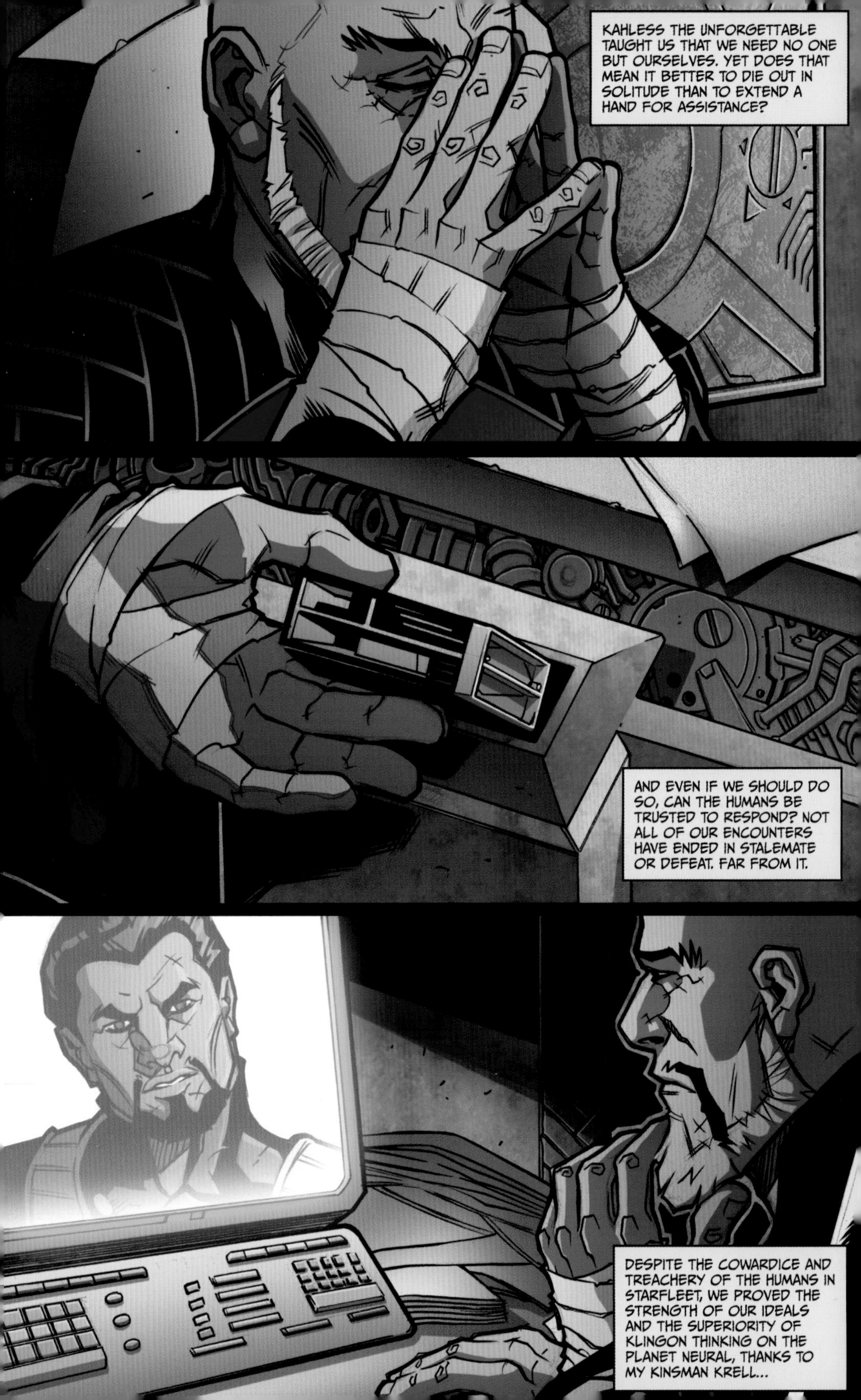
KAHLESS THE UNFORGETTABLE TAUGHT US THAT WE NEED NO ONE BUT OURSELVES. YET DOES THAT MEAN IT BETTER TO DIE OUT IN SOLITUDE THAN TO EXTEND A HAND FOR ASSISTANCE?
AND EVEN IF WE SHOULD DO SO, CAN THE HUMANS BE TRUSTED TO RESPOND? NOT ALL OF OUR ENCOUNTERS HAVE ENDED IN STALEMATE OR DEFEAT. FAR FROM IT.
DESPITE THE COWARDICE AND TREACHERY OF THE HUMANS IN STARFLEET, WE PROVED THE STRENGTH OF OUR IDEALS AND THE SUPERIORITY OF KLINGON THINKING ON THE PLANET NEURAL, THANKS TO MY KINSMAN KRELL...

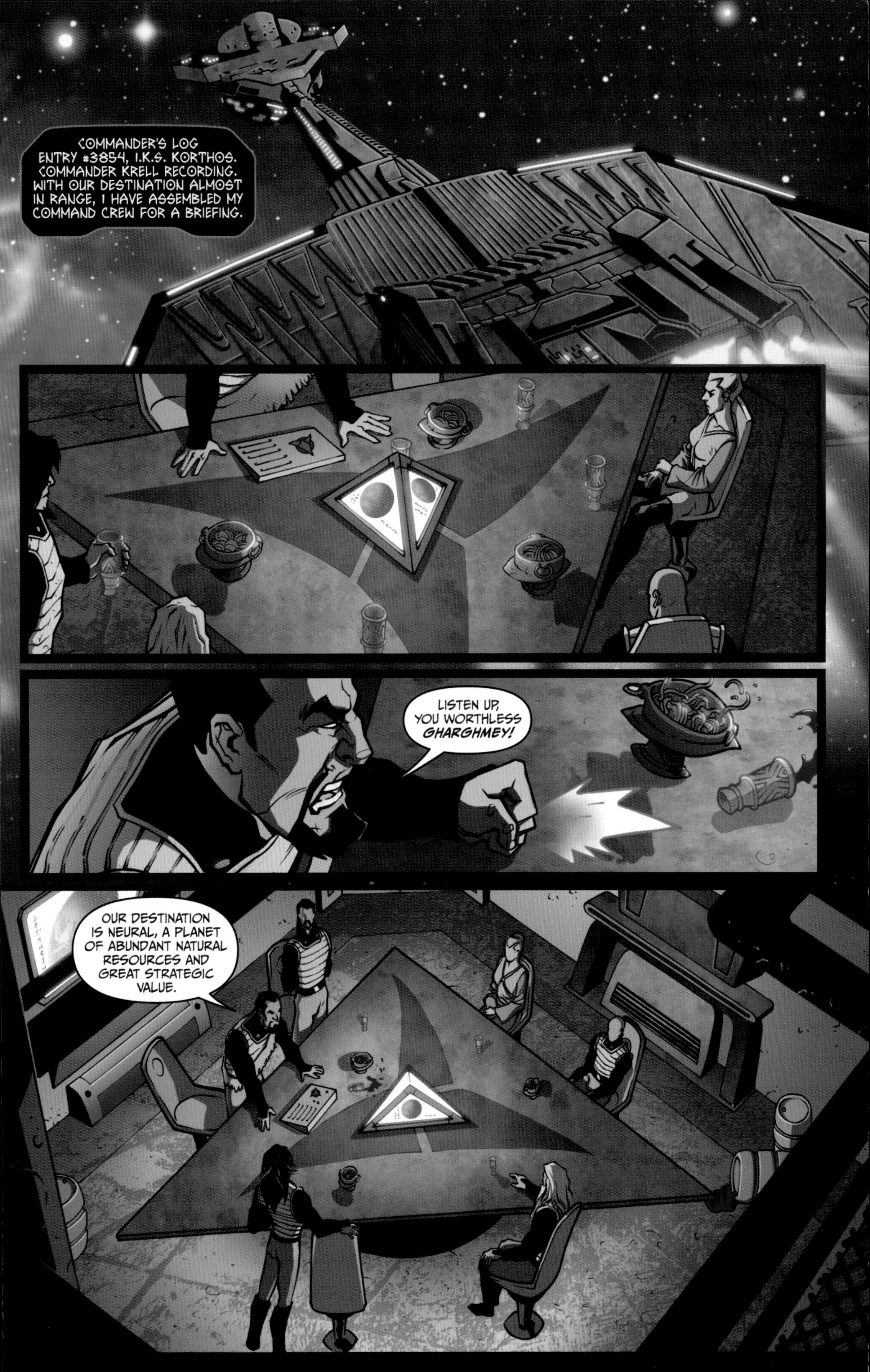
COMMANDER'S LOG ENTRY #3854, I.K.S. KORTHOS. COMMANDER KRELL RECORDING. WITH OUR DESTINATION ALMOST IN RANGE, I HAVE ASSEMBLED MY COMMAND CREW FOR A BRIEFING.
LISTEN UP, YOU WORTHLESS GHARGHMEY!
OUR DESTINATION IS NEURAL, A PLANET OF ABUNDANT NATURAL RESOURCES AND GREAT STRATEGIC VALUE.

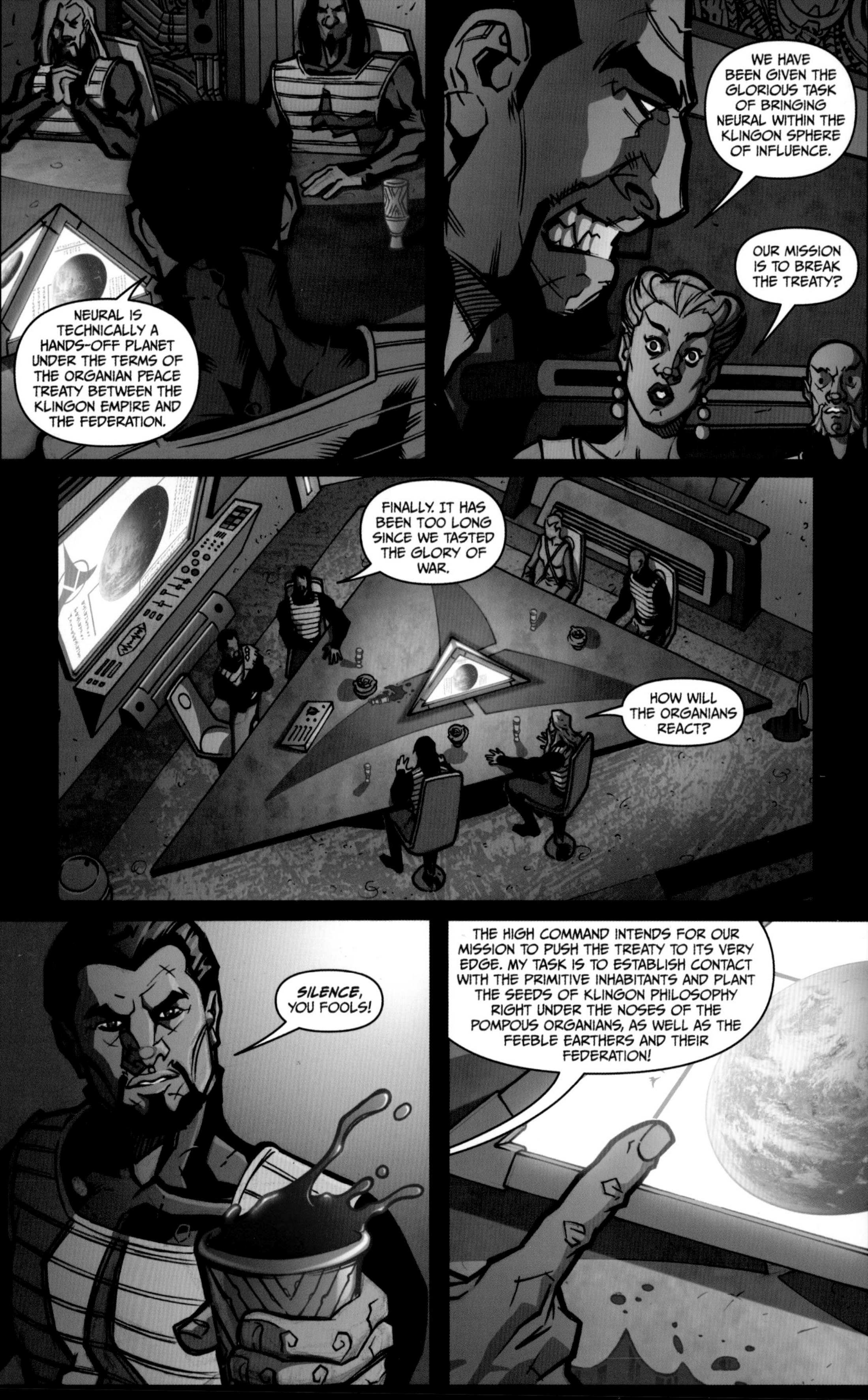
NEURAL IS TECHNICALLY A HANDS-OFF PLANET UNDER THE TERMS OF THE ORGANIAN PEACE TREATY BETWEEN THE KLINGON EMPIRE AND THE FEDERATION.
WE HAVE BEEN GIVEN THE GLORIOUS TASK OF BRINGING NEURAL WITHIN THE KLINGON SPHERE OF INFLUENCE.
OUR MISSION IS TO BREAK THE TREATY?
FINALLY. IT HAS BEEN TOO LONG SINCE WE TASTED THE GLORY OF WAR.
HOW WILL THE ORGANIANS REACT?
SILENCE, YOU FOOLS!
THE HIGH COMMAND INTENDS FOR OUR MISSION TO PUSH THE TREATY TO ITS VERY EDGE. MY TASK IS TO ESTABLISH CONTACT WITH THE PRIMITIVE INHABITANTS AND PLANT THE SEEDS OF KLINGON PHILOSOPHY RIGHT UNDER THE NOSES OF THE POMPOUS ORGANIANS, AS WELL AS THE FEEBLE EARTHERS AND THEIR FEDERATION!

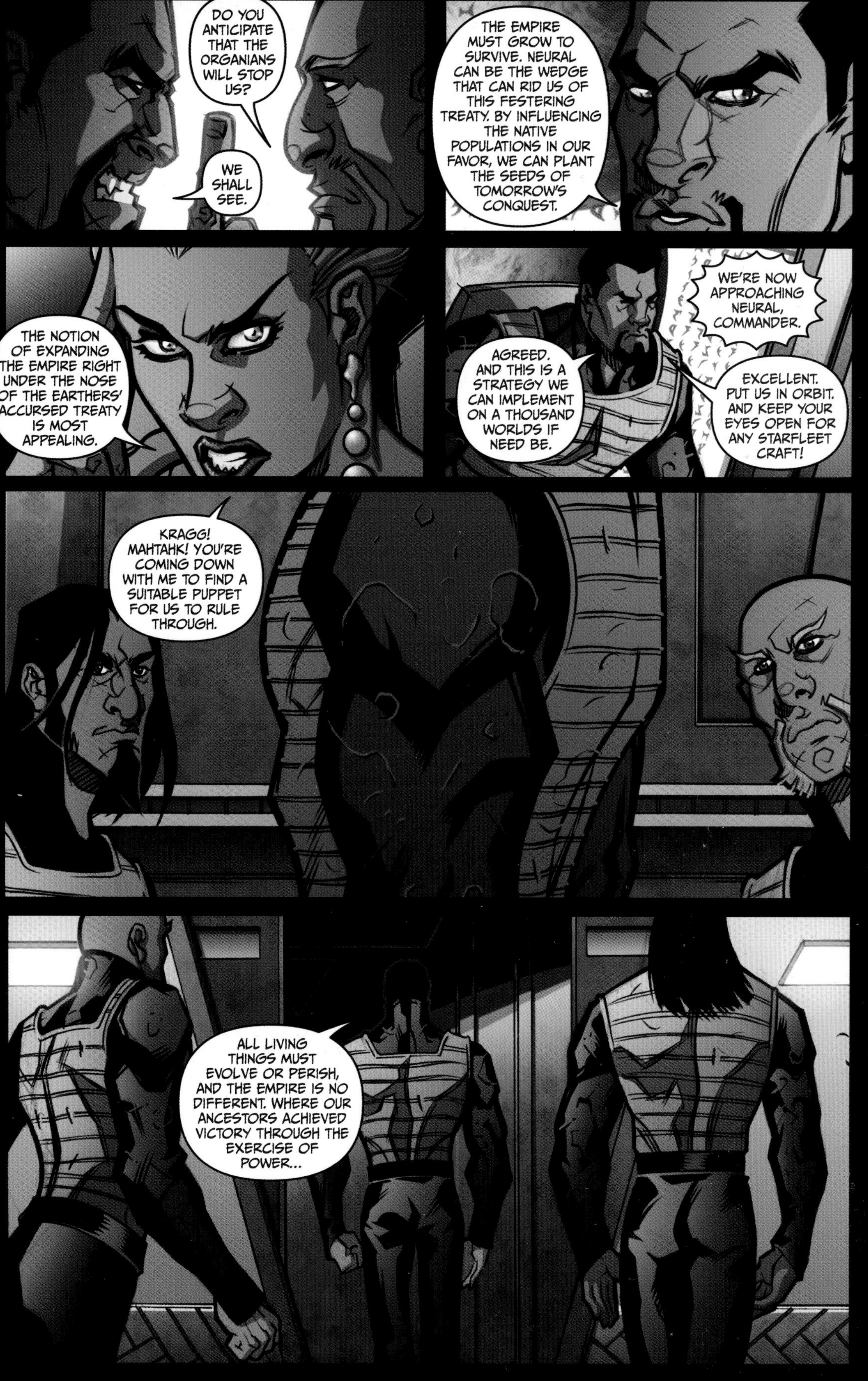
DO YOU ANTICIPATE THAT THE ORGANIANS WILL STOP US?
WE SHALL SEE.
THE EMPIRE MUST GROW TO SURVIVE. NEURAL CAN BE THE WEDGE THAT CAN RID US OF THIS FESTERING TREATY. BY INFLUENCING THE NATIVE POPULATIONS IN OUR FAVOR, WE CAN PLANT THE SEEDS OF TOMORROW'S CONQUEST.
THE NOTION OF EXPANDING THE EMPIRE RIGHT UNDER THE NOSE OF THE EARTHERS' ACCURSED TREATY IS MOST APPEALING.
WE'RE NOW APPROACHING NEURAL, COMMANDER.
AGREED. AND THIS IS A STRATEGY WE CAN IMPLEMENT ON A THOUSAND WORLDS IF NEED BE.
EXCELLENT. PUT US IN ORBIT. AND KEEP YOUR EYES OPEN FOR ANY STARFLEET CRAFT!
KRAGG! MAHTAHK! YOU'RE COMING DOWN WITH ME TO FIND A SUITABLE PUPPET FOR US TO RULE THROUGH.
ALL LIVING THINGS MUST EVOLVE OR PERISH, AND THE EMPIRE IS NO DIFFERENT. WHERE OUR ANCESTORS ACHIEVED VICTORY THROUGH THE EXERCISE OF POWER...

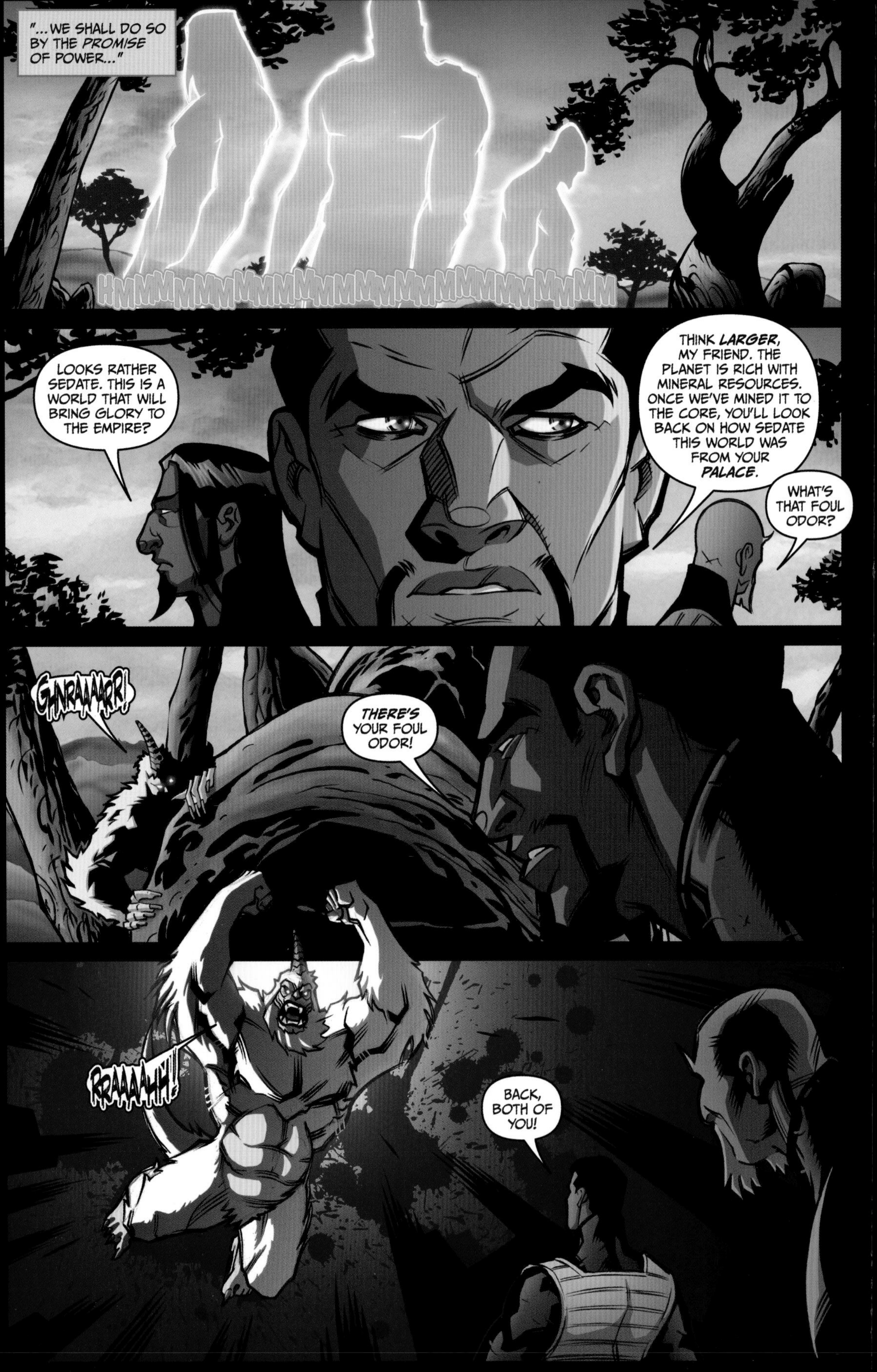
"...WE SHALL DO SO BY THE *PROMISE* OF POWER..."
HMMMMMMMMMMMMMMMMMMMMMMMMMMM
LOOKS RATHER SEDATE. THIS IS A WORLD THAT WILL BRING GLORY TO THE EMPIRE?
THINK *LARGER*, MY FRIEND. THE PLANET IS RICH WITH MINERAL RESOURCES. ONCE WE'VE MINED IT TO THE CORE, YOU'LL LOOK BACK ON HOW SEDATE THIS WORLD WAS FROM YOUR *PALACE*.
WHAT'S THAT FOUL ODOR?
GHNRAAAARR!
THERE'S YOUR FOUL ODOR!
RRAAAAHH!
BACK, BOTH OF YOU!

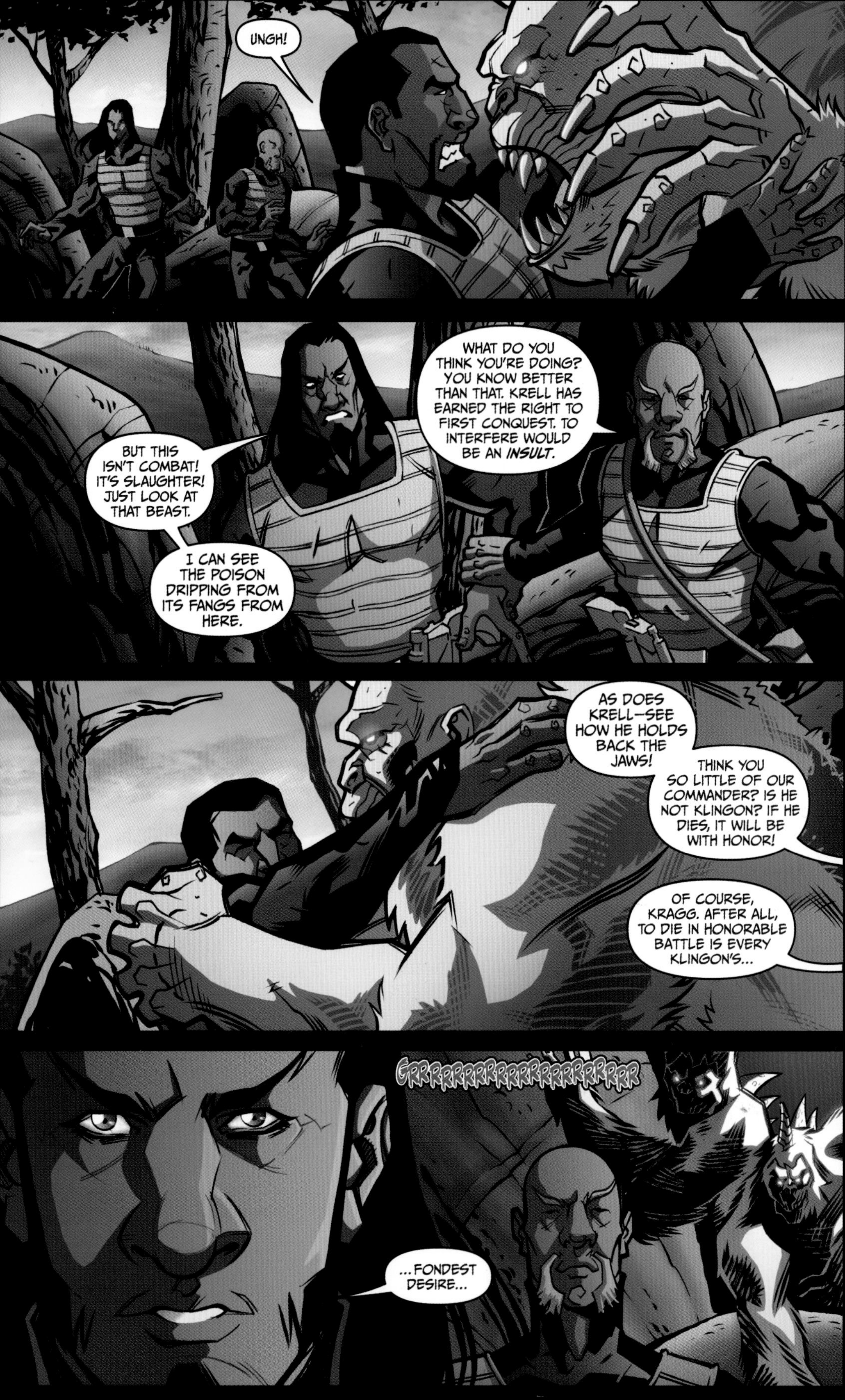
UNGH!
BUT THIS ISN'T COMBAT! IT'S SLAUGHTER! JUST LOOK AT THAT BEAST.
I CAN SEE THE POISON DRIPPING FROM ITS FANGS FROM HERE.
WHAT DO YOU THINK YOU'RE DOING? YOU KNOW BETTER THAN THAT. KRELL HAS EARNED THE RIGHT TO FIRST CONQUEST. TO INTERFERE WOULD BE AN INSULT.
AS DOES KRELL--SEE HOW HE HOLDS BACK THE JAWS!
THINK YOU SO LITTLE OF OUR COMMANDER? IS HE NOT KLINGON? IF HE DIES, IT WILL BE WITH HONOR!
OF COURSE, KRAGG. AFTER ALL, TO DIE IN HONORABLE BATTLE IS EVERY KLINGON'S...
GRRRRRRRRRRRRRRRRRRRRRR
...FONDEST DESIRE...

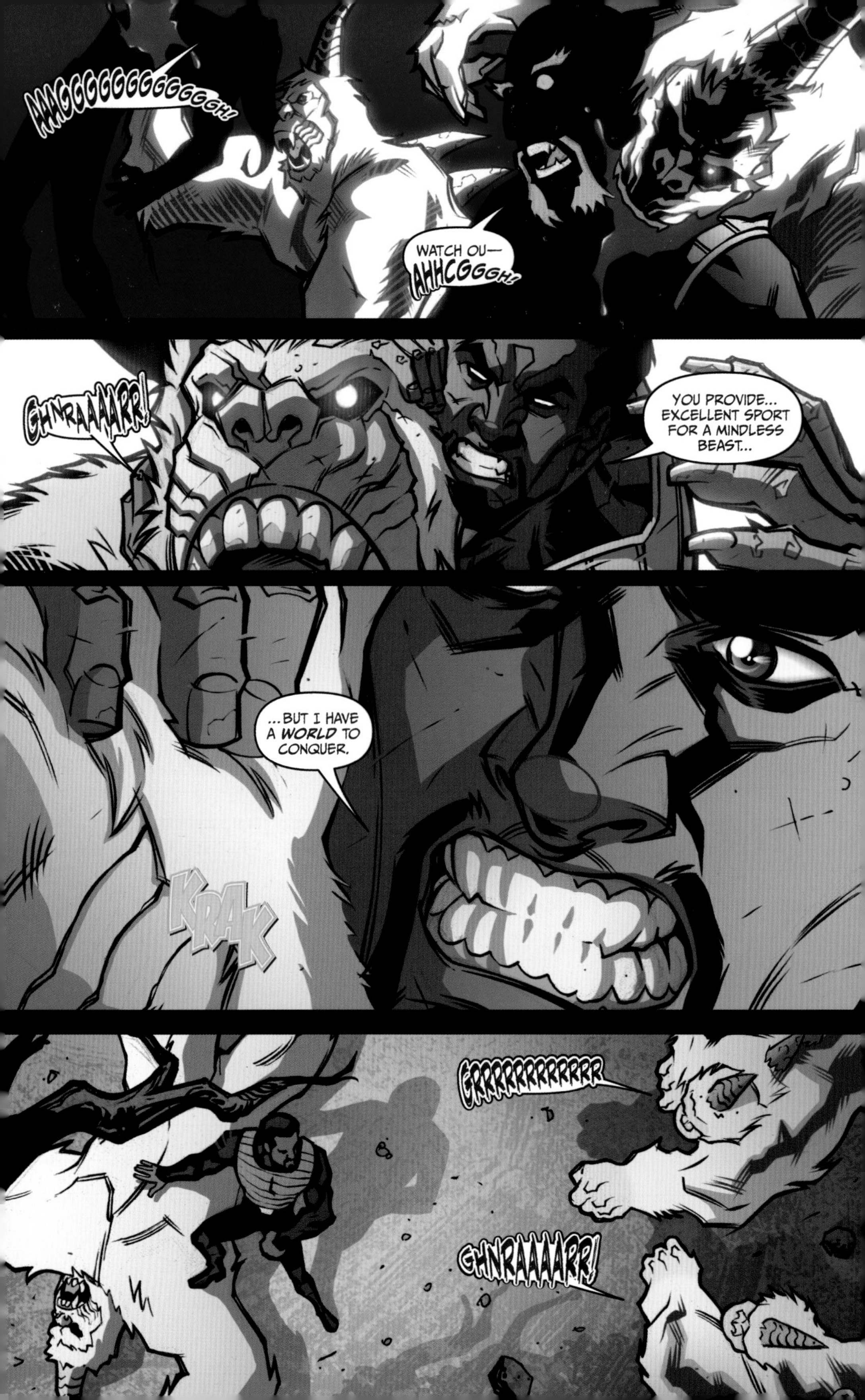
AAAGGGGGGGGGGGGGH!
WATCH OU— AHHCGGGH!
GHNRAAAARR!
YOU PROVIDE... EXCELLENT SPORT FOR A MINDLESS BEAST...
...BUT I HAVE A WORLD TO CONQUER.
KRAK
GRRRRRRRRRRR
GHNRAAAARR!

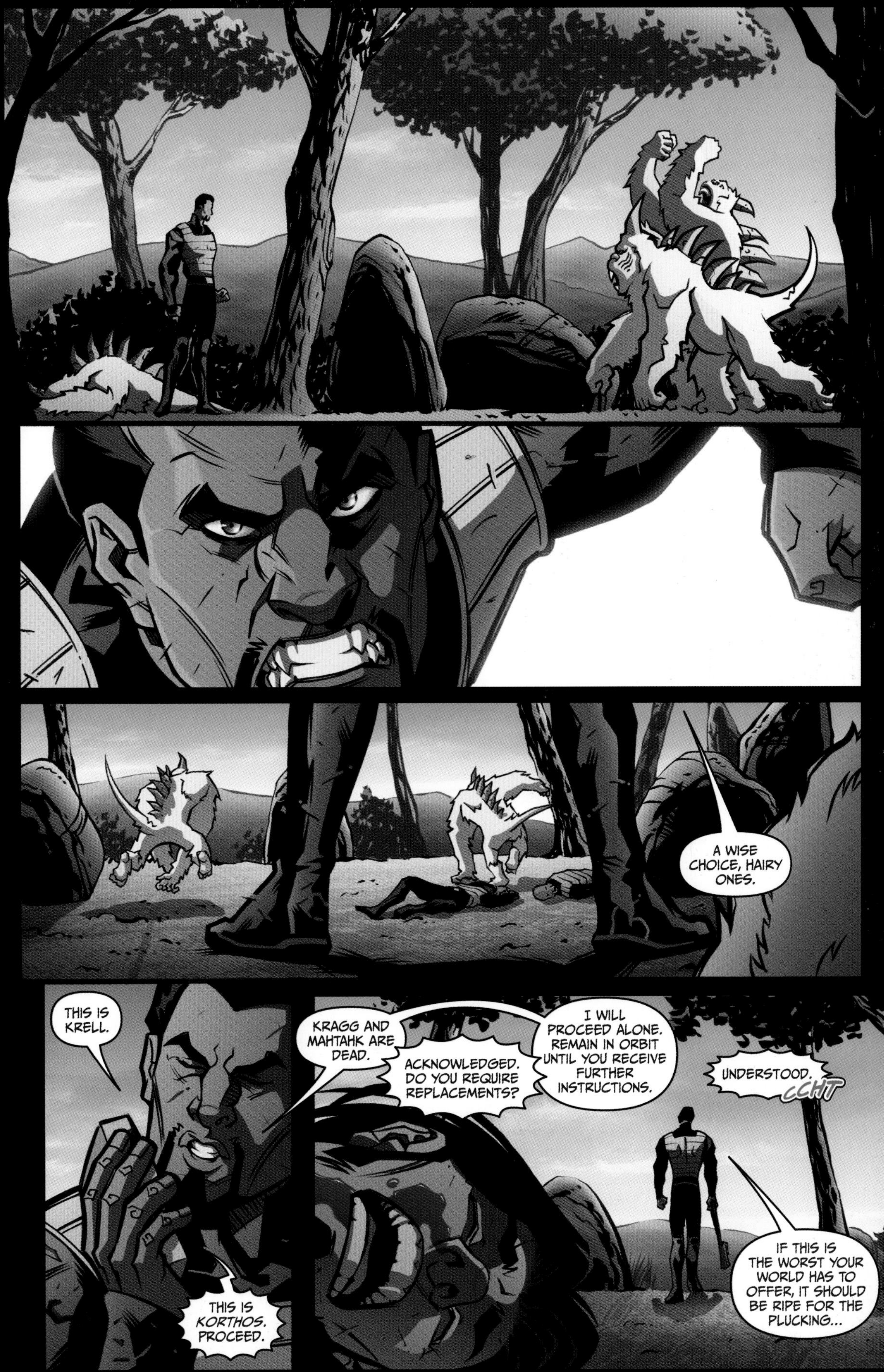
A WISE CHOICE, HAIRY ONES.
THIS IS KRELL.
KRAGG AND MAHTAHK ARE DEAD.
ACKNOWLEDGED. DO YOU REQUIRE REPLACEMENTS?
I WILL PROCEED ALONE. REMAIN IN ORBIT UNTIL YOU RECEIVE FURTHER INSTRUCTIONS.
UNDERSTOOD.
CCHT
THIS IS KORTHOS. PROCEED.
IF THIS IS THE WORST YOUR WORLD HAS TO OFFER, IT SHOULD BE RIPE FOR THE PLUCKING...

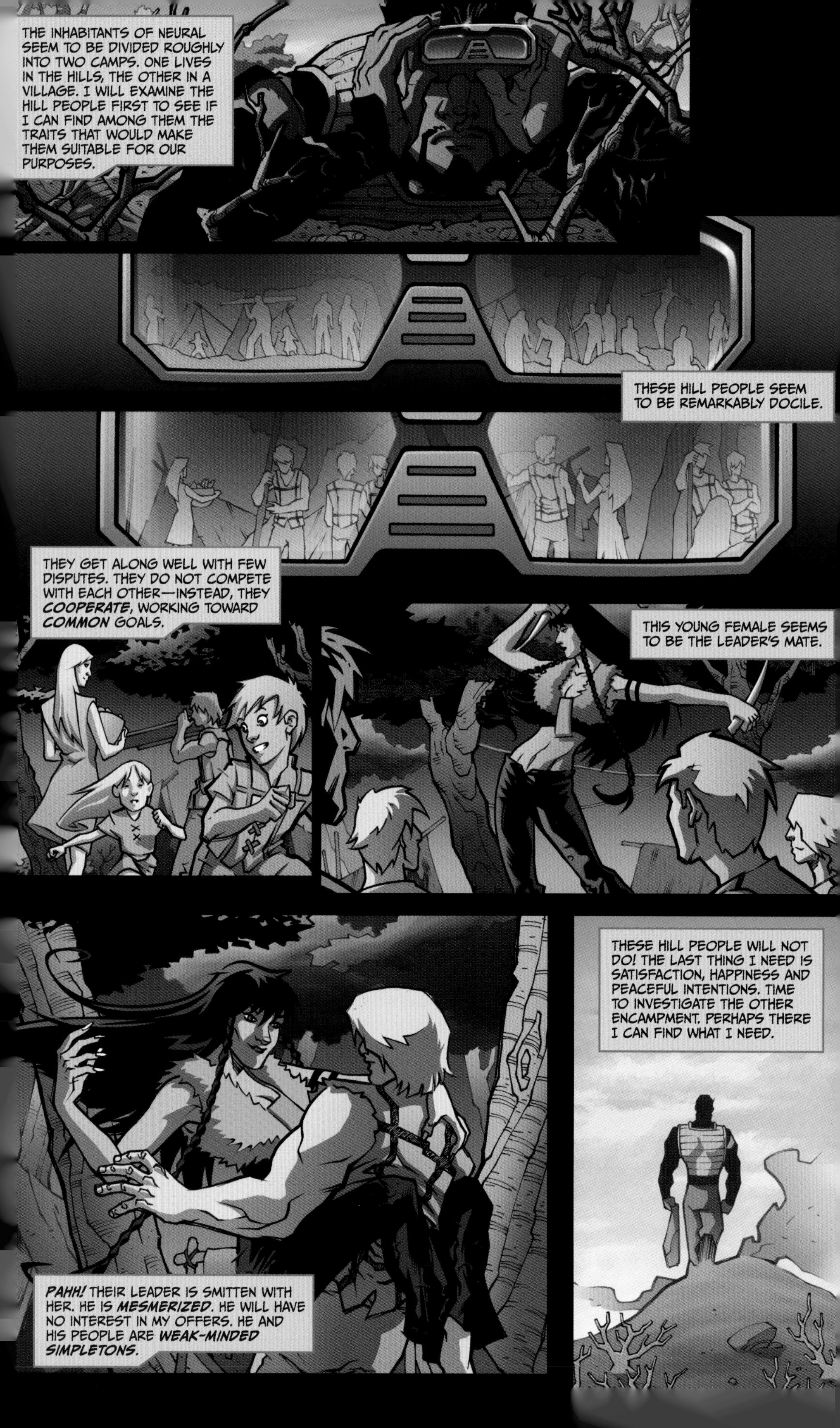
THE INHABITANTS OF NEURAL SEEM TO BE DIVIDED ROUGHLY INTO TWO CAMPS. ONE LIVES IN THE HILLS, THE OTHER IN A VILLAGE. I WILL EXAMINE THE HILL PEOPLE FIRST TO SEE IF I CAN FIND AMONG THEM THE TRAITS THAT WOULD MAKE THEM SUITABLE FOR OUR PURPOSES.
THESE HILL PEOPLE SEEM TO BE REMARKABLY DOCILE.
THEY GET ALONG WELL WITH FEW DISPUTES. THEY DO NOT COMPETE WITH EACH OTHER—INSTEAD, THEY *COOPERATE*, WORKING TOWARD *COMMON* GOALS.
THIS YOUNG FEMALE SEEMS TO BE THE LEADER'S MATE.
PAHH! THEIR LEADER IS SMITTEN WITH HER. HE IS *MESMERIZED*. HE WILL HAVE NO INTEREST IN MY OFFERS. HE AND HIS PEOPLE ARE *WEAK-MINDED SIMPLETONS*.
THESE HILL PEOPLE WILL NOT DO! THE LAST THING I NEED IS SATISFACTION, HAPPINESS AND PEACEFUL INTENTIONS. TIME TO INVESTIGATE THE OTHER ENCAMPMENT. PERHAPS THERE I CAN FIND WHAT I NEED.

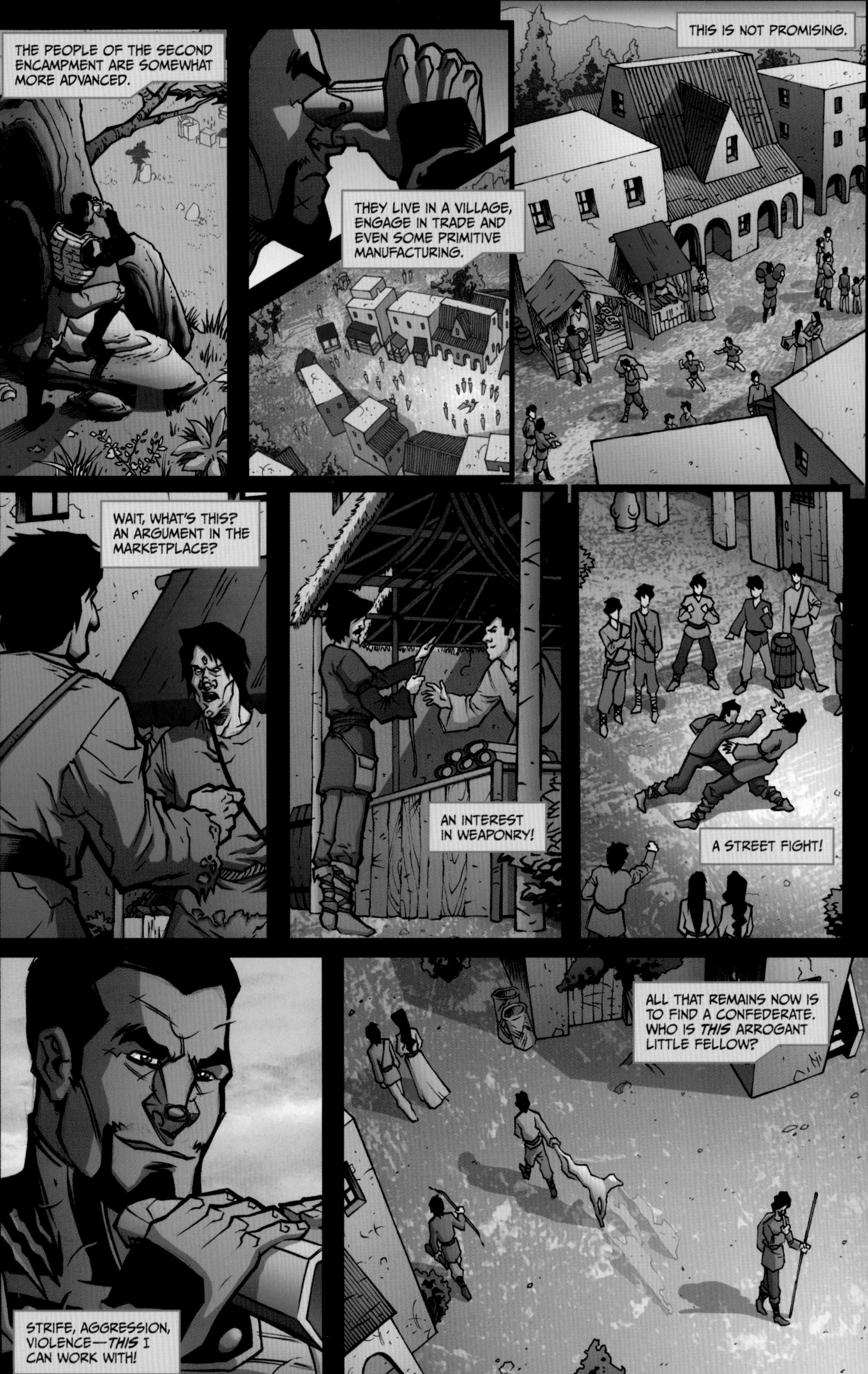

THE PEOPLE OF THE SECOND ENCAMPMENT ARE SOMEWHAT MORE ADVANCED.
THEY LIVE IN A VILLAGE, ENGAGE IN TRADE AND EVEN SOME PRIMITIVE MANUFACTURING.
THIS IS NOT PROMISING.
WAIT, WHAT'S THIS? AN ARGUMENT IN THE MARKETPLACE?
AN INTEREST IN WEAPONRY!
A STREET FIGHT!
STRIFE, AGGRESSION, VIOLENCE—*THIS* I CAN WORK WITH!
ALL THAT REMAINS NOW IS TO FIND A CONFEDERATE. WHO IS *THIS* ARROGANT LITTLE FELLOW?

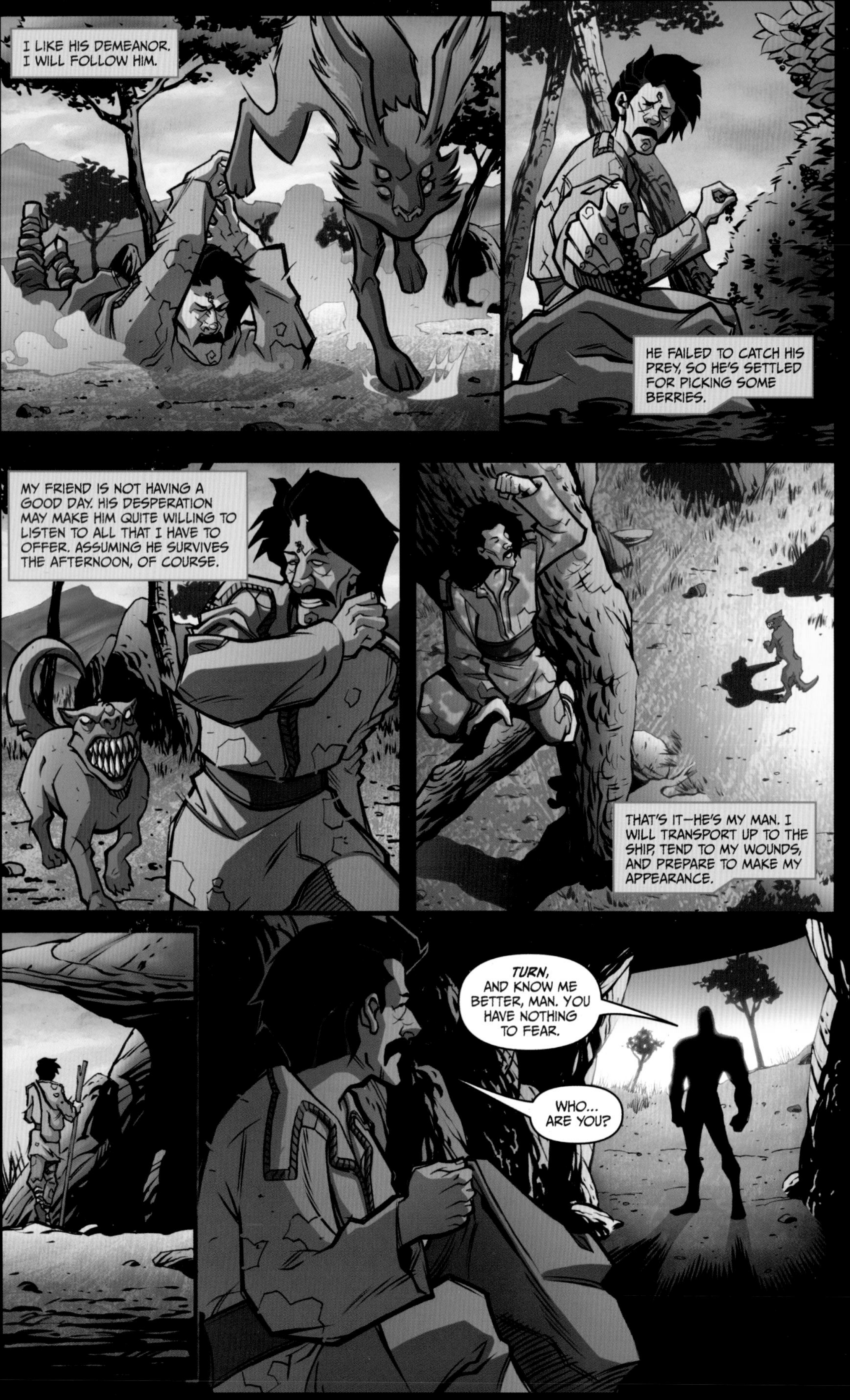

I LIKE HIS DEMEANOR. I WILL FOLLOW HIM.
HE FAILED TO CATCH HIS PREY, SO HE'S SETTLED FOR PICKING SOME BERRIES.
MY FRIEND IS NOT HAVING A GOOD DAY. HIS DESPERATION MAY MAKE HIM QUITE WILLING TO LISTEN TO ALL THAT I HAVE TO OFFER. ASSUMING HE SURVIVES THE AFTERNOON, OF COURSE.
THAT'S IT—HE'S MY MAN. I WILL TRANSPORT UP TO THE SHIP, TEND TO MY WOUNDS, AND PREPARE TO MAKE MY APPEARANCE.
TURN, AND KNOW ME BETTER, MAN. YOU HAVE NOTHING TO FEAR.
WHO... ARE YOU?

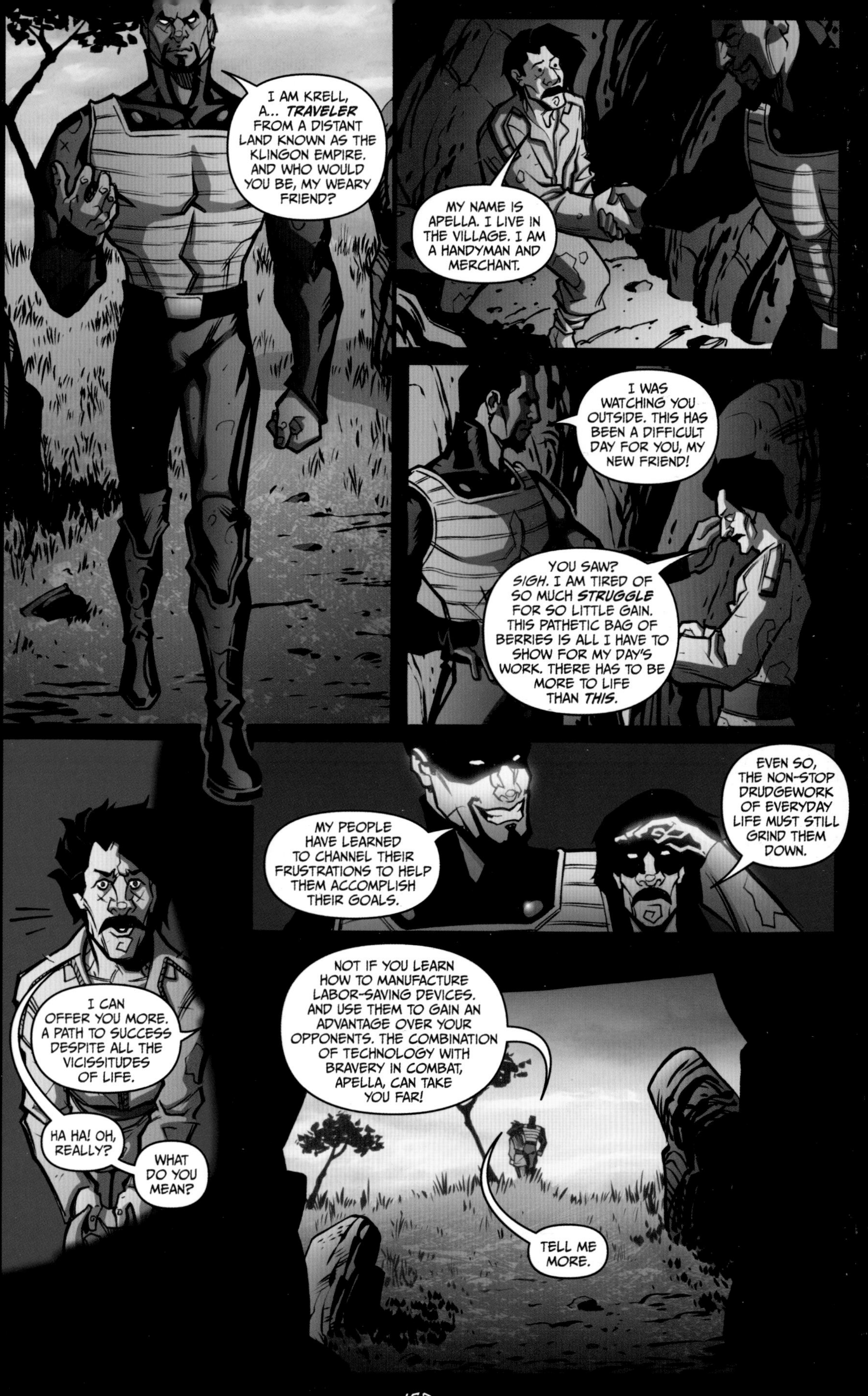

I AM KRELL, A... TRAVELER FROM A DISTANT LAND KNOWN AS THE KLINGON EMPIRE. AND WHO WOULD YOU BE, MY WEARY FRIEND?
MY NAME IS APELLA. I LIVE IN THE VILLAGE. I AM A HANDYMAN AND MERCHANT.
I WAS WATCHING YOU OUTSIDE. THIS HAS BEEN A DIFFICULT DAY FOR YOU, MY NEW FRIEND!
YOU SAW? SIGH. I AM TIRED OF SO MUCH STRUGGLE FOR SO LITTLE GAIN. THIS PATHETIC BAG OF BERRIES IS ALL I HAVE TO SHOW FOR MY DAY'S WORK. THERE HAS TO BE MORE TO LIFE THAN THIS.
MY PEOPLE HAVE LEARNED TO CHANNEL THEIR FRUSTRATIONS TO HELP THEM ACCOMPLISH THEIR GOALS.
EVEN SO, THE NON-STOP DRUDGEWORK OF EVERYDAY LIFE MUST STILL GRIND THEM DOWN.
I CAN OFFER YOU MORE. A PATH TO SUCCESS DESPITE ALL THE VICISSITUDES OF LIFE.
HA HA! OH, REALLY?
WHAT DO YOU MEAN?
NOT IF YOU LEARN HOW TO MANUFACTURE LABOR-SAVING DEVICES. AND USE THEM TO GAIN AN ADVANTAGE OVER YOUR OPPONENTS. THE COMBINATION OF TECHNOLOGY WITH BRAVERY IN COMBAT, APELLA, CAN TAKE YOU FAR!
TELL ME MORE.

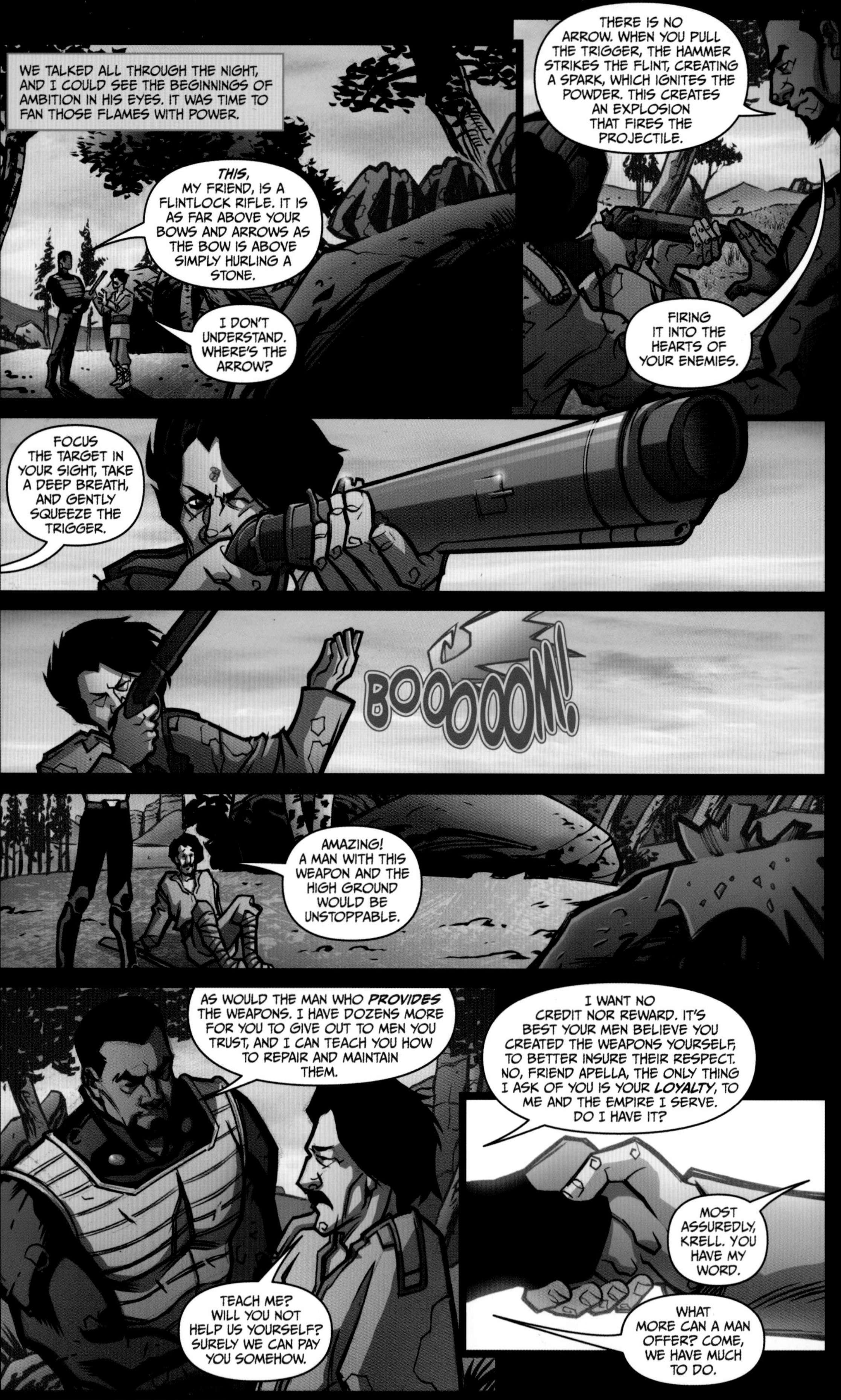
WE TALKED ALL THROUGH THE NIGHT, AND I COULD SEE THE BEGINNINGS OF AMBITION IN HIS EYES. IT WAS TIME TO FAN THOSE FLAMES WITH POWER.
THIS, MY FRIEND, IS A FLINTLOCK RIFLE. IT IS AS FAR ABOVE YOUR BOWS AND ARROWS AS THE BOW IS ABOVE SIMPLY HURLING A STONE.
I DON'T UNDERSTAND. WHERE'S THE ARROW?
THERE IS NO ARROW. WHEN YOU PULL THE TRIGGER, THE HAMMER STRIKES THE FLINT, CREATING A SPARK, WHICH IGNITES THE POWDER. THIS CREATES AN EXPLOSION THAT FIRES THE PROJECTILE.
FIRING IT INTO THE HEARTS OF YOUR ENEMIES.
FOCUS THE TARGET IN YOUR SIGHT, TAKE A DEEP BREATH, AND GENTLY SQUEEZE THE TRIGGER.
BOOOOOM!
AMAZING! A MAN WITH THIS WEAPON AND THE HIGH GROUND WOULD BE UNSTOPPABLE.
AS WOULD THE MAN WHO *PROVIDES* THE WEAPONS. I HAVE DOZENS MORE FOR YOU TO GIVE OUT TO MEN YOU TRUST, AND I CAN TEACH YOU HOW TO REPAIR AND MAINTAIN THEM.
TEACH ME? WILL YOU NOT HELP US YOURSELF? SURELY WE CAN PAY YOU SOMEHOW.
I WANT NO CREDIT NOR REWARD. IT'S BEST YOUR MEN BELIEVE YOU CREATED THE WEAPONS YOURSELF, TO BETTER INSURE THEIR RESPECT. NO, FRIEND APELLA, THE ONLY THING I ASK OF YOU IS YOUR *LOYALTY*, TO ME AND THE EMPIRE I SERVE. DO I HAVE IT?
MOST ASSUREDLY, KRELL. YOU HAVE MY WORD.
WHAT MORE CAN A MAN OFFER? COME, WE HAVE MUCH TO DO.

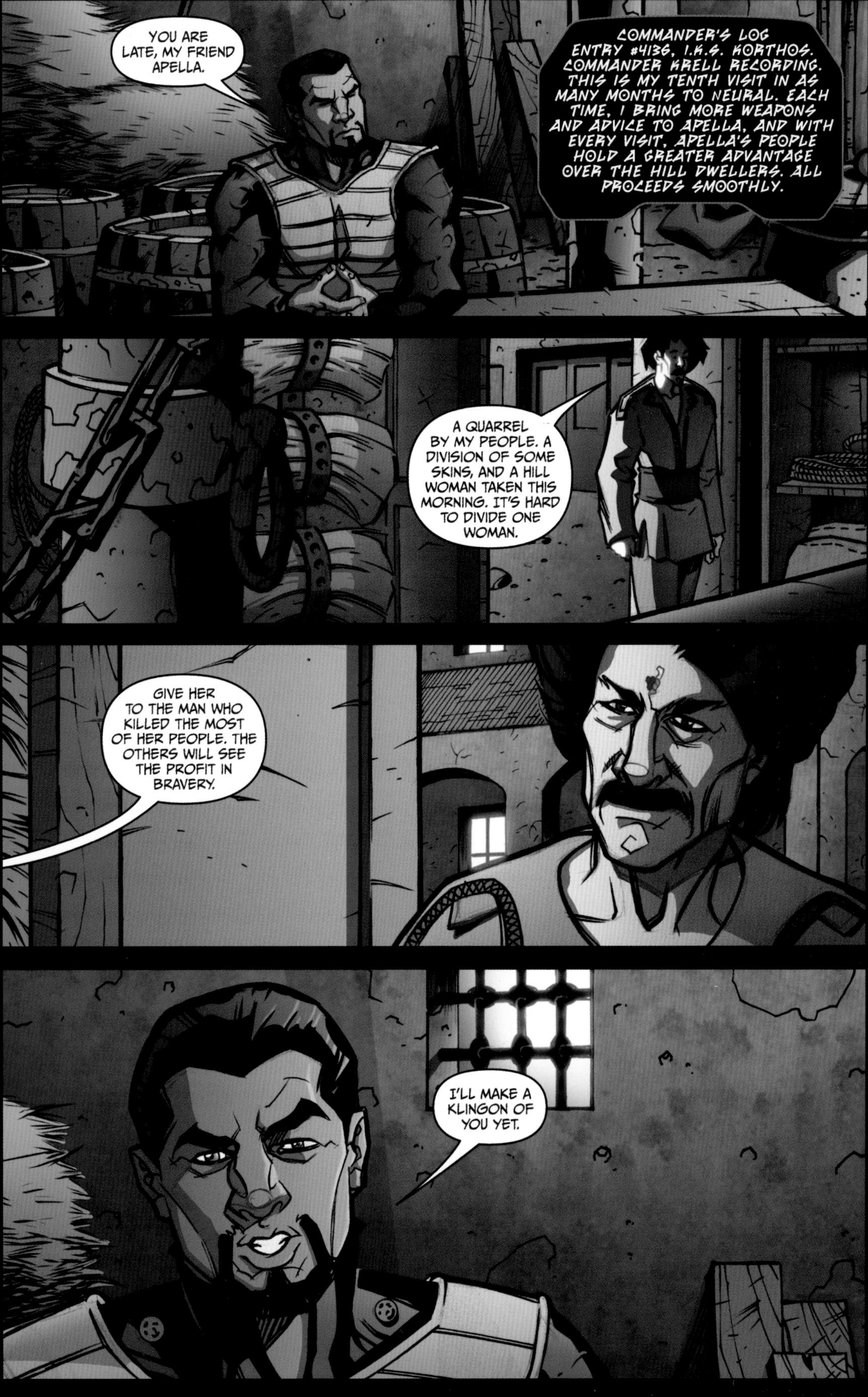
YOU ARE LATE, MY FRIEND APELLA.
COMMANDER'S LOG ENTRY #4136, I.K.S. KORTHOS. COMMANDER KRELL RECORDING. THIS IS MY TENTH VISIT IN AS MANY MONTHS TO NEURAL. EACH TIME, I BRING MORE WEAPONS AND ADVICE TO APELLA, AND WITH EVERY VISIT, APELLA'S PEOPLE HOLD A GREATER ADVANTAGE OVER THE HILL DWELLERS. ALL PROCEEDS SMOOTHLY.
A QUARREL BY MY PEOPLE. A DIVISION OF SOME SKINS, AND A HILL WOMAN TAKEN THIS MORNING. IT'S HARD TO DIVIDE ONE WOMAN.
GIVE HER TO THE MAN WHO KILLED THE MOST OF HER PEOPLE. THE OTHERS WILL SEE THE PROFIT IN BRAVERY.
I'LL MAKE A KLINGON OF YOU YET.

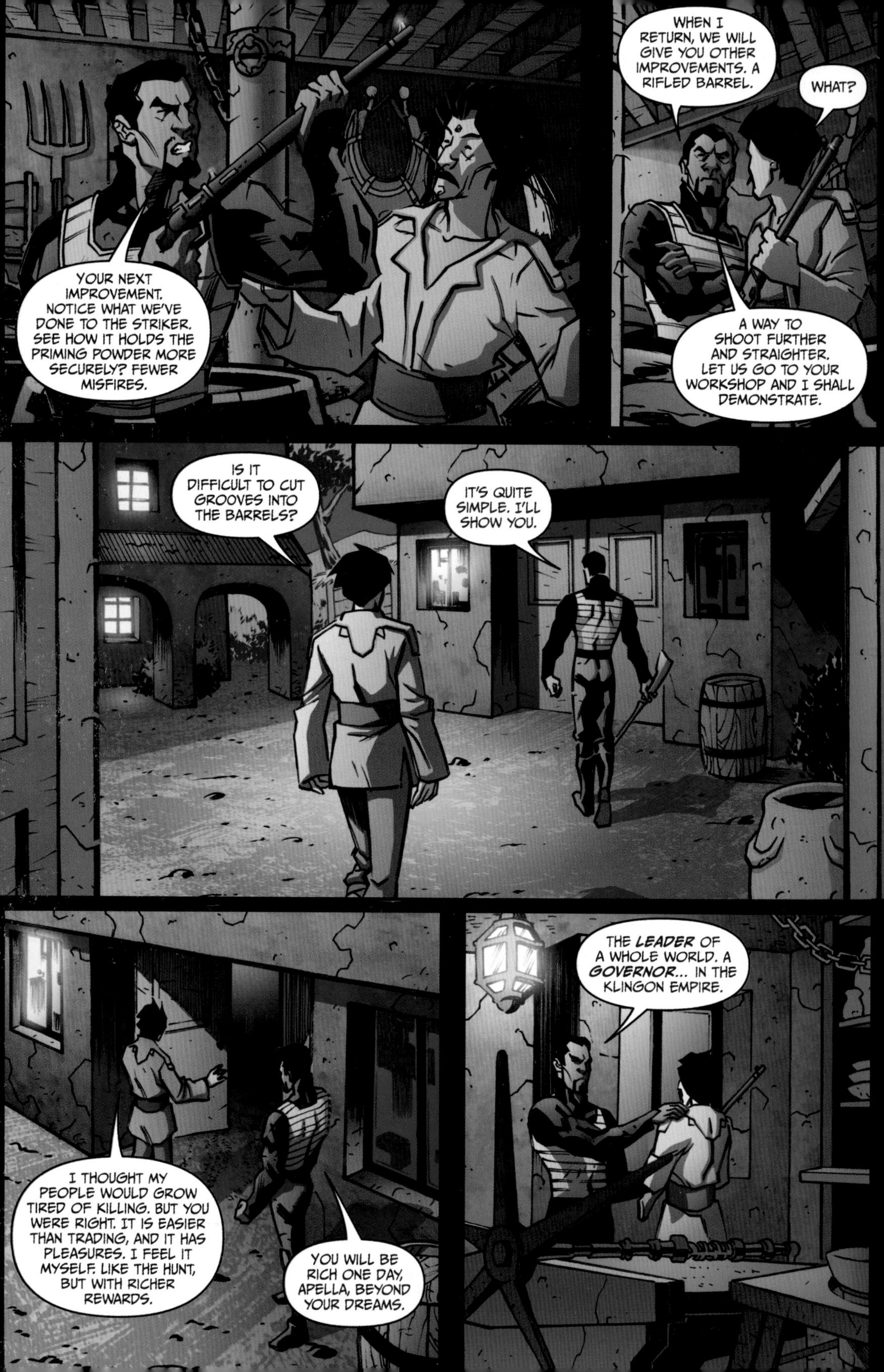
YOUR NEXT IMPROVEMENT. NOTICE WHAT WE'VE DONE TO THE STRIKER. SEE HOW IT HOLDS THE PRIMING POWDER MORE SECURELY? FEWER MISFIRES.
WHEN I RETURN, WE WILL GIVE YOU OTHER IMPROVEMENTS. A RIFLED BARREL.
WHAT?
A WAY TO SHOOT FURTHER AND STRAIGHTER. LET US GO TO YOUR WORKSHOP AND I SHALL DEMONSTRATE.
IS IT DIFFICULT TO CUT GROOVES INTO THE BARRELS?
IT'S QUITE SIMPLE. I'LL SHOW YOU.
I THOUGHT MY PEOPLE WOULD GROW TIRED OF KILLING. BUT YOU WERE RIGHT. IT IS EASIER THAN TRADING, AND IT HAS PLEASURES. I FEEL IT MYSELF. LIKE THE HUNT, BUT WITH RICHER REWARDS.
YOU WILL BE RICH ONE DAY, APELLA, BEYOND YOUR DREAMS.
THE *LEADER* OF A WHOLE WORLD. A *GOVERNOR*... IN THE KLINGON EMPIRE.

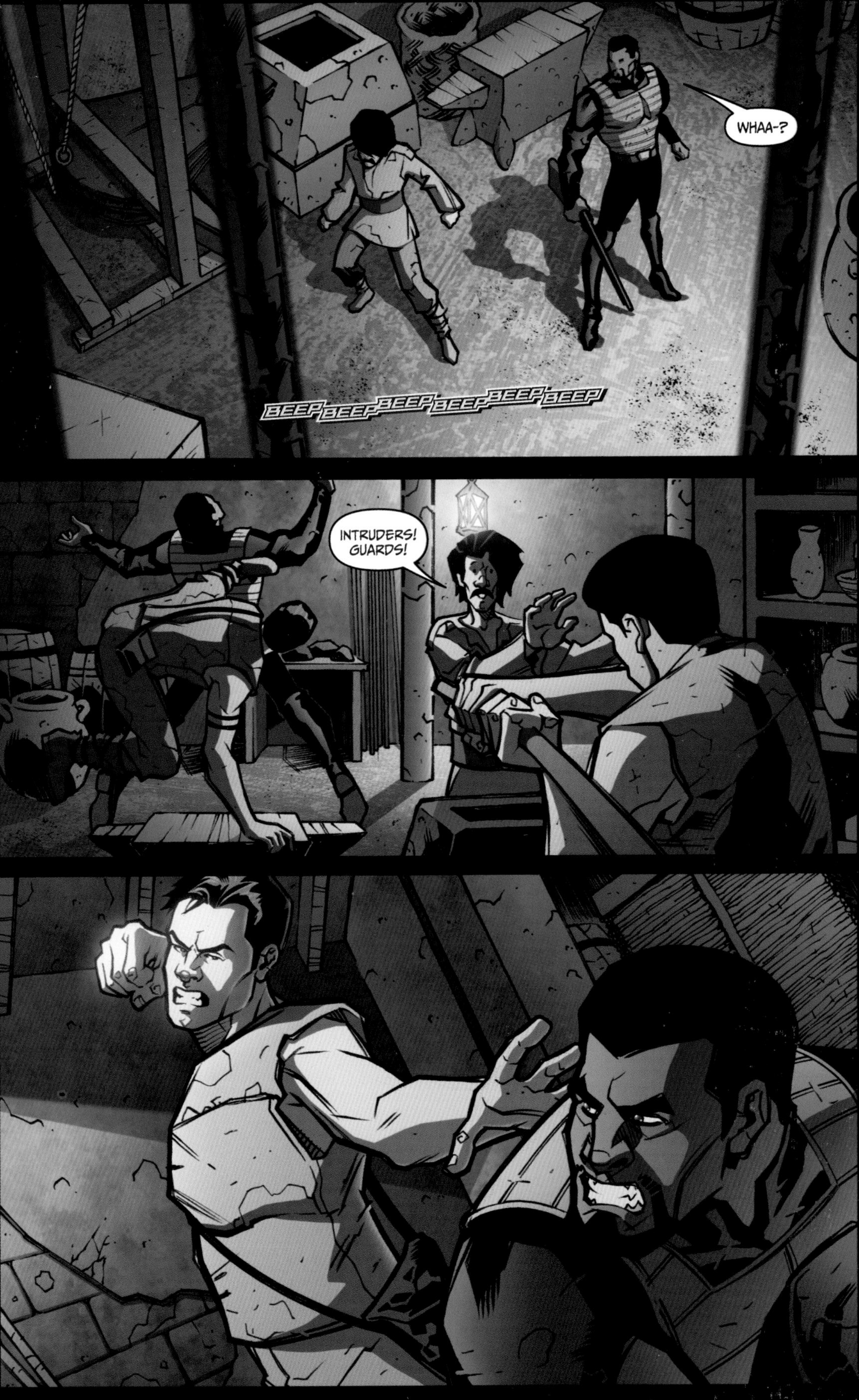
WHAA-?
BEEP BEEP BEEP BEEP BEEP BEEP
INTRUDERS! GUARDS!

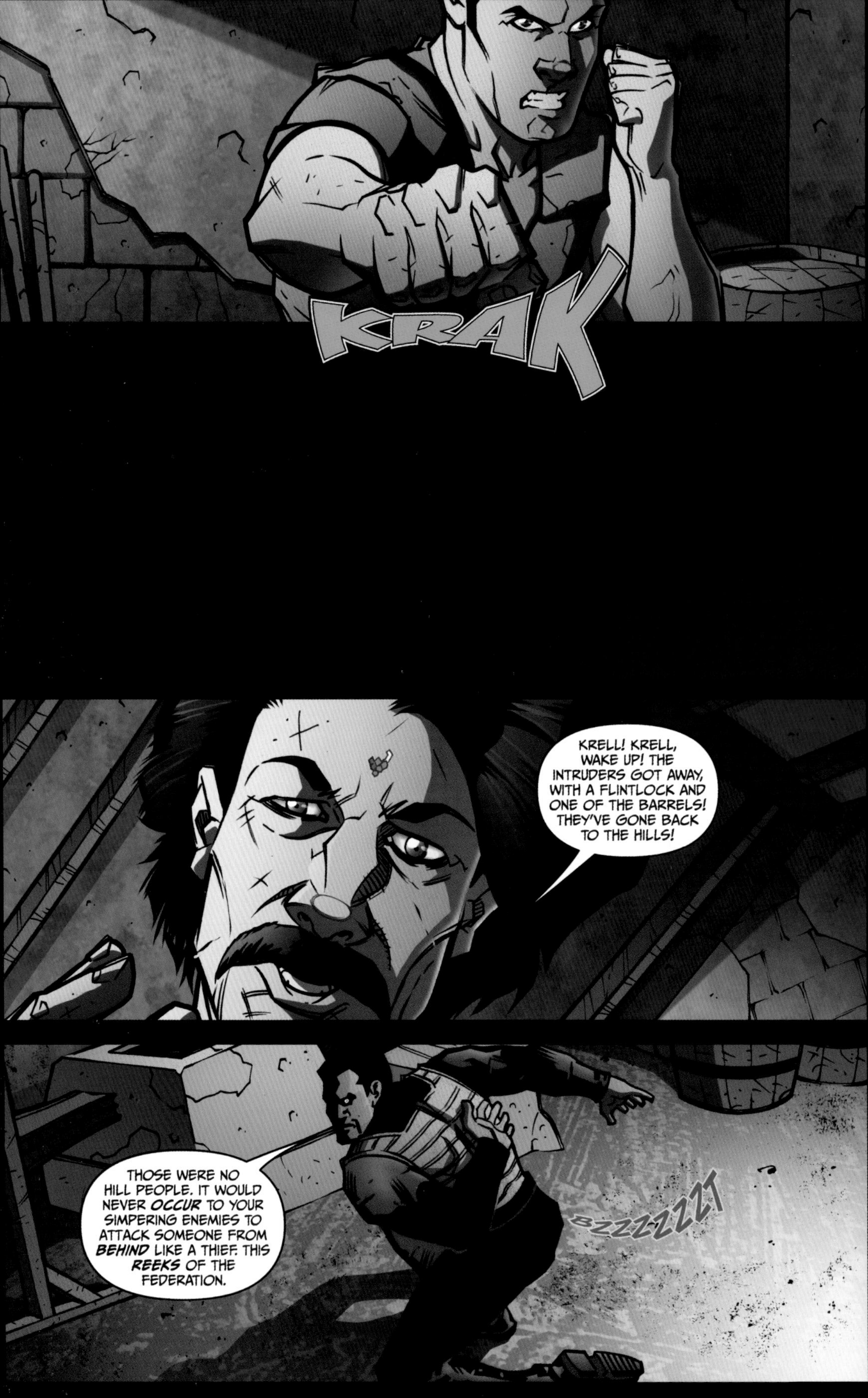
KRAK
KRELL! KRELL, WAKE UP! THE INTRUDERS GOT AWAY, WITH A FLINTLOCK AND ONE OF THE BARRELS! THEY'VE GONE BACK TO THE HILLS!
THOSE WERE NO HILL PEOPLE. IT WOULD NEVER *OCCUR* TO YOUR SIMPERING ENEMIES TO ATTACK SOMEONE FROM *BEHIND* LIKE A THIEF. THIS *REEKS* OF THE FEDERATION.
BZZZZZZT

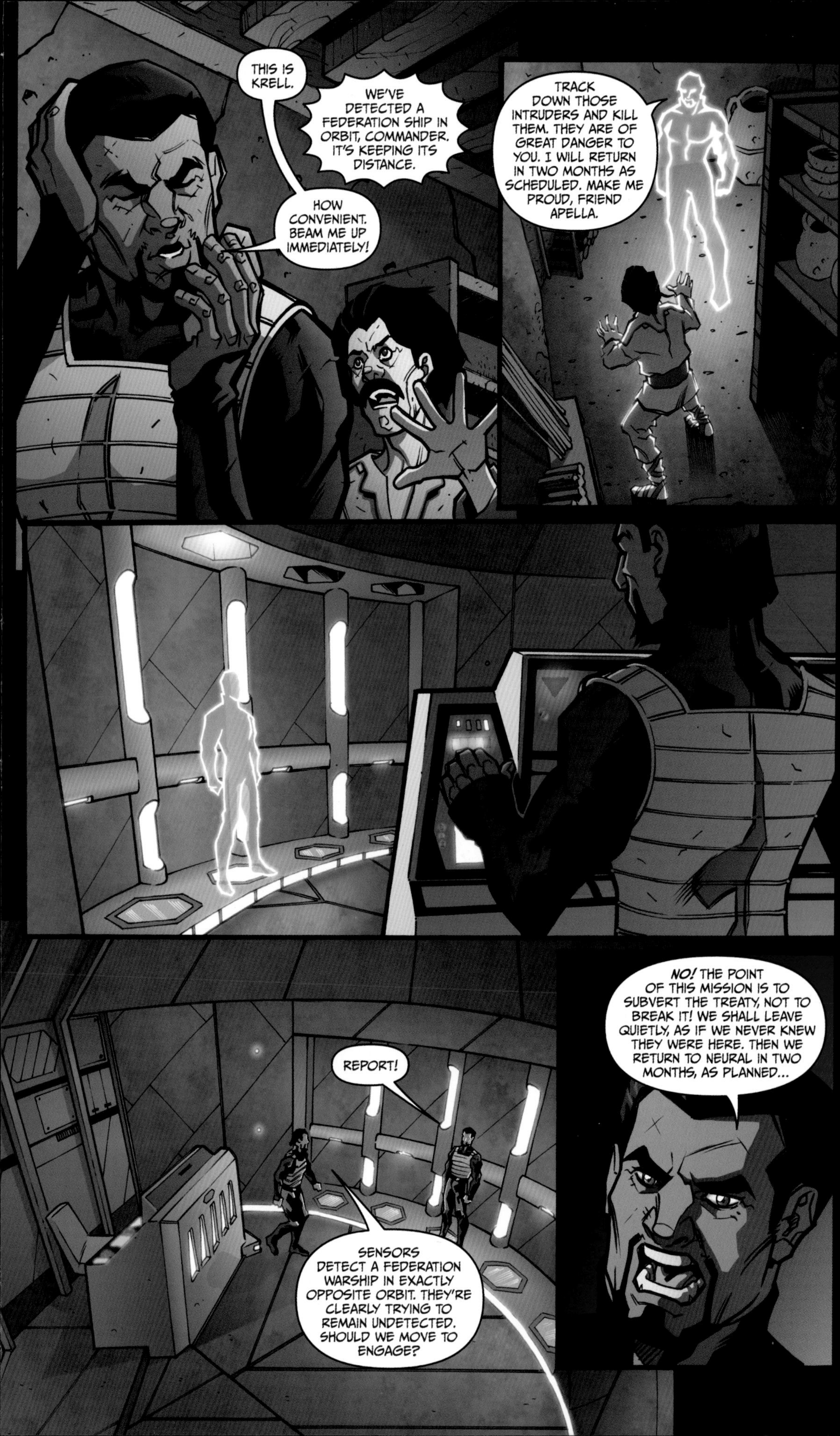
THIS IS KRELL.
WE'VE DETECTED A FEDERATION SHIP IN ORBIT, COMMANDER. IT'S KEEPING ITS DISTANCE.
HOW CONVENIENT. BEAM ME UP IMMEDIATELY!
TRACK DOWN THOSE INTRUDERS AND KILL THEM. THEY ARE OF GREAT DANGER TO YOU. I WILL RETURN IN TWO MONTHS AS SCHEDULED. MAKE ME PROUD, FRIEND APELLA.
REPORT!
SENSORS DETECT A FEDERATION WARSHIP IN EXACTLY OPPOSITE ORBIT. THEY'RE CLEARLY TRYING TO REMAIN UNDETECTED. SHOULD WE MOVE TO ENGAGE?
NO! THE POINT OF THIS MISSION IS TO SUBVERT THE TREATY, NOT TO BREAK IT! WE SHALL LEAVE QUIETLY, AS IF WE NEVER KNEW THEY WERE HERE. THEN WE RETURN TO NEURAL IN TWO MONTHS, AS PLANNED...

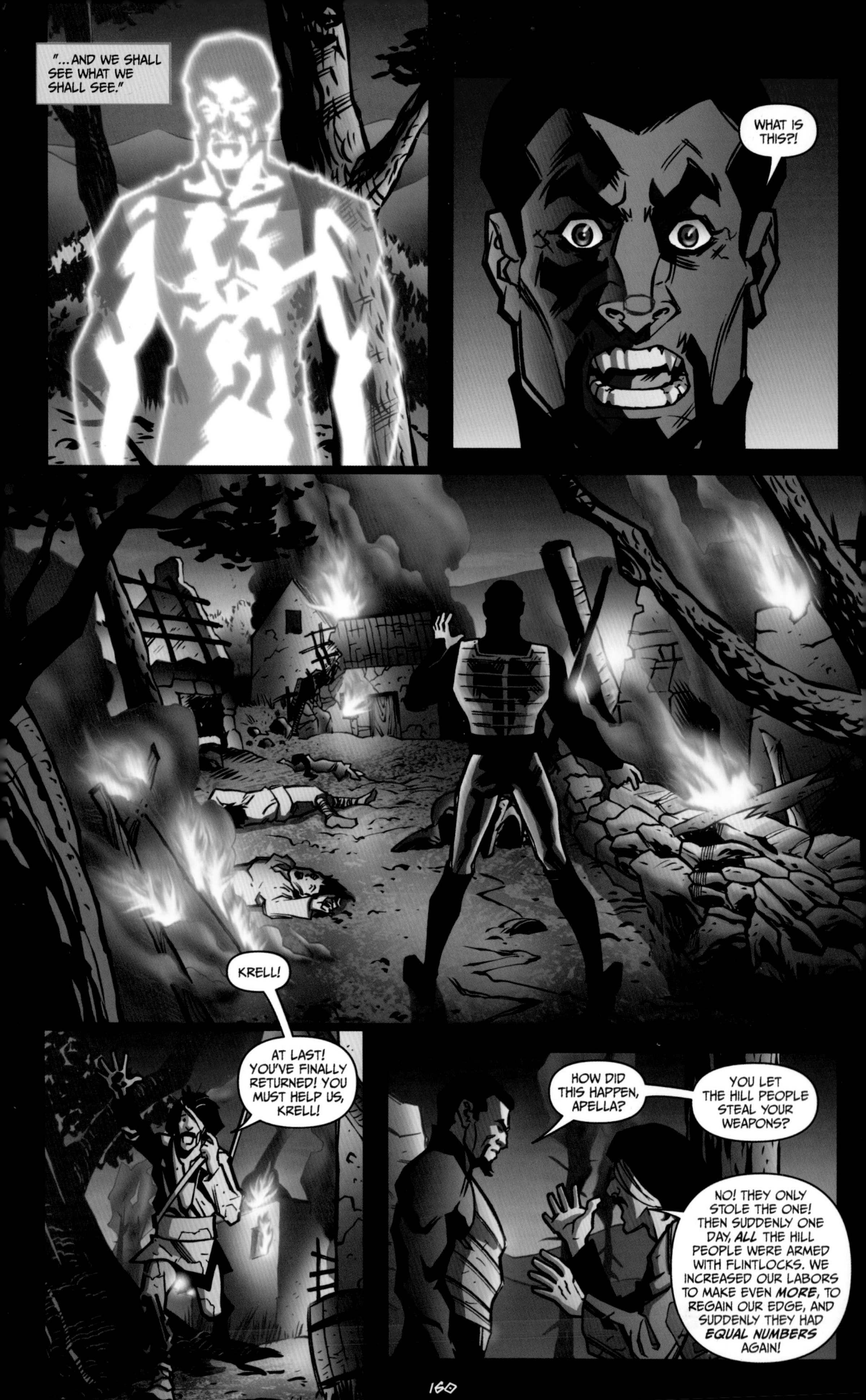
"...AND WE SHALL SEE WHAT WE SHALL SEE."
WHAT IS THIS?!
KRELL!
AT LAST! YOU'VE FINALLY RETURNED! YOU MUST HELP US, KRELL!
HOW DID THIS HAPPEN, APELLA?
YOU LET THE HILL PEOPLE STEAL YOUR WEAPONS?
NO! THEY ONLY STOLE THE ONE! THEN SUDDENLY ONE DAY, ***ALL*** THE HILL PEOPLE WERE ARMED WITH FLINTLOCKS. WE INCREASED OUR LABORS TO MAKE EVEN ***MORE***, TO REGAIN OUR EDGE, AND SUDDENLY THEY HAD ***EQUAL NUMBERS*** AGAIN!

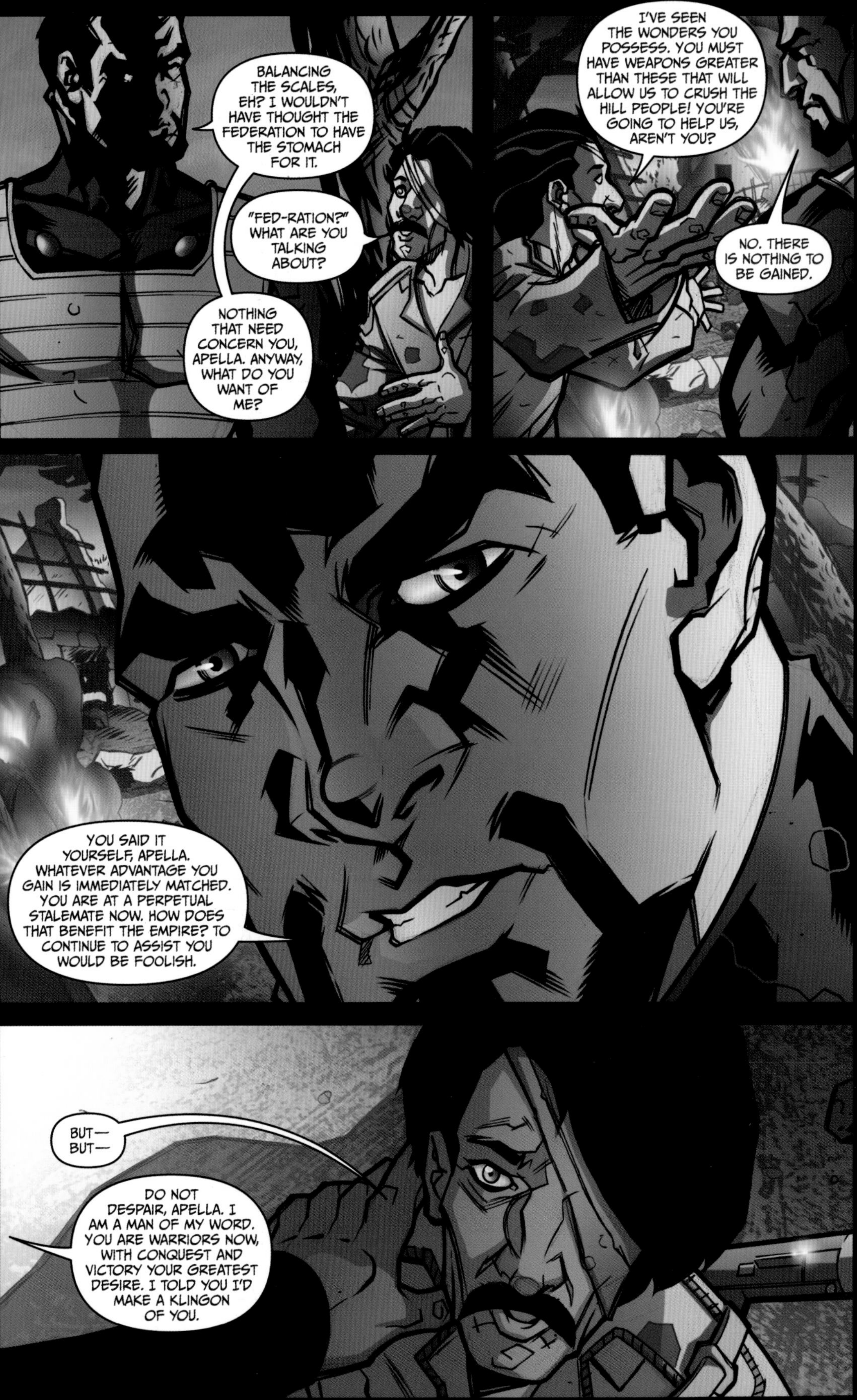
BALANCING THE SCALES, EH? I WOULDN'T HAVE THOUGHT THE FEDERATION TO HAVE THE STOMACH FOR IT.
"FED-RATION?" WHAT ARE YOU TALKING ABOUT?
NOTHING THAT NEED CONCERN YOU, APELLA. ANYWAY, WHAT DO YOU WANT OF ME?
I'VE SEEN THE WONDERS YOU POSSESS. YOU MUST HAVE WEAPONS GREATER THAN THESE THAT WILL ALLOW US TO CRUSH THE HILL PEOPLE! YOU'RE GOING TO HELP US, AREN'T YOU?
NO. THERE IS NOTHING TO BE GAINED.
YOU SAID IT YOURSELF, APELLA. WHATEVER ADVANTAGE YOU GAIN IS IMMEDIATELY MATCHED. YOU ARE AT A PERPETUAL STALEMATE NOW. HOW DOES THAT BENEFIT THE EMPIRE? TO CONTINUE TO ASSIST YOU WOULD BE FOOLISH.
BUT— BUT—
DO NOT DESPAIR, APELLA. I AM A MAN OF MY WORD. YOU ARE WARRIORS NOW, WITH CONQUEST AND VICTORY YOUR GREATEST DESIRE. I TOLD YOU I'D MAKE A KLINGON OF YOU.

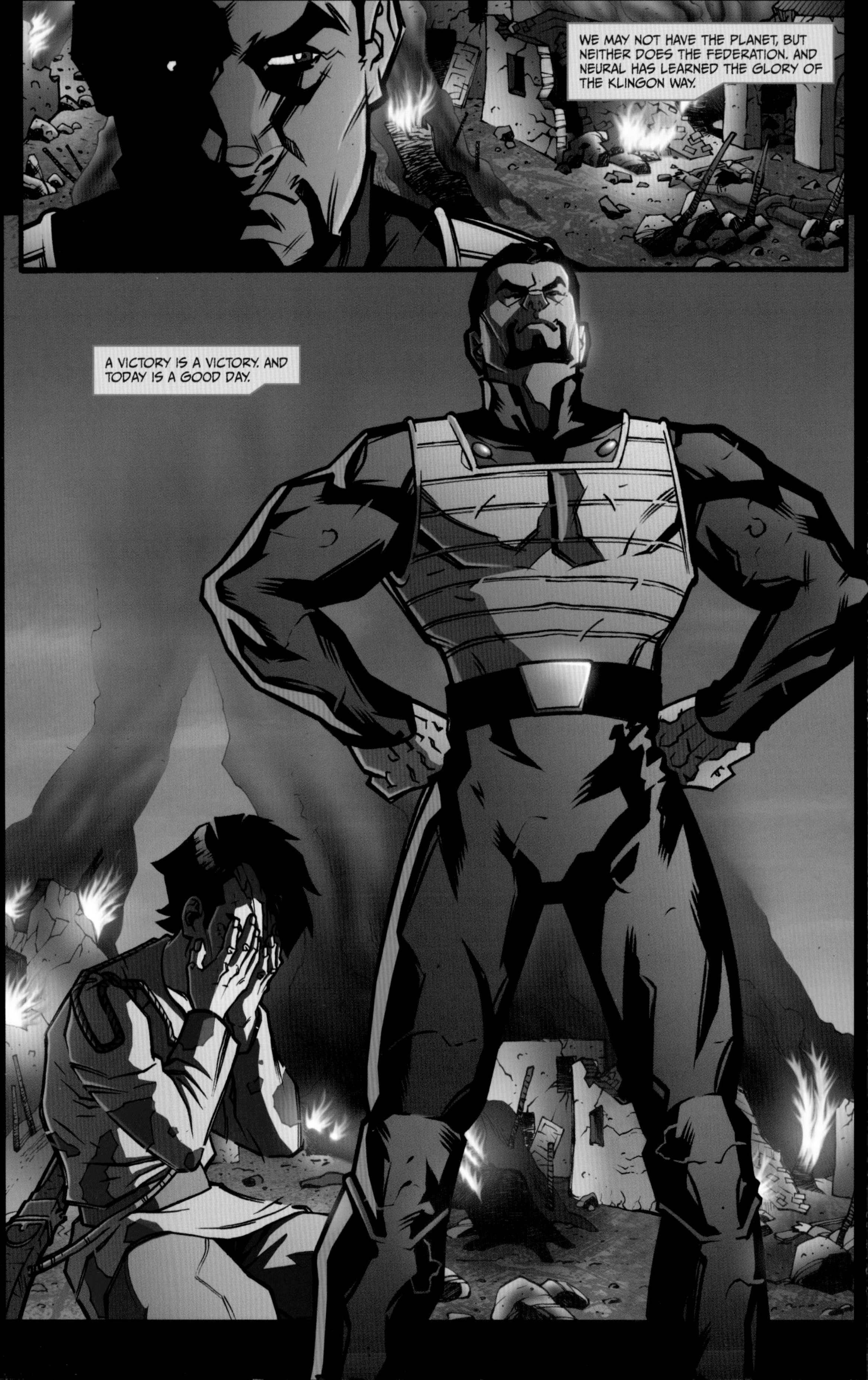
WE MAY NOT HAVE THE PLANET, BUT NEITHER DOES THE FEDERATION. AND NEURAL HAS LEARNED THE GLORY OF THE KLINGON WAY.
A VICTORY IS A VICTORY. AND TODAY IS A GOOD DAY.

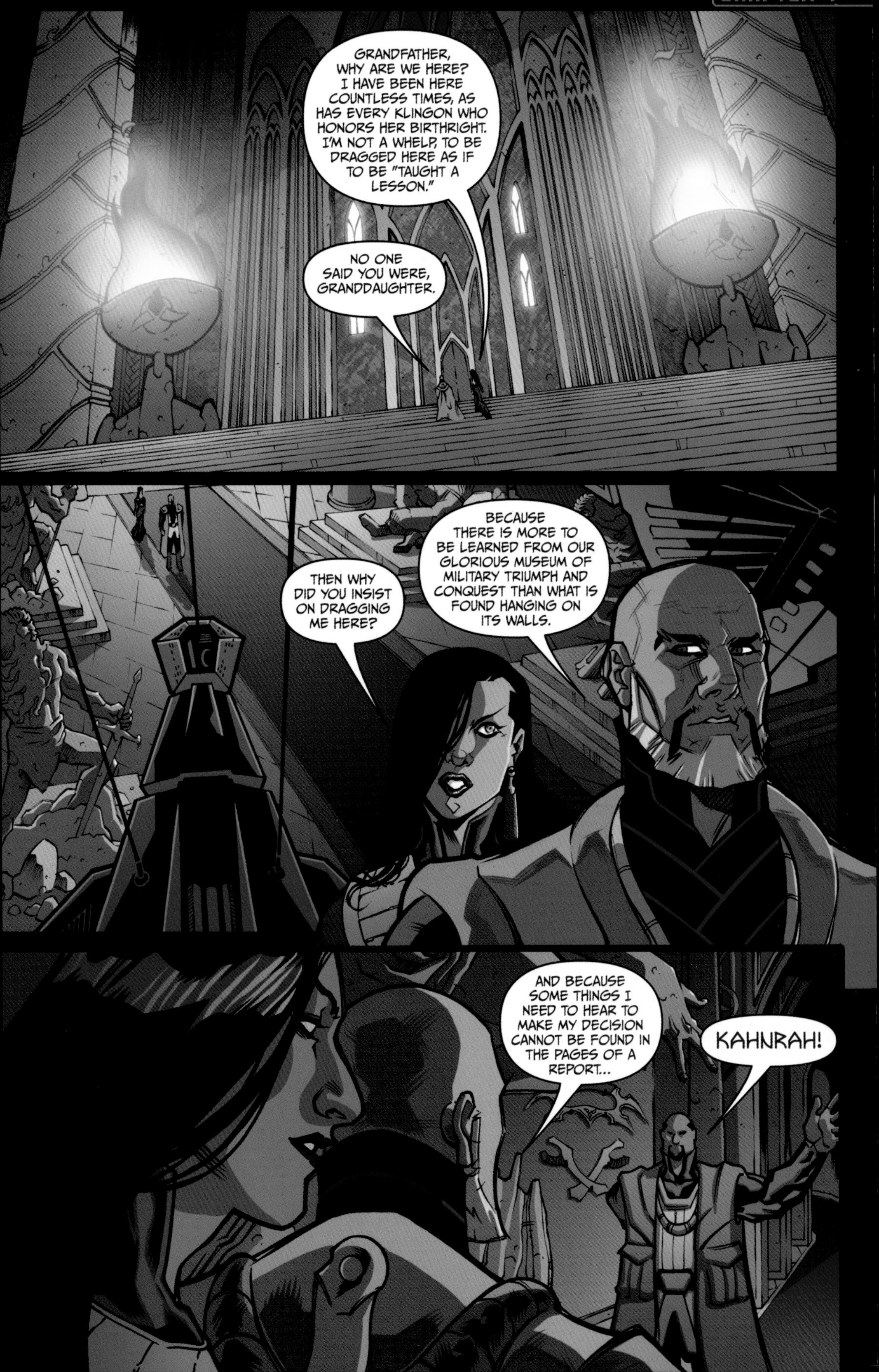
GRANDFATHER, WHY ARE WE HERE? I HAVE BEEN HERE COUNTLESS TIMES, AS HAS EVERY KLINGON WHO HONORS HER BIRTHRIGHT. I'M NOT A WHELP, TO BE DRAGGED HERE AS IF TO BE "TAUGHT A LESSON."
NO ONE SAID YOU WERE, GRANDDAUGHTER.
THEN WHY DID YOU INSIST ON DRAGGING ME HERE?
BECAUSE THERE IS MORE TO BE LEARNED FROM OUR GLORIOUS MUSEUM OF MILITARY TRIUMPH AND CONQUEST THAN WHAT IS FOUND HANGING ON ITS WALLS.
AND BECAUSE SOME THINGS I NEED TO HEAR TO MAKE MY DECISION CANNOT BE FOUND IN THE PAGES OF A REPORT...
KAHNRAH!

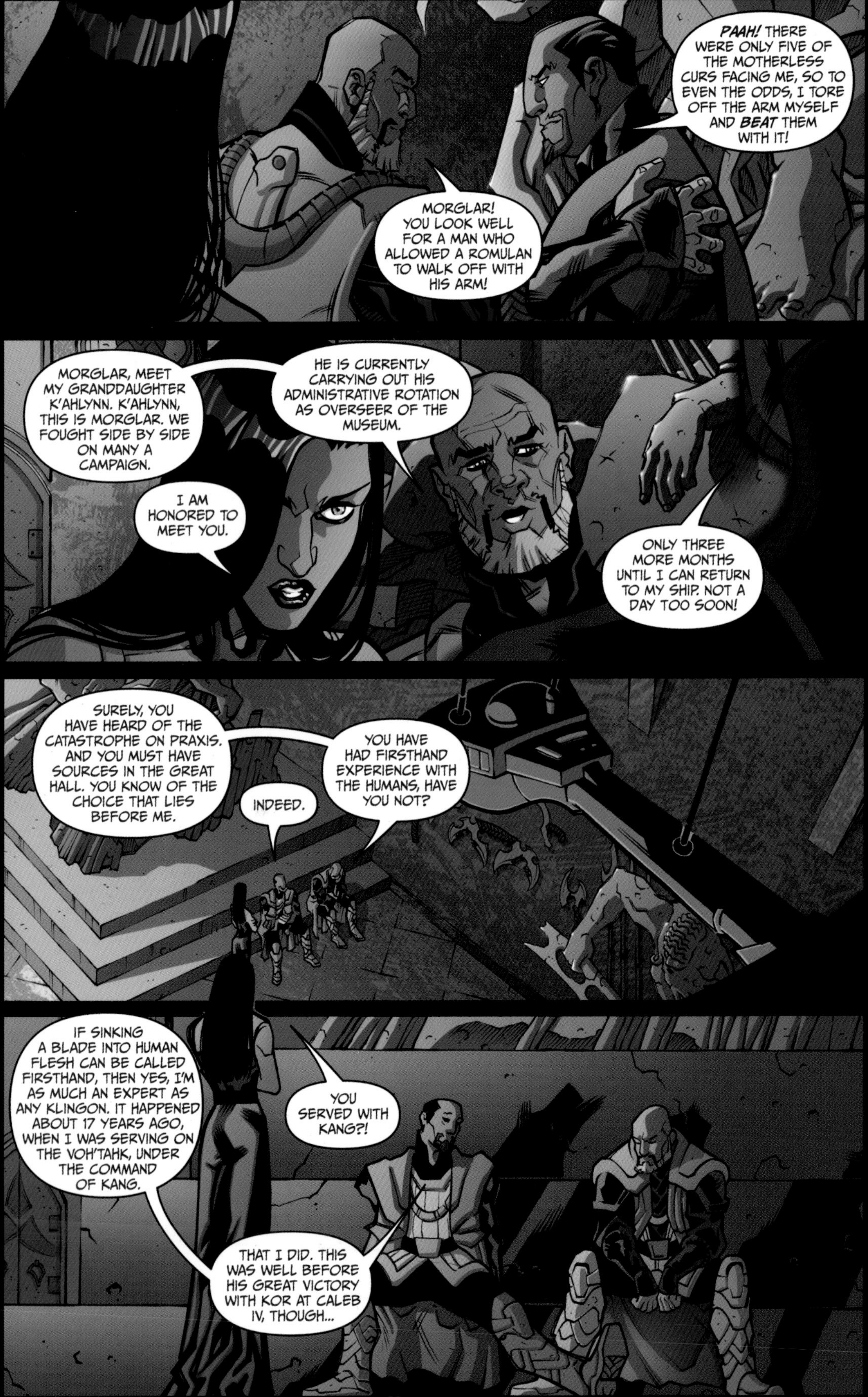
PAAH! THERE WERE ONLY FIVE OF THE MOTHERLESS CURS FACING ME, SO TO EVEN THE ODDS, I TORE OFF THE ARM MYSELF AND BEAT THEM WITH IT!
MORGLAR! YOU LOOK WELL FOR A MAN WHO ALLOWED A ROMULAN TO WALK OFF WITH HIS ARM!
MORGLAR, MEET MY GRANDDAUGHTER K'AHLYNN. K'AHLYNN, THIS IS MORGLAR. WE FOUGHT SIDE BY SIDE ON MANY A CAMPAIGN.
HE IS CURRENTLY CARRYING OUT HIS ADMINISTRATIVE ROTATION AS OVERSEER OF THE MUSEUM.
I AM HONORED TO MEET YOU.
ONLY THREE MORE MONTHS UNTIL I CAN RETURN TO MY SHIP. NOT A DAY TOO SOON!
SURELY, YOU HAVE HEARD OF THE CATASTROPHE ON PRAXIS. AND YOU MUST HAVE SOURCES IN THE GREAT HALL. YOU KNOW OF THE CHOICE THAT LIES BEFORE ME.
INDEED.
YOU HAVE HAD FIRSTHAND EXPERIENCE WITH THE HUMANS, HAVE YOU NOT?
IF SINKING A BLADE INTO HUMAN FLESH CAN BE CALLED FIRSTHAND, THEN YES, I'M AS MUCH AN EXPERT AS ANY KLINGON. IT HAPPENED ABOUT 17 YEARS AGO, WHEN I WAS SERVING ON THE VOH'TAHK, UNDER THE COMMAND OF KANG.
YOU SERVED WITH KANG?!
THAT I DID. THIS WAS WELL BEFORE HIS GREAT VICTORY WITH KOR AT CALEB IV, THOUGH...

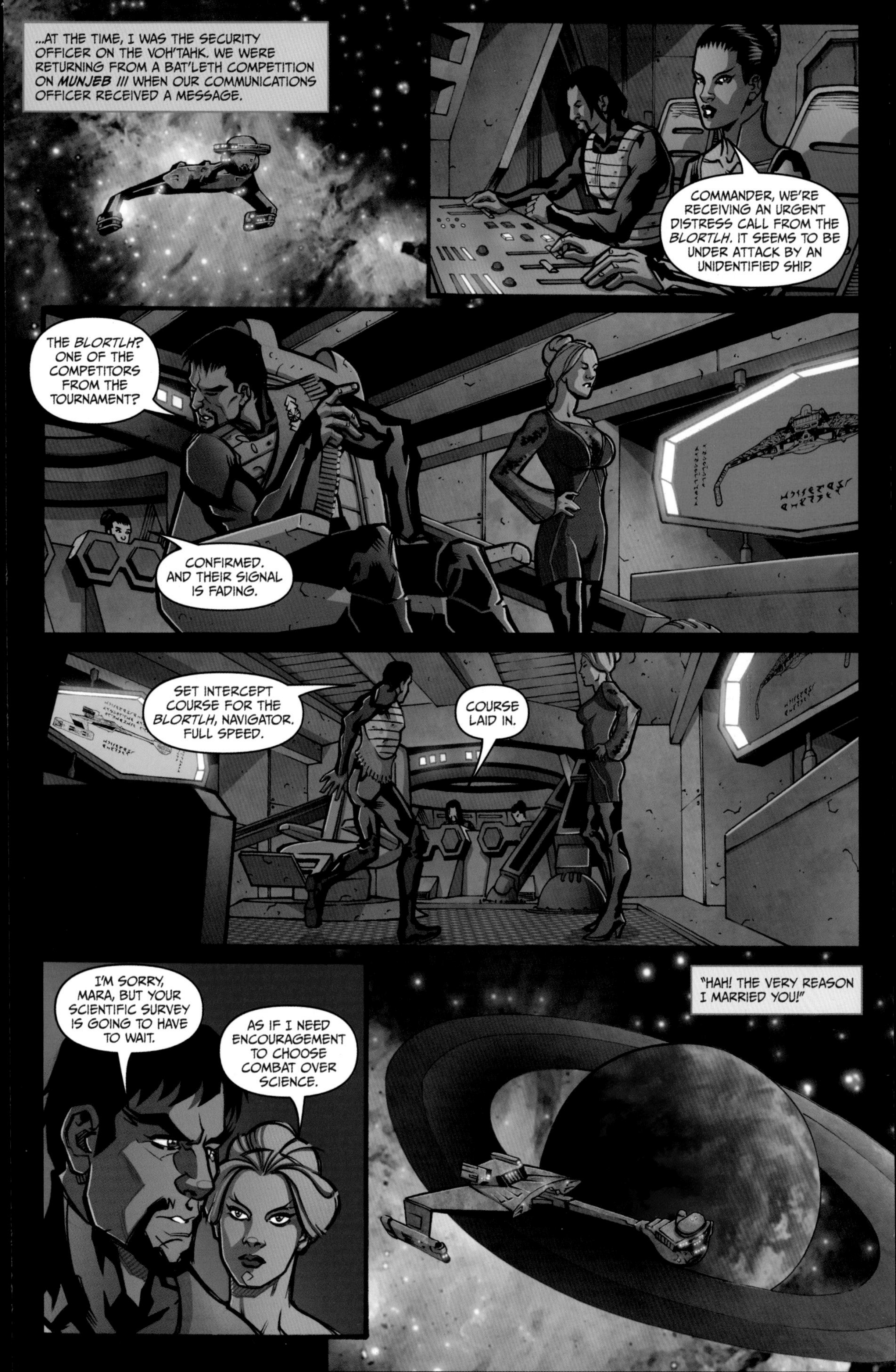

...AT THE TIME, I WAS THE SECURITY OFFICER ON THE VOH'TAHK. WE WERE RETURNING FROM A BAT'LETH COMPETITION ON *MUNJEB III* WHEN OUR COMMUNICATIONS OFFICER RECEIVED A MESSAGE.
COMMANDER, WE'RE RECEIVING AN URGENT DISTRESS CALL FROM THE *BLORTLH*. IT SEEMS TO BE UNDER ATTACK BY AN UNIDENTIFIED SHIP.
THE *BLORTLH*? ONE OF THE COMPETITORS FROM THE TOURNAMENT?
CONFIRMED. AND THEIR SIGNAL IS FADING.
SET INTERCEPT COURSE FOR THE *BLORTLH*, NAVIGATOR. FULL SPEED.
COURSE LAID IN.
I'M SORRY, MARA, BUT YOUR SCIENTIFIC SURVEY IS GOING TO HAVE TO WAIT.
AS IF I NEED ENCOURAGEMENT TO CHOOSE COMBAT OVER SCIENCE.
"HAH! THE VERY REASON I MARRIED YOU!"

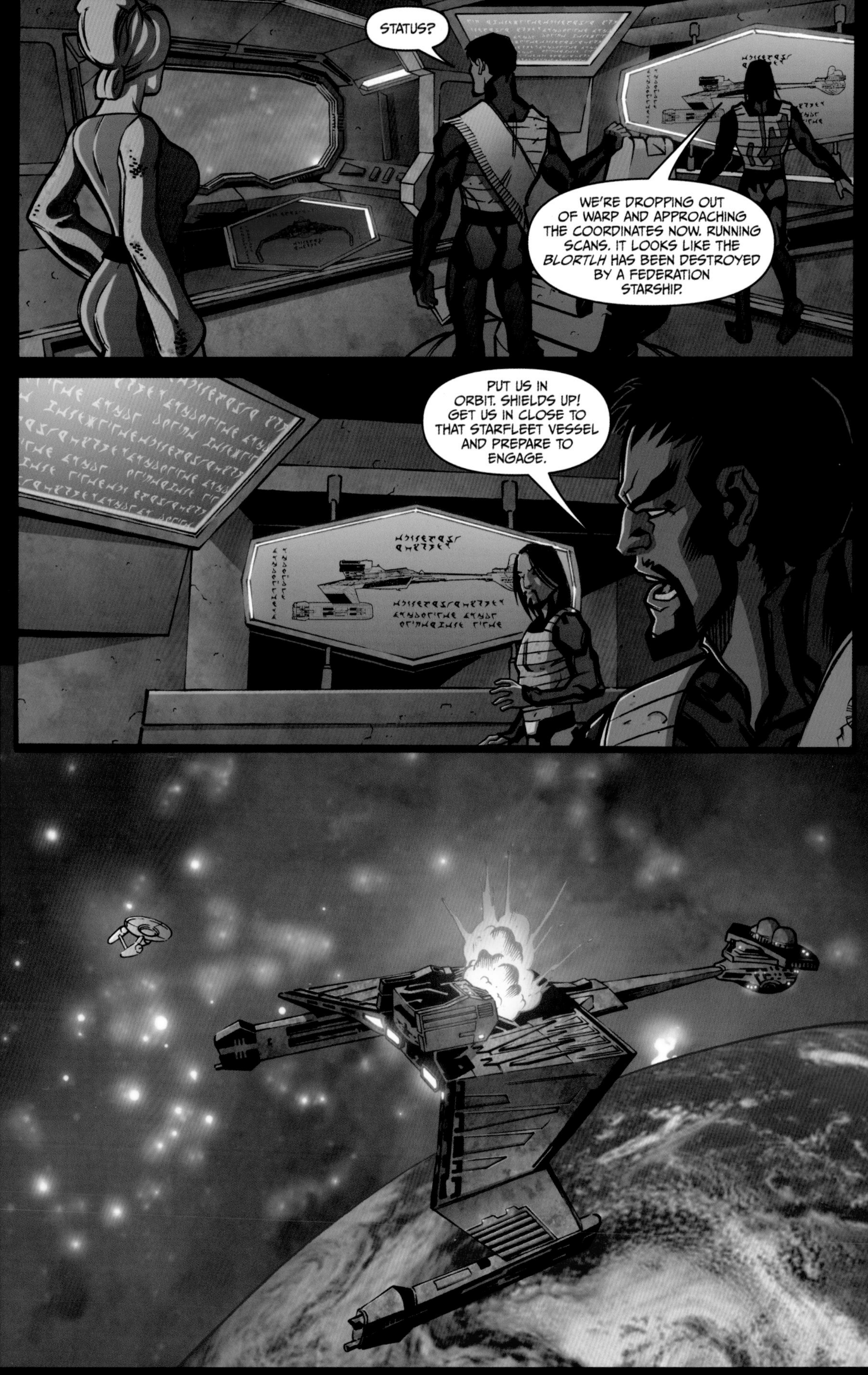
STATUS?
WE'RE DROPPING OUT OF WARP AND APPROACHING THE COORDINATES NOW. RUNNING SCANS. IT LOOKS LIKE THE *BLORTLH* HAS BEEN DESTROYED BY A FEDERATION STARSHIP.
PUT US IN ORBIT. SHIELDS UP! GET US IN CLOSE TO THAT STARFLEET VESSEL AND PREPARE TO ENGAGE.

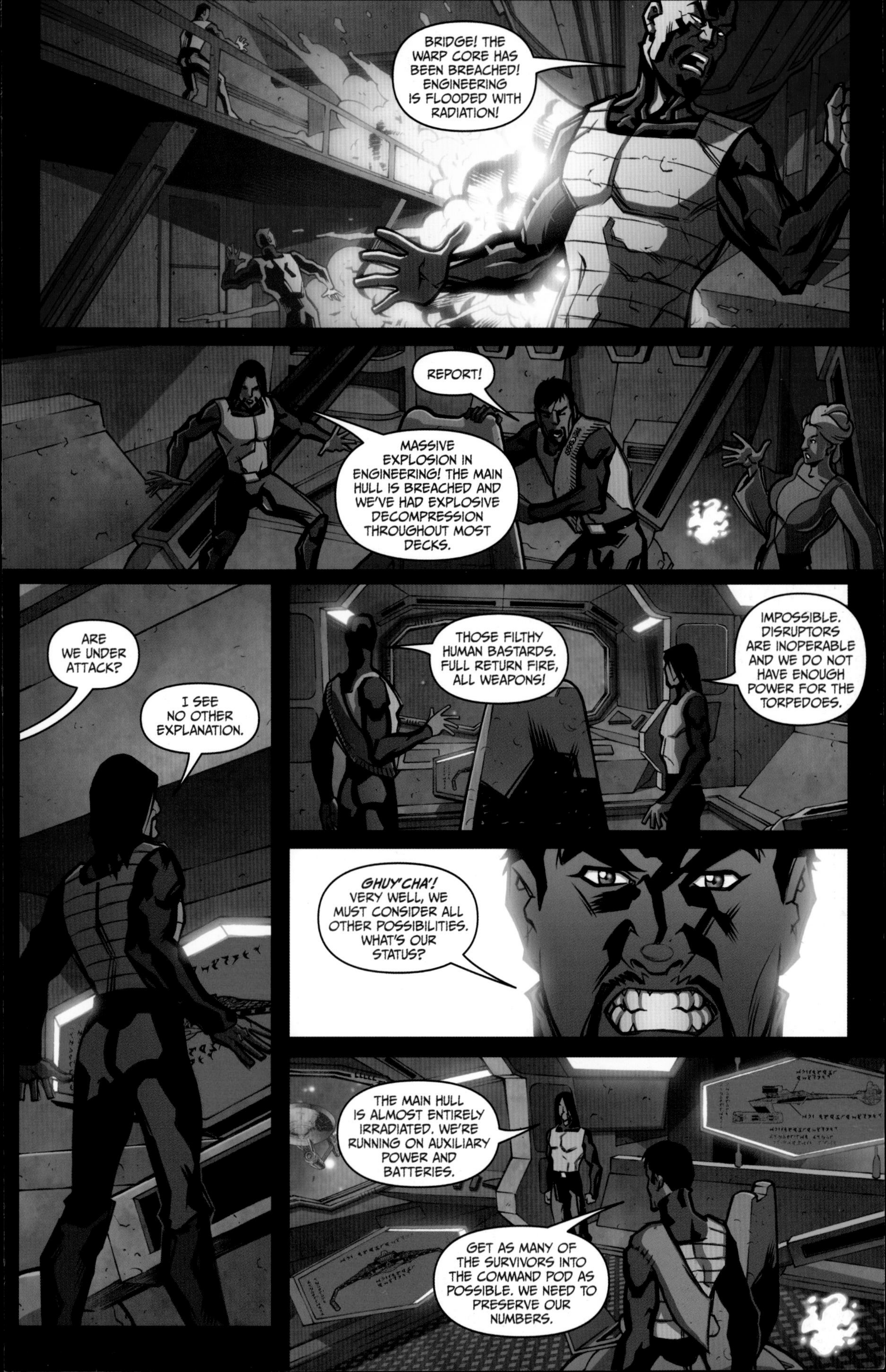
BRIDGE! THE WARP CORE HAS BEEN BREACHED! ENGINEERING IS FLOODED WITH RADIATION!
REPORT!
MASSIVE EXPLOSION IN ENGINEERING! THE MAIN HULL IS BREACHED AND WE'VE HAD EXPLOSIVE DECOMPRESSION THROUGHOUT MOST DECKS.
ARE WE UNDER ATTACK?
I SEE NO OTHER EXPLANATION.
THOSE FILTHY HUMAN BASTARDS. FULL RETURN FIRE, ALL WEAPONS!
IMPOSSIBLE. DISRUPTORS ARE INOPERABLE AND WE DO NOT HAVE ENOUGH POWER FOR THE TORPEDOES.
GHUY'CHA'! VERY WELL, WE MUST CONSIDER ALL OTHER POSSIBILITIES. WHAT'S OUR STATUS?
THE MAIN HULL IS ALMOST ENTIRELY IRRADIATED. WE'RE RUNNING ON AUXILIARY POWER AND BATTERIES.
GET AS MANY OF THE SURVIVORS INTO THE COMMAND POD AS POSSIBLE. WE NEED TO PRESERVE OUR NUMBERS.

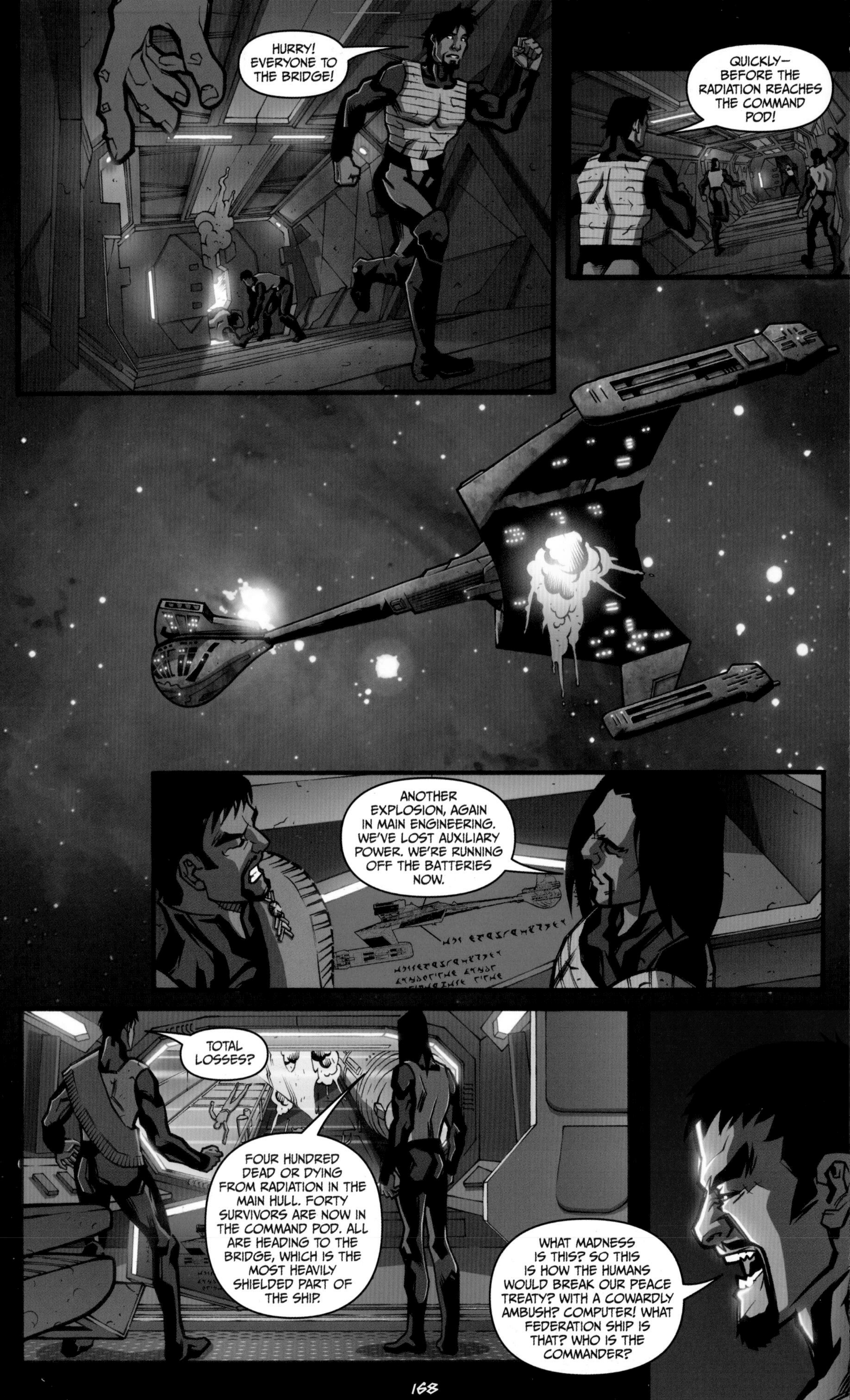
HURRY! EVERYONE TO THE BRIDGE!
QUICKLY— BEFORE THE RADIATION REACHES THE COMMAND POD!
ANOTHER EXPLOSION, AGAIN IN MAIN ENGINEERING. WE'VE LOST AUXILIARY POWER. WE'RE RUNNING OFF THE BATTERIES NOW.
TOTAL LOSSES?
FOUR HUNDRED DEAD OR DYING FROM RADIATION IN THE MAIN HULL. FORTY SURVIVORS ARE NOW IN THE COMMAND POD. ALL ARE HEADING TO THE BRIDGE, WHICH IS THE MOST HEAVILY SHIELDED PART OF THE SHIP.
WHAT MADNESS IS THIS? SO THIS IS HOW THE HUMANS WOULD BREAK OUR PEACE TREATY? WITH A COWARDLY AMBUSH? COMPUTER! WHAT FEDERATION SHIP IS THAT? WHO IS THE COMMANDER?

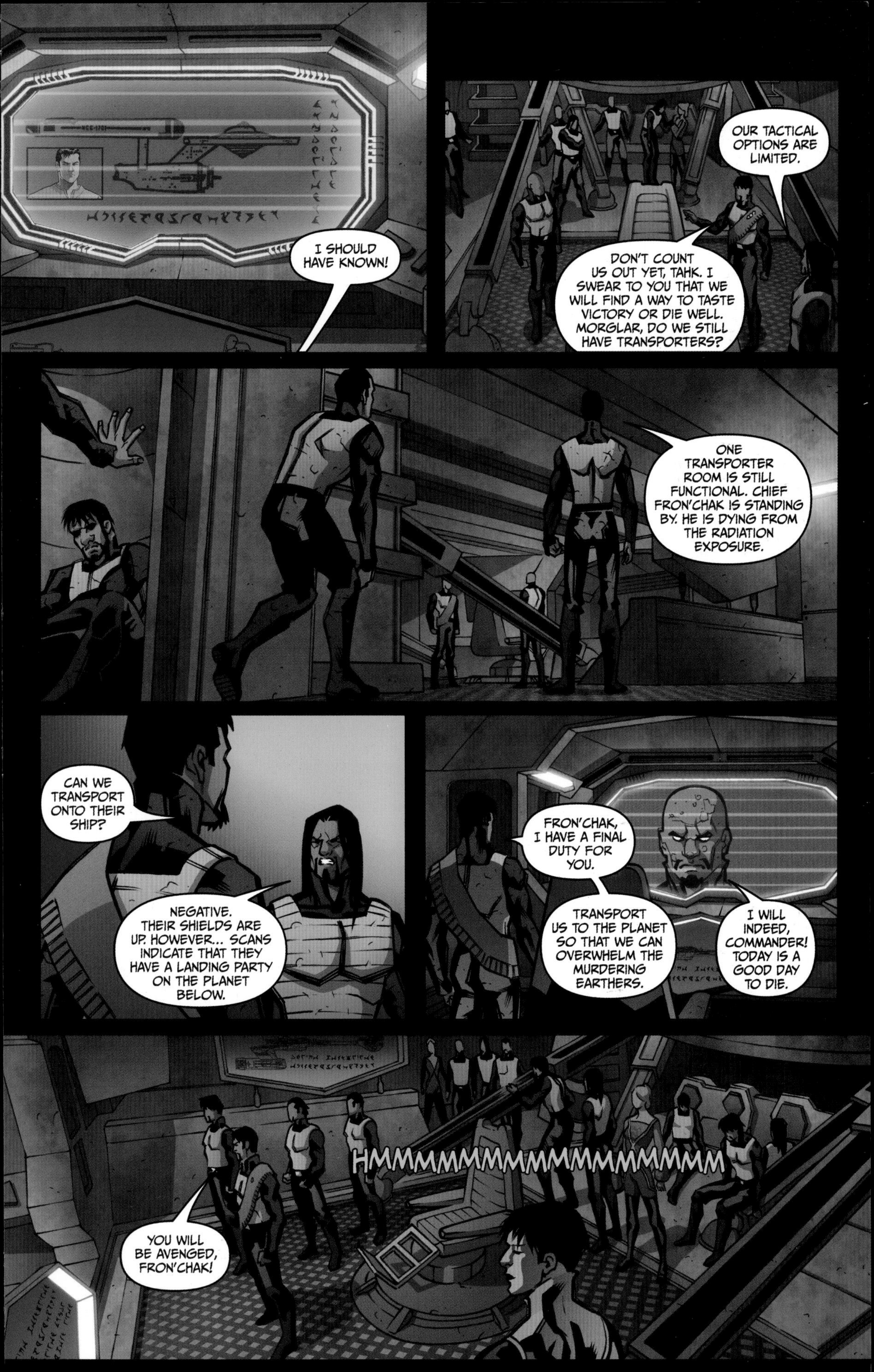
I SHOULD HAVE KNOWN!
OUR TACTICAL OPTIONS ARE LIMITED.
DON'T COUNT US OUT YET, TAHK. I SWEAR TO YOU THAT WE WILL FIND A WAY TO TASTE VICTORY OR DIE WELL. MORGLAR, DO WE STILL HAVE TRANSPORTERS?
ONE TRANSPORTER ROOM IS STILL FUNCTIONAL. CHIEF FRON'CHAK IS STANDING BY. HE IS DYING FROM THE RADIATION EXPOSURE.
CAN WE TRANSPORT ONTO THEIR SHIP?
NEGATIVE. THEIR SHIELDS ARE UP. HOWEVER... SCANS INDICATE THAT THEY HAVE A LANDING PARTY ON THE PLANET BELOW.
FRON'CHAK, I HAVE A FINAL DUTY FOR YOU.
TRANSPORT US TO THE PLANET SO THAT WE CAN OVERWHELM THE MURDERING EARTHERS.
I WILL INDEED, COMMANDER! TODAY IS A GOOD DAY TO DIE.
HMMMMMMMMMMMMMMMMMM
YOU WILL BE AVENGED, FRON'CHAK!

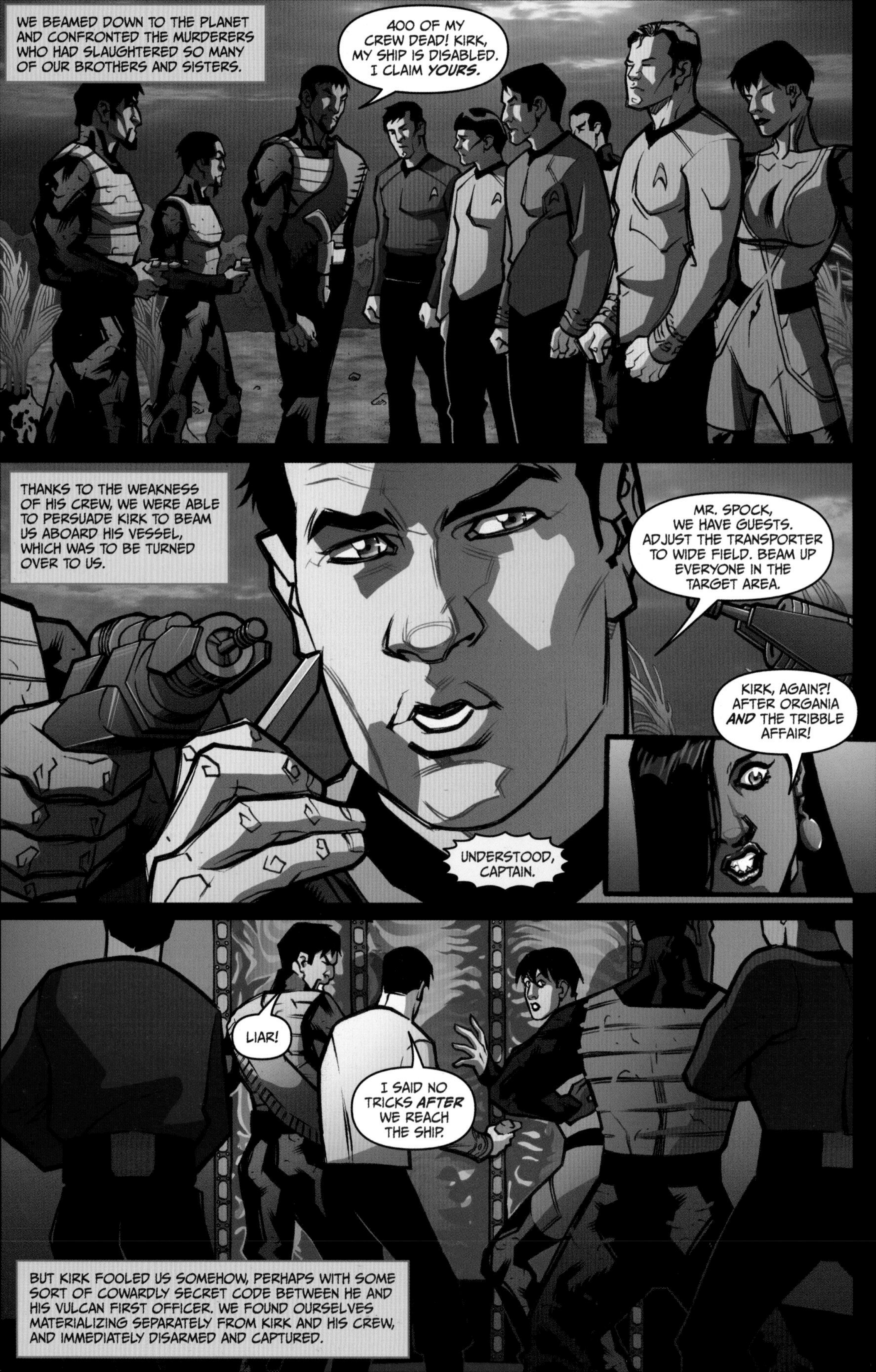
WE BEAMED DOWN TO THE PLANET AND CONFRONTED THE MURDERERS WHO HAD SLAUGHTERED SO MANY OF OUR BROTHERS AND SISTERS.
400 OF MY CREW DEAD! KIRK, MY SHIP IS DISABLED. I CLAIM *YOURS.*
THANKS TO THE WEAKNESS OF HIS CREW, WE WERE ABLE TO PERSUADE KIRK TO BEAM US ABOARD HIS VESSEL, WHICH WAS TO BE TURNED OVER TO US.
MR. SPOCK, WE HAVE GUESTS. ADJUST THE TRANSPORTER TO WIDE FIELD. BEAM UP EVERYONE IN THE TARGET AREA.
KIRK, AGAIN?! AFTER ORGANIA ***AND*** THE TRIBBLE AFFAIR!
UNDERSTOOD, CAPTAIN.
LIAR!
I SAID NO TRICKS ***AFTER*** WE REACH THE SHIP.
BUT KIRK FOOLED US SOMEHOW, PERHAPS WITH SOME SORT OF COWARDLY SECRET CODE BETWEEN HE AND HIS VULCAN FIRST OFFICER. WE FOUND OURSELVES MATERIALIZING SEPARATELY FROM KIRK AND HIS CREW, AND IMMEDIATELY DISARMED AND CAPTURED.

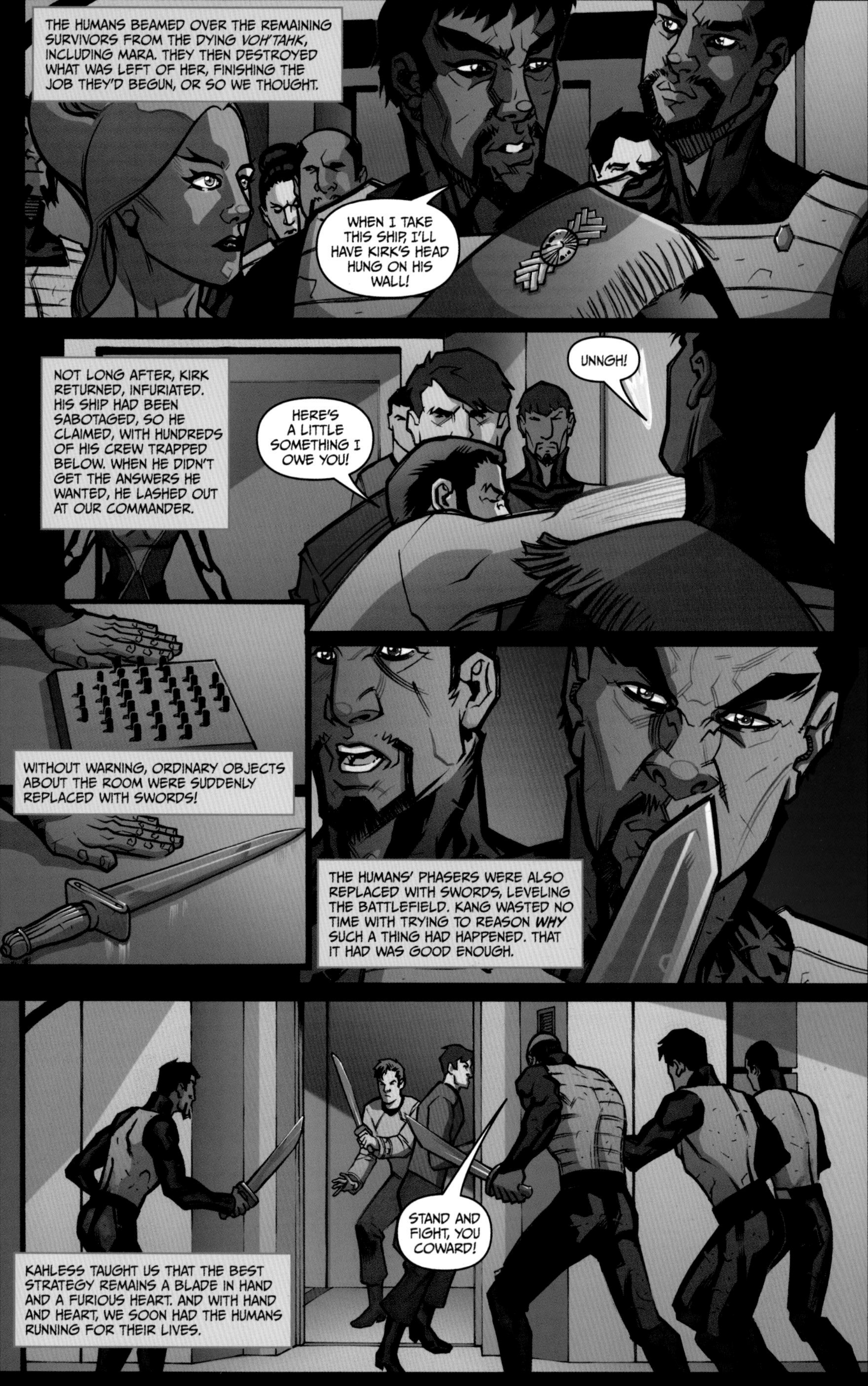
THE HUMANS BEAMED OVER THE REMAINING SURVIVORS FROM THE DYING *VOH'TAHK*, INCLUDING MARA. THEY THEN DESTROYED WHAT WAS LEFT OF HER, FINISHING THE JOB THEY'D BEGUN, OR SO WE THOUGHT.
WHEN I TAKE THIS SHIP, I'LL HAVE KIRK'S HEAD HUNG ON HIS WALL!
NOT LONG AFTER, KIRK RETURNED, INFURIATED. HIS SHIP HAD BEEN SABOTAGED, SO HE CLAIMED, WITH HUNDREDS OF HIS CREW TRAPPED BELOW. WHEN HE DIDN'T GET THE ANSWERS HE WANTED, HE LASHED OUT AT OUR COMMANDER.
HERE'S A LITTLE SOMETHING I OWE YOU!
UNNGH!
WITHOUT WARNING, ORDINARY OBJECTS ABOUT THE ROOM WERE SUDDENLY REPLACED WITH SWORDS!
THE HUMANS' PHASERS WERE ALSO REPLACED WITH SWORDS, LEVELING THE BATTLEFIELD. KANG WASTED NO TIME WITH TRYING TO REASON ***WHY*** SUCH A THING HAD HAPPENED. THAT IT HAD WAS GOOD ENOUGH.
KAHLESS TAUGHT US THAT THE BEST STRATEGY REMAINS A BLADE IN HAND AND A FURIOUS HEART. AND WITH HAND AND HEART, WE SOON HAD THE HUMANS RUNNING FOR THEIR LIVES.
STAND AND FIGHT, YOU COWARD!

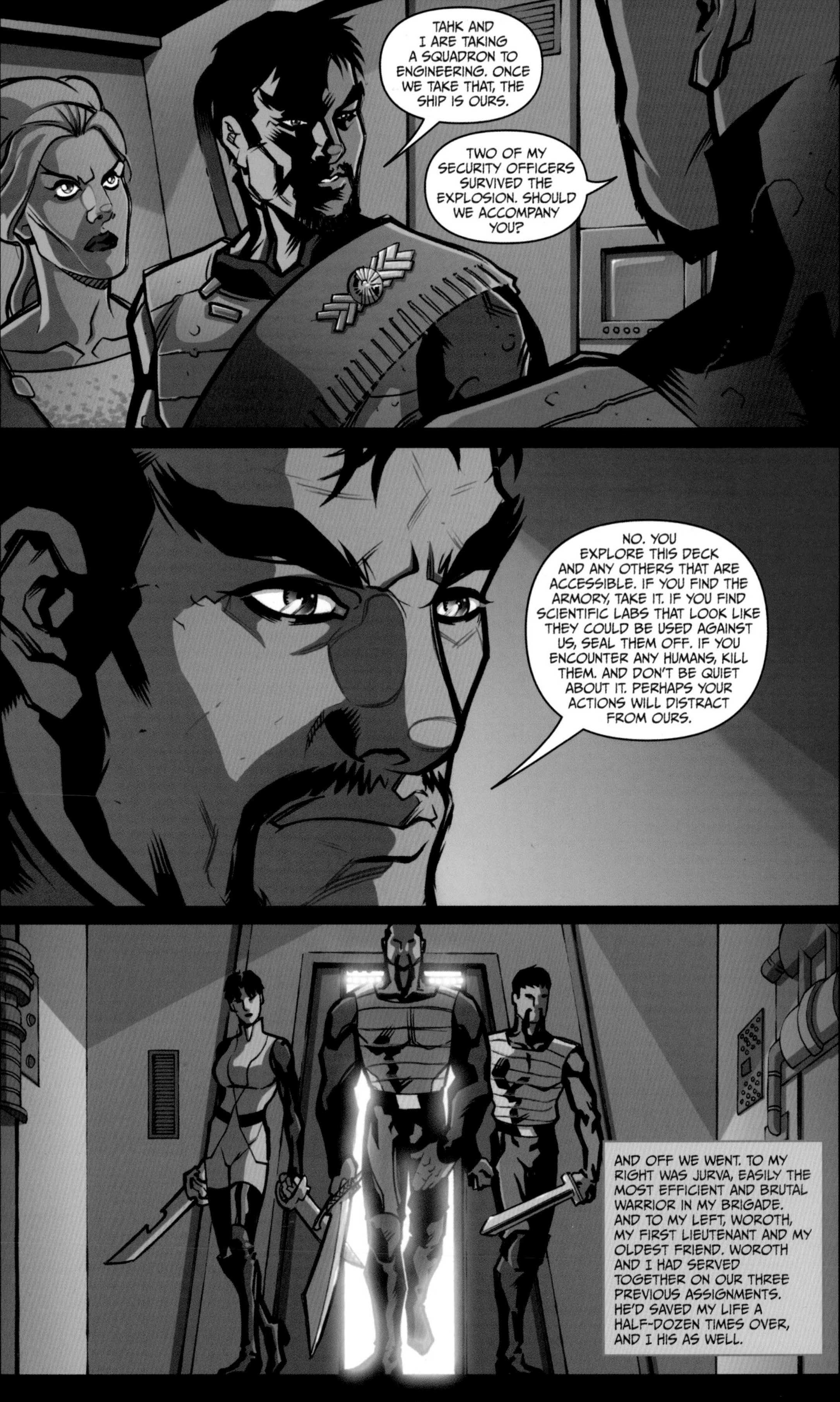
TAHK AND I ARE TAKING A SQUADRON TO ENGINEERING. ONCE WE TAKE THAT, THE SHIP IS OURS.
TWO OF MY SECURITY OFFICERS SURVIVED THE EXPLOSION. SHOULD WE ACCOMPANY YOU?
NO. YOU EXPLORE THIS DECK AND ANY OTHERS THAT ARE ACCESSIBLE. IF YOU FIND THE ARMORY, TAKE IT. IF YOU FIND SCIENTIFIC LABS THAT LOOK LIKE THEY COULD BE USED AGAINST US, SEAL THEM OFF. IF YOU ENCOUNTER ANY HUMANS, KILL THEM. AND DON'T BE QUIET ABOUT IT. PERHAPS YOUR ACTIONS WILL DISTRACT FROM OURS.
AND OFF WE WENT. TO MY RIGHT WAS JURVA, EASILY THE MOST EFFICIENT AND BRUTAL WARRIOR IN MY BRIGADE. AND TO MY LEFT, WOROTH, MY FIRST LIEUTENANT AND MY OLDEST FRIEND. WOROTH AND I HAD SERVED TOGETHER ON OUR THREE PREVIOUS ASSIGNMENTS. HE'D SAVED MY LIFE A HALF-DOZEN TIMES OVER, AND I HIS AS WELL.

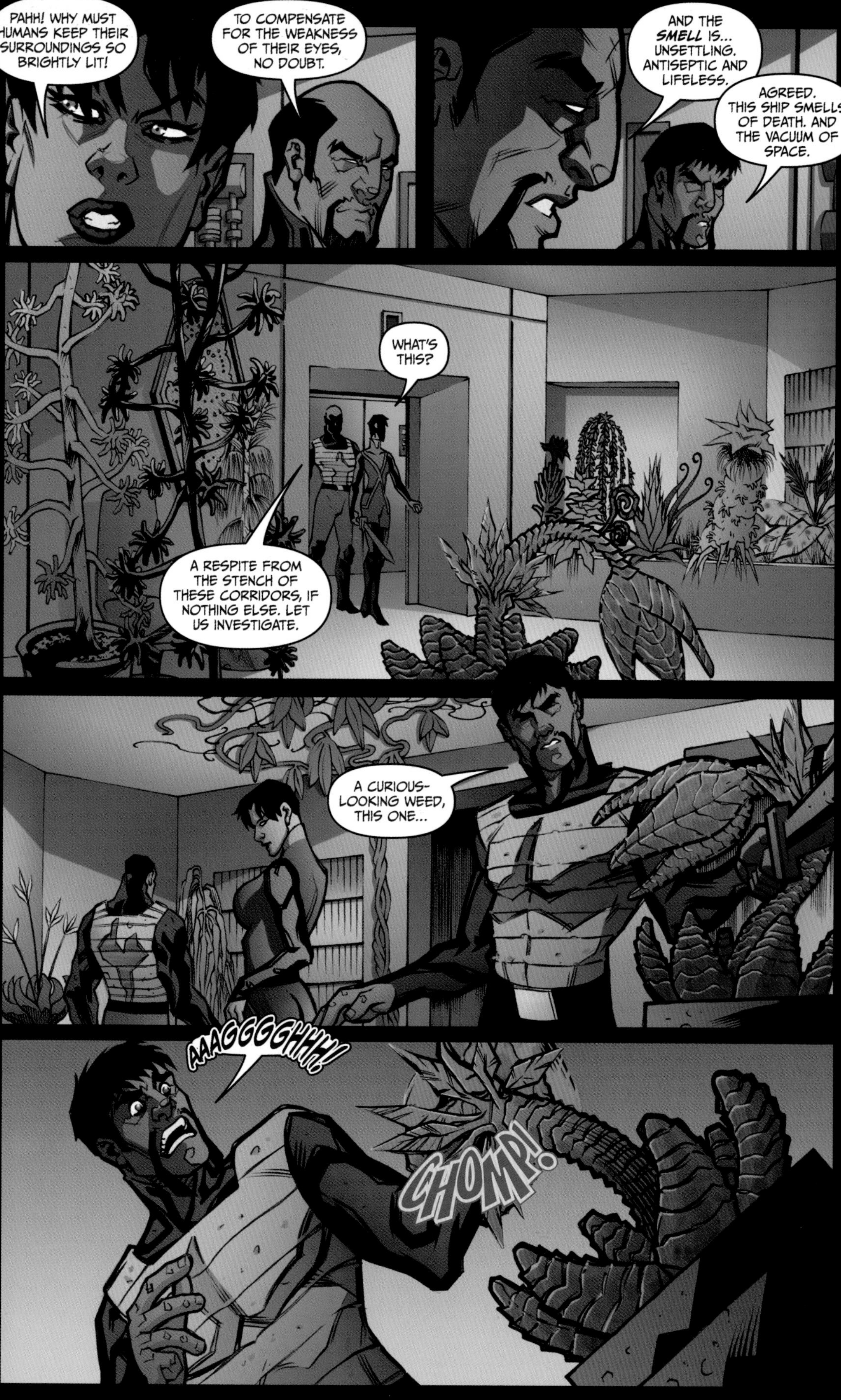
PAHH! WHY MUST HUMANS KEEP THEIR SURROUNDINGS SO BRIGHTLY LIT!
TO COMPENSATE FOR THE WEAKNESS OF THEIR EYES, NO DOUBT.
AND THE SMELL IS... UNSETTLING. ANTISEPTIC AND LIFELESS.
AGREED. THIS SHIP SMELLS OF DEATH. AND THE VACUUM OF SPACE.
WHAT'S THIS?
A RESPITE FROM THE STENCH OF THESE CORRIDORS, IF NOTHING ELSE. LET US INVESTIGATE.
A CURIOUS-LOOKING WEED, THIS ONE...
AAAGGGGHHH!
CHOMP!

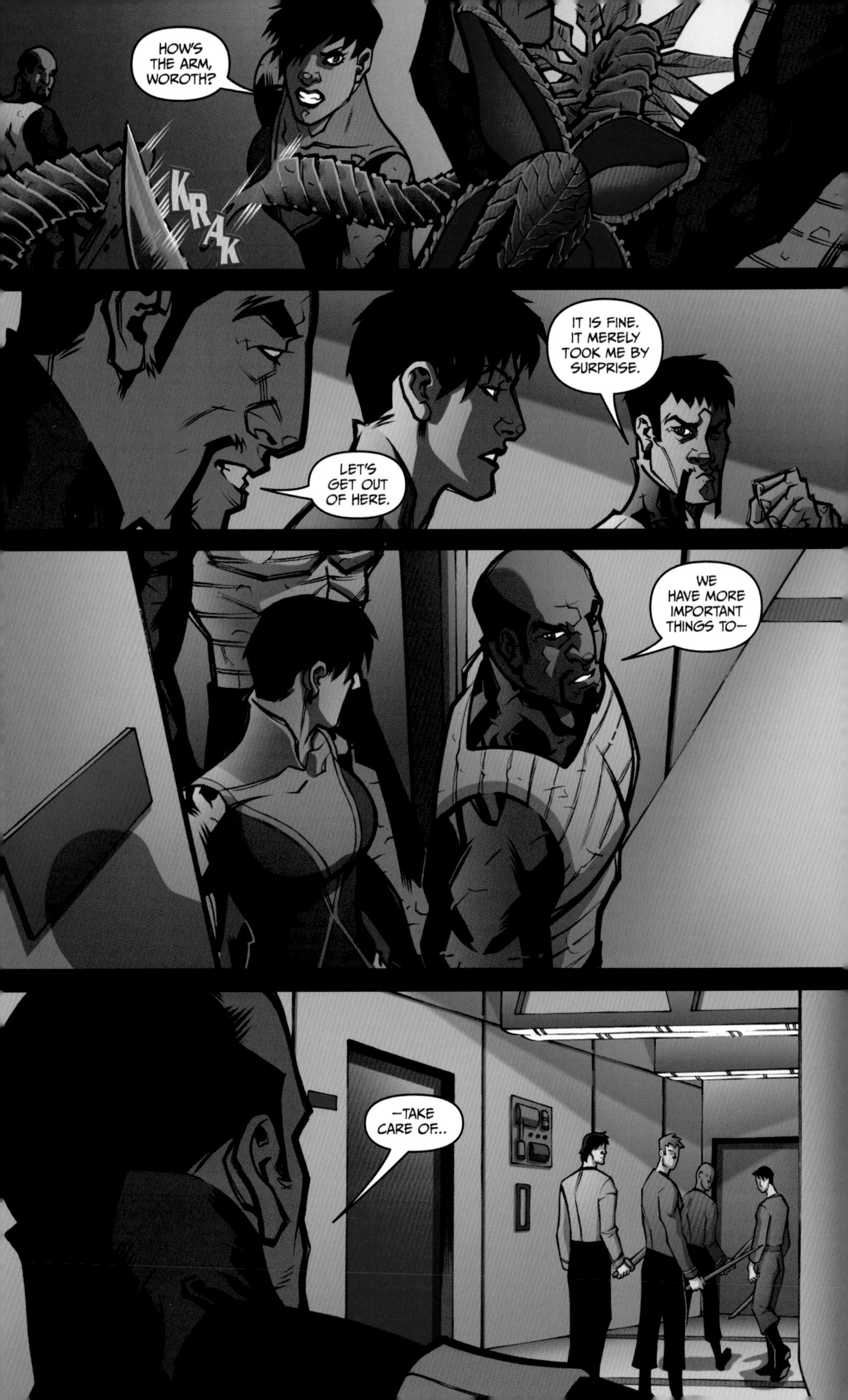
HOW'S THE ARM, WOROTH?
KRAK
IT IS FINE. IT MERELY TOOK ME BY SURPRISE.
LET'S GET OUT OF HERE.
WE HAVE MORE IMPORTANT THINGS TO—
—TAKE CARE OF...

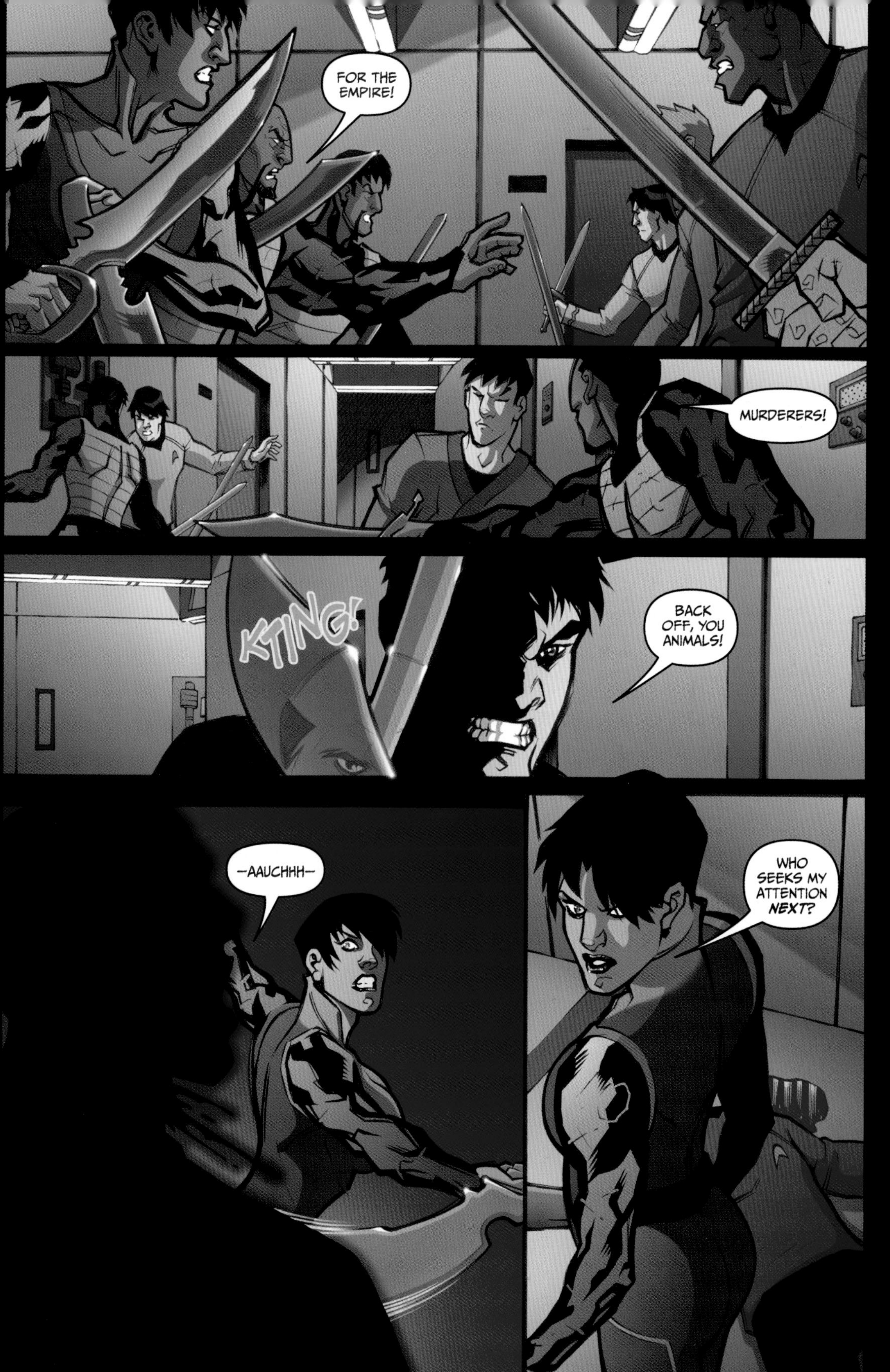
FOR THE EMPIRE!
MURDERERS!
KTING!
BACK OFF, YOU ANIMALS!
—AAUCHHH—
WHO SEEKS MY ATTENTION *NEXT?*

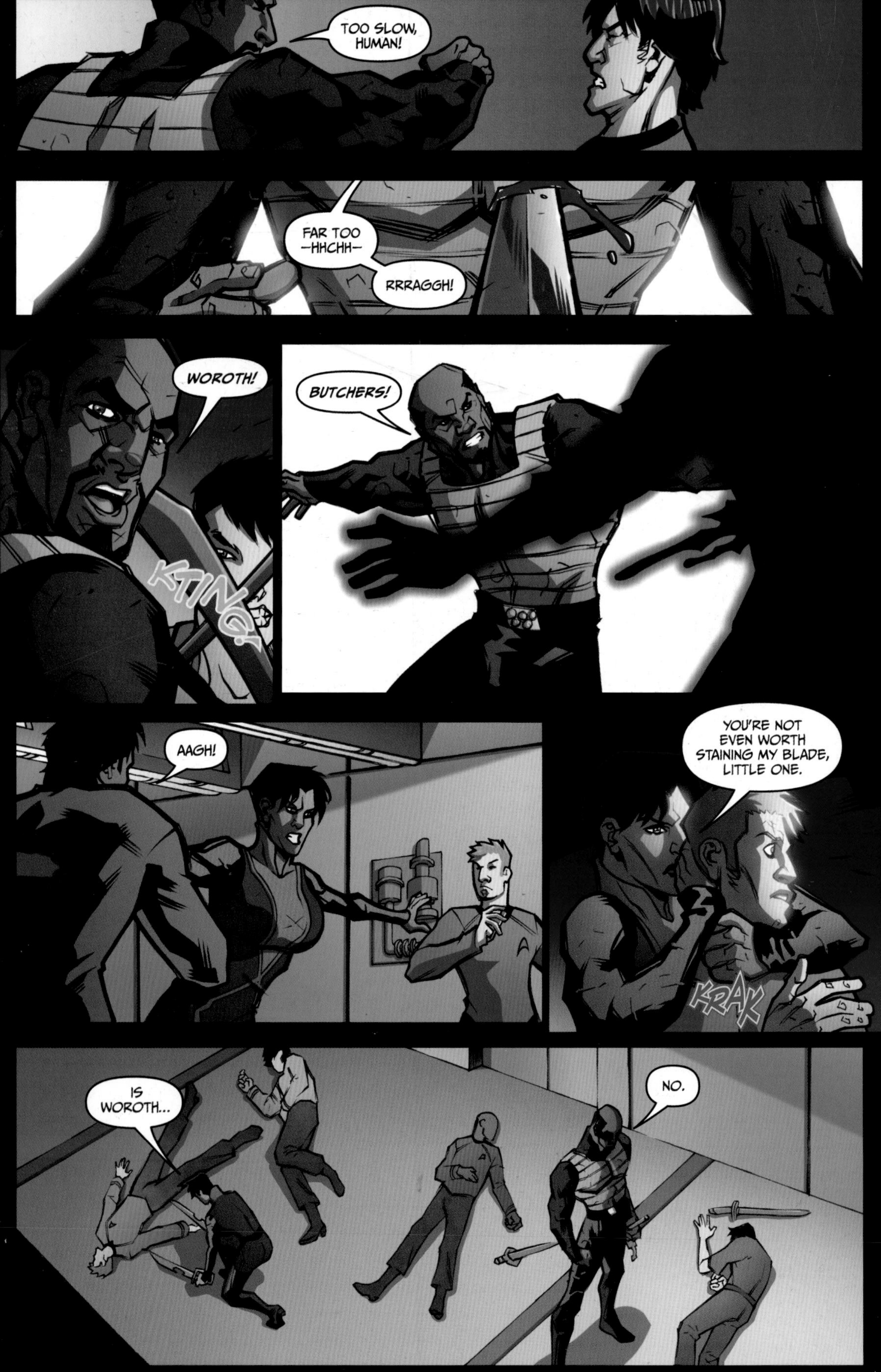
TOO SLOW, HUMAN!
FAR TOO —HHCHH—
RRRAGGH!
WOROTH!
KTING!
BUTCHERS!
AAGH!
YOU'RE NOT EVEN WORTH STAINING MY BLADE, LITTLE ONE.
KRAK
IS WOROTH...
NO.

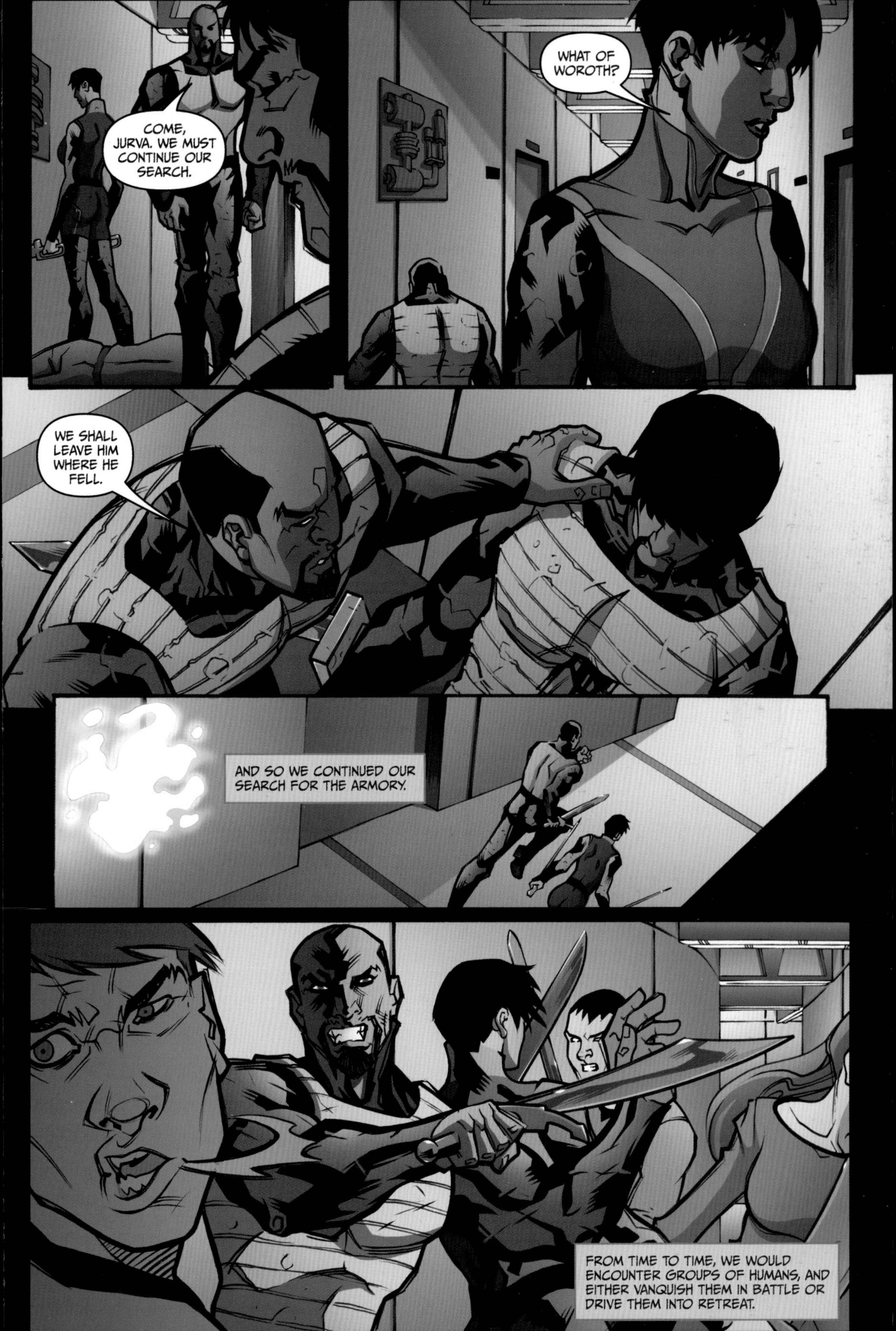
COME, JURVA. WE MUST CONTINUE OUR SEARCH.
WHAT OF WOROTH?
WE SHALL LEAVE HIM WHERE HE FELL.
AND SO WE CONTINUED OUR SEARCH FOR THE ARMORY.
FROM TIME TO TIME, WE WOULD ENCOUNTER GROUPS OF HUMANS, AND EITHER VANQUISH THEM IN BATTLE OR DRIVE THEM INTO RETREAT.

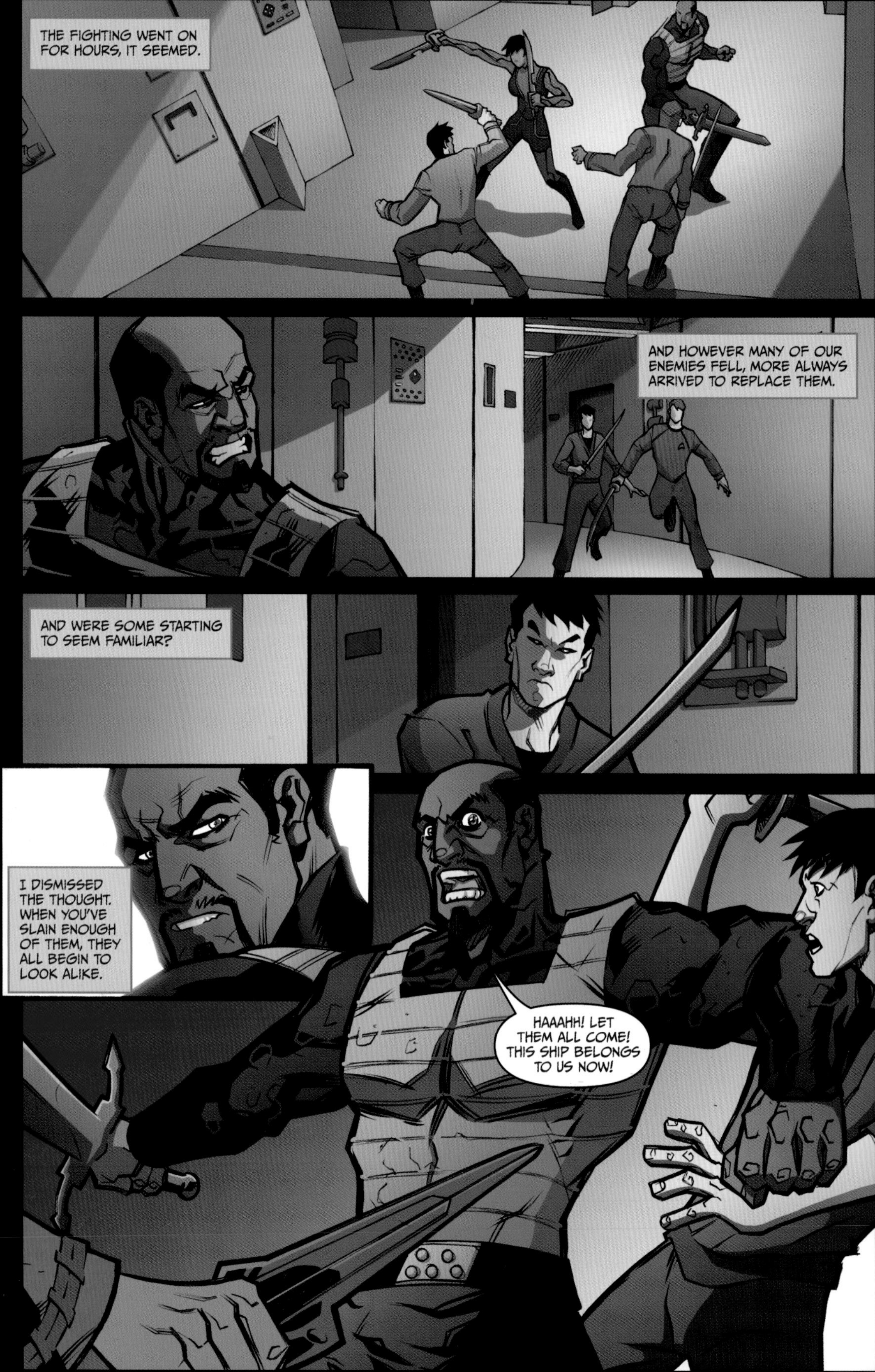
THE FIGHTING WENT ON FOR HOURS, IT SEEMED.
AND HOWEVER MANY OF OUR ENEMIES FELL, MORE ALWAYS ARRIVED TO REPLACE THEM.
AND WERE SOME STARTING TO SEEM FAMILIAR?
I DISMISSED THE THOUGHT. WHEN YOU'VE SLAIN ENOUGH OF THEM, THEY ALL BEGIN TO LOOK ALIKE.
HAAAHH! LET THEM ALL COME! THIS SHIP BELONGS TO US NOW!

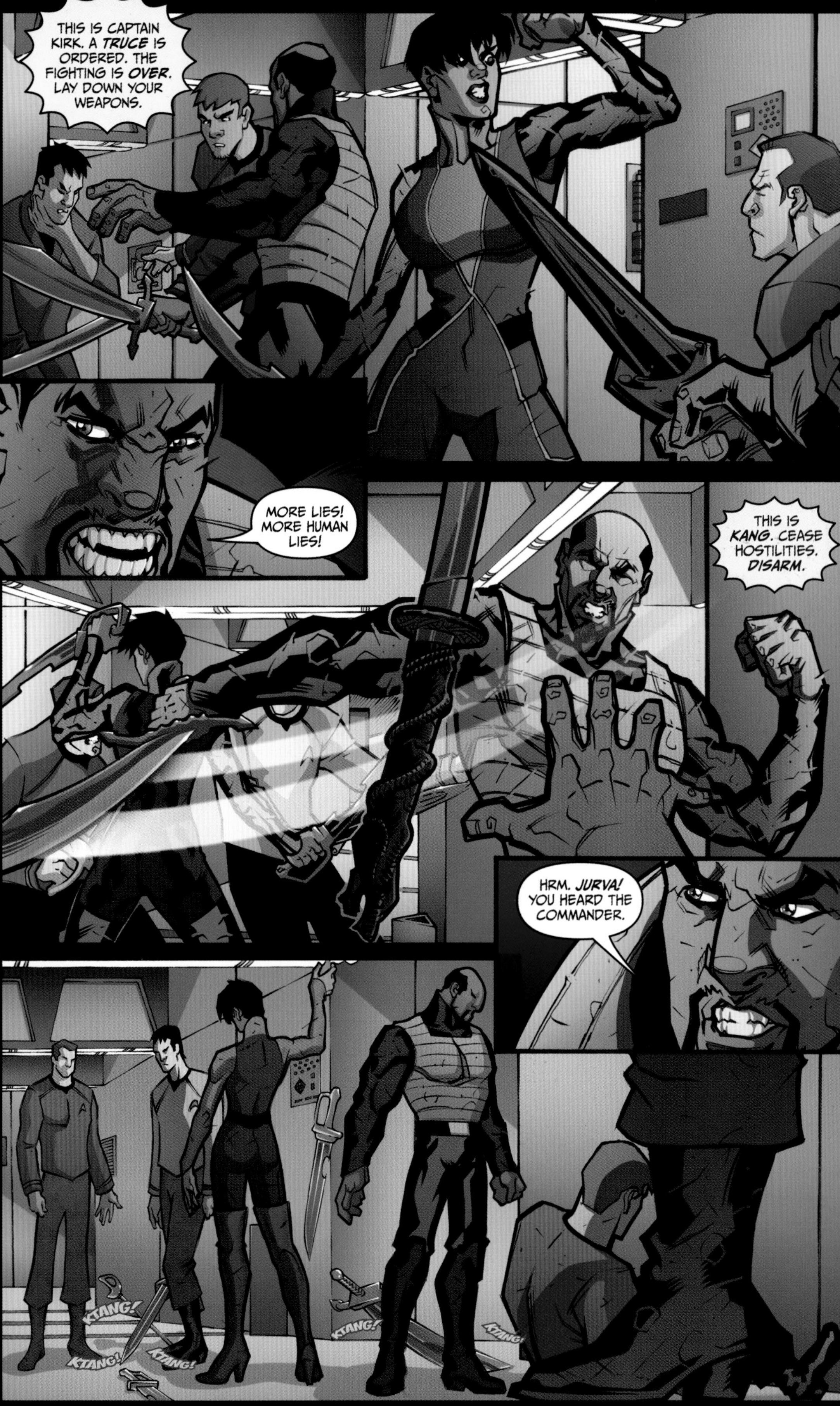
THIS IS CAPTAIN KIRK. A TRUCE IS ORDERED. THE FIGHTING IS OVER. LAY DOWN YOUR WEAPONS.
MORE LIES! MORE HUMAN LIES!
THIS IS KANG. CEASE HOSTILITIES. DISARM.
HRM. JURVA! YOU HEARD THE COMMANDER.
KTANG!
KTANG!
KTANG!
KTANG!
KTANG!

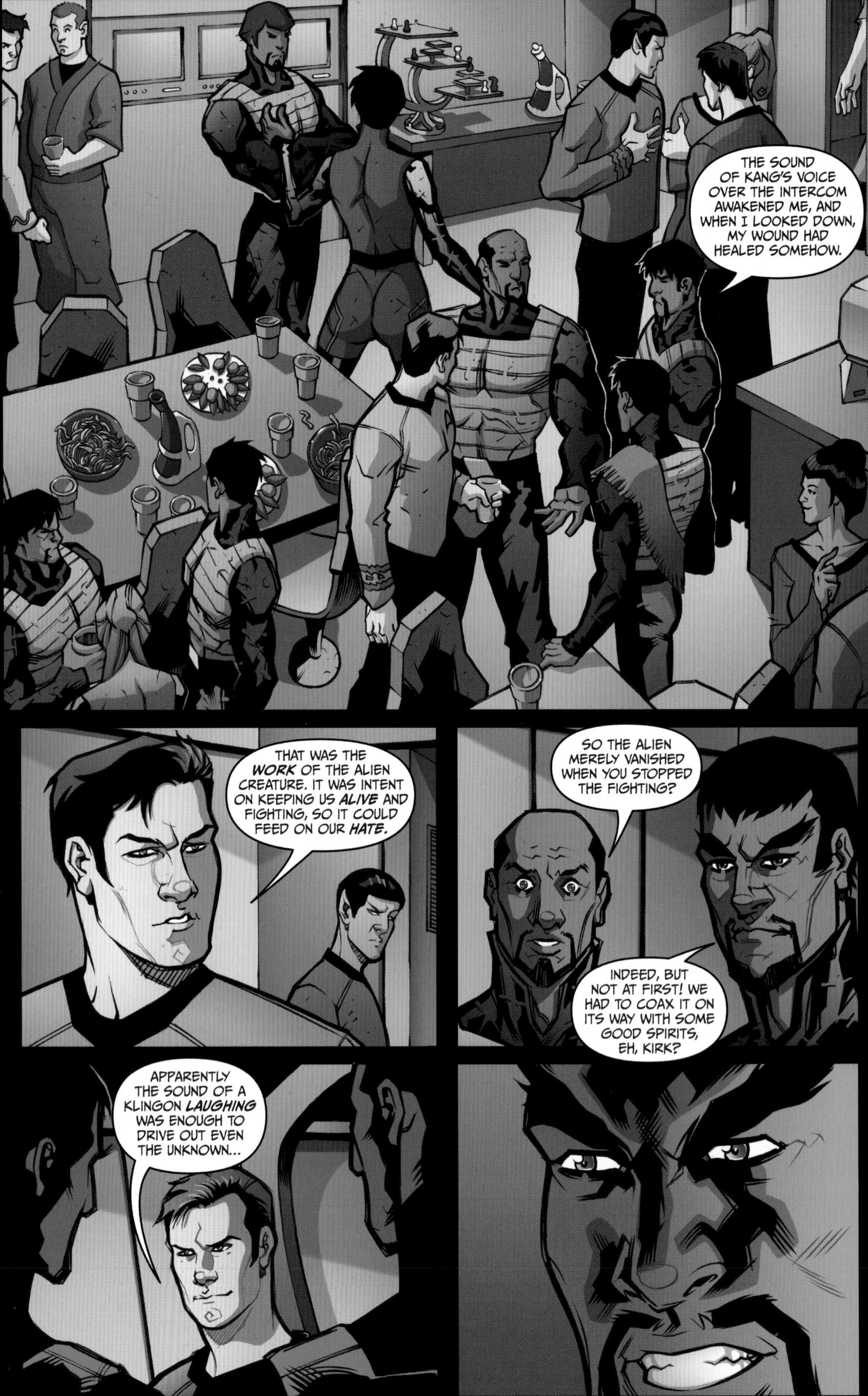
THE SOUND OF KANG'S VOICE OVER THE INTERCOM AWAKENED ME, AND WHEN I LOOKED DOWN, MY WOUND HAD HEALED SOMEHOW.
THAT WAS THE WORK OF THE ALIEN CREATURE. IT WAS INTENT ON KEEPING US ALIVE AND FIGHTING, SO IT COULD FEED ON OUR HATE.
SO THE ALIEN MERELY VANISHED WHEN YOU STOPPED THE FIGHTING?
INDEED, BUT NOT AT FIRST! WE HAD TO COAX IT ON ITS WAY WITH SOME GOOD SPIRITS, EH, KIRK?
APPARENTLY THE SOUND OF A KLINGON LAUGHING WAS ENOUGH TO DRIVE OUT EVEN THE UNKNOWN...

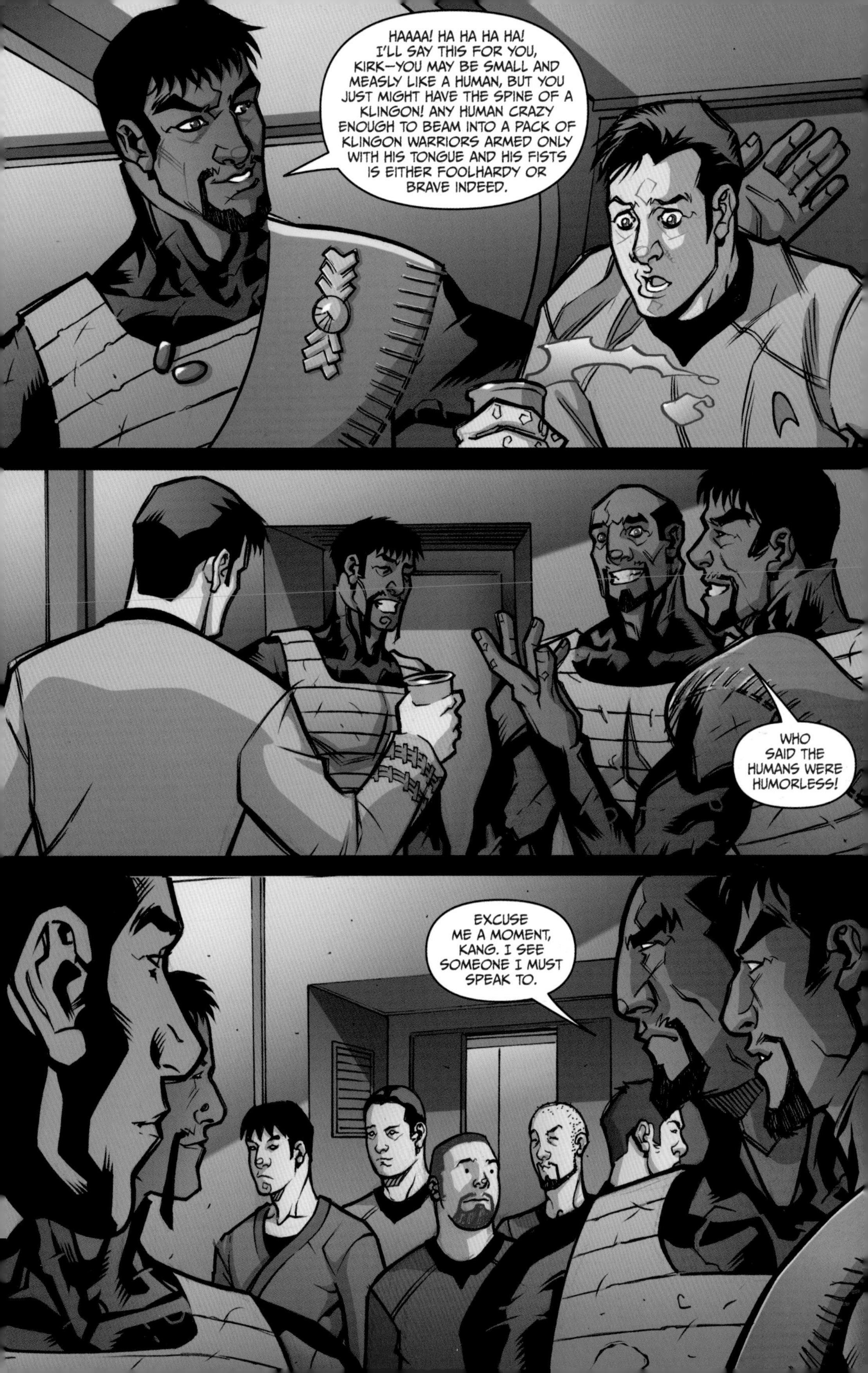
HAAAA! HA HA HA HA! I'LL SAY THIS FOR YOU, KIRK—YOU MAY BE SMALL AND MEASLY LIKE A HUMAN, BUT YOU JUST MIGHT HAVE THE SPINE OF A KLINGON! ANY HUMAN CRAZY ENOUGH TO BEAM INTO A PACK OF KLINGON WARRIORS ARMED ONLY WITH HIS TONGUE AND HIS FISTS IS EITHER FOOLHARDY OR BRAVE INDEED.
WHO SAID THE HUMANS WERE HUMORLESS!
EXCUSE ME A MOMENT, KANG. I SEE SOMEONE I MUST SPEAK TO.

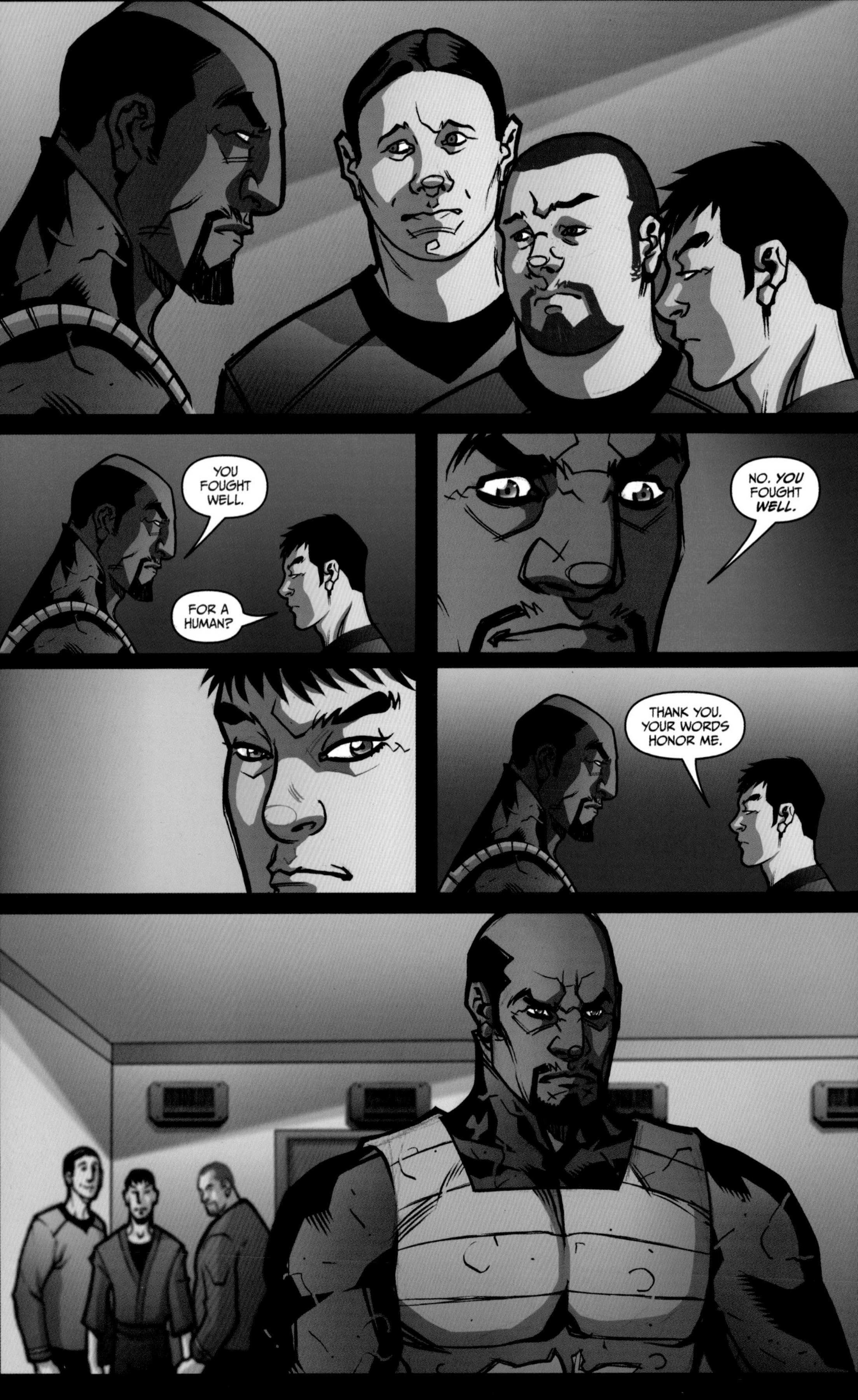
YOU FOUGHT WELL.
FOR A HUMAN?
NO. *YOU* FOUGHT ***WELL.***
THANK YOU. YOUR WORDS HONOR ME.

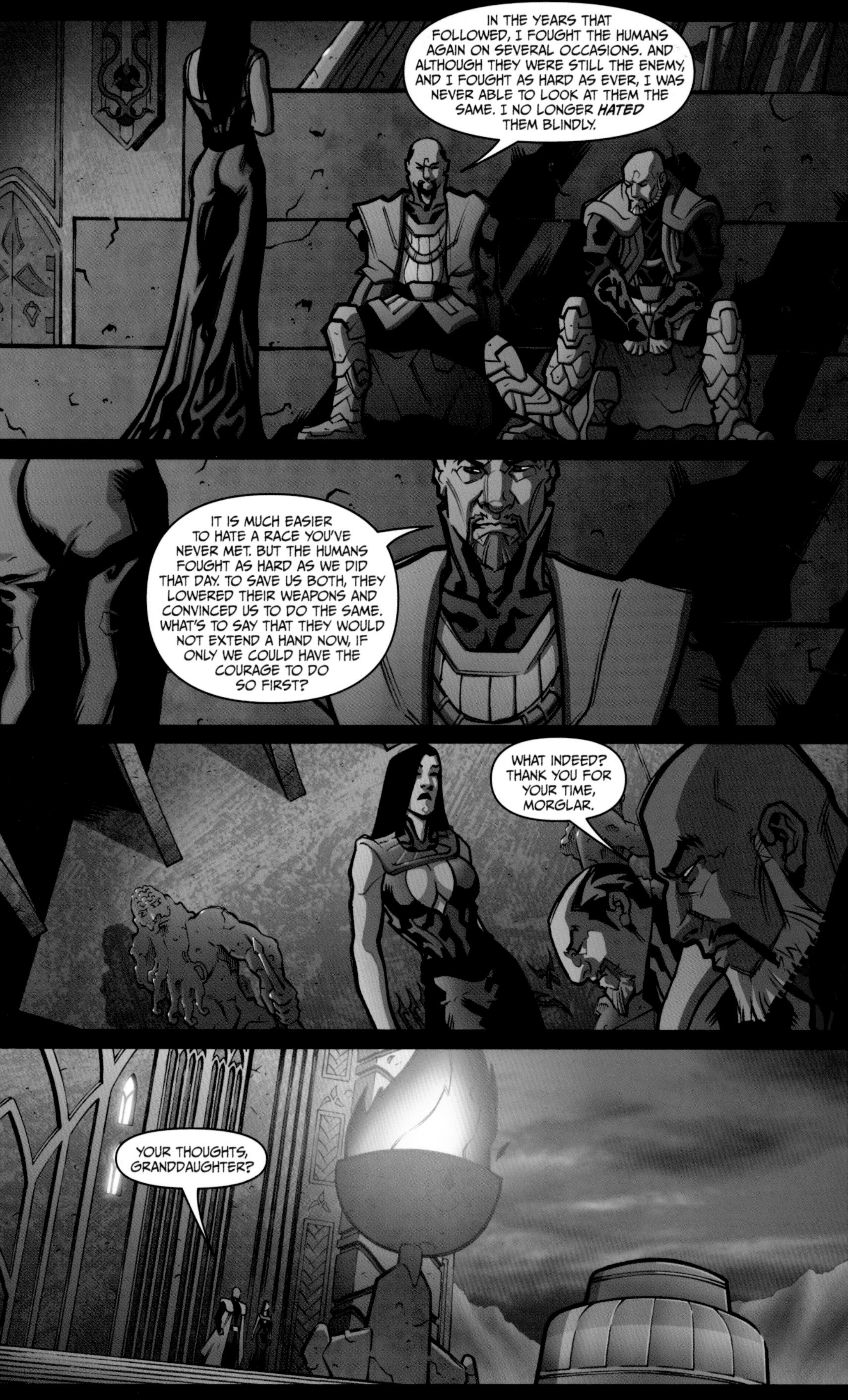
IN THE YEARS THAT FOLLOWED, I FOUGHT THE HUMANS AGAIN ON SEVERAL OCCASIONS. AND ALTHOUGH THEY WERE STILL THE ENEMY, AND I FOUGHT AS HARD AS EVER, I WAS NEVER ABLE TO LOOK AT THEM THE SAME. I NO LONGER *HATED* THEM BLINDLY.
IT IS MUCH EASIER TO HATE A RACE YOU'VE NEVER MET. BUT THE HUMANS FOUGHT AS HARD AS WE DID THAT DAY. TO SAVE US BOTH, THEY LOWERED THEIR WEAPONS AND CONVINCED US TO DO THE SAME. WHAT'S TO SAY THAT THEY WOULD NOT EXTEND A HAND NOW, IF ONLY WE COULD HAVE THE COURAGE TO DO SO FIRST?
WHAT INDEED? THANK YOU FOR YOUR TIME, MORGLAR.
YOUR THOUGHTS, GRANDDAUGHTER?

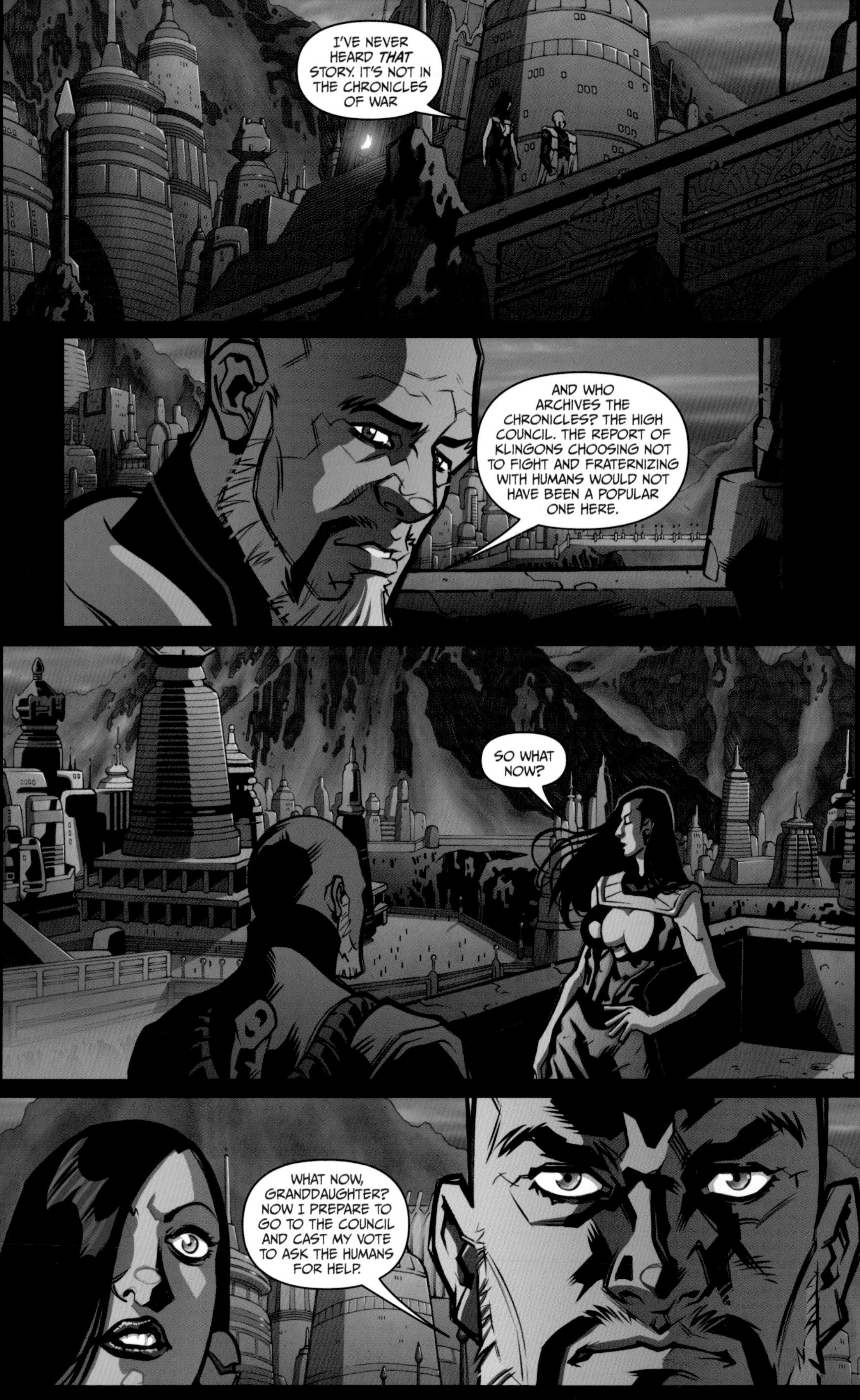
I'VE NEVER HEARD *THAT* STORY. IT'S NOT IN THE CHRONICLES OF WAR
AND WHO ARCHIVES THE CHRONICLES? THE HIGH COUNCIL. THE REPORT OF KLINGONS CHOOSING NOT TO FIGHT AND FRATERNIZING WITH HUMANS WOULD NOT HAVE BEEN A POPULAR ONE HERE.
SO WHAT NOW?
WHAT NOW, GRANDDAUGHTER? NOW I PREPARE TO GO TO THE COUNCIL AND CAST MY VOTE TO ASK THE HUMANS FOR HELP.

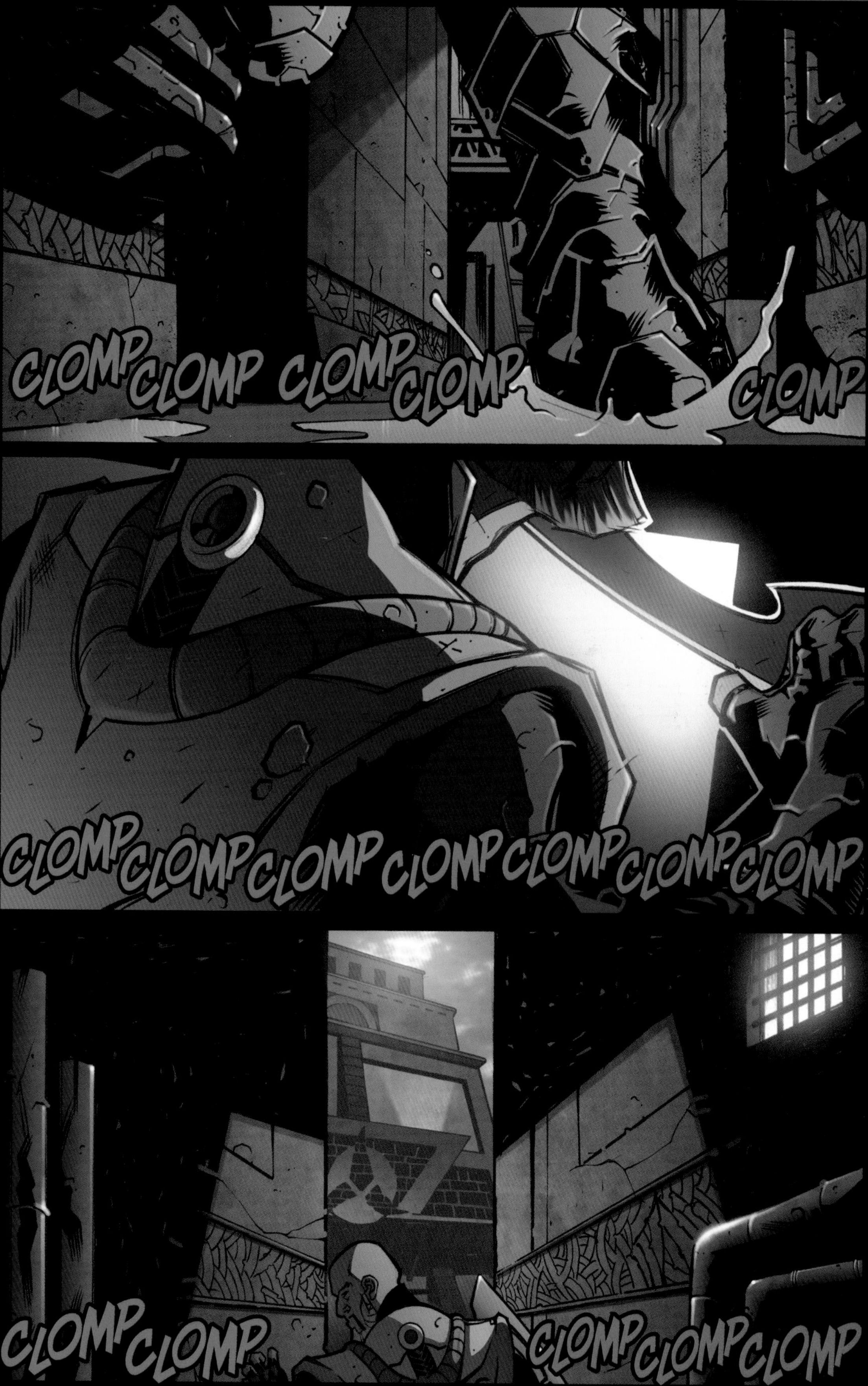
CLOMP CLOMP CLOMP CLOMP CLOMP
CLOMP CLOMP CLOMP CLOMP CLOMP CLOMP CLOMP
CLOMP CLOMP CLOMP CLOMP CLOMP

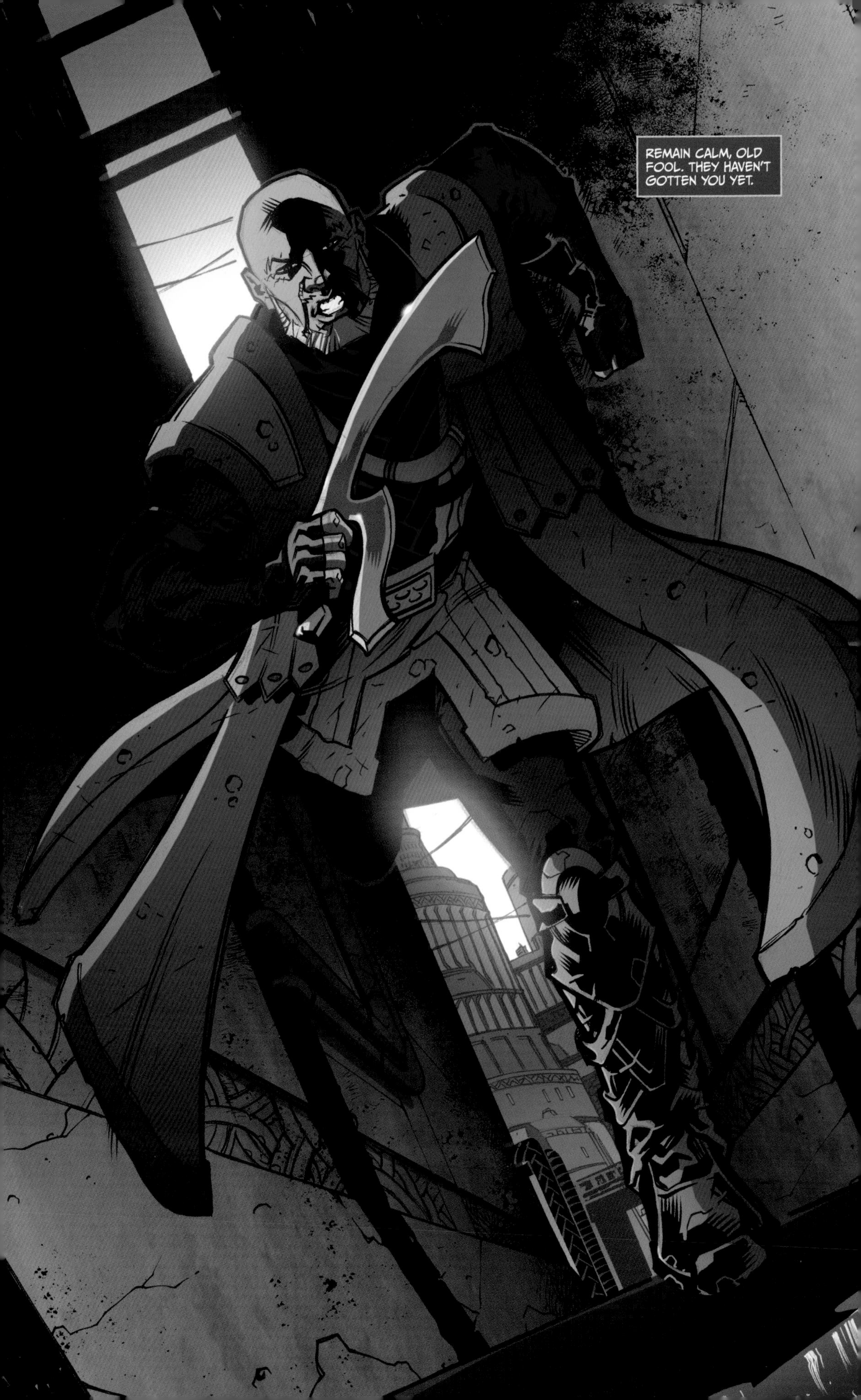
REMAIN CALM, OLD FOOL. THEY HAVEN'T GOTTEN YOU YET.

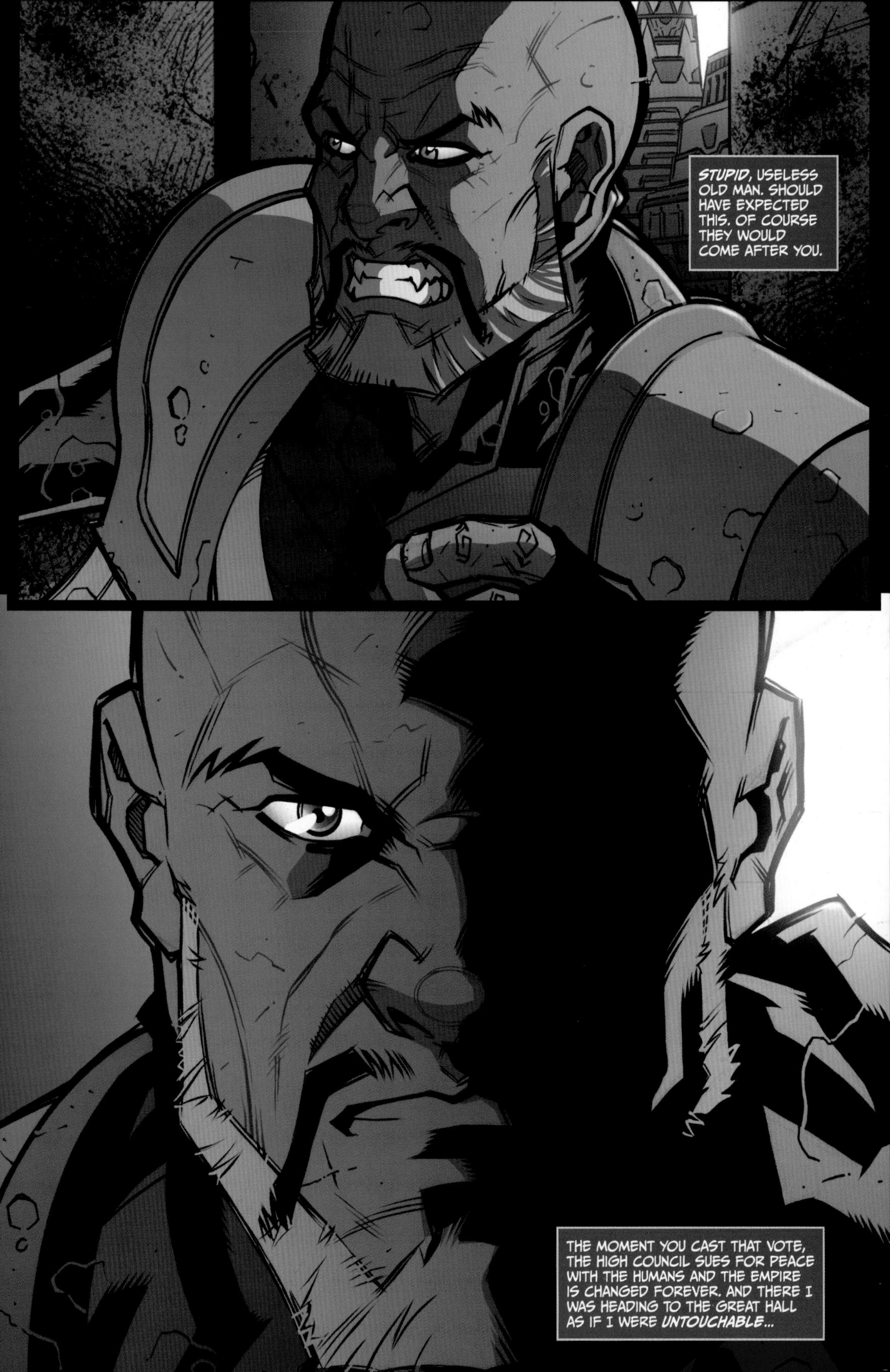
STUPID, USELESS OLD MAN. SHOULD HAVE EXPECTED THIS. OF COURSE THEY WOULD COME AFTER YOU.
THE MOMENT YOU CAST THAT VOTE, THE HIGH COUNCIL SUES FOR PEACE WITH THE HUMANS AND THE EMPIRE IS CHANGED FOREVER. AND THERE I WAS HEADING TO THE GREAT HALL AS IF I WERE UNTOUCHABLE...

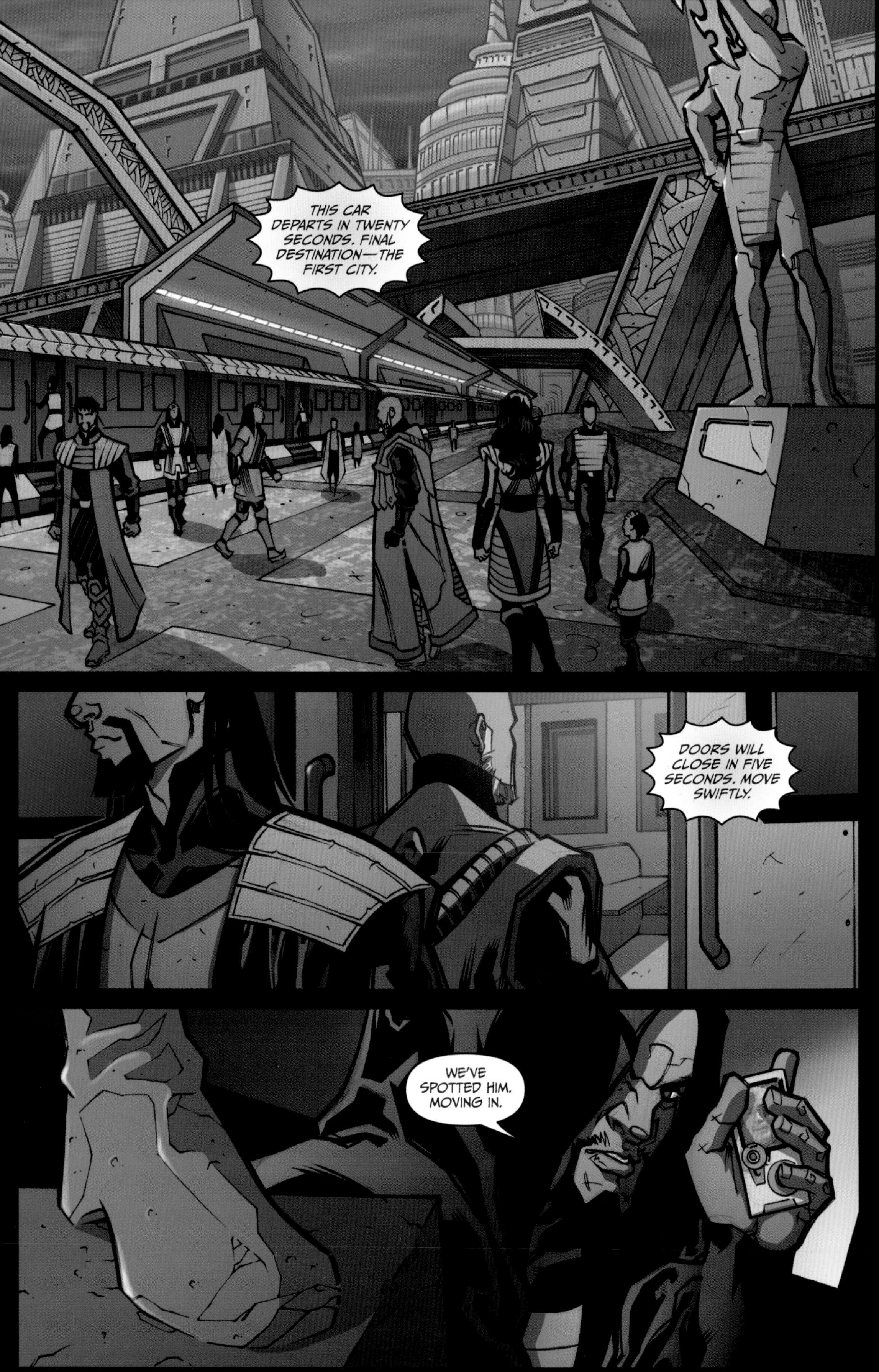
THIS CAR DEPARTS IN TWENTY SECONDS. FINAL DESTINATION—THE FIRST CITY.
DOORS WILL CLOSE IN FIVE SECONDS. MOVE SWIFTLY.
WE'VE SPOTTED HIM. MOVING IN.

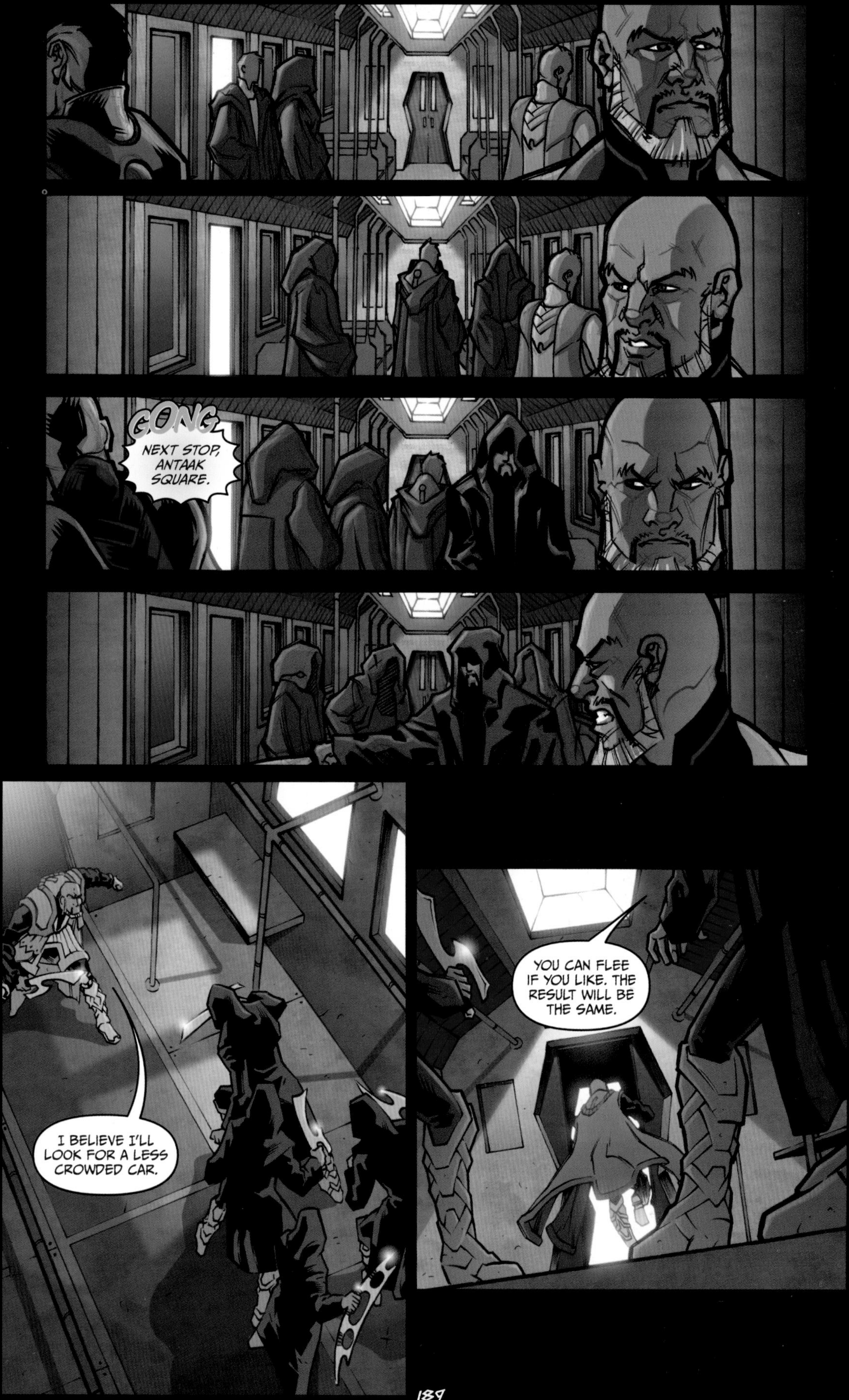
GONG
NEXT STOP, ANTAAK SQUARE.
I BELIEVE I'LL LOOK FOR A LESS CROWDED CAR.
YOU CAN FLEE IF YOU LIKE. THE RESULT WILL BE THE SAME.

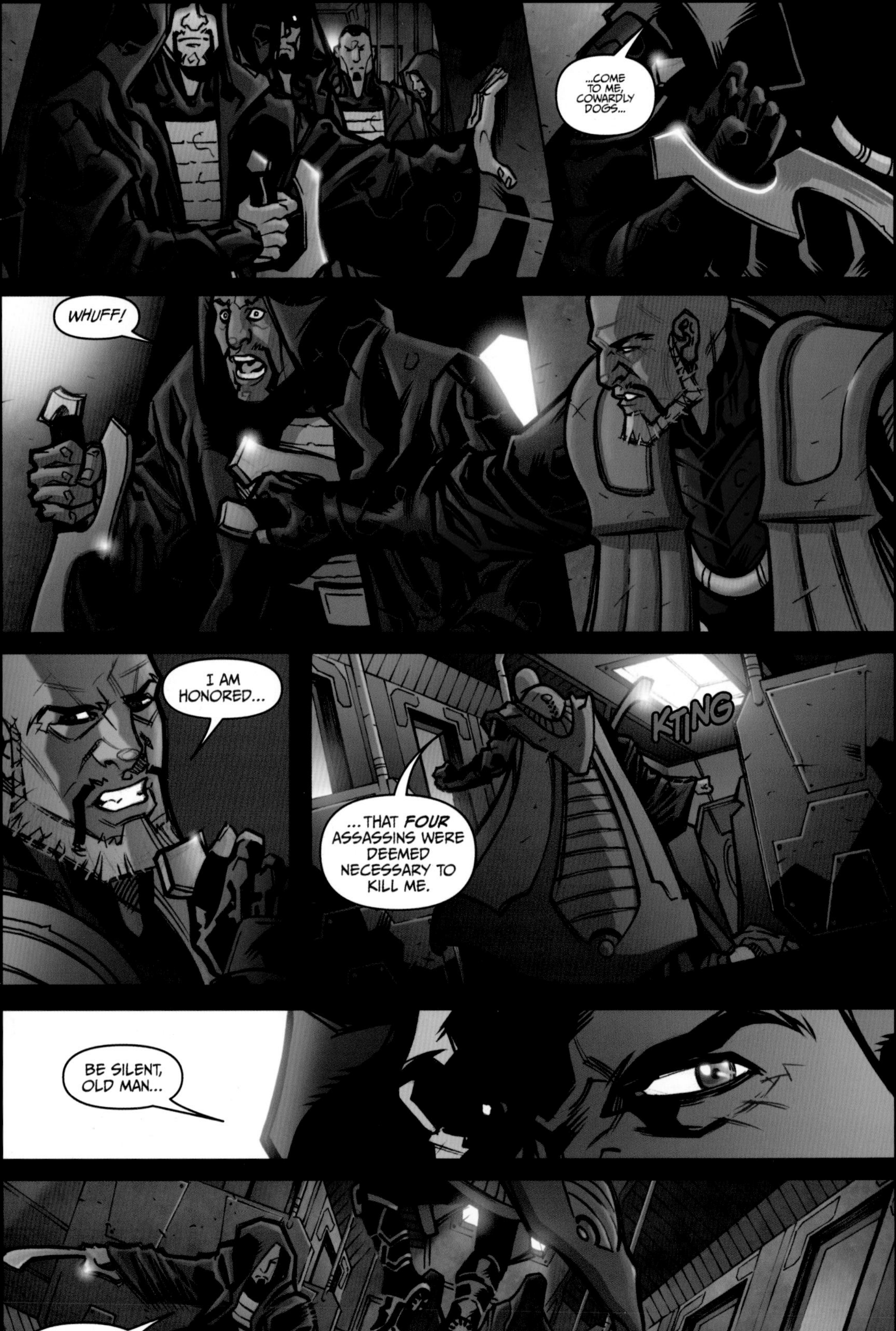
...COME TO ME, COWARDLY DOGS...
WHUFF!
I AM HONORED...
KTING
...THAT *FOUR* ASSASSINS WERE DEEMED NECESSARY TO KILL ME.
BE SILENT, OLD MAN...
...AND LET US CONDUCT OUR TASK WITH DIGNITY.

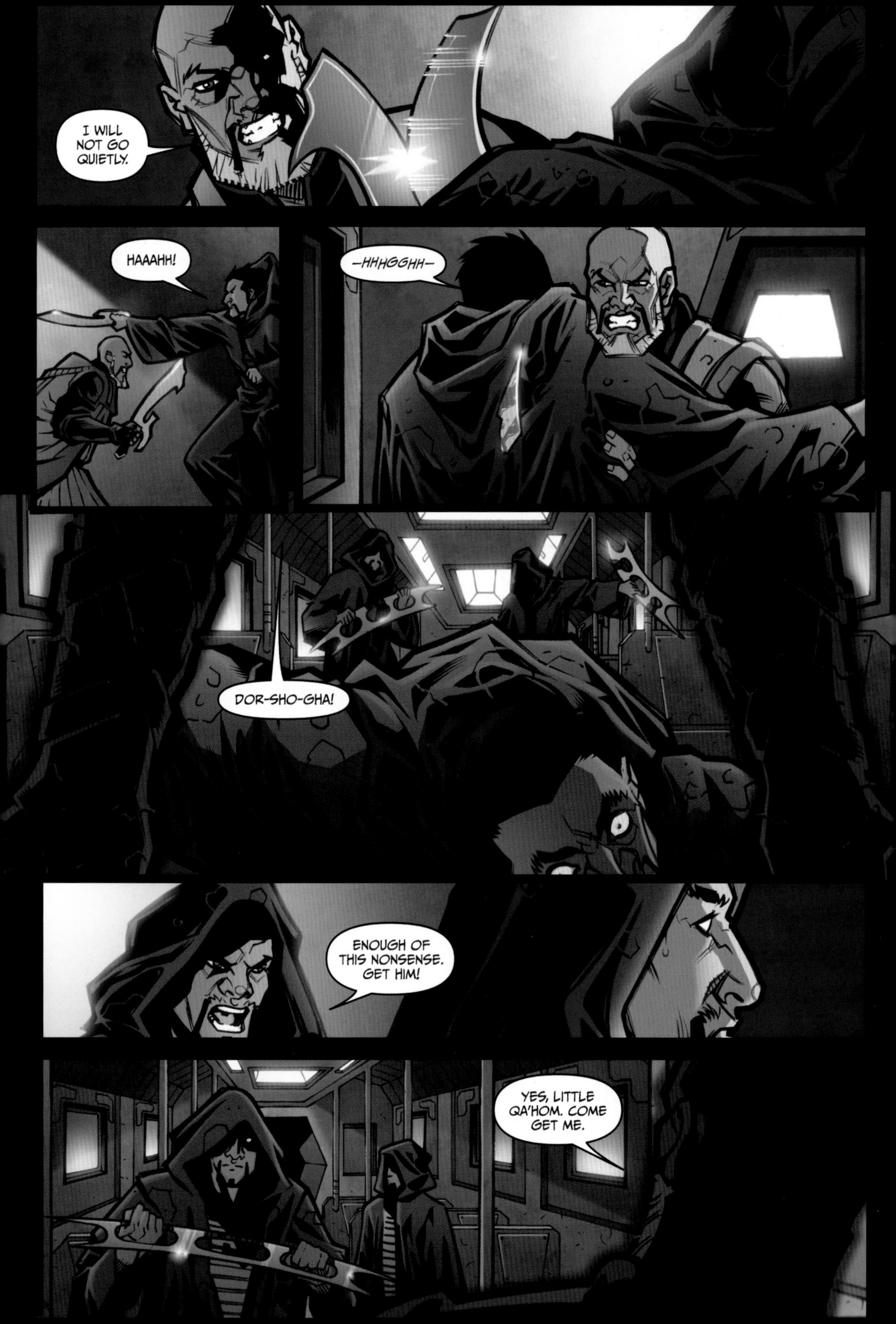
I WILL NOT GO QUIETLY.
HAAAHH!
-HHHGGHH-
DOR-SHO-GHA!
ENOUGH OF THIS NONSENSE. GET HIM!
YES, LITTLE QA'HOM. COME GET ME.

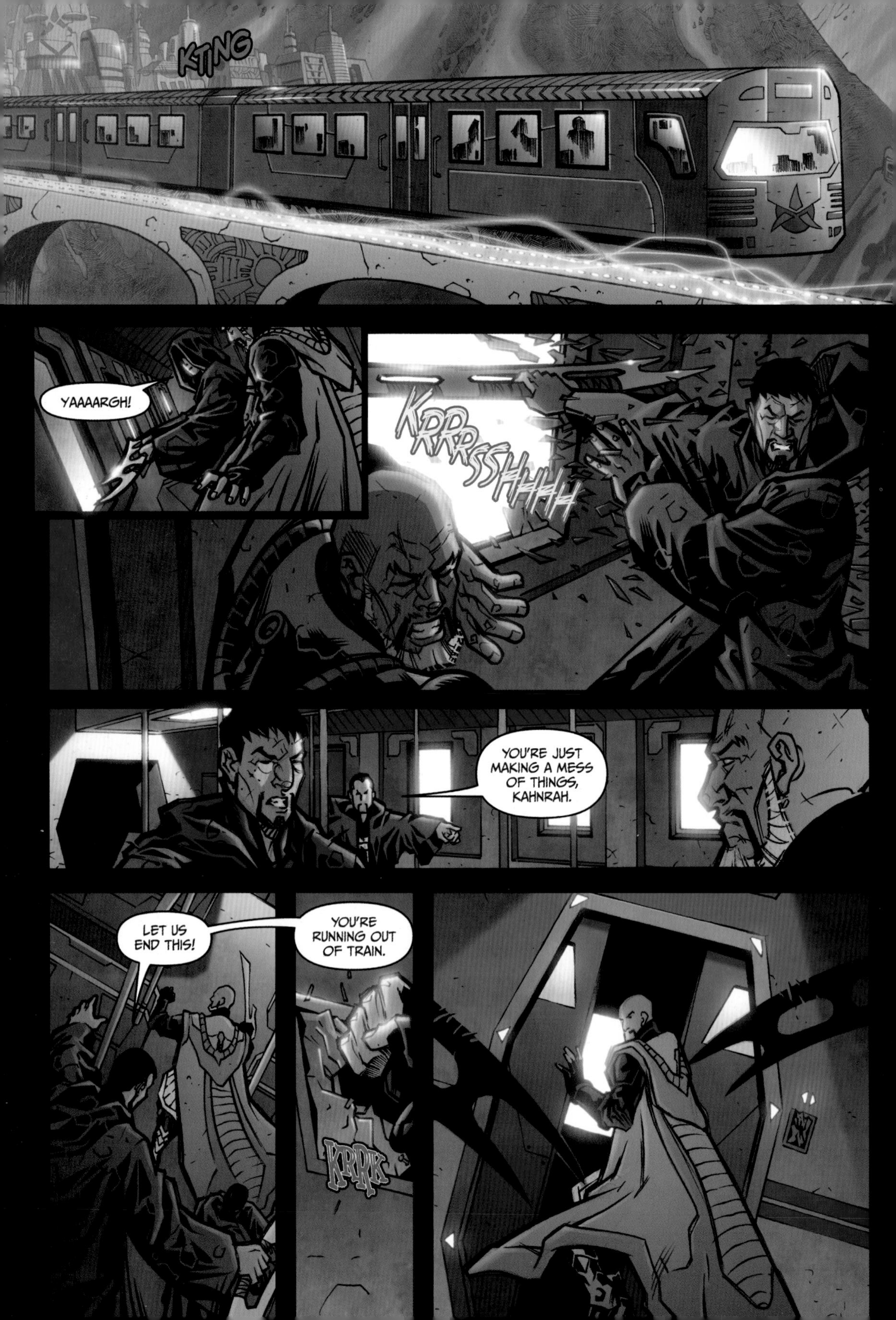
KTING
YAAAARGH!
KRRRSSHHHH
YOU'RE JUST MAKING A MESS OF THINGS, KAHNRAH.
LET US END THIS!
YOU'RE RUNNING OUT OF TRAIN.
KRRK

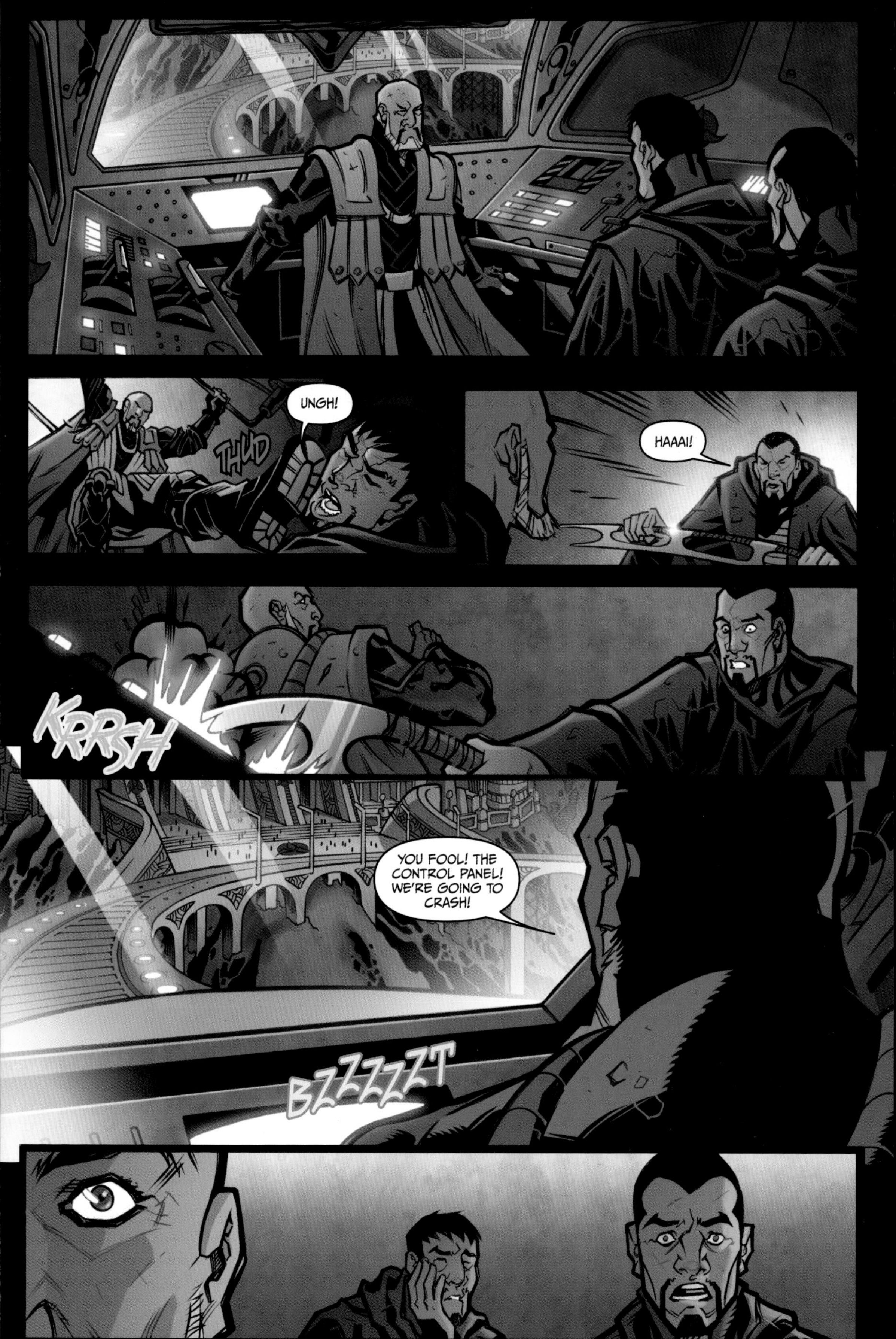
UNGH!
THUD
HAAAI!
KRRSH
YOU FOOL! THE CONTROL PANEL! WE'RE GOING TO CRASH!
BZZZZZT

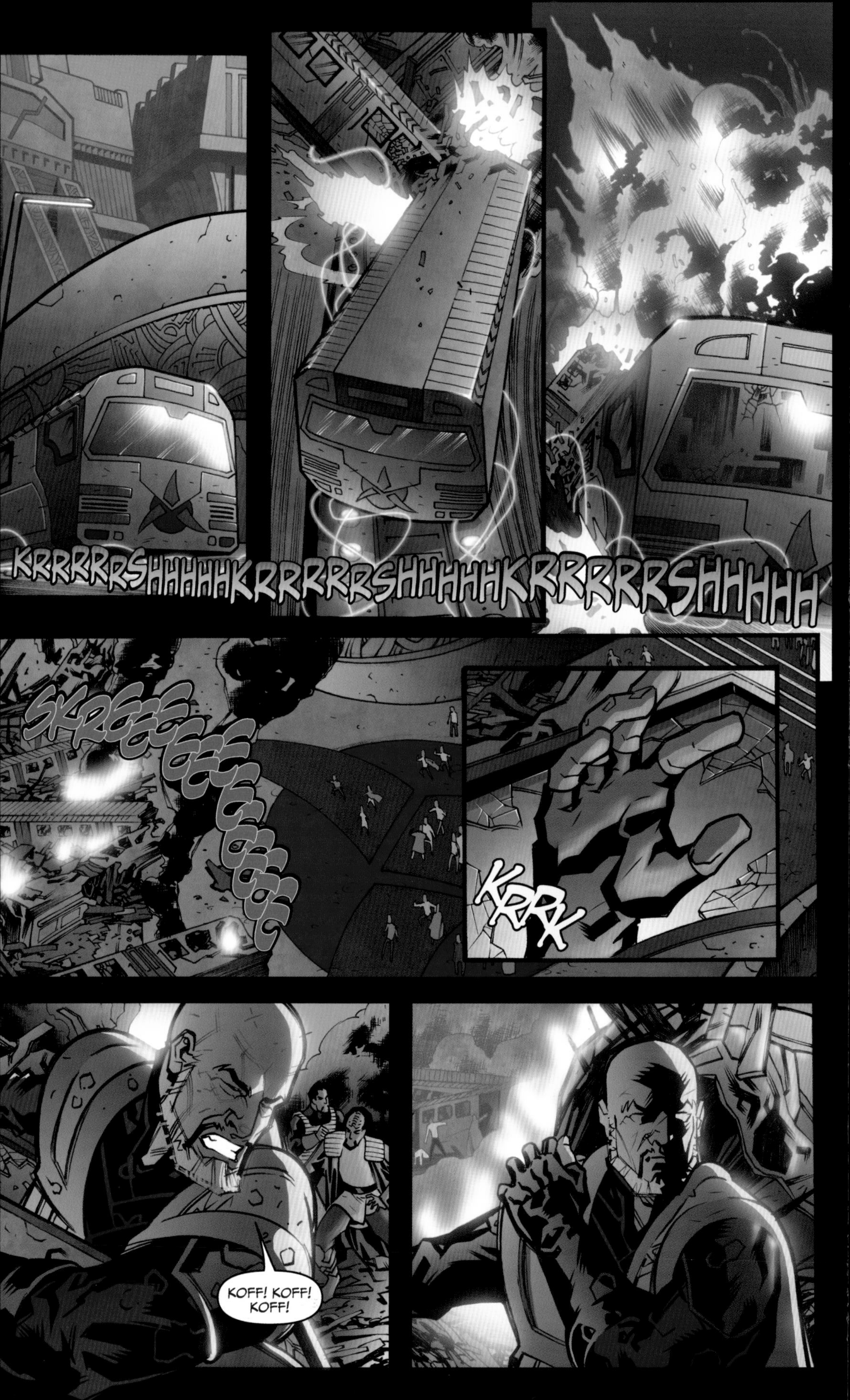
KRRRRRSHHHHHKRRRRRSHHHHHKRRRRRSHHHHH
SKREEEEEEEEEEEEEEEEEEE
KRRK
KOFF! KOFF! KOFF!

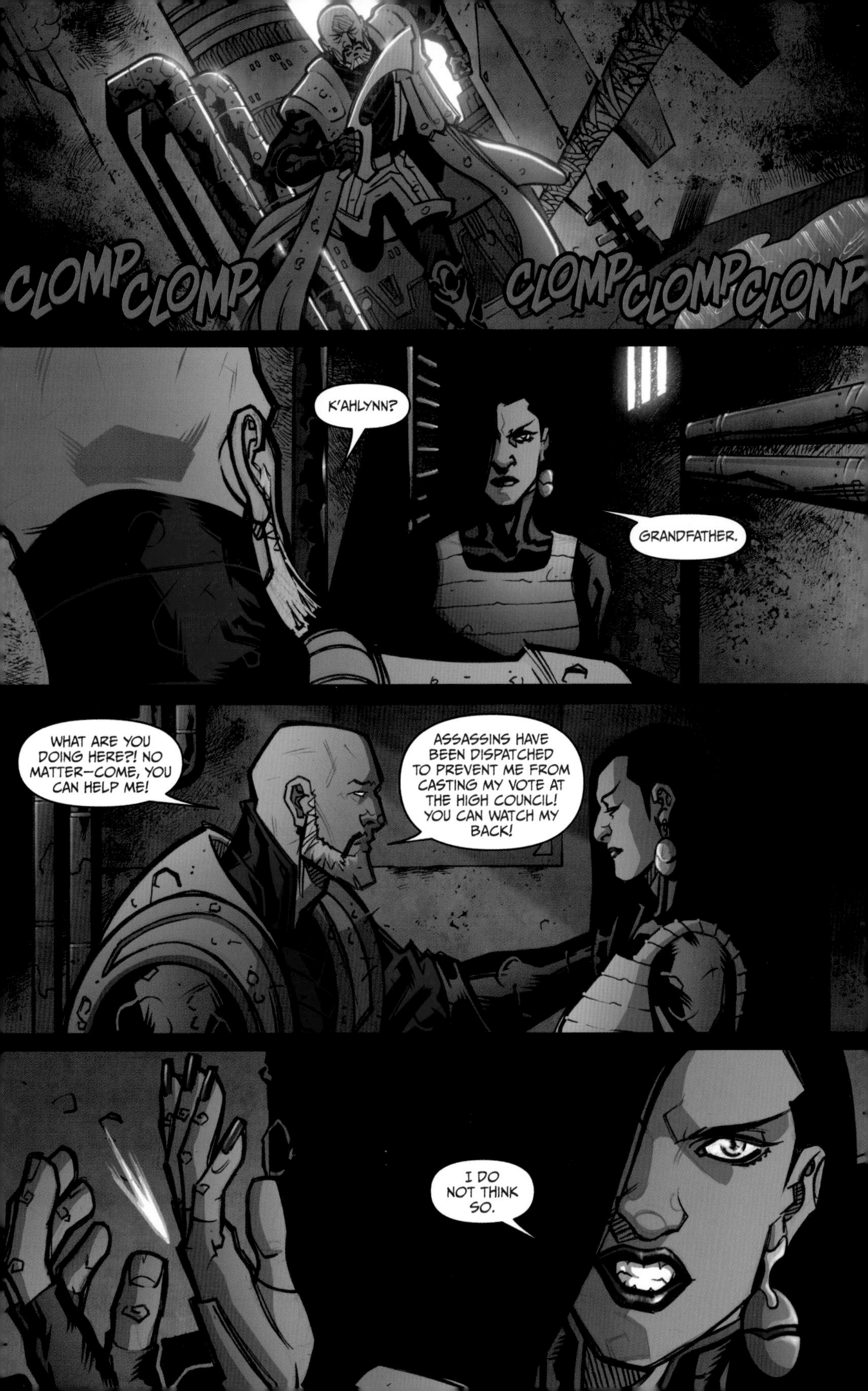
CLOMP CLOMP
CLOMP CLOMP CLOMP
K'AHLYNN?
GRANDFATHER.
WHAT ARE YOU DOING HERE?! NO MATTER—COME, YOU CAN HELP ME!
ASSASSINS HAVE BEEN DISPATCHED TO PREVENT ME FROM CASTING MY VOTE AT THE HIGH COUNCIL! YOU CAN WATCH MY BACK!
I DO NOT THINK SO.

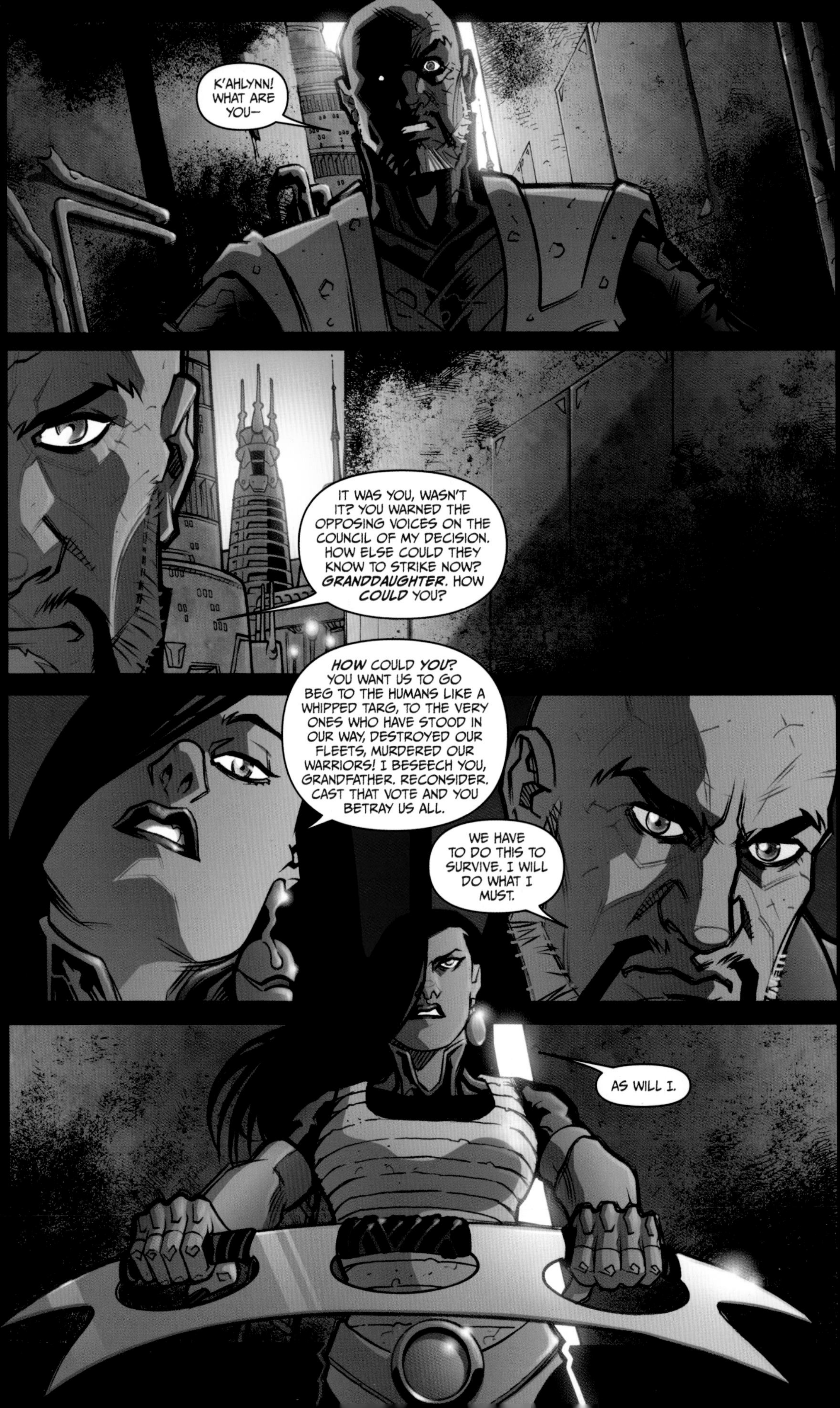
K'AHLYNN! WHAT ARE YOU—
IT WAS YOU, WASN'T IT? YOU WARNED THE OPPOSING VOICES ON THE COUNCIL OF MY DECISION. HOW ELSE COULD THEY KNOW TO STRIKE NOW? GRANDDAUGHTER. HOW COULD YOU?
HOW COULD YOU? YOU WANT US TO GO BEG TO THE HUMANS LIKE A WHIPPED TARG, TO THE VERY ONES WHO HAVE STOOD IN OUR WAY, DESTROYED OUR FLEETS, MURDERED OUR WARRIORS! I BESEECH YOU, GRANDFATHER. RECONSIDER. CAST THAT VOTE AND YOU BETRAY US ALL.
WE HAVE TO DO THIS TO SURVIVE. I WILL DO WHAT I MUST.
AS WILL I.

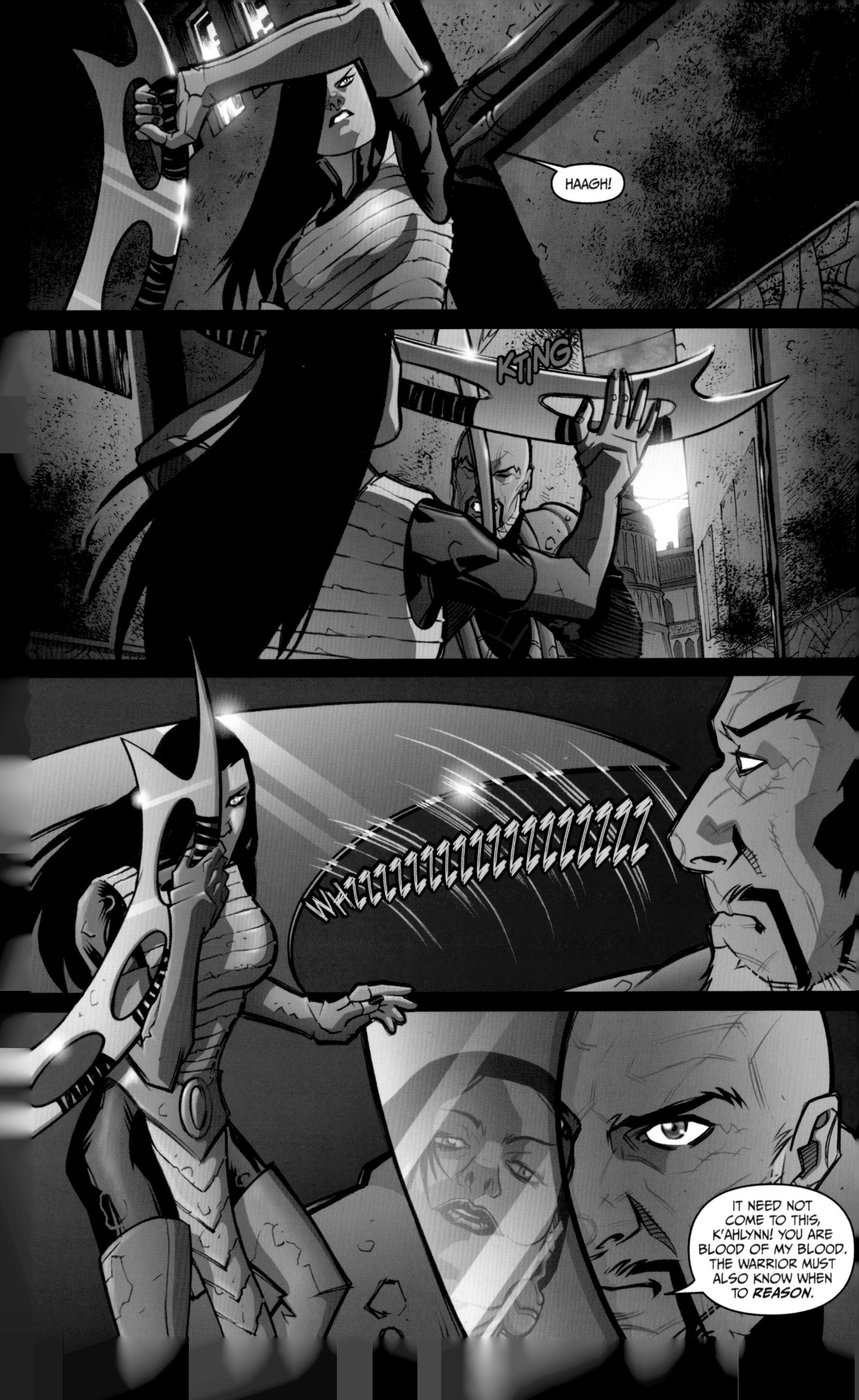
HAAGH!
KTING
WHZZZZZZZZZZZZZZZZZZZZZ
IT NEED NOT COME TO THIS, K'AHLYNN! YOU ARE BLOOD OF MY BLOOD. THE WARRIOR MUST ALSO KNOW WHEN TO *REASON*.

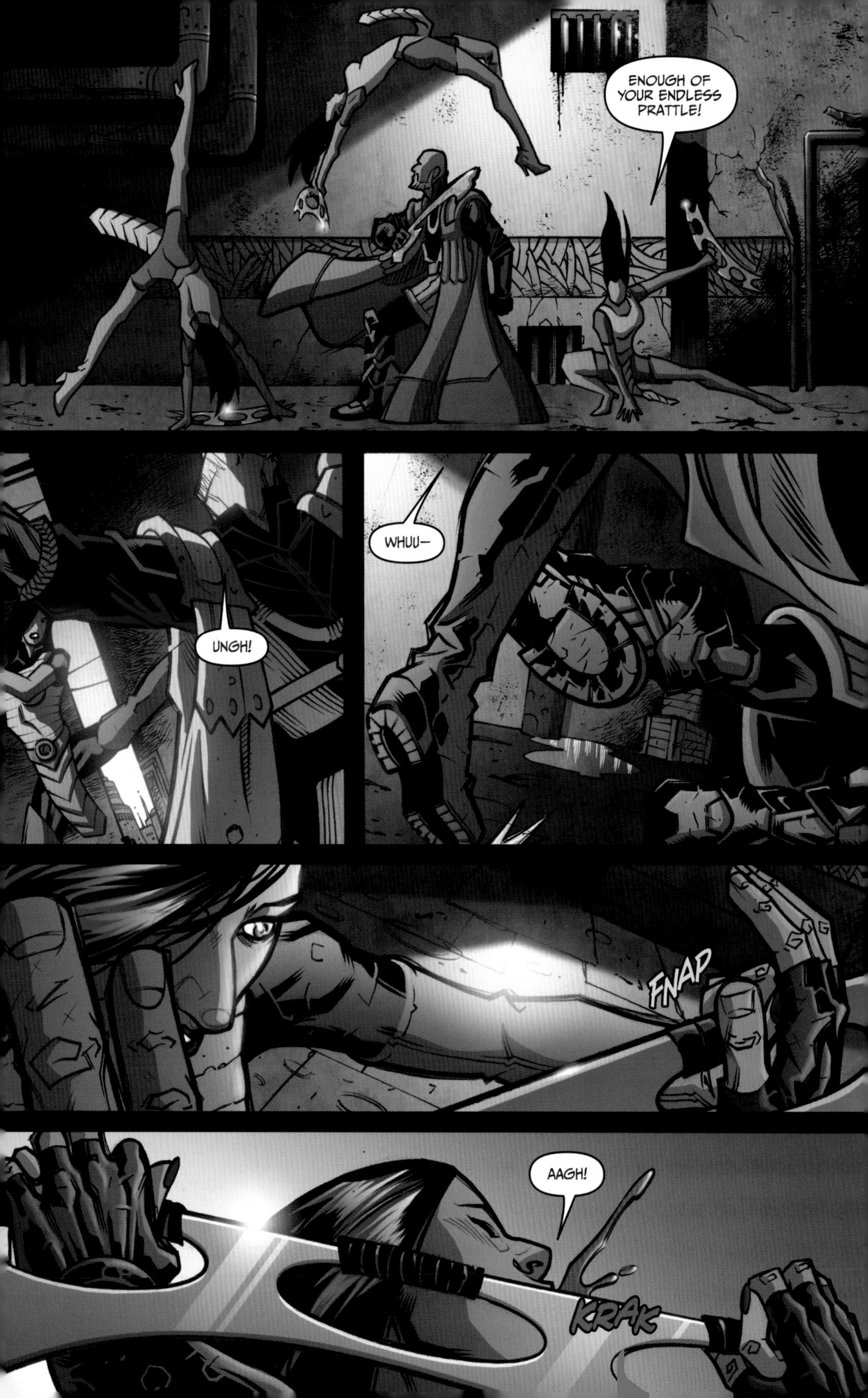
ENOUGH OF YOUR ENDLESS PRATTLE!
UNGH!
WHUU–
FNAP
AAGH!
KRAK

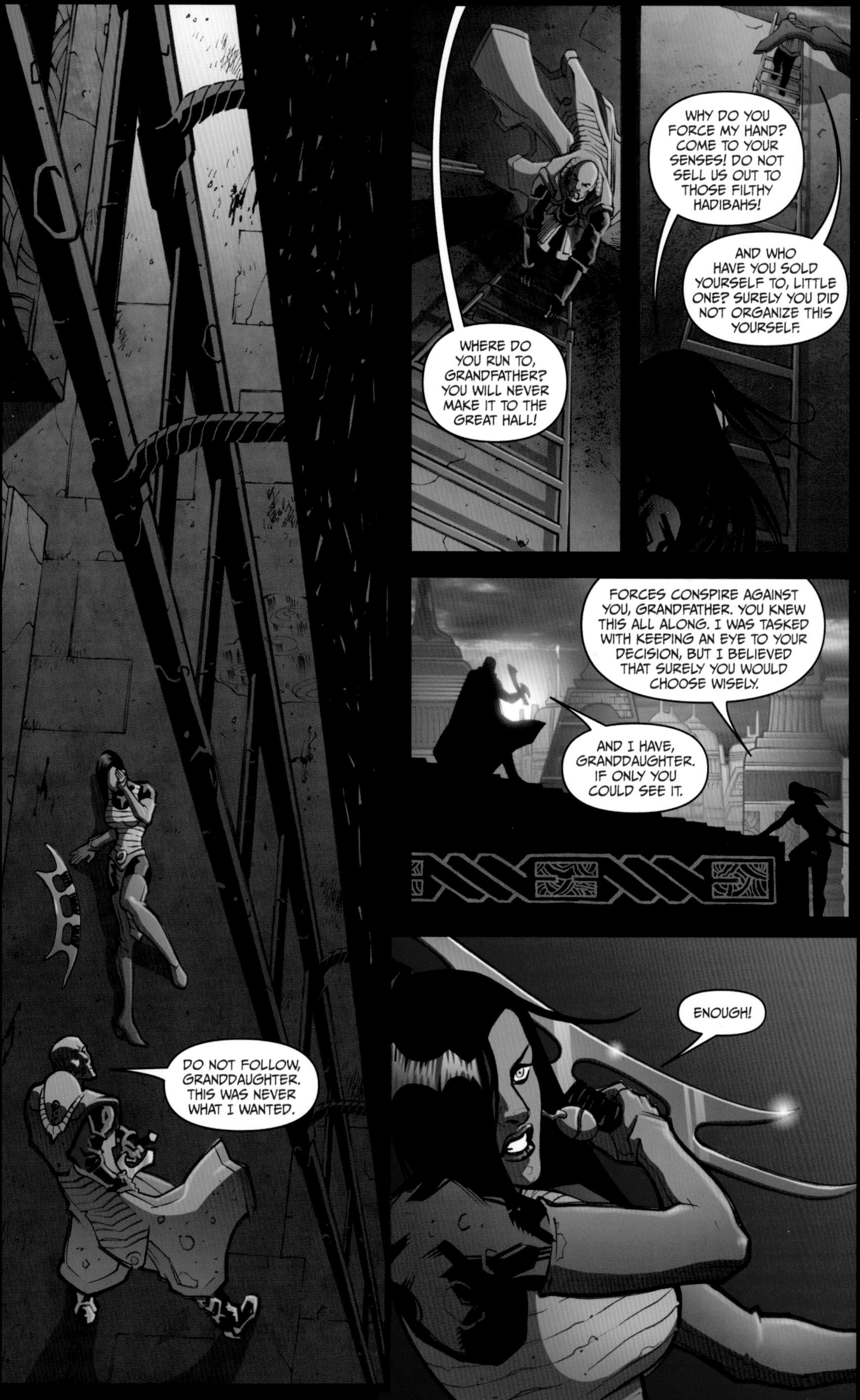

WHERE DO YOU RUN TO, GRANDFATHER? YOU WILL NEVER MAKE IT TO THE GREAT HALL!
WHY DO YOU FORCE MY HAND? COME TO YOUR SENSES! DO NOT SELL US OUT TO THOSE FILTHY HADIBAHS!
AND WHO HAVE YOU SOLD YOURSELF TO, LITTLE ONE? SURELY YOU DID NOT ORGANIZE THIS YOURSELF.
FORCES CONSPIRE AGAINST YOU, GRANDFATHER. YOU KNEW THIS ALL ALONG. I WAS TASKED WITH KEEPING AN EYE TO YOUR DECISION, BUT I BELIEVED THAT SURELY YOU WOULD CHOOSE WISELY.
AND I HAVE, GRANDDAUGHTER. IF ONLY YOU COULD SEE IT.
DO NOT FOLLOW, GRANDDAUGHTER. THIS WAS NEVER WHAT I WANTED.
ENOUGH!

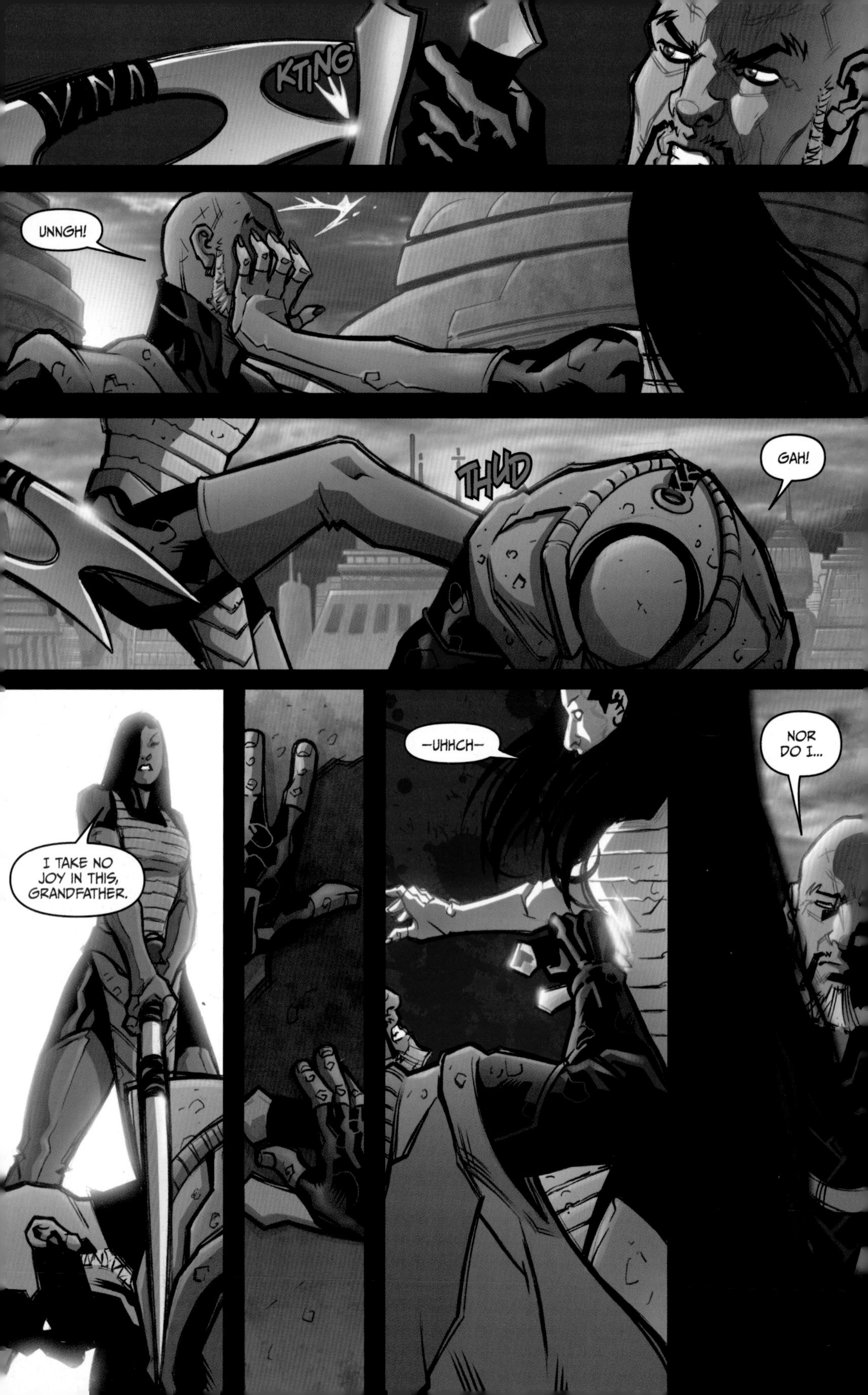
KTING
UNNGH!
THUD
GAH!
I TAKE NO JOY IN THIS, GRANDFATHER.
—UHHCH—
NOR DO I...

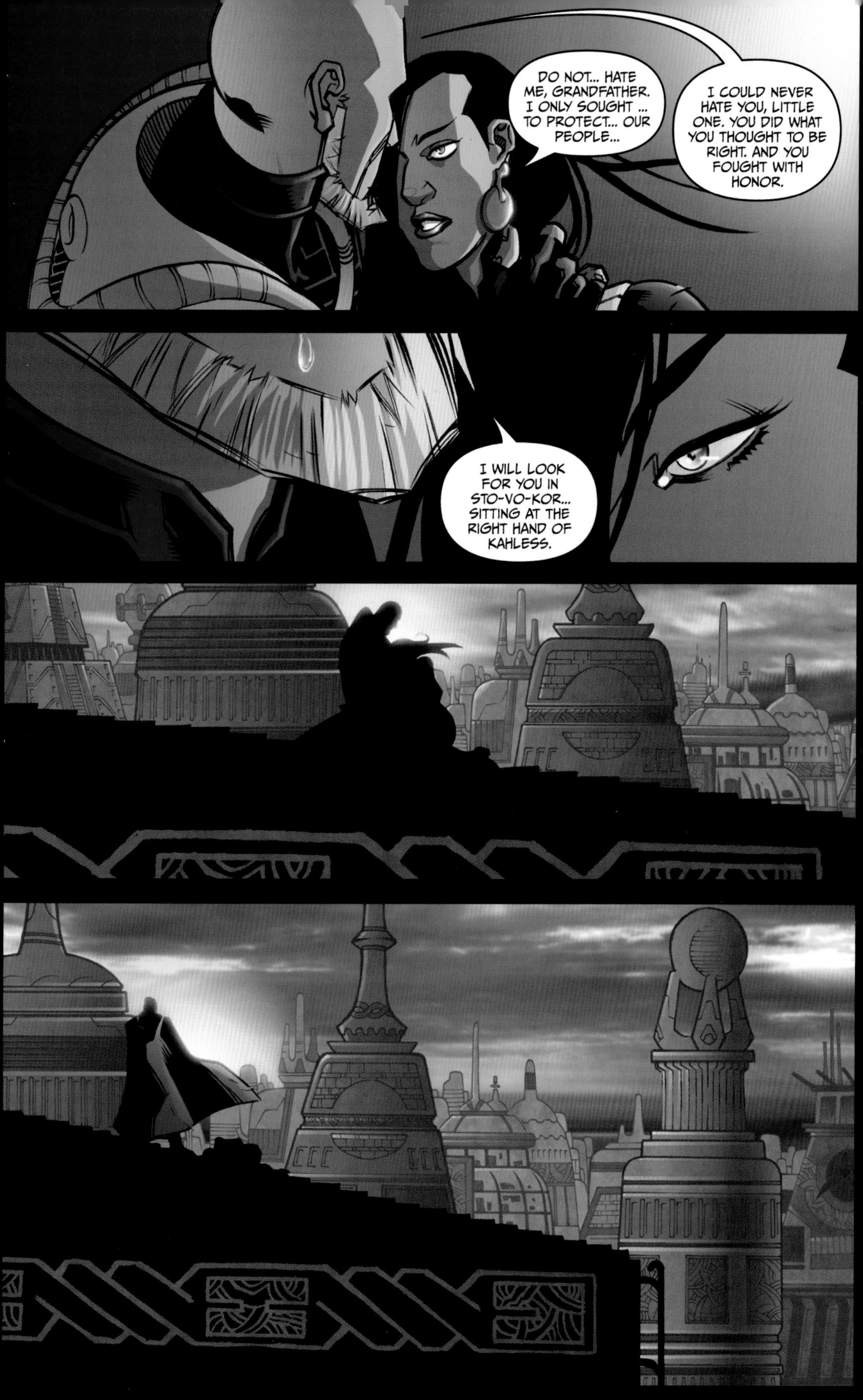
DO NOT... HATE ME, GRANDFATHER. I ONLY SOUGHT ... TO PROTECT... OUR PEOPLE...
I COULD NEVER HATE YOU, LITTLE ONE. YOU DID WHAT YOU THOUGHT TO BE RIGHT. AND YOU FOUGHT WITH HONOR.
I WILL LOOK FOR YOU IN STO-VO-KOR... SITTING AT THE RIGHT HAND OF KAHLESS.

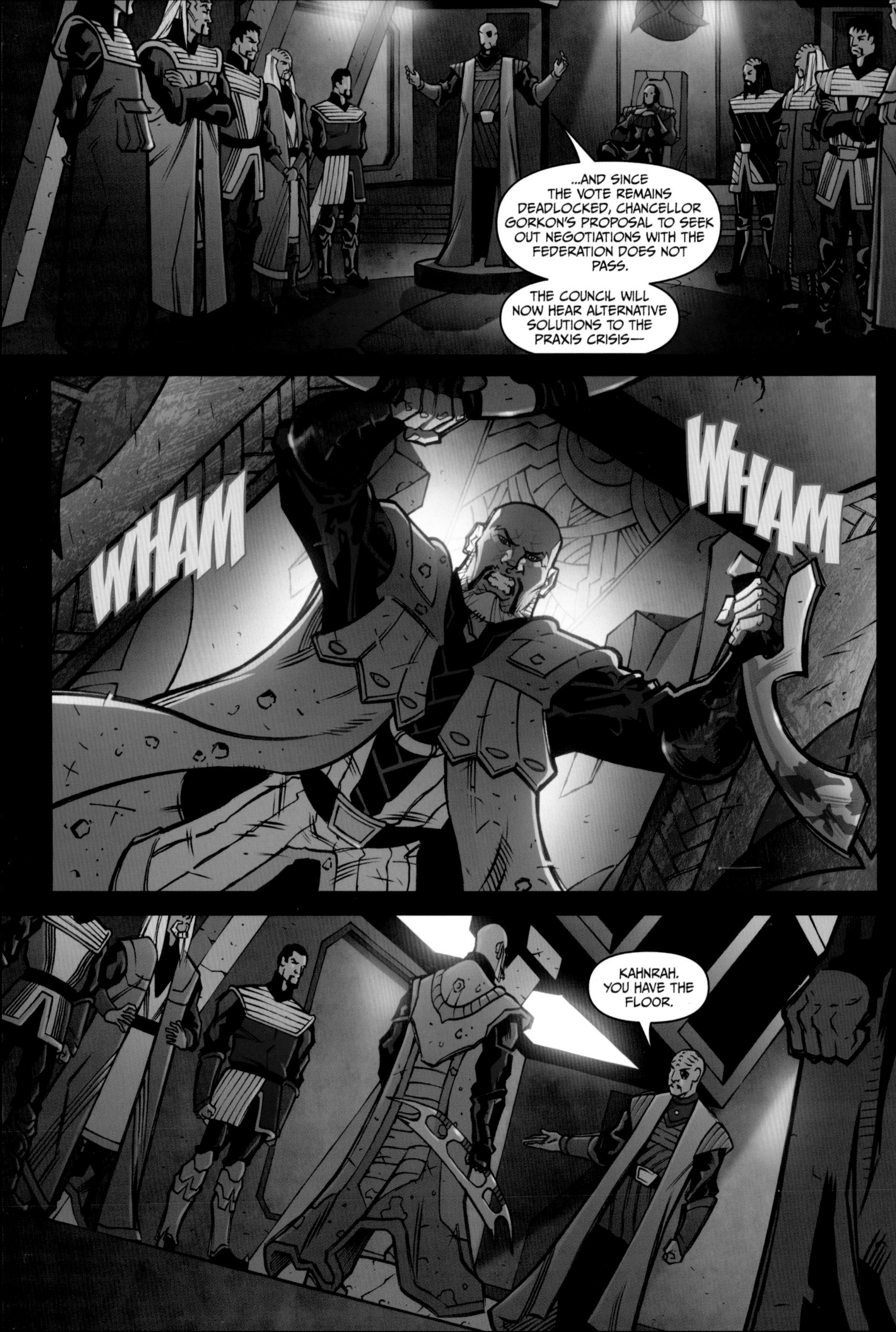
...AND SINCE THE VOTE REMAINS DEADLOCKED, CHANCELLOR GORKON'S PROPOSAL TO SEEK OUT NEGOTIATIONS WITH THE FEDERATION DOES NOT PASS.
THE COUNCIL WILL NOW HEAR ALTERNATIVE SOLUTIONS TO THE PRAXIS CRISIS—
WHAM
WHAM
KAHNRAH. YOU HAVE THE FLOOR.

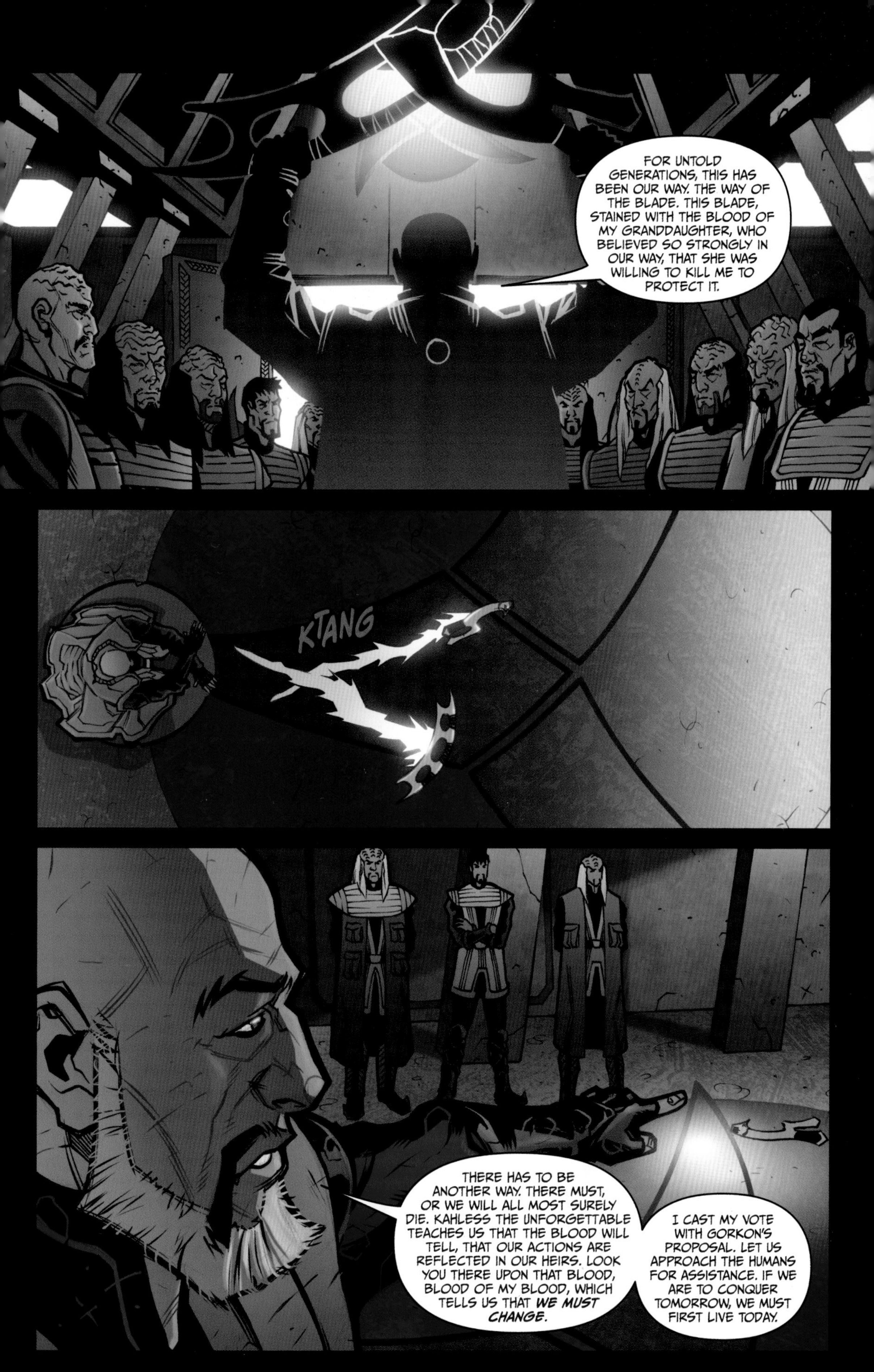
FOR UNTOLD GENERATIONS, THIS HAS BEEN OUR WAY. THE WAY OF THE BLADE. THIS BLADE, STAINED WITH THE BLOOD OF MY GRANDDAUGHTER, WHO BELIEVED SO STRONGLY IN OUR WAY, THAT SHE WAS WILLING TO KILL ME TO PROTECT IT.
KTANG
THERE HAS TO BE ANOTHER WAY. THERE MUST, OR WE WILL ALL MOST SURELY DIE. KAHLESS THE UNFORGETTABLE TEACHES US THAT THE BLOOD WILL TELL, THAT OUR ACTIONS ARE REFLECTED IN OUR HEIRS. LOOK YOU THERE UPON THAT BLOOD, BLOOD OF MY BLOOD, WHICH TELLS US THAT *WE MUST CHANGE.*
I CAST MY VOTE WITH GORKON'S PROPOSAL. LET US APPROACH THE HUMANS FOR ASSISTANCE. IF WE ARE TO CONQUER TOMORROW, WE MUST FIRST LIVE TODAY.

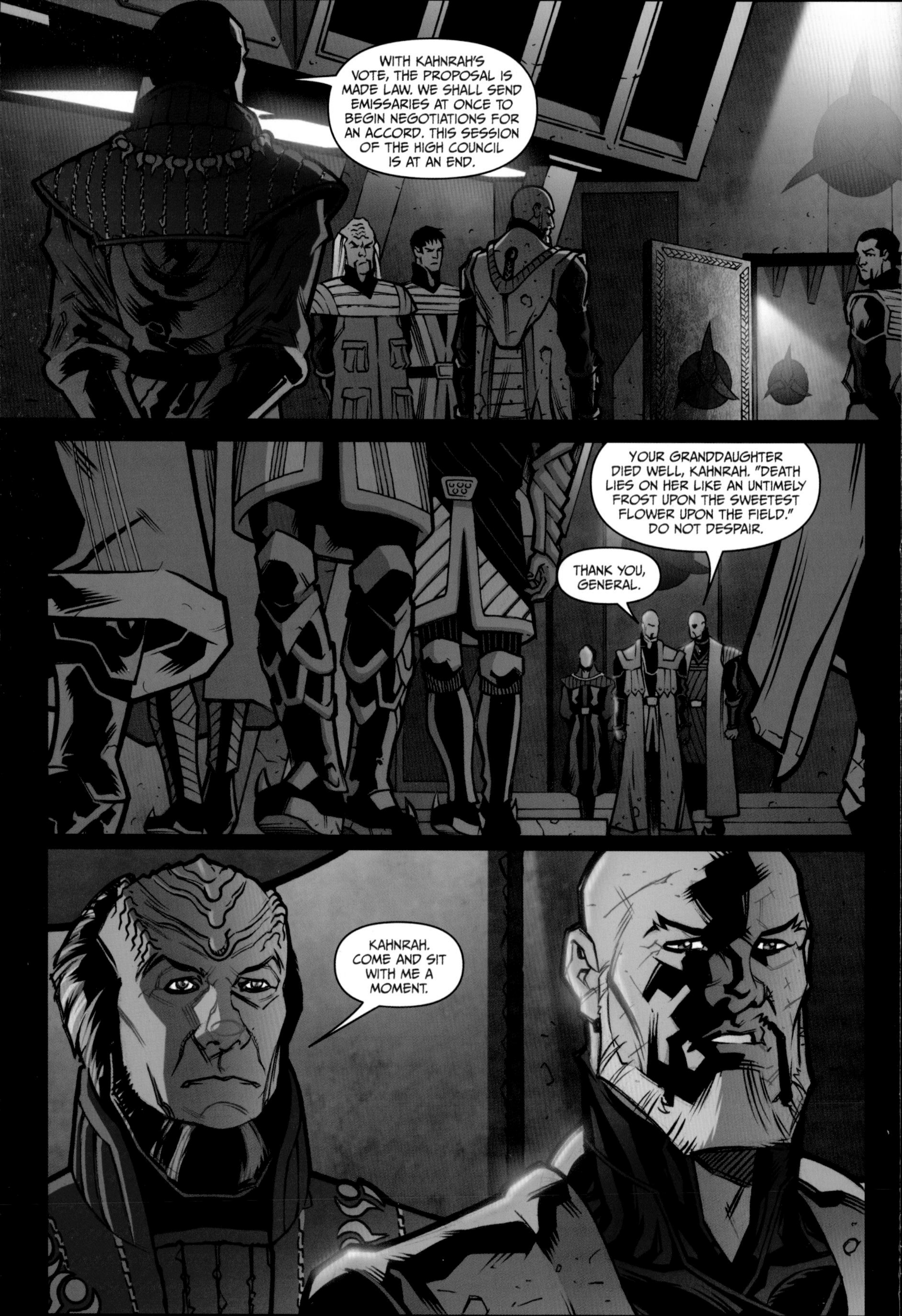
WITH KAHNRAH'S VOTE, THE PROPOSAL IS MADE LAW. WE SHALL SEND EMISSARIES AT ONCE TO BEGIN NEGOTIATIONS FOR AN ACCORD. THIS SESSION OF THE HIGH COUNCIL IS AT AN END.
YOUR GRANDDAUGHTER DIED WELL, KAHNRAH. "DEATH LIES ON HER LIKE AN UNTIMELY FROST UPON THE SWEETEST FLOWER UPON THE FIELD." DO NOT DESPAIR.
THANK YOU, GENERAL.
KAHNRAH. COME AND SIT WITH ME A MOMENT.

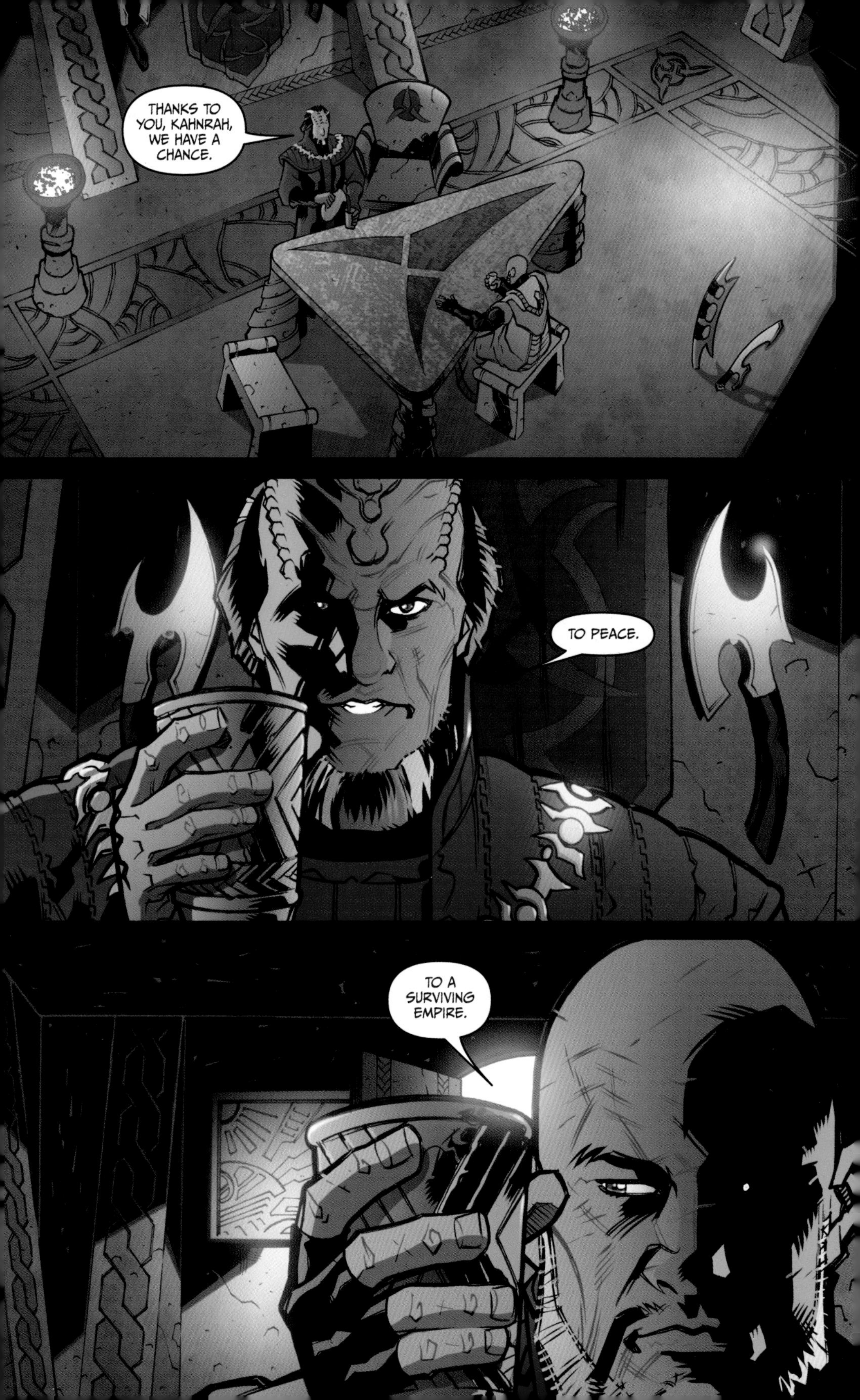
THANKS TO YOU, KAHNRAH, WE HAVE A CHANCE.
TO PEACE.
TO A SURVIVING EMPIRE.

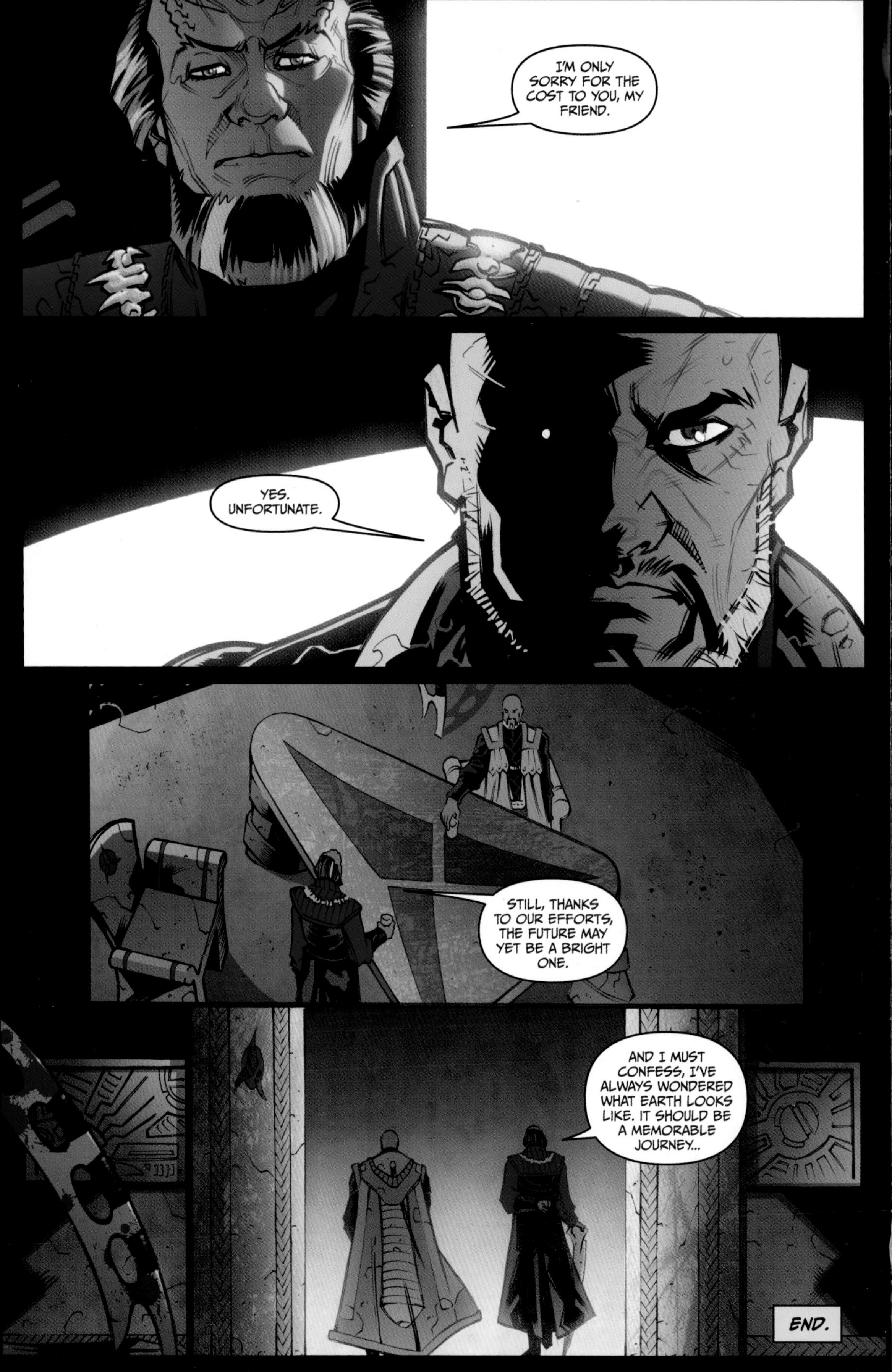
I'M ONLY SORRY FOR THE COST TO YOU, MY FRIEND.
YES. UNFORTUNATE.
STILL, THANKS TO OUR EFFORTS, THE FUTURE MAY YET BE A BRIGHT ONE.
AND I MUST CONFESS, I'VE ALWAYS WONDERED WHAT EARTH LOOKS LIKE. IT SHOULD BE A MEMORABLE JOURNEY...
END.